Worldwide Praise for the Erotica of John Patrick and STARbooks!

"John Patrick is a modern master of the genre!
...This writing is what being brave is all about.
It brings up the kinds of things that are usually kept so private that you think you're the only one who experiences them."
– *Gay Times, London*

"'Barely Legal' is a great potpourri...
and the coverboy is gorgeous!"
– *Ian Young, Torso magazine*

"A huge collection of highly erotic, short and steamy one-handed tales. Perfect bedtime reading, though you probably won't get much sleep! Prepare to be shocked!
Highly recommended!"
– *Vulcan magazine*

"Tantalizing tales of porn stars, hustlers, and other lost boys...John Patrick set the pace with 'Angel!'"
- *The Weekly News, Miami*

"...Some readers may find some of the scenes too explicit; others will enjoy the sudden, graphic sensations each page brings. Each of these romans á clef is written with sustained intensity. 'Angel' offers a strange, often poetic vision of sexual obsession. I recommend it to you."
- *Nouveau Midwest*

"Self-absorbed, sexually-addicted bombshell Stacy flounced onto the scene in 'Angel' and here he is again, engaged in further, distinctly 'non-literary' adventures...lots of action!"
- *Prinz Eisenherz Book Review, Germany*

"'Angel' is mouthwatering and enticing..."
- *Rouge Magazine, London*

"'Superstars' is a fast read...if you'd like a nice round of fireworks before the Fourth, read this aloud at your next church picnic..."
- *Welcomat, Philadelphia*

"For those who share Mr. Patrick's appreciation for cute young men, 'Legends' is a delightfully readable book...I am a fan of John Patrick's...His writing is clear and straight-forward and should be better known in the gay community."
- *Ian Young, Torso Magazine*

"'BOY TOY' is splendid..."
– *J.C., Illinois*

"...'Billy & David' is frank, intelligent, disarming. Few books approach the government's failure to respond to crisis in such a realistic, powerful manner."
- *RG Magazine, Montreal, Canada*

"...Touching and gallant in its concern for the sexually addicted, 'Angel' becomes a wonderfully seductive investigation of the mysterious disparity between lust and passion, obsession and desire."
-*Lambda Book Report*

"Each page of John Patrick's 'Angel' was like a sponge and I was slowly sucked into the works. 'The Kid' had the same effect on me and now 'What Went Wrong?' has blown me away!"
-*P. K. New York*

"John Patrick has one of the best jobs a gay male writer could have. In his fiction, he tells tales of rampant sexuality. His non-fiction involves first person explorations of adult male video stars. Talk about choice assignments!"
-*Southern Exposure*

"The title for 'Boys of Spring' is taken from a poem by Dylan Thomas, so you can count on high caliber imagery throughout."
- *Walter Vatter, Editor, A Different Light Review*

"'Boys of Spring' is Patrick's latest piece of erotic imagination in overdrive!"
-*Zipperstore, London*

*Book of the Month Selections in Europe and the U.K.
And Featured By A Different Light,
Lambda Rising and GR, Australia
And Available at Fine Booksellers Everywhere*

He's waiting for you ...

IN THE BOY ZONE

A New Collection of Erotic Tales
Edited By
JOHN PATRICK

STARbooks Press
Sarasota, FL

Books by John Patrick

Non-Fiction
A Charmed Life: Vince Cobretti
Lowe Down: Tim Lowe
The Best of the Superstars 1990
The Best of the Superstars 1991
The Best of the Superstars 1992
The Best of the Superstars 1993
The Best of the Superstars 1994
The Best of the Superstars 1995
The Best of the Superstars 1996
What Went Wrong?
When Boys Are Bad
& Sex Goes Wrong
Legends: The World's Sexiest
Men, Vols. 1 & 2
Legends (Third Edition)
Tarnished Angels (Ed.)

Fiction
Billy & David: A Deadly Minuet
The Bigger They Are...
The Younger They Are...
The Harder They Are...
Angel: The Complete Trilogy
Angel II: Stacy's Story
Angel: The Complete Quintet
Angel: The Complete Quintet
(Expanded International Ed.)
A Natural Beauty (Editor)
The Kid (with Joe Leslie)
HUGE (Editor)
Strip: He Danced Alone
The Boys of Spring
Big Boys/Little Lies (Editor)
Boy Toy
Seduced (Editor)
Insatiable/Unforgettable (Editor)
Heartthrobs
Runaways/Kid Stuff (Editor)
Dangerous Boys/Rent Boys
(Editor)
Barely Legal (Editor)
Country Boys/City Boys (Editor)
My Three Boys (Editor)
Mad About the Boys (Editor)
Lover Boys (Editor)
In the BOY ZONE (Editor)
Boys of the Night (Editor)

Entire Contents Copyrighted © 1995 by John Patrick, Sarasota, FL. All rights reserved. No part of this book may be reproduced or transmitted in any form by any means, electronic or mechanical, including photocopying, recording, or any information storage and retrieval system, without expressed written consent from the publisher. Every effort has been made to credit copyrighted material. The author and the publisher regret any omissions and will correct them in future editions. Note: While the words "boy," "girl," "young man," "youngster," "gal," "kid," "student," "guy," "son," "youth," "fella," and other such terms are occasionally used in text, this work is generally about persons who are at least 18 years of age, unless otherwise noted.

First Edition Published in the U.S. in July 1996
Library of Congress Card Catalogue No. 95-072420
ISBN No. 1-877978-62-0

Contents

INTRODUCTION:
TROUBLE IN THE BOY ZONE

THE KIDS
AT THE MALL
John Patrick
HEAT
John Patrick
BANJEE BOY
Chris Leslie
THE SEX FEST
J. Nagle
PICKING UP TOLLY
Jarred Goodall
THE CARRIAGE BOY
Michael Bates
PUNK'S COLLATERAL
Thomas C. Humphrey
MY FIRST TUTOR
James Wilton
THE TUTOR,
THE TOURIST & ME
James Wilton
HEAVEN
Nigel Christopher
KEVIN'S ASS
John C. Douglas
GOING PLACES
Edward Bangor
FUCKING FRED
John Patrick
HE DIDN'T DO VIRGINS
Bert McKenzie
ENTER THE DRAGON
Dan Veen
THE ORGASMIC RESUME
Thom Nickels
A LOVELY LAD
Rudy Roberts
SEX AT THE QUARRY
Leo Cardini
RANDY & SWEET PETE
Grant Adams
FLETCHER'S BOYS
Grant Adams
THE FULL TREATMENT
Keith Davis

TRUCKER'S SPECIAL
William Cozad
THE TOUCH OF THE
STRANGER
John Patrick
THE REFUGEE
John C. Douglas
IN THE BOY ZONE
Jesse Monteagudo
THE WRESTLER
David Olivera
THE INTRUDER
Ken Smith
FAXING OFF
David Laurents
FREE INSTALLATION
L. Amore
TAKE YOUR TIME
Antler
THE GLORY HOLE
Ken Anderson
ROADSIDE STAND
Edmund Miller
QUICK MIRACLES IN THE
ALLEY
Christopher Thomas

ALL IN THE FAMILY
A Series of Stories
TRADITION
Greg Bowden
TIES THAT BIND
Duncan P. Allen
A FAMILY AFFAIR IN RIO
Daniel Dee
TRIO
Dan Veen
LOVING UNCLE
John Patrick

GETTING OFF
The Search for Orgasm
An Expose by John Patrick
Including Climax in Excelis
Getting Off Around the World
A Lust for Leather
Beyond Orgasm

Editor's Note

Most of the stories appearing in this book take place prior to the years of The Plague; the editor and each of the authors represented herein advocate the practice of safe sex at all times.

And, because these stories trespass the boundaries of fiction and non-fiction, to respect the privacy of those involved, we've changed all of the names and other identifying details.

he banged me in the alley
it's where he led me
this messiah claiming to be an artist
i didn't want to know about him
until he brought me into his van
parked there by first avenue

the dealers clocked our work
hoping to clear the smoked-out windows
just to make a score
i heard them knocking

drifting anyway
i've tasted this urban landscape
in my forearm, my intestines
met this godhead pumping religion
into my stomach many times before

he made me swallow
i spit it back at him
after i stole his wallet
when he wouldn't deliver
on the promise
nobody ever does

*– Excerpted from "Boy of the Americas,"
by William Freeburg*

INTRODUCTION: TROUBLE IN THE BOY ZONE

John Patrick

*"Got me a big old dick and I
I like to have fun
held against your forehead
I'll make you suck it
maybe I'll put a hole in your head
you know, just for the fuck of it
I can reduce you if I want"
– Song lyrics by the group Nine Inch Nails*

"I didn't aim to get in no trouble," a boy of the streets said to me once, "but I guess I sure wasn't aiming to run away from any, either." My first inclination was to run away from him, but, of course, like the moth to the flame, I hung in there and I was rewarded with a couple of nights of pleasure before I left town. Looking back on it now, I guess I was one of the lucky ones, because, in the Boy Zone, predators lurk.

The Boys of Boise

In his book *The Boys of Boise*, about the homosexual scandal in Boise, Idaho, in the Fifties, John Gerassi demonstrates how much trouble you can get into going to the Boy Zone: "Without too much flair for fantasy, one could visualize a central headquarters with files on all the homosexuals of Boise – the underworld – as well as long lists of available teen-age boys, with price tags next to their names. One can even understand how the people of Boise, reading about their town in a tight little story in *Time*, could think that wealthy millionaires from all over America, indeed from all over the world, were flying into Boise because only there could they select fresh young boys for their favors. I even heard one woman tell me very seriously that there was so much homosexual traffic into Boise that United Airlines (which is the main airline covering Boise) 'had put special flights into operation during the busy season – the summer.'"

And although Boise began to be known as "Boysy" or "Boys' town" around the Northwest, even as far as San Francisco, it was due to the publicity that the cases received, not to the facts. Naturally there were homosexuals in Boise, but no more so than anywhere else.

"We used to watch these guys in the YMCA, in the toilet of the bus depot, in Julia Davis Park," a member of law enforcement said. "You've seen that park. There are roads going through it, and the homos would cruise around waiting for a kid to go into or come out of the toilet. They'd stop him, start a conversation, offer to drive him home, then hand him a drink. In one toilet, which had no partitions between johns, we caught a guy sitting on one john reaching over for the genitals of a boy sitting on another. It wasn't very nice work, believe me."

But it got results. First a high school teacher was arrested. Then a high school janitor. Then a pianist. A clothing salesman. "Thus," Gerassi reported, "by the time that the *Time* issue of December 12 hit Boise's stands, there seemed to be good reason to suspect that a whole underworld of homosexuals had indeed been preying on hundreds of teen-age boys. And those arrested talked."

The cop said, "'We know about you,' we would tell 'em and before long the homos would sign a confession, or talk a confession into the tape. And boy, would they talk. Like women. Look, we didn't have arrest warrants. But homosexuals are like that, perhaps more so. They tend to exaggerate those feminine qualities they admire, like cleanliness, primness, hospitality. My God, these homosexuals would sit and tell us about every guy they could think of. 'Have you talked to so-and-so?' they'd ask. So we had another name to investigate. By the time we were told to stop the investigation, we had so many names – with evidence – we could have probably gotten convictions on all of them.

"There was only one guy we didn't get," he went on, "and that wasn't because he refused to see us. He was a lawyer and knew how to stick to his denials even when presented with overwhelming circumstantial evidence."

The cop indicated that he and his helpers had the boy that this lawyer had supposedly seduced. The boy was brought into the room. The lawyer was asked if he had ever seen him. He said no. The boy then described the lawyer's office, detail by detail, and insisted that it was in that office that the two of them had committed the homosexual act. The lawyer still refused to concede, insisting that someone else must have previously described the office to the boy. (Incidentally, the boy, who was over eighteen, had been involved in a previous case when he was only fourteen, at which time the adult was found guilty and jailed for ninety days.)"

On the Boardwalk at Daytona Beach

On a street next to the Boardwalk at Daytona Beach, juvenile and adult male prostitutes have openly conducted business, even engaging in public sex, for 25 years. People familiar with the area, Ora Street Park, call it Fag Hill and have dubbed a nearby McDonald's the Pedophile Cafe because abusers have hung out there.

As the once grand Boardwalk area began to decline in the '60s, it drew runaways and troubled local kids. Predators followed. That, in turn, spawned more decline. Despite several phases of decay and repair, eradication proved elusive for several reasons.

Authorities say that victims remain reluctant to testify against the men who use them, and those who do come forward often have criminal records and a history of drug abuse that make them easy targets for defense attorneys to discredit.

Still, tales of certain boys can be disturbing.

"On a recent night," Christopher Quinn reported in the *Orlando Sentinel*, "a 15-year-old was walking by himself down a Jacksonville street, headed for Daytona Beach. He was on his way to becoming just another of the estimated 6,000 runaways who pass through the resort town every year.

"But he never made it that night. It began when a man in a red BMW noticed the solitary teen trudging down the road. He tapped his brakes and pulled alongside.

"Did the boy need a ride?

"Sure did. As it turned out, he needed a ride very badly. He was a runaway from a mental health center, and he wanted to go to Daytona Beach to hide.

"It must have seemed like a lucky break to the kid. He hopped inside the BMW.

"Before long, the driver pulled into a rest stop and had sex with the boy. When it was over, the man left him on the side of the road.

"As the BMW pulled away, the teenager saw the driver grab his car phone and put it to his ear. Minutes later, a man in a white Firebird pulled up.

"Unbeknownst to the boy, it was a friend of the first man.

"The second driver took him back to his house in Bunnell, north of Daytona Beach, where he and his roommate assaulted the boy repeatedly.

"Then, they gave him to two other men in Daytona Beach.

"Eventually, the boy spoke out to save himself. Armed with that testimony, police raided the first home and hauled away a 6-by-12-foot trailer loaded with stomach-turning pornography, involving sexual sadism and teen-age boys.

"That 15-year-old was not the first boy the men had so thoroughly degraded, although they didn't see it as abuse. They saw it as taking a youth into their family. One of the men boasted to an undercover agent of 'adopting' five similar boys.

"'None of them ever complained,' he said. 'They all liked what we did, and I could tell.'"

One man, who runs an eatery on the Boardwalk, recalls that when he was a child, his father pointed out two men he should avoid.

Twenty years later, still working in his father's business, he saw the same men approaching boys on the Boardwalk. This time, there were no fathers to warn them.

The men targeted by police as predators have included hotel operators, schoolteachers, a retired medical examiner, a church leader, a former TV anchorman, an airline pilot, a construction worker, a car salesman and the independently wealthy. But arrests remain few. Predators know plenty of tricks to keep from getting caught. "They tell each other: Don't have two boys in bed. The two could corroborate each other's testimony," Quinn relates. "With one boy, it's just the word of a minor against an adult. And predators use drugs and alcohol to lower resistance and weaken the will. When an unsuspecting boy enters this world, he is likely to wake up from a drug-induced fog to find himself raped.

"Sick, hungry, with nowhere to turn, the boys find themselves at the mercy of their abusers. Nonetheless - and predators seem to know this - the confused kids may feel grateful for a place to stay.

"Starved for attention at home they may even feel happy about being around an adult who offers rides in big cars and fast boats or plunks down a fistful of quarters for fun at the arcades.

"At least, for a while."

One victim - now a husband and father - says he was passed to pedophiles up and down the East Coast from Key West to Cape Cod, and had sex with at least 75 men. When he grew too old for their tastes, he lured other boys into the network.

Now, after more than two decades, perhaps it was inevitable that the saga of the Boardwalk would turn bloody.

In August 1994, a 15-year-old shot and killed Olen Lee Hepler jr., a 47-year-old car salesman whom prosecutors termed a "sexual predator."

A Florida Department of Law Enforcement investigation named Hepler as one of three main players in predatory activities around Daytona Beach. But, according to the *Sentinel*, a judge ruled his background could not be introduced into the trial because it was deemed irrelevant.

Hepler was shot in the back of the head while he lay on a couch in his Ormond-by-the-Sea home.

His accused killer, Mark Berrios, had run away from a juvenile detention home in Jacksonville. He called Hepler, whom he had met previously, for help.

Hepler drove up to get him, brought him back to his Ormondby-the-Sea home, bought him new clothes and took him camping at state parks.

Hepler became sexually aggressive, Berrios claimed, so he fired in self-defense.

But several of the teen's friends said he bragged about the

shooting. And prosecutors claimed the motive was robbery.

When arrested, Berrios had Hepler's Chevrolet Blazer and had withdrawn about $1,200 using the dead man's automatic teller machine card.

In December, a jury found him guilty of first-degree murder.

The conviction came just two months after a second killing. In October 1994, a 16-year-old boy stabbed to death a 40-year-old man he met near the Boardwalk.

The two drove in the man's car to a woods north of Ormond Beach where the violence occurred. Floyd Merritt, a probation officer who once monitored predators, was stabbed in the chest.

The teen-ager, Jofre Miller, took Merritt's Honda Prelude and drove himself to the hospital, where he was treated for a punctured lung and superficial cuts.

A passer-by spotted the wounded Merritt, who was taken to the hospital by emergency workers but could not be saved.

Deputy sheriffs said Miller tried to attack the man and stabbed him, but Miller maintains he fought back in self-defense. He told his stepmother that he carried a knife because another man had tried to pick him up for sex and became violent.

As we write this, Miller is awaiting trial.

But murder can work both ways, of course. In his book *Midnight in the Garden of Good and Evil*, John Berendt's sharply observed narrative about the death of hustler Danny Hansford, the facts seemed to lend credence to antiques dealer Jim Williams's claim of killing the boy in self-defense: "Hansford had been in and out of juvenile homes and mental hospitals," Berendt says. "He had dropped out of school in the eighth grade and had a history of violence and getting into trouble with the police. Williams himself had bailed him out of jail nine times in the past ten months. Skipper Dunn, a horticulturist, who had once lived in the same rooming house as Hansford, described him as a dangerous psychotic. 'He was a berserker,' Dunn said. 'I saw him run amok twice, breaking things, reaching for knives. It took two people to pin him down. You could look into his eyes and see there was no person left, only rage and violence. It was easy to see that he might try to kill someone some day.' Hansford had once torn a door off its hinges in an effort to get at his sister and beat her up. His own mother had sworn out a police warrant against him, declaring that she was afraid he would do bodily harm to her and her family.

"In his interview with the *Georgia Gazette*, Williams described Hansford as severely disturbed. He said Hansford had once told him, 'I'm alone in this world. No one cares about me. I don't have anything to live for.' With a strange sort of detachment, Williams saw himself as Danny Hansford's savior rather than his nemesis, much less his murderer: 'I was determined to save him from himself,' he said. 'He had given up on being alive.' Though Williams's view was unabashedly self-serving, it was compelling in its detail. Hansford had developed a fascination with death, he said. He would frequently go to Bonaventure Cemetery with friends and point to the grave markers and say that the small ones were for poor people, and the big ones were for rich people, and that if he died in Mercer House he would get a big one. Hansford had twice tried to commit suicide at Mercer House by taking drug overdoses. The second time, he had written a note: 'If this stuff does the job, at least I'll get a decent tombstone.' Williams had rushed him to the hospital both times. All of that was a matter of record.

"Beyond saying Danny Hansford was an employee, Williams never fully explained their relationship. But it soon became known that Hansford had been a part-time male hustler who loitered in the squares along Bull Street.

"'Oh, we knew,' said John Myers. 'Of course we knew. We weren't aware of the details, naturally, because Jim exercised discretion, which was the right thing to do. But all along we'd congratulated ourselves about Jim's social success because of what it seemed to say about us. We thought it proved Savannah was cosmopolitan, that we were sophisticated enough to accept a gay man socially.'

"'Oh, Jim Williams will probably get off,' said Prentiss Crowe, a Savannah aristocrat, 'but he'll still face a few problems. There is bound to be a certain *resentment* about his having killed that boy – that boy in particular, I mean. Danny Hansford was a very accomplished hustler, from all accounts, very good at his trade, and very much appreciated by both men and women. The trouble is he hadn't quite finished making the rounds. A fair number of men and women were looking forward to having their turn with him. Of course, now that Jim's shot him they never will. Naturally, they'll hold this against Jim, and that's what I mean when I say 'resentment.' Danny Hansford was known to be a good time . . . but a good time not yet had by all.'

"At the bar in the Oglethorpe Club, Sonny Clark put it more bluntly: 'You know what they're saying about Jim Williams, don't you? They're saying he shot the best piece of ass in Savannah!'"

Quentin Lovejoy, a soft-spoken classics scholar in his mid-sixties who lives with his maiden aunt in a high-Victorian townhouse, told Berendt, "All this talk about Danny Hansford being a violent, brutal criminal! Jim Williams does himself no credit blaspheming the boy that way."

"But Quentin," his aunt protests, "Danny Hansford beat up his sister! His mother took out a police warrant against him. He'd been arrested umpteen times. He'd been in jail. He was a common criminal!"

"Not at all," says Mr. Lovejoy in a voice slightly louder than a whisper. "The only crime that boy ever committed was turnin' twenty."

Eventually, Williams decided to come clean. On cross-examination, the prosecutor asked Williams, "So he was a street kid and had been since fourteen years of age, I think you indicated?"

"Oh, yes."

"An eighth-grade dropout, and something on the order of twenty years old, is that right?"

"He was twenty-one. He was no child."

"I wouldn't, of course, dispute your right to have any relationship you wanted to. But you were fifty-two and he was twenty-one. Was that a natural and normal relationship?"

"Mm-hmmm. I was fifty-two years old, but he had fifty-two years' worth of mileage on him."

In Manhattan's Loop

Through the many years I've been pursuing boys I have found that, by and large, if you have trouble with them, chances are it's *your* fault. Of course, in the days before crack cocaine, dealing with youths was much easier. But even during the summer of 1965, Jim Carroll relates in *The Basketball Diaries*, the fag hustling scene in Manhattn was getting "hairier and hairier all the time."

"I mean," Carroll says, "what happened to the old fashioned homo who just wanted to take you home and suck your dick? They're getting more and more like those seals up in Alaska I signed a petition for at school the other day, a species going down at an incredible rate. You just don't know what the next trick you pick up is gonna whip out of his attache case these days...

"Handcuffs, masks, snakes (yeah, that's right, real ones), chains, whips, last week a guy had a pet parrot that he had eat grapes out of my pubic hair. (He had a leather 'muff' for my cock to insure me against any danger of the dumb bird getting smart and snatching off my main asset). It's all out of hand as far as I'm concerned, I'm taking a vacation for a few weeks before I go zoo. ...I'd rather go back to ripping off old ladies or something sensible.

"Let's start with Dave, not the strangest of the last two weeks but a man with a definite problem. He picks me up on the 'meat rack' on Third Avenue and does he want to suck dick? No way. Dave is a fifty-five-year-old well off V.P. of a popular yogurt company and he's got an executive box at Yankee Stadium ... and Dave is going to pay me fifty bills if I attend the day's double header with him. This *really* happened ... I bullshit you not... I am sane, it takes a little dope now and then ... but I have maintained sanity. Every little leaguer in N.Y. is on his old man to get good seats for a ball game and I'm getting paid for it... besides the extra satisfaction for me of sitting there watching and remembering the years I slave labored around that joint selling popcorn in 90 degrees and cold drinks at 33 degrees; I felt great having old Dave buying me beers from all those oldtime hawkers there who used to call me a lazy bastard and give me shit... I even saw my old foreman who fired me and gave him a nice big gesture in front of his crew. But to tell you the truth I'm no big baseball fan and staying to the last out of a whole double header was one of the most boring scenes that ever went down. Dave was a fanatic, really laying on the old 'fan' bullshit ... I had to fake it along for the four and a half hours just like I got to fake it in bed ... but I'd rather get a boring blow job for half an hour any time instead of this crap, in fact I tapped the price up to seventy-five before the second game began, because "It was taking up precious time and money." Dave forked over an even hundred. It didn't really surprise me... how can anything surprise you in the middle of a scene like that? I have no idea what the fruit's motive was in all this... he did give me a squeeze on the thigh whenever a Yankee got a hit but that was as far as it went. I guess he was just another lonely man ... but why the bread? When he let me out of the cab at the 'Rack' I gave the souvenir Yankee cap he bought me to this drag queen on the scene there who's got the hots for Mickey Mantle "in those tight pinstripe pants he wears on the field."

"A few days before my day at the ball park some CPA gets me up to his hotel room and leads me into the bathroom. He's got a cat tied to the seat of the toilet and a bubble bath all set for someone to jump in. I excused myself for a second and went over to the kitchenette and popped a couple of Valiums... I was already loaded on junk but I could see this was going to be strictly from fruit. When I got back in the john he was already naked and in the tub frosted in bubbles... the poor cat was still chained to the john seat, yelping away. The guy laid his plan on me. He wants me to whip the cat dead after I first piss on him in his bubble bath, then when the cat has had it I'm to jerk off into his mouth while he's still in the tub. Out from under the bubbles he hands me a whip, a tiny cat size whip with leather fringes laced with broken ends of razors. I did not like this man. I didn't like him at all, and too bad for him I was very stoned and in a cat-loving mood so I decided to express my dislike. I untied the cat, he tried to get up and stop me, I punched his chump face, he landed back on his ass in the tub and I gave him the whip across the chest... a nasty wound. He was a little dazed now... I grabbed his hair, opened his mouth and pissed in it... he spit it out, the piss mixing with the blood oozing from his lip from the punch and he let out a slow motion yell at the sting of urine dripping into the cuts on his chest. He sank under water to cool the burn, I rifled his wallet for sixty bucks, picked up the kitty and split.

"If there were, say, a book like 'The Pervert's Guide To New York City,' the bathroom at Grand Central Terminal should, without any doubts, figure in it. The bathrooms in the subways themselves are bad enough, but at least you've got the Transit fuzz popping in and out of them often enough so the pervies are uptight to directly take a grab at you, but not so at old Grand Central, where anything might go. I was catching a train up to Rye, N.Y. tonight to visit old neighborhood chum Willie at, I'd say, just after five-thirty p.m. Man, all those business cats just lined up along the piss machines (there must be forty machines, whatever the hell you call them, that's right, urinals, lined next to each other) and then along with them the usual seedy dudes, hustlers, etc. and all these eyes peeking down at the guy next to me who's peeking down at me along with the guy on my other side and jacking off like madmen, forty arms like pistons pumping back and forth at incredible rates. Not a bit of class in the entire place, just a bunch of office worker closet queens getting off their rocks before they miss the 5:50. Any of those Westchester housewives that ain't had too much lately can come down here and find out why. But the peeky-boo scene is old hat and that goes on in any john, it's just that here you suddenly feel a hand moving across your leg and grabbing your fucking cock. No raised eyebrows about it from anyone, fuck, I'm beginning to think I'm the only person in the place that came down just for normal body functions. I jumped back in the middle of pissing while this stately chap grabbed me ancl I wound up spraying all over the Brooks Brothers number the guy is wearing. I had to move down to another whatever they are to finish it off. Same bit. This cat next to me now I thought for a second was going to pull out a pair of binoculars. It's true, guys even sucking dick down there right in front of other cases if the 'attendant' isn't looking. Shit, what am I gonna do, complain to this 'attendant' about what's happening. He looks like he might pull my jeans down and bugger me on the spot. Besides, rarely these days do I complain about anything.

"The businessmen are the worst, no doubt. And they all have a thing about checking out the young guys. I've seen cats who are probably vice-presidents of toothpaste firms or shit fighting over the piss machine next to me. This form of flattery will get them nowhere with me. Spades too, they dig getting next to the spades and tuning in on a little black stuff. Don't ever let your kiddie go pee-pee in that joint by himself, and if you do and he comes back up the stairs smiling, I suggest you have a little chat with the boy."

When Jim was about nine he and his friend Kenny would spend a lot of time hanging around the cellar of their apartment house, mostly tossing a ball back and forth or listening to the radio. "The superintendent of the place, Buddy, was a jolly dude who was the laziest bastard on earth but who, when bugged enough, would and could fix anything any tenant had a bitch over. He's an on and off drunk who is totally on lately, so his job seems hanging on pretty thin wire. He digs us though, and let us hang around like the older cats who would play big card games in the boiler room. It was a seedy and dark, smelly place now that I think about it. I guess that's why I dug it. I know these other guys, in fact, that hung around in an old busted down news truck for about two years without once realizing what a boring idea it was."

Now, thirty years later, New York City remains an amazing place, even though it "ain't what it used to be."

"I walked down a street I thought I knew recently and didn't know it: East 53rd Street between Second and Third Avenues," says playwright Daniel Haben Clark, author of "Tiny Tim and the Size Queen." "Refurbished rather than rebuilt. Only one new building, but the change was total, from raunchy to sedate. Almost elegant, almost quiet. I had dinner a block further east at the Mayfair, where I was informed there had been a major crackdown. This was confirmed at the G.H. Club, a geriatric gay bar known as the Wrinkle Room. They'd closed Rounds, where the high-priced hustlers plied their trade and chased the cheaper street boys away as well. Who were *they*? Probably the Giuliani administration at the behest of gentrifying local landlords. After four decades of infamy, one of the planet's most notorious meat racks was empty. Hustlers Row was recycled. The Walk of Shame had halted. The Loop had closed.

"Who named it The Loop? I'm not sure but it became official when the *New York Post* did a big spread on it a decade ago. Male prostitution flourished there from the '50s till early this year. The original Loop was larger, circling 53rd to 55th Streets, from Second Avenue to Third. In recent years it had been condensed into the above-mentioned block with occasional spillage eastward, but that short strip really jumped. No man was safe from importunement there. A straight man holding hands with his wife and pushing a baby carriage might well be solicited anyway. My eighty-year-old grandfather was nearly tackled when he went there to buy a newspaper. He was visiting me. I was never a hustler – rumors to the contrary – and I'm still not a John – amazing, but true– but I lived a block away and had to walk through the area to get anywhere. An acquaintance, photographer Conrad Ward, lived right on the block and had to fight his way in and out of his studio/apartment.

"Who were the denizens of The Loop? Runaway kids. Retired pugilists. Absentee firemen, full-time bodybuilders, struggling actors (several future stars), laid-off construction workers, serial killers, and a few freak cases like the millionaire who wanted to be loved for his flesh, not his cash. Andy Warhol showed this block in his hustler movie starring Joe Dallesandro. There was a male madame who offered memberships in a 'Fruit of the Month Club': Rumor had it that for $120 per annum you would receive monthly visits from 'A clean boy wearing cologne!' That's right! Ten dollars a shot! That was back around 1960. Inflation and drug habits drove the prices per trick up considerably in recent years. Open drug dealing was seen on the street towards the end. So were female hookers (or were they?). All this may have hastened the crackdown. Something did.

"Where did all these people go? To other streets, other bars. To the back pages of magazines. To the 800 and 900 telephone lines. And given the times we live in, to early graves. I'd often wondered what became of hustlers once built-in obsolescence caught up with them."

Many novels use New York as their setting, of course,

depending on the ready availability of boys. In Thomas M. Disch's novel *The Priest*, for instance, Father Bryce and those who shared his fleshly needs are viewed by the pillars of the church as "diseased members fit only for amputation."

"They were the sheep, and he was a goat. Their love was holy and redeeming, and his stank of shit. And there was a part of him that agreed with them, that shared their contempt for and horror of the acts he was compelled to perform."

But with Donny the priest, heaven help him, began to feel the madness of love: "Before Donny his sexual feelings had been like the weather, with longer and shorter stretches of calm and of stormy weather. Once he had initiated a boy into the rudiments of sexuality, Father Bryce tended to lose interest. Their innocence was the wine for which he thirsted; once he'd slaked his thirst, the boys were like empty bottles, an embarrassment to be tidied away. He would insist on hearing their confessions and then, under the seal of the sacrament, swear them to a secrecy they were usually all too eager to agree to.

"But Donny Petrosky had been different. Donny would not be coerced into postcoital shame. He declared himself to be in love with Father Bryce, and called him on the phone at all hours, and appeared as a communicant each morning at Mass, even after Father Bryce had told him he could no longer serve as an altar boy. At first Father Bryce had been alarmed and angered, but then the boy's obsession began to kindle similar feelings in himself. He invented reasons why Donny had to spend the night at the rectory. He took him on fishing trips to Rush Lake. He bought clothes for him and helped fabricate lies that would account for his frequent absences from the Petrosky dinner table. He interceded with Sister Fidelis, Donny's seventh-grade teacher, so that Donny would not be required to take a summer course in remedial math as a condition of advancing to eighth grade. Donny began to speak of the possibility that he might have a calling to the priesthood, inspired by his mentor's example. Father Bryce felt a strange joy at the thought of Donny's vocation, a feeling that was at once priestly and paternal.

"And then Donny Petrosky exploded. Father Bryce never knew what triggered the outburst, for there had been nothing amiss between them. The boy had had an argument with his parents, who'd told him he would not be allowed out of the house after dinner for the rest of the summer. Donny set the Petrosky house on fire the same night. Fortunately, the fire department prevented any serious damage, but Donny was sent by a family court judge for psychiatric evaluation, and the cat was out of the bag. Donny told the psychiatrist about Father Bryce, the psychiatrist told Donny's parents, they hired a lawyer, and the lawyer went not to the OLM rectory but directly to the diocese of Minneapolis. Only a month earlier Father Bryce's erstwhile friend and longtime nemesis, Father Massey, had been appointed Bishop of Minneapolis.

"Massey made the most of his opportunity. He was all love and concern and prurient interest. He did not pry directly into the sexual details, but delegated that task to his vicar-general Alexis Clareson. Father Clareson was the most openly gay member of the Chancery staff, but was probably true to his vow of celibacy, being quite obese and confined to a wheelchair. Though Father Clareson displayed curiosity about everything Father Bryce had done with Donny, he never tried to ferret out the names of other boys who might have led the priest into the same temptations, for had he done so, the diocese would have been obliged to seek out the victims and offer, at the very least, to pay for their therapy.

"Once Father Bryce had returned to the diocese from his mandatory term of treatment at a Church-run clinic in Arizona that specialized in the rehabilitation of pedophile priests, Bishop Massey astonished him with his new assignment: He was to become the pastor of St. Bernardine's Church in suburban Willowville.

"...Father Bryce had learned in Arizona that it was not quite accurate to think of himself as a pedophile. Pedophiles love prepubescent children. He was an ephebophile, from the Greek *ephebos*, which meant 'young man.' Arizona had not changed him in that respect. Like convicts who learn in prison to refine their skills at safecracking, Father Bryce had learned many things during his group therapy sessions that he was now able to apply in his day-to-day life as the pastor of St. Bernardine's. He took to heart the advice of Father William Laroche of St. John de Matha Church in Opelousas, Louisiana, who testified to the effectiveness of foot massage and shiatsu in overcoming a boy's initial shyness. He bought a video recorder that used a peculiar kind of tape that could not be played back on ordinary equipment, thus insuring against his private videos becoming mixed up with ordinary VCR tapes in the rectory – a confusion that had got more than one of his fellow priests in hot water. He even learned of two pickup places in the Twin Cities area that he'd never heard of before. One of them was Papa Bear's, the bar near Stillwater...

"The other was the Fun Fun Fun video arcade, where he discovered Lance Kramer, the boy for whom Donny had been merely a warm-up session, the boy he knew, almost from the moment he got into the car, would be his undoing. Father Bryce had never patronized male prostitutes before. He thought it demeaning to pay money to someone in order to have sex with him. Wasn't it the same as admitting (he'd asked those priests in therapy who favored sex that could be bought and sold) that one was simply too old, or too fat, or too homely to be desired for one's own sake? Those who favored 'fast food' as against 'home cooking' had protested that paying for sex was part of the excitement. Of course, its primary advantage was the safety and convenience. The boy got in the car, he blew you, he got out, you drove away. Whereas, when you seduced children from your own parish, there was always the possibility that you might wind up repenting your sins and biding your time in a rehab in Arizona's heat. Such counsels had made sense, and so Father Bryce, without completely abandoning the children of Willowville, had tried out the Fun Fun Fun arcade.

"At first Fun Fun Fun had fulfilled the promise of the advocates of fast food. For a modest twenty dollars a pop, Father Bryce was able to get his rocks off a couple of nights a week without the risk of exposure (if also without the excitement that came with the risk). Then he met Lance. With his corn-silk, summer-blond hair; his newly minted swimmer's physique, plumped with steroids. The smoothness of him. The coltish ungainliness. The intensity of his need to please – and his facility in doing so. The fast-food advocates had certainly got that part right. Young as he was, the boy knew his business.

"Father Bryce could not get enough. When he returned to

Fun Fun Fun it was only for Lance's sake. If Lance was not there, he would wait in his parked car, fuming. Lance claimed to have no phone number he could be reached at. He would not give Father Bryce his address. He refused to go to motels. 'If you want to do it in a bed,' he told Father Bryce, 'we can do it in your bed, at your own home. Otherwise, the car's okay.' Neither liquor nor pot could change the boy's mind in that respect. At last, one night when Father Bryce knew that Father Cogling had driven to the Shrine and would be staying there overnight, he brought Lance to the St. Bernardine's rectory. Lance already knew he was a priest, but that fact had not impressed him. 'You're not the first priest I've had,' the boy declared, with his air of being the world's weariest sinner. 'There was three before you. That I know of.' Even so, Lance got off on it. They had sex in the confessional, and in front of the altar. Lance loved to see himself on videotape wearing one of his silly heavy-metal T-shirts while Father Bryce, in full clerical rig, gave him a blow job.

"Lance considered himself a Satanist, and was surprised when Father Bryce professed to have no interest in the occult and its mysteries. 'I mean, you dig us fucking right there in front of the big crucifix. And you did that thing with the wafers--that was your own idea.'

"'Well, yes. But I thought it was something that would turn you on. It did, didn't it?'

"'You know what your problem is, Father – your problem is you don't have faith. And I got the solution to your problem.'

"'Yes, I know you do,' Father Bryce said, ruffing his hair.

"'No, seriously,' the boy said, pulling back from his caress. 'Acid. That's what's going to do it for you. You've never tripped, have you?'

"Father Bryce shook his head. The idea of using hallucinogens did not appeal to him. But Lance had persisted, assuring him that the sex that you had when taking acid was like no other sex in the world.

"A week later they had their trip, and it was a disaster. Father Bryce's misgivings had not been without foundation. Usually, even when sex wasn't the top priority, Father Bryce was able to turn in a creditable performance. But the acid seemed to short-circuit his sexual capabilities. He couldn't get an erection, and couldn't get interested in making the effort. Everything started to turn sinister, including Lance, whose acne suddenly became not just noticeable but increasingly a source of dismay and then of alarm. It had not occurred to Father Bryce until just this moment that the boy, with all his sexual contacts, probably was HIV-positive. He had to get Lance out of the rectory, but Father Bryce was in no condition to drive the car, and he couldn't phone for a taxi to come and take Lance away, and Willowville was a good thirty miles from the video arcade, so Lance couldn't simply be turned out onto the street.

"They reached a compromise. Lance was mollified with a sundae of vanilla ice cream swimming in creme de menthe and was given the use of the VCR and Father Bryce's library of tapes while the priest went into the bathroom, poured himself a tubful of hot water to calm down, got into it, and promptly blacked out. When he came to five hours later, Lance was gone, along with the VCR, four of the tapes, and an expensive ivory crucifix from the vestibule. Lance had also drawn a pentagram in creme de menthe on the felt of the billiard table in the rec room.

"Father Bryce waited for the blackmail note that he was certain would be the next penalty to be exacted for his sins, but there was only silence. He considered returning to Fun Fun Fun and demanding that Lance give back the things he had stolen. But his was not a confrontational nature. He preferred to let sleeping dogs lie.

"He vowed to reform. In the future he would satisfy his sexual needs without taking the risks inherent in pursuing minors. He'd been assured that Papa Bear's, the bar in Stillwater, was a virtual harem of hunky, available collegiate types. Not hustlers, necessarily, but young men who had a sense that there could be some long-term advantage to be gained by associating with those more mature. Networking, it is called nowadays."

Some of us are luckier than others when it comes to getting off in the Boy Zone. Or perhaps some just have more patience. Consider Allen Ginsberg's journal entry for Feb. 16, 1956, at the beginning of his affair with the much younger Peter Orlovsky:

"...Miss bus to Peter's, walk & wandering thru 22nd St & 3rd up Sierra hill to Peter's new apartment, fence, night back of Potrero hill, Kafka welfare project homes, can't find his # on door, finally do, house dark, knock, wake him up, he comes to door in sleep shirt & shorts to his crotch & bare legs like a dancer or Knight of projects, he hugs me, says 'Allen,' welcomes, I am taken in his openness, I am awkward, like a 'ghost' he later says, neurotic ghost of lacklove & Gary argument & coldness – look over his house, I work next day, sleep there that night again, go walking that next eve & ride to North Beach, see La Vigne, borrow $2 from 2 different people, return sleep together; then move to different beds, begs, Lafcadio welcoming me hospitably, then hitch to Berkeley, Peter goes to Napa for his girl, Sheila, Whalen & Gary here, we drink, Peter returns we wander to Oakland & hear Jazz rock & roll, return, sit talk sleep, he reads me Miller, then once in bed, Gary Phil 8; Girl N come in, singing, I sit up & so does Peter, I take off covers, during songs slowly drift off Peter's Covers, clothing, he rises, drinks, dances naked out of bathroom, I disrobe & dance Indian dance while Gary plays naked, expressive wild rhythmical jumpings till my heart beats & breath exhausted, & dance with N naked, Gary takes her home, Peter & I go to bed naked, my head against his shoulder, 'Are you hot?' he asks, masturbating himself, my hand on his stomach hair, 'Yes, let me blow you,' I go down on him, we play that way, I take it in all the way, drunken, to my back of throat, 'Are you swallowing it?' Yes, I say, watch: –take it down again, sucking wildly & sweetly solid in my back of throat, reaching around to his buttocks & thighs, 'Get the Vaseline' – I haven't any – oh yes, the olive oil, I jump out to kitchen & get olive oil, come back, blow him & then grease his cock & he turns me on my side facing out, & sticks it in me, easy, I am open, finally gets it all in deep all the way, satisfying to my belly, I begin shoving in and out, then I try to get on my stomach but he holds me there, I bend forward, he says ah that feels good and fucks away I am overjoyed, turn on my belly, he's got me, & drives rubbery down, & builds up, not coming.

"Gary enters the door. Peter does not stop but stays with me fucking, but after Gary asks for his sleeping bag (we are on it) I give it to him from head top of bed Peter turns me over his cock slipped out uncome & grabs my cock to make me come, my back to him holds me around chest right hand & left hand moves round my belly & up to my cock head I grab his hand to make him go faster I say ah that's it, go on, he sez 'Now you've got it...'

"Humiliate me!
Let me lick your ass
Fuck me
Let me suck your cock
humiliate me
Please,
Ah
I'm coming."

Most sexologists agree that sexual tendencies are defined in the human being at a very early age. Ivan Bloch, the pioneer European sexologist, was convinced that the direction of sexual instinct is clear long before puberty. Kinsey and his associates said that homosexuality becomes dominant between the ages of five and fifteen. Freud thought it was even earlier.

Bloch said, "They are really long past their sexual boyhood: if they are presently engaging in homosexual behavior, it is quite likely that they have been doing so almost since onset of puberty – at which time they were not so much led 'astray' by others as *propelled* into the homosexual situation by forces within their own psyches: conversely, if they have not by age sixteen consciously experienced homosexual desire, chances are extremely slim that they ever will."

In their study, the Institute for Sex Research found that homosexual offenders against children almost never used force (whereas many of the heterosexual offenders against children did), that half the time they were friends with the children, and that in half of the cases, according to the court records (therefore, presumably, much more frequently in fact), the boys encouraged the offenders."

Interviewed specifically on the question of homosexual child molesters, Dr. Wardell P. Pomeroy, who worked on both Kinsey reports, as the findings of Indiana University's Institute for Sex Research are called, said: "Any man who is attracted to children, male or female, is a problem. Legally a minor may be eighteen or twenty-one. Actually, many children sixteen, or even fourteen, or twelve, are adult enough to know exactly what they are doing. Frankly, if it were up to me, no man involved with a minor where no compulsion or force was used would ever be punished. I don't believe it hurts either party. But if compulsion is used or if the male seeks out children repeatedly I would place him under the charge of a psychiatrist or psychologist."

"Before Sigmund Freud shattered the myth, a child was considered an innocent and pure creature," Lore Dickenstein says in her review of David Grossman's *The Book of Intimate Grammar*. "Ignorant of the raging sexuality of the adult world, the child existed in a heavenly bower of bliss, unsullied and free of sin. It is no accident that angels – think of those adorable cherubs and *putti*, rosy-cheeked and hairless – are usually portrayed as children. But the cradle fell from the bough long ago, and writers have been picking up the pieces ever since."

In Grossman's novel, prepubescent Aron Kleinfeld, omniscient, wise beyond his years but wracked with terror and inchoate longing, joins the line of hypersensitive literary juveniles that includes Oskar Matzerath in Gunter Grass's "Tin Drum" and David Schearl in Henry Roth's "Call It Sleep." "This is not the kind of company a mother would want her child to keep," Dickstein says. "These children bring trouble and grief; they know too much..."

Cruising the Boy Zone means venturing into a dangerous but exciting penile jungle, according to *Drummer*. How can you reduce the dangers? The magazine asked Dr. Norman Greenstein, an expert in the field, so to speak, and here's what he says:

"You're alone, you're horny, you want some action. Maybe you're a single guy or your lover's out of town. Maybe you feel the need to be disciplined severely and your regular boyfriend is a bottom who doesn't switch. Maybe your master would like some help with a scene and has sent you out to attract and bring home another topman. Whatever the reason, you are in cruise mode.

"Cruising can be exhilarating, terrifying, or both. It doesn't matter where you cruise, but before approaching this object of lust, consider:

"1. Don't pick up somebody when either of you is too drunk or high to have good judgment. If a guy is really attractive but there is doubt as to whether he's sober enough to consent to what you want to do, he'll still be just as cute when he's sober. Don't get him on his knees, get his phone number.

"2. Remember that being in bottom space and maintaining limits you've set for yourself are compatible. Don't allow a top to pressure you into something you don't feel safe doing, especially an unknown top you are cruising. This goes for submission, masochism, and vanilla sex.

"3. Being in top space does not require you to behave like a public utility. Don't allow a bottom to pressure you into something you don't feel safe doing.

"4. Don't avoid negotiating your limits because you're afraid you'll scare off a potential trick.

"5. Don't play beyond your limits because you are trying to impress someone.

"6. The supply of available men is, for all intents and purposes, infinite. It may not seem like it at the time but it is better to go home alone than to pick up someone who turns you off. Your emotional and physical safety depend on honesty. It's very hard to be open and honest with someone to whom you are pretending to be attracted because you were too insecure, or too desperate, or too horny to wait for someone you wanted more.

"7. Select cruising areas judiciously. Gay bashing is on the rise, especially in urban areas with large queer communities. Each person must choose for himself where to draw the line between hiding out indoors all the time and cruising in public parks. Self-defense classes, especially classes such as 'Model Mugging,' can help decrease your risk of being injured if you do get unlucky. If there are areas in your town where gay bashing is especially frequent, don't walk there alone in the middle of the night in drag or full leather. Maintaining queer visibility is not important enough to risk getting injured or killed."

THE KIDS AT THE MALL
(& KENNY FROM KENTUCKY)

John Patrick

"Oh those kids at the mall, I just love 'em," my friend Steve gushed over the phone. He'd just returned from "shopping." But Steve never bought anything, he just cruised the shoppers, specifically the kids. "Why don't you write about 'em?" he asked.

"I write about what I know. I don't know any kids at the mall. In fact, I hate malls. I hate to shop, period."

"Well, you're missing something."

Not wanting to miss *anything* in this short life, on my next trip to Fort Lauderdale I decided to go shopping. The weather conspired to force me to do this; it was raining and I decided to go to the Galleria. At least I could park under the building and not get soaked.

Not too many kids seemed to go to the Galleria to shop at Saks or Cartier but I walked the entire length of it and back again just so I wouldn't miss anything. I found the most horrifying thing about the kids I did see was their hair. Every generation takes their rebellion out on their hair but this I thought was going a bit too far. Some shaved it completely, some had it shaved in funny ways but, thankfully, most wore baseball caps (mostly turned backward) so it was difficult to tell. At least no kid at the Galleria had dyed his hair magenta like Macaulay Culkin has. Now that would have been the limit.

Another horrifying thing was that kids today certainly don't want to show anything off. They wear baggy shorts and oversized T-shirts, usually commemorating the last rock concert they went to. And why do their sneakers have to be so big and black?

I decided what I'd really like to see was some of these kids in the showers at school. Now that would be *awesome*, as they say.

On the way back to my hotel, I drove along the Ocean. I was

dismayed to find that where Marlin Beach Hotel (the site of many of my more decadent revels in the Seventies and the Eighties) once towered over its neighbors was now just a dirt field. A sign informed me that on this site would soon be Beachplace, with more places to shop, including a Gap and a Banana Republic. Now that's progress!

After this revelation, I was badly in need of a drink but wanted to try the new masseur from Texas. I discovered J.R. (that's what he advertised himself as) gave a wonderful massage and, wouldn't you know it, had a "hankerin' for big, uncut cocks." At least somebody likes me for something. I left refreshed but still in need of a drink.

The Bus Stop bar was practically deserted at five on a Friday afternoon. I wondered where all the boys had gone but was too polite to ask. Suddenly the door opened and in popped a youth who could easily have been one of those kids from the mall, except his oversized T-shirt was emblazoned, "I'll Do Anything, Just Ask." No kid at the mall would be so bold. Unfortunately, he was being closely pursued by a gent wearing a tie who was at least 75. They sat across from me and the boy lighted a cigarette. Now I noticed he had a loop and two studs in his left ear. I forgave him both those transgressions because he was cute and seemed so friendly, chatting up all the older gents near them. I figured him for a regular. Just as their drinks were served, he returned to talking with the man with the tie and ignored me. Suddenly, almost as quickly as they came it seems, they were gone.

A few minutes later, clutching the latest issue of *Hot Spots*, I made my own exit. No one urged me to stay or even to "come back soon."

I left the parking lot and was forced by the signs to turn right. As I approached the next intersection, who should be waiting at a *real* bus stop but "I'll Do Anything!" I made a quick turn into the parking lot and lowered the window.

He looked over at me and smiled. He seemed to recognize me. He was now carrying a boom box, blessedly turned off.

"Need a lift?" I offered.

"Yeah, sure," he said with a wide grin, ambling over.

He was a bit taller than I usually go for but he did have dirty blond hair and the slender body I prefer.

When he was seated in the car, with his boom box stowed in the back seat, I said, "I thought you were with the guy with tie."

"Hank? Oh, no. A friend of mine borrowed my radio, brought it up here and pawned it."

"Nice friends."

"Well, Hank helped me get it out of hock."

"Now he *is* a friend. But no sex?"

"No. He says he's too old, that he might have a heart attack."

"Boys need at least one friend like that."

By this time I was headed back to my hotel. Still, I wanted to get things straight, so to speak. "How much do you charge?"

"Depends. What do you like to do?"

"Oh, I'm easy."

He smiled. "I usually get forty."

Forty? Oh, yes, it is off-season, I hastened to remind myself. You always get a bargain in the off-season. "Do you have a regular job?"

"During season, at the Sheraton. Now I just hang out."

Now he was massaging my groin. He was either in a hurry or he really got into this.

I pulled into the hotel's parking lot as he was unzipping my pants, eager to get to the hard-on he had caused.

"Wait," I said. "We're here."

I needed to know his name; I asked.

"Kenny."

Perfect.

Moments later, he was on the bed, me kneeling over his naked chest.

"Hmmm, I love uncut cocks," he sighed, pulling the foreskin back and examining the head of the erection closely. The second natural man fan that day. Truly amazing. He began nibbling on my cock. He was hungry. Soon he was sucking like there was no tomorrow.

"Where did you learn to do that?" I finally asked.

"You know how it is back in the hills of Kentucky."

"No, not really, but I wish I did. When did you start suckin' dick?"

"When I was six."

"*Six?*"

"Yeah. It was a lot of fun until my brothers discovered they were straight."

"That occurs at about fourteen or fifteen. Older if you're lucky."

Talk about luck! An incredible spark of lust and excitement jolted up through my cock. He reamed and twisted and slammed my dick deep down his throat until I felt my load quickly boiling up. I was so close, yet I held back, feeling swept away by a maelstrom of fears and joys beyond my understanding. A low groan of pleasure escaped my lips and I knew for certain I wanted this Kentucky babe to do more than just this. His hand on my thigh slid slowly upward, sending shivers up my spine. He stopped inches from my balls and started backing down again, murmuring something to himself about softness. Next his left hand reached out to glide across my hairy chest. His nearly hairless chest was dappled with sweat. His eyes slipped shut as he tweaked my nipples while he continued sucking my cock with world-class fervor, as if he was determined to suck up every possible ounce of cum I could muster. He kept screwing my right tit and then my left until they both were numb. I felt my body shiver and thrash, my hips convulsing upward as they fucked his mouth. The more I moaned and groaned, the faster his mouth worked and the more self-satisfied his grunts of pleasure became. Finally, I stopped resisting the inevitable and began coming. His grunts of appreciation grew louder as he unleashed my cock from his mouth and watched it spurt on his chest. My own groans of pleasure rivaled his, and then, exhausted, I lifted myself from him and lay on my back next to him. He gave my spent cock one last squeeze and then bounded off the bed and hurried into the bathroom. I heard the shower running and then, in seconds it seemed, he was back, nude this time, with what at that moment I thought was the hardest, meanest-looking uncut dick I'd ever seen. His huge balls hung low and heavy between his legs, swaying slightly as he stood silently before me – waiting for further instructions.

I am selective when it comes to cocksucking but I am always ready to be butt-fucked, and Kenny had the perfect tool for the job. I rolled over, saying, "You know where I want that, Kenny."

I had several condoms on the nightstand and he helped himself. Suddenly, one thrust followed another, each fiercer, more sadistic than the last. My ass arched upward, driving his dick even deeper into me. I looked behind me to see he had closed his eyes, tilted his head back, and had slipped into a world of his own. He shivered in a spasm of shattering sensuality so intense it made me jealous for a moment. His huge prick changed its angle of entry just enough to slam hard into me on nearly every stroke, and I ground my ass into his crotch. Suddenly, it seemed he was having a seizure as his massive manmeat exploded. As he came down from his high, he continued ramming my butt, hugging me to him.

Finally, slowly, as though relishing a slight delay to intensify his ultimate pleasure, his cock popped from the opening and I dropped to the mattress.

"Wow, you sure learned a lot back in Kentucky," I said.

"You liked it?"

"Loved it."

He took another shower and quickly dressed. He didn't say so but I presumed I was to return him to the bus stop. I threw on a part of shorts and followed him, carrying his radio, to the car.

As we arrived at our destination, I asked, "Haven't you forgotten something?"

I pulled a fifty out of my pocket.

He chuckled. "Oh, sometimes I have such a good time I forget."

I still couldn't believe this. Was he for real, or was I only dreaming?

"How long you in town for?" he asked.

"Just tonight." I really didn't know, but it was better to play it safe.

He said he'd take the bus south. He drew the boom box from its resting place in the back.

"Oh – " I started.

"Yeah?" he asked hopefully, his big brown cow eyes meeting mine. Damn, I *liked* him. I wanted to ask him to stay, and yet I didn't. I'd had what I came to town for – in spades.

I didn't need any more.

"Do you ever go to the mall?" I asked.

"Which mall?"

"Any mall."

He shook his head. "No, not if I can help it."

I smiled and handed him another fifty. "Good boy."

The author's Fort Lauderdale adventures continue in the anthology "Boys of the Night," with the story, "Sunglasses After Dark"

HEAT

John Patrick

A look of interest. Jerry can read it. The boy's eyes reveal everything. As if without thinking, Jerry casually rubs his fingertips across the bulge in his jeans. "It's hotter than hell in here."

"Yes, it'll be awhile." The boy's eyes are fixed on the bulge. Then his eyes move upward, and when they meet Jerry's, his gaze does not waver.

The boy is Jerry's type: pretty and blond, his body delectable. Jerry says, "You're gorgeous."

The boy smiles, comes forward. Jerry kisses him, a warm kiss on the boy's sensual lips. The boy's mouth opens immediately. For an instant, the kiss blazes between them as Jerry gently passes his hand across the boy's firm buns.

The boy pulls away.

"Stay with me," Jerry urges.

"In an hour."

"Do you promise?"

"Yes, I get off work in an hour."

The boy hurries out, his toolbox in his hand.

"Oh, and thanks for fixing my air," Jerry calls after him.

After the boy leaves, Jerry trembles at his own audacity. Never in his life has he attempted anything like this. The Florida heat has made him daring. And the boy. That film of sweat on his upper lip. That splendid ass as he bent over the air conditioning controls. Nothing ventured, nothing gained, Jerry thinks. He hasn't taken this vacation to be celibate. Jerry hates celibacy. And to think how upset he'd been when he couldn't get the air to work! Just think what he would have missed if it *had* worked!

Jerry passes an hour in sexual heat. He plays with his swollen cock but doesn't want to come. Pre-cum forms on the head and he wipes it away, tastes it.

An hour passes but it seems like ten hours to Jerry. Finally, there's a gentle tap on the door.

The boy looks both ways before entering the now frigid room.

"If they catch me, I'm fired."

"I understand," Jerry says. Jerry put on his jeans ten minutes ago. His cock is still hard. The boy's hand goes to it immediately.

There will be no preliminaries. Jerry's jeans are opened, yanked down, his erection devoured. He has been so close to coming for so long, it is impossible for him not to come now. The boy is a superb cocksucker. Just as Jerry is about to explode, the boy releases the cock and starts sucking Jerry's big balls. The cum gushes from the cock and splatters on the carpet.

"Wow," the boy moans. "Big dick, big come."

Jerry pulls him up, kisses him.

Holding the boy tightly, Jerry says, "I don't even know your name."

"Ken."

"Ken," Jerry repeats it several times, as if he is savoring it. He goes back to the lips, shoves his tongue in Ken's mouth.

They part. Ken gives Jerry a coy smile as he strips off his shirt and jeans. He wears no underwear. "I don't even know *your* name," Ken says, mimicking Jerry.

"Jerry."

The boy nods. "The man in room 101."

As Ken turns his back a moment, Jerry is transfixed by the boy's buttocks: lovely, irresistible. He feels a tightening in his belly, his cock coming to attention again, rising awake and standing tall. Never mind the book he'd planned to read tonight; his hunger is too sharp.

Ken walks over to Jerry, smiles. The boy's face is too thin and angular to be handsome, but sweetness is there. And the eagerness. Jerry reaches up to pinch a pink nipple, then pushing at Ken's hip to make the boy turn around.

The boy knows what Jerry wants. It's what they all want. What he is happy to give them. After parting his legs, he bends forward a bit to offer himself, to show himself from the rear.

God, I love his, Jerry thinks, his fingertips gliding across the smooth skin. Just a tickling touch, first one globe and then the other. Then he spits on his cockhead and gets inside quickly, no preliminaries, the head sliding into the tight anus.

Ken groans. He had already lubricated his ass in the lavatory of the maintenance shop. That is something his father had taught him: always be prepared. Ken groans again, squirming his rear on Jerry's cock, shaking his hips, shuddering from head to toe as the cock is worked in and out. He jacks off and comes quickly, his sweetness spilling on the floor. He is shaking again when Jerry comes again.

But Jerry's cock does not leave the ass. Ken remains bent over like a bitch-dog in heat, his ass open and vulnerable, ready for whatever Jerry wants.

"You want more?"

"Please."

Jerry pulls his cock from Ken and shoves his thumb in the opening.

"Wiggle it. Wiggle it on my thumb."

Ken churns his hips, rolling his ass, his anus gripping Jerry's thumb as the other fingers of Jerry's hand remained on the outside of his wet ass, stroking it

Suddenly Jerry pulls his hand away and rises.

"Don't move."

Ken remains where he is, bent over, as Jerry goes to his suitcase in the alcove.

Jerry returns to the room with a huge black dildo.

"My traveling companion," Jerry explains. "I call him Rufus." The boy looks at it, his eyes hotter than ever because getting fucked by Jerry's cock was something special, but to get fucked by Jerry's foot-long traveling companion is something else again.

"Oh, God," Ken moans.

Without dawdling, Jerry moves in and uses his hand to guide the round knob of the dildo to Ken's anus.

Ken groans as it goes in. He relaxes and opens himself. He spreads his knees farther apart on the bed and groans again as he feels Jerry's hands grasp his buttocks.

"Easy, man."

"Feel good?"

"Yeah. God, yeah."

Jerry starts fucking him slowly, watching the black shaft as it slides in and out of the boy's stretched anus, the hole like a round mouth sucking on the black cylinder. He slides a hand under the dildo to find Ken's hard-on. He works it as he continues thrusting. Ken begins a continuous moaning and trembles as he comes. Finally Jerry pulls Rufus out and makes Ken turn around.

"Go on, get it in your mouth," Jerry says, his voice coaxing.

With a soft cry, Jerry suckles Rufus. Jerry is hard again, watching Ken suck his dildo.

Ken's face flushes and he moans, his eyes on Jerry's cock, his legs trembling as he realizes how much he wants it, how much he wants to be completely dominated by this startling man. His ass throbs. In Siesta Beach. Of all places in the world, this had to happen in Siesta Beach.

"What do you want?" Jerry asks softly.

"I want you to make love to me."

"No, I won't do that."

Ken's heart sinks. He stares at Jerry. "Why not?"

"I'll fuck you, but I won't make love to you. We don't know each well enough for love."

Ken begs. "Please – "

"What?"

"I don't know."

"Do you want my fuck again?"

"Yes."

Ken shudders as Jerry spreads his cheeks apart and enters him again, still from behind. Jerry will not take the boy in his arms and make love to him. Not yet.

Ken is hard again. Is this really happening? He feels so helpless with this stud, his mind whirling with his need to have Jerry ravish his body.

After Jerry comes again, he lies back on the bed. Ken gets up. Jerry takes a couple of deep breaths as his eyes follow Ken across the room to the bathroom. He is so hot he hardly knows what to do. He pours a drink for himself from the bottle of bourbon on the nightstand. The ice cubes in the bucket have all melted. He gulps the drink as he tries to regain his composure, wondering if the kid will ever emerge from the bathroom again and what he will do if he does. Jerry finishes his drink and lies back down on the bed.

Then after a few minutes he sees Ken coming back across the floor, walking cool and slow and sultry, and, oh, God, he stands over the bed, a look of desire still in his emerald green eyes.

"I liked that. I want more," Ken says.

Jerry takes Ken by the hand, reaches up and puts his arms around his neck and turns his mouth to his. Their tongues dance around each other as their bodies meld together, and Jerry feels his cock swelling again.

Ken returns the caress, pinching and rolling Jerry's nipples between his fingers. Jerry probes his mouth with his tongue as they kiss, and runs his hands down the firm muscles of Ken's back to cup his ass in his hands.

Oh, Jerry knows what Ken wants. And now he is willing to give it to him. He will make love to this boy as no one else ever has.

Ken slowly sinks to his knees next to the bed and licks up the insides of Jerry's thighs to where his cock waits, hard, hot, inviting. He grabs it with his lips. He presses against Jerry and moans deeply. He drinks him in, really going to work on that long, cut cock. As he nuzzles and laps, swirls and twirls it in his mouth, his cock seems to grow. Jerry thrusts his hips against Ken's mouth, Ken jerks in rhythm as he face-fucks him, and growls, a long, low sound in his throat as his passion increased.

Ken feels Jerry's orgasm coming on and backs off. He lowers himself over the throbbing prick. He moans and heaves against Jerry.

The hot flush of Ken's face rubs against Jerry's face. He cannot refuse. He is too excited, too overcome with an intense desire not to submit. Jerry has never been as wildly aroused. He's amazed at himself. He came to the beach depressed, not expecting anything to happen. His lover of five years had left him for another four months ago and he hadn't had any luck after that. He thought a little vacation would be good for him. Little did he realize how good.

Ken bends his head and turns it sideways. His warm wet mouth captures a succulent nipple.

Jerry moans as he cradles Ken's head in his hands.

Ken moves from one pec to the other, his tongue working,

his lips sucking and nibbling. Jerry feels a glorious ache in his nipples. His cock is ready. He wonders whether Ken is as excited as he is. Ken continues licking and nibbling at Jerry's pecs.

Jerry comes. He cannot stop it. Jerry feels marvelously wanton and voluptuous. All through Jerry's orgasm, Ken is kissing him all over his face and neck and shoulders. Ken's lips touch Jerry's eyelids, the tip of his nose, his cheeks, his jawline, the point of his chin, and then his mouth slides back down to his pecs.

Jerry has never felt so adored. His last lover certainly never showered him with affection like this. Ken's touch is so deft. He knows exactly how to kiss every part of him to produce the most incredible sensations. Now in dawns on Jerry that Ken must have a lover. He is too young to be such a marvelous lover without some training. Somone has taught him well.

As they lie in each other's arms, Jerry asks, "Can I meet your lover?"

"My lover?"

"You must have a lover."

"Well, sort of – "

. . .

Jerry is filled with great passion as he gazes down at Jimmy's proffered ass. Yesterday he'd had Ken almost exactly the same way. But this was different. Jimmy is dark-haired and hairy, mature, his masculinity fully developed. Jerry finds the wet asshole with his thumb and enters it without delay. Ken is sitting next to where Jimmy is kneeling on the bed and he takes Jerry's hand and sucks his fingers. After a few moments, Jerry pulls his thumb out and replaces it with the three fingers Ken has been sucking.

Jimmy moans as he feels Jerry's fingers push inside his ass, the strong digits filling him, stretching his passage. "Is this what you want?"

"Oh, yes," Jimmy cries.

All Jerry is certain of is an intense desire to please his new friend Ken by fucking his fuck buddy.

Jerry steps away for a moment and pulls a long,

double-ended dildo from his case.

Ken's eyes bulge. "The dildo king!" he cries.

In moments, Jerry has inserted one end into Ken and one end into Jimmy.

Ken starts moving at once – tightening his legs up near his waist. Each time he moves, the other end of the dildo pushes into Jimmy.

Jerry squats next to them and begins manipulating both their cocks at the same time.

"Now," he says, "here we go."

His expert fingers fill both boys with the most incredible pleasure, their cocks pounding in direct response to his constant motion.

Within seconds, Jimmy is arching up, slamming down onto that dildo – no longer certain of Ken's movements – only aware of that dildo ramming into him over and over.

"Nice, boys, very nice," Jerry says, continually massaging their cocks.

Jimmy bursts into an orgasm that has him racked in pleasure, jamming that dildo – fucking it – imagining his childhood friend Ken on the other end – causing resistance with his tight, tight ass.

Surrounded by the boys' scents, feeling their heat Jerry arches into ecstasy. He comes hard, so hard he is screaming, "Yes, oh yes, so fuckin' hot!"

His body tightens and then suddenly he relaxes, totally spent.

He opens his eyes. Jimmy has removed the end of the dildo that had been inserted in him and is ramming the other end into Ken at a furious pace. Ken, moaning, is jacking off, on the edge. Jerry goes to him, caresses him, sucks his nipples.

Ken's orgasm starts building immediately. He gasps and makes a plaintive sound as he feels Jimmy penetrating his anus, Jerry sucking his skin.

Ken cries out as his cock explodes. Jerry holds him as the orgasm racks his body from head to toe. Jimmy leans over and kisses Ken on his neck as he brings Ken down gently with his probing dildo until Ken finishes.

Jerry backs off. Now he feels awkward. He wants to throw himself into Ken's arms, but Jimmy is doing that now. Jerry knows so little about these youths. His heart beats more rapidly as he remembers yesterday afternoon. So unexpected. First that rush just inside the door, but a cool distance as Ken went about adjusting the air conditioner.

Watching the boys lie together, kissing each other, Jerry blushes, pours himself another bourbon. "God, it's hotter than hell in here." He chuckles.

"It's not hot enough," Ken says. "Come over here. Put your drink down and come closer."

His pulse racing again, Jerry places his drink on the nightstand and slides across the bed to get closer to the fuck buddies.

"That's better," Ken says, draping his left arm around Jerry's shoulders, and then he bends his head to kiss Jerry's cheek.

His head lifting as he feels the tingling kiss, Jerry moans. He slumps against the back of the bed as Ken continues kissing him. Then he feels Jimmy's fingers grip his penis. His eyes closed, Jerry shudders as he feels Ken's fingers rubbing his nipples, rubbing the stiff points until they seem to burn like two flames.

Jerry opens his eyes, blushing as he gazes at Jimmy manipulating his cock. His cock is soon swollen with his excitement.

"Oh, boys..."

"Yes?"

"Make love to me!"

With a satisfied throaty murmur, Ken drops down to take a burning-hard nipple between his teeth.

Jimmy takes Jerry's cock in his mouth and Jerry shudders, happy, so happy he can scarcely believe it.

Jimmy reaches for the dildo, Rufus, the ebony marvel from San Francisco. The cock is perfect: not too long, pliant enough to take any angle, and thick enough to make a man groan.

The boys want Jerry groaning. Jimmy reaches out and gently strokes Jerry's firm buttocks. Jerry visibly trembles as Rufus slides into his anus. Ken runs his fingertips over Jerry's erection, already coated with a milky gloss.

His eyes hot, Jerry continues looking. Ken fondles the cock and they all groan as Jimmy pushes Rufus forward to fill Jerry's passage. Jerry groans.

Ken breathes against Jerry's ear. "Like it?"

"Oh, yes!"

Jimmy works the dildo, thrusting, churning in the tight ass. "Come on, man."

"Fuck me, Jimmy!"

Ken cries, "Come on, come on, come in my hand."

Ken watches Jerry's face as the orgasm ripples through Jerry's body. Jimmy keeps the dildo moving, more gently now, a slow stroking as Jerry comes down to earth again and slumps against Ken's shoulder.

When the boys have dressed and are ready to leave, Jerry tells them he has only one more day of vacation. They agree to meet the next evening. Jerry has already made plans to return to Siesta Beach in six months.

"Well, sir, I hope you won't have any more trouble with your air, but if you do, just call maintenance," Ken says.

Then he turns and winks at Jerry as he leaves.

BANJEE BOY

Chris Leslie

I started out cruising in Brooklyn's Prospect Park just after midnight. A spring shower had washed the sidewalks and left a clean scent lingering in the air.

I walked along Prospect Park West, checking out the many men hanging out there. The foliage was just returning to the trees, and there was just enough cover. The regulars were checking out an area that they hadn't been able to cruise since the leaves fell. I looked them over and, finding no one to hang out with, I continued on to the bridge.

I cruised the shadows under the bridge to no avail. But as I stepped out of the tunnel a cute Puerto Rican-looking guy was entering. He was along the lines of what I was looking for, with a fade and sharply shaved facial hair. He was a few inches shorter than me, and was wearing a football team jersey over a long-sleeve T-shirt. Most importantly, he gave off an aura of street-smartness that was out of place here; he was more the type I'd seen hanging out on a Lower East Side street corner, drinking a 40 with his friends, than the kind of kid you find cruising the park. I was immediately smitten.

I stopped and watched him as he passed me, but he hardly looked my way. Encountering him changed my relationship to the park. Suddenly, I was the one drooling at the young, aloof banjee kid. But that did stop me from cruising him. I turned around to see if he looked back to give me an indication to follow him, but he didn't, so I shrugged my shoulders and continued on my way. I knew that he would most likely find nothing in the tunnel and continue on to where I was headed, the small meadow with the reflecting pools (known as "Mount Prospect Park").

As I crossed the street above the bridge and got onto the path he was right behind me. I slowed down, on the pretense of lighting a cigarette, and he tried to check me out in the darkness. I grabbed the crotch of my pants and walked slowly without looking at him, letting him check me out.

We walked together for a few feet in silence until he spoke.

"What's up?" he asked, giving me full borough realness in just two words (one word, actually, considering the way he said it).

"Nothing," I said. "Just hanging out."

"Me too."

We walked in silence along the path, about five feet apart, strolling slowly and silently - that banjee thing where two best friends walk down the street without speaking that I picked up from watching fierce boys walk down the avenues in Manhattan. The two of us together looked a little rough, and we scared a few guys who happened by as we walked. Instead of cruising us as we passed, they moved to the other side of the path and looked the other way. We made one guy so nervous that he walked off the path and crashed through the underbrush until he reached the safety of the road, and then watched us pass with a quizzical look on his face. Being part of a small posse gave me a rush, and I started to get a hard-on.

I looked at the boy, and this time he spoke. "So what do you get into?" I was instantly cautious, because this is the way a boy tries to convince another boy that sex is where one guy services another, rather than a free-for-all session. "I like to get my dick sucked," I said, with a deep and quiet voice.

He stopped short and looked like he was about to walk away. "You don't suck cock?" he asked. We were standing near a street light, and I checked him out carefully while I considered the situation. He looked really, really fit – his face was slim, and his shoulders nearly filled out his oversized football jersey. His baggy jeans gave little definition to anything but his ass, which was small and round. He looked like a fairly-well-off inner city kid.

"Do you suck dick, or not?" he demanded, growing impatient.

He was cute, no doubt about it, and I didn't want him to get away. "Not usually, but I'll suck your dick," I said, trying to give him the idea that he was a special circumstance.

He nodded and looked me up and down, as if he wasn't sure yet if he wanted me to. "I don't get into sucking dick or anything. Got it?"

I nodded, giving him my best open-mouthed poker face. But when he walked off into the underbrush, I rolled my eyes and stuck my tongue out at him.

We walked until we couldn't be seen from the path, then searched for a place to hang out. We were walking near a fallen tree, and I led us over to it. This looked like the right spot, and we stood and looked at each other for a moment. Just for kicks, I said, "You don't suck dick at all?" and looked back the way we came, pretending to be uncertain. There were a lot of other guys out there, and I easily could have found someone to do me the favor.

He knew this, and pondered the situation. "Well, maybe a little," he said. He was waffling, but all I really wanted was for him to admit that he would. Since we had called each other's bluff, I decided to continue to play the game. But not before I grinned at him. He looked away with an out-of-character smile for a few seconds.

When he regained his composure, he motioned for me to have a seat on the stump. I sat down and he sat down on the tree trunk, which put his dick right in my face. One of nature's small wonders – a blowjob seat better than in any sex club anywhere, in the middle of Prospect Park. He put his hands on his sides, leaned back, and waited. I reached up and massaged his crotch, feeling around until I found his dick. I was finally up close to him, and I used the opportunity to check out his labels. He was wearing Guess? painter pants, about three sizes too big, and dark brown Dr. Martens. He had the whole outfit down.

It took quite a bit of rubbing to get him hard, which gave me even more banjee realness. When his dick finally stiffened, it snaked off toward his left pocket. It wasn't real long, but it was certainly a handful.

I unzipped his pants and continued to stroke his dick, now through his underwear – which turned out to be white Calvins. Another anomaly; I was expecting bikini briefs. This boy had seemed to be a pretty rough street kid, but I was starting to have serious doubts. I know that appearances can be deceiving: If those kids who come up to me on the street and start to talk to me in Spanish only knew that I was a white kid from a farm town in upstate New York, I'd never get laid.

"Suck my dick already," he said. He was right; this was no time to be musing about cultural appropriateness. I took his dick into my mouth. "That's right. Suck that dick."

His dick was now hard, and it twitched lightly as I started to work on it. It was just big enough for me to call big, but not so big that I couldn't get it into my mouth. It had a loose-fitting foreskin that he pulled out of the way with one hand. A light smell of cum drifted from his open fly. I wondered if he had jerked off, or had already had sex with someone tonight.

I sucked his dick slowly, and he muttered encouragement. It tasted good, and it had a thicker spot toward the middle that felt good as it slipped in and out of my lips. I reached up and pulled down his briefs a bit, letting his balls hang free. They were shaved, leaving a light sprinkling of hair above his dick and between his legs. Shaved balls on a banjee boy? I don't think so. This was a gay boy, I was certain now, no doubt about it. But instead of turning me off, strangely it made me really hot – somehow the idea of one poser sucking off another turned me on. I massaged his balls and worked up and down on the entire length of his dick.

I pulled up his shirt, and, as I guessed, he had a tight, cut stomach. I rubbed his belly button, which like his thighs was covered with a light sprinkling of hair, and a small piece of lint came out. He was watching and saw, and with an embarrassed laugh brushed it off his stomach. I continued rubbing his stomach with his dick seated at the back of my throat.

"You like suckin' my dick, don't you," he said gruffly. I grabbed the base of his dick and worked his foreskin up, then sucked on his protected head. He liked that, and started to breathe heavy.

"I want to cum. Do you want my load?"

"Yeah, give it to me."

"Jerk me off and suck the skin," he said. I started jerking him off, lightly and quickly with two fingers, while sucking on his foreskin. Pre-cum was pulsing out of his dick, filling my mouth with a sweet flavor. This boy tasted so good, and I could hardly wait for him to let his load fly.

It didn't take long. His dick started to twitch, and I slowed my pace. "Oh, yeah. Take my load," he said, coming. His sweet load spurted into my mouth, and I didn't stop jerking him off until the final spasm of his orgasm squeezed the last drop of cum out of his dick.

I moved off of his dick and looked at him. He was sitting

back, with his mouth open and his eyes closed. I smiled as I leaned over and quietly spat the cum to the side. He opened his eyes and rubbed the top of my head. "That felt really good." He leaned over and gave me a peck on the cheek.

I stood up and fixed my still-hard dick, which was poking out of the top of my pants. "Are you okay?" he asked, motioning to the bulge.

"Yeah, I'm fine." I'm sure he would have sucked me off, but I didn't want to kill the moment. He stood up and pecked me on my cheek again, smiling, as he zipped up. I stood and wiped off my chin, and smiled back.

"Are you sure you're okay?" he asked again.

"Yeah," I said.

"You didn't get to cum."

No straight boy worries about such things, and I smiled. "Don't worry about it. I'm pretty beat, anyway."

"Me, too. Do you want to get going?"

"Yeah."

We took the road out of the park, barely speaking except to introduce ourselves (he said his name was Octavio). We stopped walking when we reached the road that turns off and heads toward Grand Army Plaza. I kicked a few pebbles as we stood, not knowing what to say to each other. Finally, he spoke.

"I'm not usually that way."

"You mean you don't come here that often?"

"That's not what I said," he said with a grin.

"What do you mean?"

"I don't know. I'm usually the other way." He wasn't being very clear. I looked at him with a question on my face. "You know. I'm usually in your shoes." Playing stupid, I looked at my feet. "No," he said, laughing. He gave up on trying to continue the charade, lost his accent and said in a clear voice, "I'm usually more of a bottom."

I looked at him sharply, as if I was shocked to hear him speak that way. He was taking a bit of a risk; after all, other than the fact that I liked to suck his dick, I hadn't given him any clues as to my feelings about my sexuality. He saw the rough look on my face and looked away, embarrassed.

"That's all right," I said. "I'm usually more of a top."

"Really? That's funny." A few guys were walking in our direction, so to maintain appearances I stepped up on a rail-road tie and put my hands in my pockets, looking at my feet as I walked for affect. We were nearing the entrance to the park. "If you're a top, why were you doing all of the work?" he asked.

I didn't have a good answer to that so I kept silent and shrugged my shoulders. Truth be told, I am certainly not into the "top" and "bottom" thing – he was a cute guy, had a beautiful dick, and I was certainly more than happy to suck it.

There was a cold wind blowing through the plaza, and I was starting to shiver. "Let's get going," I said. We walked to the spires that circle the Sailors and Soldiers monument and hesitated. He watched the cars go around the circle, I studied the monument. It's an awkward thing to ask for someone's number after a sleazy encounter in Prospect Park, yet I wanted to ask for his, and he for mine. But after a minute we looked at each other, and he offered his hand.

"So maybe I will see you again?" he said. I shook his hand and said I hoped I would. He walked off toward the subway and I walked down Flatbush Avenue toward home...

THE SEX FEST

J. Nagle

Yes, here you are again. I had been wondering if you would be here tonight. You were seated, alone and small, at a table in the front room as I passed you. You looked directly at me, with interest, even, but appeared not to recognize me.

When I passed you in the next room, I felt myself exhale. A fine mist of sweat covered my neck and armpits, and my heart was pounding. I remembered to breathe deeply. When I reached the door to the bathroom, I opened and closed it on the crowded room behind me. The face in the mirror looked slightly distraught. I consciously breathed the tension out of each part of my body. Ten shakes, I told myself. I inhaled deeply and shook everything I could muster through my shoulders and down the length of body. No, I would not hold this energy in my body throughout the night; I would stay with the intent I brought in. I was here to fulfill my own desires, period.

When I felt grounded, I moved into the main room of the sex fest. So many bodies taking pleasure before, with, on and about one another. I was sure you and I would lose each other in the crowd. We hadn't spoken in so long, I didn't think this setting was the right one to reconnect anyway. The wounds still felt fresh.

So, yes, here you are again, indeed. We may well have been dancing toward this place all night. If the truth be known, I did think it more than pure coincidence that you appeared in my line of vision whenever I was just getting turned on and would have most appreciated your furtive, curious gaze. Your presence raised my heat several degrees, in spite of myself.

And, when you walked in on my bare, freshly showered ass in the locker rooms, we both turned and suppressed an involuntary smile. If there is a Creator, he's enjoying a good laugh over our awkwardness – or perhaps our chance meetings were really a Blessing. It would be difficult, after all, for buck naked, sex-crazed boys to fixate on anything but the pleasures at hand, so to speak. In this setting, our falling-out seemed crazy.

Still, I am more than a little surprised to find you here intentionally, once again, damned if either of us knows top from bottom, or cares for that matter, but rather, only that your mouth is now on my cock, pleasuring me. I am beyond surprised to find you so ready to work me, to use your knowledge and skill for the highest of purposes, my pleasure.

As you put me in the sling, my gaze moves from your green eyes that pierce like a needle to your strong shoulders, your tight pecs, down your muscular stomach to your burgeoning crotch. My equilibrium falters. How unsettling is my attraction for you!

Damn, I forgot you had such a big dick. I remember I once said I didn't really care to hear about just how big it was, and how the guys at the baths begged to suck it. Such things are trivial. But that was before.

Now I can feel my mouth twitching to suck on your prize cock slowly, like a teething baby, sucking for its life's sweet nourishment. You are waiting for me to tell you to take off your jockstrap, whose fabric is already stretched beyond capacity. And don't think this fact is lost on Essex and his new friend Jared, whose nipple rings are clanking into each other nearby, they are watching you suck my dick and jerking one other off, looking into each other's eyes, then back to your cock. Essex wants to slide his uncut number between your beautiful, firm, tight ass cheeks while you fuck me – I can read that in his gaze, and I find my hips bucking toward the ceiling at the thought of such a sandwich. Jared wants to kneel at your feet and worship your cock. When he sees a cock like that, he goes into a sort of trance on the way down to his knees. And I know how you hate that. But Essex won't release him just now – he has other plans for Jared's hungry mouth.

Jared looks a little like Sly Stallone but smarter and prettier. I was lucky enough to have had my hand in the very same glove that found its way into Jared's beautiful ass and fucked him gently, then rather firmly while he sucked Essex's cock earlier in the party. They had said that I would have my turn, that they were going to watch me get fucked tonight, that I would be their entertainment, that they would jerk off to me. Were they psychic, or what?

Two gay boys, jerking off to me getting fucked by this most unlikely suspect. I wanted to burst out laughing. I wanted to come really hard.

Now I want to incinerate your jockstrap and suck you silly right now – but I'd rather beg you. I think it's taking every ounce of control I have to be this nasty with myself. I sit up, wrap my legs around you and squeeze you close, feeling your fabric-constrained erection against my stomach. Your eyes are getting glassy and unfocused. I gently flick your nipples with my wet thumbs. A guttural moan escapes your mouth.

"Don't fuck me until I say," I sigh.

You frown slightly, then nod. I don't know that I'm any surer than you what I'm up to. I feel as though I am taking direction from some Other Place.

I must do something about your huge, engorged cock. I peel off the white contraption from your cramped, swaying phallus with my toes, and toss it to Essex and Jared. It may be all they get of you tonight, because for right now, and until I am completely spent, you are mine. They move spontaneously into some sort of erotic improvisation, with the jock as their prop, like some sacred fuck object, sniffing it, sliding it across their cocks, into their ass cracks like a g-string. Any excuse for art. Or are they making fun of me? It looks to me like they'd genuinely like to fuck you. I'm tempted to make you bend over and be their toy while I jerk off to you taking it up your tight, cock-virgin ass – but not tempted enough. Next party! Besides, I'd enjoy the relaxed, unrushed process of personally working your tight little asshole up to taking a real, live cock. I take that back. Enjoy isn't a strong enough word.

Spasming with the thought of colonizing your canal, I slide back into the sling, reposition my legs, and press my wet asshole up against your cock, all the way up to the quivering head. "Fuck me," I whisper, smiling with mischief. You look at me, raise an arched eyebrow, and a large, tattooed hand slides a turbo condom down your horse shaft. The shaved head of a stranger suddenly encloses your cock for a few moments, sucking and sliding up and down. Your eyes gloss over. The man leaves quickly, distracted by a new lover, and you look at me expectantly. "Fuck me," I say again, this time a little louder. You push the sling up and tuck the head of your dick barely inside my asshole, just as far in as you know you're allowed. You know this will drive me mad within moments. I reach for my cock, but you pull my hand away clamping it into a restraint. As you lean forward, you press against my asshole, and I let out a little gasp of pleasure. You move away immediately. You didn't mean for me to have that...yet.

You pride yourself on your discipline, and want to hide your desire for this scene. But I know better, and I can see every hair's breadth of your increased want, and that alone could make me come. Do you know that? Maybe you're purposely flashing your desire to turn me on, or maybe you just can't contain it. I don't know which thought is more thrilling.

Jared is sucking Essex really fast now. Bite him real soft for me, I think toward them. Essex is pulling on his own nipple rings, which are connected by a string of pearls. Essex is such an artsy fag with those pearls and I want to tug on those pearls and watch his irises disappear, like before.

You resume position, just barely inside me, moving in and out, scarcely a centimeter of depth – you have one hand on your cock guiding it in circles almost inside me, and another stroking my hard cock. After a few minutes of this, I mutter, "Fuck me..." and you move in a full inch, and I let out a sharp cry.

"Oh, god, fuck me, fuck me, please, please god, I can't stand it!"

You move away entirely for a moment, and I feel on the verge.

Then I feel your warm, soft, strong hands pressing my tits hard into my rib cage, and then bearing down my torso, first softly, almost tickling then in long, slow scratches. I am shuddering, on the brink of incoherence. You are smiling fiendishly.

I feel pre-orgasmic rushes, and consciously absorb this energy back into my body. I am now hypersensitized to your touch and the desire in your gaze; I am on an edge where I could linger for any length of time – depending on what you do to me. I am on the tips of your fingers, and you can play me hard or soft, I am your toy, your instrument. I am singing and moaning and gasping entirely in response to you. I have surrendered all notions that I have any control over what's happening here –

My insides are twitching madly to the thought of you deep inside me. "Please," I whimper.

You lean forward and lovingly catch the tear in your lips, smiling. "Please what?" you ask, with wide-eyed mock innocence.

"Please...please, I need you..."

As you lean over me, I embrace you gently, finding your warm, almost hot cock in the swirl of soft thick hair. I suck gently, my lips and teeth finding your pleasure points. You bellow out loud, and let me begin steadily stroking your wet, insistent cock. In my fingers, your cock swells even more. Could I have imagined you this hard, full to bursting, my hand straining to contain you?

I stroke you harder, in rhythm to the music, and sliding out of the sling, we fall to the floor, surrounded by soft lights. You wrap your whole body around me, which I can barely stand. I begin to scream and thrash, "Fuck me, now," I demand, and by now the whole room wants you to fuck me, and probably them, too. Essex and Jared have ceased their duet completely and are watching us with incredulousness. Why, they must be wondering, won't he fuck that boy? Maybe they both want to fuck me. Maybe I'll be gang-banged tonight!

You roll me onto my back and pin my arms above my head, locking your blazing eyes knowingly with mine, just grazing my nipples. I am nearly unconscious with desire. I think I may pass out.

As you finally enter me fully I burst into tears and you hold me there, nuzzling my neck. I grab your ass cheeks and shove. You concede a scant extra inch to my plea. I am thrusting madly against you.

Your body, tensed, suddenly relaxes, and you slide in and out of me easily.

And of course I grip you with all the suction I can muster, and throw my legs around you, locking you in. You are moving in circles, and the long, slow surge that began somewhere at the base of my spine is traveling up my body.

Grinding your face into mine, you are kissing me into fierce demanding contractions, but you have taken your cock away.

"What was it you wanted?" you whisper.

"Oh, god," I moan.

With a knowing smile, you slide slowly halfway in and stop. I wrestle my arms free and take your ass in my hands and shove. I don't stop, I can't stop. We are rocking and coming but you still feel hard inside me and the whole room is giving us energy and I am completely locked around you, I roll over on top, easily pinning you, and I bounce up and down on your cock...

We are alone now, no longer at the party. I barely remember the ride home.

I'm here, stretched out on my own bed. Your body is very warm. Yes, you are lying beside me fast asleep.

I recall that I began this fantasy once, and thought then that I could never finish it. That, instead, the depths of my own desire would drown me, would finish me off for good. Now I am considering the possibility that I was right. My mouth is open and wet on your smooth chest and your stray tendrils caress my neck. I realize I am drooling on you. We change position, and I feel your warm breath in my ear, your warm hand on my cock...

I think we have actually been here for several hours now. I touch your creamy cheek. You remain still. I watch your buttocks rise, perfect moons lighting the dim, two cool scoops of vanilla ice cream. A faint hiss rises from between them. I quickly exit the bed.

On the way to the bathroom, the image in the mirror stops me. Looking back at me is somebody beautiful. I am warm flesh capable of mind- and body-splitting desire and pleasure whose depths I have yet to fully comprehend or possibly even experience. I can let the kite soar into the universe, holding tightly to the string. I can even court lightning because now I am learning how to harness it. And I can relinquish the string to you, because yours are, after all, hands that I trust. Or perhaps it is myself I have come to trust. I whisper a prayer of thanks for our time together. Just thinking about it has given me a hard-on.

I go back to the bedroom, my cock bobbing ahead of me, and see that you are awake and gazing intently in my direction behind a radiant almost-grin. I wonder how long you have been watching me. I slowly slide onto the bed next to you. Your hand slips around my cock.

Our eyes lock, faces break into smiles. "Does this mean we're talking again?" I whisper in your ear.

You laugh, then look at me sideways. "It depends. Do I get my turn now?"

Before I can answer, you pull me onto you, hand gripping hard my cock and invading my mouth with relentless and unconstrained kisses.

– This story has been adapted by the editor from the original especially for this anthology.

PICKING UP TOLLY

Jarred Goodall

It was the sort of day when you felt right from the start that something just had to happen – soft morning mists with birds chirping out territories and advertising love-nests, hazy sun, the light scent of cut grass coming in the window to blend with the smell of bacon and slightly burnt toast. Surely a thunderstorm at the very least would break the sultry heat.

In the living room the phone rang and I carried my coffee over to it.

"Um... Mister Addams? Mister Joe Addams?" An adolescent voice, light, unsure.

"Speaking."

"I'm Tolly Weddock."

The name meant nothing to me. "Yes?" I said, sipping my coffee.

"I'm at the bus station and I wonder if you could come down and pick me up. I'm sorta short of cash. Oh, yeah, I'm Billy's brother."

"Billy?" I didn't know a Billy Weddock either, as best as I could recall.

"Sorry, Billy Neil. I changed my name to our step-father's; Billy didn't."

Now I remembered: the Neil "problem family" with its ill-clad children of different parentages spilling out onto the rotten porch of a near-derelict home in the poor part of town. One of the boys had grown into the beautiful Billy, who in his last high school years, had supported his hetero love-life by exploding his cock into the mouths of, among others, paying men.

"I thought your family had moved away," I said.

"We did, only my sister Angela married a local guy and now she's having a baby and that's why I've come back. Really, Mr. Addams, could you pick me up?"

Why me? Surely the family had closer ties in the community than to one of Billy's old casual customers. And yet... I've always had a soft heart – and a hard prick – for youths in need. "Give me ten minutes," I told him. "How am I going to recognize you?"

"Don't worry, Mister Addams, I'll recognize you."

And he did. I'd parked outside the bus station, gone in, and there he was, putting out his hand, a long, lanky, good-looking boy in his late teens with sun-streaked brown hair falling to his shoulders, clad in tattered blue denims, rude sweatshirt and wearing a formidable backpack. I looked for resemblances to his older brother, found a few; like Billy, this kid in himself was handsome, in an innocent, unaffected way. I congratulated myself on a good decision in coming to his rescue.

We went to my car, stowed his back-pack in the trunk. I watched him maneuver his long legs under the dashboard, his crotch (so trim, obviously so well stuffed) already alluring.

"You probably don't remember," he said, once we were under way, "but sometimes when Billy came to visit you he brought me along and I sat and watched television in your living room while you and Billy went off and... you know."

Now I did remember: a cute little smiley kid who worshipped his big brother to the point where Billy often had a hard time getting rid of him. That little smiley kid had put on years, height (a good inch on me already), a whole lot of muscle and good looks.

"Okay... Tolly, is it? Where are we going? To your sister's place?"

"Um, not yet, 'cause it's a small house and everyone's running around being intense. I'm not supposed to go there until the contractions start."

"So... you staying with a buddy or something?"

Tolly looked at me, uneasily. "I was hoping... Billy said, 'cause you were the nicest grown-up man he knew back then and the only one he trusted..."

"Yes?"

"I mean, I got my sleeping bag and all and I don't take up much room and I'll stay out of the way, I really will, and maybe I can help you, like shopping and stuff... will you?"

I laughed. "Yes." I couldn't wait to find out the rest of this tempting teenager's agenda.

We parked in my driveway. Tolly retrieved his back pack and lugged it through my front door. "Just leave it there," I told him. "We'll worry about what to do with it later. How about some food?"

"Oh yes!" Like most teenagers, he was starved.

A frozen pizza, quickly microwaved, was fine. It slid down his throat (what a beautiful mouth he had, what full lips, strong white teeth!) with a rinse of Coke and a minimum of mastication.

By now we had ensconced ourselves at opposite sides of the kitchen table. He began reminiscing about the good old days which hadn't been all that good, it seemed. "But Billy was there for me, what really mattered. He was strict. Sometimes he was awful strict, but, man, I couldn't have lived without him. You knew how great Billy was, didn't you?"

Billy had been a nice boy, and certainly good at what he did for what now seemed a pitifully small payment. "I can imagine he was a wonderful big brother," I said.

"Wonderful is the word. He's working on fish boats in Alaska. He and Marilyn have a baby girl."

"Do you visit him?"

Tolly shook his head. Then he took a letter out of his pocket and laid it down on the table. "I got this last week. I'd written him a lot of questions. He told me to go to you for the answers."

"To me?" As I suspected, there was more to Tolly's presence in our town than his sister's impending delivery. "What sort of questions?"

Tolly blinked and sighed. "Oh, Jesus, Mister Addams, I never did any of those things Billy did. Billy told me not to, so I didn't. I don't know anything. I've done nothing, leastways not with anybody else."

"So you dated girls?"

He shook his head. "There was never enough money."

"Wasn't that sort of frustrating?"

"Sometimes. Only... I just didn't let myself think about it much."

"And you never... how shall I say... jerked off or got it on with Billy?"

Tolly's eyes grew big. "Especially not with Billy."

This was incredible – and sad. "Man, you're sixteen, seventeen..."

"Seventeen a couple of weeks ago."

"...and you never, in your whole life, in all those years, got that thing out of your pants and did something sexy with any other human being?"

"That's right. At first it wasn't so bad, when I was thirteen and fourteen." Our eyes met and I could see there were tears in his. "Then I got older, and now it's about tearing me up."

Obviously this was a plea, not just for information but for experience. Obviously, too, I'd been selected -- by the boy's big brother.

What should I do? How fast should I go, where should I lead him? "Is it a girl you want, Tolly?"

He shook his head. "Not at first. Not right away. anyhow." A kind of crooked smile twisted his mouth. "You ever had a 17-year-old virgin on your hands before, Mister Addams?"

I moved around the table and sat down in the chair next to him and wrapped an arm around his shoulders.

"Billy said you could help me." Tolly closed his eyes and slumped down in the chair a bit. "It's in his letter..."

Billy's letter would have to wait. I dropped a hand onto his humid crotch where I could feel an ardent hard-on pressing upwards the blue denim. He sucked in air between his teeth.

"Let's get this out in the open," I said.

I loosened his belt, a flamboyant hand-tooled leather affair with a silver cowboy buckle big as a fist, then ran down the zipper and parted the fly over a triangle of white skivvies. The scent of him rose into the air, the intimate odor of a bargain-basement teenage traveller unable to change clothes for several days, the arousing smell of scrotum and penis sweat caught and trapped in soft cotton, the light stink of certain minor leakages both fore and aft.

"Raise your butt," I whispered.

He did. I slid his denims and undershorts down to his knees.

Now exposed (for the first time to other eyes?) was his fine circumcized cock in arousal. Whoever had carved it had worked with good stock. A lovely lilac glans rose to a double mound in front, half-hiding the urethral eye which was already weeping a crystal tear, then rolled smoothly back. The shaft below was straight, hard, blue veins threading through the loose skin like suckers of some climbing vine. Beneath, the scrotum was tight, the balls in it moving a little, as though in gentle anticipation that now, at long last, their effervescence might be appreciated.

What a shame that this magnificent apparatus hadn't yet realized its potential for joy, received and given. What a wonderful stroke of luck that I was there, at this particular time and at this very place, with the encouragement of a beloved brother, to end the drought.

I wrapped my fingers around Tolly's cock and squeezed. Again came the sound of inhaled air hissing through clenched teeth.

"You don't know how I've wanted this," he whispered.

Ours may not have been the easiest position or greatest setting for a boy's First Time, but obviously Tolly had to be done right now, or he would simply explode.

"Jesus, Mister Addams, please don't let go!"

"I won't. Now, sit back and think anything you want. Your cock's in a very experienced hand."

I started to move Tolly's loose foreskin back and forth over the oak-hard penis core. He began to tremble lightly. The muscles, the tendons in his thighs tensed and relaxed, tensed and relaxed.

"It's not going to be very long," he whispered.

"Want me to slow up?"

"No, I couldn't take that."

"Just tell me when you're getting close and we'll go for broke."

His breathing became harsh and uneven. The light body tremors turned into spasms. He gulped. He gasped. His head jerked from side to side, up and down, with no rhyme or reason or coordination with my stroke.

"I'm getting close," he whispered hoarsely.

I increased the pace, and with the fingers of my other hand I dobbed some saliva onto his glans and let it trickle down to where his frenulum snuggled upon my index finger.

"Oh, fuck, oh shit, that feels so sweet!" he gasped. "What'dja do?"

Hadn't this virgin boy discovered the increased pleasure of masturbatory lubrication?

"Don't worry about it," I said. "Just..."

And then, incredibly, the doorbell rang.

Tolly's face paled to the color of spilt sperm. He shot up to his feet, knocking the chair over backwards, pre-ejaculatory sperm oozing out of his urethra. "What the fuck is that?"

"I'll get rid of whoever it is."

Tolly worked manfully to put his messy cock away, pull up his underwear and bluejeans over it, raise the zipper. He looked at me helplessly, then turned to the wall, still struggling.

At the front door were three neighborhood boys who always seemed to be driving, or more often pushing, a tail-finned 1950s Dodge that had miraculously survived four decades of adolescent owners.

"Hello, sir. Was that Tolly Weddock we saw getting out of your car?" one of them asked.

"And if it was?" I said.

"Well, we're old classmates. Can we come in?"

"No."

"Oh, okay. It's just that, if it was Tolly, we'd like to say hello."

"If it was and he wanted to see you, I'm sure he'll be in touch."

I shut the door on their puzzled faces and went back to my guest. He still hadn't managed to close his trousers. "Who was it?" he asked.

I told him their names, and he seemed relieved. "They're not bad guys. They used to be in trouble all the time, but not mean trouble."

But Tolly had more important things to deal with. His denims, still open at the fly, hung about his hips. His hard-on was no match for his skivvies -- more than a bit of his purple glans peeped out above.

It was obviously best to take him to my bedroom. "You think you can make it up the stairs without an... accident?"

"I dunno," he said shakily.

"Come on, I'll help you."

We released his cock once again, then I took his elbow and steered him in the right direction. He climbed the stairs bent like an old man who had peed his pants.

I laid him out on my bed and went about stripping him down for action. He kept looking at me, like a puppy-dog, or a suppliant, or simply a kid so spaced out from sex he didn't know what to do.

I had him naked in less than a minute, his cowboy boots tossed into a corner, dirty jeans and skivs and socks and "Kiss My Ass" sweatshirt in a puddle beside the bed. What a lovely sight he was, with the blush of advanced lust touching his cheeks and coloring his breasts, his long sun-streaked brown hair feathering out beside his face on my pillow, his strong, utterly hairless chest, a navel that actually seemed to protrude, narrow waist and legs dusted in golden down. And, of course, the trim pubic bush out of which that leaking, dominating cock rose, and the smooth, crenulated mounds of his scrotum below.

I parted his legs a bit and knelt between them. His strong smell filled my head, the musky odor of aroused adolescent penis mingling with hints of darker exudations from behind his balls. I grasped his cock and moistened my lips.

At the first touch of my tongue, Tolly nearly jumped out of his skin. "Jesus, Mr. Addams, whatcha doin'? I mean... that's my penis, for Chrissake, you're lickin'!"

"Shut up and enjoy it," I said, then added, to give everything the seal of approval, "Billy always did."

"Billy liked that?"

I nodded. He'd liked it... and how!

"All right..." Tolly said, but not without an uncertain tremor in his voice.

Now I could really get down to work, moistening first this side, then the other of his salty, sweaty cock shaft, then its back. When it was all slick and wet, I closed my lips over its purple tip and sucked out some oily ooze of pre-cum. I swished my tongue around the softish glans, then worked down, sucking all the while, to find by feel the little frenular nerve embedded in his foreskin and tickled it with the tip of my tongue.

"Man alive!" he gasped.

His hands came to my head and began to stroke my hair. I started to move my head up and down, drawing in his cock so its tip probed deep into my throat, then letting his penis slide almost all of the way out to let that same tip snuggle between my lips, softly pulsating.

From this point on his conversation degenerated to a series of groaned-out expletives: "Shit!... Fuck!... God!...," even, to my surprise, "Catatonic!", mixed with "oooos" and "ughs" and "aaaaahhhs" and groans and gasps which would tax the limits of any linguist's ability to render them in print. It wasn't so much that he was enjoying the blow-job; he was transfixed by it, blasted off into outer space and a whole new galaxy of feeling.

The final rise began. His body went into a series of terminal shudders. Legs thrashed about under me and beside me; fingers tangled in my hair and pulled to the point of pain. A kind of death rattle came out of his throat, and then his urethra stiffened and filled with semen and began the orgasmic clicks that sent sperm jetting into the back of my throat, flooding it, the wonderful ejaculate even rising up uncomfortably into my nose before I managed to swallow. I gulped gratefully at Tolly's first gift ever to anyone of his own teeming gametophore life.

Afterwards he lay back on my bed absolutely shattered, eyes closed, without even a smile crossing his lips. "How was it?" I asked.

"I couldn't begin to tell you."

"Well, we'll take a break. I'll put these clothes in the washer. Is there other stuff in your back-pack?"

A nod.

"You don't mind me pawing through your private things?"

He shook his head. "You know all about me now."

But did I? I pulled a comforter over him and left him to his own ruminations, or sleep.

There was a lot of dirty clothes in his backpack, as well as a copy of a motor magazine folded and rolled up to a double-page advertisement showing a half dozen handsome youths in swim suits clustered around a girl dispensing Cokes. Something for a surreptitious jack-off on the bus? And if so, had he been lusting after the boys or the girl – or both in a great maelstrom of adolescent omnivorousness?

I set the washing machine to work on his clothes and went to the kitchen to make a pot of coffee for us, and some light snacks: Oreo cookies, graham crackers, a couple of wedges of Aunt Mary's famous cherry pie. When all was ready I brought everything up to my bedroom and found Tolly, far from asleep, sitting up in bed and idly stroking a resurrected cock. "When I was thirteen," he said, "when I jacked off, I always went for three."

"Let's leave that thing alone for a bit," I urged. "I brought reinforcements."

"Aw, you didn't have to do that, Mister Addams!" But already his eyes had greedily glommed onto his share of the spoils. Sometimes it's hard to know which organ dominates a teenage boy more ruthlessly: his cock or his stomach.

We showered – together, something he had been used to doing with Billy, it seemed. Later while I shaved he blow-dried his hair until it glowed like a freshly hatched horse chestnut. "How's that?" he said, presenting himself for inspection.

"Fantastic."

He reached for my cock, which was already beginning to rise. "Now I'm really ready for lesson two," he said. "But you'll have to teach me what I'm supposed to do with this..." – squeezing "this" with boyish enthusiasm and affection.

Now he smelled sweet, all of him, of soap and shampoo, his breath redolent of Pepsodent. We lay on the bed, on our sides, in loose embrace. Having found my cock he wouldn't let go of it. "It's real nice," he said, naively surprised. "I mean, what's so great is it's like this for me."

"Lick your lips," I told him.

"Huh?"

"Just do it."

"Jeez, Mr. Addams, okay!"

"Don't you think you could call me Joe by now?" I took hold of his cock and gave it a gentle squeeze.

"Uh..." He shook his head. "I don't think so. Billy never did. It wouldn't seem right."

"Then never mind. You ever kissed?" A little spark of alarm came into his eyes. "Do guys do that?"

"All the time. It's the same as with a girl."

"I never kissed a girl."

"Tolly, it's going to be a pleasure teaching you. Lick your lips. Make them soft."

He did. I pressed my mouth against his. At first there was resistance, with little moany sounds coming out of his throat, but after a while his lips gave up their stiffness and allowed me to glide mine over them, sucking lightly, feeling just the tips of his teeth.

An arm come around my neck. Pretty soon he was pressing my face harder against his. Our lips made wider and wetter excursions -- over chin and nose and cheeks and eyelids. His breathing was beginning to become excited again.

Suddenly he drew back and looked at me. "How we going to... do it this time?"

"Whatever way you want."

"I don't know as I'm ready to..."

"Give me a blow job?"

"Uh huh. I'm afraid I'd fuck things up."

"We don't have to try everything this afternoon."

He looked relieved. "Thanks, Mister Addams."

"Some things take a little getting used to."

"I remember when I was at home and there was a good TV program on and I was lying on my stomach on the floor watching it, I'd sort of fuck the floor, making up stories about the people on the screen – me and those people. Can two guys do that, one on top of the other?"

"It's called rubbing off. And you don't have to make up any stories."

He rolled onto his back and patted his stomach. "Come on up and rub off on me – if you want."

There was a time, I'm told, when all the shrinks were saying that if married couples wanted to maintain good sexual relations they had to "achieve simultaneous orgasm." When you consider how differently women are made from us and how much less intense their involvement in sex is, there must have been a lot of potentially happy heterosexual couples who were troubled by the fact that Jack invariably got his orgasm first and Jill had to be worked up subsequently to hers with loving digital manipulation.

Between guys, simultaneous orgasm is more achievable, but, really, how often does it happen? How often do we want it to happen?

But this time between Tolly and me it did. We didn't think about it, couldn't think about it. It just happened, because it couldn't have gone any other way. We both moistened our cocks from our mouths and then I lay on him – and, oh, how beautiful it was to melt into his warm but excited embrace.

We began the first gentle oscillations, Tolly picking up

without any instruction the need for equal but opposite movements. There were pauses, to postpone and enjoy, then the sliding was resumed, each time more strongly, until in the rumpled sheets of my groaning bed I was actually pounding down on him with my hips as he moved in counter rhythm, stabbing upwards with his cock against the taut muscles of my lower abdomen, everything between us lubricated by sweat and spit and our two oozing sources of pre-come. One of my arms was around his back beneath him; with my other hand I was running my fingers through his beautiful hair, holding his head steady while I kissed him, kissed all over his face, licked his face as though it was an ice-cream bar, as he groaned and snorted and tried to chew on one of my ears.

I didn't have to say anything. I was right there, and I knew he was right there. His arms about my back tightened, one fist started hammering on my shoulder blades. He gasped, gurgled, wailed, as the sperm started pouring out, the orgasm seeming to go on and on (somebody had written somewhere that crayfish had 24-hour orgasms when they mated!) and only slowly started to ebb away.

We came back down to earth... to the sound of applause!

I snapped my head around. It couldn't have come from my bedroom TV, which was off. Then I looked out the window. An old sycamore tree grew in my back yard, shading my house from the fiercest of the summer sun. In its ample crotches sat the three youths of the tail-fin Dodge.

"Way to go!" one of them called, a youngster named Alan who lived almost across the street.

"That looked like a good one," said another.

"Give the old Tolster our congratulations," said Alan. "We figured he'd keep up Billy's tradition."

"Just didn't know till now you were part of it."

I stalked off the bed, cock swinging and dripping milky streamers, pulled the curtains, then stuck my head out between them. "What in God's name do you boys think you're doing?" I croaked.

"Lookin'. You guys was better than a porno tape any day."

I glanced back to the bed. Tolly was dying of embarrassment. "It's okay," I whispered to him. "They're not going to get mean."

Which confirmed what Alan next said. "We have a party at my place tonight – weed, beer if you bring it. Tell Tolly he's invited. And, oh yeah, there'll be this foxy lady that'll do anything!"

"At a party," said one of the other boys, "you just can't wear her out."

"Tell the Tolster. Maybe he'll want to change his luck."

They were climbing down the tree now, laughing, talking excitedly. In a flash they were gone.

I went back to my bed and looked down at Tolly who had a hand thrown across his eyes recovering from his second great shock and embarrassment.

"This has been some day," he said.

"For me, too. What do you think about the party?"

"Come down and lie beside me."

I did and we snuggled for a spell, absently caressing, occasionally licking, getting hard again.

"You know what?" Tolly finally said. "I have a good feeling about today. I think I'll go to that party and see what's up."

"You think it'll be up to that foxy lady?"

He grinned. "Sure, if she does all the work."

I grilled steaks out under the old sycamore and then I showed Tolly where my emergency back door key was hidden outside. When I sent him away to the party across the street he looked keyed-up and very, very sexy in his clean clothes. I offered a silent prayer to whatever pagan gods might be listening that he be well treated there, that events not become too much for him. Then I went upstairs and climbed into bed and, since we'd made love three times that afternoon, I fell quickly asleep.

At earliest dawn I felt Tolly climbing into my bed and taking me into a firm grip from behind. He'd stripped right down – for cuddling or action or maybe both.

"How was it? Your party." I mumbled.

"Wild. Those guys do everything, in front of everybody."

"Did you loose your innocence with the foxy lady?"

"I'm afraid so."

"Was it good?"

"Old Alan had to grab me and roll a thing on my thing. He said, 'Tolly, you don't know nothing from nothing, do you?'

which isn't far from the truth."

"I'm glad you're back."

"Whew, so am I. This is just a lot less... stressful." He snuggled his face against my shoulders and started licking the back of my neck. I was quickly becoming warmly, sleepily aroused again.

"What was so nice, you know, was the feeling," he said dreamily. "It was all warm in there and tight and slippery. Everything seemed to work so well."

"You liked it better than what you and I did?"

"Well... she was a party-party girl and all giggly. Not my type." His hard cock had found its way into the crack between my buttocks and was starting to slide in the ooze of his renewed excitement. "I hear you can also do that with a guy. Alan said sometimes the feel was even better..."

My mind snapped out of its sleepy daze and began to think. Until a few hours ago Tolly had been a virgin. They'd put a rubber on him when he'd had sex with the foxy lady. Surely there could be no risk of infection to me if he wanted to test Alan's claim. And I knew there was no risk to him..."

"Tolly, would you like to fuck me?" I asked.

He froze, tongue caught somewhere between one of my ear-lobes and shoulder tendons, cock poised in the valley, if not at the target, of our conversation.

"Yes, Sir," he breathed. "I really would."

"And so would I."

The preparations were surprisingly simple and affectionately done: the application of saliva and pre-lube to cock and anus, the positioning by my hand of Tolly's soft-hard penis tip at the roseate entrance, the command to exert pressure, the slow breakdown of resistance, sliding in and Tolly's groan of satisfaction – and my own as his still-lubricated hand closed around my cock and squeezed.

"Now wait just a bit," I whispered.

"Sure," he said.

I knew I couldn't keep him on hold forever, but it had been several months since anything other than a thermometer had been where Tolly's cock now was. Slowly I found myself relaxing, regaining my power of anal grip.

"Man, whatcha doing?" Tolly whispered after a couple of

my contractions. "That feels... just so good!"

"You can begin now – gently at first."

He rolled back slightly with his hips, drawing his cock part-way out, then slid it smoothly back in. His mouth gave up a great happy sigh, then fastened again onto my neck, biting slightly at the base of my hairline. He drew his cock partly out again and then slipped it snugly back in.

Is there anything more wonderful than the feel of a friendly youth's hard-on gripped by your anal ring, moving in and out among the spasms of your sphincter, sliding against the hidden joy-spot and forcing that reservoir to relinquish some of its brew? It is the little paradise, a foretaste of heaven (should such an unlikely place exist), the most wonderful feeling a human being can ever have. I revelled in my submission, the miraculous reversal of roles that takes place when the wise old man makes himself open to the bare physical lust of the unpracticed youth.

Of course Tolly couldn't last very long. Nobody can at that age. He quickly went wild. He gasped and pounded and gripped me in a death-lock. I thought he would take a whole mouthful of flesh out of my shoulder when he came.

And once again, when he came so did I, both of us gushing, me into my bed-sheets and spilling over his tight-gripping knuckles, he into some dark, secret place deep inside my bowels. The orgasm seemed to go on and on and on.

We relaxed in a great sweating, sighing, locked-together heap under my covers. I thanked his still-hard cock with a couple of nice anal squeezes.

"It must have been a long night for you," I said.

"Yup," he said. "And this was about the best part." He yawned. Nice warm breath flowing over my shoulders. Then reality. "I found out, when I telephoned over at the party, that they've taken my sis to the hospital. So this morning I guess I'll have to leave."

"So soon?"

"Yeah, I'm afraid so. I'm supposed to help paint the new baby room."

What a chilly come-down from our shared bliss! For youth, all experience is outward expansion. At my age a man is consolidating; he knows that life is tricky; his instinct is to keep precious things close to him as long as possible.

"I'll miss you," I said. Then added, "And this."

"I'll miss you, too, but... I think you'll be pretty well fixed up for guy-sex."

"With you staying at your sister's house and painting nurseries and things?"

Tolly started gently licking my shoulders and rubbing his nose in the wetness it made. "Alan'll be coming over here tomorrow afternoon," he said.

"Alan? He will? For what?"

Tolly just chuckled. "And Wally and Jim both said they'd like to have a crack at doing things with you, too."

My God, I couldn't believe what Tolly was saying: there was a plethora of kids out there – neighborhood kids, wild but decent kids, good looking kids, kids just my type, kids with perpetual hard-ons and holes in their pockets. It seemed that old Dodge (my new ally?) needed an awful lot of replacement parts.

"You up to another fuck before we go to sleep," Tolly asked shyly, "or do you want me to pull out now?"

THE CARRIAGE BOY

Michael Bates

Not far outside the bustling port city of Valparaiso in Chile lies the community of Vina del Mar; an area that enjoys the reputation of being a premiere resort for visitors from all around the country and foreigners alike. While my ship was in port I had gone there to explore the plethora of quaint shops nestled among the narrow streets and avenues, look at the beaches arching around the great curve of Valparaiso Bay, and, of course, do plenty of cruising.

It was while strolling casually past the gardens adjacent to the casino that my attention was drawn to a young Chilean man reclining on the gently sloping lawn in the shade of a flowering tree. He didn't notice my stare as I passed, which allowed me plenty of time for a long, leisurely look. He appeared to be in his late teens or early twenties and had the chocolate brown skin and shiny black hair mixed with the subtle European features that so commonly resulted from the mixing of genes between the Spaniards and Indians so many generations ago. His arms and face appeared further darkened by the intense sunshine so prevalent during these summer months. With his arms crossed behind his head, he was smiling and staring skyward while softly humming a song as I passed, and seemed in a world of his very own. I stepped between the horses and carts lined along the roadway, and crossed the street. Sitting on the low sea wall, with my back to the drumming surf, I made a pretense of watching the tourists going off in the horse-drawn buggies for little sightseeing circuits around the park, but my eyes were glued to this handsome youth reclining in the background. He frequently looked out toward the horses, and I wondered if he might notice my staring, but his attention never came entirely my way. While I was contemplating a way of approaching him with some sort of conversation, without looking too bold, yet fearing my poor Spanish would make my aggression appear even more unusual, he suddenly stood up and approached one of the parked buggies. He lifted the seat and produced a small cassette player, with its own miniature speaker, and set it up on the rear seat so he could listen to it. I realized then that he must own the horse and buggy! Or at least he was in charge of it. But he didn't seem particularly interested in promoting his business. While the other buggy operators came and went, he seemed totally void of business. Well, his buggy did look a bit more run down than the rest, and it didn't sport as much polished brass or shiny leather-work. This boy was wearing only baggy blue jeans and a white shirt casually rolled up at the sleeves, compared to the more spiffy uniforms of some of the other drivers. But I could see the form of a trim, fit body under those clothes, and to me he was the handsomest of the lot.

On an impulse I re-crossed the street and approached him. "Buenos tardes."

He looked up in surprise. "Buenos tardes, senor." Up close my first impression was that he was a country person; totally out of place even in these rural gardens of the city. His hands were rough and callused and his young face looked more leathery than from a distance. His lips were chapped and peeling from the sun. Faint smells of manure and hay and wood smoke lingered around him as we stood next to the horse and carriage. He casually rubbed the horse's neck as I tried to communicate, and his brown skin and lean muscles contrasted very pleasantly against the light gray mane of the horse.

I used what little Spanish I knew to ask him about the rides he offered, how much they cost, etc. Apparently it wasn't good enough, I thought, because he turned suddenly to a nearby driver and spoke rapidly in Spanish. I feared he may be trying to refer me to someone else who spoke English. But instead he was handed a laminated price card which he in turn passed on to me. Although it was all in Spanish, I could easily decipher it, and learned that besides the minimum tour around the casino gardens, you could hire the buggies by the hour, and the price was surprisingly cheap. I indicated that I wanted to hire his buggy for an hour and have him drive me around. I also indicated that I wished to sit up on the driver's seat instead of in the back passenger seat. We climbed aboard and off we went, clop-clop-clopping along the narrow street, winding amongst the parked cars, and letting others pass us as they could. It was just sunset, and the cool evening breeze felt refreshing to my sun-baked skin. I learned his name was Rene. Armed with my dictionary, I managed to make a decipherable conversation, although it was certainly far from being anything academic.

The driver's bench was small, and we sat close to one another, our legs nearly touching. It seemed joyous to have such a wonderful view, looking over the cars we passed and out toward the pinkening horizon over the sea. It was ever more enchanting having this young vaquero sitting next to me, our legs occasionally touching with the jostling of the wagon. I proposed we stop and have something to eat, which he agreed to, but when we stopped in front of a restaurant, it was clear he had misunderstood, as he indicated I should get down and he would wait. As I tried explaining that I wished him to join me a waiter came out, dressed in white coat and slacks, presumably to see what was going on with this horse and buggy parked in front of his establishment. He spoke some English, and I explained that we wished to eat there, but he said that unless the boy stayed with the cart and horse we couldn't leave it parked where it was. We circled the block looking for a place to leave it, but with car parking at a premium, finding a place for a horse and buggy is even more difficult! By the time we located a suitable spot, and Rene had strapped the feed bag over the horse's muzzle, we were far from the restaurant. But there were many others to choose from in that area, and we found a quiet, family-run place nearby. It was obvious Rene had eaten very little, if anything, that day as he wolfed down everything that was set before him. Even though there wasn't much in the way of conversation, this was still so much better than dining alone. I sipped my dry, Chilean red wine for dessert as Rene polished off a big bowl of ice cream. Throughout the meal he had animatedly called me his amigo, and I could see he was enjoying himself more than with just an ordinary fare. Returning to the buggy we stopped at a kiosk where I bought him a packet of cigarettes.

I indicated that I wanted to continue "hiring" him for another hour or two so he could show me around Vina del Mar some more, and as I did so, I slipped some peso notes in his pocket to amply cover the cost of the tour plus a little tip for himself. He beamed a smile of thanks.

By now it was well after dark, and I asked him to take some of the quiet back streets, away from the hustle and bustle of the nightclubs and beach front activities. Rene urged the horse along with little clucking sounds and words of encouragement in Spanish. He used the reins to turn and guide him and occasionally hurried him up with a smack of his whip. The horse's name was Prieta. "Divergir!" he said, seeming to understand my intentions about finding more quiet and secluded surroundings. We found ourselves on a shadowy avenue not far away, and he slowed the horse down to a walk. No words were spoken, as he smoked quietly. I could feel his lean leg pressing steadily against my own. Was it intentional or was I simply reading too much into something I vaguely hoped for? I pressed my own leg back subtly, but harder. He didn't move. A stirring of excitement began in my groin. I desperately wanted to make a move, but feared doing something that might be offensive to him.

"Amigo," I said. Then I slid my hand from my own leg onto his, resting it lightly on his thigh. He turned with a slight look of surprise, then looked ahead again and I could see the realization dawning on his shadowed face. I squeezed gently and moved my hand ever so slightly upward. My own heart was pounding with excitement and I could feel the blood in turn bulging into my crotch. "Okay?" I said.

Rene slowly shook his head from side to side, still looking straight ahead. I didn't remove my hand, though, and he made no move to stop me. He even held the reigns higher off his lap to allow room for my hand.

Thinking I had misunderstood I asked again, "okay?" He merely shrugged his shoulders this time. My hand remained. Then I slid it further up and closer between his legs. It was a pleasant surprise when I came across the hard shape of his cock. It wasn't overly huge, but the stiffened rod was rock hard. It pointed down his inseam. Rene shifted slightly when I touched it, but still did nothing to stop me. He reigned back on the horse, and we stopped.

"Uno momento," he said, hopping down and motioning for me to do the same. He lifted the driver's seat and took out the little cassette player and speaker. Then he carefully set them up on the floor in the back of the buggy. He extended the awning up over the back seat and climbed aboard as if he were a passenger. I did the same. We were parked with the back of the buggy toward the nearest house; its awning now blocking any possible view within. The lights in the house across the street were all darkened.

Guitar music wafted lightly up from the floorboards and Rene sprawled back listening to it with his legs casually spread apart. I took this as an invitation to continue, and again laid my hand on his thigh. His young cock had retracted to an almost imperceptible lump in his crotch. Rene surprised me by reaching down and unzipping his trousers. He wasn't wearing any underwear. I delved my fingers into the warm recess of his crotch and fished out his still limp member. It was uncut, and began immediately growing at my touch. I fingered and twiddled the soft lips of his foreskin as the hardening head reared toward the opening. Already it felt slippery with juices. A musty aroma drifted upward. My own cock was swollen with excitement and straining to be freed. I gently took hold of Rene's hand and laid it on my stiffened rod to show him my excitement, but he immediately pulled it away. Undaunted, I unbuttoned my own fly and slipped out my own meat. I squeezed and stroked both our hardened cocks in rhythm, sliding Rene's foreskin up and down over the slippery head, then for a few moments I leaned down and licked his shaft up and down with my warm tongue. At this he squirmed and moaned ever so lightly and I felt his hands take hold of my head to urge me on. Releasing my own meat I slid his shirt up to expose and rub his flat, trim stomach. With his shaft slick with my saliva and the juice oozing from his pumped up cockhead, I continued jacking up and down his shaft. The tempo picked up and I knew my own excited dick wouldn't hold out much longer.

Rene must have felt the same as he was breathing more and more rapidly and rolling his head from side to side on the seat back. I knew when he started coming as his entire body tensed up and he thrust his head to one side. His cockhead began pumping out spasm after spasm of jism, first spitting some long shots onto his bare stomach and then oozing down over my hand. The musky smell of his come, combined with its warm, sticky feel, sent me over the edge, and my own cock erupted.

Jets of my jism splattered down onto the floor of the coach. I hoped I missed the cassette player.

As though suddenly waking up, Rene hurriedly fastened up his pants, glanced quickly around, and then gestured that we should return to the driver's seat again. Riding slowly back to the gardens by the sea, Rene turned to me and said quietly, "amigo."

"Si," I said, and slipped more peso notes into his pocket. It was getting late and time for me to return to my ship.

The last I saw Rene, the carriage boy, he was standing next to Prieta, stroking the horse's neck with his strong brown hands, and humming quietly to himself.

PUNK'S COLLATERAL

Thomas C. Humphrey

Jimmy Radovitch had punk stamped all over him.

He posed arrogantly against the door jamb, his eyes glazed from dope, the expression on his face somewhere between a question and a challenge. Neither of us spoke as my eyes slowly took him in. Shaved head. Four tandem gold hoops in his left ear. Gold ring dangling provocatively from a quarter-sized chocolate nipple. Symmetrical arcs of molded, hairless pecs artfully displayed by an open denim vest. Firm, rippled abdomen with a soft brown fuzz circling the navel. Beltless, worn jeans hugging narrow hips and caressing substantial thighs. Polished black shitkicking boots.

"How you doing, Mike?" he said after allowing me time to absorb the impact of him.

"Apparently not feeling as good as you, but making it, Jimmy. Making it," I replied. "What you up to?"

His smooth face softened and his normally hard blue eyes became soulful. "I need to ask a big favor," he said.

"Then shoot. Never hurts to ask," I encouraged.

"Can I come in, maybe for a soda?" he hedged.

"That's your big favor? Hell, Jimmy, many times as you've been here, you hardly need to ask. Come on in," I said, stepping back into the room. "You know your way to the fridge. And bring me a beer. But you drink soda."

"You know I don't drink that bull piss anyway," he said, rummaging in the refrigerator.

"No, you'd rather suck on that weed and travel outer space," I said.

"Hey, don't knock it, man. No hangover next morning," he said, handing me a beer and melting onto the couch.

Jimmy meant trouble with a capital "t," and I knew it---had known it for a long time. For the past five years, since he was fourteen, he had lived with his mother and whichever of her long string of boyfriends in the apartment complex where I was the live-in maintenance man.

From the beginning, he had been a pain in the ass. At first

he had run with a skateboard crowd and sported the weird hair style and funky clothes that was their totem. High on weed, he and his friends would tear around the complex on their boards, terrorizing the elderly residents and chipping hell out of curbings and planters. After the police were called during a particularly wild rampage, he and his friends retaliated by sinking all the lawn furniture in the pool. He spent the night in Juvenile Detention for that.

A couple of years later, he had outgrown skateboarding and graduated to gangsta rap. Dressed in the latest ill-fitting hip hop fashion statement, he would loll around the complex with his boom box blasting out mega-decibels of Snoop Doggy Dogg's obscenities to the horror of staid matrons, and the conversations of him and his buddies became loaded with "motherfucker" and "whore" and "bitch." About this time, they discovered spray paint and decorated laundry rooms and walls and sidewalks with their territorial marks.

Again, Jimmy went to Detention for shoplifting rap tapes he was not old enough to buy legally, and then a third time for trashing the apartment of a resident who dared chastise his crowd for their behavior. The fourth and fifth times were for possession of marijuana. After that, I lost count.

The current skinhead image was relatively new, and the nipple ring had been added since I'd seen him last. Knowing Jimmy, I fully expected that, unless something else captured his attention, his involvement would escalate until he had swastikas tattooed on his forehead and used his shiny boots on some Jew or black or fag.

He was the kind of kid I was very ambivalent toward. He had always been courteous and cooperative with me and obviously liked me and found excuses to hang around me a good bit. But the forms of his adolescent rebellion made me want to kick his ass and force him to get himself straight and start to earn his way through life. This urge brought me very close to actively disliking him sometimes. Yet I knew enough about teenagers to sense that somewhere beneath his tough exterior was a decent kid crying out for relief from whatever inner hell he was going through.

Not that this awareness made me want to become his daddy or big brother, or even role model. Judging by the quality of most of the men his mother took up with, I figured the influence of role models was ninety per cent of his problem. I was concerned enough, though, to take up a little time with him and to tease and prod him into at least taking a good look at himself.

"Why'd you get your tit pierced?" I goaded as he sat staring into space and the silence lengthened.

"Something to do," he shrugged. "And chicks flip over it."

"Why, because they can lead you around by it?"

"Nobody leads me around by anything, man," he bristled. "Especially not some dumb bitch."

"Yeah," I laughed. "They can wiggle their ass and grab you by your little dick without even touching you and lead you anywhere they want." Jimmy and I had dealt in sexual innuendo since he was fifteen, and I sometimes felt we both wanted to progress beyond verbal play. I had to admit that physically he was very tantalizing, and, now that he was legal, I held off only because I didn't want any part of the emotional baggage that would come with the beautiful body.

"Shit, I get laid so much I'm bored with it," he boasted. He hesitated and then asked, "All right if I smoke a joint?"

"Sure, light up," I said. "You probably get off on it more than you do sex, anyway." I don't smoke the stuff myself, but I've lived long enough and become cynical enough not to hold other people's vices against them. As he moved through the ritual of shredding the weed and picking out seeds, I went to the kitchen for another beer, self-conscious of my slight limp from a three-story fall on a construction site which had ended my career and driven me into maintenance work. As I grabbed a beer, I wondered why only the presence of an attractive young guy made me think about the limp. Vanity, I supposed. It wasn't enough that I was middle-aged, now I was crippled, too.

After I waved away his offer of a hit, Jimmy toked deeply, sucking in as far as he could go, and then, like every pot head I've ever known, insisted on trying to talk while holding his breath to keep the smoke trapped as long as possible. When he'd finished about half the big joint, he stubbed it out and leaned back contentedly. "Wow, what a buzz!" he said. "This is really good shit. You ought to try it, Mike."

"Not my kind of poison," I said.

"About that favor," he said.

"Yeah?" I encouraged.

"I hate to ask," he apologized, "but I'm supposed to meet some people at the county fair later. Mom took off for the weekend with that dickhead who's living with us and didn't leave me any money. I was wondering if you could let me hold thirty or forty bucks."

"That's a lot of money to advance on nothing but your good looks," I said.

"I'll pay you back, Mike," he pleaded. "You know I'm good for it."

"I know your mom'll come back totally broke, and you can't raise it on your own. For that kind of money I'd need a guarantee. What kind of collateral you got?"

"How about if I help you with maintenance next week?"

"Get real, Jimmy. How many times have we tried that and you always invent some excuse to wiggle out of it?"

"We ought to be able to work something out," he said, cupping his crotch in such a calculated move and grinning so knowingly that I suddenly was confident of where we were headed.

"I'm open to suggestions," I said, my racing pulse telling me that this time I was going to play the game as far as he wanted.

"How about if I'm my own collateral?"

"What the hell am I going to do with a drugged-up punk like you?" I said, laughing. "I couldn't even rent you out."

"You're a tough bastard to deal with, Mike. You're going to make me spell it out, aren't you?"

"You need the favor, I don't," I said. I was pretty confident that more than just the need for money had brought him to my door, and I was determined not to make it easy for him.

He shifted around as if waging some kind of inner battle, and then licked his lips nervously. "Why haven't you ever come on to me, Mike?" he asked. "There's been enough talk that I know you like guys, and I've caught the way you look at me sometimes since I was fifteen. I know you're interested, so why haven't you made a move?"

"I figured you knew about me, Jimmy. I suspected a couple of guys probably couldn't keep their mouths shut," I said.

"And, yeah, you're a damned attractive kid, but for most of the time I've known you, that's exactly what you were – a kid. And lately all I hear is how much pussy you're getting and how much you hate fags. Despite your pretty little ass, you spell too much trouble for me."

"Aw, Mike, that's all just talk to keep up my image," he said, massaging his crotch, which now seemed fuller. "You know I respect you as a man; I don't mind that you're gay. I'm not screwing that regular, and I've had gay sex before, and I'm not exactly a kid. What do you say, Mike?"

"So you're willing to get fucked for forty bucks?" I put it to him bluntly.

"I don't know about that," he stammered. "I don't much go for that. Usually I'm the fucker, not the fuckee."

"Usually – that's an interesting way you put it," I said. "But that's not the way I play. If we get it on, and that's an awful big if, you can be the '-er' as much as you want, but, Jimmy my boy, you're also going to roll over and be the '-ee.' I know you can go downtown and find some old man desperate enough to pay just to watch you jerk off, but I'm not desperate. If it's not mutual, to me it's not sex, and it's not worth it, whether or not money is involved." I paused to let it sink in. "It's your call, Jimbo."

His eyes darted around the room, focusing on everything but me, and he squirmed around on the couch for a few seconds. Then he squeezed his obvious hard-on and met my gaze. "You are a hard-assed bastard, Mike," he said, grinning. "But hell, I'm game."

In the bedroom, after he took off his boots, I stood him up and took my time undressing him, determined that this was not going to be hurried and impersonal. I pushed my crotch tightly into his and ran both hands up from his navel, spread his open vest, and grasped his ample pecs. He closed his eyes and threw his head back slightly as I massaged his chest and dug at his nipples with both thumbs. He stood rigidly still, hands at his sides, but a tremor ran through him as I leaned down to brush his chest lightly with my lips. He inhaled with a quick rush of air when I sucked a nipple into my mouth, and his legs trembled against my thighs.

Still sucking his nipple, I twisted the ring in the other one sharply and he flinched back. "That hurts!" he complained.

"Oh, you like a little pain, Jimmy," I said. "That's why you got the ring. I bet you pull on it harder than that every time you jack off, don't you?" I gave it another tug. "Don't you?"

"Sometimes," he groaned.

I kept twisting and pulling on the ring and started nibbling on the other nipple fairly hard. Instead of pulling away, he stepped into me and ground his crotch against me. I ran my hands around to his back and pulled him even closer as I moved up to kiss and nibble at his neck, just under his ear. "You can touch me, Jimmy," I whispered. "Enjoying it won't make you queer."

I slid the vest over his shoulders and trailed it down his arms and dropped it to the floor. I massaged his muscled back and kissed my way across his face until I brushed his lips. I expected him to pull away or protest, but his arms slid up my back tentatively and his lips parted against mine. Seizing the opportunity, I pushed my tongue between them. He opened his mouth with a groan, and his tongue battled mine as he pressed his chest against me tightly and squeezed me to him with his arms.

Kissing him voraciously, I shoved one hand between our bodies and worked it down until his cock throbbed against it. When I first made contact, he sounded a long "Ooooh!" and his knees buckled. I ran my fingers along his shaft, helping him unbunch it, until it lay straight out along his thigh, throbbing violently under my touch. The way he was sighing and moaning and squirming around, I was afraid he was going to come then and there.

I broke our embrace and stepped back. "Let's get rid of some clothes," I said. He reached to unsnap the top of his jeans. "Uh-uh," I said, pushing his hand away. "Undress me first."

He worked my shirt over my head and tossed it aside as I pried off my shoes with my toes. He ran his hand over my chest lightly. "I like hairy chests," he said timidly, as if he were a little kid caught doing something he knew he shouldn't. His fingers trembled as he mastered my belt and slid my pants down my thighs. I pushed them on down and kicked them across the room. He stood uncertainly, waiting for me to make a move. "Underwear, too," I said. He hooked his thumbs in the elastic and slid them down, allowing my stiff cock to jut straight out. "Man, you're hung," he said with a touch of awe.

"Hold it and get a feel for it," I said. He circled it lightly with his fingers and moved his hand back and forth slowly.

"Feels good, huh?" I said.

"Uh-huh," he replied, tightening his grip.

"You're going to like it a lot better before we're through, Jimmy. I promise you that," I said. I unzipped his jeans and slid them down to his knees, then ran both hands down inside the back of his briefs and cupped his firm orbs at the juncture of ass and thighs, fingers of both hands easing into the crack and spreading his cheeks, one finger probing for the opening.

"Ummm," he purred. His hand moved faster on my dick, and he nestled his head against my neck.

I stepped back and slid his briefs down for my first view of his cock. It stood proud at a forty-five degree angle, and it was pretty – the only word I could think to describe it. It was barely six inches long and not very thick, but it was straight and evenly formed from base to tip. The foreskin barely covered the rim of its bullet-shaped head, and the shaft was as creamy white and smooth as marble, with no prominent veins marring the surface.

I knelt in front of him without touching it and worked his jeans and briefs down his legs and over his feet. As I inched my hand up his downy thigh, a nervous tingle vibrated through his flesh. When I cupped his nearly hairless, tight ballsac, he grabbed my shoulders, shoved his pelvis forward, and pushed his dick in my face. "Suck it, man," he urged.

Ignoring his prick for the time being, I forced his legs apart and nibbled at his inner thigh and then on a loose fold of his nutsac before I sucked one of his balls into my mouth and swirled it around. I caught some saliva on one finger and gradually worked it into his ass. His legs were quivering, and he clawed frantically at my head and shoulders. As the sensations of my excitant tongue and probing finger intensified, he kept moaning, "Oh, man! Oh, man! Oh, man!" and his fingers knotted and twisted in my hair.

When I finally took his rod in my mouth, I thought he was going to collapse. "Oh, god, yeah!" he moaned. "Suck that dick!" He grabbed my head and shoved his pole even deeper into my mouth and pistoned in and out with rapid fire speed.

I twisted away from his grasp and freed my mouth. "Whoa, slow down and enjoy it," I cautioned. "You're like a rabbit. At this rate, you'll be done in half a minute."

I backed him against the bed and pushed on his shoulders until he sat. I leaned down to kiss him and caress his cheek, then moved in and pushed my boner in his face. He turned his head. "I don't – " he started to say, but I twisted him back around and pressed my cockhead against his lips and moved it back and forth. Slowly his lips parted to accept it. He wasn't a master at it, but his mouth wasn't virgin, either. As I rotated my pole in his mouth and caressed his chest and shoulders, he quickly added some pretty good tongue action that had my nuts tightening in no time.

When I couldn't take much more, I tumbled him onto the bed and stretched full-length on top of him and crammed my tongue down his throat. His arms circled my back tightly and he hunched his dick into my abdomen.

"You're pretty good collateral," I said. "Just how straight are you?"

"I don't really know what I am," he said. "But guys never have turned me on like this."

"This is just the beginning, Jimmy boy. I'm going to rocket you deeper into space than those drugs ever carry you," I promised. "Hell, when I'm through with you, you might decide your drugs are too tame."

"Convince me," he said.

I reached into the bedside table for lubricant and rubbers and then straddled his chest and fed my cock back into his mouth. As he tongued it, I reached back and worked a big dollop of lube into his asshole and teased it with my fingers. I eased my dick out of his mouth and dropped a rubber on his chest. "Put this on me," I said, and went back to fingering his ass while he slid the rubber down my shaft.

"I don't think I can take this thing, Mike," he said, squeezing my tool to measure its thickness.

"Oh, yeah, Jimbo, you're going to take it. You're going to be begging for it," I said.

I kneeled between his legs and hoisted them onto my shoulders and then went down on his cock. As I worked it over with my tongue, I squeezed his balls in one hand and fucked his ass with the other, getting two fingers all the way in him. I inched forward until I had him bent almost double, released his dick, and rubbed my cockhead around the surface of his asshole. He sighed and relaxed and I pushed the tip of my cock into him.

Immediately, he tightened up and retreated. "Don't," he said. "It's too damn big. I can't take it."

I rapped his ass cheek sharply with my open palm, hard enough to leave prints. He gasped in surprise and relaxed his ass muscles long enough for me to ease half way into him before he knew what had happened. When he clinched his sphincter to block further invasion, I threw my weight against his upper thighs to hold him immobile and started pinching his nipples.

"Come on, Jimbo, don't fight it," I urged.

"It's too fucking thick," he complained.

I reached up to caress his cheek. "Just relax, Jimmy," I soothed. "I won't hurt you. If you really can't take it, I'll quit. I promise. But give it a try, okay?"

"Okay," he said, not at all certain.

I tugged on the nipple ring hard enough to take his mind off my intrusive cock and shoved in another inch before he clamped down on it again. "You're going to split my ass open," he protested.

"We're almost there, Jimbo," I said. I gave his ass a couple of quick slaps and buried my long pole completely in his nearly virgin hole.

He sucked in air sharply and contorted his face. "Oh, shit, it feels like a goddamned telephone pole," he moaned.

I massaged his pecs and caressed his cheeks for a few seconds to let him get used to my prick, and then I had him lock his legs around my back and stretched out on top of him, a good bit of my weight on his chest, his cock wedged tightly between us.

"Get ready for blast-off," I told him before I kissed him and began moving inside him.

From long years of practice, I patiently shifted position and gently probed his ass until my prick located his prostate, which he didn't know he had until I discovered it for him. The first time I brushed against it, he almost came off the bed, despite my weight on him. "Holy shit!" he moaned. "What're you doing to me?"

"Showing you what butt-fucking is all about, son," I said, massaging the gland again with a couple of quick strokes.

Using the only virtue of age that I know – the ability to fuck forever without coming – for the next thirty minutes I turned my beautiful punk into a quivering mass of sensitized nerve endings beneath me and had him begging me alternately to fuck him harder and to end his agony by letting him get off. We were both drenched with sweat. He had clawed at my back so hard I feared I was bleeding, and I had sucked at his lips so much they were bruised and swollen.

Finally, he bucked and hunched beneath me, his ass spasmed tightly around my cock almost prohibiting my thrusts, his dick throbbed and pulsed between our bodies, and he exploded in torrents. "Oh, shit! Oh, shit yeah!" he kept saying as his hot come seeped across our abdomens. A few seconds later, I humped his ass with several quick lunges and shot my load unendingly into the rubber before I collapsed on him in exhaustion.

We rested and fucked, and then rested and fucked again before showering together, teasing and caressing all the while. It had been a long time since I had felt so completely relaxed and fulfilled, and from Jimmy's playful behavior, I suspected he was experiencing a completely new euphoria.

"Well, Jimmy," I said as I toweled off some droplets he had missed between his shoulder blades, "I don't know exactly what you are, but I know what you're not, and that's completely straight. No straight guy fucks like you do."

"If it's always this good, maybe I'll have to keep coming over until you teach me where I stand," he said.

"Not at forty bucks a lesson, I won't," I said.

"This wasn't a trade. I'm just collateral, remember? You have a claim on me until I pay you back." He fingered my shrunken cock, which couldn't possibly come back to life for hours. "I've got a feeling it's going to take me a long time to raise that forty bucks," he said.

"In that case, maybe you will have to come back. I can teach you a lot, maybe even how to grow hair," I said, scrubbing his bald head with a knuckle.

"I may just do that, too. I need a new image, and I know a hard-assed construction guy I wouldn't mind being like," he said, poking me in the ribs.

"If you can see well enough to find me after the fair closes tonight, maybe you should come wake me up, and we'll get in a couple more lessons then," I suggested.

"You said girls could lead me around without touching my dick. Well, now that you have touched it, I can find my way back stoned and blindfolded. I'll be here for my lessons," he said as he slipped on his jeans.

As I watched him finish dressing with that promise hanging between us, I knew I had opened myself up to a pack of future trouble, but I also was pretty sure I had launched us both on a very long and rewarding journey.

MY FIRST TUTOR

James Wilton

Looking back now, it's hard to believe I was so closeted. That's not to say that I didn't know what I wanted to do, just that I was afraid to do anything about it. Then one Saturday afternoon, I was walking home from the mall and a man offered me a ride home. Once we got about a block from my house, he said his name was Mark and he asked me if I wanted to party before going home. I nodded, hesitant but enthusiastic at the same time.

When we arrived at his place on the other side of town, he got two beers and his smoking paraphernalia and I had my first chance to really check him out. He must have been in his early thirties, well-built but not overly muscular, about six feet tall, glossy black hair, clean shaven. I thought he was the handsomest man I'd ever seen.

Mark sat down close to me and lit up. After several hits each we sat back and listened to the stereo. His knee was bouncing to the music and rubbing against my leg. It felt good. The smoke, having a man so close to me, and the friction on my leg woke up my dick and I began to throw a boner. It really felt fine. I was worried that I might get caught but decided that his eyes were closed and there wasn't anything I could do without drawing attention to my tenting slacks so I lay still and enjoyed the sensation.

The next thing I felt was my friend's hand tapping the rhythm on his knee. Soon it was between our knees, then fully on my knee. What was I going to do? At this point I caught on to what he was after but I still wasn't ready to admit to anyone, not even a man putting the make on me, that I was gay. I froze. Soon his hand was on my thigh. The feeling was wild. My cock was jumping in my pants. Up and up the leg he moved until his little finger rubbed against my balls. It was like a shot of lightning. I bolted up and slid away from him.

Mark gave me a real surprised look and asked what the problem was. When I said that he had gone too far (I felt like the prude in all those Frankie and Annette movies) he laughed and said that it was obvious that I was enjoying it. Anyway, he asked, why had I come home with him in the first place? My attempts at an answer were so foolish that he quickly caught on that I was a closet-case. When he then asked me if I was virgin, my silence said it all.

Mark seemed like a trustworthy sort so I decided to spill the beans for the first time in my life and admit that I was gay, a virgin, and hot for him.

Now, looking back at the incident, I realize how Mark must have felt. There I was, a goodlooking, in-shape, twenty-five-year-old virgin with a rod shooting up in my pants. It's a wonder he didn't jump all over me on the spot. Instead he talked through my sexuality and fears. Satisfied that I really was ready to have sex with a man he guided me into the joys I had only dreamt about.

Mark knew that I wanted to try it all but that I was too unsure of myself to initiate much so he took control and told me what to do. First he had me touch him. We started with his firm chest. I learned that I was not the only man to get erect nipples. After making him groan while tickling those little buttons through his shirt I ran my hands over his pecs, abs, and biceps. After years of admiring men's muscles I was finally feeling them. Being too shy to go below the belt, I was glad when Mark took my hand and placed it over his crotch. As soon as I moved my fingers to explore the mound, I felt his cock jerk. This was almost too much for me to take without blowing my own load. I think I would have shot at the lightest touch just then. I found the balls, shaft and dickhead inside those slacks. Meanwhile Mark was leaning back and moaning to the manipulation I was giving him. His hips began to rise as he humped up into my hand.

With my other hand I began to explore his face and hair. I ran my fingers through his glistening black hair. Then I traced his jawline and around the dimple on his chin. I outlined his lips and was surprised when his tongue shot out and licked my index finger. His mouth opened and sucked the whole finger in. I had never considered fingerfucking a mouth but Mark's tongue and sucking lips got me pistoning him. I was too excited to realize it but Mark had reached behind my head, rolled me toward him, and gently brought my lips down to his. My tongue replaced my finger as I began frenching a man for the first time. Meanwhile I was lying on top of him and feeling his hard basket against mine.

This had me so turned on that after only one or two humps of my crotch against Mark's, I shot in my pants. During the orgasm I nearly swallowed his tongue as I ground my lips against his. I was immediately sorry that I had come, thinking that our session was over. Mark laughed at my apology and said that we could then get into some longer-lasting play.

To my total surprise, he rolled me onto my back, took off my shirt and pants, and cleaned up my jizz with his tongue. Before he was half done I was back to full staff. His actions changed from licking the surface of my dick to sucking the shaft into his mouth. I was having my first blowjob. Since I had just creamed I was able to enjoy it for much longer than I would have earlier. It was heaven. Mark knew his way around a man's organ. He tongued the edge of my head, nibbled the underside of the shaft, deep-throated the whole thing and all the time played with my balls in his hand.

After a pleasurable eternity, Mark returned to his tutoring. He stood us up and had me undress him. Needless to say, I needed little direction. I luxuriated in the feel of hot velvetlike skin as I eased his shirt off the broad shoulders. I palmed his pecs and felt the nipples tickle my hands. Next I opened his belt and fly like a kid with a Christmas present. As I slid his underwear down I watched the trail of hair from the navel narrow down to a thin strip before widening at the bush. The base of his rigid cock and the mound of his buns stopped my progress. I pulled the elastic forward and peered down into his drawers.

There was that erection I knew I was going to learn to love. As I lowered the pants his member jumped out into the air. It was a fat, uncut beauty that looked a little longer than my seven inches. It bobbed and swayed, inviting my touch. Not needing any encouragement, I gently took it in my hand, feeling its warmth and hardness. It jumped to my touch. Ever since early puberty I had wanted to feel another man's penis in my hand and here it was happening. The emotions overwhelmed me and I leaned up into another long kiss with

Mark.

The dick felt wonderful. It was thick, velvety, throbbing, and hot. My hand naturally slid the skin back and forth along its length. As I pulled the skin away from his belly, it fully hooded his dickhead. I had clearly never played with an uncut dick and that gave an extra element of excitement to my explorations. As I gently drew the skin back and forth, watching the crown appear and disappear, Mark's dick got harder and harder and redder and redder. Without realizing it I was masturbating his beauty. He grabbed my hand before I caused an explosion in my face. As he drew me into another kiss I pressed my body into his and we began some hot body humping. He grabbed my wrists and placed my palms on his ass cheeks. These furry, hard mounds reminded me of all the hot man-asses I had ogled over the years. They stuck out far from his lower back and curved down and back into his upper thigh in nearly perfect hemispheres. I then ran my hands up his back and felt that deep valley over his spine, between the strong back muscles. Finally to his broad shoulders and defined biceps. It all felt better than I had ever dreamed it might.

While my hands were enjoying their excursion across paradise, our bodies were pressed tightly together. Our dicks were dueling, balls bouncing against each other, and our nipples were stimulating the others. Mark's hands were kneading my buns and tickling the puckered hole in between. Here was another erotic zone I didn't even know I had. The feel of this man's finger circling my anus and gently pressing against the entrance had me moaning yet another time.

My tutor decided it was time for me to experience another pleasure so he reached up and gently pushed me down to my knees where I found his hooded rocket looking me right in the eye. Our humping and extended foreplay had him dripping. My first oral act was to taste the pearl drops at the opening of his piss slit. It tasted smooth and only slightly salty. I was eager for more new treats so I licked around the edge of his foreskin which was still half covering the head. This had an obvious and immediate effect on Mark. His dick jumped skyward, he gasped, and another drop of precum oozed out of his slit. With this kind of encouragement I went for even more. Grabbing his shaft, I pulled the skin back to fully expose his head and ran my tongue around the rim of his helmet. It tasted mild and felt great so I took the head into my mouth and tried to go down on his whole length. I was quickly brought up short when his head hit the back of my mouth and I was only about half way down. It was only later in life, after considerable more practice, that I learned to deepthroat an erection. Nonetheless I enjoyed swirling the dick around in my mouth and bobbing my head back and forth in my first, crude blowjob. The novelty of the experience, rather than my skill, must have kept Mark aroused.

As I got into a rhythm of sucking I found my hands. One went down to play with Mark's loose sack and its hefty balls. The other ran up his hard stomach and tickled his nipples. Mark took my fingers in his and pinched his nips hard. I caught on quick and began sending him further toward the heights.

He asked if I was ready to take his load and, even though the idea of a mouthful of cum was a turnoff, there was no way I was going to let go of the beauty I had between my lips. He took my silence as a 'go' and began humping my sucking mouth. It took just a few thrusts to push him over the top. First his balls pulled up from my hands and nestled high in his crotch.

I soon felt his dick stiffen that little bit more. Then I felt it pulsate as the ejaculation began. Finally the back of my mouth was blasted by spurts of his juice. His hands on the back of my head forced me as far down on the length as I could take and my mouth began to fill up with his white load. I was excited beyond words. There was no way I was going to let a drop of this elixir out of my lips. Mark seemed to be having a dozen-shot orgasm and I was reveling in the feel, the sounds of him grunting, and the sight of the massive body in front of my face writhing in the joy of relief.

After the fireworks ended, Mark kept his cock deep in my mouth as he recovered his breath. Gradually I felt his cock soften and shrink. Finally he drew it out and I could savor the taste of the offering he had left in my mouth. It was unique and indescribable but I knew I loved it and wanted to have many more helpings.

Mark quickly told me not to swallow and pulled me up into a deep kiss where he got to taste his own jism in my mouth. Without swallowing, himself, he began to deposit his sperm on my lips, chin, and cheeks. I was squirming with delight as he licked my neck and ears. He worked his way down to my nipples and gave them a touch of the roughness he had taught me. All these pleasure zones had me stiff as a rod. My hard-on was resting against his chest and I was so horny I was humping his body, leaving a trail of precum down his front.

Mark took his time licking my chest, navel, stomach, and thighs but not touching any of the important places. I finally couldn't take the torture and, grabbing him by the sides of his head, I aimed my dick into his mouth. Being experienced, he was able to take me all the way so that my pubes were against his lips. I wanted more but all the humping in the world wasn't going to get me any deeper in his throat.

Mark took control by holding me by the hips and slowly eased my cock out of his mouth. The trip out was even more arousing than the trip in. As I was about to leave his lips his tongue swirled around my head and Mark nibbled his way down my vein to my ball sack where he gave me another new thrill by sucking one and then the other ball into his mouth. I was so excited that I tried to fist my own dick but Mark kept swatting my hand away. He knew what he was doing and he knew that this slow torture was driving me wild.

After a seeming eternity of ball play, Mark finally returned to the center of my being. He lightly ran his tongue up and down one side and then the other, around the cockhead, into the piss slit and then along the vein. Seeing that he had me real close to the edge, Mark finally took my dick into his mouth and began rocking my hips so that I was fucking his face. In less than six thrusts I was cumming into this man's mouth. My knees felt like jelly and I experienced the ejaculations throughout my body.

Before Mark even released my softening cock from his mouth I crumpled down onto him in a weak embrace. He eased me to the floor and covered me with his body as we exchanged leisurely kisses. My first time was truly an exhausting experience and I reveled in cuddling with my new mentor.

Once I had regained myself and got ready to leave, Mark and I both decided that we needed to meet again, real soon. He had an eager learner to play with and I had at least ten years of suppressed desire to catch up on. Not being afraid to appear too eager, I suggested the next afternoon and he agreed.

All that night and the next day I ran over my experiences in my head. I had trouble concentrating on work and probably had an erection most of the day. I kept wondering if I was exaggerating the pleasure I remembered or Mark's good looks. Was my memory filtered by all those years of denial?

After work, I drove the short distance from the commuter lot to Mark's house and waited nervously for him to answer the door. I had no need to worry. He was as exceptionally hot as I remembered. And, he seemed genuinely eager to see me. He ushered me into his living room and my inexperience took over: I jumped him and grabbed his crotch. Mark backed away, explaining that we would soon get to that but we did have some pleasantries to get out of the way. Sheepishly, I sat back and went through the normal civil exchange, all the time mentally undressing the hunk before my eyes. My host went off to get drinks and bring the smoking paraphernalia.

After a few tokes, I was in no mood to wait on convention. I put my hand on Mark's thigh and leaned into a kiss. This time he was ready to reciprocate and the session began. Since I had already been invited to explore his body, I was less shy about my actions. I wanted to return to the chest I had enjoyed, so I felt it through his shirt. It truly was hard and well defined with erect nipples catching the cloth as I ran my hands across its expanse. I ran my hands down his hard belly to his packed basket and felt it jump to my touch. Knowing that I was turning this man on, I ran my fingers up and down his thigh while watching the effect on his crotch. Mark just lay back and enjoyed the attention. Soon I tired of all the fabric and began to unbutton his shirt, unfasten his belt, and work open his fly. He was perfectly willing to facilitate my unwrapping and lifted his hips so I could lower his jeans and jockeys.

There it was, the perfect body I had remembered. My erotic recollections hadn't distorted reality. He really was a hunky specimen. That chest really was wide and tight. His skin really was velvety and smooth. There really was just a wisp of hair around those erect nipples and an inviting line from the navel to the bush. Those balls really were big and hung low in a silky-soft sack. His cock really was uncut and at least eight thick inches long and it was aiming straight up at me. To Mark's obvious pleasure I palmed his erection and felt the head rest along my wrist. I felt the dick stiffen, saw it give off a drop of precum, and heard this hot man moan in ecstasy. With my thumb I spread nature's lubricant around his dickhead and felt his thrust him hips upward to fuck my fist.

In my excitement, I woke him from his pleasures by deep kissing his inviting lips. At this point he took over the controls; without breaking off the kiss he began to disrobe me. In no time I had his hand rhythmically squeezing my dick until I thought I would cum. Next he played with my balls while rubbing that ridge of cockroot below the sack with his middle finger. Each passage got a little lower until he was massaging my asshole.

Like the day before, this gave me an incredibly unexpected sensation. I found myself spreading my thighs and raising my hips to meet his manipulations. As one hand rose to play with my erection, he wet the middle finger of the other hand and began a gentle invasion of my sphincter. Every fraction of an inch combined a little discomfort and a lot of erotic pleasure. I found myself rotating my hips to ease his entrance. My willingness encouraged Mark to lubricate the entrance a little more and work his finger further and further into my anus. I had assumed that gay guys let themselves get fucked because it felt good but I had never expected it to feel quite this good. And this was only his finger.

With some deep kissing and tit play to distract me, Mark began working another finger in with the first. Again, more discomfort overshadowed by more pleasure. At this point Mark was getting pretty aroused himself and I could feel his boner poking my thigh as he continued the kissing and the assplay.

Miraculously, a tube of K-Y appeared and Mark began to lube my hole. This felt even better and there was no feeling of discomfort. Without realizing it I was acquiescing to a man fucking me. And, this was with a dick I couldn't even fit down my throat. Mark swiveled me around on the sofa and raised my legs to give him access to my ass. He was fingerfucking me with one, then two, and finally three fingers. It had me squirming and writhing. When he withdrew I felt empty and bolted upright at the feeling. Laughing at my look of disappointment, Mark knelt over his more-than-willing partner and greased up his beautiful tool. I was mesmerized by the sight of that staff. The lotion made it glisten, his manipulation made the hood slide back and forth over the head, and the ball sack swayed to and fro with the action. I would have been content to watch this operation for hours if I weren't so eager to feel such a rod replace the fingers in my ass.

With soothing words of encouragement, Mark raised my knees to my shoulders and massaged the entrance to my anus with his cockhead. I was apprehensive and eager at the same time. Clearly this was bigger than a finger but it also promised a much more intimate contact with this hunk. With a look of concentration, Mark began the easy pressure against my portal. After the finger play, I was pretty loose and his head entered without much trouble. However, there was a bright pain. Mark must have seen it in my face because he froze in place. With one hand he brought my softening cock back to erection and at the same time caused my anus to relax. Feeling the change, he began his slow glide down my chute. Just as I began to feel his cockhead press against a wall, I felt his bush press against my asscheeks and his balls bounce against my lower back. He had hit bottom. I felt luxuriously full. Looking up, I saw that Mark was also in the throes of excitement. His eyes were shut tight and his nostrils were flaring. I was causing exquisite pleasure to this hunk.

As he came back to his senses and our eyes met, he began a slow withdrawal. The friction on my anus was stimulating but the feeling of emptiness was a disappointment that was to last only a brief moment. Just as the cockhead was about to escape, Mark reversed his motion and slowly filled me up, again. This time the withdrawal came quicker and he built into a pistoning movement. I grabbed his hips and pulled him into me harder. The pleasure became more intense as the actions became more forceful. I wanted him to batter my ass. My hands rubbed his pulsing butt and powerful back as I felt those muscles make his body fuck me. Without even a touch, I suddenly became aware of my own cock as it jumped to attention and sprayed jism over Mark and me. My ejaculation must have given that extra stimulation to him because I felt his cock stiffen as he bucked up against my tail with a mighty grunt and came in my gut, ramming forward for that extra bit of penetration.

When he was done, Mark collapsed his sweaty body on my chest. I felt his cock soften and slowly slip out of my ass. The gradual withdrawal added a last new thrill to the whole experience. We stayed wrapped in each others arms for a long time as we kissed and fondled. I had never imagined that a fuck could feel so good to the man doing the bottoming.

They say we never forget our first sex partner. I guess I was real lucky to have such a patient and sexy teacher. I know I'll never forget him.

THE TUTOR, THE TOURIST & ME

James Wilton

Through my house here in Florida, a variety of young men have passed. Most stayed briefly, but one long-term resident was Mike. He was worldly, older than his tender years. He was just my type: slim, dark-haired, nicely hung, agreeable. We had a very fulfilling sexual relationship. Or so I thought. Then one day, Mike asked if we could get into kinkier sex. The question came just after I had come, and I was too exhausted to ask what he meant. I merely said, "Sure."

A few nights later I found out what *kinky* meant to Mike. This was the night Mike found Ramon at Charlie's, the local cruise bar. His tight body and sparkling black eyes caught my attention first. I bought him a drink, knowing he was a newcomer and probably a tourist. I was only being my sociable self, the way I can get after a few brews. After a brief chat, Ramon excused himself to go to the john. Mike said, "Well, how about it?"

"How 'bout what?"

"Is Ramon submissive enough for you?"

"For *me*? This isn't about me. This is about *you*," I said, finishing my beer.

As we made our way to my car, Ramon seemed to be more interested in me than Mike, so my lover decided to drive. Ramon sat in the front seat between us and while he fondled my crotch, I had the chance to run my hands over his loevly body. His chest was very well defined with his nips popping hard into the jersey material. These were clearly going to be a source of serious action later on I decided. I ran my hand further down his hard belly to his crotch where I felt a long, hard tube stretching across his right thigh. At the end was a wet spot where the boy was evincing his excitement about his situation. As I felt my way around his generous endowment, Ramon arched his back and thrust his pelvis up to hump my hand.

Mike turned on us, making a scary show of his displeasure

with our antics. "Hey, you assholes, slow down."

We sat in stony silence for the next five minutes before we mercifully rolled into the driveway.

At home, Mike took over. He grabbed the collar of Ramon's T-shirt, lowering his head and dragging him from the car to the laundry room. There, the exposed beams and pipes served as hooks to tie our guest up. The tenting of the front of his pants let us know that we were doing just what he wanted. I was ready to get into it.

Using sections of clothesline, Mike tied Ramon's wrists to the overhead pipes, opening this stud to our whims. Once he was incapacitated, Mike began his torment by firmly grabbing his victim's basket and squeezing the equipment, making Ramon squeal and try to withdraw into a fetal position. As the boy's ass backed my way I got into the action by giving him a loud whack across his hard buns. This straightened him up. I stepped up behind him and humped my excited crotch into his ass as I felt his firm chest through his shirt. I was quickly realizing that this kind of sexual dominance really turned me on.

Meanwhile, Mike began some verbal torment by reminding Ramon of his vulnerability and telling him all we wanted to do to him. The raunch rap seemed to have the same effect on Ramon it was having on me. I could hear him moan and feel his nipples harden as he rubbed his buns across my stiff dick. While Mike moved up and gave Ramon some intense nibble action, I renewed my familiarity with the boy's crotch. His dick was still hard but the damp spot at its tip had gotten much bigger. He was so hot that he tried to hump my exploring hand but, not wanting to please him, I eased the pressure as he pushed forward, giving him nothing to press against.

It was time to unwrap our sex package. After opening his shorts, I slipped them down to his ankles, leaving his midsection covered only by his tight-stretched briefs. Mike raised the T-shirt over Ramon's head exposing his hairless chest and the small patches of hair in his armpits. We both stepped back to admire our toy. His buns fully filled the fabric like two half globes. His chest was smooth and well defined. His thighs were as muscular as most gymboys' upper arms. And, his crotch promised a long, thick cock above sizeable balls.

Sensing my arousal, Mike began massaging my erection through my jeans as he talked about the fun we were going to have with this gorgeous sex object. With his other hand he accented his plans with pokes and tweaks at Ramon's anatomy: a flick at the tip of his dick, a pinch on his nipple, a jab into the crack in his briefs, and a loud slap across his buns. Each time the boy tried pathetically to back away from his tormentor. Finally Mike decided that Ramon had been decent too long and yanked his briefs down, totally exposing him to our eyes and hands.

I was right, we had picked up a remarkable piece of dick. Ramon had a small, dark bush over an equally dark set of equipment. Otherwise, there was almost no hair anywhere on his crotch. The cock itself jutted up at a forty-five degree angle with no curve at all. The large balls hung low in a silky sack. After removing the clothes from around his ankles we spread Ramon's ankles and the scrotum hung free from his thighs. With a jab at the back of the sack, Mike got the balls to swing back and forth like a pendulum. He was able to make a fist around the sack between the base of the dick and the balls, themselves. This handle let him tug the boy's erection down by the root and make it flap nearly all the way from his belly to his thighs. Meanwhile drops of precum oozed out of the pee slit and created a fine thread down to the floor.

The view from the back was almost as incredible; those buns were totally hairless except for a little fur showing in his crack. His balls were clearly visible from behind in their lowhanging bag. His back muscles were as defined as his chest and his torso formed a vee from his narrow waist to his broad shoulders. While I was enjoying the rear view, Mike was arguing that Ramon's dripping cock was proof that the boy was getting into this domination. While threatening various forms of bondage and pain he was swatting the dick back and forth. Ramon tried to pretend pain but the increased flow of precum belied his complaints.

Knowing that there was another beautiful cock in the room that I couldn't see, I suggested to Mike that we strip too. In a flash I was treated to my handsome friend's magnificent body and a hard cock telling me that he was getting turned on by having this guest at our disposal and watching me enjoy this new experience. Grabbing him by that erect member, I drew him crotch-to-crotch with Ramon. Their dicks were about the same length but Mike's was both lighter colored and thicker.

However, Ramon's balls were considerably larger and lower. I fought to grasp both cocks together in one hand as I played with the ballsacks with the other. After a few jags on the combined dickflesh, the boys took over the action and humped against each other and into my fist.

Before the action got out of hand, I withdrew and slapped our toy hard on his ass. Mike stepped back and renewed his attack on Ramon's nipples. I took this chance to step up behind the boy and slip my hardon up between his thighs. I felt his scrotum move as I humped forward and heard him gasp with each jab. Meanwhile his torso was writhing under Mike's manipulations and my chest was being given a massage by the victim's muscular back. I reached around his narrow hips and ran my hands down his tight thighs. As he moved I could feel the muscles bulge under my fingers. While my cock was being excited by the tops of Ramon's legs, I reached in front of him and grabbed hold of Mike's cock. He was obviously enjoying himself because his dickhead was dripping with precum, making a nice, slimy fist for him to fuck. I watched his nostrils flair and his eyes glaze over as he enjoyed my manipulation of his member.

I was tiring of dryhumping Ramon's crotch and withdrew enough to poke at his rectum. With the slime on my dickhead I probably could have jabbed my way in. Instead I stepped back and wet my middle finger as a replacement for my cock. As I began to massage his pucker, Ramon let out a long sigh and backed into the pleasant feeling. I took this as a signal to burst into that hole with my longest finger. It was incredibly tight and hot. I could feel Ramon working his ass muscles and massaging my digit while he writhed in pleasure against my hand. This was going to be one great fuck receptacle.

Mike had had enough. Here we were exciting this bottom when he was supposed to be showing me how to inflict pain. Looking around the laundry room for implements, he started with more clothes line. First, he tied Ramon's ankles to opposite walls, spreading his legs wide. Then he began wrapping another length around Ramon's sack, forcing his balls further and further away from his dick. I watched with fascination as I kept twisting my finger around up our guest's cute ass. Next, Mike tied a partially filled bottle of bleach to the trussed balls and let it swing between his legs. This got to Ramon who tried to lower his body as much as possible to relieve the downward pressure. Mike's dick, which had deflated during all the mechanical work, was back to full erection as he watched the dancer writhe in his restraints. To Ramon's obvious pleasure, we removed the bottle, which was sure to get in the way.

Mike then turned to the bag of clothespins. I was fascinated as he attached them to various parts of Ramon's anatomy causing groans of pain. First each nipple, then pinches of skin in his crotch and underarms. With such a tight body, he had trouble finding places loose enough to grab. Despite the yowls, Ramon's dick told us he was thoroughly enjoying himself.

My domination instructor had yet one more torture to make his victim endure. Mike brought candles from the dining room table and gave me one. Ramon's eyes bulged and he begged us not to hurt him. This was a mistake because it got Mike even more fired up and spurred him on to further verbal abuse.

First we pulled Ramon's ankles backward so he lost his balance and hung by his wrists. This gave us his backside to dribble on. With the first drop of hot paraffin on his ass cheeks, the boy jerked and shrieked. Wondering if this may have been too much, I reached around to check his dickmeter and found it at full enjoyment so we continued. The droplets of pain caused an inspired and very erotic dance by our little dancer. After covering much of his back with wax droppings I jammed my extinguished candle up his ass and stepped back to look over our creation. In my excitement I reached over to Mike and enjoyed a brief makeout session with him. We were both really turned on and stopped soon before we caused an ejaculation.

Next, to the front of our friend. This was even more fun since there were several more erotic targets to hit. Every drop on his scrotum, dick, and nipples caused jolts and cries but also spasms of his everhard dick and continuous drops of precum from his slit.

Mike and I agreed that the punishment stage was complete and it was time for our pleasure. I enjoyed yet another feel of this hard body as we brushed most of the dried wax off Ramon and removed the clothes pins and ball restraint. We left him spread eagle to keep his ass fully exposed.

Mike gave me first crack at this orifice. He unrolled a lubed condom over my erection as he played gently with my balls. This combination got me to the height of hardness and I was ready to plow our guest's waiting hole. With Mike's hand to guide my tool and my hands grabbing Ramon's narrow hips, I gave one long lunge and fully impaled the boy. This knocked the wind out of him but he recovered quickly and his moans let me know how much he was enjoying himself. Mike encouraged me with orders to ram my hardest and push in to the hilt. Meanwhile he was nearly wrapped around me as he used one hand to massage my asshole while pushing me further toward my target. With the other he was fondling my balls. Between the excitement of all our previous activities and the overwhelming sensations of this fuck, I took no time in popping my nuts. I kept my shrinking cock inside the ass as long as I could but it eventually withdrew and I hunched back into Mike's arms in exhaustion.

Mike, however, wasn't finished. In a flash he had his condom on and was promising Ramon the rut he wouldn't soon forget. With one mighty hump this virile fucker sank all the way into the boy's ass and had him off his feet. Grabbing both thighs, he held Ramon up and pounded him from below while he was suspended off the floor. Putting him back down, Mike reached up the boy's chest and pulled down on his shoulders to increase the force of his jabs. Several times I watched him totally withdraw his cock and power fuck Ramon's ass. Wanting to be part of this action, I spit on my hand and wrapped it around Ramon's cock. As he lunged forward on Mike's attacks, he fucked the tunnel I had formed with my fist. Clearly he couldn't take much of this and on the next deep plunge Mike hit a button that made our guest's cock rise and blow its wad out into the laundry room. Ramon's ejaculation must have given Mike the stimulation he needed because he quickly howled as he jumped onto his tiptoes and lunged as far up into Ramon as he could reach. He gave him several more short jabs as he shot the last of his juice. Still hanging onto Ramon's shoulders he eased himself out and down the boy's sweaty back.

Once the cut-down and clean-up was over, we invited Ramon to stay with us for a while. He declined, and in the morning Mike drove him back to his hotel. I guess the spontaneity and mystery of a first time cannot be repeated and Ramon didn't want to diminish either his or our memory of an unforgettable evening in the laundry room.

HEAVEN

Nigel Christopher

As a youth I lived in Cambridge, near the large supermarket where I eventually went to work as a trainee manager.

About the only place to meet other guys was at the humble cottage (or tearoom). Cambridge had four main cottages, and a few smaller, less frequented ones that were mainly in the suburbs.

Although there was some daytime activity at the cottages, the bulk of the trade appeared from around five. Here came the businessmen, after a hard day at the office, were dutifully venturing home to the wife and kids, and fancied some cock action on the way. This was the time of day that the rent appeared, hanging around, in the hope that the discreet businessmen, not wanting to be seen hanging around such places, would pull up in their posh company cars and, with wallets overflowing, would make discreet eye contact at the boys, and take them to a secluded spot, usually at the direction of the rent, to enjoy the pleasure of a paid session.

Occasionally they struck it lucky, and instead of picking up the rent, they managed to attract the attention of someone like me, who like them, was there for the fun, not the money.

After about an hour and a half of this activity things quieted down until about eight when the fully-fledged gays ventured out. Now there were none of the "can't let the wife know" brigade, just like-minded guys out for cock. This was the time of day when it would not be unusual to walk into a cottage and hear the rapid scuffle of feet as people tied to attain a normal stance, as if they were just there for the intended purpose of the urinal.

That's how it was when I first came out, but my discovery of gay life started only about a year ago, just outside the most infamous cottage in Cambridge at Midsummer Common.

By that time, I had begun studies at the local college, and on a Friday we normally finished at lunchtime. In summer, before going home, I would venture down to Midsummer Common to soak up the sunrays.

On this particular Friday, in the middle of a scorching June, I took up position in a spot where I could observe the comings and goings of the guys who were regularly popping in and out of the cottage.

After a while curiosity took advantage, and I decided to go and check out why it was, when a young, spunky hunk went in, he was immediately followed by a few of the older guys who were hanging around.

As I walked towards the doorway, I noticed a young, blond, very cute guy also walking in the same direction. He was wearing only a pair of ripped jeans, which showed off his well-developed muscular chest to its full glory.

As I stood at the urinal, knowing that we were the only guys there, and with about fifteen stalls to choose from, the guy stood just one stall away from me.

I glanced across towards him, and saw that he was looking at me as well. Instinctively we smiled at each other, and I, not knowing what to do next, turned back to look at the wall rising in front of me.

The wall was not, however, the only thing rising that afternoon; my cock had started to do it's favorite trick, slowly rising to attention as my mind pondered the situation, and the vision by my side.

I did not realize that the guy was looking at me, nor did I know that he had moved along and was now standing right beside me.

"Looks like you've got one helluva problem there."

I was startled how close he was to me now.

"It often does that," I eventually managed to say. I think the nervousness in my voice, and the tremor in my legs, gave away my newness to the situation.

"I've gotta place just across the park, if it would make you feel easier."

"I don't know."

"Maybe you'd like to come in for coffee."

The phrase "come in for coffee" had a double meaning when I was at school and somewhere deep inside me I hoped this offer also had hidden depths. "OK, lets go."

As I packed everything away and followed him outside, it seemed to be hotter than it had been moments before when I had entered the building.

Slowly, we walked across the park to the row of small Victorian houses that lined the eastern side. As we walked he told me that his name was Gavin, he was 18 and was a qualified masseur, trying to make a living here in Cambridge. I was fascinated by this and asked him how he handled the sexual aspects of the job. He said he never went any further than a quickie hand job, after the massage, although many of his punters did request more. He was now building up a nice little clientele, the money was good, and he thought the job easy.

As we reached the front door, and my nerves started playing up, I did manage to introduced myself. "I'm Chris, I'm studying at the TEC."

"Take a seat," he said as we entered the living room. Motioning toward the sofa, he asked, "Coffee or a cool can of lager?"

I opted for the lager. Coffee would take longer, and I sure was ready for a drink. He returned from what I assumed was the kitchen with two cans, and he held one out to me. "You look hot, Chris. Why don't you take off your shirt, and relax?"

I placed the can on the floor, and slowly started removing my T-shirt. I noticed Gavin was studying my body. He smiled as I placed my shirt on the floor and picked up the can again. He moved next to me and stretched one arm along the back of the sofa. Gently caressing my shoulder, he asked, "You've not done this before, have you?"

I gulped. I stared at my lager. "No."

"Just so you know, I don't usually bring people back here. I do like to keep myself private, but with you, well – "

"Well, what?"

"You aren't like most of the guys I've met around here."

That was an understatement, if ever I heard one. Not only was I naive, but I was also still a virgin. "No, I guess I'm not. You see, I've never."

"Never what?"

"I've never done anything with anyone."

"I guessed as much, but don't worry, I've never gone further than a handjob with anyone."

"Oh?"

"Yeah." He finished his lager, then asked, "Why don't we go upstairs and get more comfortable?"

"I don't know."

"You look like you could do with a nice massage. You look so tense."

I chuckled now. Was I going to get his evening special for free?

He stood up and I noticed his packet, with at least eight inches of manhood throbbing away in his jeans. He looked at me as I rose, dropped his eyes, then looked back up. "Yes, I think you are tense. I think a massage is just what you need."

I followed him up the narrow stairs and, as he started to enter the bedroom, he pointed to a door to my left and informed me that that was the bathroom if I needed it.

He lay a large bath towel on the bed. "This is to stop the oil getting on the duvet," he explained, "I suggest you loose your kit." As I started to remove my jeans and trainers, he too kicked off his trainers and dropped his jeans. He didn't have any underwear on and, as the jeans fell, his cock sprung up, ready for action. I had been right in my guess it was about eight inches, and so it nicely matched what I was about to reveal. As we stood before each other naked, looking each other down and up.

For me being a first timer, I had certainly found the best tutor. He told me to lie face down on the bed and get comfortable. Then he climbed up onto the bed, and straddled me, his balls resting nicely at the top of my crack. Then I felt the cold splash of oil fall into the small of my back, followed by the sensation of his hands starting their workout over me.

As he worked me over, my cock felt like it was going to explode. Gavin must have sensed this; he said, "The towel doesn't just stop the oil, and there is a shower you can use afterward." The gentleness in his voice was so inviting I wanted to roll over and kiss him, but instead I reached down and stroked myself. The jism came quickly.

This must have turned Gavin on because, just as I finished, I felt the warm splash of his cum on my back, and there was a lot of it. "Look, no hands," he exclaimed.

On his command, I rolled over, and he lowered his face to give me a long tongue-searching kiss that started up the passion in my loins once again.

Throughout the frontal massage, he kept pawing and leaning forward to kiss me, then he slipped his hands around my raging cock, and started to lightly massage it. I could feel the second parcel getting ready for its delivery, and my hands reached up towards his silky body.

As he worked my cock into a frenzy, I returned the pleasure, and worked my hand on his cock. Then, as if by magic, both of our tools reared up and let forth mighty gushes of jism that covered us both. He then lowered his body onto mine, and with the sweet sticky mess bonding us together, we kissed and relaxed in each other's arms.

It's fair to say I was in heaven.

KEVIN'S ASS

John C. Douglas

There wasn't a girl in Mason High who didn't envy Kevin Dunn's ass. In his skintight jeans, the firm curves of his muscular buttocks were far more attractive that those of any of the admittedly lovely female bottoms. In fact, there were few girls whose facial beauty surpassed his. Only his position as a quarterback for the Mason High Raiders kept him from being dubbed a sissy.

Kevin was five-eleven, with chestnut, shoulder-length, wavy hair, and the flawless body of a young Greek god.

He was also failing my English class.

"If you flunk me, Mr. Scott," he said, "that means I can't play the last three games. We'll lose the state title for sure."

I looked at that full-lipped, sensual mouth, and my prick quivered with excitement. If I handled things just right, Kevin Dunn would soon be using that pretty mouth on it.

"You flunked yourself, Kevin," I reminded him. "Of course, I could give you another test."

"Now, you're talking!" he exclaimed. Then his shoulders sagged. "I'd probably fail it, too."

I perched on the corner of my desk, a position that pulled my slacks tight across my prominent basket, and outlined the semi-hard length of my cock. It was impossible for Kevin to miss it, and his eyes kept drifting down to examine and compare.

"How badly do you want to continue playing" I demanded.

"More than anything!" he answered quickly. "I gotta play, Mr. Scott! I just gotta!"

"Then you 'just gotta' pass my test, Kevin," I sighed. "There's no other way."

"Couldn't you fix it some way?" he asked hopefully, his slender hips squirming in the chair, the movement sending a surge of lust through my balls.

"All I can do, Kevin, is give you another test. I will not falsify your grade."

"Then I'm sunk!" he groaned. "I ain't cracked a book since last semester."

"Don't be so hasty," I said. "I'm authorized to give you any test that I deem suitable."

I moved my hand slowly up along my thigh and, making sure his eyes were on it, I cupped my crotch and gave it a deliberate squeeze.

"I could give you a test that I know you could pass, if you really wanted to. It's up to you, Kevin."

He frowned in concentration, not certain of my meaning. "This test," he asked hesitantly. "It would be in something else? I think I know what you're getting at."

"Do you, Kevin?" I said, making my voice equally soft. "Then it's up to you."

He blushed and shifted his feet nervously. "I already told you how much I wanted to play. Ain't that answer enough?"

"No," I told him. "I want a clear answer."

"You sure nobody else'll know about this?"

I nodded. "Quite sure. We'll conduct the test in my apartment tonight. Can you arrange to spend the night with a friend?"

He gave me a crooked grin, sure now of my meaning. "Yeah, I can fix that. But, Mr. Scott, I ain't never done nothing like that. How do I know you're gonna . . . I mean, you can still flunk me."

"Kevin," I assured the boy, "you'll score a perfect one hundred if you'll just cooperate."

Five hours later, I was wearing only a sashed silk robe when he knocked on my door at exactly eight o'clock, and he entered with a nervous smile. I waved him to an easy chair and busied myself at the wet bar in one corner of the living room.

"I think we should drink a toast to your success," I said, handing him a tall glass.

"I ain't passed yet," he answered, taking the glass with eagerness.

"Oh, but you will," I smiled. "You will."

He took several swallows before saying, "This is blackmail, Mr. Scott."

"Bribery, Kevin," I corrected. "In an effort to obtain a passing grade, you are bribing me, and I am accepting the bribe.

"That ain't the way it is," he complained. "You're forcing me to . . ."

"Stop!" I exclaimed. "Stop, right there!"

I strode to the door and flung it open. "You're free to go, Kevin. Good night."

He stared at me for a moment, then shrugged in resignation. "You win," he murmured. "Shut the fuckin' door."

"That's better," I said. locking the door and emptying my glass. "Now, Kevin, take off your clothes."

Without argument, he obeyed, stripping down to his jockey shorts. The sheer beauty of his young nakedness made my prick throb almost painfully.

"The shorts, too," I said quietly.

"Damn!" he grunted, baring his curly haired crotch and its sizable equipment. "I feel funny as hell doing this!"

I stood up, facing him, and threw off my robe, revealing my erection. The boy gasped.

"Jesus! I didn't know anybody was hung like that!"

"That's our test equipment, Kevin," I said, skinning my cock back and squeezing it as the youngster stared. "I think you should examine it, before we begin the actual test."

His own dick was swelling, in spite of his attitude of protest. "You mean," he demanded, "touch it?"

"We have to start somewhere," I reminded him.

Uncertainly, he moved toward me, one hand extended, and his whole body shivered as his fingers curled about my prick, warm and exciting. His own penis jerked responsively.

"Just to make it easier," I said, my voice soft, "I'll touch you. May I?"

The brown eyes had been staring down at the cock in his hand. Now, they lifted to meet mine with a strange glitter in their swirling depths. He nodded, wordless with emotion, and he tightened its grip on my cock.

I ran one hand beneath his balls, and took hold of his dick with the other. He gave a sharp gasp, his hips jerking.

"Goddamn!" he groaned. "This is crazy!"

"Let me show you just how crazy." I pulled him down to the thick rug, breaking away to arrange my body alongside his, but with my head toward his feet.

I milked the boy's dick with my fingers, and saw a pearl of

jism ooze from its slitted tip. My tongue licked it off, and his hips jerked at the touch.

I sucked Kevin's cock with all the skill of my twenty-nine years, fondling his heavy balls and teasing his sensitive anus as I worked my lips up and down the throbbing column, my tongue pressing, massaging and fluttering. His hips pumped the shaft in and out of my mouth. He was close. I wanted to take him but he had been a bad boy, really. I mounted his chest and forced open his mouth. He fought me. The harder he denied wanting it, the more intense my desire to have him experience it. I slapped his face with my cock and snarled, "If I can suck yours, you can suck mine."

"But – "

"But nothing," I said, holding his head steady with my hands. I knew if he really didn't want it, nothing would have made him open his mouth wide enough to accept it.

I forced only the head in, letting him get used to it. I did everything. His mouth was merely an instrument of my pleasure. But eventually he began to suck as if he was truly enjoying it. At times, his suction was almost painful, but I loved every minute of it. Unfortunately, the minutes were far too few because the mere thought I had Kevin sucking me off was enough to cause orgasm.

As my load gushed out, some landing on his cheek, he gasped, "Christ! Now I'm a goddamn cocksuckin' queer!"

"No!" I smiled reassuringly. "You're just one of the lucky guys who can make it either way. You'll still give the girls babies!"

He licked his lips and pressed my cock against his cheek, as cuddling a doll he had loved as a child. "Okay, did I pass the test?"

"The oral section," I grinned. "You made an A-plus! Now, there's one more part."

He stiffened in protest. "No way! I ain't gonna do that!"

"Do what?"

"I know what you queers do. No way am I gonna take it up the ass!"

"But it's such a lovely ass," I said, rolling him over on his stomach.

"I've swapped blowjobs with a few guys. But I ain't never

been screwed."

Swapped blowjobs? Well, no wonder he was so good once he got going.

"Well," I said, slapping that ass, "then, it's about time. But let's have another drink, and then move to the bedroom."

Ten minutes and one tall drink later, I had changed my mind. Kevin's cock was still nearly fully erect. It was a magnificent cock and I wanted it up my ass in the worst way.

"Tell you what," I said, getting on the bed, "why don't you push that big thing into me first?"

"What?"

"Look, you fuck pussy, just imagine it's a pussy." I lay back and pulled my knees up, spreading them wide.

"It sure as hell looks like a pussy," he said, obviously ready to fuck anything. I handed him a tube of lube and he prepared himself. His prick slid into my asshole like a well-oiled piston, all the way to his heavy balls.

"Oh, shit!" he gasped, his hips trembling. "That's better than pussy!"

"Be still a minute!" I ordered, flexing the internal muscles of my rectum. His body jerked and his cock throbbed inside my ass.

"Oh, damn!" he moaned. "That feels good!"

"Fuck me, Kevin!"

Fucking was something at which the handsome youth was quite experienced, and he rode my bucking ass like an angry stallion. I began to doubt he'd never fucked another guy before, so willing was he to do this. His cock filled and frictioned, and I worked my hips to increase the pleasure as he fucked me, hard, fast and deep.

He almost screamed when he hit the short rows, and I worked my ass in a savage circle while he rammed his dick deep, and his cream began spurting into my belly. I flexed my asshole and he cried out with ecstasy at the sensation of the tissues literally chewing and sucking his jetting cock.

"Christ!" he moaned. "I've never had a piece of pussy that good!"

"I don't think I've ever been more thoroughly fucked!" I panted. "You're quite a stud!"

He gripped my erection. "So are you. Look at that fucker."

"On your back, boy."

"Holy shit, I don't think so."

"Oh, you'll get used to it, just as I got used to you."

Briefly, I explained how he could loosen his sphincter, and the boy nodded eagerly, his knees pulled tight against his hairless chest. I felt the slight yielding as he bore down, and I slid my prick up into him.

I hadn't made a dozen strokes before his ass began jerking beneath me, and he cried, "I'm gonna come! Oh, goddamn! Do it! . . . Do it!"

Between us, his prick spurted, and his asshole convulsed about my cock as I rode him with savage thrusts. His semen arced over his belly and splattered on his chest, trickling sluggishly down into the valley of belly and chest. I kept right on fucking him with full length strokes.

"My god!" he panted, staring up at me with wide eyes as I began my orgasm deep inside him. "It feels *so* good! So *fuckin'* good!"

When Kevin returned to my apartment just three days later, there was no discussion of grade changes or any hesitancy in his surrender. He welcomed my prick into that hungry mouth just long enough to assure its ultimate hardness, then straddled my hips and impaled his torrid asshole on the throbbing prick, fucking it until we both came.

Throughout his senior year, he spent at least one night a week in my bed, and before he graduated, we had initiated a total of seven eager young studs into our special little fraternity.

GOING PLACES:
ON THE BUS TO MANCHESTER

Edward Bangor

Nicky Bailey was bored.
More than bored really, he was fed-up. Although he'd initially felt trusted to be left alone at London's Victoria Coach Station, he now realized nothing could go wrong once he'd found the correct gate number. All he had to do was sit tight with his shoulder bag on the hard plastic seat until the bus to Manchester was indicated on the video screen above the doorway. Then he'd proceed to the coach just outside, in the courtyard. His mother would be waiting at the other end. There were no stops, nor possible delays. But the bus wasn't due to leave for another four hours, and there was nothing for a teenage boy like Nicky to do.

Only thirty minutes had passed but already he'd read, and re-read the music paper he'd bought at the newsagent outside the main door. The bustling people and occasional loud announcements made it impossible for him to concentrate on the latest Christopher Pike Teen Horror novel that peeked out of the end pocket of his Head bag. Instead, Nicky settled down to his favoured game, "Watching," adding names, origins, destinations, and occupations to those within view, across the concourse. For example: At the end sat Mrs. Granny, aged about seventy, bringing sweets to her grandchildren whom she treated as though they were still in nappies, when they'd rather be inside Take That's jeans. (This was modelled on Nicky's maternal Grandmother and his reaction to her.)

Next to her sat Mr. Exchange Student touring Europe on a budget break from university. His back-pack stuffed with drugs and condoms, for those long nights in the Youth Hostels. (Based on one of Nicky's fantasies.) At the far end sat the most politically correct member of Nicky's collection. A single white mother with her black baby, her heavily made-up eyes shooting venom at anyone who looked her way, not that many did.

Between Ms. Single Mother and Mr. Exchange Student sat

two groups. The first, a family, occupied the space most directly opposite Nicky: bratty girl sat next to permanently tired teenage son, and then the constantly bickering parents. They would have faced Nicky but for, the second set, Mr. and Mrs. Middleclass, who seemed to have thought of everything for a few days out of town, including what looked suspiciously like the kitchen sink wrapped in a sack. It was that Nicky faced, the sink-in-a-sack taking care of two chairs by itself. Given the option, Nicky would have rather studied something, or someone, nearer his own age, and preferably male. The twisted position he had to take up in order to do this was far from comfortable but, from there he could study the other lad's stretched out legs. You see, Nicky, knew what he liked, and he'd never be responsible for the likes of the baby at the end of the line. Nicky was gay, and had been for as long as he could remember. Slowly, he invented a life, for the youth...

The boy, Nicky decided, was called Peter Dawson by his family and Biff by his friends, of which there were plenty. He was rapidly accelerating away from his eighteenth birthday and excelled at everything he did: Captain of Sports, especially Rugby; top of the class in all subjects; liked by his teachers and admired by the other students; the youngest person to ever lead his own Scout group; he helped his father with the car and assisted his mother with the housework - without being asked. In fact he was everything Nicky wasn't. Only on one thing did their lives cross - girls - both boys hated them.

Biff, or whatever his real name was, slouched in his seat, with baseball cap pulled low over his face, arms neatly folded across his jacket, and ankles crossed in a similar fashion. Slowly, Nicky embellished on the life he had invented for the youth, concentrating on what lay under the small hillock created by that neat row of brass buttons. In his mind's eye he conjured a picture of Biff returning from a sports field after a particularly hard championship game, his Rugby kit coated in equal amounts of sweat and mud. Entering the changing room he'd be congratulated on his virtual single-handed victory by his own team-mates, followed by the referee and opposition. In his filthy kit he'd stand before the wall of pegs holding his 501s, shirt, jacket and cap. A single foot at a time up on the bench so he could bend down and remove his boots. Long thigh muscles would swell and grow taut as his small, once white, shorts tighten across his rear to show a dark sweat line running down the centre.

Barefooted Biff turns to pull the horizontally stripped shirt over his head exposing his wide shoulders, hard flat stomach and exquisitely defined pectoral formation. Placing his shirt into his kit bag, the dream boy spins back to the wall pushing down his shorts, bending from the waist to take the tight cotton right down to his ankles. His buttocks wide and strong without an millimetre of fat on them, framed within the support of his jock-strap. The flesh tensing and relaxing as he fumbles for his towel and soap. A hand reaches out to stroke the slightly furry mounds of solid muscle. Biff laughs with a mile wide grin at the perpetrator, his face appearing, inverted, between his opening knees. Mud-stained fingers pry the buttocks apart. Between them a small hole winks at Nicky's all-seeing eye. The youth turns round, idly stretching the tense front of his jock until it stands taunt, pushed forward by the monster it hides. Hand then goes to his thin waist and hooks into the Biker-engraved elastic. Slowly the material descends...

"Will passengers for the National Express 13:30 service to Liverpool please have their tickets ready for boarding at gate number 17."

"Shit!" Nicky answered to the public address system. Why did something like that always have to happen at the best part? Nicky pulled his bag onto his lap and used it as a shield while he readjusted an awkward protuberance between his boxer shorts and trouser lining. Then, comfortable, he worked Peter "Biff" Dawson into one of his favoured fantasies, closing his eyes just in time to miss the youth open his...

Biff crouches behind a row of bushes at the edge of a wooded clearing, the cloth of his scout-issue trousers flatteringly tight over his broad rear. From beyond the vegetation drifts sounds of excited females. Biff takes a peek through the foliage, parting it with his hands. There, in the very centre of the camp, is the object of the war game, a blue flag embossed with the embalm of the Girl Guide Association. Capture that and the war is won.

Suddenly his head turns to the sound of a muffled cry from the right as Nicky enters the frame. A kerchief redesigned for an effective gag across his mouth, with the woggle protruding phallically from between his stuffed jaw. His hands tied with rope. Nicky imagines himself being stood while the rope is thrown up over his head and secured, almost hanging him, his elbows pressed into his ears, the tips of his toes making slight contact with the ground.

"Where is he?" the Guide demands, "Where's Dawson?"

They take fallen branches of birch and bamboo from the ground and whip Nicky's bare legs with them but he'd never tell, even without the gag. He'd never betray his hero, no matter what they do to him. His eyes fill with tears as his legs become stripped red raw. The girls systematically beat every single inch of the bare flesh, front and back, until the area between the top of his garter held socks and lower hem of grey shorts looks like a colourblind zebra.

Then, there's movement in the bushes. Biff is up and running for the unguarded flag. All but one of the guides panic, the youth's sister, "Stop right there, Peter!" she shouts, "Or I'll bash your little friend's balls. Then he won't be no good to you no more, will he?"

Biff doesn't stop, not until Nicky cries out in pain as a stick lashes the fly of his shorts. Pulled to a halt Biff turns. "Go on!" Nicky shouts in his mind and through the gag, adding flicks of his head, but Miss Dawson is right. Biff can't leave his young lover in pain, not for anything. "Don't hurt him." he pleads.

"I won't, if you agree to be our prisoner." the stick was laid, threateningly across Nicky's groin, "So, do you?"

"Yeah, sure!"

The pointed end of the stick pokes a young teenage crutch. Both boys catch their breath, "Say it." the elder is told.

"I'm your prisoner." Biff's hands shoot up in surrender.

"You'll do anything we - I - say?"

"Anything."

"In that case, you should be punished. Agree?"

Biff hangs his handsome head. "If you say so."

"I do. Come here, and take down your trousers."

Nicky's eyes open wider as the youth steps forward until they are face to face. The pupils swivel downwards to track Biff's hands moving onto the scouting belt on the tan trousers unfastening it, followed by the button and then the zip. The cloth falls to his ankles, baring him from shin to upper thigh.

"Right off." he is told, "Shoes and socks as well."

Biff does so. His legs, sturdy and tanned, disappear under the tails of his shirt.

"And your knickers."

Long fingers reach under the tan curtain and remove the familiar jock-strap. As they do there is only the briefest glimpse of dark curly hair.

"Bend over. Hands on the floor."

Biff seeks reassurance from Nicky before breaking their eye contact to turn around. His back arches high, his shirt riding up to expose the beginning of a crack where thighs part. Feminine fingers draw the shirt up the broad back. The buttocks, bent almost to a perfect right angle, clench tightly as their sister stripes them six times with her birch twigs. Never once does Biff cry out, though the beating must have hurt. He took to it like the hero he was. The punishment only stopping when, on the sixth blow, the birch breaks into three pieces, right across the target. Nicky was so proud of his lover, pride that showed itself in the front of his shorts.

"On your knees," Biff is kicked over but quickly recovers when informed, "Your lover seems to be missing you."

Once more the much shorter length of broken branch pokes Nicky's groin, tracing the length of his erection. "Why don't you kiss it better for him?"

"Yes, Miss."

Nicky's head falls to his chest waiting in anticipation as the half-naked scout runs his hands all over his crutch under the guise of taking down the too-short shorts. Biff leans forward and puts his lips momentarily to the swelling before the younger boy loses his lower clothing. Nicky's merit badge-emblazoned green jumper doesn't cover him as the other's shirt had done. All five inches of his barely thatched penis were plain to see. Biff held him by the hips, keeping the wriggling body still. The penis head, uncovered and damp, is rigid to Nicky's abdomen. Biff extends his tongue along its length, then

Nicky's abdomen. Biff extends his tongue along its length, then curls the tip in order to drag the captive into his mouth. However, it never gets there.

"Enough!" Miss Dawson demands, "You're enjoying it too much. It's meant to hurt."

The bottom of Biff's shirt testified to this fact, being both damp and parted.

"Fuck him!"

Immediately Biff leaps into the defence of the younger boy's (supposed) virginity. "But it's his first time and I'm so big. It'll kill him."

His sister steps forward and seizes a handful of his golden hair, twisting his head back fully on his bulging neck. "You will do it, or I will personally ram every single branch I can find up your little lover's arse until he's never able to take you up there, understand?"

Biff winces.

"I will then tell everybody at school that you did it. See how popular you are then, golden boy. As for him," she turns sharply to slap Nicky's bared bottom, "he'll be fucked by every boy in his school, from the biggest sixth former down to the lowest first year, and you'll be nowhere near to stop it. You'll be in prison having your arse and mouth filled by men three times your size, one after the other, all day and every day. That's what happens to your sort in jail, and no one gives a shit, least of all me and Mum and Dad. They'll let you rot there forever, and ever, and ever, and ever..."

"Alright!" cried Biff, "I'll do it."

Rising to his feet, he walks around Nicky's helpless body whispers, "Sorry!" into an ear below the crooked cub cap, drops his extra large scouting shirt to the ground. Hands tighten on Nicky's shoulders, slightly shaking him, "You alright?" a faraway voice asks. The smaller teenager wiggles into the embrace he knows is coming, longing to feel the long hard shaft press into his willing hole, waiting to feel the pounding column of teenage manhood ravish his near virgin hole for all it was worth. Then he lands with a thump on his arse...

"You alright, sonny?" Mrs. Granny asked for a second time

kneading Nicky's shoulder as he leaned back into the chair lip, "You just fell right off. You have a fit, or something?"

Nicky opened his eyes and groaned. His bottom hurt from the impact with the cold tiles, but that wasn't the main reason for his discomfort. The front of his underpants was sticky with cum from spontaneous combustion. "I'm okay." he lied, looking from one of the faces which now surround him to another. "I think."

"Well, I think you'd better go and freshen up. You do look a state, you know." the old lady suggested moving aside to give the boy some room, "Think you can manage?"

Nicky didn't answer. He wasn't listening. Now Mrs. Granny had moved aside he could see the real Biff once more. The youth still slouched as before only now he had a hand inserted between his spread legs and seemed to be trying to pick his underwear from out from the crack of his arse. Nicky couldn't believe his eyes. He was sure the youth was as hard as he had just been, and was in danger of going again.

At Nicky's trancelike state the old woman turned to the man behind her, "I think someone should help him. He could use the Mother and Baby room rather than walk all the way to the Gent's, don't you think?"

"Brett!" The man turned as he shouted. "Come and help the lad. You can use that first aid training you pestered so much to take."

Slowly the youth stirred. Biff, Peter, Brett, whatever his name was, he came and stood by the youngster who'd just hero-worshipped him into his underpants.

Still silent Nicky allowed himself to be helped up onto his feet and with Mrs. Granny promising to look after his bag, was led into a small room consisting of little more than a table and chair. Sitting the lad into the chair, Biff/Brett asked what he'd been meaning to for some time: "Do you often do that?"

"What? Have fits?" Nicky coloured. "No, not often."

"I meant wank in public."

"But I didn't..."

"Yes you did. I watched you sitting there rubbing yourself stupid under your bag. So do you?"

"What?"

"Do it often?"

"Not really."

"But you have done it before?"

Nicky remembered a damp, dark changing room, after school. "Sort of."

Biff/Brett turned the engaged sign on the door. "Want to do me? It's more fun with two, you know?"

"I know."

"Take it out then. Go on, it won't bite, though it may spit, if you're nice enough to it."

By now the youth stood in front of the chair and Nicky was once more captivated by the swelling in his trousers, for real. With his hand shaking, he reached for and stroked the rough denim. Brett shivered, hands on his hips. "That's good. Been a long time."

"How long?" Nicky asked absentmindedly as he struggled with the brass buttons and belt buckle.

"A whole week, would you believe? Ever since the night before we left home. Fancy, at my age, having to share a hotel room with my little sister?" He wiggled his hips to allow the 501s to descend. Beneath he didn't wear a jock-strap as Nicky had envisioned but regular white Y-fronts. Regular, that is, but for the way they jutted out to one side.

"Can I take them off?" asked Nicky, "It's always better without anything."

"Sure," Brett shrugged and dropped his jacket and shirt to the floor, but kept his baseball cap. That and his underpants. Nicky reached for the latter but was stopped by the words: "After you."

Memories made him painfully aware of the risk he was taking, nevertheless Nicky raised his arms and allowed both his hooded sweat-shirt and the T-shirt beneath it to be pulled over his head. "You've a nice body." Brett said honestly.

"I'm skinny."

"Better than being fat." Which was true enough. Not all of Brett's size was due to the muscles Nicky's imagination had given him, although he wasn't fat either, just approaching the tubby side of well-built. His underpants were well built though, about that there was no argument. Nicky pointed, "Can I, now?"

"Go on. If you can't wait." Brett sighed, "But be careful you don't snag anything."

Nicky was. His fingers inserted in the waistband and pulled out before stripping the undergarment away from what he most wanted to view. Then he was confronted by the nicest penis he'd seen in a long while. True it did still curve slightly towards Brett's left but it was silky smooth, with just a hint of criss-crossed purple and red veins along the shaft. The foreskin rolled half way down the divided head where bubbles of pre-cum decorated the tiny slit. At the other end, clusters of black curls wormed their way around the root and over the heavily sagging testicles.

"Don't just leave it," protested the erection's owner, "do something."

Nicky did this as well. It would only be the second time he'd been involved with other boys. After his previous experience he'd promised never to be involved again, but somehow, he just knew this time it would be alright. Nothing would go wrong with Brett as it had with Gary George. His left hand held the sizable weapon and peeled back the foreskin to completely expose the skinny head. Still holding it Nicky pressed his lips to the end and kissed as wetly as he knew how.

"Oh my God! You're not going to..."

Nicky already had. Finished with the kiss his lips had parted. His tongue tickled and teased the slit as the crown sunk into his welcoming mouth, instantly lips formed an airtight seal around the crown. Nicky expelled all the air from his mouth. Then, as his left hand gently frigged the remainder of the shaft, he sucked with all his worth. If only the boys at school could see him now, they'd be sorry. Especially Gary George. Fancy turning this down, just to get in with the in-crowd.

As he did a passable impression of a milking machine on his fantasy-cum-reality Nicky shivered with memories. He'd only asked his nearest school friend if he'd liked to have his dick sucked. Gary had even agreed - for a fee - and they'd arranged to meet in the changing room after school. Nicky had spent the rest of the day in a daze. All he could think about was having his mate's hard, stubby cock throbbing in his mouth, just as he now had Brett's.

First to arrive at the designated spot, Nicky had quickly

stripped naked but when Gary had entered he wasn't alone. Instead he'd brought the third-year gang with him. Quickly they'd pounced on Nicky and tied him up, on his knees, with his own shoelaces. Then they formed into a line and unzipped. For the next forty-five minutes Nicky sucked over and over on pubertal cock, from big Harry MacNally's nine-inch ponder, to Scotty Nawoy's barely-visible tiddler. Then, when all was done, he'd been re-tied between coat hooks, arms stretched. A length of three-inch-wide sticking plaster, prevented him from spitting out the thin sperm that filled his mouth. The word COCKSUCKER written across his forehead in indelible black marker pen. WANKER across his pubis, and FUCK ME on each of his buttocks. He was left with the promise that the last word would be proven if he was ever seen in the street which is why Nicky had been heading to Manchester in the first place.

Of course Brett knew none of that and he sighed as his penis was freed then, couldn't believe his ears when he was asked by the angelic creature sitting before him if he wanted to fuck him. His enforced silence didn't prevent him from answering. By the way his head pounded up and down you'd have thought he'd walked into a heavy metal concert.

In a flash Nicky was on his back across the table with his legs held out. "Strip me." he demanded, "I want to be as naked as you. Please."

The next second he was just as he wanted to be. Brett had intended to proceed slowly and take the shell suit trousers first but his fingers had caught the undershorts as well so, in one quick motion, he had the boy completely nude. Now, it was his turn to stand transfixed at the smooth barely haired boy's body laid out before him. Nicky tried to roll into a ball. On the third attempt he clasped his knees and pulled them back up to his chest. As he did so his bottom curled up from the table, parted and presented its finest point to its assailant. Directly above the puckered hole and over the cum encrusted testicles Nicky had gained his full six-and-a-half inch length. "Fuck me." he repeated. "Fuck me, now."

Snapped from his trance by the urgent words Brett got into position. In one hand he aimed his saliva-dripping organ at the offered target, with the other he steadied himself. He pushed, gave a small twist and entered. Nicky's years of practise with fingers, pens, pencils, brush stales and the armless torso of his Action Man figure gave him enough control to accept the youth's sizable prick relatively easily.

As all eight inches eased up his back passage Nicky released his legs to rest on Brett's shoulders. The youth over him bent him double. They kissed. Nicky's hands sought the toughened buttocks to work the shaft in and out of his arsehole like an expert. His own pricklet pressed into Brett's slightly flabby naval and was consumed by it. The fucking was under way.

Under the lad's guidance Brett moved his penis back and forth between the gripping sphincter. His week-long abstinence deadened his usual trigger-happy responses. His buttocks clenched in Nicky's fingers as he fought to hold back the flood which would soon be pouring forth. To some extent he succeeded, so much that, when he did finally allow his cum to spurt forth, it shot like thick, lumpy water from a high pressure hose, to flood Nicky's bowels...

"You alright, sonny?" Mrs. Granny's face barely masked her concern at Nicky's drawn expression as he, and Brett, returned to the main concourse. "You've been gone an awfully long time."

"We had a lot to get through," Brett said straight-faced, "didn't we, Nicky?"

The boy blushed and fought back the urge to rub his bottom, not that it stopped him from stiffening. Quickly he sat back down in his still vacant seat and asked for his bag.

"Here," says Brett, "I'll give it to him. I'll give him head."

Nicky snatched the bag and pressed it tightly into his groin and groaned, raising concern all around.

"It's not going to happen again, is it Brett?" asked the youth's father.

"It might. What do you think Nicky?" The lad looked as Brett patted the hip pocket of his 501's where the paper towel on which they'd exchanged addresses was stored.

Will passengers for the National Express 14:30 service to Manchester please have their tickets ready for boarding at gate number 19.

The small group scattered to collate their belongings, except the boys. "Need a hand?" Brett asked as he made to swipe Nicky's bag from his lap. Only to find the lad more recovered than he'd expected.

"Only if I can give you a hand afterwards. On the bus." Then to Brett's confused look: "We could sit together. It's four and a half hours to Manchester, we'll need something to do, to pass the time!"

"Come on Brett," the father yelled before his son could answer the tempting offer he'd just received. "We're going places."

"Can he stay with me, Mister." Nicky answered, "I might cum over all queer again and he can give me a helping hand, or kiss me better, or something."

Nicky highlighted the double entendre solely for the benefit of the youth by his side. It worked better than he expected. Ignoring the bag, Brett grabbed a small hand and had the lad on his feet in next to no time, "Come on."

"I already did - twice!"

"Never mind that, we'll have to hurry."

"Why?"

"There aren't many people," explained Brett, "so if we're quick we'll be able to get the back seat to ourselves. You know, the long back seat where – " He lowered his voice and bent closer to Nicky.

"Yeah?"

"Well, where we could lie down together. It'll be easier to give you my injection – "

Nicky beamed. "Why didn't you say?" After thrusting his ticket at the hostess, Nicky dragged the other teenager onto the bus with the words, "We're going places."

And they did. Several times. Each!

FUCKING FRED

John Patrick

He wasn't my type at all.

I like 'em blond and Fred had black hair, cut short and greased in the latest style. I like blue eyes and his were dark, mysterious. He was thin and tall, almost six foot, and I like 'em short, gym-built. He was 21 and I like 'em as young as I can get 'em.

But from the moment I walked into the Zone bar and saw Fred in his short shorts, I was smitten. Fred was the new bartender and everyone was after him, plus he had a lover. My chances were practically nil but I always love a challenge.

Then Fred got another part-time job, this time at the video store I patronize. He worked there from 11 to 2, and then went to the bar to work happy hour until eight. I started renting more videos than I could ever watch just so I could see Fred bend over and get them for me. He didn't wear his short shorts in the store, of course, but whatever he wore displayed the splendid mounds of his ass.

A fellow employee of the video store who had contributed stories to some of my anthologies mentioned that fact to Fred. This sparked Fred's interest. He told me he'd always wanted to write some stories. I'd heard that many times before, but coming from Fred it meant a lot.

One day, as Fred counted out my change, I noticed that he had the most beautiful soft skin and elegant long fingers. I wanted so much to kiss those hands and suck those fingers. The thought of it kept me hard all day.

My lust for Fred was beginning to consume me. I started bringing Fred packages, copies of my books and lists of the merchandise he could get wholesale.

Still nothing came of it. Perhaps, I thought, I was being too eager, so I backed off. After all, Fred did have a lover.

When I returned to town after a week away, Fred asked where I had been. I was delighted that he had missed me. When I mentioned I had been to the Gay Video Awards in Hollywood, his eyes flashed. He wondered if I had met anyone interesting. I explained that it was expensive to entertain a porn star, inasmuch as I like to wine 'em and dine 'em before I bed 'em, and they charge astronomical fees to begin with.

"You know," I said, my eyes fixed on his crotch, "you should try escorting. You'd make a bundle."

"Oh, no, I couldn't do that."

But it is curious how trouble can make strange bedfellows. A week later, Fred's old Volvo broke down and he needed a hundred to get it back on the road. He'd exhausted his lines of credit with all of his friends and his lover and he called me. He began gingerly, simply asking for advice. I knew where the conversation was headed but I played along. Fred was the type who needed time to consider all the options. While he explained the seriousness of his car trouble, I imagined my cock sliding between the crack of his extraordinary ass, as deep into his body as he could possibly tolerate. My revelry was interrupted when Fred asked, "Where did you say your office was?"

But without a car, it was obvious Fred would have trouble getting there. His friends and his lover could ferry him to his jobs but to my office? I quickly agreed to pick Fred up. It was Saturday, his day off. He met me at the corner of Main and Orange. In five minutes, he was sitting in my office enjoying a cold beer.

I locked all the doors and prepared to make Fred's visit as pleasant as possible for both of us. It was a rainy afternoon and when I turned out the lights the office seemed incredibly cozy. Fred reclined on the couch, sipping his beer. I lifted his legs and sat on the end of the couch. I began by massaging his legs. They were thin, lighted-furred legs and I was happy to see he was wearing the short shorts he always wore at the bar. He nervously chattered away about the problems with his car, how his lover had lost his job, and all of the other things that had made his life miserable lately. All this misery, I was sure, had dampened the lad's ardor for lovemaking, but in this new situation, it was obvious he was getting the knack of being seduced for profit: his hard-on was visible as I continued gently stroking his feet and calves, working my way up to his thighs.

He closed his eyes, as if to ignore what was happening to him. I stripped off everything but my briefs, then began to remove his shorts; he did not resist. I moved down between his legs. He arched his back, spreading his legs wider to give me better access. It was a formidable cock: about seven inches, thick, cut. It smelled of a citrus cologne. He had expected this. I began licking him, slowly, teasingly, moving in small circles with my lips and tongue, my kisses falling on him, gentle as the rain outside. His lithe body strained against my face, and when he looked down at me, he smiled devilishly. "Can I fuck you?" he asked.

It took me by surprise. With that magnificent ass, I supposed he was the fuckee in his relationships. Then I decided, perhaps he was and now he wanted a change of pace. "Oh, yes," I moaned, as if I had been waiting for it for months.

But I had to have it my way. I stripped off my briefs and applied the grease, then mounted him. He held his cock as I slid him inside me, achingly. I had never had anything so hard inside me. I held my breath as he kept coming into me. He took my erection in his hand and stroked it. Precum slid onto his fingers. I was ready to shoot.

We were breathing and then not breathing in unison, and I brought his hand up to my mouth to suck his longer fingers, one at a time, then two at a time, then three. His fingers tasted of the beer, of my own sweat, and my precum. "Suck," he said, and pushed into me, harder still, as if by trying he could disappear up inside me.

When he came his face became contorted as if it hurt him to come so hard.

We lay quietly for a while, and then he began licking my cock, making me come with his tongue, his lips, and his fingertips. His talent was incredible. I envied his lover. In fact, I *hated* his lover and I didn't even know his name.

As I came, he began kissing me. And we kissed as if to seal our fate, to finish a life together we hadn't even begun.

HE DIDN'T DO VIRGINS

Bert McKenzie

My roommate volunteered to man the gay rap line. It was a worthwhile cause and I admired him for it. The rap line was a phone line that was staffed by volunteers and provided an information clearing house and volunteer counseling option for people who called in with questions about the gay community. They might be calling for information about bars, churches or events in our area, calling to ask questions about a lifestyle they knew little about, or wanting to talk because they had just discovered their own sexuality, or uncovered that of someone close to them, be it a son or daughter, spouse or friend.

Ben was a psych major at the local university, and thought he would be doing something very noble by working the rap line. Unfortunately, it didn't turn out that way. When a volunteer was selected, the phone was forwarded to his home number so he could take calls into the night without having to journey to an office. This ensured that there would be a number of volunteers and that they could use their own phones but with complete anonymity. Well, Ben used our phone in a way that was certainly not intended by the founders of the rap line. If he got a curious virgin on the line who thought he might be gay, Ben would arrange a meeting and used the rap line to get dates. When I found this out I made him quit the rap line by threatening to turn him in.

I found out the hard way, by coming home one night and catching him in the middle of a young man, still obviously in his teens. The frightened boy bolted and Ben confessed everything to me, making me promise not to tell on them. He was genuinely more concerned for the feelings of his young partner than for his own legal and ethical problems.

Ben knew my interest in young men. In fact, I often commented and lusted over cute boys, barely out of their teens, and some still in their teens. I was an admitted chicken hawk, but one that would never act on such impulses. I was very conscious of legal ramifications to such actions. Nevertheless, this didn't stop me of dreaming about nubile young boys, sucking and fucking with me. Ben and I had often talked about such things and commented on some street tough we might see walking down the boulevard in tight cut-offs and a baseball cap, but nothing more.

After I got Ben to agree to quit the rap line, he made me an offer. He asked me if I would be interested in talking to a young man about gay sexuality. The boy was only fifteen and needed to chat with someone. I felt this was a mistake because the local child welfare laws were very specific. Such action could be misinterpreted as child abuse. But Ben said this boy was the one to initiate the call, and he really needed someone to talk with. Despite my interest I was adamant in my refusal.

Ben didn't let it rest there. About a week later the phone rang, and when I answered it, a young voice asked for me by name. I was angry with Ben when I realized what he had done. He had given my name and phone number to Javier. I politely told the boy that I was not able to talk with him and hung up. Unfortunately, Javier was much harder to discourage. He called repeatedly and always asked to speak to me. Finally in desperation, I gave in, agreeing to just talk.

To start out with, nothing sexual was said. We spoke about superficial likes and dislikes. He asked me to describe myself and I did as best I could without sounding too vain. I have a decent body from working out, long blond hair to my shoulders, and green eyes. He asked about my cock and I told him that I didn't feel comfortable talking about that. Javier surprised me by describing himself. He told me he was five-five, weighed about 115 pounds and had soft, bronzed skin, dark brown hair and brown eyes. He said he had a thin but growing patch of pubic hair surrounding his cock which he had measured at six inches when it was hard. His penis was circumcised.

Again he asked me about my body. Did I have a hairy chest, arms, legs? I told him yes, I had light-blond chest hair, and a fine coating of blond hair on my arms and legs. Javier asked about my crotch. Was I hairy down there? "Yes," I said. "I have a thick patch of blond hair completely covering my pubes and surrounding my dick."

"Are you circumcised?"

"No," I told him and felt myself coloring in embarrassment

at such a personal question.

"I've only seen one uncut cock," Javier admitted freely. "I saw the man in the locker room at the swimming pool. I wanted to look more, but he noticed me and called me a little fag. I would love to see an uncut penis up close. I would love to see how it works. Does the skin cover up the head all the time? Does it feel different?"

I explained as best I could about how things worked. I told him that the skin was loose enough to pull back out of the way. He said he really wished he could see it. Then my young friend had to go to supper. As I hung up I realized that I had a raging hard-on. I had gotten really excited describing my prick and now I unzipped my pants, taking it out for a quick jerk-off. As I was nearing my climax, Ben walked in the door and surprised us both. "Well," he said with a grin on his face. "I bet you were just talking to Javier."

"Fuck off," I replied, my face coloring a deep red.

"Love to," he retorted and unzipped his own jeans, pulling his long cock out and beginning to stroke it in my face. I leaned forward and sucked him to a quick climax, then yanked his jeans down to his ankles, spun him around and slid into his tight ass. My fucking was a bit violent, but I needed to cum quickly as well as relieve the emotional tension that had built up between us.

Two days later Javier called again and told me he was alone at home. His family had all gone off shopping and he managed to stay behind. As we chatted, he finally admitted to me that he had stripped his shorts off and was masturbating. I told him that I would be happy to talk with him another time, but he said, "No, I want to talk to you while I do it. I do it all the time and when I do I think about doing it with you."

"Javier, I'm too old for you," I explained. "You are under age, and I could get in serious trouble just talking to you about these things."

"No more trouble than you could if you and I were together and we were doing it to each other," he answered.

"Oh, yes, we could get in a lot more trouble doing that."

"Not if we were careful," he pleaded. "Not if I came over to your house where we could be alone together. I could see your uncut dick, and maybe you could let me feel it, let me try sucking on it. I've always wanted to suck on a dick ever since I heard about blowjobs."

"This isn't something we should talk about," I told him, but I had already pulled my cock out of my jeans.

"I'm rubbing my prick right now and it's all juicy," he said. "Are you rubbing yours?"

"Javier, I don't think..."

"Are you?"

"Yes," I admitted.

"Great! That makes me even harder." We continued to do our joint masturbation for a few minutes, then his breathing grew ragged and he began to moan. In seconds he was shooting his youthful sperm all over his thin body, and I matched him groan for groan as I unloaded at the same time.

What really surprised me the most was that after we climaxed together on the phone, I wasn't overcome with guilt. In fact, I felt relieved. I knew it was wrong, forbidden, taboo, but I had enjoyed it; I had enjoyed it a lot. Javier could sense the tone in my voice as we talked about the experience.

He asked me if I ever ate my cum. Did I run my fingers through it and then taste it. He told me he did this and he enjoyed the flavor. He really wanted to taste someone else. Then he asked me if we could meet.

This sent up the red flags. "Definitely not," I said firmly.

"Just to talk. I think of you as a good friend. I just want to meet my friend and just talk with him."

"Well..." My resolve was weakening.

"I will be at the baseball diamond in Central Park on Saturday."

Saturday morning as I drove to the park I realized how foolish this was. I had no idea how I would find him. His description could fit about any young Hispanic boy. But I pulled into the parking area, and knew him immediately. He was sitting alone on a big rock beside the drive. He must have recognized me as well, because no sooner had I stopped the car than he jumped up and came over to it. Without even an invitation he opened the passenger door and slid into the seat. "Let's go," he said. "I don't want any of my family to spot me getting into your car."

I was suddenly very nervous and asked if maybe he

shouldn't get out. But he said, "Just drive, man," and I did. I drove out of the lot and headed for the bypass.

"Do you live close to the park?" I asked.

"Not real close, but my little sister often likes to follow me."

"Shit."

"Hey, don't sweat it. It's cool," he said. Then he sat back and looked at me, taking a really long look. "You know, you are really hotter than I imagined."

I blushed at the compliment, but managed to glance over at him, appreciating what I saw as well. Javier was young and beautiful. He was wearing baggy denim cut-offs, a loose fitting muscle shirt and sneakers. As we drove, he reached down, grabbed the hem of his shirt and slipped it off over his head. "What are you doing?" I asked, feeling nervous panic rising in my chest.

"Just getting comfortable. You know it's really hot out there. It feels good to have the air blowing on my skin." He reached up and rubbed his chest, wiping the little bit of sweat off that had given his sternum a glistening appearance. I watched as he rubbed his tits, small little brown circles with tiny points in the center. "I wish I had a hairy chest like yours," he said and reached over to feel the hair that was curling up out of the neck of my shirt.

"I don't think you should do that," I said, feeling my body responding.

"Oh, come on. I really want to see your chest. To feel it." Javier was now rubbing my chest, unbuttoning my shirt and playing with my nipples.

"Not while I'm driving," I ordered.

"Then this would be out of the question?" he asked as he dropped his hand to my lap and felt for my growing cock.

"Don't," I said and reached down to move his hand. He gripped my wrist and guided my hand to his chest, guiding me as he worked my fingers up to his tiny nipples.

"This is really not a good idea," I said as I pulled into the driveway. I realized that I had just come home, parking beside the house.

"Is this your place?" he asked and jumped out of the car, bounding up the porch steps to my door. I followed him like a lamb to the slaughter, unlocking the door and letting him step inside.

"It feels really good in here," Javier remarked as the air conditioned interior hit our hot bodies. "I bet it feels good on all of our skin," and he began to pull his pants down.

"Javier, don't do that," I said again, but I was gazing at his tender young body, my cock throbbing in my pants.

"But I want to," he said as he dropped to his knees in front of me and tugged at my shorts, yanking then and my underwear down to my ankles. My cock bounced up into his face. "Cool! Now I get to see what an uncut dick really looks like. Wow, it's so big. Are all uncut dicks this big?" He gently wrapped his hand around my prick and pulled back, sliding the foreskin off and revealing the pink head with a drop of precum poised at the tip.

I groaned in answer to his question, then looked down to see him stick out his tongue and lick the sparkling drop from my piss slit. "Mmmmm," he breathed. "That tastes good. Kind of like salted almonds. I want some more." Javier placed his lips against my cock head and sucked.

I couldn't help myself. It was so good and so hot seeing this young, nubile boy kneeling at my feet, his lips planted firmly on my penis. I pushed forward and my dick began to slide into his mouth. The boy tried to push back, but lust overcame me and I grabbed his head, sliding my fingers into his black, curly locks and pushed into him.

My cock filled his young teenage mouth and caused him to gag. As he did, his teeth nicked my sensitive shaft and I grunted, pulling back. "Watch those teeth," I ordered. "Try to keep them out of the way and just use your lips and tongue on my cock." He obeyed and I pushed in again, this time getting my shaft all the way into him, pressing back into his throat. The boy swallowed in reflex and his tonsils massaged my dick head, causing me intense pleasure. I pulled back and let him breathe, then pushed in again, beginning to pick up a rapid fucking motion.

Javier was a natural-born cocksucker. He quickly caught on to the movement, bobbing his head in time to my thrusts, and flicking my cock with his tongue. The sound of his slurping only added to the intensity of my fucking and in no time at all I was shooting my load into him. The boy choked and gagged, my cum shooting up and out of his nose as he coughed. I pulled him to his feet and bent down to kiss him, tasting my sperm on his lips and in his mouth.

When we calmed down a bit he thanked me. "That was just what I wanted. I have never had sex with another person, but I saw that in a book once and I wanted to try it so bad. It was fun and tasted good too."

"Do you want to go home now, or do you want to try some more things?" I asked. I figured I couldn't get in any deeper now. I was already committed to sex with this hot little underaged boy.

"Please, teach me more," he begged, his deep brown eyes looking up into mine.

I couldn't resist. I swept the boy off his feet and carried him into the bedroom. Dropping him on the bed, I fell down beside him and began to worship his young body. I plunged down on that small, almost hairless cock, swallowing it in one gulp. It was much smaller than I was used to, but it still seemed to fill my mouth with firmness. In only about three slurps, the boy tensed and began to shoot his young load into me. His dick may have been on the small side, but his load was anything but. It seemed like he came forever, pumping squirt after squirt of rich spunk into my. I ewallowed as fast as I could and siphoned that flavorful Hispanic cream out of him.

The very act of sucking him off caused me to get hard again, my own dick wanting to join in our love play. But I didn't want to get another blow job. I wanted to fuck his sweet young cherry ass, yet I felt that was a bit too far for me to go. So it came as a complete surprise when Javier was the one who suggested it. "I want to feel you inside me," he said and pushed me over onto my back. "I want you to push your cock into me like I saw in that magazine."

My dick was already standing at attention, throbbing and drooling precum. Javier straddled my naked body, and squatted down, positioning his tight little butt over my shaft. "Are you sure you want this?" I asked, and in reply he fell back, sitting down on my cock. The force of gravity and the lust of the moment caused my cock to push up into him. His tiny ass opened and I slid into the tightest boy cunt I've ever had.

Javier's eyes grew wide, and I thought he must be in

incredible pain, but he took only a moment to slide further down on my prick, then a wide grin spread across his face. "I don't believe this," he whispered. "I don't believe I am here and I am sitting on your cock. I don't believe you have it up inside me." To convince him I pushed up with my hips and he gasped for a moment. "This is just what I saw my sister Rosalie doing with her boyfriend," he said as he bounced up and down on my hard prick.

His tight virginal butt quickly massaged my cock to climax and in no time at all I was unloading my cum up his guts. He fell off me and lay beside me, my hot sperm slowly oozing out of his abused asshole. "Thank you," he said over and over again.

"Thank you," I replied, glad that I had taken a chance with this Hispanic jail bait.

In a few minutes, Javier jumped off the bed and dashed out to the living room. I followed him only to find him pulling on his pants and shirt. "I gotta go," he said quickly.

"Okay," I agreed and dressed, fishing in my pocket for the car keys.

We headed back downtown in silence. I didn't know what to say and all the time I wondered if he was happy, upset or what.

Finally he said, "Stop here," and jumped out of the car in front of an old grey apartment building.

"Is this where you live?"

"No," he replied sheepishly. "This is where my sister's boyfriend lives. He said if I ever got my ass broken in proper he was willing to fuck me, but he doesn't do virgins."

THE ROOMMATE

Dylan Spaulding

Alvin unpacked the last of his books and placed them on the bookshelf next to his desk in his new dorm room. He wanted to make sure the room was neat before him. Alvin really looked forward to meeting his new roommate. His last roommate, Rick, had moved to an apartment off-campus and Alvin already missed him.

He knew his roommate's name, Howell Burns; he was a junior too. Alvin thought Howell was an unusual name. He figured that he'd like to be called "Howie" so he went around the room saying "Howie" over and over. Alvin wanted to make sure he didn't sound like a jerk, like when he stammered when he met both Morgan and Rick. These guys were so hot and hunky that Alvin had difficulty keeping his hard-on hidden.

Yeah, Alvin was gay. It didn't take too long before it was known by some of the guys on his floor. These guys would look at him with disgust and make a point of moving away from him in the showers. Alvin wished these guys wouldn't hate him so much. He'd be twenty-one in a few months. Maybe then he'd get the nerve to go to one of the gay bars downtown.

Alvin did have a few friends. Most of them were computer nerds like him. He met most of them in his classes and got to know them through the Physics Club and Computer Club. But they all wanted to have sex with girls and that was all they would talk about. They'd complain how they couldn't get laid. Alvin couldn't tell them he was more interested in getting fucked by his roommates than fucking girls. Or that he wouldn't mind sucking their cocks.

Truth be known, Alvin loved cock. He loved the feel of it in his mouth, ramming deep down his throat. He loved the taste of cum. He loved getting fucked, too, even though it had only happened three times. The first time he got fucked was with his older cousin Ken when he was about twelve. Then Brian, a guy who used to teased him while he was in high school, fucked him a couple of times. Brian used to force him to have sex, mostly blowjobs in the shower room at school. He fucked his ass once after the senior prom, then again after Brian's girlfriend dumped him. Ken and Brian were both athletic studs and that was the kind of guy Alvin got hot for.

Both Morgan and Rick were jocks, too. Morgan played basketball and Rick played baseball. Each of them had been paired with Alvin to get their grades up and Alvin did help them. But after each year was over, Morgan had gone back to his frat and Rick had decided to move in with his girlfriend.

Alvin had rushed a few frats but never got in. So he stayed in Buchanan Hall, the only all-male dorm on campus. It was sort of like a frat house, but not as raucous. Here, he could study in peace and maintain his 4.0 G.P.A. The only distraction he had was the other guys in the dorm.

There was one gang-type shower room for every floor, which Alvin loved. He took a lot more showers than he did when he was at home. And, because it was an all-male dorm, many guys walked around with little or no clothing. Alvin kept a journal of all the guys he thought were hot. He noted if he had seen them naked or in their underwear, and how big their dicks were. He had seen most of the guys on his floor naked. And most of the guys looked like they had big cocks, though he'd never seen any of them hard.

Alvin jerked off almost every night before Howie got there, recalling all the guys he'd seen naked. He usually fantasized about an orgy in the shower room, where he'd get fucked by all the guys on his floor. Sometimes he'd imagine being on his hands and knees sucking off Rick's eight-inch cock and getting fucked by Morgan's big ten at the same time. How he longed for someone to just take him down and fuck his brains out.

That Friday, Alvin got tired of waiting around for Howie so he decided to take a walk into town. When he got back, he heard thumping and things being moved around in his room. When he opened the door he saw a great altar of stereo components had been set up where the desks once were. The receiver, amplifier, CD player, cassette deck, and even a turntable was placed on top of each other on shelves, in a pyramid. Below the pyramid were stacks of C's and cassettes, hundreds of them. And on each side of the altar was a towering speaker, almost as big as the ones the they use at rock concerts.

And beside the speakers, putting them into place, was a mass of blond hair attached to a Metallica T-shirt and black jeans. Alvin was very disappointed. He had hoped for another humpy jock. Instantly, he dreaded listening to hours of Metallica, Skid Row, AC/DC, Megadeth, Queensryche and worst of all, Guns 'n' Roses. For Alvin, who listened only to classical music, it was all noise.

"Hey dude, you must be my new roommate," the hair said in a doper tone. Alvin recalled that the druggies at his high school all talked like that.

"Yes, my name is Alvin. You must be Howie."

"It's Howl, man. Like wolves do." Then he howled, throwing his head back. His hair fell back and Alvin got a look at his face. He was actually pretty cute but Alvin thought he'd probably look better with short hair.

Then another guy walked in. He had straight black hair that went down to his waist. He wasn't wearing a shirt and Alvin immediately lusted after his torso. He was lean and well defined, but not bulky. The guy's chest was smooth but there was a line of hair coming up from below his jeans to his navel. Alvin thought that was really sexy. Then he realized he was staring, something he did often around cute or hunky guys, and felt a little embarrassed.

"Dude, this is my bud, Kill. Bud man, this is my new roomie, Alvin."

"How's it going, dude?" Kill said, extending his hand. Alvin shook it.

"Pretty good." Alvin's face showed he was put off by the guy's name.

"His name is really Kelly, but that's sorta faggy, so he changed it to 'Kill.'"

Shit, Alvin thought, they hate fags. I'm as good as dead. But then Kill looked at Howl like he insulted him. Alvin didn't notice.

"It's just sounds cooler and a lot tougher, that's all," Kill explained.

"You go to school here too?" Alvin asked, a little relieved.

"No way, man," Kill replied, chuckling. "I could barely stand high school. I would've dropped out if it weren't for

Brainiac here." Kill grabbed Howl in a headlock and gave him a noogie.

Brainiac? Is Howl smart? Alvin thought. He sure doesn't look it.

"What's your major, Howl?"

"English, American Lit," he answered. "What's yours?"

"Physics and computer science," Alvin replied, a little ashamed.

"I could've guessed that," Kill said, laughing. Alvin felt like a complete nerd now. Even though Howl was a brain, at least he was cool.

"Come on, Kill, don't make fun of Alvin."

"I wasn't. He just looks like a physics dude."

"It's OK, Howl," Alvin assured him. "I can take a joke." Alvin was used to it and Kill wasn't being mean.

"Thanks, dude," Howl replied. It seemed weird to Alvin that Howl was trying to be nice to him. Morgan and Rick usually ignored him, except when they studied together. But neither of them wanted to be his friend. But Howl seemed to want that. Now Alvin was beginning to feel better. Maybe he would even grow to like heavy metal. That Dave Mustaine guy was pretty cute.

Luckily for Alvin and the other men on their floor, Howl usually listened to his music with headphones. But once in while though, he'd listen to it full blast. Alvin was beginning to like the music. He enjoyed Queensryche and Extreme, and he could listen to Metallica and some others without getting annoyed. So he and Howl were getting along.

Alvin found out just how smart Howl was. Howl told him his G.P.A. was 3.8 and he had gotten 1310 combined on the SAT, 730 verbal, 580 math. Alvin's score was almost the reverse. They helped each on their homework. Alvin would check Howl's math and science and Howl would edit Alvin's papers. And they both helped some of the guys on the floor with their homework.

Another thing Alvin liked about Howl was that Howl liked to lounge around their room in his underwear. Howl made him feel so at ease that Alvin started wearing just his boxer shorts around the room too. From what he could tell, Howl had a big cock. Once, he caught a glimpse of it hard, the tip just above the waistband of his briefs. Then Howl left all of a sudden to go to the bathroom. When he got back he was flushed and a little sweaty but Alvin didn't think anything of it.

Alvin needed to jerk off badly. He used to do it often, at least twice a day. Since Morgan and Rick often spent the night at their girlfriends' rooms or off-campus, Alvin had the room to himself a lot. He'd sneak into their laundry baskets and dig for a dirty pair of briefs or jock strap. He'd hold them to his face, breathing in the smells of a sweaty young athlete. Then he'd strip down naked and lie on his roommate's bed. He'd lube up his six-inch cock with lotion and start stroking it slowly. He'd start feeling his ass with his other hand, poking his asshole with one finger then two, imagining it was Rick or Morgan invading him with his big cock.

Often, he reran his fantasy of being gang-banged by the guys in the shower room. They'd feed him their cocks two at a time, while another guy fucked him brutally. It wouldn't be long before Alvin shot his load into a tissue. One time he shot a huge load, after he had seen Rick naked for the first time, and came all over Rick's sheets. Alvin was afraid that Rick would find out. But Alvin liked feeling anxious about being caught. Maybe Rick would be so angry that he'd force Alvin to suck his cock or he'd fuck him.

Alvin didn't have much chance to jerk off like he used to, though. Howl spent as much time as Alvin did in their room. Alvin didn't dare jerk off it the bathroom or showers. He was afraid of being caught in there. He didn't want Howl to think he was a total freak so Alvin stopped jerking off.

When he went home for a weekend Alvin finally got to beat off. He wondered what Howl planned to do while he was away. He figured he had a bunch of girls lined up to fuck. Howl said he didn't have a girlfriend and Alvin thought he was just playing the field. At home, he cranked his cock so many times he thought it'd fall off.

They both studied during the week. They spent their free time with their friends. Alvin had his friends in the physics and computer clubs, and Howl had hooked up with some other metal heads. But Alvin liked being around Howl and oddly, Howl felt the same about Alvin. They were an unusual sight on campus, a nerdy egghead and long-haired, freaky headbanger talking, eating lunch together, or just hanging out.

Alvin's popularity was also growing in the dorm. On Saturday nights, Alvin spent some of his sizable allowance on food and beer, bought by the older guys. Howl would crank up his stereo, there would be a party on their floor.

One weekend, Howl went home for a visit, leaving Alvin alone. Finally he'd get a chance to jerk off like he used to. It was getting late, so it was time for bed anyway. He locked the door, then went through Howl's laundry and got a pair of his briefs. He took out the porno video brochure he had hidden in his desk. It was the only pictures he had of guys having sex with other guys. Then he took off his clothes and lay down on Howl's bed. It didn't take long for his dick to get hard and he greased it up with lotion.

Alvin pictured Howl slowly stripping off his clothes then climbing into bed with him. Howl would kiss him all over his body. Alvin wanted Howl's thick cock up his ass desperately. The moment he pictured Howl fucking him he started to cum. He shot so much it went everywhere, splashing the wall behind the bed, on his face, on the pillow and then spurting on his chest and stomach.

Alvin was breathing heavy, recovering from one of his most intense orgasms. He was still imagining Howl pounding away at his ass. Then he drifted off into a light sleep, not even bothering to clean himself off.

Howl slipped his key into the door and turned the doorknob. Neither he nor Kill was ready for the sight they were about to witness. There was Alvin, lying naked on Howl's bed, a gay porno video brochure in one hand and a pair of Howl's dirty briefs in the other. Howl looked at Kill in disbelief.

"I can't fuckin' believe it," Kill whispered. "He's queer."

Howl said nothing and just stared at his naked roommate. He didn't know what to do.

"What're ya gonna do?"

"Let's wake him up," Howl replied. Kill nodded and they stepped over to the bed. They saw the pools of drying cum on his hairless chest and the pillow.

"Alvin," Howl said softly into Alvin's ear. "Alvin, you're in my bed, dude." Alvin shifted a little but didn't wake up.

"Alvin!" Kill shouted.

Alvin bolted awake, nearly falling out of the bed. For a moment he didn't know what was happening, where he was or what he had been doing. Then a horrible feeling swept over him, almost as intense as his orgasm, when he saw Howl and Kill staring at him. He sheepishly covered his crotch with Howl's briefs.

"Oh shoot! Howl, I'm sorry. I-I-I-I--" He couldn't think of anything that could explain what he was doing in his bed naked and covered in cum. Except the truth. "I was jerking off. I thought you weren't going to be back until tomorrow. I'm sorry."

Howl took the brochure from Alvin's hand and looked at it. "What is this?"

"It's a...well, it's a brochure for a movie."

"These are all guys." Howl said in a serious tone. "It's for a gay porno movie."

"Yeah," Alvin replied, dejected.

"So you're gay then?" Howl asked.

Alvin thought about it before he responded. Howl and Kill had been cool up to now, he thought. Maybe they'd understand.

"Yeah," Alvin sighed, "I'm a fag." Alvin turned away, waiting to be slugged, or for the guys to start laughing derisively. He was sure they would do something that would make him feel even worse than he did right at that moment.

But nothing could prepare him for what happened next. Howl put his hand on Alvin's shoulder and caressed it.

"That's cool," Howl said softly. "So are we." Then Howl kissed him. "Were you thinking of me when you were beatin' the bishop?" Howl asked as he took his underwear out of Alvin's hand.

"Uh, yeah. I was."

Howl looked at Kill and winked. Kill took off his jacket, then kicked off his shoes, then pulled off his T-shirt. Howl pushed Alvin back down onto his bed then started stripping his clothes off, too.

In a few moments, both Howl and Kill were naked. Kill had the idea of putting the two twin beds together to make a bigger bed. Alvin lay between the two headbangers, jerking their cocks. Howl kissed his roommate, their tongues wrestling.

Alvin wrapped his arms around Howl and hugged him tightly. Howl squeezed him back just as tight. Alvin never felt like he did just then. The warmth and the softness of their skin touching his were sheer ecstasy. For the first the time in a long time, Alvin felt good about himself.

Kill got between Alvin's legs and started licking around his crotch. Alvin's six inches stood straight up, harder than steel. Then Kill took the cock in his mouth and sucked it all the way down. Alvin's head reeled from the sensations. He'd never felt anything but his own hand on his dick before. Neither Ken nor Brian ever touched his cock when they fucked him. But Kill's mouth was doing things to his cock that his hand could never do. Lucky for Alvin, jerking off right before was keeping him from cumming too quickly.

Kill just kept licking and sucking while Alvin and Howl explored each other's bodies. Alvin felt up Howl's smooth chest as Howl starting kneading Alvin's ass. His fingers dug into the soft, fuzzy flesh, then started moving deeper into Alvin's crack. Alvin moaned as Howl's finger started to drill into his asshole. Man, Alvin wanted his roommate's cock up his ass.

Then Alvin started to spurt. Again, the thought of Howl fucking him pushed him over the brink and made him start shooting. He clutched Kill's head, pushing him down farther on his cock. He shot a huge load and Kill swallowed it all down. Alvin cried out and kissed Howl passionately.

"Fuck me, Howl!" he moaned. "I want your huge cock deep in my ass."

Howl smiled. His cock pulsed as he looked into Alvin's soft hazel eyes. Without his nerdy glasses, Alvin was really cute. The glasses made him look older and plain. Without his glasses, Alvin looked younger. If he'd let his hair grow out, Howl thought, he'd be damn foxy. Someone he could fall in love with.

"Yeah, I want you, Alvin," Howl said softly. "I want to make love to you."

Alvin got on his hands and knees as Howl maneuvered himself behind him. Kill moved to the side of the bed and started to slowly stroke his meat.

Alvin thought about Kill for a moment, the guy who had just given him his first blow job. Kill continued stroking his thick, heavy cock. Howl's cock was about seven inches, but Kill had the biggest dick Alvin had ever seen. Probably more than ten thick, succulent inches of headbanging hard-on hung between Kill's legs and Alvin wanted it. He needed it.

"Kill, come over here, in front of me," Alvin instructed. "I don't want you to be left out."

Kill smiled at him. He leaned forward and kissed him, jamming his tongue down deep. Kill then positioned himself in front of Alvin, spreading his long hairy legs. Alvin grabbed the guy's cock and immediately slurped it down.

Meanwhile, Howl started to get Alvin's ass ready for the ride of its young life. He grabbed the tube of something called JiffiLube he kept hidden under his bed. He squeezed out a good-size glob in the palm of his hand and started to slick up his tool. He smeared some on Alvin's hairy asshole. He jammed his finger in the tight orifice to loosen it up.

"Damn, you're tight, Alvie," Howl cooed. "Are you still a virgin?" Alvin took his face away from Kill's crotch.

"It's been a long time since anyone's even touched me there, aside from my own fingers."

It felt good to have someone penetrating his asshole like that, opening the hole, probing deep, tickling his prostate. All he wanted was to be split open. He needed the pain, that luscious, exquisite ache.

"Do it, Howl!" he begged. "Fuck me! Fuck me hard!"

Howl was shocked at Alvin's passion. For such a little guy he was damn hot. Howl wasn't about to disappoint his new lover.

Howl put his cock's bulbous head at the tight rosebud and pressed in. Damn, he thought, this guy is so fuckin' tight. Alvin let out a low guttural moan as Howl's cock slipped farther into his hot chute. Alvin's ass gripped his cock like a vise. He pushed in until his pubes were rubbing against Alvin's tight little buns. Howl realized how cute Alvin's ass was, tight and firm. His cock was all the way in and he started rockin'.

"Shit! Tight ass!" Howl cried, "Fuckin' A!" Howl slammed into Alvin's ass brutally, pulling out so the head stretched his hole then jammed it back in. Alvin loved it, getting pounded like that. Howl dug his fingers into the flesh of Alvin's hips.

Kill was enjoying the blowjob he was getting from the little guy. Alvin just sucked away at Kill's rod, taking it all the way down into his throat. He looked up at Kill, who was looking back at him. Kill had soulful brown eyes, framed by such long lashes. For just a moment, Alvin couldn't believe what was happening. His greatest fantasy, getting his ass fucked and sucking a big slab of cock at the same time, was coming true. Alvin was in heaven. His cock, achingly stiff and throbbing, slobbered pre-cum. Man, he was about to shoot for the third time in a row. He never did that, even on his horniest days.

Alvin reached down to his pulsating cock and started jacking himself off. Howl kept punching Alvin's little butt with his meat. Suddenly, Howl stopped Alvin's hand.

"Save it," he whispered into Alvin's ear. "I'm gonna need it later."

Alvin was confused but took his hand off his cock. He reached up and grabbed Kill's hard pecs. Kill moaned as Alvin pinched his little brown nipples. His glans was dancing with Alvin's tonsils, bringing him closer to the brink of orgasm.

Howl couldn't hold off much longer either. Alvin was flexing his sphincter, tightening and relaxing it around his dick. Howl never fucked an ass that did anything like that. He rammed his cock in his buddy's asshole faster and more forcefully. And Kill grabbed Alvin's head and pushed it down, jamming his cock deep into Alvin's throat.

Alvin didn't miss a beat, relaxing his throat and tightening his asshole at the same moment. Howl and Kill both growled lustfully. Alvin felt Kill's cock flutter against his tonsils, then flood his mouth with cum. Alvin swallowed as much as he could, but some spilled over his lips and dripped down his jaw.

"Aww, fuck!" Howl rasped, "Alvin, baby!" His cock spit shot after shot of cum into his roomie's hot ass. It was the most intense orgasm and damn near the biggest load Howl ever had. He collapsed onto Alvin's back, drained physically and sexually. He wrapped his arms around him and hugged him.

"Alvin, boy, you really wore me out," he gasped. "I never had a fuck like that." Howl rubbed his hands all over Alvin's skinny and hairless chest. "No offense, Kill."

Meanwhile, Kill let go of Alvin's head and Alvin let the cock slide out his mouth. He lapped up the cum from his lips and Kill's balls and savored it. It'd been so long since he had tasted another guy's juice.

Alvin bucked his ass, hoping to get Howl's softening cock to stiffen again and stay inside his asshole. But Howl wanted something else. He pulled his soft cock out of Alvin and fell beside him on the bed.

"I want you to fuck me, Alvin," Howl murmured. "I want your cock up my ass." Alvin was shocked. He'd never even thought about fucking a guy. He thought he'd always be getting fucked. But lying right there in front of him was his roommate, his legs up. Kill had squeezed out more lube and was slicking up his buddy's butthole with one hand and Alvin's cock with the other.

"Come on, Alvin," Howl cooed, "dive in."

Alvin smiled broadly and positioned himself between Howl's legs. Kill guided his cock to Howl's asshole, lining the head up. Howl sucked in a shot of air as Alvin began pushing his six-incher inside. Howl rarely got fucked and wasn't used to even Alvin's average-sized dick. Alvin continued pushing in, then slipped, forcing his cock in all at once.

"God, go slow!" Howl gasped. The pain shot through him like a knife.

Alvin stopped pushing and let Howl's asshole get used to the invasion. Alvin's brain was sent to a new level of ecstasy. His dick never felt anything like the soft, warm, tight hole it was in right then. It was even better than Kill's mouth, which was amazing. Alvin felt Howl's sphincter twitch.

"OK, Alvie," Howl whispered, "I'm ready."

Alvin smiled again, and started to rock and roll in Howl's ass. He fucked slowly at first, a little awkward, and not much rhythm. Howl moaned as Alvin's kept plugging away, building rhythm and speed.

His thrusts came harder and soon Alvin was giving Howl's ass a real pounding. Kill bent down and took Howl's cock in his mouth while jacking himself off. Alvin caressed Kill's back and ran his fingers down his crack.

This was all too much for Howl. The penetration of his ass by Alvin and Kill's mouth on his dick sent his senses reeling. And then he flooded Kill's mouth with his cum. Kill swallowed the few spurts of jism easily. The contraction of Howl's asshole pushed Alvin over the top and he started gushing his load into his rectum. Kill lay back and started jerking his cock furiously.

Alvin pumped Howl's ass a few times then fell on top of him, spent. Howl wrapped his arms around him and kissed him. It only took a few more strokes before Kill shot a small load on his stomach. He huffed a little as he caught his breath. Alvin looked at him, then reached over to his stomach and scooped up some cum with his finger. He swallowed some then got more and fed it to Howl, who lapped it up eagerly.

"Man, you love cum, don't you Alvie?" Kill chuckled.

"I can't get enough," he replied, also smiling.

"Was that the first time you ever fucked a guy?" Howl asked.

"Yeah. The only times I've had sex I either blew the guy or got fucked. I usually had to bring myself off with my hand."

"You give some bitchin' head, man," Kill said.

"So do you," Alvin answered, "dude."

ENTER THE DRAGON

Dan Veen

Did you ever see a stranger you knew you'd soon be fucking? For me, that stranger was The Dragon, a.k.a. Ipet Ur-Prong, the Kickbox Champion of Thailand.

Dammit, we should've been kissing, not kickboxing. Yet there was Ipet Ur-Prong, The Dragon, across from me in the ring, and I found myself cruising him like a trick in a Bangkok boybar. We should've been fucking in bed, not fighting in a jam-packed stadium. Blood-hungry Thais were yammering to see my American guts kicked in.

But that wasn't the sort of gut-punching I had in mind.

Ipet Ur-Prong was surrounded by his devoted stable of Thai studboys. I'd heard rumors about these boys. How the Dragon had them firmly in his thrall. These studboys popped hard-ons at the snap of his fingers, shot cum when he told them to cum. The juvenile delinquents worshipped The Dragon like a god.

And I could see why.

My Secret Weapon already uncoiled just thinking about what sort of mix'n'match orgies The Dragon had with his subservient boytoys.

But I couldn't let his looks throw me. My Secret Weapon and I fought to win.

The Dragon pranced around in his corner like Nijinsky. His snooty stuck-up butt teased my Secret Weapon out of its shell. The Dragon's head was a skullcap of fine black stubble; a five o'clock shadow ingrained his deluxe cranium. His brown body was sweat-oiled ridges of glossy muscles flexing in the stadium spotlights.

Had we met in any other place but the ring, we'd've sized each other up quick. We could've gone back to my workout room, had a no-holes-barred fuckmatch. I knew it'd be a thousand pure pleasures to stick my cock in him. His ass clinching my hard-on, I'd fuck him. Fuck him rough. Fuck him hard – the way I knew he'd love it. Then I'd spew my load all over that hairless brown kickboxer's backside.

The starting bell rang. I hardened every muscle but my heart. The crowd roared. They adored The Dragon. They loved to see big blond Americans like me get trounced in their kickboxing ring. Too bad I'd have to disappoint them.

My Secret Weapon grew harder. Ipet Ur-Prong snarled. Honest to god, I'd never felt so attracted to an opponent in my life. He was a real dragon, ferocious and sexy. Each jab at The Dragon felt orgasmic. I surprised him with a groin jab. God, why couldn't I kiss it and make it better?

Ipet retaliated with a front-kick that turned into a high behind-the-knee sweep. Damn, if he fucked as good as he kicked, it'd be like screwing a hurricane!

I kept my balance. Ipet's pretty little face took one of my roundhouse kicks. That hurt me more than it did him. Like slapping a lover.

Ipet slashed back. No emotion showed in his Buddha-smooth face. Two knee-kicks smashed my chest, breaking my heart. He swivelled his hot hips and threw a hard elbow into my kisser. Don't stop, please! I backfisted him. His right uppercut grazed the cusp of my chin. More! Do it harder! Harder! We sparred a moment, danced in crotch-close, like foreplay.

That triggered my Secret Weapon. My cock slipped its jock. For a split-fatal-second, The Dragon lost focus. His eyes shot to my crotch. My meat had jostled free and it waved at him like a big pink flag. The cockhead flopped just outside my shorts. It's a big'un – even when it's soft. Who could blame him for giving me an opening?

Flattered as I was, I took my shot. My powerhouse kick sent my would-be cocksucker to the mat.

The poor devil just lay there, devastated by my tricky dick.

His studboys screamed, cried foul. They didn't know what I'd done, but it had to be against the rules. Rules?

The Dragon was conquered. I towered above Ipet Ur-Prong. Poor cocksucker got humiliated before his worshippers, defeated by the big blond ungodly American. The Dragon lost the title before a Bangkok TV audience and nine thousand booing fans at Rajdammnern Stadium. I placed my foot on his chest, giving Ipet one last look-see up my boxing shorts, cockteasing him a little, so he could admire the throbbing manmeat that had defeated him.

I've won more than a few lovers that way. And quite a few fights.

. . .

Naturally I celebrated my victory by treating myself to the notorious Bangkok nightlife.

I cruised Patpong Road 3 (the queer district) and partied my ass through several sho-bars. Hustler traffic jammed the neoned streets. Twins offered themselves to me. One man with peroxided hair groped the love muscle between my legs. "It's as big as my arm!" he gasped. They love *farang* – foreigners. Especially tall strong blond American *farang*. Especially *farang* with money. Ah, capitalism! predatory and raw.

If you're ever in Bangkok, why not stop by Madame Adipesra-nga's Fuck Hut for a sample of the Bangkok sex industry's sophisticated-tacky accommodations? Most of mama-san's young men can be had for a two-dollar bill. Of all her studlings, I recommend Tshuri, with the most fuckable ass in Asia.

I loved hot-cocking Tshuri. Tshuri's hole was always steaming. Putting my dick into Tshuri's ass was like sending it through a mini-carwash to be lathered, rubbed, scrubbed, buffed and polished from the inside out. Service with a smile!

That humid evening, Madame Adipesra-nga's smooth, naked studboys served us dishes of sushi upon the bare backs of other naked youths, who were poised on all fours. Condiment trays for various sauces were stuck conveniently into their asses. Their ever-hard cocklets served as napkin holders. The boys' mouths were always open should you desire amusement while awaiting desert.

I treated little naked Tshuri to a sumptuous supper from these well-laid boy-tables. I regaled him with my kickboxing adventures, how I defeated The Dragon with my Secret Weapon. How all The Dragon's studboys vowed vengeance. Tshuri teehee'd and said I could've knocked'em all out with my giant farang cock when it was hard.

Tshuri was frisky for a fucking. The Madame never allows any of her boys to cum unless a patron requests it. A horny boy is good for business. So Tshuri was always pleased to get hold of my cock, and he was proud to service it. He said American cocks were the most fun to suck on. They made the nicest sounds when they went up into his ass, too, he said. Tshuri claimed to tell fortunes by reading the bumps in a cock with his sensitive ass-lining.

We went back to Tshuri's pink-lit cubbyhole for the night. Lovely, scenic ricepaper shoji screened us from Madame Adispesra-nga's other customers. Orgies of sounds penetrated our fucknest. Businessmen could be heard dumping their cumloads in the throats of their fuckboys.

Taxi-drivers loudly buttfucked their geisha guys before heading home to their loyal wives.

My own special Tshuri was a splendid cinnamony tint. He had coarse black bangs and crooked teeth. He was slight. He was lift-able, ride-able, bend-able on the winds of whim. This pliant young body had got licked smooth by a thousand tongues. His mouth tasted of the clove cigarettes he smoked when I wasn't near. Tshuri's few shortcomings made him the more exquisite – a piece of Oriental pottery intentionally flawed so that perfection might be better imagined.

Tshuri always oiled himself up before we screwed. He gave his large orchid balls generous dollops; it made him more supple and fuckable. His butthole always brimmed with edible lotions and warmed fuckjellies. Hell, I once found a peppermint up there!

Tonight Tshuri put on a 'Championship' dance for me, swaying like a barboy determined to give the whole audience a hard-on.

His nipples and baby dick jutted up erect. He was proud of his hard boy-size kazoo; not at all self-conscious of its littleness compared to mine. Tshuri's cock stuck straight out from his petite body, a hurting dowelpin of flesh, dripping oil and pre-cum. He just loved stroking his dick while he danced. He undulated and masturbated before me. Tshuri was a kewpie doll with a hard-on, an irresistible combo of cherub and slut.

When his dancing made my cock big and hard enough, Tshuri splayed his legs like a horny cheerleader and jacked his dick happily until he spurted over his tummy.

Dripping in his own cum-splatter, Tshuri deftly rolled a

mechai onto my cock. He called my meat his big bamboo fleshflute, which he wanted to play. He cooed at the hugeness of it. He sang Thai lullabies to it, and burbled and lubed my tube with the residue of his own cum. He loved fitting his hands around the full circumference of my cock.

"C'mere you randy little monkey." I worked my cockskin back and forth, revving up for his hot sucking asshole. "C'mere and get that cute butt fucked."

He perched his cute butt atop my meatstick, smiling blissfully, awaiting my say-so to sit down on it. My meat snaked up to the crater of his ass-entrance.

I nodded my head.

Finally allowed to work the fat hot roundness of my cock up his butthole, Tshuri's mouth gaped as he lowered himself down onto me. I loved watching him struggle. I loved lying back to see him fuck himself on my cock. He hissed and squirmed, panting to skewer himself upon my meat. He pulled his fat ballsac up out of the way so I could watch my cock disappear into him.

"Go ahead, kid. Fuck yourself. Use my cock." His expert asslips puckered. Amazing how fast that tiny tight ass gulped my dick. That boyhole consumed my meathead first, then the entire pink length got sucked into him like a foot going into a warm woolen sock.

He bounced lightly on my thick fucker, feeling it widen his ass canal. His own big and baggy nuts were something extra I could toy with. He smiled proudly and said he liked the music my fleshflute made.

Some Oriental men put their cocks into their boyfriend's asses and leave them there, stewing, all night, stiff and aching, till morning. (There's more to fucking than just cumming). Then they finish off with a lusty pre-breakfast fuck. It's a custom said to enhance the virility of both partners. I do it because I love keeping my big American cock up Tshuri's luscious Thai butt such a long time.

Tshuri's bursting butthole purred and dilated around my cock all night. He read me my fortune as I slow-fucked him, saying that a lot more fun was coming my way very soon.

"You got that right," I whispered as I bit his ear. No way my cock would hold out all night, what with my wet dreams of

Ipet Ur-Prong. A bout of kickboxing with a friend never seems quite finished until the loser gets fucked.

Right when I was ready to cum up Tshuri's bum, a half-dozen impolite ninja warriors crashed into our fuckhut. Shoji screens ripped, bamboo splintered.

Damn, a raid? No.

I recognized one of Ipet's grinning punks. Sure, The Dragon had vowed vengeance, but right now he was a damned nuisance.

"Take it easy, boys, there's enough of my cock for everyone, see?" I lashed out, naked and hard.

My fleshflute swung like a tempered sward unsheathed from Tshuri's asshole. I fought back at Ipet's thugees. It didn't matter that I was completely naked. I always fight with my hands and feet anyway. Two of Ipet's studkids caught it in the sweetbreads before one bastard brought out the nan-chucks.

"Shit!" I shouted, just before he knocked me cold.

. . .

"We like the way you fight, American boy."

I was flat on my back. Ipet Ur-Prong, The Dragon, towered over me in a loincloth, the attire of smart ninja warlords everywhere.

The Dragon looked like some spiteful exotic god. Firelight from torches bronzed his skin like a glazed pig's. His broad chest rose and fell rapidly; it excited him to have me in his power.

"You owe me two dollars," I spit out. "Or a fuck."

I was fit to be tied – but, hey, I *was* tied.

When he saw me struggle with the ropes, Ipet's exotic mask actually broke into a smirk. His nostrils flared at the sight of my long penis dangling between my legs. I looked around me. Near as I could tell, I'd been shanghaied to an airplane hangar abandoned since the War.

"Captain America is pissed," Ipet announced, putting his foot upon my cock and pressing ever-so-excruciatingly. Ipet reminded me of too many old boyfriends. Just my type, unfortunately.

Ipet's studboys laughed.

"Yeah, well, fuckus interuptus doesn't put me in the best of moods. I was about to cum – " I looked down at my disappointed cock, my Secret Weapon exposed, still loosely wrapped in a rubber like a snake shedding its skin.

"Today you took my honor before my disciples – "

"Well, if you hadn't been such a cocksucker – "

Ipet held his hand up accusingly. "Tonight the real fight begins. My men demand a rematch."

"Fine. Talk to my agent."

"Now. Tonight. We demand revenge!"

I looked down at my body, defenseless but for the years of muscles I'd honed and polished like armor. I was bruised, but otherwise in great shape. A grudge match? A duel? Hell, this was the one-on-one dreambout with Ipet that I'd imagined when I first saw him in the ring. No referee. No clothes. No rules. No shit.

"Of course, cute as you are," I said as his boys untied me, "I'm not going to let you win just so you can save face with your studpets."

Ipet's boyfriends tittered like munchkins. They couldn't help but brush their hands against my formidable Weapon. They were the classy kind of Thais you'd find at dogfights. Young tattooed gang toughs, silver-capped teeth flashing like switchblades. They'd fuck me as soon as look at me. Probably both.

I could see why these guys kowtowed to Ipet. He was their sex god, alright. All those dirty stories were true. The Dragon was one of those sinful acrobats you see carved on the sides of crumbling x-rated temples.

His boys made a makeshift kickboxing ring with their half-naked bodies.

We circled each other as in some ancient ritual. His boys were either chanting or placing bets. I could feel the heat rising, could see their hard-ons growing with anticipation of using them on the loser.

Ipet morphed into a half-dozen menacing stances, the spidery kabuki movements of martial arts, intending to freak me out. All that body language meant something if you were a native. I must've missed that class. It just made me more determined to fuck his flexible little ass.

I dropkicked to Ipet's midsection, only grazing his tits. He wheeled round, threw me a heel-punch like one of the Radio City Rockettes.

When the stars cleared, I was down on my knees. Ipet stood over me about to spearkick my back. Just as he aimed his blow, I aimed mine below the belt – literally.

I reached beneath his loincloth for the soft underbelly. Bingo! I clutched Ipet's Pride 'n' Joy! His Scepter of Virility – plus his Pud Pouch. I twisted his goodies like taffy, scooting under his legs, and pulling his precious jewels with me, right up behind him.

This was dirty fighting. He howled. I yanked those balls till he dropped to the floor belly first. I pressed my advantage, pulling on his cock.

I could've pulverized The Dragon's little pink fleshlizard right there. Could've made a temple priest out of him, eunichized him, but I wanted some fun with him first.

I sat on The Dragon's back now, pinned him down while I faced his butt and pulled his dick back between his legs, stretching it into the slot between his asscheeks.

"You little bastard! Nobody butts in when I'm about to cum!"

I flipped back the flap of Ipet's loincloth.

I exposed his butt to the crowd of his studboys.

They laughed as I gave it several hard smacks. It bounced in pain. Ipet screamed and yelled for mercy, crying uncle. I just gave that dick another twist, making it look like a bright red corkscrew. I felt it grow hard in my hand, but still showed it no mercy.

Ipet's punk studs went wild. Strength was their only allegiance. They loved me. There were my fans now, my studboys, my cocksuckers. They loved me, loved what I was doing to their ex-leader. Their kind would fuck any man when he's down.

Over Ipet's rattling protests, I grabbed Ipet's legs and brought them back above his spine. He was a flexible little chimp. I took both his hands and clasped behind his back to his ankles, making him rock like a contortionist. He put up a nominal fuss, almost as if he felt he deserved the humiliating positions I was forcing him into.

The gang started rattling their nan-chucks at him, warning him not to budge.

"I guess they want to see what I'm going to do to you next, cocksucker!"

I posed over him, letting my cock stand out big before his wide eyes. He was putty in my hands. "Now I've won the use of your ass, fair and square. Looks like you've bossed these boys too many times, Dragonshit. They want to see you get what's coming to you. And I'm the big American with the big American cock that's going to do it."

The boys watched me jack my dick. They rooted for me now, cheered me on.

Ipet's nostrils flared. He wanted this too.

"You guys like to see this puny dickwad get fucked by my big all-American cock? Here you go, boys! Take a look at it!"

I stormed the perimeters of the crowd. My cock swung as I strutted. It felt good showing it off to all those envious eyes. They imagined what it would feel like to take my cock up their own asses, wondered if their mouths could open wide enough to suck it. They rubbed their butts and tweaked their tits. They wanted it. They wanted to lick my balls, worship my cock.

"Hold those ankles like I told you, asswipe!" I snarled at Ipet. He fearfully kept the position I'd put him in.

With his ankles back over his head, he was practically immobile, except that he swayed back and forth like a rocking horse, bug-eyed with anticipation of what I'd do to him next. I yanked off the loincloth that covered him.

His gang hooted. Ipet's butt flinched and blushed with embarrassment. I couldn't wait to get up that perfect ass.

I moved round to his frightened face and gave his raised forehead a contemptuous push with the heel of my foot. His boys jeered at him as he rocked helplessly back and forth.

He yelled out but took it, knowing that his punishment would be far worse if he unbowed himself.

When he rocked forward, I popped my big toe into his mouth. The very weapon which kickboxers respect the most, the thing which had defeated him, I made him suck on it. It was like making him suck on a gun. I rocked him back and forth some more with my toe in his mouth.

He tongue-washed my feet. He mouthed my toe while I held

it out to him. He didn't dare stop worshipping it. He seemed to want to keep it in his mouth. This was all part of what he deserved for his humiliation.

His tongue lolled around. It started to lick the balls of my feet, slurping in between the toes, as he sucked hard and obediently with his cute oval mouth. His hungry, efficient licking didn't stop till I popped my big toe out and smeared it over his lips.

I moved behind him. With his legs bent backwards, thighs suspended in the air, his prong hung down against his curved belly. It was a dark drooling slug of a dick, depositing its slime into his belly button. He was turned-on by the toe-job he'd given me. I spun him around once just so everyone could have a good laugh.

"You're ready for anything now, aren't you, asswipe!"

I made him release his ankles. He sprawled out flat on his tummy.

I spanked him again, harder this time, hard and longer and louder. I beat those buttmounds like they were bongos. It was then I saw the light stencilled dragon flowing from buttcheek to buttcheek like a magazine centerfold. You had to part the valley of Ipet's twitching ass to get the full picture of the dragon tattoo enfolded between his gorgeous mounds.

"Oh sweet Jeezus, you're gonna be one pleasure to fuck," I grunted.

Ipet's horny buddies were ready too. They grew quiet and respectful once they saw how huge my cock had gotten.

Ipet gasped.

My thick cockhead nuzzled between his buttcheeks.

"Hmm, bet you've never had one up the ass before, have you?" He was probably one of those top men who complained about back problems whenever somebody tried to fuck him. Now I would give him a real back problem.

Ipet moaned something.

"Hm? You ever get a big fat cock up your prissypuckered poothole before?"

I slapped him like a maniac masseur, all over his backside. "Spread those knees, fuckhole! Farther! Spread'em!"

Ipet stretched his knees so wide he was pressed out frog-fashion.

"That's it, Dragon shit, come to poppa. Open up your oily little bunghole for this big ol' cock. I'm gonna fuck it. Here it comes."

Ipet moaned and prayed or begged. He pushed his asscheeks up to my shoving dick. The butthole was practically kissing on it. Something in Ipet complied; succumbed to the inevitable; he couldn't resist. He desired my cock now. The anxious tremor of his asscheeks welcomed my meat. He wanted screwing bad, needed it in the worst way.

"Watch this, boy. This is what a real cock can do!" I pushed Ipet's pelvis down further, squashing his dick in the dirt and widening his ass entrance. "Gather round and watch your boss get fucked!"

They all had their cocks out. They liked watching their master get fucked. I could hear the simultaneous stretching and mushing of their dickskins.

And I stuck my cock in slow, aligned it with that dragon tattoo and screwed it in to the snatch. I pierced the delicious slit of his sweaty ass.

"Feelin' hot and sweet already, boys. Gonna make sure he feels every inch!"

They all sighed, I suppose imagining my giant tool fucking them all. Their hands worked their dicks furiously.

"Yeah, this butt can handle a hot cock. You can ride me right up to my balls, can't you, boy? Can't you?"

I ground it in slow so that we all relished every humpy inch as my meat wrecked him. Ipet's hands clawed the floor. My cock smoothed out the lining of his asshole.

My cock smelled virgin butt territory. I could tell by the glove-tight feel up there, snug as another ribbed mechai wrapped around my dick.

"How's that feel?"

Ipet's butt rippled in reply. He heaved against the floor.

Another shove or two and I was mashing my crotch flat against his buns.

He arched his back in response to my gently jabbing cock. He rubbed his shoulder blades against the hairs on my chest. Cuddling up to me now like a horny pussycat.

I got him up on his hands and knees and cockwalked him around the circle of boys, letting 'em wipe their dicks' pre-cum on him.

"Look at your hero, boys!" I pushed and fucked him at the same time. "He may be the Dragon, but I'm the Dragon Fucker!"

They each gave his butt a slap. They poked at his pingpong balls and laughed whenever he groaned at my fucking him.

Finally I body-slammed my hot cum into him. As I finished, I reached under for that tubby pork-filled eggroll of his. It had already splashed cumdrops all over the floor.

I gave him a final jostle on my cock, and he lay there like I'd crushed him. The squirt vise-gripped my cockmeat gratefully. All around us, I heard the slapping of Thai balls.

"You hear that? They want to fuck you now." These horny ninja studs liked what they saw.

"And I'm gonna let them."

I figured they deserved it - and so did Ipet.

I spread Ipet's asscheeks apart, exposed that battered dragon tattoo, showed 'em Ipet's well-fucked hole. It gaped like a fish's mouth now - open for more.

I slapped each cheek.

"Spread 'em!" I ordered.

He spread, showed all the boys that they could fuck him.

I tapped the ring of his ass.

"Open!"

He opened it up, wider than ever.

"There you go, boys. Help your horny little selves to some prime pink ass! This'll really suck the spunk out of you!"

They lined up.

"You can fuck him now. After that, maybe you can have a go at a real cock. The one who fucks him the hardest, and makes him yell, can have a go at sitting on my cock."

This gave them just the incentive they needed, and we lost count how many times Ipet got dicked up the ass by his boys - or how many times Ipet came. Pretty soon, Ipet was just the gang's fuckhole. He'd gone past orgasm, into cocklover's nirvana. His dick just dribbled a constant ooze of cum.

When we finished fucking him all we wanted, one of the boys produced a leather dildo almost the size of my cock. They had a great time holding Ipet down and putting it up him till nothing showed but a long leather string hanging out him. The

Dragon would be a lot more controllable now that he was on a leash.

They called me The Dragonfucker after that. It became a manhood test for the boys to take my cock up their asses. They'd smile when they got my meat stuffed all the way up inside them. They'd spread their legs, triumphantly showing their buddies the buttfuck they'd accomplished.

I called the cumshots now. Tshuri became my Number One Fuckboy. He would love being in charge of the festivities, devising ways for the Dragon to service us all. After all, I was the Dragonfucker, and it would be a while before a bigger man could screw me out of my position.

THE ORGASMIC RESUME

Thom Nickels

A couple of years ago I was working at a resume office in downtown Philadelphia owned by a man named Lenny. As the owner of twenty quick-print shops in the city, Lenny was glad to have a sports columnist for one of Philly's big newspapers manage his pilot project. Lenny hired me before do-it-yourself resume writing kits became the rage and before high schools and colleges created courses in resume writing.

The office was part of a mini-mall in the foyer of a twenty-story office building. Across the hall was a yogurt store, a jeweler's, a tailor and a card and gift emporium. These shops attracted a fair amount of traffic.

"Resume Place" looked like a Swiss chalet with its floor-to-ceiling paneled windows. There were no curtains or blinds on the windows so the overall effect reminded me of a fish tank. Since I had no intention of being on display, my first official act as manager was to order a large set of curtains. This was necessary because I knew that many of my customers would be hot young men I didn't want passers-by spying on as I conducted interviews or watched as they filled out resume application forms.

My first day on the job was spent arranging the office furniture to please my cock-hungry eye. I repositioned the desk so that it faced the long sofa on the other side of the room (in case men should be sitting there), and I put the client interview chair to the left of my desk in a small corner niche, out of the viewing range of people passing in the hall. To protect my privacy, I posted huge signs advertising my services on the front window, then walked the hallway to see what was visible from that vantage point. I was glad to discover that my desk was hidden by the posters, and that the interview/seduction chair was invisible to anyone but those already in the office. Next, I ordered curtains to be put behind the ads so that the office would have a dark, cozy and seductive feel to it.

The first few weeks were slow: I waited in vain for nice-looking men or college boys. The only people who seemed to show up were women. Women in Marketing. Women graduates of Wharton. Nurses. Waitresses. Mothers. Yuppie wannabes in pony tails and baseball caps who drank bottled water. I was getting frustrated.

The first male customer appeared one day just as I was about to go to lunch. He was blond, maybe 22, Italian, with a buzz cut that reminded me of an inflated penis head. He wore white cut-offs, sandals without socks, a T-shirt. He was cute, though his pursed lips reminded me of an anal-retentive sort, a spoiled brat with a stick up his ass. I just knew he was the kind of guy who wouldn't welcome advances from hip, urban gay males.

He told me he was a roofer but was thinking about switching careers. "Can you quote me a price?" he asked, not sure whether to sit down or keep standing but somehow wanting me to tell him what to do.

"I'm affordable," I said, trying to take my eyes off the huge soft cock bulge snug against his right leg. The bulge was so big I guessed his penis length to be about ten or eleven inches when erect.

"I like to keep price options open. Have a seat and we can talk about it," I said, indicating the seduction chair.

When he walked, his penis did a position change: the mammoth head moved in a slow downward curve, creating a phenomenal arc. During the few seconds it took him to get to the chair, it shook from side-to-side, making me think of rock slides and wild things under wraps.

Seated, he leaned back and opened his legs so that the cock-bulge looked larger than ever. I guessed he wasn't wearing underwear because the thing had a dangling looseness: his balls danced as he shifted in the chair, and his fat cockhead came into sharper focus.

The way he was sitting – legs spread far apart as he slouched against the back of the chair – suggested he knew I was staring at him and that he was responding to my sexual radar. So much for first impressions.

In a quivering voice, I quoted the price list, careful to let him see the direction of my roving eye. As he asked to see resume samples, I leaned forward and did something I'd never thought I'd do: I told him we could work out a deal if we got to know each other better. "In this space, you can lean back and relax and fill out the form in a leisurely fashion. Then we can see what's what," I said, giving his crotch an intense eye caress.

Having him fill out forms gave him plenty of time to slouch forward and get into the body language thing. I was hoping he'd get a full erection and give me a show. After that, I'd cop a feel and coax him into the backroom. Or maybe I'd just hang my "be back in ten minutes" sign on the front door and do him in the niche. Only later would I bring up the free (or reduced) resume package.

The office was perfect for gropes, foot massages and blowjobs because it had an empty storage area in the back. This was a big space my boss talked about renovating and renting out as an additional business. I had already figured out that if I met someone I could take them back there, or into the partitioned area leading to the backroom, which was sometimes used as an office for Lenny's wedding card displays. This small enclosure had two desks and two chairs. Best of all, it was walled off so even people in the shop couldn't see into it entirely.

As the roofer worked on the form, I leaned forward, a Thesaurus in my hands so I'd have a prop in case someone walked in. I was leaning into his crotch in a hunched over pose nerds assume when they don't want to sit back and spread their legs (in another office I did plenty of resumes for this type of guy). The roofer was writing with his left hand, the questionnaire propped on his raised left knee (bruised recently, he said, from a roller blading accident). His other leg was spread out considerably, providing a crotch valley for my hands should he decide to do something outrageous – like take his cock out and slap it against his leg.

Occasionally, I'd close the Thesaurus and stare into that manly valley, moving closer in lurching spasms only an idiot would fail to notice the meaning of.

I soon began taking many small liberties: I let my left arm dangle in the area in front of his crotch, careful to cup my hand and swing it back and forth in a jerk-off motion. Then I swooped my arm upward in a half-ferris wheel swoop that stopped at the level where his penis was. My fingers circled round as if they held a thick knockwurst and in three or four violent strokes I made blatant milking motions. He didn't let on that he noticed this as he continued to write. It occurred to me that he noticed this as he continued to write. It occurred to me that I was being ignored, and that here was another indifferent twenty-something who knew all of life's sexual hints and signals but, like the rock of Gibraltar – and the hopelessly heterosexual – would not budge.

I was getting pissed. I want people to be like pieces of furniture so I can move them around at will.

Just then he bolted upright and clasped his legs shut. The shock of this movement jerked my body back. I continued to lean into him, thinking that a quick move away would look suspicious – even during the best body language displays, a little decorum is necessary. The questionnaire, which was on a clipboard, now totally blocked his crotch.

Not a good sign by any means. I adopted a wait-and-see attitude, thinking perhaps he didn't want to move too fast. "Perhaps he wants to hear the low price or the word 'free' before he gives me total access." I said to myself.

I sat back in my desk and assumed a professional pose, not an unwise move considering that potential customers or one of the bosses – especially Lenny's wife – could enter the store at any time. I figured I'd give the roofer ten minutes to reposition himself..If that didn't happen, I'd get the clipboard from him somehow, or do something to make him reposition his body. I wanted his legs open, come what may. He was not going to sit there like a church lady, not in my office anyway.

Ten minutes later I came to the awful realization that his legs were shut for good. "He has eyes for nookie only," I surmised. "And resumes."

"Look, how about if I fill the form out for you?" I offered. "Sometimes words and ideas flow faster when a customer doesn't have to write and think at the same time." What helped me in this analysis was that someone once told me that roof tar aroma was known to kill human brain cells: Was that why he was taking so long to complete the form? He had inhaled too much roof tar? Or was it to tease me? "Let me ask you questions about your work history and write them down myself. Here, why don't you give me the clipboard?"

I held my hand out, my fingers cupped as if they were holding a cucumber. If he was really a victim of roof tar, he'd need colorful hints.

He handed me the clipboard and once again I had a full view of his crotch. The penis bulge seemed squeezed down between the lower portion of his legs. For a micro-second it looked like he didn't have any cock at all. Had he tucked it under something when I had my head turned? Had he stuffed it up his ass? I could only see the upper outlines and a portion of the cockhead – a frustrating view considering what I'd glimpsed previously. I knew I had to get him to spread his legs. But how? Patience was one answer: I waited for him to slouch down in the chair but he kept his legs closed, his pursed lips frozen in a sour Puritan cast. He wasn't giving me anything.

If I were Caligula and my office ancient Rome, I'd have him flogged – or worse.

I plied him with questions as my eyes took Kamikaze-like dives into his crotch. Was there no way to get him to relax? Did I have to do the unthinkable: grab his cock in one violent swoop?

I thought he moved a leg, a motion that shifted his cockhead into view. I thought it was erect because there seemed to be a discreet, pulsating motion there. Then I realized that his genitals were just shifting in his cut-offs. He gave me what I wanted when he slid down on the chair and opened his legs in a scissor wide-angle. I saw the big lump in its primal glory. Cockhead. Low-hanging balls. A million fresh pecker tracks in cut-offs. I wanted to taste his salty dog and lap up his body juices. I wanted him, in-coming customer notwithstanding. And I was prepared to take a major risk.

I half-expected him to grope himself and say something crude, but he just sat there, a bump on a log. It was hard to remain professional as I finished the interview.

I leaned forward, confident our cocks were speaking the same language. My face was in his lap when he repositioned his legs and sat up. The Caligula in me tied his roofer limbs to two horses and had the horses run in different directions. I watched as he broke into six parts. Next, I forced him to get on all fours as Sumo-sized wrestlers fucked him without a lubricant. Then I made him tell me he was nothing but a piece of furniture.

"Why don't you take the form?" I suggested, handing him

the clipboard. "I think with your personality it's best that you do it yourself." My plan was to cop an underhanded feel.

He took the clipboard and put it over his crotch. I couldn't see anything but his hairy legs, though I still leaned into his lap. He didn't seem to notice anything but continued writing.

I faked a question as I grabbed the clipboard, my right hand pressing into his stomach in a jab that might be dismissed as accidental had there not been so much crotch gazing. I hadn't touched his cock but a small portion of his stomach.

"Take your fucking resume and shove it," he said, standing up and slamming the clipboard on my desk. "You fucking dick! I came here for a resume. You fucking dick! I'm going to tell people about you and you're going to be sorry. You fucking dick."

What did he know about a fucking dick! His was all bunched up inside his cut-offs – a dead deal.

I expected shingles to fly and roofer's tar to feather me all over. Foul-mouthed and ignorant, here was one of Philly's eloquent underclass, a yahoo on the warpath.

"You fucking dick!" he screamed again. He was so loud the yogurt shop people looked over to see what was happening. I held my breath and faked a look of shock, as if I'd come upon a nut case. He backed out of the store as I stole one last look at his crotch.

"Loose hanging sausage, cockhead for nookie only," was a phrase that crossed my mind as he left the office.

Several days after roofer incident, I discovered the pleasures of a local chat line. Soon I was spending many happy hours connecting with men I'd sometimes invite to the shop. Some men never showed up, as is the usual case with chat line connections, but several did. This was a great alternative to having to wait for sexy male customers to walk in by chance. The chat line also helped to alleviate the boring stretches between resume customers.

Chat line men who showed up at the shop were usually well behaved. If there were customers present, they'd usually wait quietly on the sofa, pretending they were customers (most did their best to hide hard-ons). They'd introduce themselves to me once we were alone.

"Hi, I'm Jeff. Six-one, 165 pounds, brown hair, blue eyes, eight 'cut.'"

Usually I'd take them to a friend's apartment several blocks away, but there were exceptions.

A gangly (six-five), dark-haired businessman walked in and introduced himself as Joe. His face had the peculiar markings of a compulsive masturbator – thick, lippy lips, sunken eyes, flat nose, high forehead. Everything about the man oozed sex. He whipped out his twelve inches when he walked up to my desk. I was beside myself. Nobody had ever done that before. I was about to direct him towards the rear of the shop when he noticed the backroom and walked back there himself, shaking his dick the whole time.

He expected me to follow him in a doggie-style toddle. But I was so amazed at his behavior – acting as if this were his shop and not mine – I just observed him in a kind of trance. I couldn't believe the size of his cock and the way he kept beating it against the back door. The "thump thump" sounded like a light hammer.

I searched his sex crazed gaze for a semblance of sanity as he began a race-against-death masturbation session, his long spindly legs crouched forward and his polished size-13 businessman's shoes at a wide duck angle. No sooner had he begun to grunt and approach what seemed to be an orgasm when in walked Lenny's wife, a thin, Florida-tanned millionairess with houses up and down the east coast. She seemed to sense something amiss in the shop (the motor-scent of a fast whack off?) as soon as she opened the door. He beat a hasty retreat behind the backdoor, the tip of his long dick the last part of his body to slip from view.

She missed seeing something by a hair.

"How's business?" she said, the look in her eyes seeming to pick up the strange something she couldn't quite grasp.

"Consistently slow, but people *are* coming," I said, peeking towards the back. I panicked when she went near the backroom to poke around. She was known for poking around in spots most people in her family ignored. When she bent over a box of stationery, her back to the door where the businessman was hiding, I expected the worst. I hoped he'd have the good sense to get out from behind the door and walk to the far end of the hidden room in case she decided to check the room with a cursory glance. I'd already had him pegged as a exhibitionist, so I feared his dick was throbbing and erect and pointing straight out for the first taker, be it a Florida matron or a frantic resume writer fearing for his job.

"Nothing in here," she said, heading out. "Okay, sweetie, have a nice day."

I thanked my lucky stars.

When she left, he was out of there in a flash, without so much as a wave or good-bye. Just the sort of behavior I'd come to expect from closeted businessmen in the City of Brotherly Ambivalence.

In the days that followed, I interviewed several men, mostly lawyers in monkey suits. Some were sexy. Most were overweight. Sexy men I relegated to the corner chair; women were told to fill out forms on the sofa, though some insisted on the chair. With the men, I followed the same procedure I started with the roofer: pretend to leaf through a book or flip through a folder while stealing looks at their crotch. Most of the time I never saw any noteworthy crotches, since most men were only interested in their resumes. I had learned to be careful and not stare too long or lean over too close, and I made it a rule that I would never grab a customer unless they gave me a blatant sign.

Slouching back in the interview chair was the sign I always looked for. If a man slouched, that meant he was probably open and free. If he sat crab-like and continued to sit like that even after I stared at his crotch, he was hopeless – hooked to nookie.

A hand-lettered sign above my desk offered hints: "Relax – sit back – I'm not the dentist." This never failed to elicit at least a chuckle from even the most nervous.

One day I came back from lunch to find a tall, blond Temple student sitting in my office. He was on the sofa across from the desk, legs spread in a wide inverted V, the ends of his gym shorts ballooned out so that anyone at the desk could see inside. My heart raced as I listened to him say that Lenny's son had directed him to me after giving him an application.

He was already filling it out, so there was no way I could

move him to the chair. As I sat at my desk, I could see that his ballooning gym shorts revealed much more than I bargained for: a section of pubic hair and a chunk of flaccid, thick penis, the color of fine Italian marble.

Red-faced, fidgeting with paper clips and pencils, I leaned forward in a preying, menacing pose, hoping he'd pick up my sexual radar and whip out his cock. The overall effect he had on me was uncanny; it wasn't long before I felt like the businessman-exhibitionist who wanted things to happen instantly. I was tired of waiting, tired of being patient. "The time is NOW," I said to myself. Call it sex fever at its highest.

No matter how I preened, licked my lips in a loud smack or cocked my head, the student, barely legal, never looked up or made direct eye contact.

The flaccid penis, I soon realized, was something I'd have to crawl towards and grab – Caligula - style.

"Nice shorts," I said, at which point he seemed to open his legs wider, his penis head very visible, the long slit seeming to wink at me.

"Let me jack you off and pump out your blond boy stuff and a typeset resume with 150 free copies is yours! Only a fool would resist such an offer." I rehearsed these lines over and over, measuring how he'd respond, examining his face for yahoo character flaws and hints of meanness.

He seemed to be reading my mind as he put on a pair of sunglasses and slid down on the sofa. In a second he was stretched out all the way, his big feet touching the front of my desk as he moved his legs in a sideways erotic whirl. Why the sudden change? Cynical about quick reversals – I've been fooled by too many cock-teasers – here was this blond bombshell (in a city of dark-haired men), getting his cock hard so that it pointed straight up towards his navel in rocket-launch mode.

I could scarcely believe the miracle that had taken place when he said "Aren't you going to lock the door?"

...An orgasmic resume at last!

A LOVELY LAD

Rudy Roberts

"If it be a sin to love a lovely lad,
Oh then sin I."
— Richard Barnfield

It took me two weeks of intense searching, but I finally found it. I had looked everywhere I could think of and had spoken to every person I knew, trying to locate another place to live, suitable in both size and price. Everything in the city seemed to be well beyond my means. It hadn't been my choice, after all, to move. I would sooner have stayed put in my old flat but the landlord had decided to sell the place. My options quickly disappeared.

But then, one evening, I spoke with a bartender at one of the clubs I frequented and got an interesting lead on a place that would be coming available soon – on the second floor of a house out in the west end. I had my doubts at first, to be honest, when he described the place to me: away from the downtown core; no private entrance; no laundry facilities; and poor water pressure. But, with some desperation, I went to investigate the place. And, to my utter astonishment, I found the place to be quite charming: roomy, bright, clean, quiet and relatively inexpensive. I also thought that this would be a nice change from my usual downtown place. So, I contacted the landlord for an interview and, within a few days, I was the new tenant.

And no sooner did I get things arranged when I saw *him*. He lived across the road. There was a curve in the street that partially obscured his house. But, if I strained, I could see him: a young, Italian boy, perhaps all of eighteen. I had always had this weakness for Italians, finding their swarthy, dark looks irresistible. This boy in particular had curly, dark locks, smooth, clear skin, and a body that should have been registered as a lethal weapon. He was broad-shouldered, with a tapering and muscular torso that ran into one of the most spectacular butts

I'd ever laid eyes on – so curved, so round and so tight. And his legs – long, muscular limbs – were hairless and defined. He must have been a runner from the looks and succulent shape of those calves and thighs. But his face betrayed that manly body. He was too young, I quickly decided. I had to resist.

And resist I did. No, I did not notice him sitting on the front porch of his parents' house, wearing little more than a worn and faded pair of Adidas shorts and a tight-fitting T-shirt. I never once noticed how his thighs flexed involuntarily, even if all he were doing was sitting in a deck chair, reading. I didn't even consider watching him from my living room window, catching the occasional genital adjustment, watching as he would scratch the sometimes itchy pectoral or rub the taut thigh. Thank *Christ* I didn't take heed of him or he would have most assuredly driven me mad. And it's a damned good thing, too, that I didn't notice the immense oak tree outside my window which offered perfect and sturdy concealment. No, and the fact that I had recently purchased a pair of high-power binoculars made no impression upon me whatsoever. I was oblivious to him.

But he was certainly a challenge to oblivion. After spending an evening vigil by my window, I finally allowed my curiosity – fortified by a tumbler of scotch – to direct me outside my fantasy *and* outside my living room window. I soon found myself perched precariously upon the sturdiest branch of that nearby oak. I was instantly frightened that the rustle of leaves would betray me. But nobody seemed to have heard. And there I was, grasping daringly to an enormous tree limb, binoculars pressed to my face to prevent their falling. And there *he* was, sitting across the street on his front porch, wearing those cursed Adidas shorts -- adjusting, scratching, rubbing.

And what reward do I get for my troubles? He decided, for whatever reasons, to go inside. And he snapped off the porch light, throwing the entire house into darkness. I pulled the binoculars away from my face then and checked my watch, squinting in the darkness.

"Shit!" I exclaimed to myself. "It's *only* eleven-thirty, kid! What's the big deal?!"

Just as I was about to crawl back inside, a light went on

upstairs. And there he stood, in full view, with or without my binoculars, inside his bedroom. I silently prayed that he wouldn't dash to the windows and pull his curtains shut. Because *then* I would most emphatically be nothing more than a lecherous voyeur, hanging out on a limb, left with nothing but a stomach in knots from anticipation and underwear full of a raging hard-on.

I plugged the binoculars back up to my eyes then and observed him across the street, standing tall. Taking a deep breath, he crossed his arms and peeled the tight-fitting T-shirt up and off, tossing it aside. His torso was as I'd imagined it would be: smooth, hairless, glowing, heavy with young muscle, rigid with firm abdominals, dark from the sun and his heritage. I took a sharp breath then, accompanied by a painful twinge inside my shorts. Then he walked over to his window and gazed outwards. One hand fell to his crotch, making more than a mere adjustment. The bulge expanded; he seemed to have the most delicious aversion to underwear of any kind. When he reached for the window, I was certain that he was going to draw the curtains. And, fighting back a yell, I watched, sure that I would soon have to climb back inside, leaving this peculiar vigil for another time. But instead of closing the curtains, he opened the window wider and then turned back.

I re-focused my lenses and readjusted my position on the branch, having quickly abandoned my despair and readying for some sort of show. But then the bedroom light went out, plunging the entire house once more into total blackness. I stared past those fluttering curtains for a few moments longer, hoping to catch a glimpse of something, anything; I was so horny. Fortunately, though, I didn't have to wait long. A bedside lamp was switched on and there he was, spread-eagled atop his rumpled bed, one hand relinquishing a glossy magazine, the other stuffed inside his shorts, playing with his mighty phallus.

He plopped the magazine down beside him, thumbing the pages with eager anticipation. Upon finding a particularly desired photograph, he settled back into his pillows, bringing the magazine up to cover his face. This picture seemed to capture his attention at whichever angle he chose. Although unable to see his face and his expressions, I was fortunately able to see the impact of that picture upon his swollen cock. His chest and biceps began to shine with perspiration. His flat stomach clenched. And his thighs flexed, spreading even wider. I gulped, not wishing to miss a thing.

As I fiddled with the dials on the binoculars, trying to ascertain the title of the magazine that had captured his attention so completely, a car pulled around the corner into the street. I pulled my eyes away briefly, and recognized the car as that of my landlord downstairs. Wide-eyed with terror at the prospect of being caught like this, I held my breath, frantically thinking up an excuse should I be unceremoniously caught. The only thing that I could think of was claiming that I was an amateur astronomer, gazing into the night sky at a star cluster in the north-west quadrant of the heavens. Fortunately, however, the landlord simply climbed out of his car and went inside, not once turning his attention to his new tenant high above him in that magnificent and shivering oak. Letting out a sigh of relief, I resumed my vigil.

It's amazing what a person can miss in just a moment's time. In the time that I'd taken thinking up an excuse for my landlord, I'd missed the action across the road. There he was, spread out on top of his dishevelled sheets, totally naked now, the shorts finally having been abandoned, perspiring and writhing with desire, his fingers curled around his tumescent penis, frantically tugging at the dark flesh with both hands. I gulped hard, eyes wide at the sight.

"Holy shit!" I screamed to myself, unable to believe my eyes. My own erection was stiffly rammed against the trunk of the tree, extremely uncomfortable yet alert. I didn't dare touch it, even to adjust it into a more comfortable position, for fear of falling or of shooting off. Instead, I focused upon the scene unfolding rapidly across the road.

His cock was large – quite thick – and his balls were truly massive, jumping around as he forcefully yanked on his dick. His chest and arms were slick with sweat now, well-defined in their young musculature. Despite the fact that this boy indeed had a boy's face, he most emphatically had a man's body. Knowing that I'd be witnessing him shoot his load made me squirm, shivering in the tree, rustling more and more leaves. But at that point I didn't care whether the entire *street* could see me. I was determined to watch this boy jerk off.

I returned my attention to the magazine for a moment, straining to see what picture had stimulated him so immensely. Unfortunately, though, he had closed the magazine. But, upon closer scrutiny, I did happen to recognize the cover. Oddly enough, it was one of the magazines I'd just recently bought, so the cover was familiar to me. I continued to watch the boy's hands racing up and down the length of his fat, engorged cock, recalling that the magazine was resplendent with glossy photographs that showed an immensely hot black man skewering his latin companion with his formidable cock. Other photos included ecstatic orgasms, valiant blowjobs, and one wild scene of auto-fellatio by a well-endowed stud.

The thought that this boy was jerking off crazily to those particular photos made my head spin. Before long, he was reaching the edge of his endurance and shot off a voluminous blast of cum up and across his chest. Stream after stream shot from the shining tip of his cock, landing on his biceps, his neck, his shoulders, his nipples, and his textured belly. Finally, after what seemed like an inordinate amount of time to be spent unleashing a volley of cum, his orgasm subsided. His fingers were slick and dribbling. His chest was heaving, glistening with cum and sweat, thick gobs of semen puddling and dribbling. Then he reached down beside his bed and produced a towel. Before he commenced cleaning up, I saw him do the truly amazing – he wiped the last glob of cum from the glowing tip of his softening erection and stuffed the fingers into his mouth.

That was enough for me. I quickly emptied a pent-up load of my own into my underwear, almost convulsing myself into a nose-dive into the peonies below. Regaining my composure, I looked across to see him reaching for the lamp, a look of exhausted satisfaction smeared upon his handsome face. I could tell that he was headed for sleep. And I also knew that *I* was headed for trouble.

The next day he resumed his regular post on the front porch. After awhile, though, things began to get somewhat boring – nothing more than the occasional rub or scratch. And after having witnessed the scene from last night, I was no longer satisfied with mere suggestions. I wanted to see more. His mother, from the looks of things, spent most of her time at home, cleaning and cooking, the traditional Italian wife. She seemed somewhat old, though, to be the mother of such a radiant, young beauty as that boy. But mid-life babies are common in Europe, and have been for years, I reminded myself. His father, on the other hand, looked ready to draw a pension. Their interaction was difficult to imagine.

I would have simply pulled myself away from the window had the cyclist not distracted me. He, too, was young and lithe, supple and tautly muscled, wearing shorts and a T-shirt. His hair was a dark blond, straight, and blowing behind him as he whirred down the street. I was beginning to wonder why the previous tenant had given up this place. After all, the view was startling.

To my pleasant surprise, the boy on the bicycle pulled into the driveway across the street and dismounted. He talked with Adidas (as I'd dubbed him for want of a name) for a few minutes, occasionally laughing. I couldn't – however much I strained – make out their conversation. And then they went inside.

After several moments, I decided to go get a coffee, trying not to spend all my valuable free time staring across the street with hopeful expectation on my face, waiting for sexual antics.

When I returned with my coffee, however, I tossed another casual glance out the window and was once more drawn into the bedroom of my young neighbour. They had made their way upstairs, it seemed, Adidas sitting cross-legged on the bed while the cyclist stood at arms length. Presently, Adidas broke into an hysterical fit of laughter; I could hear it faintly through the open window.

During this lull, the cyclist brought his hands flatly down upon Adidas' thighs, rubbing and petting the flesh with great familiarity and comfort. This didn't seem to annoy Adidas in the least. In fact, he lay back on the bed and uncrossed his legs, spreading them enough to allow the cyclist access.

Then the cyclist moved into position between the outstretched knees, still rubbing, only now growing closer to that phenomenally swollen crotch. Adidas managed to wrap his legs around the other boy's waist, drawing him tighter, closer, between his legs.

The hands then began to make their way up past the crotch

to the T-shirt, slid underneath the thin fabric, and journeyed upwards over the flat stomach to the heavy, rounded pectorals. Adidas' head was lolling from side to side as this friendly assault continued. With a quick yank, Adidas had managed to strip his T-shirt off, tossing it onto the bed beside him. The other boy slowly followed suit. But before he managed to get his head clear of his shirt, Adidas had grabbed his arms and held them in place while he leaned close and sucked one of the boy's flesh-coloured nipples into his mouth. Soon their limbs were entwined and they were kissing and licking everywhere.

This was astonishing! And to think that I used to *hate* moving! This was quickly proving to be one of the *best* moves I'd made in my entire life!

Before I realized it, Adidas had the boy on the bed naked, on his back, his cock fully-erect and aloft. Adidas, now off the bed and on his knees, grabbed the other boy's cock with his eager fingers and slowly started to jerk it.

Within moments, Adidas dipped his head lower and opened his mouth wide to accept the boy's ample dick-flesh. Obviously he had done this sort of thing before. The cyclist, although not enormous, was well-endowed for a kid his age. And, not missing a beat, Adidas continued to suck, bobbing his head up and down the length of that hard, wet cock, while slipping those shorts off once more.

A frenzy of outstretched hands reached for that fat, Italian meat. The cyclist heaved his body across the bed, making himself available for mutual satisfaction. Adidas' cock, however, was too large for the boy to take entirely home, but he made a valiant attempt. It didn't take long, no matter how much or how little would fit inside, to bring Adidas off to a thunderous climax. And then the other boy's cock blew its load shortly thereafter. They spent the next short while cleaning each other's spent cocks, sucking and licking at the last vestiges of their youthful orgasms. And I was all too soon making a mess of my wardrobe.

Off to the bathroom I trundled, pulling my pants down and grabbing a nearby towel to clean up the mess I'd once again made inside my shorts. Tired but satisfied, I went back to the window in time to see the cyclist rolling off down the street, disappearing around the curve in the road, waving full-armed.

Adidas had resumed his spot on the porch, still waiting but happier.

I fell onto my bed and dozed. A few hours later, the telephone rang, waking me from quite pleasant reveries. But it was a wrong number. I contemplated rejoining my already-begun dream, but one glance at the clock propelled me out of bed. It was nearly eight-thirty! I'd slept for more than four hours! Instinctively, I ran to the living room, the last glints of sunlight striping the floor. Across the road sat Adidas with his elderly parents. He seemed to be a well-read individual, if nothing else. Perhaps it was all a cover-up to avoid having to speak with his folks. When he gave his crotch a random nudge, I smiled. He seemed golden in the fading sun. I sighed, just staring at his body. Another whir caught my attention as I turned and saw the young cyclist return along the street, waving and smiling as before. His legs were slender, longer than I remembered. I wondered if he just roamed around the city from one friend's place to another, giving head. The thought of such a summer pastime made my dick twitch anew.

I was becoming rather hungry, so pulled myself into the kitchen to prepare some supper before resuming my night-time vigil out on that limb.

After a hearty meal of chicken, I returned to my living room, turning off the lights as I went.

At the window, binoculars strapped around my neck, I noticed, to my horror, that the lights in Adidas' room were indeed on but that the curtains had been closed. I sighed again, this time in genuine frustration, and sat in front of the television watching mindless programs until I could stand it no longer.

It was a warm night. One of the bonuses of my last place had been the air conditioning. And, as fate would have it, the only way I got any air was through the open windows and a noisy, oscillating fan. I slowly trotted back to my bedroom and disrobed, returning to the weird, flickering television light of the living room.

Those glances across the road were becoming habitual already. But, finally, my waiting paid off. Because there he was, across the way, once more tugging on his proud cock. I sighed and reached for my binoculars. And, as though highly practised, I climbed out of my window onto the limb of the tree and resumed my vigil.

Adidas was firing his hand along the length of his cock then, almost a blur, bringing himself close to the edge. Suddenly, I caught a reflection of myself in a nearby window, hugging the limb of a tree, binoculars glued to my face, watching a boy across the road jerking off. And the sight was all too much for me. I let out a laugh, followed by another. And another.

Sometimes there are just too many things to juggle when you're up in a tree – laughter, an erection *and* binoculars. One of them had to go. Quite often, I was beginning to discover, it was usually the erection that blew first. But the binoculars were a different matter altogether. Almost as if in slow motion, I watched as they slipped from around my neck, falling and crashing to the ground below. I was helpless, horny and hysterical with laughter. Nothing could have avoided the accident, I realized. But I was immediately silenced and sobered upon hearing shattering glass. One of the lenses had popped from its casing and had broken. And another had rolled out into the driveway, singing in circles, attesting to a presence among this once-believed private haven. I held my breath and waited.

Across the street, I could make out Adidas sitting up on his bed, his erection in hand. Obviously he had heard the breaking glass. With furrowed brow, he rose and approached the window, looking across the street to a place where he believed the noise originated. And, slowly, he worked his way upwards to the top of the tree. I stopped breathing altogether. He paused, straining to see clearly, and then broke into a broad grin. And he waved.

I realized how this all must have looked. Still, despite the fears of exposure as being an incredible pervert, I waved back, suppressing my laughter with little success. I could see his teeth smiling back at me. And then I could hear the faint laughter as he threw back his head. My laughter made it extremely difficult to crawl back inside. But, once safely back in my living room, I took one last look across the road. And there stood Adidas, looking into *my* windows now. And he waved again, friendly and bold. His smile was large, enveloping his entire face. I smiled back and returned the greeting. He made some sort of gesture, pointing down, and shrugged. I assumed it meant that he couldn't come out and play because of his parents. But then he stepped back into the light and showed me his heavy penis, hefting the bullish balls for my inspection. And, with a simple wave, he turned out his light and went to bed.

Before I went to bed, though, I realized that my shattered binoculars were still outside in the peonies and across the driveway. So, I pulled on some track pants and a T-shirt and scurried downstairs. I certainly didn't want my landlord to come home and drive over my lens. I wasn't at all prepared to explain myself to him after *that* night. Fortunately, he wasn't home yet. So, I had to work quickly to retrieve the debris, everything, down to that betraying round of glass lying at the foot of the front steps. I breathed a sigh, somewhat of relief, and went in to bed, exhausted.

The next morning, I awoke with clouded memory. Then it all came flooding back to me and I felt instant shame. Out on the kitchen table was the mangled pair of binoculars. They were still under warranty, at least. I smiled and chuckled to myself.

Still in my housecoat, I went out into the living room, a mug of steaming coffee in hand, and unfolded the newspaper. I'd almost finished my first cup, feeling somewhat human and awake, when I sensed that I was being watched. And there he stood, resplendent, in his window across the road, wearing just those goddamned Adidas shorts and nothing else. He waved at me, full-armed. And I waved back, smiling sleepily. He yawned, having just got up as well, it seemed. I motioned for him to come over, not totally sure what else to do. And then I raised my mug and pointed to my coffee, as though that should be the irresistible factor that would have him pounding on my door within seconds. He, in turn, nodded and hefted his ample crotch.

Within five minutes, there was a loud knock at the door. I put down my mug and went to the stairs. I tied the belt of my house-coat tighter and descended calmly, my heart racing despite my cool exterior. Then I opened the door and stepped aside as he entered. His presence seemed to fill the entire front hall. I noticed that he'd put on a pair of sandals and a Coca Cola T-shirt to accompany those shorts. He smelled of straw, with the faint, sweet smell of sweat. He smelled good. I followed him up the stairs, still as yet not uttering a word one to the other. One good thing about being the host -- you get the best view of your guests as you follow them up the stairs.

"My name's Peter," I said, hand outstretched.

"John." (The shorts finally had a name.) His smile was dazzling. His lips looked as though they were always wet. Up close, I could see just how dark and sparkling those eyes really were. Small curls played at the corners of his mouth. His nose was straight and perfect. His hair was a mass of soft curls. He was taller than I'd imagined, poking about an inch or so above my head. But his body was as I'd recalled -- broad and thick with muscle. For someone who appeared to do little more than sit on his front porch and read, he had managed to develop a phenomenal body.

I saw him glance across my body then and back up to my eyes. I smiled confidently, knowing that I was no slouch in the physique department either. I could tell that he enjoyed what he saw, even though partially obscured by the robe.

He pulled a hand out from behind his back then and handed me a thin, black strap.

"Is this yours?" he asked, smirking. "I found it in the driveway out front."

I smiled, blushed and took the strap from him, realizing that I'd missed it in all the turmoil of the night before. And I thanked him.

"I, ah, I suppose I owe you some sort of an explanation," I began, gesturing him into the living room.

"No need. I guess if I had binoculars, I'd be taking a gander around the neighbourhood myself."

"Ya, well, I feel a bit ... well, *perverse* about it. I had this constant fear of being caught by my *landlord* but I never expected to be caught by *you*."

"Well, I'm glad it was just the binoculars that fell. It would've been far worse if it had been *you*." He sat down on the sofa, crossing his legs.

"I've just made a fresh pot of coffee," I announced. "Can I get you a cup?"

"Sure, that'd be great."

Off to the kitchen I padded, anxious to overcome the formalities and get to more serious business. Part of me was absolutely delighted to have this boy within my grasp. But another part of me still winced at the tender age of my young guest.

I poured a steamy mug of coffee for John and refilled my own before calling out, "Cream and sugar?"

"I just like lots of cream," he called back, a laugh in his voice.

I smiled and thought, "I bet you do!" before carrying the mug back into the living room.

"So," John said, sipping, "you're new to the neighbourhood. When did you move in?"

"Just last week," I replied. "Still getting unpacked."

"Well, it's generally a pretty quiet area," he added, raising an eyebrow, a smile curling on his supple lips. "Not much happens. I guess you've already noticed that."

I blushed and looked into my cup, watching the swirling steam. Smiling, I asked, "And what do you do for amusement?"

"You tell me," John replied, raising his mug in a mock toast.

I chuckled. "You seem to have a rather ... interesting hobby, at least."

"Oh, well, it passes the time."

"While you wait for friends to come over and play," I added, smirking mischievously now.

"Someone's been busy."

"Just doing my homework."

John then giggled, putting me at ease. I wasn't entirely sure that my admission about his encounter with the cyclist would go over well with him, but his laughter assured me that he found my actions highly amusing.

"Well," John said, "you certainly go about getting to know your neighbours in an interesting way." He shifted on the sofa then, bringing one leg up under the other. I noticed that his crotch was bloated. I took another sip, taking more than the occasional glance between those beefy, smooth thighs.

"So, John," I resumed, "how are you enjoying your summer so far?"

"Fine. You?"

"Oh, very well, thank you. Very well, indeed. And, um, what do you do in your spare time to keep you ... occupied?"

"Well, I like to read. And, of course, I work out every now and then. And I've got a part-time job three days a week. The usual stuff."

"You must work out a fair deal," I added, tossing a glance down to his arms. "You've got a nice body."

"I use the gym at school."

"Oh, really? You're still in school?"

"I'm going into my senior year."

"Really," I replied, not wanting to sound as shocked as I feared I might. I took another gulp of coffee and looked out the window. "I've never known somebody your age to be so sure of himself, of his ... sexuality."

I looked back at him and he nodded his approval, smiling.

"How long have you been out?" I asked.

"Coupla of years now."

"And where does a young boy go for good times when he comes out of the closet?! That must've been mighty tough."

"Well, there's a youth group downtown that I go to. They've been really helpful, actually. I've made a few friends there and have been able to ... discover a few things about myself."

"Oh? Like what?"

"Oh, just about ... you know, like sex and stuff like that. About what I like to do and have done. That sorta thing."

"They discuss all that at these youth groups?!"

"Ya," he nodded, continuing, "along with counselling and confidence-building. All that kinda stuff."

"Do your folks know about all this?" I asked, genuinely curious now.

"No," he said, shaking his head, as though I'd touched a nerve ending, "they'd kick my ass out so fast, I wouldn't know what hit me."

"Those kind old people?!" I asked, not entirely convinced that they had it in them to be so cruel.

"Yes, those kind old people. You forget one important thing, Peter – they're Italian. *No* Italians are gay. Italian men are supposed to be pigs and chase after chicks in hot rods all night long and use really great words like 'Ehh' and blow snot out their noses. Things like admitting you like to suck cock don't go over very well in an Italian family, let me tell you."

I laughed as his description ripened. "So, you go to these

groups, meet friends, discuss what it's like to be gay, and then go out afterwards and ... well, do whatever it is you do?!" I, too, put my coffee mug down, leaning back into the couch to listen further to this boy talk about his sexual awareness.

"Something like that, yes," he said, smiling broadly. His dimples were glorious.

"What was your first time like?"

"My *first*?" he asked, trying to recall. "Well, it was two summers ago, and it was with a friend I'd met at the youth group. He thought I was about twenty-one; I guess I look older than I am."

"Yes, *that* you do. Well, in some respects you still look your age. You've got a boy's face. But you've definitely developed a man's body." With that comment, I noticed that his cock seemed to swell even more inside those damned shorts. Things were progressing better than I'd at first anticipated. He seemed pleased to have caught me staring into his straining crotch.

"So, anyway, this guy asked me if I wanted to go out for awhile after one of our meetings. We went for a bite to eat. And then we went off to this park; I don't remember exactly where. And we sat on a bench for awhile, discussing our mutual coming out experiences. And before I knew it, his hand was on my knee. And then it just happened, right there in the park. It just seemed so natural, you know, to be having sex with this guy. And that was the first time I ever sucked cock."

"Now, I trust that these meetings discuss safe sex with you as well?!" I interjected, instantly cautious and concerned.

"Oh, ya, they don't miss a beat, those guys. They're a great bunch of counsellors."

"Well, it seems that you've got yourself an early start. That's nice. Some of us weren't that lucky."

"Ya? Why, what happened with you?"

"Well, it's a long story. Let's just say that I didn't really come to terms with my homosexuality until I was almost twenty-one, *after* my engagement had fallen through."

"You were engaged?!" he exclaimed, sitting forward. "To a girl?!"

"Yep," I nodded, smiling at his excitement. "Bought her the ring and everything. My folks had been after me since I'd started dating her back in high school to pop the question. It seemed the thing to do at the time. If they'd known that I was hot for her *brother* and not for her, it would have been a different matter, no doubt."

"So, what did you do? How'd you get out of it?"

"It was three weeks before the wedding and I was beginning to get really nervous about the whole thing. I mean, I knew I liked guys better, but I was absolutely scared shitless to admit it to anyone. And then this one night I was driving around town, just thinking, when I picked up this guy hitch-hiking. He didn't really *look* down on his luck, but he told me that he didn't have very much money with him, that he was trying to find a place to stay for the night. And I was living at the university dorm at the time; just finishing up my second year. So, I told him that he could stay in my room if he wanted for a couple of days. He seemed nice enough. And my roommate had dropped out at the start of the second semester, so there was an extra bed.

"Well, he agreed, but told me that he had to repay me somehow. I told him not to worry about it for the time being and we went back to the dorm. I had some food there and we ate a little, and talked, and drank. I'd picked up a case of beer just the night before and we went through about half of it. And then I went to bed; I had an early class the next day. And he climbed into bed across the room.

"I guess it wasn't until after midnight that I first felt something. When I sat up, I couldn't make out what was going on; I was still pretty groggy. And then it hit me -- this guy was down on all fours on the floor beside my bed with one hand up under the covers feeling my leg. I asked him what he was doing and he said that he didn't know any other way to repay me other than to give me a blow-job. Well, I went instantly hard and he threw back the covers and began to give me my first blow-job. Man, it was amazing! Before either of us knew what was happening, we were making love. It was beautiful. And, well, to make a long story short, he stayed with me for about three more weeks before he moved on; he was backpacking across the country and had to get to Montreal to meet up with some friends. But in that time, he taught me almost everything I needed to know about making another guy feel good sexually. And that was it. I called the wedding off, told my folks that I was gay, and went about leading my present lifestyle."

"That's *wild*! How did your *folks* react?" John asked, intrigued by my tale.

"Well, at first they were furious with me. I mean, who wouldn't be?! But after we talked it out, they understood that it's more important for *me* to be happy with myself than to continue lying to everyone about everything. Understandably, though, my ex hasn't spoken to me since. And neither have her parents; we were pretty close before all this happened. It was rough, but I'm infinitely glad I made the choice."

"What a wild story," John said, nodding his approval. "I always like a happy ending."

"Ya, it was kinda neat," I agreed.

"So, I guess you've got more than a few men lined up now?"

I shook my head, smiling. "Well, no, I don't, really. I just got out of a relationship about six months ago and that's taken a little while to get over. No, I'm pretty much a free man these days. What about you?"

"No one special," he replied, resting a hand on his thigh then.

"Well, then, maybe we should ... um ... I dunno, take up a bit of each other's time," I suggested, provocatively loosening the knot in my bathrobe.

"Sounds like a reasonable idea," John replied, bringing his hand up higher, nudging his turgid balls through the thin fabric of his Adidas shorts.

"I've been noticing," I said, gesturing with my head, "that you seem to be slightly confined down there."

"Oh, it gives me some trouble sometimes," he said, removing his hand, exposing the entire, throbbing mound.

"Well, why don't you get comfortable, then?" I suggested, using my spreading thighs to part my robe further.

John's eyes dropped down to catch a glimpse past the folds of my robe.

"See something that interests you?" I asked.

"It's hiding in the dark," he replied, craning his neck to see past the folds in my robe. All the while, he had a hand placed over the bulge in the front of his snug-fitting shorts.

I slowly spread my thighs apart then, opening the dark gap between my legs. John's eyes grew enormous, sparkling delightfully, as they encountered my raging hard-on for the first time.

"It's beautiful!" he whispered, rubbing at his own swollen pouch.

"Do you need some help with that?" I asked, nodding towards his strained crotch.

"I think so," he replied, removing his hands. A wet spot had formed, about the size of a quarter.

"Stand up," I said. He rose, bringing his crotch closer. I looked up into his face, smiling, reached out for the draw-string and pulled. He let out a sigh of ecstasy as some of the pressure had been released. "Feel better?"

He just nodded, hands dangling at his sides, fingers working absently in the air.

"You appear to be quite the lovely lad," I said, grinning. Then I loosened the waist of his shorts and began to work them down over his tight butt and hard, smooth thighs.

As I worked, he bent over me and slid my robe off my shoulders. It fell behind me on the sofa, revealing a tanned and muscled torso. My upper arms and shoulders flexed as I worked his shorts down and off.

Finally, his cock sprang free of its confines, the balls and shaft heavy and dangling, the scent of his arousal heady and intoxicating. He gasped out of a release of pressure. And I gasped out of arousal.

"Get that shirt off fast!" I exclaimed, wrapping my hand around the base of his thick, Italian cock.

Wordlessly, without hesitation, John peeled his T-shirt up and off, standing before me totally and gloriously naked. His flesh glowed in the early-morning light. I gulped.

"God, but you look good," I said, my voice husky and low.

"From what I can see, you look pretty fine, too."

I pulled my arms free of the bathrobe then and stood up, our cocks rubbing, sending sparks of excitement through our bodies. My hands fell to his butt, cupping the tight cheeks, clenching and kneading the hard flesh. His hands circled my neck, his fingers tangling in my hair, and he pressed his lips eagerly against mine.

That first kiss was explosive. Nothing subtle about it, we stuck our hungry tongues into our respective maws and sloshed around inside. With our lips, we nibbled at each other, slurping on the wet, hot muscles inside our mouths. His ass was slick in my grasp. I could feel a thin trickle of sweat making its way down his back.

He broke for air shortly, having enfolded me in a manly embrace. Our cocks were painfully wedged between our grinding bellies.

"Sure is hot for first thing in the morning, isn't it?" I joked, licking my lips.

"You're hot at any time of the day, Peter," he replied, stepping back to relieve the pain and erotic pressure of our duelling cocks.

"Maybe I should take your temperature," I said, slowly falling to my knees, my hands dragging across his hot, slippery body.

"If you think it's best," he agreed, putting up no struggle whatsoever.

I was suddenly face to face with that monstrous cock. I grinned and opened wide to accept it in my mouth. John let out a deep, sensuous moan as soon as my lips closed around the fat head. I dug my tongue into his piss slit, tasting the salty pre-cum that had already begun to dribble its way out. Then I pressed more of his thick shaft inside, feeling the knobby head brush against the back of my constricting throat. I had sucked several cocks in my time and understood the need to concentrate on relaxing one's throat muscles to prevent gagging. But this was not something that I could readily do with John's massive cock.

I twisted his balls with one free hand and reached through his slightly-spread thighs to the dark, sweaty crack of his ass beyond. John's hands found their way back to my head again, cupping my skull, urging me further onto his fleshy lance. I slurped and sloshed around that fat dick, sucking fiercely, inhaling painfully through my nostrils to fill my aching lungs.

"Fuck, you're hot!" he hissed, shoving the last of his cock into my throat. His coarse pubic hairs scratched at my chin and nose. But I didn't relinquish one millimetre of that dick.

I slid my fingers into his crack then, coming into immediate contact with his puckered, dark asshole. This made his knees quake and I thought that he'd collapse upon me at once.

"Maybe I'd better sit down," he said, his voice breathy and rough.

I didn't want to pull off, so we moved in sequence, in tandem, to bring John back down to the sofa. We were soon resuming our previous course of action without having missed a beat. Unfortunately, though, I couldn't get my fingers back into that delicious crack of his.

"Can you bring yours over here?" he said, stroking my shoulders and back as I sucked. My cheeks were concave and sharp smacking sounds burst from my lips.

But I didn't want to pass up the opportunity of feeling this boy suck on my own raging pecker. So, I manoeuvred around, bringing my drooling dick up towards his gaping mouth. He swallowed it instantly, taking it effortlessly, greedily.

Within moments, we were sucking with abandon, our hands roaming across our sweating bodies, feeling our tense muscles, stroking nipples, cupping asses, sucking and guzzling each other's turgid and bloated penis. I knew that it wouldn't be long before I'd be spraying his throat with my hot cream.

Slowly, I pulled back off his cock, holding just the plump head past my hugging lips. His cock held a perfect arch, dark and tantalizing. He moaned with sensual pleasure as I focused my oral attention on the sensitive cockhead. But it wasn't enough. I had to feel that ass again.

Deftly, almost desperately, I pried my fingers under his body, feeling for his hot asshole. Finally, sucking ferociously on his impaling cock, I struck gold and jammed an insistent digit into his puckered hole. Wriggling it further inside, I managed to ram it up to the third knuckle. And that's when he lost control.

He moaned loudly, deeply, and shot off a heavy load, sending jets of steaming cum into my slurping, hot mouth. I, too, shot my load into his humming throat, spraying him relentlessly with one of the largest loads in recent memory. I couldn't stop cumming. But, then again, neither could he. I swallowed and swallowed as more of his hot, salty cum spurted forth from the shiny tip of his cock. His moan vibrated through the entire length of my aching pecker.

Finally, after much cleaning and with some hesitation to relinquish that succulent flesh, I pulled off, administering one last kiss, wet and hot, before sitting back up. John, too, finished cleaning me up and allowed my semi-erect, softening dick-flesh to slip out of his tight, hot mouth.

Smacking our lips, we began to breathe again with some regularity, fondling and kissing each other's bodies. Our cocks were still half-erect, but our energy had been diminished somewhat.

"I have to go," he suddenly said, breaking the sensuous mood of mutual fondling. "I told my mother I'd only be a little while."

He rose to his feet then, grabbing his clothes and putting them back on. "But I'll be back later, if that's okay with you?"

"You are kidding," I said, pulling a stray pubic hair from between my teeth. "I can't wait."

He dressed quickly and slipped back into his sandals. I pulled the robe over my naked and pleased body and followed him down the stairs. At the door, he turned and kissed me hard, rubbing my chest tenderly.

"Now, you take it easy today," he said, opening the door to leave. "We can't have you falling out of that tree!"

"You got it," I agreed.

"See ya later," he called back, dashing across the street. "Oh, and Peter? Welcome to the neighbourhood!"

And he went home, laughing the whole way. There was a wet trail down his back. I smiled, licked my lips, and closed the door.

SEX AT THE QUARRY

Leo Cardini

The smooth, flat slab of granite pressed sun-warm against my body as I lay ass-vulnerable with spread-apart legs by the abandoned, water-filled quarry in the middle of the woods. My right cheek rested on my crossed forearms. With half-open eyes I gazed lazily across the quarry, scanning its placid surface glistening in the mellow, late-morning sun. My eyes finally came to rest when they reached the opposite side where the quarry ended in a steep cliff about fifty yards high, ascending into the lush greenery of Vermont's Green Mountains.

Ian, kneeling between my legs, was massaging my tanned asscheeks, his thumbs slowly inching their way towards my asshole. With his expert hands that knew every inch of my body, he slowly pulled my asscheeks apart, exposing my hole, making it itch for his touch, knowing perfectly well that if he kept this up, he would drive me crazy with desire.

How much time had Ian and I spent together during this past July? During how many hours and in how many ways had we made love to each other in this idyllic setting where the days sauntered by with only the rising and setting of the sun to remind us of time, and where civilization ceased its encroachment several miles down a dirt road where half a dozen houses and one small general store called themselves a town.

In response to Ian's massage, my cock grew hard, sliding into the dark, snug, tunnel it insistently created for itself as it wriggled its way towards full erection. And as my cock grew, I became aware of the delicious heaviness of my balls in my slightly contracting ballsac, and of the warm sliver of sunlight that heated them from behind.

My asshole involuntarily twitched in begging anticipation of Ian's touch. I knew he could see this, and I knew he could interpret with perfect accuracy this and the thousand and one other tacit disclosures of my desires of which my body was capable. He had become as familiar with them as I had become of all the physical cues his body employed to lure me into our mutual sexual satisfaction.

I felt his sure hands pull my asscheeks apart and hold them there. Then, a pause. I groaned in response to the sweet, urgent, begging-for-more feeling of my exposed, slightly stretched asshole. I could tell from the shifting pressure of his hands that he was changing position. I knew what was coming next.

And there it was, that familiar, probing tongue snaking its way into my asshole, alleviating my itch, and sending waves of pleasure throughout my body.

I closed my eyes, moaned again, and entered that private universe where only Ian and I existed; naked man kneeling and naked man prone, contact of tongue and asshole, union refined and familiar, stretching across so many afternoons. And I marvelled at the turn my life had taken during this past month.

This was during 1969. I was spending the summer at Goddard College - or rather I had intended to spend it there. Goddard's this small, independent-study college, nestled in the Green Mountains. It's on the outskirts of Plainfield, a town of about five hundred people.

Actually, I didn't go to Goddard. I was a music major at Boston University, originally planning on a career as a concert pianist, but questioning my goals and values as I watched from the sidelines while so many of my generation entered a bright, innocent, and hopeful new world of peace and love, where you got high with a little help from your friends and celebrated the dawning of the Age of Aquarius.

Jon, my closest college buddy, was spending the summer at Goddard to be with his girlfriend. He had asked me if I would like to come along. I jumped at the opportunity. Goddard had the reputation of being the hippest college on the East Coast. I'd no longer be on the sidelines. I'd be right in the middle of what was happening.

Life was so easy that summer. I worked mornings at Sam's General Store. This gave me all the money I needed to support myself. For reasons I now forget, I was crashing in the lighting booth in the Haybarn, Goddard's theatre, which was connected to the Community Center, the hub of campus activity. I had a sleeping bag and a knapsack, which in those days meant I had everything; everything being mobility, those few possessions you really couldn't live without (like Tarot cards wrapped in silk the color of your astrological sign), and freedom from crass middle-class materialism. And as for living in the lighting booth - well, no one really cared. It was cool. That's what Goddard was like.

What a world Goddard was! There were no classrooms. Everyone designed his own program of study and everyone was very heavily into the counterculture. And the dorms were small (sixteen students each), co-ed and specialized. For example, there was the transcendental meditation dorm, the organic food dorm, the voluntary fire department dorm, and the nudist colony dorm. Each was painted a different color, and they were referred to collectively as the "Rainbow Village."

Here I was in the middle of all this, and yet I still felt like I was only acting a role - that I wasn't really part of what was happening. I discovered that being on the sidelines isn't a matter of physical position. It's a matter of headset. Sure, I parted my straight brown hair in the middle and wore it down to my shoulders, and I wore the requisite sandals, bandannas, tie-died T-shirts and lo-rise, embroidered bell-bottoms. Sure I was into transcendental meditation, began every morning consulting the I Ching, and sought guidance and inspiration from the Hesse novels and Nin's diaries. Sure, I smoked grass and took psychedelics for fun and religious experiences, and grooved on the current music. But while everyone around me seemed so free of conventional behavior and values, I always felt like deep inside I never could fully let go and drop out, no matter how much I wanted to.

One day in early June during my second week at Goddard, Jon and I were in the cafeteria eating lunch. When I was done, I brought my tray up to the rectangular window that opened onto the dishwashing section of the cafeteria. Two hands reached out to take my tray. The obviously tall tray-taker's head and neck were cut off by the window, but I did see his shirtless, broad, muscled chest crested with two tantalizing, penny-sized nipples, and covered with a sprinkling of golden blond hair. My eyes traveled down his torso, following its taper to his firm narrow waist. Then they followed the route of his body hair as it descended below his navel in a thin trail across his hard, flat abdomen to the uppermost border of his lush forest of pubic hair. All else was hidden by the press of his body against the inside counter as he leaned forward to take my tray.

He wasn't wearing any clothes!

In my surprise and curiosity, I forgot to let go of my tray. In response, the owner of this sublime torso leaned forward and sideways to look out at me.

His silken, shoulder-length hair spilled onto the counter. He focused his deep blue eyes on me and smiled a wide, open smile, revealing the whitest teeth I swear I have ever seen, and setting the features of his handsome face in joyful, good-natured play.

I was so taken aback by this sudden confrontation with masculine nudity and beauty that I didn't do or say a thing - except I think my mouth fell open.

Then, with one of those general, undirected laughs I had come to associate with being high on grass, he took the tray from me and turned around in the direction of the industrial-size dishwasher against the opposite wall.

As he moved toward it, I could see he was indeed naked. He was tanned, and he had no tan line. Like a photographer taking a snapshot to capture a precious moment, I stored in my mind the beauty of this magnificently tall hippie with the perfectly proportioned body of a Greek god, and the head of blond hair spilling onto his shoulders and down his back And below, those two firm, sun-browned asscheeks lightly sprinkled with curly blond hairs.

I marvelled at the robust play of his muscles as he nonchalantly sent another load of dishes through the machine, so sublimely unconcerned about his nudity.

In those few seconds of precious observation, my mind wrote a scenario for my desires. I wanted to run into the dishwashing area, strip off my clothes, and approach him from behind, taking him by passionate, irresistible surprise as I pressed my body against his. I wanted to wrap my arms around his torso and finger the hard, pointed nubs of his tight, brown nipples. I wanted to feel my abdomen against his buttocks, and my chest against his broad-shouldered back. And I wanted to nestle my stiff, standing-up dick in the crevice of his asscheeks.

But that was not the kind of thing I could ever do. I felt

myself once more on the sidelines at this college where the prime directive was to "do your own thing."

It was an effort to pull myself away from the window. I reluctantly walked back to Jon, aware of the heaviness of my cock as it repeatedly repositioned itself in my lo-rise bell-bottoms with every step I took. At that moment, I felt like the center of the universe was my slightly-hardened cock broadcasting my carnal desires to everyone in the cafeteria. But no one seemed to notice.

Except Jon, who could always read me like a book.

He looked up from the orange he was carefully peeling, perfecting the art of removing the peel in one Escher-like piece.

"What's up man?"

"The guy washing dishes..."

"Yeah?"

"He's not wearing any clothes."

"Hmh. Wanna join him?"

"Nah." Like it was no big deal to me.

But it was, believe me.

Later that day, I found out that sometimes there'd be a "naked dish crew" day, which usually ended up in a massive water fight that other students would join in, stripping off their clothes as they ran through the cafeteria, streaking by the no-longer-shocked middle-aged ladies from Plainfield who cooked and served the meals.

Here at Goddard, nudity was no big deal. That's how free every one was. Except me. And this tall, blond-haired hippie working dish crew in the cafeteria lingered in my mind as the epitome of this counterculture. Imagine being so liberated, you could do dish crew naked!

To my great disappointment, I never saw that nude dishwasher in the cafeteria again.

But during the nights, resting on my sleeping bag in the lighting booth, he was there with me whenever I wanted him. While the indistinct conversations outside the window announced the casual come and go of students about their business, I lay naked in the darkness with my hard dick in my hand, and played out scenes in which this hippie dishwasher and I did dish crew together in the nude. We battled each other with the jets of water that sprayed out of the nozzles on the long cleaning hoses, our bodies dripping wet, our hair soaked, and our cocks and balls swinging between our legs as we abandoned ourselves to the exhilaration of the moment.

And then the wrestling that would ensue! We would discard our hoses as he struggled to force me into surrender, his body pressed against mine. I would imagine, in slow motion, every movement of our struggle, every variation of flesh against flesh and muscle against muscle as he ultimately straddled me between his strong, muscled legs, pinned my arms back against the wet floor, and laughingly insisted I holler "uncle."

In the lighting booth, still imagining being pinned down beneath him, I was free to vicariously savor the feel of his cock and balls resting on my chest, and the weight and firmness of his ass pressing against my hips, his asshole just inches away from my cock; so close, in fact, that if I got a hard-on, I could've slipped my cock right up his ass.

Cherishing these thoughts, I would stroke my cock until I became a willing, helpless slave to my own passion, and shot my cum all over my chest, letting those warm, milky-white pools dry on me as I drifted off to sleep with amorous recollections of this hippie dishwasher receding in my consciousness.

One afternoon in early July, Jon and I took his VW van up to Burlington on an errand. Driving back through the rolling, green Vermont countryside, high and mellow from the joint we'd smoked just after leaving Burlington, Jon asked, "Any plans for the afternoon?"

Like scheduling your time really meant much of anything up at Goddard if it got in the way of doing your own thing.

"Not really."

"You wanna go to the quarry?"

"Sure!"

I'd never been to the quarry, but I'd heard about it. The quarry, which had been abandoned years ago, was a favorite swimming hole deep in the Vermont woods. Everyone went swimming there in the nude.

Now, there was no way I could imagine having the guts to hang out naked with who knows who might happen to be there. And it wasn't like I had to option of wearing a bathing suit or briefs, because that wouldn't have been cool. With a certain amount of cynicism I had grown to realize that "doing your own thing," had its own constraints. Some things were simply not done. And I knew that wearing a bathing suit or briefs at the quarry would definitely be one of them.

But as apprehensive as I was, I wanted to prove to myself that I could be as cool as the next guy - though I was scared stiff I'd get an erection. I mean, just the thought of seeing all these guys lying around in the sun bareass with their cocks dangling between their legs was giving me a hard-on right there in Jon's VW. And I don't get the type of erection that is easily concealed. My cock grows to about eight inches. It gets absolutely rock hard and it sticks right up, curving slightly towards me, like its trying to kiss my navel.

Jon took the Stowe exit and drove along country roads that brought us further and further into rural Vermont. Soon the roads were dirt, and the small towns separated by acres of fields and woodland were replaced by the occasional farmhouse looking like it was taking an afternoon nap under the shade of the tall old trees that surrounded it.

Eventually, we turned onto a road overgrown with vegetation, the forest on either side threatening to reclaim it when no one was looking. We drove for about half a slow, bumpy mile, and stopped when we came to three parked cars I recognized from Goddard.

Leaving the VW behind - windows down, doors unlocked, like the other vehicles there - Jon led me into the woods. I followed him along a practically invisible path that you could just barely make out a few yards ahead of you at a time.

After a few hundred yards, the path suddenly ascended. Abruptly, we emerged into a shock of sunlight. And there, in the middle of the woods, was the quarry.

An irregular oval in shape, it must have measured a hundred by a hundred and fifty yards. The far side ascended straight up. At the highest point it must've been about fifty yards above the water-filled quarry. But the side we were on was just a few feet above the cool, inviting water. Slabs of granite bordered the quarry in a series of haphazard terraces.

To the right, a sole flower child sat in a full lotus position chanting "Om." Two guys treading water in the middle of the quarry watched another, Rainbow Carl, a local artist/dropout, climb up the far side of the quarry and ascend to its highest point.

And directly in front of us, Ted, Art and Herb - friends of ours from Goddard - sat together Indian style on one large slab of granite. They passed around a joint while talking about this rock concert in Woodstock that almost everyone at Goddard was planning to attend.

They looked up at us. We all exchanged laid back hellos. Art held up the joint to share it with us. A typical Goddard greeting, which Jon accepted.

Everyone at the quarry was bareass.

What an idyllic scene. And all I could think of was, "How will I ever get up the guts to strip? And what if I get a hard-on!" Everyone there was so cool and casual, except for uptight me trapped in a private prison of anxiety.

Jon passed the joint to me. I inhaled and passed it on to Ted.

From across the quarry a loud whoop resounded as Rainbow Carl jumped off the cliff and descended feet first into the water, sending up a tall splash where he disappeared below the water's surface. All heads turned, waiting for him to emerge. Seconds later, his head appeared, he shook the hair out of his eyes and yelled, "Oh, my balls!"

A sprinkle of laugher drifted through the quarry, as fleeting and ephemeral as the smoke from the joint being passed around. Then everyone went back to what they were doing.

The conversation drifted back to Woodstock.

Jon already had his sneakers off. He pulled his tee shirt over his head. His torso stretched with the exercise. Muscles arranged and rearranged. I knew I'd also be expected to do strip.

On one hand, there was no way I could take off my clothes. On the other, there was no way I couldn't.

The joint came my way again. I inhaled slowly and deeply, stretching the moment out for as long as possible.

When I passed the joint on and faced the inevitable, I felt like I'd stepped out of myself and the moment. I looked on as I pulled my tee shirt over my head, forced my sneakers off, left toe against right heel, right toe against left heel, and finally, unbuttoned and unzipped my bell-bottoms and pulled them off. I wasn't wearing any underwear, a secret that would shock a mother, but who the hell would care here?

When I stood up again, naked in front of all these unconcerned guys, I had never felt such a delicious sense of freedom. I could feel my feet planted on the warm granite. The air caressed my body, teasing my sensitive nipples. I quickly glanced at my crotch. In my rapidly-getting-really-stoned state, I surreptitiously admired my soft, heavy-hanging dick. From the lush amazon jungle of my pubic hair, my pale brown cockshaft emerged, free from the confines of my bell-bottoms, basking in the unaccustomed warmth of the sun.

I stood there savoring my nudity and new-found freedom, astonished that less than a moment ago I couldn't possibly imagine myself like this. But now, in this setting, it seemed unnatural to even think of wearing clothing.

Jon sat down Indian style with the other guys. I followed suit.

By now we were all getting noticeably stoned. The sharp edges of reality were wearing smooth. The conversation drifted, occasionally abandoned while each of us went inside his own head, held in the communal grasp of the circulating joint, and the shared experience of this ideal afternoon.

I watched Jon sitting there arched over, elbows on his knees, his tight-muscled chest and abdomen covered with a profuse spread of silky, dark-brown hair that progressed below his navel into the forest of his pubic hair. His thick, heavy cock pushed his balls out on either side of it, and his cockhead rested on the granite like a sleepy monster.

I had seen Jon naked many times before. Although he was straight, we jacked off together now and then. He was the only straight guy whose body I dared to admire without feeling I had to conceal it. He really didn't mind. That's how liberated he was. Actually, I think he kind of got off on it.

The joint passed my way again. When I took another toke and passed it on, I became very aware of the feeling of my balls pressing down against the sun-warmed granite. I swear I could feel every ballsac hair tingle as they rested crushed between my balls and the rough granite surface. My dick hung soft between my legs, and my cockslit pressed against the hard rock in a prolonged, wanton kiss.

"We could take my VW to Woodstock," Jon said, reviving

the conversation. "Get there in six or seven hours. Eight at the most."

While the conversation that seemed miles and miles away from me meandered on and plans somehow got made, I looked at each guy here like I was looking at him for the first time, impressed with each variation of the male body.

There was short, brawny, brown-haired Teddy, whose bubble-butt always looked so inviting pressing against the seat of his jeans; square-jawed Art with the blond curly hair and the boxer's build; and tall, lean Herb with that huge uncut horsedick that looked several sizes too large for him.

Shit! I could feel the first stirrings of a hard-on! I looked down between my legs. Yes, my cockslit had broken off its kiss and was rising up. I leaned forward to conceal my erection.

The conversation droned on. No one had noticed. And no one was aware of the sudden stab of anxiety in my chest that yanked me away out of my welcomed, new-found sense of liberation.

I looked around, desperately scanning the quarry for anything to distract me. Then, high up on the opposite side someone emerged from the trees and bushes that bordered it.

I abandoned my marginal attention to my friends, forced my mind away from my cock, and watched.

Everything happened in slow motion stonedom. I was watching a movie. It was an old Tarzan movie, like I'd seen on TV on lazy Saturday mornings when I was a kid. Only it was in color. And Tarzan emerged from the jungle wearing no loincloth. Tarzan was tall and tan, with shoulder-length blond hair.

Tarzan was the same hippie I'd seen doing dish crew naked a few weeks ago!

He stood above the quarry for a few seconds, surveying the scene. Then he dived in. I watched as this perfectly proportioned manchild of nature descended, cutting neatly into the water. A few seconds later, he emerged in the center of the quarry. He treaded water while he shook his hair away from his squinting eyes, and then swam over to us.

Dripping wet, he emerged from the quarry. With his hands on the rock, he pressed upwards. One leg left the water. Then the other. His thick, light brown cock and two large balls ascended into view, swinging between his legs in response to the exquisite play of his body as he pulled himself out of the quarry, finally standing there in front of us, a smiling, tanned Adonis, stepping out of a Greek myth and into my life.

After everyone had exchanged greetings, he looked over at me.

"Hi. You're name's Ron, isn't it?"

"Yeah. Hi."

How did he know?

He moved over to me, extended his right hand, and introduced himself.

"Ian."

I stood up and took his hand.

Did his eyes travel up and down my body, taking it all in and evaluating it in the same way I would when sizing up some potential sex partner in a gay bar? Or was I just stoned and hoping, still writing my own scenario?

With our hands still clasped, his eyes travelled up to mine again. The second of silence between seemed like an eternity. But while I stood there feeling awkward, Ian just smiled broadly and commenced to sit down, joining our group. I sat next to him, so aware of his body so close to mine that I could practically feel his presence.

Ted passed Ian a newly-lit joint. He inhaled a slow, deep toke, lifting and expanding his marvellous chest, causing his pecs to stand out more prominently, his two tight, erect nipples perfectly displayed, making me ache for the contact of tongue and tit.

After holding the smoke in as long as he could, he exhaled and asked everyone, "So what's happening at Goddard?"

Why wouldn't he know?

The other guys proceeded to tell him about events that were yesterday's news at Goddard, and about all the plans to go to the rock concert at Woodstock.

Engaged in their stoned conversation, did any one of them notice how I observed Ian with covert desire? I would constantly turn away to stare at the water, pretending I was drifting off into my own stoned thoughts as I tried desperately to distract myself with mundane pre-occupations. But I always returned to Ian, to watch that open, smiling face with the serene, dark blue eyes, that wonderful expanse of his broad shoulders tapering down to his slim waist as he bent forward, his forearms resting on his thighs. Did anyone notice my quick glances between his crossed legs, watching that ample treasure of cock and balls that rested on the granite, tantalizingly repositioned with his every little movement.

What would the other guys have said if they could have read my thoughts, discovering I was much less interested in filling Ian in on what was going on at Goddard than in contemplating the enviable contact between his asscheeks and the rough-surfaced granite they pressed against, the granite so close to that shady crevice between his buttocks where my tongued longed to roam.

Or did anyone notice my quick glances at my own cock, monitoring myself for any signs of the dreaded, uncool advent of a hard-on announcing to one and all my admiration of Ian's body?

Repeatedly, I found myself irresistibly drawn to the thin line of blond hair that travelled from Ian's navel to the overgrowth of his pubic hair glistening with droplets of quarry water lodged in its curly embrace. What I wouldn't give to nestle my nose in that bristly damp forest and inhale!

Time and time again I pulled my eyes away from Ian's body, looking up at one face or another, feigning interest in the conversation.

But after one episode of crotch contemplation, when I was studying the route of the fine blue veins that travelled over the surface of his cockshaft, I looked up and my gaze met his. He'd caught me looking at him! But he just smiled and winked. Yes, he actually winked!

Then he broke the moment by passing the joint to me.

After I'd taken another toke and passed it on to Herb, I looked down at my own crotch. My cock gave one slow lazy twitch, like a waking animal stretching out before rising. The hard-on I had so dreadfully feared was on its way.

When it comes to erections, my cock has a mind of its own. I knew I had to take immediate action to save myself from embarrassment, so I quickly jumped up, walked towards the water's edge, and asked, "Anyone wanna join me?"

After a few headshakes and a couple of "nahs," I dived in.

I welcomed the cool embrace and silent darkness of the water. I swam under its surface, leaving behind that world of frustrating desire.

When I emerged in the center of the quarry and shook my hair away from my face, I could see that Ian had gotten up and was standing there, hands on his hips, looking at the water. Was he looking at me?

On seeing Ian, my thoughts went to my crotch again, and I realized I had never swum naked before. The feeling was so perfect, so natural. I felt such an exhilarating sense of liberation at that moment that even a bikini brief seemed like Victorian overdress.

I turned and swam to the far side of the quarry, just left of its steep ascent, getting off on the physical high of feeling the play of my muscles as they executed clean, precise swimstrokes. I had done quite a lot of swimming in high school and I had never lost my skill, or the tightly-muscled body I had developed.

When I reached the other side, I pulled myself up and sat on the edge of the quarry, resting my feet on a narrow ledge that was submerged in about half a foot of water.

I looked across the shimmering water at the group I had just left. Ian was still standing there. This time I was sure he was looking at me.

Then he dived in and swam straight towards me. When he was about a yard away, he treaded water in front of me. I was acutely aware of my cock and balls hanging down between my legs, suspended over the water-covered ledge in front of me.

"You're a pretty good swimmer," he said.

"Thanks. Not any better than you, though."

"Yeah, I did a lot of swimming in high school. I've never really been into competitive sports."

"Same here."

He lifted himself out of the water and sat on the ledge. His cockhead floated on the surface of the water like an exotic lily.

"How come I never see you around Goddard," I asked.

"I decided to spend the summer here."

"Here?"

"Yeah."

He pointed to the mountain behind the quarry.

"Up there. I was going to spend the summer hanging around Goddard, but the first time I came here, about a month ago, it felt so liberating running around bare-assed in the middle of the woods that I thought, 'Why don't I really drop out?' So I got a tent, a sleeping bag and whatever else I thought I'd need, and set up camp. I've always thought it'd be really far out to be a nudist, so I didn't bring a any of clothing with me. Not a stitch."

Then he drifted off into his own thoughts as he looked out across the water.

To drop out so fully! Images of what his life might be like here carouseled through my mind. I saw him standing on a mountain top, looking into the distance at a brilliant, orange setting sun. I saw him on his haunches contemplating the delicate beauty of a lady-slipper. I saw him lying on a soft bed of pine needles in the shade of the forest, legs spread apart and jacking himself off...and I knew I'd better direct my thoughts to a less arousing subject.

But before I could, he asked - well, it was more of a statement, actually - "You're gay, aren't you?"

"How'd you know?"

"You kidding? At Goddard everyone knows everything."

"Yeah?" I replied after a brief pause, hoping to gain access to his thoughts."

"Like I was just thinking - you know Doctor Reed at the infirmary?"

"I've seen him around. Why, is he gay?"

Ian leaned back, resting his elbows on the granite behind him, and looked up at me, squinting against the sunlight.

"Well, he's new here. Just since last April. But in May, when I had to have a physical check-up? As he was putting on a rubber glove for my rectal exam, he said, 'I'm sure you'll like this, Ian, though I guess my finger's a poor substitute for the real thing.' Now, how did he know I liked cock up my ass?

"Well, I figured if he felt like he could say something like that to me - you know, it was kind of tacky, but I could tell he meant it to be friendly - well then, I could be fresh, too. So, as soon as he had his finger all the way up my ass, I said, 'You're right. It is a poor substitute for the real thing. So how about sticking your dick up there instead, huh?'

"I thought that'd freak him out, but after he removed his finger, he just stood there, not doing or saying a thing. I was still bent over his examination table, so I turned my head around, and, you know, he looked like he was actually thinking about it."

Ian looked towards the water again.

"So I said, 'C'mon doc. You're wife won't know.' 'Nah,' he said real slow. But he was still contemplating my asshole. And to tell the truth, I was getting a hard-on just thinking about it.

"'Look at it as a learning experience. I mean, that's what Goddard's all about, isn't it? And you'd really be doing me a big favor."

"So he did - right in there in his examination room. Pants and briefs down to his ankles. Shirt unbuttoned. Funny thing is, he insisted on putting a rubber on first.

"It really felt good. He was so slow and careful, like he was afraid he'd hurt me. And when I felt him coming, I reached down for my cock and jacked myself off. I was so hot and horny feeling his dick up my ass that I came so quickly I shot my load before he even pulled out of me."

While Ian was talking, it was like he'd drifted into this recollection and was telling it as much to relive it as to share it with me.

I relived it with him, picturing him prone and ass-vulnerable. My cock grew hard and sprang up between my legs. But all my fears of a detectable hard-on were long gone.

What an exercise in liberation this afternoon was turning into. First I'd overcome my embarrassment of hanging out nude, and now I wasn't even ashamed of my erect cock proclaiming my interest in Ian and his story.

Between Ian's submerged legs, his dick was slowly coming to life. In my stoned state, I watched as the lily that was his cockhead slowly transformed itself into a magnificent, jumbo mushroom that rose above the water.

Then he turned his head and looked directly at my hard-on.

A faint, awed, "Wow," was all he said, though.

And then, after a brief, silent contemplation of my cock, he jumped to his feet, totally unashamed of his stiff cock bouncing up and down in front of him as he moved.

"C'mon," he said.

"C'mon where?"

"Just c'mon, man."

"Uh..."

"So what? Even if anyone sees your hard-on, they're not going to care."

I got up and followed, my rigid cock spearheading my progress.

Ian led me along a narrow ascending path through the foliage that edged the quarry. By the time we emerged into full view again at the top of the quarry we had fortunately lost our erections. Everyone on the other side of the quarry looked so small below. We paused to watch for a few moments. Then Ian wordlessly led me back into the foliage.

We ascended, diagonally making our way around the mountain. The quarry was left behind. Every step was a step into freedom; my clothes, identification, money, and the pre-occupations and hang-ups that make up my life left far behind at the quarry, entrusted to a small circle of stoned friends grooving on the afternoon. All that existed for me at that moment was the physical high of naked man following naked man up a mountain, trusting in Ian, my guide into freedom.

Eventually, when we were almost half way around the mountain we arrived at a small, grassy plateau. It couldn't have been more than ten yards long and five yards wide. On three sides it ascended practically straight up. Hardy, stubborn vegetation clung to it. But the outermost side looked onto a breathtaking view of miles and miles of gently rolling Vermont countryside, the lush carpet of greenery obscuring the small towns nestled in it.

"This is home."

"No kidding!"

"No kidding. See? Tent, sleeping bag, campfire, utensils. Everything I need. And you know, you don't really need much."

"What about food?"

"I get friends to pick up supplies for me on their way over here every now and then. It all works out. Hell, I could survive on all the blueberries alone around here, if I had to."

"Sposin' something happened to you?"

"I can take care of myself. Besides, dropping out is about taking chances. If something happens, I'll deal with it. I've been here a month and I've had no problems yet. Never even opened my first aid kit. It's sure gonna feel funny in September wearing clothing again.

I looked around me, piecing together Ian's simple, back-to-nature life style.

After a pause, like he could read my thoughts, he said, "Yeah, it's really something, up here. Except for the afternoons, there's no one around. It was such a turn-on being able to do anything I wanted that the first week I was here I must've jacked off ten times a day. Like, I'd sit over there on the ledge and jack off while I'd look out at the scenery. Then I'd let the cum dry on me and I'd go down to some of the blueberry bushes, stain my body with their juices and jack off again. Then I'd go over to the quarry, actually kinda hoping someone would be there to see what I looked like, and dive in and clean myself off again.

"I guess the only thing that bothers me sometimes is the nights. They can get lonely."

He crossed his arms, his face turned sad, and I could tell he was dwelling on the loneliness of his nights.

Then, as if to pull himself out of his thoughts, he shook his splendid head of hair, uncrossed his arms, and stepped over to the ledge. He shaded his eyes with his right hand and looked out at the view.

I joined him, standing on his right. I didn't know what to say or do. I could feel his palpable presence on every inch of my body and I ached to touch him.

Then I felt Ian's left hand slowly slide across my waist from the back until it rested on my hip.

I turned my face toward him. He was still looking out at the scenery.

I leaned over and kissed him on the shoulder. My lips pressed against his smooth, sunbrown skin. I could smell the heady aroma of the slight coat of perspiration that covered his body. My cock twitched.

"Mmm," he said, still looking out at the scenery, sliding his hand slowly down across my left asscheek.

I turned slightly toward him and slowly ran my left hand

across his abdomen, feeling every inch of its firm, tight-muscled terrain. My cock twitched again and grew harder until it was sticking straight up.

Simultaneously, we turned to each other and hugged. His powerful arms encircled me, pulling me into his embrace. I was overwhelmed with aching desire. I felt the underside of my cockhead press against his body. It ascended his abdomen traversing that same territory my hand had just explored, rising towards his navel until it was finally forced to rest trapped between our two bodies.

His own heavy-hanging cock pushed forward between my legs. The topside of his cockshaft pressed against my balls as his cockhead tunneled towards my willing asshole.

Pressing Ian closer to me, I tilted my head back, closed my eyes and opened my mouth. His tongue slid in and probed about as he lowered his hands to my asscheeks, pulling me towards him, crotch against crotch.

He withdrew his tongue and sucked my own into his mouth, greedily taking possession of me. I fell into the moment, all lust and passion for this hippie god who lived on the mountain.

When we finally broke tongue contact, I kissed him wetly all over his throat. He groaned as he tilted his head back to receive me as, kiss by kiss, I slowly descended to his chest.

My lips reached his left pec. I stuck my tongue all the way out and slowly ascended his pec, feeling every detail of that smooth, masculine mound of muscle.

He inhaled, with a prolonged "Ahh," expanding his chest. On my left, the Green Mountains rolled into the background. On my right, Ian's mountain rose high above us. And in front of me, his mountainous pec expanded with his incoming breath, forcing the hard, erect nub that crested his nipple against my tongue.

"Oh, man!" he said in a low voice as he slowly exhaled.

He put his hands on either side of my head and pulled my face away. He looked into my eyes.

"It's been so long since I've been with another man. You don't know how many times I've jacked off imagining what it would be like to make it up here with another guy. But I never thought it'd be someone like you."

"That day I saw you in the cafeteria, Ian?"

"Yeah?"

"You don't know how many times after that I jacked off at the thought of you doing dish crew naked. And now..."

I looked at his pec, hungry to continue where I'd left off.

Reading my thoughts, he took my head in his hands and gently pressed me back onto it.

With the tip of my tongue I teased his hard, erect nub. Yet every time I bent it, it stood up straight again, like a stalwart soldier.

I took it between my teeth, holding it in place with a gentle bite while I continued to play with it.

From above, I could hear Ian moan with pleasure.

I moved to his right pec and continued my worship of his magnificent chest. Ian took my own nipples between his thumbs and forefingers, gently squeezing and tugging at them.

I reached down with my left hand and took his large, low-hanging balls in my cupped hand, feeling their exquisite heaviness. Then I let them hang free again and explored the way they jostled around in his ballsac as I stroked them with my fingers.

Kiss by kiss, my lips travelled down to his navel. When I reached it, I probed it with my tongue. Then I continued my descent, savoring the hard flatness of his abdomen and the narrow line of hair that descended into that lush pubic forest that had so fascinated me when we were sitting cross-legged by the quarry.

Then I got down on my knees in front of him. He had opened his eyes once again and he was looking down at me, smiling.

My face was about a foot away from his cock. His sun-browned dick had stiffened into nine inches of thick, cut cock that hung in front of me occasionally twitching, laboring under the force of gravity.

I grabbed my own dick and stroked it while I moved my mouth onto Ian's, taking it in, feeling every bit of it filling my mouth, moving steadily forward, lips circling his treetrunk cockshaft, until I felt my nose buried in his pubic hair. I inhaled, smelling the funky odor of his crotchsweat.

I slowly sucked on his cock while my free hand returned to his balls to continue stroking them, feeling their bigness in his large, low-hanging ballsac and the sparse, bristly hair that covered them.

I lost myself in Ian's crotch. Eyes closed, the center of my universe became this huge, gorgeous cock, this contact of solid manmeat and tongue and mouth and throat sending waves of pleasure throughout my entire body.

Eventually, I felt Ian's hands hook under my arms, pulling me up, his cock slipping out of my mouth, my eyes touring the terrain of his body as I ascended.

When he had pulled me up, he said nothing. He just looked into my eyes with a half-smile on his face.

Then he got down on his knees in front of me. With his hands on my calves, he indicated that I should spread my feet apart. I eagerly accommodated his wishes.

My cock was sticking almost straight up and my balls were deliciously sensitive to the very feel of the air between my legs. I looked down and watched the way he stared at my crotch, studying it, open-mouthed with fascination.

He leaned forward and stuck out his tongue. But he didn't lick my cock, as I had expected him to. Instead, he moved down to my balls and licked; first one, then the other, his tongue moving back and forth between them, driving me crazy with rush after rush of the sweetest sensations I swear I have ever experienced. No one had ever licked my balls before. It had never even occurred to me that this could be the source of such ecstasy.

And then he took them into his mouth. I felt the slight tug on my ballsac as he gently pulled on them, and the flicker of his tongue as he teased them with pinpricks of pleasure. I had never felt such a delectable sensation between my legs.

Then he removed his mouth, repositioned himself so his face was once more in front of my cock. He paused to admire it again. I looked down at him, fascinated with watching the watcher who was contemplating my cock.

He opened his mouth and licked the length of my cockshaft, ending at my cockslit, delicately and repeatedly teasing it with just the tip of his tongue, making it bob up and down in front of his face.

Ian was so full of surprises. I had never had my balls licked before, and I had never had anyone spend so much time concentrating on my cockslit, isolating it from the rest of my cock, telegraphing waves of pleasure through the whole of it through his fond and detailed attention to that one little area.

He removed his tongue, pulled back and stared again as my cock twitched, begging for a continuation of his fine tongue worship. He looked at it amused and contemplative.

Then he pulled me down onto the soft carpet of grass. We locked in manly embrace and kissed with greedy, passionate abandon as we rolled around. I felt his body on top of mine, the wonderful weight of his frame pressing down. Then I was on top of him, legs spread apart, thrusting my hips forward to feel my cock slide between his legs to nestle under his balls.

For a precious eternity on this idyllic plateau in the middle of Vermont, we rolled on and off each other's bodies, feeling the warm sun above us, and the cool, soft grass below. Finally, at one point, when Ian was on top, he dismounted and kneeled between my legs.

"You just lie back and relax."

He repositioned me so my legs were spread apart and my knees were in the air.

I clasped my hands behind my neck and looked up into the infinity of pale blue sky above me where only the occasional wisp of cloud lazily drifted by.

Ian licked me way under my balls, darting his tongue down between my legs teasingly close to my asshole. His tongue gradually moved up to the swollen hardness below my balls. Then a long, ascending tongue-stroke to the left of that hardness. Next, one to the right of it. Then a repeat. And another and another. I got lost in the ecstasy of this hippie god between my legs making me feel hot, sweet and horny.

He finally ascended to my balls, taking them both into his mouth and giving them a good tonguing, occasionally tugging at them.

I sat up on my elbows and watched. With his mouth full of my ballsac, and his right hand stroking his swollen cock, he looked up into my eyes. My cock kept twitching, jumping up between our eyehold like it was trying to gain our attention.

"Ian. No one's ever done that to me before."

He released my balls and sat up, resting his hands on his thighs.

"Goddard College, the school of independent study. You like it?"

My cock jerked upwards again.

"That answer your question?"

"Sometimes I have these fantasies, like how it would feel to be a jockstrap. Like, imagine if I were yours. You'd put me on, and for hours on end I feel your balls inside me..."

His hand went to his cock and he stroked himself while he continued talking.

"...pressing against me, stretching me into shape around them. And whatever you did, I'd be there to witness it in the force of your balls against me."

"Wow! What a trip! Let me tell you one my own fantasies."

"Okay."

"I pretend my tongue's this very, very small person. Like a Lilliputian?"

"Uh, huh."

"And what it likes most in the world is to go spelunking."

"Huh? What's that?"

"I was hoping you'd ask, because now I'll have to show you."

I got up.

"Okay, lie on your stomach."

When he did, he sat up on his elbows and twisted his head back to watch me. I spread his legs apart and kneeled between them. I ran my lands along his calves and thighs, feeling their muscled contour. I surveyed the way his two firm asscheeks descended to the small of his back, and the way his back then broadened to his wide shoulders.

He smiled at me and said, "Now what are you up to?"

"You'll see."

I placed my hands on his asscheeks and pulled them apart, exposing the silken, lightly-haired darkness of his asscrack, and his pink, puckered asshole.

"A spelunker is someone who likes to explore caves. Like this."

I suddenly pulled his asscheeks ever further apart, leaned forward, and snaked my tongue up his asshole.

"Ah!"

Further.

Further.

"Ahh!

A little more.

"Oh! You're driving me crazy, man!"

"Anyone ever do that to you before?"

"Shit. Never."

"I was hoping I'd be the first."

I pulled his asscheeks apart, closed my eyes, and bent over. My entire being poured into my tongue as it continued to explore Ian's asshole.

And Ian kept up ahhing and shaking his head in pleasure as he forced his butt up and out to make my access to his hole all the easier.

When I finally withdrew my face from Ian's butt crevice and sat up, Ian was looking at me with this desperate, heavy-lidded look on his face.

"Fuck me, Ron. Please! That tongue of yours in my asshole has made me so horny I feel like I'll die if you don't fill me up with that hard cock of yours and shoot your cum inside me."

Ian turned around and lay on his back. He held his legs up and apart with his forearms.

"You gotta do this for me!"

I tongued some spit onto my hand, rubbed it on my eager cock, and then pushed his bent legs up by the crook behind his knees until they were nearly by his ears and mounted him. The tip of my cock pressed against his asshole. I pushed forward and it slid in easily.

"Yeah! That's it!"

I slowly inched my cock inside him until my lower abdomen pressed against his asscheeks and I was all the way up his ass.

"Oh, Ron. This past month has been Nirvana. But you don't know how much I've missed feeling cock up my ass."

I slowly withdrew my cock until just my cockhead remained inside him. Then I shoved it all the way in again.

In no time I found the pace that suited the both of us, and I was rhythmically pumping in and out Ian's asshole with ease. He held his cock in his right hand and irregularly stroked it, clearly holding off orgasm. I watched the rise and fall of his balls as he stroked his dick, and the way he shook his head back and forth, eyes closed, a look of agonizingly exquisite pleasure on his face.

Finally, I could feel the sweet advent of cum below my balls. I worked my cock all the faster in and out Ian's asshole.

He could tell I was coming and worked on his dick with abandon.

The cum shot out of my cock and up his asshole. Wave after wave of pleasure coursed throughout my body as I became a helpless slave to the ecstasy of the moment, discharging my juices into Ian.

At the same time, I heard a long, prolonged "Ahhh!" from Ian as he shot his cum all over his chest in abundant, arching spurts.

When we finally came to rest, I withdrew my cock from him, lowered his legs, and rested on top of him. He embraced me, I pressed my lips against his, and we stretched out one long and lazy open-mouthed, tongue-probing kiss.

Finally, I dismounted him and we lay side by side, silently looking up at the vast blue sky above us.

"Oh, man," he said, still looking up, "this summer's been a real trip. But sometimes, especially at night, I think how far out it'd be if I could share it with one other guy. Now having you here like this, I don't know how I'm gonna get through the night."

Then he fell silent again and we each fell into our own thoughts.

After a while I leaned over, ran my fingers through his hair and lightly kissed him on the lips.

"Can I come and visit you again?"

"You kidding? Anytime you want."

"As soon as I can," I promised, kissing him again.

I got up. Ian raised himself onto his left elbow and turned to look at me. The smile had left his face.

"I really hate to see you go, man."

"Yeah. Me too. But I shouldn't be holding Jon up like this. See you soon. I promise"

"Yeah. Kiss me again before you leave."

Our mouths joined in a final, anguished kiss.

Then I got up, we exchanged see ya's, and I turned away took the path back to the quarry.

But Ian remained in my thoughts; that smiling, handsome

and my aching admiration of his liberated lifestyle.

When I reached the quarry, everyone but Jon had left.

"Where've ya been?" Jon asked.

"With Ian."

"Oh. Ready to go?"

I stood there for a second, and finalized the decision I had been turning over in my mind all the way back to the quarry.

"Do me a favor, huh?" I asked Jon.

"What's that?"

I pointed to my clothes.

"Take them with you? And will you be sure to pick me up in September in time to go back to Boston?"

"Right on!"

Jon jumped up, and gave me the thumbs up sign with both hands, and then hugged me.

"Thanks, Jon."

I smiled broadly at him, flashed him a victory sign, and then dove into the quarry, leaving everything behind me, swimming towards a greater liberation than I had ever thought myself capable of, and towards a summer of lovemaking with Ian.

RANDY & SWEET PETE

Grant Adams

Peter, or Sweet Pete as his few close friends called him, lay on his bed, his back propped up by several king-sized pillows, watching the first of two male porn tapes he had rented at the local video store that evening. The one he had just started was a new release which had been praised in the current fag-rags. But thirty minutes into it, he wasn't that taken with what he was seeing. And forget what he was hearing, the usual mumblings of inarticulate studs who spoke as if they were using English as a second or third language.

He had to laugh at himself for sounding like the English teacher he was and had been for the past fifteen years. He worked full time at a local community college, and he supplemented his meager income by teaching an adult education class two nights a week. Some of his hunkier male students managed to tempt him to such an extent that he often stopped to rent a video or two on his way home to the studio apartment he shared with his aging cat in North Hollywood.

But who rented these tapes for the dialogue? he asked himself. Who cared what was being said or how it was being said? Shouldn't the action speak for itself, though? And shouldn't any reasonably normal fag get aroused and erected within a reasonable length of time? But Pete was finding this increasingly difficult lately. He was tired of the shaved bodies, the shaved genitals, and the obligatory tattoo. He was also tired of their sex-by-the-numbers routines, so predictable and so passionless. If they weren't having a ball, how could he? Pete thought. Yes, most of the boys were pretty enough. Their bodies were choice, and their cocks were dandy. Those were givens. But Pete found that most of these so-called actors were little more than models who did far more posing than performing and who seldom showed any genuine excitement in their sexual antics.

Pete much preferred some of the old, grainy tapes in his extensive collection before the shaving and the posturing and the awful dialogue became the trend. The tapes when the boys got carried away and thrillingly fulfilled every possible homosexual fantasy. Then the past icons of gay sex were able and even eager to suck as well as be sucked and to be fucked as well as fuck. But now the industry seemed almost dominated by these stunning, sexless creatures who epitomized the new generation of tiresome trade. Pete found them irritating and tedious and even resented their being paid handsomely for just lying back to be blown or for fucking some young man with all the enthusiasm of a mannequin. That's what they were, he thought, mannequins whose skin even had that strange plastic quality of an inanimate dummy and whose eyes were cold and expressionless, like marbles.

Then the burly and brawny leading man appeared in the video. He had been featured in many of the fag-rags lately, and he was impressive. No doubt about that. Over six feet of prime beef topped by a glowing crown of golden hair (surely dyed since the color couldn't exist naturally), steel blue eyes that looked equally unnatural, and one of the more massive cocks in the business. But he was so shaven, so plastic, and so overbearing as he slowly stripped and then stroked his cock to its erected length that Pete started to fast forward to the next sequence. But then another actor entered the scene, and Pete found himself riveted.

The object of his attention was as young as he was beautiful, surely at least 18 but looking more like 16. He was also quite short but powerfully built as his tight T-shirt and cutoffs revealed. His close cropped hair was a light brown, almost wheat-colored, much like the fine hair that covered his arms and legs. His large brown eyes, set in an angelic yet sensual face, lit up with curiosity and apprehension as the star stud pulled the boy over to him and pushed him to his knees so that his face was inches from the engorged and glistening cock.

"Suck on this!" he ordered, and the boy tried to comply but found it difficult to get his mouth around the enormous glans. With a great deal of effort, he finally got the head and a couple of inches into his mouth, but his discomfort was apparent.

"Yeah, that's it. Take that big fucking cock!" the stud demanded, pushing the boy's head further down on his cock mercilessly and ripping off his T-shirt to reveal a perfectly proportioned back. Luckily for the boy, the stud soon withdrew and shot his load all over the boy's astonished face. Would the stud now fuck the boy? Pete wondered, hoping that he wouldn't for the boy's sake but also hoping that he would so Pete could get a glimpse of the boy's bare buns as well as his cock which was still bound tightly in denim but whose bulge was both provocative and promising.

The scene abruptly shifted to another sequence in a bar, and Pete quickly hit the Fast Forward button to see if there were any other episodes involving this delectable wonder. He hadn't even seen the boy's body and, consequently, felt cheated. But the boy never appeared again in the video. Disappointed but still aroused, Pete replayed again and again the one sequence in which he had seen the boy, and with this image to feed his fantasy, he beat off his own formidable cock, shooting his load across his chest and beyond his head. He wasn't called Sweet Pete for nothing.

. . .

Several nights later Pete went to meet his new night class for the first time. Even though he had extensive experience as a teacher, he still felt a certain anxiety with a new class. He wondered if they would like him, if they would even listen to him, if he could share his knowledge without wasting their time and effort and money. He knew he was a successful teacher; his student evaluations attested to that as well as his popularity. But he was also strict in his approach and demanding in his methods. To be otherwise would be irresponsible and unprofessional, he firmly believed. The classroom was not an open house or an entertainment center. A few students had resented him and his guidelines, but most came to respect him and learn from him.

His chairman had told him earlier in the day that the class would be larger than usual due to budget cuts and heavy enrollment, but Pete hadn't anticipated the forty or more students who were crammed into his classroom when he entered.

A silence fell over the multitude as he went to the desk, took a deep breath, and began the class.

Once he had assembled a roll sheet and gotten the preliminaries out of the way, Pete started in on the first lesson having to do with sentence structure, something so few students understood or applied correctly. He was in the midst of explaining the independent clause when the classroom door opened and a young man entered. Pete looked toward the newcomer and immediately recognized him as his dreamboat in the flesh. And what fine flesh it was! But was it possible? This must be someone who resembles the boy in the video. But, no, this was the boy himself. Pete had watched that particular sequence so many times, even buying his own copy, that he had memorized every feature of the boy's extraordinary face and muscular yet graceful body. He was even wearing a tight T-shirt and cutoffs in spite of the chilly evening.

Moments passed, maybe even minutes, before Pete could breathe properly or speak. "Come in," he finally managed to utter. The boy smiled at him, and Pete thought he was going to expire on the spot. Since there were no vacant desks in the room, the boy sat on the floor near the door. Pete apologized for this inconvenience, but the boy kept smiling as if he couldn't be happier with the arrangement. God, those eyes, that face, that body. With considerable difficulty, Pete returned to the clause.

When the ninety-minute class ended, several students came to the desk to ask the usual questions about the course and the assignments. The room soon cleared and Pete sat down in something of a stupor. He closed his eyes to relax for a moment.

"Excuse me, sir," he heard. Looking up, he saw the boy and that smile. "I never gave you my name. And I want to apologize for coming in late, but I got lost trying to find the right building." Pete just stared, mesmerized. "My name is Randy Luck. I know that's weird, but that's really my name." And still Pete sat speechless. "Is anything wrong, Mr. Potter?"

"No," Pete stammered, trying to regain his composure. "Not at all. I guess I'm just . . . tired."

"I'm sure you must be," Randy agreed. "You gave a terrific lesson. I learned a lot. I've never been very good at English, but I really want to learn. Some kids over in the Commons said you were the best, and now I can see why."

Pete flushed. "I try to do what I can."

Randy extended his hand which Pete took hesitantly. "Thank you, sir," Randy said and shook Pete's hand firmly.

Delighting in Randy's touch and not wanting to let go, Pete said, "I promise to get you a proper desk. We can't have you sitting on the floor." I'd love to have you sitting on my face, Pete thought to himself, then quickly put his raunchy imagination on hold.

Randy grinned, almost as if he had read Pete's mind. "Don't worry about it." he said. "I was fine." With that, he waved good-bye and went whistling out of the room.

As Pete gathered his materials together to put in his briefcase, he again questioned the validity of his assumption. Certainly it was possible that this boy was and is the boy in the video, but it was just too unbelievable to be true. This is the stuff that dreams are made of, he thought. This is not reality.

He walked out of the building and into the cool night air thinking he was either the luckiest man in the world to have his fantasy materialize or the unluckiest for having to endure Randy's presence in his classroom without being able to act on his desires.

"Get hold of yourself, " he said aloud to himself as he got into his Toyota. Then he smiled, realizing that's just what he would do when he got home and once again popped his favorite video into the VCR. But tonight there would be a difference; he would have not only the filmed image of Randy to behold but also the real image imprinted indelibly into his mind.

. . .

Several weeks passed, and Randy proved to be a hard-working and fairly bright student. He seldom spoke in class, but he always came by Pete's desk at the end of class to thank him for the lesson, an unusual but pleasant gesture and one which Pete always looked forward to and appreciated. It also gave him the opportunity to be near Randy, to drink in his beauty up close. In one of the papers Randy wrote, he mentioned that he had done some things in his past that he wasn't proud of but that he hoped he had learned from the experiences. Pete wondered if Randy was referring to the video.

Then he wondered if Randy was even gay. Perhaps he had hated sucking that stud's cock and had made the video only because he was desperate for the money it paid him. Certainly he was as masculine looking as any heterosexual student, but this meant nothing. Randy did have an unmistakable sensitivity that combined a charming shyness and vulnerability with an extraordinary eagerness to please, but this also meant nothing.

Realizing how obsessed he was becoming, Pete tried not to think about the boy, and he forced himself to stop watching the video. He even stopped looking at Randy in class and ignored those few times when Randy would raise his hand with a question. Pete also found himself hurrying out of the classroom before Randy could talk to him at the end of the class. But none of this worked. Pete still thought about him constantly, and his head was filled with his image and the sound of his voice each night when he turned out his bedside lamp.

He had a major crush on the boy. That's all it was, he tried to convince himself. And like all crushes, this would come to an end. But when? He couldn't go on much longer with this torment and frustration. And he couldn't act on his desires. As a teacher, he had never made it with a student. He considered this unethical and very dangerous. Yes, he had been tempted . . . often . . . but he had always managed to redirect the temptation. What he needed was a good romp in the sack, he decided. It had been too long since he had reaped the rewards of the flesh.

No longer knowing anyone he could call on for this kind of assistance, he phoned a masseur after looking through the countless ads in one of the gay newspapers. The man had advertised himself as being young and good-looking, but he was neither. He did have a good, firm body though, and when he dropped his jock, Pete was impressed with his cock. But in spite of the masseur's efforts to arouse Pete and bring him to climax, Pete's cock refused to harden. It was only when Pete closed his eyes and imagined himself in Randy's hands did his cock cooperate and swell to its imposing girth. In moments he was shooting his cum onto himself and the masseur, wishing it was Randy he was anointing with the seed of his passion.

That night in bed Pete felt ungratified and wished he had never spent the sixty or so to have some stranger jack him off. He could have done that himself – and more efficiently. Putting aside his previous resolution, he again looked at Randy's video as he stroked himself to climax and then to sleep.

Another Saturday came and two of Pete's oldest friends, who were also lovers, invited him to dinner. Not having any other plans, Pete accepted. He went to a new hair stylist that morning and had his hair shortened. To look younger? he wondered. He also took a particularly long time in the bathroom before his dinner engagement, taking far more care with his grooming than usual. In fact, for some years, Pete hadn't paid much attention to his appearance. He was always clean shaven and neat, but his clothes were old, and he no longer went to the gym on a regular basis.

After his shower he looked in the full-length mirror in his bedroom before dressing, and what he saw didn't displease him. He was 38 but could pass for a half dozen years younger. His dark brown hair was full and rich, his complexion was flawless, and his body was tight and well-proportioned. He then ran his hand lovingly down his broad, hairy chest until it came to rest on his flaccid cock, impressive even in this state. Yes, he liked what he saw and promised himself to start using his attributes to greater advantage. There was no reason for his not having a more active sex life. He had been out of the loop too long and would no longer avoid the bars and the gay parties he was often invited to. Then this obsession with Randy would end.

. . .

Pete left his friends' house after enjoying a gourmet dinner and several hours of "remember when." It was just past 11:00, and he was eager for some action. He certainly wasn't going to answer another of those ads. He wanted something more personal, friendlier, more satisfying. So he found himself driving to a gay bar he used to frequent in years past. He had given up the bar scene some time ago because he became so bored looking for Mr. Right and always finding Mr. Wrong.

Maybe his standards were too high. That's what his friends told him.

He parked in the crowded lot at The Alcove which looked as if it had been recently repainted a garish green. When he entered, he saw that it was as dark and gloomy as ever, but he was determined to stay. He found one of the few empty stools at the bar and ordered a beer. As his eyes became accustomed to the dismal surroundings, he noticed how young the crowd was, and his self-confidence began to ebb. He drank his beer quickly, wanting to leave and retreat to the warmth and safety of his own apartment.

Just then he heard the laughter of a group of young men as they came into the bar. They were obviously having a raucous time together, and he momentarily envied their high spirits and their youth. They approached the bar, and suddenly Pete recognized Randy among them, in his regulation T-shirt and cutoffs, looking as adorable as ever. Pete choked on his beer, jumped from his stool, and headed for the back door, hoping against hope that Randy hadn't seen him.

That's all he'd need for one of his students to see him in a gay bar. He practically ran to his car and zoomed out of the lot in a panic.

He didn't see you, he kept telling himself. It was too dark. Stop worrying. But then he wondered why Randy would be in such a place if he weren't gay. He's got to be gay, Pete wanted to believe. Or maybe he's just trade and hopes to pick up a few bucks on a Saturday night. God knows he has plenty to sell, and it couldn't be packaged more appealingly. But what the fuck does it matter one way or the other, Pete thought. He's forbidden fruit under any circumstances.

Arriving at his apartment feeling physically and emotionally exhausted, Pete climbed into bed, aching with an unfulfilled desire which even masturbation failed to subdue.

. . .

Sunday began with fog and continued with light rain. It was almost noon before Pete even got out of bed. He had had a restless, troubling night and awoke depressed. Seldom had he felt so alone as he brewed his coffee and fed his cat.

He took his coffee and *The Times* back to bed with him, not wanting to even open his bedroom blinds.

As he read his paper and drank his coffee, he heard what sounded like a light rapping at his front door. Maybe it was at the next apartment, he thought, and ignored it. But, no, there it was again, and it was his door. He hated drop-in company, and all of his friends knew this. He wouldn't answer it, he decided, but then the knocking became louder, more insistent. He pulled his robe around his buffed bod and went to the door. Peering through the peep-hole, he almost fainted away when he saw Randy Luck.

He took a deep breath, tried to steady his hand, and opened the door slightly.

"Sorry to bother you, Mr. Potter," Randy said smiling. "But I thought you'd be up by now." The rain had increased, and Randy was getting wet.

"Come in, come in," Pete said opening the door for him. The two of them stood looking at each other before Pete broke the awkward silence. "You're wet."

"Just a little," Randy said apologetically. "I hope I didn't wake you."

"No, no. I just haven't dressed yet. I'll get you a towel," Pete said and hurried from the room, eager to get away for a moment to compose himself. Why was Randy here? What did he want? In the bathroom Pete ran a comb through his hair and grabbed a clean towel which he took to Randy who had removed his windbreaker and revealed his customary uniform. Randy took the towel and rubbed it quickly over his face and hair and arms, seemingly unaware that Pete was admiring his every graceful move.

"Thanks a lot," he said, handing the towel back to Pete. "I guess you're wondering why I'm here." Pete nodded. "I won't be long. I promise." Pete hoped that Randy couldn't hear his heart pounding. Randy continued: "I've just been so bothered by something, and I wanted to talk to you about it." Randy looked into Pete's eyes. "Can I do that?"

"Yes, of course, you can. Sit down." The two of them sat on the sofa, Randy almost too close for comfort. "How did you know where I lived?"

"I followed you home one night."

Pete was stunned. "Why?"

"I wanted to know where you lived."

Becoming more and more flustered and confused, Pete said, "I don't understand."

"I'm what I guess you could call a loner, Mr. Potter. My dad died when I was a kid, and my mother lives back East. I moved here last summer, and I know just a few people here in L. A., and I wouldn't call any of them friends." He paused and stretched back on the sofa, accentuating the thrust of his ample crotch.

What's going on here, Pete wondered, but said nothing.

Randy averted his eyes from Pete's and said, "I've been so impressed with you as a teacher . . . and as a man, I just wanted to find out something." He paused, seemingly unable to articulate his thought. "Now I feel so ridiculous coming over here like this." He quickly rose. "I'd better go."

Pete took his arm. "No, wait. You haven't told me why you've come. What is it, Randy? Tell me." Pete wondered if it was the concerned teacher talking or the lovesick fag?

Randy sat back down on the sofa's edge and said, "I thought you liked me. I even thought we could be friends, but then you started acting . . . strange . . . as if I did something awful." He then stared into Pete's eyes. "What did I do, Mr. Potter?" he pleaded. "And what can I do to make it right?" His beautiful brown eyes were moist with emotion.

Without thinking, Pete took Randy's hand. "You didn't do anything wrong, Randy. I promise you that. It's just that . . . well, I've had sort of a personal problem lately, and I'm afraid it's affected too many of my actions. I'm sorry." He squeezed Randy's hand. "Please forgive me."

Randy spontaneously threw his arms around Pete and hugged him. Then just as quickly he drew back , feeling clumsy and embarrassed. "Sorry about that. I'm just so relieved that I'm not the problem," he said, wiping his eyes with his hand.

If you only knew, Pete said to himself. And then to Randy, "I usually don't bring my personal problems into the classroom, but I apparently slipped up. At your expense."

Randy stood up and said, "Thanks, Mr. Potter, for letting me disturb you like this. And for listening. I'll leave now and let you get on with your Sunday. You must have a hundred things to do." He extended his hand.

Pete shook Randy's hand and held it in his own. He then spoke his next thought aloud. "I have nothing."

They looked into each other's eyes, connecting and yet not quite connecting. Randy moved a little closer to Pete who could now feel the boy's warm breath on his face. Finally Randy said, almost in a whisper, "I saw you at The Alcove last night." Pete sank to the sofa, his hands shaking, his worst fears realized. "Did you see me?" Randy asked.

"Yes," Pete muttered, trying to control his panic.

"Why did you leave in such a hurry?"

"I was . . . afraid."

"Of what?" Randy asked, sitting down and taking Pete's hands into his. "Of me? Why were you afraid of me?"

"Randy, for God's sake, you're a student. I'm a teacher. Your teacher. Think about it." Pete couldn't understand his sudden anger. Nor could Randy. "Now would you please leave."

Pete tried to release his hands, but Randy held them tightly and said, "We're also two people who could like each other. What's the problem?"

"You're a child, Randy. A beautiful, wonderful, desirable child, but a child nonetheless. And I'm . . . . "

"A wonderful, desirable man," Randy finished for him. Then after a long pause, Randy added, "I think I'm in love with you. I think I have been since that first night in your class." This can't be happening, Pete thought. I'm dreaming. I'm still asleep and I'm dreaming. "I followed you home a lot of times and would even drive by on the weekends wondering if you lived alone or if you had a wife or a lover. Some nights I couldn't even sleep thinking about you. Then last night when I saw you in the bar, I was so glad to find out that you were like me . . . you know. . . gay." He moved still closer to Pete who was in a state of shock and disbelief. "And I'm not a child. I look younger than I am, if that's what's bothering you. I'm nineteen." Suddenly Randy stopped and looked down. "I guess I'm making a fool out of myself?" But he continued, piercing Pete with his eyes. "Do you like me at all?"

Instead of answering with words, Pete took Randy's face

into his hands and brought the boy's luscious, full lips to his own. Their mouths met and opened to mutually receive the first confirmation of their desire for one another. For minutes they clung to each other, loathe to separate, wanting to hold the moment forever. And the moment didn't end; it was merely extended and enhanced as Randy slowly separated Pete's robe in order to kiss his neck and then his chest, working his way deliciously down to Pete's warm groin and fully erected cock. Randy sampled it tentatively, teasingly, licking enticingly around the glans and then kissing the perfectly pear-shaped head.

"Oh, Randy," Pete moaned. "I can't believe this."

Randy then swallowed Pete to the root and held him deep in his throat, gradually withdrawing his mouth before plunging down again and again, increasing his tempo as well as his suction, until Pete screamed out his release and filled Randy's anxious mouth with hot, heavy come, the first fully satisfying orgasm he had had in weeks and the best he had ever had. At last Pete's hardness waned and Randy reluctantly released his cock, kissing it gently as he then began his meticulous journey up Pete's stomach and chest and finally to Pete's mouth where he lovingly shared the residue of Pete's rich cream.

No longer able to control his eagerness to explore Randy's physical attributes, Pete flipped him over on the couch, removed his damp T-shirt, and dove for his pointed nipples which he massaged passionately with his tongue, first one and then the other. Without relinquishing their sweetness, he hastily unbuttoned Randy's cutoffs and liberated his firm young cock, fondling its exceptional length and texture before moving down to more fully appreciate its splendor.

Pete wanted to cry, he was so overcome with joy. He kissed the cockhead, then took it gradually into his mouth, savoring its taste and texture. Thoroughly exploring its silky surface with his tongue and delighting in the discovery, Pete suddenly felt the cock throb and thicken, and he knew what was coming. Unable to restrain his desperate urge a moment longer, Randy burst forth and copiously filled Pete's mouth with what Pete considered the nectar of the gods. Nothing had ever tasted so deliciously gratifying to him, and he was both surprised and pleased with its abundance.

. . .

Later in bed, after they had thoroughly investigated each other's bodies and after each had taken the other lovingly and lustfully into his ass, they lay blissfully in each other's arms, aware of having created their own world and delighting in the satisfacrtion and comfort it provided.

Pete pulled slightly back from Randy to say, "I've thought of nothing else but you for weeks. And I've played your video over and over and over, at least one of your videos. I never could find out if you made any more."

Randy struck his forehead with the palm of his hand and laughed, rolling onto his back. "Oh, God, that video. What a mess that turned out to be." Then he sat up in bed and explained that a guy he had met in The Alcove had talked him into meeting this producer who made gay fuck films. The producer liked him and signed him on immediately. Everything went well the day of the shoot until Randy got a look at the mammoth meat he was supposed to suck, and he panicked.

"I've never been so scared," Randy confessed, "but thankfully the guy came in a hurry and put an end to my agony. Don't get me wrong. I like a big cock." He squeezed Pete's, "as I'm sure you know by now. But this guy was so damned rough and so fucking mean. A real son-of-a-bitch."

"I was afraid he was going to fuck you," Pete said.

"He was supposed to and he tried, but I just couldn't take his cock or his bullshit so I left. I just walked out without even getting paid." He laughed. "I guess that's the end of my big movie career."

Pete drew Randy more tightly into his arms. "I'm glad you walked out. I wouldn't want anyone to hurt your perfect little ass in any way." He snuggled into Randy's neck, nuzzling him with his nose and lips, still doubting the dream, yet thrilled with its reality.

And again the two made love with Randy sitting on Pete's cock, rocking slowly back and forth until each erupted the evidence of their passion. Crooning his satisfaction, Randy collapsed onto Pete's chest and was sound asleep in moments, his head cradled beneath Pete's chin.

As the boy dozed, Pete softly stroked Randy's superbly molded back and cupped his apple-firm buttocks in the palm of his hand. He was also sleepy after the several hours of ecstatic sex he had just experienced, but he didn't want to sleep. He didn't want to miss a minute of this dream come true, a dream that may not last but a short time. After all, Randy was just a youngster, and he would surely move on to other adventures, other conquests.

But for the time being this was more than enough, and Pete counted himself among the luckiest of men to have drunk this deeply of Randy's many charms.

FLETCHER'S BOYS

Grant Adams

Jason sat waiting in the over-heated lobby of his Boston hotel that was his home away from home while he attended a three-day sales conference financed by the large corporation he worked for in Arizona. Fletcher wasn't due for ten minutes, and Jason regretted ever having set up this dinner engagement with his ex-roommate from college. Actually they had lived together in Fletcher's swank apartment for only a few months.

Jason remembered being apprehensive about moving in with Fletcher initially, and his closest buddies at the time tried to talk him out of it. He should have listened. Not that Fletcher was unlikable. Most everyone thought he was a kick – friendly, funny, and rich, always insisting on picking up the check regardless of its size. But Fletcher never dated, seemed interested in only movies and music, and his apartment had been decorated by some swish from Boston where his parents' chain of upper-cut department stores was based. For these reasons he was labeled an eccentric by some and as a fag by others, though Jason refused to accept this as fact. Fletcher was too regular a guy, a little peculiar maybe but certainly not gay.

For weeks Fletcher kept after Jason to move in with him, telling him the apartment was too big for just one person. When Fletcher finally offered to pay Jason's portion of the hefty rent, Jason agreed, unable to refuse such an attractive proposition.

All went well until late one night after Jason returned from a dinner date. He was feeling no pain, having had too many martinis before dinner followed by too much wine during dinner, and he was sloshed and barely able to stagger to his room, throwing his clothes to the floor as he stumbled to his bed. He fell into a deep sleep almost immediately, but during the night he was awakened by someone lapping at his long, limp cock. At first he thought he was dreaming but soon realized he was awake. He struggled away from the intruder, clicked on his bedside lamp, and saw Fletcher crouched between his legs. Jason was outraged and demanded that demanded that Fletcher leave his room. Fletcher started to cry and begged Jason to forgive him, telling Jason he had always loved him and that he couldn't live another moment without expressing that love. Jason told him to fuck off in so many words, and Fletcher left.

No longer comfortable in the apartment and unable to get back to sleep, Jason threw some clothes in an overnight bag and left. Several days later he heard that Fletcher had dropped out of school and returned to Boston. And that was the last of their friendship. Or so Jason thought.

Then a couple of years ago, a smoked turkey and a case of fine champagne arrived at Christmas. They were from Fletcher wishing Jason and his family good cheer. Jason's wife Sally wanted to know all about this generous friend from the past whom Jason had never mentioned previously, but Jason told her very little, saying he really didn't know him that well in college and wondering how Fletcher had found him. Sally insisted that he send Fletcher a thank-you note which Jason did. Then the gifts kept coming, only on holidays at first and then almost monthly: wine, hams, sweet delicacies, dozens of roses, even a 32-inch TV with a built-in VCR. Fletcher's ostentation began to annoy and embarrass Jason, and he wrote Fletcher asking him to stop, that he couldn't and wouldn't accept any more gifts. And the gifts did stop for a while. Then the following Christmas two large crates of expensive toys arrived for Jason's two young children. His wife had unpacked the beautifully gift-wrapped packages and had them arranged under the tree when Jason got in from his office. He was angry and took it out on Sally who went to bed in tears.

What was Fletcher trying to prove? he had asked himself. What did he want? Then he began to feel guilty for suspecting some ulterior motive. He and Fletcher had been friends, and their friendship had ended badly. Maybe this was just Fletcher's whimsical way of saying he was sorry for that late-night invasion so many years ago.

Jason checked his watch again. Fletcher was due in about five minutes now. Ironically their reunion had not been arranged by Fletcher but by Jason himself. Several months ago when his boss had told him about this trip, Jason decided to drop Fletcher a note to tell him he'd be in Boston for a few days and would like to take Fletcher to dinner. Now he regretted this decision, worrying that he would feel awkward in Fletcher's presence. Their lives were so different now with no common ground to share. Fletcher was a multimillionaire who moved in the rarefied circles of the very rich and high finance whereas Jason could hardly make ends meet for his family. No, I should never have contacted him, he thought.

"Paging Mr. Jason Pierce!" someone was calling. Jason jumped to his feet, thinking and hoping that perhaps Fletcher couldn't make it after all.

A bellhop approached Jason and said, "There's a car waiting for you at the front entrance, sir." Why was Fletcher waiting for him outside? Jason wondered. He had told Fletcher they would eat here at the hotel.

Jason hurried out into the cool night air and was greeted by a liveried young chauffeur who was holding the rear door open for him, the rear door of the longest limousine Jason had ever seen. The chauffeur tipped his cap and said, "Mr. Crenshaw regrets he couldn't come personally, but he asked me to drive you to his home." Without knowing how to react, Jason slipped into the luxurious leather interior. Soft music was playing, and someone was sitting opposite him, another handsome young man, only a boy really. "I'm to take care of your every desire, Mr. Pierce," the boy said, opening the well-stocked bar complete with crystal decanters and glasses. "What's your pleasure?" the boy asked with a smile. Jason had a Scotch, the best Scotch he had ever tasted. And then he had another as he was driven outside of Boston to a gated estate which overwhelmed him. Why shouldn't Fletcher live well? he asked himself. He had always had more money than he knew what to do with.

Jason was impressed though, not ever having seen such splendor first-hand. And he wondered if Fletcher hadn't arranged all of this to impress him, to somehow make him regret his rejection of the past. As the limo pulled to a stop and his door was opened, he became aware of an indefinable fear. Not knowing what to expect next, he told himself he could handle any situation that arose.

. . .

A uniformed butler opened the heavy glass front door to the ornate foyer filled with orchids of every variety. The butler was also young and good-looking, just like the chauffeur and the boy in the limo, and he led Jason into what appeared to be a library. The roaring fireplace was fully seven feet across and five feet high, and the walls were lined with built-in bookcases, their polished wood veneers reflecting the dancing light from the fire. "Mr. Crenshaw will be with you soon," the butler said. "He's on the phone to Japan. May I pour you a drink?" Against his better judgment, Jason had still another Scotch.

When Jason was left alone in the room, he noticed several heavy leather-bound books on one of the large tables. Assuming they were photo albums, he opened one and was surprised to discover artistic photographs of adolescent boys in various stages of undress. Flipping further into the book, he found other boys, all naked and all sporting erections. Some were even sexually coupled with a companion. He slammed the book shut when a door opened and Fletcher appeared, all smiles and sincerely apologetic for having kept Jason waiting.

When the two of them settled down in front of the fire, Fletcher said, "Since my father's death a year ago, I've had to assume much more responsibility, often working an absurd twelve-to fifteen-hour day – and night. I don't know that I enjoy the work I do, but for some reason which escapes me, as well as others, I'm quite good at it." He poured Jason another drink before continuing. "You look wonderful, Jason, all health and happiness, it seems. And I do appreciate your asking me to dinner. But business kept me from joining you in town." He then paused for a moment. "I thought you'd never want to see me again."

Jason protested. "That's not fair, Fletcher."

"Perhaps not," Fletcher said, "but fairly accurate, I'll warrant."

Jason tried to explain. "That last night we saw each other was awkward for us both. And I felt somehow responsible for you leaving school. Then all those gifts started arriving. You shouldn't have sent them."

"They were nothing," Fletcher said. "I'm rich, Jason, richer than you can imagine, and I'm getting richer every day. I have no family except my mother, who has even more money than

I, and I'm her only heir. What's a few gifts among friends?"

Fletcher moved to stand near the fireplace, and Jason realized what a distinguished-looking man he had become. He had always been elegant, even in college, but in his maturity he was strikingly handsome. Even the premature gray at his temples was flattering.

"You are my friend, aren't you, Jason?" Fletcher asked almost timidly. "I sincerely hope I didn't spoil that all those years ago."

"Of course, I'm your friend. I wouldn't have gotten in touch with you otherwise." And for a moment Jason regretted his earlier wish to cancel his evening with Fletcher whom he was genuinely glad to see, to be with after all this time. But the photos he had seen bothered him. Fletcher was gay, Jason assumed, but the openly displayed pictures seemed inappropriate. Then it occurred to Jason that the photograph albums might have been left there for his benefit. Jason decided he shouldn't drink anymore, to keep his wits about him, not knowing what the evening would bring.

. . .

The excellent dinner featured a crown pork roast with artfully arranged miniature vegetables. Jason wished Sally could see the dazzling beauty of the table and the food. The service was equally impressive with two young men attending to their every possible need. Finally Jason succumbed to Fletcher's persuasive powers and sampled the superb wine. Then a full glass. And then a second and third. The dinner concluded with a flaming dessert which tasted faintly of raspberries and cognac. The rich do indeed live differently, Jason thought to himself.

During dessert Jason began to realize that he was having trouble concentrating on what Fletcher was saying. Surely I'm not getting smashed, Jason said to himself. He didn't really feel drunk, just light-headed and somehow disconnected from the real world around him. But the world around him wasn't real, all glitter and gold and seductive in its utter extravagance. Jason became aware of Fletcher smiling at him and asking him something. But Jason hadn't heard the question. He tried to say something, but his mouth wouldn't work. He wanted to excuse himself, to go to a bathroom in order to orient himself. But he couldn't seem to stand up, yet he also felt as if he were floating. He had never felt this way before, but he couldn't complain. The sensation he was experiencing wasn't unpleasant, just strange and illusory. His eyes closed, and he drifted into a warm, soothing oblivion.

. . .

Jason was finally able to open his eyes, and he saw candlelight reflected in mirrors. He heard distant music, and he felt soft fur beneath his body. He then realized his body was naked and that he was stretched out on some sort of bed. He tried to stir, to sit up, but he couldn't. Hands held both his ankles as well as his wrists. He wanted to speak, but again his mouth wouldn't cooperate. As his eyes became more adjusted to the dimly lit room, he saw his captors more clearly. They were boys, and they too were naked. Did he recognize the chauffeur? The butler? The waiters? Possibly.

His mind couldn't seem to grasp what was happening. Or why. Was this some sick joke Fletcher was having at his expense? Was this Fletcher's carefully plotted revenge for that night fifteen years ago?

He then felt warm hands begin to caress and rub his body with some sort of almond-scented ointment. First his face and neck, then his arms and chest, then to his feet and legs, and finally to his inner thighs, barely touching his balls as fingers burrowed into the hot crack of his ass. Jason struggled in vain, frightened by what the boys were planning to do next. He had to admit though that he was getting the greatest massage of his life. But how often does a massage consist of seven or eight pairs of hands, all knowing just what to do and where to do it? He felt the young bodies touching his – smooth, firm flesh rubbing against him. It was strangely comforting and highly sensual. Then he felt their hardened cocks touching his legs, his arms, his chest. He knew also that his own cock was rising. But he couldn't understand why he was so sexually stirred. These were boys, he told himself. And he knew he didn't have a gay bone in his body. But he also realized that his cock couldn't make such a distinction, that it could become easily aroused under the most diverse and unusual of circumstances. But to this extent?

Then he felt a warm mouth on the head of his cock. This unexpected sensation electrified him, and he threw his head back against another boy, another hard cock at the back of his neck. The eager mouth suckled more and more of him until hungry lips met his pubic hair. God, this was fantastic. He loved a good blowjob but hadn't had one in years. He had tried to get Sally to go down on him during their first years of marriage, but she had always gagged, and he knew that she hated it. But the person blowing him now was a fucking expert, teasing his cock with an incredible tongue that knew all the right moves. He was about to blow, but suddenly his cock was abandoned, much to his disappointment. The idea of blasting off into someone's mouth had always thrilled him. Even a boy's mouth.

Jason's cock wasn't neglected for long though. The mouth was soon replaced by tight, muscular flesh pushing down on his cock, and he realized someone was sitting on him, thrusting down on his dick until it popped into a constricted hole and found its way into a soft, seething interior. He was ass-fucking someone, for the first time, and it was unbelievably sensational. He bucked his hips forward to drive more of his prick into his willing recipient. This must be another of Fletcher's boys, he thought, but when he raised his head to look up, he saw Fletcher himself straddled across his hips, moaning lowly with his eyes closed.

So this was the plan, Jason assumed. To be drugged and then raped. But how could rape feel so fucking good. As he was thoroughly enjoying Fletcher's tight, clenching ass, a beautiful boy jumped upon his chest, his young, stiff prick at Jason's chin. He smiled down at Jason and took his head in his hands, gently pulling forward until his cock was at Jason's closed lips. No, Jason thought, I'm not sucking this cock. I'm not a cock-sucker. I'm not gay. But as he was mentally protesting, other hands behind him pushed his head forward until the young man on his chest was able to get his cockhead between Jason's lips. The boy then rubbed his sweet-smelling cock against Jason's clenched teeth. The cock was firm yet velvety soft, and after a few moments Jason opened his teeth to permit the boy to enter his mouth slightly. Jason licked his tongue across the head tentatively, feeling the pisshole and the pronounced ridges which framed the large, slick glans. He was shocked he was letting this boy face-fuck him, and even more shocked that he didn't really mind it, telling himself he was just too turned on to know what he was doing or why.

His wrists were finally released, and each of his freed hands was placed on a hard prick. Their size was impressive, and Jason manipulated their appealing texture, occasionally reaching for and squeezing the big balls beneath them. Two ravaging mouths began to suck his toes while still others licked his legs. He felt as if he were being consumed, eaten alive. He didn't really know where to concentrate his attention--on the cock in his mouth, the ones in his hands, or on his own in Fletcher's burning ass.

Jason's heart began to beat faster and faster, and his body quivered with excruciating passion. He had never had such an amazing sexual experience, and he felt that he was devouring and being devoured all at the same time. He was then astounded by what happened next.

He was lifted from the bed along with Fletcher and the boy he was blowing by countless strong hands, and someone crawled beneath him. When he was again lowered, he felt a hard prick poking at his ass and then prying its way into him, slowly but surely. He tried to break free from this invader, but too many hands held him fast. He was helpless to prevent the painful penetration, and he wondered if it would kill him. More and more of the seemingly endless prick sank into him as the hands pushed him down upon his intruder. Then everyone was quite still. There was no movement at all, only the flickering candles reflected in the mirrors. And the heavy breathing. And the music.

Jason felt the pain ease somewhat, and as he recovered from his shock, Fletcher and his boys began a slow, easy rhythm, coordinating their maneuvers to bring Jason the maximum pleasure. Everyone was grunting and sighing and moaning, and the pace increased. Jason hadn't even realized that the boy on his chest had managed to get most of his cock into his mouth, and he was sucking it wildly, delighting in its taste and pulsing hardness. He even began to clamp his anal muscles around the cock in his ass to enhance this new and ecstatic sensation.

He heard Fletcher mumble something to the boys, and they all moved in closer to Jason, their cocks and tongues and hands everywhere on his writhing body. Jason felt his own cock expand in Fletcher and knew he would shoot his load in seconds. Apparently that's just what Fletcher wanted because he started riding Jason frantically, twisting and turning his ass in a frenzy of sexual excitement. Jason screamed a silent scream as he burst into his friend.

Then each of the boys, as well as Fletcher, announced their mutual orgasms with a shout. They pumped their offerings of rich sperm onto Jason's body and up into his ass and into his mouth. Cum was everywhere, and the pungent smell filled the room. Jason swallowed what he could of the sweet salty love lotion being pumped into his mouth, amazed at the amount the boy kept giving him.

Finally the boy withdrew from his mouth and hopped from his chest. Jason could now see Fletcher smiling down at him, coming closer to him until their lips met and Fletcher inserted his tongue into Jason's cum-filled mouth. Jason released the dripping cocks in his hands and put his arms around Fletcher, holding him tightly as the boys continued licking every part of his available body.

. . .

Later, in Fletcher's canopied bed, after a shower and a soak in the hot tub, Jason turned to his host, who was lying beside him, and asked, "Weren't you taking a terrible risk setting all this up? What if I hadn't cooperated? What if I had fought you off, even tried to hurt you in some way?"

"You weren't able to do any of those things. You were powerless and greatly outnumbered," Fletcher replied smiling. "And I knew from the first time I met you that you could be seduced under the right circumstances. It was in your beautiful eyes, in the way you moved your hands, even in the way you walked. But I was so clumsy that night in our apartment. I let my eagerness get the better of me and drove you away. Tonight I was determined to make the most of my second chance."

"But was it worth it? The limousine, the elaborate dinner, and all those boys acting out their parts in your elaborate orgy?"

Fletcher drew Jason into his arms. "Of course, it was worth it. I wanted your first time to be memorable. I've never stopped loving you, Jason. Or wanting you. And after tonight I hope I'll be able to express that love from time to time, in and out of bed." He kissed Jason's cheek and threw his naked leg over Jason's, an invitation to further dalliance.

As Fletcher kissed and tongued his way to Jason's stiffening cock, ready again for action, Jason relaxed into the moment, aware that he would see Fletcher again, that what he had discovered about himself this night would demand attention and satisfaction in the future. He would remain married, fulfilling his role as husband and father. After all, he did love his wife and children, and he was responsible for them. But he would play another role as well, one that Fletcher had cast him in and one that he now accepted, even embraced, a little frightened but thoroughly fascinated by this new and exciting dimension in his life.

He pulled Fletcher to his lips, kissing him tenderly, appreciatively, then swiveled his body to take his new lover's cock into his mouth as his own cock was being suckled lovingly. Yes, he thought, as he began to explore Fletcher's impressive prick with his tongue, this is what I want, and this is what I can and will share. Fletcher and his boys had turned his life around. And he was in their debt forever.

THE FULL TREATMENT

Keith Davis

"Submissive, attractive young men interested in having their ass and bush shaved by an older, attractive daddy-type, call Mike at... "

I figured with summer on its way, I needed to get a light pre-Fire Island trim. I like to look my best. You know me: I'm just one of the kids in the bar with a fake ID. Like most of 'em, I don't give anyone the time of day. If I'm low on cash, I'll take the drinks that someone will buy me, but that's it. I won't let an old leach sniff my big boy-dick in the toilet, let alone allow his dirty hands anywhere near my cherry hole.

When I arrive at Mike's, I find he's forty-five, bearded and hairy, with a brawny physique that puts my gym-built body to shame. Oh, daddy! I'm thinking, standing here at the threshold with my mouth open.

"So, uh, you have permission to enter, boy," he growls.

"What?"

"Come on in, kid."

"Oh, yeah... Sure."

Tom of Finland prints, hot drawings of hung, muscular, macho men submitting to other men, decorate every wall.

"You want a beer?"

I am admiring the pictures. "What?"

"A beer, kid. Beer? I see we're going to have to work on your manners."

"Oh, sorry. A beer would be great." Then, as an afterthought, I add "Sir."

Why not give the daddy a little of what he thinks he'll get from me? I take the beer and kick back. Mike pulls out what is at least a dime bag, and begins to roll a joint.

"You smoke dope, kid?"

"Sure."

"You want to smoke my fucking dope? You want to be in my fucking house? You start showing me some of the goddamned respect I deserve. You got that?"

I jump at the force of his words and, in spite of myself, I say,

"I'm sorry, Sir. It won't happen again, Sir."

Growing up without a father around, I've always wanted to call a man "sir," if I could find one I could respect. Mike lights the joint, and I begin to tell him what's what. "You can shave my ass, but I just want a little trim around my cock." Mike just stares at me, so I quickly add, "Sir."

"Well, fucker, first I gotta see if you're worth my time." He barks, "Strip, faggot."

Worth his while? Guys of all ages drool over my bulging basket and bubblebum. Many have been in my face, too, fucker. I've seen others trying to sneak a peek at my cock in the john. Well, shit, I can't blame the old bastards, or him. I'd wanna see me naked, too. So, I peel off my T-shirt and 501's, and stand before him in my swelling jockstrap. Faggots love that. Nothing gets them hotter than a young jock like me, trying to restrain the monster between my legs with the thin cotton fabric of an Ace jockstrap.

I turn around, pretending to fold my clothes. I want him to get a good, long look at my backdoor. Mike's a cool dude. I might let him sniff around a bit there. Maybe I'll let him stick his tongue up my chute. It's clean. I always use an enema before going out.

Suddenly, Mike slams me against the wall. The wind gets knocked out of me, and I can't speak. I feel a cold, steel blade against my back.

"Motherfucker," I think, "you'll be sorry."

I realize that it's a straight razor, and Mike's cutting my jock strap off me. He backs off, and I spin around. I start to speak when I see him holding my jock like an Injun's scalp, and I'm awed by the sheer balls it took to do that. I say nothing.

"Next time, boy, when I tell you to do something, you'll do it quickly. Won't you, boy?"

"Yes, Sir."

"Put your hands behind your back, boy."

I obey immediately.

"When I ask you for something, what do you say?"

"Yes, Sir."

"That's right, fucker. Seems to me you've had a lot of trouble with that. Well, until you learn to speak respectfully, you won't speak at all."

With that, Mike stuffs my own jockstrap in my mouth. The smell of my own crotch fills my nostrils. I can taste the pre-cum that I leaked onto the pouch.

"You don't move while I set things up." Mike disappears into the bedroom. I think I should bag, but I don't move. Standing naked in this man's apartment, chewing on my own funky strap has given me a rod of steel. A thick dribble of dickjuice dangles from my cock.

Mike re-enters. "Glad to see you didn't move, fucker." He snaps a leather dog collar around my neck. "You're wearing a collar now, boy. Do you know what that means?"

I shake my head.

"It means you belong to me now. You're my property, so get any of those fucking pretty boy 'I won't do that' fantasies out of your head. Is that clear?"

I nod.

Mike snaps a leash to the collar and leads me like a dog to the bedroom. My mind is reeling from the smoke and the collar and the jockstrap in my mouth. Mike's bedroom is lit by at least 100 candles, with mirrored walls multiplying it into the thousands. I glimpse at myself, and feel both ashamed at being treated no better than a piece of meat, yet proud that a mature, macho man like Mike deems me worthy of his attention.

In the corner, Mike unsnaps the leash and lowers me back into the sling hanging from the ceiling. I've never been in one before, but a sling immediately feels like the most natural place for me. My legs are spread and raised with my hands above my head. I feel at home.

Mike looks perfect in his leather harness and chaps. Both tits are sporting large, heavy rings, and between his legs is the biggest cock I've ever seen. Now, I've been with many hung studs, and seen plenty of porno flicks, but never have I seen such a monument to mankind. Mike is a stunning pillar of flesh, deserving of adoration and worship.

I snap out of the hypnotic stare as Mike slaps hot water and shaving cream on my ass and prick. The straight razor scraping across my asscrack replaces any fantasies of servitude with concern about how I'd appear tomorrow in the locker room.

I mumble with my mouth full that I wanmt him to be careful.

Mike pulls the jock from my mouth. "What the fuck did you

say, boy'?" He grabs my balls – tight – and begins pulling and twisting them.

"Owww! Please stop. You're hurting me," I cry.

Mike begins pummeling my dick and ball-sac. "Who you talking to, boy? I know you're not talking to me. Not like that."

I'm not talking, now. I'm screaming. "Please stop! Please stop smacking my dick."

Mike just hits me harder. My cock glows redder than usual as Mike punishes the underside of my shaft. Tears well in my eyes from the punishment my manhood's taking. The breath goes out of me as Mike lands a good one on my ball-sac. Jesus, what does he want? I resign myself to letting Mike use my pole as a whipping post. I figure I'll play his game. Mike brings his hand down hard on the head of my dick, and I scream out, in both pain and pleasure, "Thank you, Sir. May I have another?"

"What did you call me, boy?"

"Sir."

"That's right, boy. I told you I'd teach you some respect." He begins to massage my stinging cock. I'm strangely proud that I can take his abuse. Just as I'm lulled back into some sense of security, Mike grabs my cock and balls at the base and twists them. He then starts rubbing the flat end of the razor along my dick. "Now, boy, we're going to discuss these family jewels."

I'm terrified. Mike is staring me in the eye, and not watching what he's doing with the razor.

"Now, boy. Who do you belong to?"

"You, Sir."

"That's right, boy. And if you belong to me, who do these family jewels belong to?"

"You, Sir."

"Very good, boy. Now, then, it is not your decision how much hair I shave off, is it, boy?"

"No, Sir."

"All right, then. Let's get back to work."

With that, the thick black bush I'd begun sprouting nine years ago begins to hit the floor. I watch the tufts of hair disappear from around my perpetually hard cock. I realize that I'd best not fuck with this guy. That's for sure. I don't know what he'd do if I tangled with him. I figure I am in no position to disagree with a sharp razor.

Hairy balls and a full bush are the privilege of manhood. With the disappearing curly strands goes the sham of my manhood. But I can't argue. I don't care. I'm in a situation in which I've never been before. I'm not in command. I'm getting forced into servitude to a man. But in an odd way, I experience a sense of relief. Giving up my selfish wants might just not be too bad.

Mike has finished denuding my pubes, and is carefully shaving my pits. "Tell me how you feel, boy."

"I'm scared, Sir." I decide that answering truthfully would be best.

"You want to stop?"

"Not really, Sir."

"That's my boy." He pats my head, and I can't help grinning. "Shit, you're tight, boy."

"No one's been there before, Sir," I say through clenched teeth.

"You mean you've been waiting for someone like me to come along and open this up?'

"Yes, Sir."

"You want me inside that ass of yours?

"It's not my ass, Sir." I decide it best to keep playing his game.

"What?"

"It's yours, Sir."

Mike grins. "You're a fast learner, boy." He gives my ass a good hard pull, "Yells, I'm going to enjoy this piece of meat."

I'm nervous now about his intentions.

"Well, you know your Daddy would never do anything to hurt his boy. He loves his boy and wants to take care of him. Don't worry, son, that boy-pussy of yours is going to see a lot of your daddy's manmeat. But for now, I'm going to take it slow."

Mike reached onto the table next to me and grabs a white latex glove.

"Like I said, boy, your Daddy would never hurt you. I'm always safe."

I carefully watch as Mike stretches the latex over his massive right hand. My butthole quivers at the thought of any one of his massive digits trying to get back in.

"Before we get started," Mike says, "we've got to do something about those tits of yours."

I look down at my nipples. They look ridiculously small and childlike compared with the masterpieces on Mike. My pecs are big, but my tits could never sport the manly jewelry Mike wears.

"These are from a snakebite kit," he whispers as he slips the suction cups onto my nipples. "They'll help your nipples get nice and big in case we, I mean I, decide I want to pierce them later," and he slaps at my cock, "or that."

To help me relax, Mike brings me a can of Bud, and another joint. "Don't get the idea I'm going to be fucking serving you all the time, boy. But since this is your first time, it's going to be special."

I close my eyes and try to will myself to relax. The booze and grass help lull me to accept what's coming. My frame of mind still fights the submissive position in which I find myself. I can only take what Mike decides to give me. I feel the cold, wet lube smearing against my pucker-hole. I realize that I will no longer have a man's asshole. After today, I won't be calling it that. Boy-pussy. Fuckhole. Boy-cunt. That's what Mike's gonna turn my asshole into. Boy-pussy, that's me.

"Yeah, I'm gonna fucking love this," Mike purrs.

He thrusts his middle digit into my hole. It hurts like hell. Mike's not content just to fingerfuck me. Once inside, he thoroughly explores my anus, bending and twisting inside me. I writhe as Mike jabs pleasure points I never dreamt existed.

"What are you thinking, boy?"

"Thank you, Sir! " I could think of nothing else to say. I felt Mike stretch my hole a little wider.

"That's two fingers you got inside you now, boy. You like that? You like giving up your little ass to your Daddy? You enjoy being his fucktoy and spreading your hairless little asshole for me?"

"I love it, Sir. I love it!" And strangely enough, I do.

Suddenly, I feel Mike's fingers abandon my hole. For so long, I've been proud that no one has penetrated my booty. Now, I feel such emptiness. I try to speak but can only cry, "No."

"Don't worry, boy. I'm just putting on some more lube." He shoves his gloved hand under my nose. "Smell your pussyjuice, boy." I wince.

Mike slaps my face a few times.

"Pussyboy, come to my house and not show me the respect I deserve. Look at you now."

Mike slaps me again.

"Not so cocky now, are you? What would all your friends say if they could see you now?"

He smacks me again and again, as I observe my skin begin to redden.

"How'd your mama like to see her little boy acting like a fucking slut pussy-hole?"

"I don't care, Sir," I whimper.

"I'll make you care. I'll send you home to mama, and your fag friends."

"I don't have a mama," I cry. "Only a Daddy, Sir. And that's you."

"I'll bet you're sorry you didn't show your Daddy respect."

"I'm not sorry for anything. I have to be taught. Teach me more, Sir."

"What do you want, son?"

"Use me. I want you to use me. Please do what you want to me, Sir."

Fingers penetrate my hole. My face gets smeared with lube and funk.

"You love that feeling don't you, boy? You love your Daddy being inside your ass."

"It's your ass, Daddy. It's your property, and you can do whatever you want with it, and with me."

"You want another finger?"

"Yes, Sir."

"I want it, too. That's four fingers I got up your butt. Bet you never thought you could open up so wide. Oh, yeah. You're opening up nicely, boy. This is your destiny. This is what you were born for."

"Another finger," I scream. "Please, Sir. Another finger."

"You want all five up there?"

"Yes, open me, Sir. You have to. I was born for this."

"That's my son."

Five fingers! From a virgin to five fingers in one night. I don't care. I don't regret it. In fact, I am beginning to enjoy my role.

Maybe I've wasted my time being a top. And here I am – shaved, slapped, and slinged. I never have really felt more alive, or more at home.

"You've got five fingers, boy. I'm really proud of you. I didn't think you'd take that many the first time."

"More, Sir. Please, more."

"What does Daddy's little boy want? You want me to fist your ass? Do you want your Daddy's big manfist all the way inside your little boy-butt?"

"It's your butt. Fist it! Fist it! Make me a fucking whore for your hand."

The pressure is so fucking intense. My ass strains. It's not going to work. My ass is too small for his massive hands. But it must work. I close my eyes and I remember what I have become – a slave. This will be my lot in life from this day forward. I must serve my master well. With that, my sphincter relaxes, and the last of Mike's knuckles pushes past into my intestines. Mike's now in me up to the wrist.

"Oh, fuck, yeah, boy. You did it. Your first fucking time. I'm fistfucking you, boy. I got my hand all the way inside. You feel that, boy? You feel your Daddy's fist inside you?"

I begin to cry. Is it happiness? Is it my loss of pride? I grind my slave-ass onto his fist. I want it up to his elbow. Nothing has ever felt so good. No sensation has ever been so intense. No subjugation has ever been so complete. Then, without warning, and without me touching it, my nine inches of thick, beautiful boycock begins spurting rope after rope of thick manjuice. Glob after glob hits my filthy fag-face. I taste my own seed, as a thick, sweet spun lands in my open mouth.

"I'm sorry, Sir." I whimper. "I didn't mean to. Please forgive me. I didn't mean to come . . ."

"Don't worry, boy. I was just working you from the inside. Bet you didn't know I could make you do that. You've got buttons and glands you don't even know exist in there, boy. They're just waiting for me to use and abuse."

I'm shaking. My body is hairless. My face is smeared with tears and cum and bunjuice. Mike's fist still sits inside me, splitting my cheeks open. My worthless sphincter muscle is stretched to the breaking point. With his free hand Milce scoops up my slimy jism. He puts it under my nose. What else can I do? I lick Mike's hand clean of my own scum. This is the only nourishment I need - except for my daddy's love.

I quit school. What need was there in completing my education? Anything I need to know, Mike tells me. Though it is not my place, I feel proud when we walk into a bar. Mike is dressed in full leather, and I'm clad in as little as possible - except for the red hanky in my right pocket. I love it when people look at me and know that I'm a fistfucking slut. Mike now owns my hole, and has stretched it wide open by long sessions of punch fucking. My nipples, too, are larger now, and they sport large metal rings - just like my cock. Ocasionally, we see one of the friends I used to know. They just look away - in embarrassment, but with a little awe.

I still see others drooling in the bar, as their lustful eyes draw across my hairless body. Some still glare as they ogle my young meat by the urinal. I still won't give anyone the time of day. I belong to one man, now. I'm his property, but don't despair - just ask Mike. It's his ass. If he wants to rent it out to any fucker, I can't say anything. I don't like it, but it's not my decision. I wouldn't have it any other way.

TRUCKER'S SPECIAL

William Cozad

On my way home from college for spring break, I pulled my clunker into the truck stop just off Interstate 80. I figured truckers knew where to get good food since they could stop almost anywhere.

In the cafe, I was out of my element. I must have stuck out like a sore thumb with my college-boy drag of baggy short pants, oversized T-shirt, baseball cap turned around backwards and high-tops. The other guys at the counter were much older, wearing jeans, plaid shirts and boots.

I ordered the trucker's special from the menu. It was only a hamburger and fries with a salad, but it was greasy and delicious. I washed it down with a soda.

Sitting at the counter, I heard some of the truckers talking about "smokes" stopping them, checking their manifests and logs, and about the loads they were hauling, from tires to almonds.

The waitress was a friendly older woman. Maybe she thought I was a trucker's son. I remembered a joke on campus about a new law that all truck-stop waitresses had to have at least three teeth. She was at least four ahead of that requirement.

While I ate, I listened to the music playing on the jukebox, country and western singers like Johnny Cash and Willie Nelson, songs about loneliness. Most country music seemed to be about a man with a pickup, a dog and a broken romance. The sound was a far cry from the rap music that blasted from stereos in the dorm, about offing the cops and street "boyz" hanging out in the 'hood.

It was time to be on the road again, like Willie was singing now on the jukebox. I still had some miles to cover and my folks were expecting me. But I didn't think they missed me that much, not as much as I'd missed them. At home it was like my younger brother Jimmy was an only child. It was springtime and the track season. Jimmy was the star runner. I used to tease him that running was for horses. I was kind of jealous from all the attention he got, his picture in the paper and everything.

Coming home from college, I was still an eighteen-year-old virgin. Probably the only boy on campus who was, from the stories I heard, but most of those sounded like bullshit. My roomie was a regular Don Juan, a legend in his own mind. He even put a sign on our door that said: "Do Not Disturb – Except To Party."

I paid my tab and stopped in the toilet next to the front door. The greasy food had made my stomach queasy.

I went into the middle stall because the other two were occupied. I tried to take a dump, but it was only gas. The man on the left side flushed and left without washing his hands.

There was a lot of graffiti on the wall. Shit like "Call Donna for a good time," with a phone number. "Here I sit broken-hearted, came to shit but only farted." Like me. "Blowjobs for truckers, call Al."

In the middle of the wall, I noticed a small hole. I leaned over and peeked through it. To my surprise, I saw a man who was masturbating.

I figured truckers got horny like anyone else, all those long hours tooling down the highway. College boys like me had to.be the horniest breed on earth. I had a perpetual hard-on it seemed. Sometimes I'd even whack off in the johns on campus to make my dick go down. It was difficult to schedule jack-off sessions in my room with my roomie popping in and out. At night, I succumbed to beating my meat under the covers, just like at home, so that I could get some sleep.

The trucker had to be the hairiest man I'd ever seen. I mean, his chest looked like a grizzly's and he had whiskers on his face. His dick was fascinating: long, thick and stiff, with a thin cowl of foreskin. He was a lefty pumper.

Watching him choke the chicken, spank the monkey, beat his meat, gave me a big boner. He stroked leisurely, rolling the skin over the crown and wiping away the seeping clear pre-cum from his piss-slit with his other hand. Then he jerked his prick fast and furious.

Suddenly, he stared at the peephole and caught me watching him. I bolted upright on the throne.

"You're just a chicken-boy. Look kinda tasty. Watching Big Daddy pleasure himself. Maybe you'd like to feel my big dick."

I was shocked by his words. No one had ever spoken to me that way in my life. I didn't know whether to shit or go blind. I thought I should leave but my hard pecker begged me to stay.

"I'm sorry, sir. I just wondered if you were all right, from the noise you were making."

Before I realized what I was getting myself in for, the big, hairy man knelt on the floor and showed me his huge, hard dick up close from under the partition.

There was no one else in the toilet. Through the crack in the stall door, the mirrors over the sink gave a panoramic view of the room. But someone could come in at any minute and catch us. Like the highway patrol. I didn't want to go to jail like those guys in the paper, arrested for lewd conduct and homo activity in rest stop public toilets.

I'd fantasized about that scene myself. College boys didn't do it for me. Like it or not, I knew I was gay and I was attracted to older men like some of my profs, but they were not interested in my charms. Not only that, I thought blue-collar men like my dad were the real men. That hairy trucker was beefcake to me, as much as a girlie mag centerfold was cheesecake to straight boys.

For the first time in my life, I was faced with real temptation. To make it worse, I had the biggest stinking hard-on I could remember.

"Go ahead, feel it, baby. Feel Daddy's boner." The hairy trucker waved his big meat under the stall at me.

Without even thinking about it, I reached down and grabbed the big, uncut dick. It was hot and rubbery. I frigged the skin over the crimson, glossy cockhead.

"Oh, yeah. Jack it," he moaned.

I tugged on the turgid prick and goo bubbled out of the piss-slit.

"Kiss it, baby. Kiss Daddy's dick."

I was stunned by the request, which sounded more like an order with the trucker's deep, husky voice. It was one thing to touch a man's dick, but quite another to kiss it.

What the hell was wrong with me? I'd been waiting all my *life* for a homosexual experience. The fuzzy trucker was like a Greek god to me. Why did I hold back? Jesus, if I let myself go, I could suck every trucker's dick in the cafe, have them line up at the door to my stall.

My instincts--my horny urges--took over. Kneeling on the dirty tile floor, I cupped those big, hairy trucker nuts with one hand while I kissed the bloated, blushing crown which turned purple. I tasted the tangy cockcheese and lube.

"Lick it, baby. Lick Daddy's dick."

Sticking out my tongue, I swabbed the satiny crown, licking off the cheesy residue.

"Suck it. Suck it for Daddy."

I did it. Opening my mouth, I engulfed the head and gobbled up the shaft until I almost gagged.

"Oh, yeah, baby. That's great," the trucker groaned, "suck Daddy's dick."

All these "daddy" references seemed weird, but they excited me. Like we were related and loved each other. Even if my real pop never showed me much affection. When I graduated second in my high school class, he only shook my hand. The boy who got top honors – because he took only the easy courses – was hugged and kissed by his father. Again I felt like a loser in my dad's eyes. To him, only being *numero uno* counted. Like when Jimmy won the state prep mile as a junior. I was as jealous as Baby Jane.

With a real macho man's big dick in my mouth, I felt like a champ. He wanted me. Even if I was a gangly college freshie without a jock's muscular body. And I wanted him.

Suck the big guy's dick I did. I laved it with spit. I gorged on his drooling dick. I gobbled up as much of it as I could, greedily sucking away like I'd been doing it all my life.

The trucker pulled his dick out. I was real disappointed.

"Easy with the chops, baby."

"I'm sorry, sir. It's my first time." I was ashamed.

"I thought you was a greenhorn. But hey, that's okay. You're a little doll. Get Daddy's engine revved up again. Suck on his balls."

I'd do anything he wanted if he'd only let me get my mouth on his throbbing dick again. Somehow, I managed to stuff both of those dangling, hairy balls into my mouth. I sloshed them around until he groaned with delight.

Spitting out his nuts, I got my mouth back on his towering prick. I sucked slowly at first, doing my best not to graze my teeth on his stiffer.

When his dick got hard as a rock, he clamped his big, hairy paws on my head and humped my face. I thought for sure I'd be choked to death. His was indeed the dick of death, but what a way to go. Somehow I hung on while he battered my tonsils with his ramrod.

"Oh, baby, here goes! Take it all, baby. Swallow it! Swallow this trucker's wad!"

I thought I'd shot some big wads. *Holy fuck!* The trucker's cock went off like Old Faithful, a gusher of the creamiest spunk you could imagine. It tasted like buttermilk and left a scum ring in my throat. But I liked it. I liked it because it was the big trucker's jizz.

All of a sudden, the outside door to the crapper flew open, then the inner door.

I hopped back up on the throne. It took the trucker a little more time. But the two beefy truckers who entered didn't seem to notice. In the mirrors, I watched their big rumps while they whizzed in the urinals near the sinks. They left pronto.

"Whoa! That was a close call. Dangerous, but you're worth the risk. How'd you like to see my truck?" My anonymous partner offered.

"Yeah, I'd like to." I was so hard it hurt.

I stuffed my stiff dick into an upright position in my short pants.

I left the john with the big, hairy trucker. He was in his mid-thirties, but that's old to a teenager like me. He told me his name was Sam. I noticed the silver wedding band, so I knew he was married. I was surprised when he told me his oldest boy was about my age. He was a cross-country trucker, an independent.

Sam was a giant, about six-two, well over two hundred pounds. He had brown hair and the bluest eyes I'd ever seen. Like Sinatra's, they lit up the room. He was from the East Coast.

Out on the blacktop, I walked with him to the rows of big trucks parked just inside the truck stop, near the frontage road. His rig was red with chrome wheels, a tractor and trailer.

"So what are you hauling?" I asked.

"Dynamite, so don't light that cigarette," he joked.

"For real?"

"Just teasing," he chuckled. "Actually it's container cargo from the Orient that I picked up in Seattle. Electronic gear, which I'm taking down to L.A. before getting a load to take back to New York."

"You like trucking, huh?"

"Been doing it ever since I got out of the Army. Whatcha wanna be, kid?"

"I'm in college, I dunno." This was beginning to mirror all the conversations I had with my dad about my future. I was anxious to get into some more action.

"Well, you got plenty of time to decide. C'mon, climb into the cab."

I'd never been in a big truck before and was fascinated by it, all the gauges and the CB radio crackling.

"This is somethin' else," I said.

"Wanna see the sleeper?"

I nodded.

"Go ahead. Climb back."

That's what I was hoping for, some more sex. My nuts were full of cum since I hadn't taken time to wank off before leaving campus.

Climbing-back into the sleeper, I was followed by Sam. He gave me a bear hug like I never had before.

Right away, he started stripping off my clothes. That's what I wanted, to show Sam my smooth, teenaged body. I already knew that I made him hot to trot. I could tell by that lusty look in his blue eyes.

There I was in all my naked glory, posing for the appreciative trucker.

"You're a beautiful boy. Natural build. Cute as can be. Didn't expect you to be hung so big."

"Runs in the family, I guess."

I didn't say it but I was secretly pleased that my dick was bigger than my jock brother's, if only by an inch. Once we'd measured them on a bet, while horsing around.

"Your butt, that's the prize. It's perfect."

Sam took my hand and placed it on the lump of dickmeat in his denims. I squeezed and kneaded it until it was stiff. Then I unzipped his fly and freed his cock. The crown was out of the hood and the curved, veiny shaft throbbed.

I felt so vulnerable naked while Sam was fully dressed, but I knew he wouldn't harm me. I trusted him totally. He was a nice guy, a family man. Just lonesome out on the road. I knew the feeling, being away from home for the first time.

When he rolled me over onto my belly, I wasn't sure what to expect. I figured maybe he'd like to give me a blowjob. Boy, would I ever like that. Of course I was on the wrong side for a blowjob, being on my belly, unless he sucked me from behind with my butt up in the air.

Looking over my shoulder, I watched him. I got bold.

"Unbutton your shirt, Sam. Let me look at that hairy chest, like you had it open in the toilet."

He grinned knowingly and opened his shirt, letting my eyes gaze on his fuzzy chest.

What Sam did to me I never expected.

"That's some ass you got, kid."

With his big, callused paws, he spread my fleshy ass cheeks. Then he dove in with his tongue. He lapped at my crack, slurping and slobbering on it. My whole body shivered. His beard stubble grazed my cheeks and that sensation aroused me even more.

Coming up for air, the trucker stuck his middle finger all the way up my tight, lubed hole. I moaned and squeezed his finger with my butthole.

"Tight, cherry hole. Primo boy pussy."

It didn't take long for me to realize what Sam had in mind. I was about to get my cherry busted. I wanted it, true. But I was plenty intimidated by the size of that monster trucker dick that Sam was fisting when he mounted me.

I cradled my head in my arms. I couldn't watch. He'd split me in two with that massive, uncut pecker.

Straddling my thighs, he slapped his boner against my smooth buns. It felt like a red-hot poker. I could feel sticky cum oozing from his piss-slit.

When he pried open my rosebud with that club swinging between his legs I let out a bloody scream. I couldn't help myself. The pain was searing.

"Relax, baby. Let Daddy in. You'll like it, once you relax your ass. Push back at it, that'll make it go easier."

I did what he said but I thought I'd die.

Soon, I was moaning while Sam was grunting and humping my boy-butt. The pain vanished and it felt as pleasurable as an itch being scratched when he humped me.

Backing up on his giant prick until I felt his brown pubic hairs scratch my buns, I moved around underneath him and bucked back.

"Fuck me, Big Daddy. Fuck me hard!"

Knowing that I could take it and wanted it, Sam crammed my ass with cock, with his bull-nuts slapping against my tender ass cheeks.

It was the most pleasurable sensation I'd ever felt. Knowing that I was pleasing Sam and could get him off with my tight boy-butt made me determined to do so.

While he prodded lustily, I clenched my butt muscles around that monster meat that relentlessly slammed into me.

"Oh, baby, you got the best butt I ever fucked! Gonna get me off. Gonna make Daddy blow his wad!"

Without warning, it just happened. My boner had been rubbing against the mattress but all the sensation seemed to be in my ass. That's when my hard dick started spurting ball juice. At the same time, my butthole spasmed around the trucker's dick.

"Oh, baby, here it comes!"

If I thought Sam flooded my throat earlier, he now flushed his nuts deep into my guts.

When he pulled his dick out, my butthole was sore and throbbing. He kissed my crack, then licked my hole clean with his tongue – it was wild.

Before I left, I had to do it. Turning around, I dove into Sam's hairy chest and licked it with my tongue. I even sucked on his big nips. He held my head against his chest and kissed it, giving me the love and attention I'd wanted all my life from another man.

Although it had been the most joyous experience of my life with the hot trucker man, it made me sad, knowing I'd never see him again.

THE TOUCH OF THE STRANGER
The Further Adventures of the Saint

John Patrick

Wilbur sat by the azure sea and it seemed the air shimmered, a kind of blurred, fractional movement, like a heat haze, making the boy in the dunes appear as if in a vision.

"Or is it my eyes?" he thought.

Wilbur had been coming to this beach three times a year for longer than he cared to admit. He always brought books with him, from the spring, autumn, and summer best-seller lists, and always he brought a companion. He had just picked up the phone; there were always boys ready to flee Boston for Florida, if the price were right. But the last companion, Johnnie, was so deeply into drugs that he became uncontrollable, disappeared the day after they arrived and, as far as Wilbur knew, hasn't been seen since. No, this time he had decided he would sample the local offerings.

Wilbur got up from his chair and walked towards the boy, who was adjusting the crotch of his sky-blue Speedo. Wilbur had been here for a week no one had paid him any attention. Nor had he seen anyone who truly excited him. Now a godlike young stud was walking directly toward him. No, Wilbur's eyes were not deceiving him. This was no apparition. Wilbur didn't mind the obviousness: he knew where he stood. However, the boy merely nodded at Wilbur as he passed and broke into a sprint for the water.

Wilbur watched the boy dive into the warm water of the gulf and begin swimming. The boy was a powerful swimmer. Wilbur shrugged and returned to his place on the beach. The boy swam for several minutes and then, just as Wilbur became absorbed again in his book, a figure was blocking the sun.

"Got an extra towel?"

"Why, yes," Wilbur said, reaching into his beach bag. "I was saving it for you."

"Thanks," the boy said.

The towel covered the boy's face and permitted Wilbur's eyes to feast on the boy's nearly hairless swimmers body, and the abundant crotch directly in his face.

"Wow," Wilbur said under his breath. Wilbur could make out the head of the penis, and some of the shaft, as if the cock was semi-hard. Maybe it was, Wilbur thought, the idea of driving an older man wild somehow appealed to this kid.

"There, that's better," the boy said, dropping the towel to the sand and spreading it.

Wilbur was immobile in his lounge chair, staring, a benign smile on his face.

"My name's Terry," the boy said, extending his hand.

Wilbur introduced himself, using his now-preferred nickname of "Wil."

As Terry sat on the towel, Wilbur gulped. He was dumbfounded. He had never had anyone ingratiate themselves in this way, and wasn't sure what was expected. He picked up the book he had been reading. Terry noticed it, asked what it was.

"*Sexual Outlaw*, by John Rechy," Wilbur responded. "This trip I'm catching up on a lot of the old ones."

As Terry nodded and Wilbur handed him the paperback, the long plumes of the sea oats lined up behind them bobbed drowsily.

Soon Terry was scowling prettily into the sun, pretending to read the book Wilbur had chosen for him, waggling his toes in the sand. Wilbur, elegant and jaunty in his straw sun hat, stared down at him, and sighed. But they were getting so young, he thought, while admiring Terry's sculpted face even in its petulant frown.

The beauty didn't have to be here, Wilbur told himself, looking away momentarily. He could at any time be back in the city, in the world, with friends, and admired. Oh, how admired. "Yes, he would hate me," he thought, now looking at Terry with thirsty eyes.

Tourists swarmed and splashed and smiled around them and sometimes they stared, as if pointing at them, the slim man with his much younger companion, the beauty with the soft, angelic face. Wilbur smiled at them as if he knew them and he found they smiled back at him. Terry paid no attention, engrossed in the book. Wilbur pushed his hat over his eyes and lost Terry's face, but when he lifted it again, there he was again, like a sun over the horizon, glowing. Wilbur bit his lip, and looked away, then quickly back again.

Terry stretched his fine legs, elongated his spine, cattishly, for the world to see. It was as if he paraded his beauty.

Another group of tourists walked quickly past, self-conscious and stiff-necked.

"They're probably thinking he's young enough to be my son," thought Wilbur, "if I weren't so well-preserved." And he was. Wilbur had taken care of himself.

The smooth-limbed youth pushed himself up onto one elbow and lifted his head from the book with learned insouciance. Said Terry, "Gives me a hard-on reading about guys getting off." The bulge in his trunks lengthened and thickened, the plump, uncut head now peeping over the waistband. Wilbur's eyes widened.

A sudden salty gust stung Terry's legs with sand as he shoved his cockhead back inside the fabric. "My best feature," Terry snickered, seeing Wilbur had noticed. "Everyone says."

"Yes," Wilbur said, blushing and averting his eyes.

Now Terry rolled away from him, as if teasing him.

The smell of the sea, the chatter and fresh breeze faded, giving way to a heavy, tropical silence.

Finally, Terry rolled back towards Wilbur, asked the time. Wilbur checked his watch. It was nearly five.

"I've got to be going," Terry said.

"Me, too," Wilbur said.

Wilbur folded his chair and put his things in his beach bag.

They followed a path into the dunes, hung over by sharp, shiny fronds and almost concealed from the sky. The air was dank, and under their feet the ground was creepily soft. Strong, wet leaves brushed against their faces and arms; there was the noise of water dripping; the undergrowth rustled as they passed. Finally they came to a clearing and some parked cars. Terry had not stopped, made no move to leave the path, find a thicket where Wilbur could suck him.

They arrived at a new white LeBaron convertible. The boy stopped. "Well – " he started, allowing Wilbur his opening.

"Well," Wilbur stammered, "will you have dinner with me?"

Terry smiled as he unlocked the door of the convertible. "Of course."

Wilbur stood beside the car, his breath caught sharply in his throat. He held back his head and smiled up to the sun, in case tears rolled out.

As Wilbur climbed into the passenger seat, he picked up the rental contract. Terry turned the ignition and "I'm So Excited" by the Pointer Sisters blasted from the speakers. Terry turned down the volume. Wilbur chuckled.

At Wilbur's condo in the tall building overlooking the beach where they had just met, Wilbur offered Terry the guest bathroom to shower and change. Wilbur went to the master suite and began undressing. When he heard the water running in the guest bath, his cock grew hard. It had been months, perhaps years, since he had been this excited. He started humming "I'm So Excited."

They went to the French Hearth, a cafe a block from Wilbur's condo. The same waiter Wilbur had taken a liking to showed them to their table. When the young man, whose name was Paul, saw Terry, he seemed to show new interest in Wilbur, even calling him by his name for the first time.

Once they were seated, Wilbur ordered a martini. Terry had a Perrier. As the waiter moved away, Wilbur said, "It's so strange – "

"What?" Terry asked, reaching for the bread basket.

"My vacation is almost over and I hadn't met anyone and now – "

"Now what?" Terry teased.

"Well, I'd given up, I guess. I suppose it's an ethereal thing. When you seek it out, you get nowhere, get nothing." He nodded. "Yeah, it's an ethereal thing."

"Little do you know," Terry chuckled, "just how ethereal."

As Wilbur sipped his martini, Terry said, "You look so sad sometimes."

"I haven't been well."

"Oh?"

"Yes, depressed. My entire department was laid off. I was moved into another position. I'm secure, but the – "

"You had a whole department?"

"I'm in computer programming. All forty people were out of work in a day. Corporate downsizing they call it."

"I have heard of that. Where I come from they call it greed."

"And where is that you do come from?"

"Oh, here, there, everywhere."

"Very mysterious."

"Yeah, guys like that."

"I imagine. I mean, I know."

Terry buttered his bread. "So you are sad."

"Been sad. I should have taken the whole department and set up my own company."

"Why didn't you?"

"Oh, I'm too old to do that now."

"You're never too old – for anything."

Wilbur shook his head. "If you say so."

Terry smiled. "If I promise to go to bed with you tonight, will you start your own company and take those forty people with you?"

"What?" Wilbur couldn't believe his ears.

"That's all I ask."

"You're kidding, of course, but I just don't know. If you think I could do it – "

"I *know* you can do it. Trust me." Terry reached his hand across the table, touched Wilbur's. The hand lingered, toyed, teased.

Wilbur smiled. "Somehow I do. I can't figure it, but somehow I do."

Over the next hour, here with Terry, Wilbur found his anger, his thwarted spite, had gone and that he felt instead a kind of longing, an exquisite, gentle longing for sex with this beautiful boy. His cock stirred in spite of himself.

At the end of the dinner, Wilbur ordered French champagne. Paul brought it grinningly. As Terry filled and refilled Wilbur's flute (he took nothing for himself) his hand roved up and down his own empty glass and he fixed on the older man those startling, greenish blue eyes. It seemed the boy was desiring him, as much as he desired the boy, and the gesture stripped him of years more surely than his hair dye had ever done. Finally, Wilbur took the bottle from Terry and let their hands touch when he filled Terry's empty glass.

As the waiter brought the check and hovered at their elbows, Wilbur noticed Terry showed no interest in Paul. His eyes were only for him.

When they left the restaurant, the streets teemed with people, young, ardent, untouched, all of them, and the men and women alike were sleek-haired and shining with youth. With Terry at his arm, Wilbur was in splendid isolation, as if in a dream.

At the condo, Wilbur sat on the balcony with his robe half open. The wind was lower, the moon swelling in the indigo sky, the air sticky, balmy with a steady beating heat. For the first time in months, Wilbur had an erection that would not go down. It seemed he was drugged. The touch of the stranger had made him high. His bare feet danced on the warm rose tiles. The lazy slap of the waves, the murmuring in the trees, the sound of Terry taking another shower lulled Wilbur into a euphoric state.

Terry had a towel wrapped around his waist when he came onto the balcony. Saying nothing, he guided Wilbur into the master suite, sat him down on the bed. Wilbur stared up at him as if he'd never seen him before, biting back his full lower lip. Terry, looking at him intensely, reached his hand and hauled it to his sex. Wilbur's fingers trembled as they were invited to touch the incredible hardness. Terry lifted Wilbur's chin, commanding him to look at his face. Terry bent and gave Wilbur a kiss, the tenderest kiss the older man had ever known.

Wilbur smiled, then gasped as he stroked the sizeable cock through the terrycloth towel. Terry loosened the towel and let it drop to the floor. Wilbur moaned in appreciation and buried himself in Terry's crotch, enfolding himself, losing himself in its great heaviness.

"Oh," Terry cried softly.

Tears ran freely down Wilbur's cheeks, his mouth gaping, choking on, drinking in Terry's eight inches of uncut cock.

In the noise of the night, of the waves, the far-off fading

music and murmuring of the trees, Terry kept saying "Oh," with occasional gasps of indrawn breath. This was followed by Wilbur's full and choking, "Oh, God."

After a few minutes of sucking, Wilbur begged Terry to put it in him. Wilbur wanted it from behind and got on his stomach on the bed. Terry poured himself into the older man, arching over him, quite lost, as Wilbur gasped beneath him. His ass was incredibly welcoming. Wilbur could not help it. Terry's plunges hurt him, taking him by the scruff as if he were a rag, shaking him.

After a time, Terry's breathing changed, became regular, quieter, listening. Then, panting a little, he tensed briefly inside Wilbur. Terry lifted Wilbur and clutched the older man's erection. Wilbur's eyes widened in acquiescence. Both of Terry's hands were coursing and roving – Wilbur's stretched body working, busy, frantically coming. Terry's movements become faster and more frantic, feverish even, his head thrown far back. His right hand continued to play with Wilbur's now-spent cock. Wilbur's hand covered his. Terry's kind, strong hands, laid on a warm, hard place, had pleasured Wilbur. Terry's head remained thrown back and his eyes tight shut, as if possessed. He came again, groaning.

When he was capable, Terry disposed of the condom and lay down beside Wilbur, facing him. Their sweat had begun to cool and they got under the covers.

"I don't think I've ever come together with somebody the first time," Wilbur said. He burrowed his face into the curve of Terry's collarbone.

"You were good. So good, I want some more."

Wilbur shook off his tiredness and leaned over to examine Terry's prick, which was hard again. He was soon sucking continuously – licking, drinking in the sweetness. Drunk from the taste, he desperately took the entire shaft into his mouth and buried his face deeper and deeper into the reddish pubic hair.

As Wilbur ravenously devoured him, Terry began fingering his own asshole, then fucked himself with one digit, then two.

Suddenly, Terry let out a loud moan. He grabbed Wilbur's hair. Bucking wildly in deep pleasure, his entire body shuddered as he entered into another orgasm, moaning, "Yes, baby! Oh yes, baby!"

Wilbur continued to suck madly on Terry's throbbing prick. Barely able to breathe, Wilbur sank his entire face back into Terry's crotch, hardly conscious of anything else but the delicious tangy taste, the musky inviting scent. This was it, heaven, as far as Wilbur was concerned. It had been a most unbelievable night.

But it was not over. Now Terry wanted to get fucked. Soon he was on his back on the bed, his legs spread, jacking his cock.

"Come on," Terry whispered.

"Oh, I can't. I haven't done that to anybody in years."

"Oh, come on," Terry begged. "Give me that big dick."

Wilbur did have an erection, the hardest erection he could remember. He knelt between the outstretched thighs, and began applying grease to Terry's anal lips.

"That's right," Terry was moaning.

As Wilbur entered him, Terry said, "Oh, that's just what I want."

Wilbur could not believe how hot Terry felt as he allowed the head to lie in the throbbing anus. "Go ahead, go ahead!" Terry pleaded, and Wilbur sunk his fat, hardened prick all the way in. Now Wilbur was crying, "Yes," half breathing and half whispering in Terry's ear, echoing him. Wilbur's heart was pounding, almost into his throat, it seemed. He finally remembered to breathe deeply. He inhaled and shook everything he could muster through his shoulders and down the length of body. No, he would not hold this energy in his body any longer. He would fulfill his own pent-up desires at last.

He held the firm, freshly showered ass in his hands and fucked it. If there is a Creator, he thought, he's enjoying a good laugh over his awkward gyrations – or perhaps their chance meeting was really a Blessing. Damned if either of them knew now top from bottom, or cared for that matter, but rather Wilbur knew only that Terry's palms and manicured nails were playing all over his skin. It felt so surreal.

"Is it okay?" Wilbur was foolish enough to ask. He was beyond surprised to find Terry so ready to be fucked, to use his knowledge and skill as a top and a bottom for the purpose of

Wilbur's pleasure.

Wilbur backed up to look at Terry again, the strong shoulders, the tight pecs, down his muscular stomach to his again burgeoning crotch. Suddenly Wilbur's equilibrium faltered and his cock slipped from the hole. He held Terry's body still and shoved it in again, then began long, hard surges. He would no longer be scared of it. If this boy wanted to get fucked, Wilbur was ready.

"God, it's so big," Terry moaned.

Wilbur had forgotten just how big he was. He remembered the days, years ago, when the guys at the baths begged to suck it. But nobody ever wanted it inside them the way Terry seemed to. Wilbur could now feel Terry's ass twitching to keep the cock in him.

Terry grabbed Wilbur's asscheeks to force Wilbur in all the way. Wilbur was thrusting madly and surprised at his own strength. Terry's lips were inches from Wilbur's, his eyes searching with a fierceness.

"So you want me, eh?" Wilbur cried, then kissed Terry, so hard it almost seemed as if he was trying to absorb Terry's beautiful face into him, as if he felt beyond any hope of relief.

Suddenly, Terry's body tensed, and he gripped Wilbur, throwing his legs around him, locking him in.

Terry began grinding his face into Wilbur's, kissing him into fierce, demanding thrusts of release. To Wilbur's bursting delight Terry was making him come harder and harder.

"I can't stop," Wilbur cried at last, rocking and coming and lifting Terry with all his might. Terry bucked against him and that made Wilbur surge one last time. Terry was completely locked around him, and he rolled over on top, easily pinning Wilbur, and he kissed him violently on the mouth.

Wilbur was completely exhausted. He thought he must now be dead. He felt merely a ghost of himself, weightless. His mouth was open and wet on Terry's smooth chest.

Terry pulled away and Wilbur watched as the buttocks rose, perfect moons lighting the dim, two cool scoops of vanilla ice cream. A faint hiss rose from between them.

On the way to the bathroom, the image in the mirror stopped Terry. Wilbur could see the reflection and Terry appeared rosy, perfect, more beautiful than ever before. Not a religious man,

Wilbur was stunned to find himself whispering a prayer of deep thanks for their short time together.

He looked up to see Terry gazing intently in his direction behind a radiant almost-grin, and then he vanished behind the bathroom door. Presently Wilbur fell asleep. He dreamed vaguely of music that, in the dream, had a very important and perfectly obvious meaning but faded away and could not be recalled when he later tried to translate it into words.

Dawn light, rose-hued and clear, filled the bedroom of the spacious master suite. Wilbur frowned at the empty space beside him and eased out of bed. He threw a robe around himself and went through the condo, looking for the boy. The air was cool and silent, the rooms empty.

He returned to the bedroom, stared at the bed as if Terry might have reappeared during his search. Then he noticed the two hundred-dollar bills were still on the bureau where he had left them for Terry.

Wilbur went out to the balcony and looked down at the parking lot. The convertible was gone. Wilbur blinked. No, he thought, it *did* happen. The boy *was* here. It *wasn't* a dream. In seeming desperation, Wilbur called the boy's name, and a soft, cool breeze from the direction of the dunes touched his sun-burned face.

– *The Saint first appeared in* Runaways/Kid Stuff *and visited another mortal in* Lover Boys.

THE REFUGEE

John C. Douglas

"Refugee: one that flees for safety."
Webster's Dictionary

I saw him when I was still twenty feet from my big black Buick sedan. Evidently he had just climbed into the car and was ducking down behind the back of the front seat. I got only a glimpse of blond curls and a near-naked torso, but my trained eyes registered a girlishly-pretty face, and a pair of dainty nipples on a perfectly sculptured, hairless chest. He looked to be about fifteen, maybe younger. The skimpy cutoffs hugged a deliciously large basket, and my imagination filled in the details.

Christ, the kid must be freezing. A cold, late November wind whipped down the almost deserted avenue of the once-posh neighborhood, dropping the chill factor to near zero.

I had parked almost directly opposite the liquor store, and glancing to my left, I saw the faded sign on the front of a time-worn, three story brick building with barred windows: HOLY GHOST CORRECTIONAL REFUGE, REV. CARL MATTINGLY, DIRECTOR.

In my business, you have to learn a little about a lot, and a lot about a little. Either that, or you learn what it's like to be dead, and that was a bit of info I wasn't ready for. But I had heard a few rumors about Mattingly and his so-called refuge, all bad. According to gossip on the street, the preacher forced some of his charges, boys from five to seventeen, to do whatever he wanted, especially the very young ones. There were also reports that he farmed the boys out to some highly placed politicians.

I shifted the heavy sack to my left arm, feeling the comforting pressure of the holstered magnum against my ribcage, and fished the car keys from my overcoat pocket.

Opening the Buick's trunk, I wedged the sack between two large suitcases and closed the lid. The metal was like dry ice.

I heard them approaching, and watched their movements out of the corner of my right eye. There was a heavy blanket and several packages on the car's rear seat, and I hoped the kid was smart enough to hide himself. I instinctively knew that the approaching pair was looking for him. I turned to face them.

It wasn't hard to figure which one was the preacher, even if I hadn't seen him on television. He was a dapper, not unhandsome man in his late thirties or early forties. The other guy could have doubled for King Kong. Big, ugly and obviously mean.

"Open it up!" he growled menacingly, waving a huge paw at the trunk.

"Go fuck yourself, shithead!" I said in a flat tone. Ugly took a step toward me, giving an animal-like growl.

The preacher placed a restraining hand on an arm only a little larger than my thigh.

"Peace, Wilbur," he urged in a quiet, oily tone. "Let's ask the man nicely."

Turning to me, he said, "Forgive my friend, won't you? It's just that he's terribly worried about a young man who has wandered away from our little fold."

"Your friend had better worry about losing his teeth," I grated. "Where did you find this ugly son of a bitch, anyway?"

My words had exactly the effect I intended. Ugly shook himself free from the man's light grasp, and lunged at me like a demented bull.

It was too easy. I quickly sidestepped and brought my right hand down across the back of Ugly's neck as he sailed by. His own momentum and my added blow carried him face-first into the heavy rear bumper of the Buick. There was a gratifying sound of smashing flesh and shattering teeth before Ugly slid to the pavement. He didn't even have time to grunt.

"Oh, my!" Mattingly exclaimed, his hands raised as if he expected me to attack him. "What have you done?"

"Removed an obstacle," I answered, poking the body with the toe of my shoe. "When he comes to, put him on a shorter leash. The next guy may not be as patient as me."

Without waiting for a response, I climbed into the Buick, keyed the ignition, and pulled away. In the rear-view mirror, I saw the preacher writing down my license number.

Two blocks down the street, I said, "You can come up, kid. I don't think anyone's behind us."

There was a flurry of movement, and the blond curls appeared in the rear view mirror, followed by a sensuously pretty face. Full lips parted for the tip of a moist tongue.

"What did you do to Wilbur?" the boy asked in a breathless voice. "My God! I was afraid he'd kill you when you called him that name."

I shrugged, patting the seat beside me. "Climb up here, kid," I suggested. "What the hell was going on back there?"

There was a glimpse of smooth, young flesh, slender legs and narrow hips, as the youngster crawled over the back of the seat and settled his delightfully curved rump beside me. I felt an overwhelming rush of desire as my eyes drank in the sight of those exquisitely shaped thighs, revealed by the denim cutoffs almost to the bulge of his crotch.

I'm highly partial to young pretty boys, and this kid was a real beauty. In the light from the dash, his full lips glistened, moist and inviting. His belly was smoothly muscled and the well-developed pectorals sported a pair of mouthwatering nipples.

"The preacher was fixing to give me a beating," the boy explained. "But I got loose and jumped out a window before he could call Wilbur in. That's why I ain't got nothing on but these shorts. I was about to freeze till I saw your car was unlocked."

He peered at me in the semi-darkness. "You ain't gonna make me go back, are you?"

Instead of answering, I asked, "What's your name, kid?"

"Randy," he answered readily. "It's really Randolph, but I hate that."

"I'm Bill," I grinned. "Bill Lawson. No, Randy, I'm not going to send you back to that place."

He slid closer on the seat, his thigh pressing mine, and my prick jerked impatiently. I took one hand off the wheel and dropped it almost casually onto his left thigh, my fingers curling about the exquisitely curved smoothness.

To my delight, the boy let his knees drift apart, as if inviting me to explore between those lovely legs. I had to force myself not to slide my hand upward.

"Can I stay with you, Bill?" he asked hopefully. "I ain't got nowhere to go."

"Where are your parents?

"They just took off," he shrugged, "about two months ago. They got into drugs and stuff, and I guess they got tired of having me around. Some damn social worker took me to the preacher, and I been there ever since."

"Why was he going to beat you, Randy?" I asked. I still had my hand on his leg and now I felt his fingers cover mine, squeezing gently.

"Me and Greg - he's my buddy - was fooling around, and the preacher caught us." he said innocently.

"Fooling around?"

"Yeah, you know, feeling of each other." He hesitated. "You think that's wrong?"

"Is that all you were planning to do?" I demanded. "Just feel of each other?"

He hesitated. "No. We was gonna do it to each other, but the preacher caught us before we could."

"Had you and this Greg done it before?"

"A few times. Not really done it. We never did really do it to each other. This time, we was gonna really goin' all the way."

"You mean you've never done it at all?"

"Just a few times," he admitted. "And I've . . . you know . . . played with myself a lot. I've always liked boys, ever since I was just a kid." Again he peered at my face, and his fingers tugged at my hand, trying to pull it higher on his thigh . "Do you like boys, Bill?"

My fingers curled about a surprisingly large bulge between his almost naked thighs, and the boy pushed his hips upward to increase the erotic contact. I felt a surge of lust.

"Yes, Randy," I said, and noted that my voice was suddenly very husky. "I like boys. But, you don't have to do anything just because I pulled you out of that mess back there."

"That ain't why I asked," he said carefully. "You're a good looking guy and you're nice."

I forced myself to take my hand away from his crotch, but his hand stole into my lap and groped for the bulge he found there. He drew a sharp breath.

"Holy shit!" he exclaimed. "Is that for real?"

"It's real." I assured the boy. "Think you can handle it?"

He gave my prick a gentle squeeze as he answered, "Hell, yes! It's just what I've always wanted."

I enjoyed the feel of his warm hand for a moment before I asked, "How old are you, Randy?"

"Old enough to know I want some of that," he replied, his fingers searching for my zipper. "In this state, they can put you in that damn place unless you're twenty-one." He turned toward me and used both hands to slide the fastener down. His right hand slipped inside the fly and found its target.

"Damn! That's a big dick!"

I moved my hips cooperatively as he fished it out of my trousers. The shaft thrust up past the rim of the steering wheel, the head dark in the dashlight. Randy's fingers worked the uncut foreskin up and down, capping and uncapping the glans.

He bent over, his cheek rubbing my chest, and I shifted my right arm from the wheel to his bare shoulders, urging his face down toward my rearing cock. I felt his warm moist breath bathe the sensitive tip.

"Christ, kid!" I groaned. "Are you sure you want to do this?"

"Yeah!" His voice was muffled, for he chose that moment to press his parted lips against the head of my prick and run his tongue over the slitted tip, flicking it across that delicate triangle just below. "Ummmmm!" he murmured.

My hips pushed upward and his mouth claimed my cock. Hot wetness surrounded the throbbing head and slid down the thick shaft, his tongue swirling against the ventral vein as he drew me deep into his throat in one delicious engulfment.

"Jesus!" I groaned. "You know how it's done!"

Technically, he was probably too young. But a stiff cock doesn't have a conscience, and if Randy wanted to suck my dick, I wasn't about to deny him that pleasure. To do so, considering his obvious hunger, would constitute child abuse.

I ran my fingers through his blond hair and forced his head up and his mouth off of my prick.

"I'm on my way to my vacation cabin, Randy," I told the boy. "The preacher took down my license number, so it's just as well we're not going back to my apartment. Want to spend a few days with me?"

"Can't I suck you off now?" he asked plaintively. The boy had a one-track mind.

"It'll be a lot better," I said, "if we're both naked and on a bed. Okay?"

His fingers gripped my dick and he kissed the head, wetly and noisily. "Okay!" he agreed. "Man, your cock tastes good! I could suck on it all night!"

Reluctantly, the boy freed me, and I managed to work the big shaft inside my trousers, not bothering to zip up the fly. It was only twenty miles to my mountain cabin, and the roads were deserted, letting me give the big Buick its head.

His full name was Randy Prescott, he told me. His parents were both hooked on drugs and alcohol, and hated him because of his sexual bent. And he insisted that he was older than he looked. Eighteen, but he couldn't prove it, which was why they locked him away in the so-called shelter.

"They call me queer and faggot," he said angrily. "Then the old man rents my mom out for money, enough for another hit." "You're okay for now, Randy," I said, giving his bare thigh a gentle squeeze. "Later, we'll see what we can do to get you straightened out."

"Right now," he murmured, "I want to be your boy, Bill. I want to do everything you want me to."

I wheeled the Buick off the sideroad and onto the narrow lane that led to my cabin. The headlights parted the darkness like rolling back a black curtain.

A mile from the road, the cabin perched on a gentle slope, and I parked the car behind it.

"Let me get the heater fired up inside," I told the lad. "You stay here where it's warm."

I took a flashlight from the glove compartment and rounded the cabin, unlocking the door and flicking the switch inside, flooding the large room with light.

It took only seconds to ignite the gas heater and the heat began chasing the bitter cold from the place.

I plucked a heavy parka from a wall hook, and carried it out to the car. I opened the door and handed it to the boy.

"Put this on, and wait for me inside. I've got some stuff in the trunk."

In spite of my protests, he waited and carried the heavier of my two bags, while I retrieved the paper bags and the second suitcase.

Inside, we deposited the bags and faced each other, our eyes exploring and his arms going about my neck as he pressed that slender body against mine. His warm sweet breath bathed my lips as he tilted his face up to be kissed.

"I feel safe with you," he said. "Jesus! The way you got rid of old Wilbur! How did you do that?"

His lithe hips gyrated, rubbing the hard bulge of his prick over mine. I clasped his shapely ass with both hands and pulled him even closer.

"In my business," I said, my voice husky, "you learn a few tricks."

His eyes widened as he said, "You a spy?"

"No," I lied. "Nothing quite that glamorous.

His arms went about my neck again, and he shoved his hips against mine, his face tilting up invitingly. "I'd like to stay with you," he said, almost whispering.

Slowly, deliberately, I kissed that delicious mouth, and began working his shorts down over those slender hips. The boy responded by undressing me, while between tongue-swirling kisses, we made our way toward the bed. I pushed the naked kid down onto the bed, and straddled his waist, my big cock thrusting up over his chest and lower face.

Leaning forward, I braced my hands on the headboard of the bed and arched my hips over his excited features. He licked his lips, his eyes almost crossing as he stared at the head of my cock, and he opened his mouth wide when I lowered my hips and inserted the oozing tip of the prick between his even teeth.

I gasped as I felt his tongue lash the head of my dick and his lips tighten about the shaft, beginning a rhythmical nursing that sent shivers of pleasure back to my heavy balls. With a groan of ecstacy, I pushed my cock farther into the boy's mouth.

I was not getting a virgin. This kid knew all there was to know about sucking a dick, and he was putting all of his knowledge to use. Not only was he letting me fuck his mouth, Randy was actually lifting his head to meet my thrusts to make sure that he got every inch of my shaft, which meant that he was taking nine inches of hard dick down his throat and not gagging.

There's nothing that feels any better than ramming the head of your cock down a boy's throat and feeling it spasm, all hot and wet. It makes you want to just hold it there, but you can't do that without choking the kid.

But Randy could keep it lodged there for several seconds, and while it was there, he actually swallowed, making the slippery tissues squeeze and massage the head of my dick. It felt so good that I had to cry out, and it made me fuck his mouth even harder, my balls slapping his chin and throat as my cock slid in and out between those greedy lips.

"I'm gonna come, Randy!" I gasped, my hips pounding his face. "Take it, kid! Take it!"

My balls seemed to turn to liquid and come spurting out of the tip of my dick. My semen spilled into Randy's mouth, jetting against his tongue and palate, for I pulled back to let him suck as I shot my load.

The boy grunted as he claimed the creamy load, gulping audibly as he swallowed the ropy sperm. His tongue lashed the spitting knob, and he sucked eagerly as volley after volley bathed his hungry throat.

He was in no hurry to release me, even when he was sure that he had the last drop of my cum. He sucked gently then, knowing that my prick was sensitive, and I eased it in and out a few times to let him milk it, just in case there was one final surge of orgasmic thrill left in the still-hard shaft.

Finally, slowly and reluctantly, I raised my hips and drew my cock out of the boy's mouth, hovering over his pretty face as he gave the head one final caress with his warm, wet tongue.

"Ummmmm!" he murmured, his hands stroking my ass, and his breath caressing my glans. "That was good, Bill! You really know how to fuck a guy's mouth. Most fellows are afraid to ram it in. But that's when it's good."

I slid down between his legs and lowered my chest to his, tasting my own cum on his lips as I kissed him, long and deep, our tongues dancing and probing.

"You give good head, Randy," I whispered into his open mouth. "If you can fuck like you suck, I just may keep you around a long time."

"I hope you do, Bill," he whispered back. "I want more of that big dick! Any way you want to give it to me!"

"Let me get some K-Y on this!" I said, starting to lift my hips.

His hands grasped and held me in place. "No, don't use anything! Just put the big thing in!"

On knees and elbows, I stared down into his pretty face. "I don't want to hurt you."

"I *want* it to hurt!" He lifted his legs, his knees almost touching his chest, offering that shapely ass. "Fuck it!"

"No way!" I said, rubbing the head of my cock against his anal circle. It was tempting, but I honestly did not want to harm the eager boy. Some men get off by deliberately hurting their partners, and some kids like to be hurt. That's a matter of personal preference, and I try to avoid it. I found myself reaching to the bedside table, opening the drawer, and withdrawing a tube of lubricant. With one hand, I snapped the cap and squeezed a glob of the jelly onto my cock, smearing it about the head and down the shaft. I tossed the tube aside and touched his thigh with tenderness.

"Now," I said, my voice husky. "I don't want to hurt you but I want that ass! Spread your legs!"

Eagerly, he rolled onto his belly, his slender and perfectly shaped legs parting as I knelt between them and guided my cock into position.

He didn't wait for me to put it in. With a soft cry of excitement, his hips thrust upward, forcing the lips of his asshole onto the head of my cock. He was tight, and even with both of us pushing, it was an effort to force the flared rim of the glans past his protesting sphincter.

"UHHHHH!" he cried as the swollen knob snapped through the spasming ring and into his waiting colon. "OHHH, GODDDD!"

It was obvious that the boy had never taken a dick as big as mine, and it was equally obvious that, even though I was giving him all he could handle, Randy was loving every inch of it.

I didn't try to get it all in. Just enough to enable me to begin fucking that hot, tight asshole. I pulled my cock almost out, making him gasp as it frictioned the tender membranes and massaged his prostate, then drove it in, even deeper than before.

"HUUUUNNNHHH!" he yelped as I explored new territory, and his hips writhed beneath me, his rectal muscles convulsing as I again pulled back until only the head remained inside his anus. Then, in again, all the way, my balls pressing his as I short stroked him, keeping my cock deep inside his ass, and fucking him with little jabs that made him cry out again and again as my dick rubbed those tender tissues. But they were cries of pleasure, and Randy was clawing at the sheet and grinding his hips to make sure he felt every inch of my prick.

"You like being fucked," I grunted, hunching in and out of the writhing youth. "Don't you, boy?"

"Yessssss!" he hissed, his rectal muscles tightening each time I pulled my prick back for another thrust. "It never felt that good before. All I ever done it with was just kids. Your cock's so big!"

I love to watch a boy's face while I'm screwing him in the ass, and though Randy's head was turned and his face was half buried in the pillow, I could tell that his lips were drawn back from clenched teeth, and his pretty face was contorted with strain and passion. Now and then, his eyes would close tightly, and he would work his ass in a grinding circle that made it feel as if his rectum was chewing on my cock.

I must have fucked him for five minutes without letup, driving my dick to the balls and pulling it back until only the head remained inside him, again and again.

"I'm gonna come, Bill!" he panted, his whole body quivering with the thrills spreading out from my massage of his prostate gland, and the frictioning of his nerve-laced anus. "I can't wait!"

"Not yet!" I grated, quickly pulling my cock out of his asshole and urging him onto his back. "Pull your knees up, Randy!"

His legs lifted and I hooked one with each arm, gripping his slender ankles and spreading his limbs wide, working my hips about until the head of my prick found that hot little circle again.

"UHHHHH!" he yelped, for I plunged into him all the way to my balls, filling his ass. "OOOHHH!"

I fucked him hard and fast, driving my cock in and out with savage thrusts, making him cry out each time I slammed up into his spasming colon, my balls bumping his tailbone.

"Here it comes, Randy!" I gasped, feeling the first delightful spasms deep in my belly.

"Give it to me!" he half-screamed, his hips writhing as my prick swelled and jerked inside him.

His own dick, almost touching his chest in the curved position of his body, quivered and bobbed, and I felt his asshole tighten as a glob of cum jetted from the swollen cock.

"UUUNNGGHH!" he keened, his hips twisting and bucking as I shot my load into his butt, and he spilled his own semen onto his quivering belly.

It was well past midnight when I let him take a hot shower, then fix a couple of tall bourbons while I felt the stinging spray wash the residue of our frolic from my own body. Then, we sat across the table from each other while he told me about the so-called shelter, and I began making plans to blow the whistle on Mattingly and his crew.

"I want to suck your dick again, Bill," Randy said hopefully, his eyes bright.

"How about a little sixty-nine?" I suggested.

His smile broadened. "You don't have to."

I nodded. "I know, but I want to."

We polished off our drinks, and I stood up, waiting on the boy to join me. Soon he was pressing that warm body against mine, his arms about my neck, and that hot, hard prick jammed between my thighs, my cock pressing his warm belly.

Our mouths fused, tongues swirling, and our hips writhed to massage our dicks as we kissed. Then, more eagerly than before, we entered the bedroom and scrambled into position on the big bed, each claiming the other's prick in fierce hunger.

Tomorrow, I promised myself, I would get the boy some clothing, and stake him to a fresh start. For the present, however, that writhing body required my full attention.

IN THE BOY ZONE

Jesse Monteagudo

My name is Perry Hibbert. I joined the Social Services division of the Fort Lauderdale Police Department in 1976, when I was fresh out of college. In addition to a law enforcement degree I have degrees in psychology and social work. This makes me uniquely qualified for my position, which tries to reduce crime by curbing its causes. Consequently, though I carry a gun and a badge, I never wear a uniform.

No sooner had I gotten through my training period and settled down than I was summoned by Captain Floyd Bucket, the bald, portly, middle-aged head of my division. I found Capt. Bucket behind his desk, smoking a fat cigar and glancing at a thick dossier that lay before him. He waved at me to sit down and, having done so, he tossed the dossier at me.

"What you see before you, Hibbert, is the combined report of the department's vice squad, juvenile division and beach patrol. Those guys can't stand each other but they worked together on this one. Do you know why?"

"I don't know. Free tickets to the Dolphins' game, maybe?"

"Very funny. Do you ever go to the beach?"

"Sometimes. I burn easily, though."

"Then you might know that the beach is crawling with young male prostitutes, hundreds of them, some as young as fourteen. The kids come here because it's Fort Lauderdale, Spring Break and all that, and they stay because they get hooked on drugs and can't afford to go back home. They in turn attract queers from all over, who are itching for some young stuff. The kids give the johns their dick or ass in return for money to buy drugs, chicks, clothes or what have you. And they keep coming down faster than we can arrest them, or chase them away."

"It seems our reputation precedes them."

"Exactly. In fact, the strip at Fort Lauderdale Beach is known all over the world as the Boy Zone, which is how it's advertised in all the gay papers." Bucket pulled out a New York bar rag and began to read from it. "Fort Lauderdale is the fun and *son* capital of the world. If you have a taste for chicken, come down to the Boy Zone, hang outside the Marlena Hotel, and wave a few dollars around. Before you know it the boys will *cum* your way." My boss dropped the magazine, as if to avoid contamination.

"You said you tried arresting them," I said. Picking up the rag, I began to glance at it. "Did it work?"

"We conducted a raid that would make J. Edgar Hoover proud. Arrested a whole bunch of them. But then some big shot lawyer came over and claimed the kids were 'abused youngsters' from 'broken homes' who weren't really selling their bodies but just looking for a place to stay the night. So the judge let them off with a slap on the wrist and a promise of good behavior. Good behavior my ass! Instead of going to the youth shelter the way they were supposed to, they went back at the Zone the very next day, doing what they were doing before." My boss expressed his disgust by blowing a ring of smoke in my direction. I put down the magazine.

"Did you talk to the Marlena Hotel management?"

"They claim they have nothing to do with the whole situation. But we made them nervous enough to start doing something about it, if only to save face. Now they "officially" keep hustlers out of the hotel. That's a laugh! If a john stays at the hotel all he has to do is walk outside, pick up a hustler, and take him up to his hotel room as *his* guest." But then the hotel's hands are clean.

"So what are you going to do next?"

"That's where *you* come in, Hibbert. The Mayor has been pestering me to try the "nice guy" approach so I guess I'll give it a try. I want you to go down to the Boy Zone and talk to some of the boys. Find out where they come from. Tell them we'll drop all charges if they quit hustling, go back home or to the youth shelter, and in short get out of our hair. If they need to, get them to join a drug rehabilitation center or go on welfare."

"Now you sound like that big shot lawyer."

"Well, he might have something there. Maybe if the kids get off the street, give up drugs and go back to school, then they might stop selling their bodies. It might work, and if it does, we'll get the credit for it." Bucket smiled, no doubt entertaining thoughts of an impeding promotion and a service medal.

"Hibbert, you are the officer who's most qualified to do this. You are an expert on social work, psychology and law enforcement. You wrote a thesis on teenage runaways that was praised all over. You are a young man, which would help you reach those kids. If anybody can do the job, you can."

"When do I start."

"Right away. I want you to talk to those kids, take notes, and report back to me. At least you'll keep them off the streets while you're talking to them. To make it easier for you, I'll get the vice squad to lay low for a while."

I nodded. The job, to say the least, appealed to me. My assignment would involve something I knew about, it was less violent than investigating crack houses or gambling dens, and it got me outdoors. Not waiting for a reply, Bucket continued:

"I want you to start with a guy named David Shaw. He's just nineteen, but he has been hustling since he was ten. Most of the kids look up to him as their leader and the ones who don't are smart enough to stay out of his way. He's been arrested a few times but always manages to get out. He's street-smart, savvy, and if you get him on your side your job is half done."

"What do you want me to tell him."

"Just tell him that if he gives up hustling, and works with us, we'll drop all charges against him. He'll help you get to the other kids. Working together, you two might clean up the Zone."

"Consider it done, Boss," I said, shaking Bucket's hand as I rose out of my seat. "It's off to the Boy Zone, to save David Shaw and Company from a fate worse than death." I was out the door before I could hear Bucket's reply. I was going to enjoy my job.

When I arrived at the Boy Zone that night, the place was hopping. There was not a woman in sight, and except for an occasional tourist or cop, the place was full of young hustlers and older johns. Except for their common interest in each other, the two groups had little in common. While virtually all of the johns were white, the hustlers represented every race and ethnic mixture. Most of the johns were dressed like me, in shirt-sleeves, pants and shoes, while the boys were largely attired in tight-fitting tank tops and shorts that left nothing to the imagination.

Though a couple of the boys cruised me, I managed to ignore them. I was in search of the elusive David Shaw, and with that in mind I walked over to the Marlena Hotel. I was standing in front of the hotel door, wondering whether or not to go in, when I was struck in the stomach by a short blond that came running out of the hotel, followed by a very angry hotel manager in hot pursuit.

"I told you not to come in here anymore! We don't want hustlers in here!" Doing my job as preserver of the peace, I grabbed the kid and held him in place. Dealing with the hotel manager was easier: I just gave him a stern look and flashed my badge at his face.

"Officer, you got do something about those hustlers. They come here and cause trouble. They rob our guests and beat them up."

I took a look at the young troublemaker, doubting that this skinny twerp could beat up anybody. But the man had a point. If they let this boy in they'll have to let them all in.

"Don't worry. I'll make sure this one doesn't bother you again." Though the hotel manager gave me a dubious look, he apparently took my word, for he turned around and went back in.

"Whatcha gonna do with me?" yelled the kid, trying like hell to get away. This only made me hold on to him even tighter.

"I am not going to do anything, not if you cooperate. Now come with me." Wishing to avoid a crowd, I pulled the kid out of the main drag and onto a side street. We stopped under a street light. "Now if you know what's good for you you'll listen to me. What's your name?"

"Butch." Sure. And my name is Jimmy Carter.

"Listen, Butch, or whatever your name is. I want you out of the streets tonight. Go to a youth shelter. Here is the address." I gave him a card. "Now, if you know what's good for you, you'd go there and spend the night. And tomorrow night you go back home."

"But I ain't doing nothing!", Butch protested.

"Sure you 'ain't.' And I'm going to make sure you 'ain't

gonna' do it tonight. But before you go, I want to ask you a question. Do you know a guy named David Shaw?" The mention of his name brought a smile to Butch's face.

"Sure I do. He's right behind you!" With that the kid shot out like a rocket, out of my hands and down the street. Startled, I turned around, only to come face to face with David Shaw.

I was surprised. Where I expected an underfed urchin I found a hunk of machinery. Shaw was taller than I was, over six feet tall, and had a powerful, muscular build. He had long red hair that went down his back; fair, freckled skin; green eyes, an expressive nose and sensuous lips. He looked like Huck Finn on steroids. Like most of the hustlers at the Boy Zone, he wore a tight tank top, even tighter shorts, socks and gym shoes. A bulge in his crotch promised untold pleasure.

"What do you want from me?"

I showed him my badge. Shaw was obviously a take-charge, no-nonsense kind of a guy, a world away from punks like Butch. Only a strong man could survive in the dog-eat-dog world of the Zone. Though just nineteen, David not only survived but prevailed. He was regarded by the other hustlers with awe, by the johns with fear and desire, and by the police with trepidation. Though my feelings were decidedly mixed, I hid my emotions and began my spiel.

"I'm Perry Hibbert. I was sent by the department to clean up the Zone. They told me you were the one I should talk to."

"Why me? Why should I talk to you?"

"Because you are the one who can help me. Because if you don't I might have to arrest you." That gave him pause. At best it would make him listen. At worst, it might make him want to beat me up, at which time I hope I would be able to deal with it.

"Come with me." I followed David down the street to a small apartment building. Entering the building, we went down the hall to an efficiency apartment located near the back. David turned on the lights to reveal a sparse, undecorated room, with a bed, a table and two chairs which we proceeded to sit on.

"The owner is always out of town. He lets me stay here and I let him suck my dick once in a while." Not a bad deal. I decided to get down to the point.

"Listen, you're a big shot to the other kids here. You can do a lot for them. Get them off drugs. Off the streets. Back to school." That sounded corny, even for me. David just laughed.

"You're kidding! Those kids ain't gonna do what I tell 'em. And *I* ain't gonna do what you tell me!" This was going nowhere, so I changed the topic.

"Why do you hustle?"

"I hustle because I'm good at it, and because I got a hot bod and a big dick! There's no man around who wouldn't want to swing on my dick. Even the straight ones. Even you." As if to make his point, Shaw stood up, unzipped his shorts and pulled out a huge, uncircumcised sausage that was at least ten inches long. I was speechless. Shaw smiled as he stroked his cock to a full erection.

"That's okay, Officer. You can play with it." As I stood up, David grabbed my hand and placed it over his now-erect genital. "You like it, don't you? Now, let me see you play with it!" Before I knew it, David had me down on my knees, face-to-cock with his enormous organ. The sight of David's powerful prick, and the strong, masculine smell that flowed out of it made me lose all self-control. My own cock stood erect inside my pants.

"I knew you were a fag," said David, as he noted my own erection. "Now suck my cock. I know you know how to do it, you fag." I took David's enormous *pinga* in my hand, pulled back the thick foreskin and began to lick the head with my tongue. Not satisfied, David pushed his manhood into my mouth, almost choking me as it went down my mouth and throat. David was in control, holding me down with his strong hands while thrusting his thick prick inside me with ever-increasing force. Just when I thought David might reach the point of no return, he stopped.

"Now take your clothes off."

We stripped. David's muscular body was covered with peach fuzz, and his pubic hair was as red as the long hair on his head. He had low-hanging balls; thick, muscular thighs and calves; and two beautiful, masculine feet that matched his cock inch by inch. Now naked, David sat down on the bed, his legs spread apart. I reached for his crotch but David held me back.

"Start with my feet. Lick them wet. Then work your way up

to my cock," he ordered. Here I was, an officer on duty, naked and on my knees in front of a young hustler. But I did not care. I craved David's monster dick and I would do anything to get it. I also craved young, masculine feet, and David's were the best I've ever seen. I took David's strong, right foot in my hand, and began to give his toes a tongue bath. David smiled as I made love to his feet with my grateful hands and tongue. I then began to work my way up, licking and massaging my young lover's powerful calf and his massive thigh. Before long I reached the object of my desire, and began to suck on it as if my life depended on it. But David had something else in mind.

"I want you to play with your ass. I want you to finger your asshole, loosen it up and get it ready for my cock. I'm going to fuck your manpussy, and I want you to get it ready for me!" His wish was my command. After licking my fingers wet with my spit, I reached back towards my waiting asshole. I played around the rim of my rectum with my fingers before I shoved one inside me. I fingerfucked my restless asshole, getting it ready for things to come, while I continued to swing on David's juicy manmeat. David's hard cock in my mouth, and my own finger up my ass, kept my own cock fully erect.

"Now get over here," David ordered, as he pulled me up and threw me face down on the bed. "Now I'm gonna to fuck the shit out of you!" He wasn't joking. No sooner had I hit the bed that I felt spit on my asshole and David's huge prick begin its massive assault on my tender rectum. I held on to the bed for dear life as my lover shoved his ten-incher deep inside my ass. Pain mingled with pleasure as David began his savage thrusts into my bunghole.

Sweat fell down our faces as David continued to ravage my manhole. David's long hair fell on my face as he held me tight, squeezing my tits hard as he pounded me with ever-increasing pressure. We were two young savages, indulging in the most primal of endeavors, man fucking man. I was no longer a cop/social worker/ psychologist on a mission. I was a willing sex object for a young dude, who used my ass for his own pleasure. As David's cock continued to pound my insides, my own dick pushed against the bed repeatedly, driving me insane with pent-up, erotic energy.

"Fuck me David!," I yelled. "Fuck me!"

Soon we were at the point of no return. With a savage thrust, David pulled me off the bed as he shot his manload deep inside my hole. I immediately took hold of my own throbbing cock, which I began to stroke with ever-increasing force. David held me in his strong arms as I shot my jism all over the bed.

"Are you still going to arrest me?" said David, as we sat down on the bed. He smiled. I smiled too.

"I guess not. But I'll tell you what I am going to do. I am going to tell the department that I spoke to you and that you agreed to work with me. But it's going to take some time, so it would be better if they let you and the boys alone for the time being. That would keep the cops away from you and your friends."

"And in return?" asked David, who already knew the answer.

"In return I want more of what you gave me tonight. I want your hot sausage in my mouth and in my ass, and I want it often. So what do you say?

"I'd say you're crazy. But it won't be the first time I 'paid' a cop to leave me alone. So go for it."

"It's all in a day's work," I said, diving into David's bulging crotch. And I am going to enjoy my job.

THE INTRUDER

Ken Smith

Brad bent and rubbed his ankle. He hadn't considered how high the branch of the oak tree really was. "That was some jump!" he muttered, sucking blood from his grazed leg muscle.

Momentarily, he was limping through the woods but soon his ankle was functioning again and he began to race up the steep, leafy bank; dodging between rhododendron bushes which were in full flower, sending wafts of their sweet perfume into his nostrils as he sucked in extra air in order to reach the summit.

From this vantage point Brad could view his kingdom of bushes, trees, flowers and ferns but the huge electricity pylons, cutting a swath through the woodland, spoiled the tranquil scene and their constant hum did not blend well with the singing birds and other sounds of the wildlife which surrounded him.

He would have very much liked to share his wooded paradise with a special friend but there was only a scattering of cottages in the vicinity, about twenty in all, and he knew of a couple with babies and one with young girls, but none had a boy.

It was a lonely life for a spirited youth, living miles from anyone his own age, but he was content playing in the woods, tracking down wild animals, and hunting for bird's eggs.

Occasionally, he would see strangers or local inhabitants out on country walks and would observe them from the tops of trees or from one of his many secret hide-outs.

Young lovers were often an excellent source of entertainment and he had seen, on occasion, how sexual acts between men and women took place; often becoming aroused and aware of his own sexual needs and desires. But, at his age, both sexes seemed to appeal to him.

Over the Easter holidays, he did invite one of his cousins over but he was a 'Townie' and, unbelievably to Brad, wasn't at all impressed by the countryside. When Brad had persuaded him to follow the herd on their way to the farm to be milked, his cousin found it quite repulsive.

Brad, however, found it fun as he skated in the fresh cow-pats, turning his green wellies brown with the rich-smelling substance. But even bird-nesting didn't appeal to his cousin who was scared of everything, even stinging nettles and brambles. Brad never invited his cousin again.

And Malcolm Pike, his best buddy at school, brought strange sexual feelings to the surface on certain memorable occasions, but Brad was not overly concerned about them.

It was such a scorcher of a day that Brad stripped down to his white briefs and lay on the leafy bank, sunning his slim but quite muscular frame; watching the birds cut across the blue sky above. A hawk in the distance held his attention for some while as it searched for food, every now and then falling like a stone onto its prey.

Beside him was a large mound belonging to a family of wood ants. Brad giggled as the occasional one strayed and ventured over his naked body. They didn't bite or sting and one particular ant had taken a liking to his navel, doing several circuits of the indentation before venturing down to his briefs and over his bulge; Brad keeping a wary eye on it lest it find a way beneath them.

Brad's slender young body was browning beautifully under the baking afternoon sun and for a while he removed his briefs, tanning the one remaining white part of his youthful torso. Perhaps slightly overdone, especially the freshly exposed skin, Brad decided he needed to cool down. Being the ruler of his kingdom, he was privileged to know places in the area that others would never know and secreted in the vast woodland he had many hide-outs.

But one very special place, known only to himself, was a clear pool supplied by an underground spring, and this was where he was headed. Brad loved to skinny-dip and the water was always crystal clear and now almost as hot as a bath.

Replacing his briefs but carrying his T-shirt and shorts, he headed through the maze of undergrowth passages, many of which were made by badgers or other wild animals and barely big enough for him to crawl through.

In one sunny spot, he stopped short when confronted by an adder. He knew to leave well enough alone but they weren't dangerous if not disturbed and would soon slither away. Cautiously, he moved around the snake, so as not to upset it, its tongue darting out in sharp jabs. Brad stuck out his own tongue, teasingly, as he passed, mimicking the adder, then disappeared down a steep slope, sliding on his buttocks and dirtying his pants.

After half-an-hour of twisting paths, steep climbs and even steeper slopes to slide down, he arrived at the welcoming water, a slight mist of steam hovering just above it. A sweet smell of pine cones had been trapped in the hollow and several half-eaten cones, which the squirrels had been feasting upon, lay scattered about. Brad sucked in the fresh pine smell before plunging into the pleasantly warm water.

Carefully, he washed the dirt from his pants before removing them (he didn't want to get into trouble with Mum), then hooked them onto a nearby twig to dry. Blissfully, he bathed in the four feet of water; ducking under several times, flattening his long, blonde hair against his head. The pool wasn't wide enough for a swim but about five strokes would take him from bank to bank.

For ten minutes he floated on his back watching a solitary, fluffy cloud make its slow journey across a clear blue sky. It was constantly changing shape: a ship, a face and then an animal. He wondered where it was headed and if it would survive its journey or evaporate.

As he lay, peacefully relaxed in his surroundings, his mind wandered over a variety of things, eventually settling on visions of Malc in the showers. He never knew why these thoughts happened but they often did. Predictably, he became aroused as sexual thoughts of Malc, and Malc with girls, surfaced and seduced him. For some odd reason, he never pictured himself with these girls; it was always Malc. This was perhaps due to the size of Malc's sex, so much bigger than his own. Often when they wrestled, he would find himself drawn to that area of Malc and would become aroused, wishing to touch it; and when they showered, after sports, Brad would bring his body close to Malc's, hoping for their soft skins to touch and observe Malc's penis grow larger as he soaped his body. Few other boys had this effect on him, but the boy who explained what sperm was and showed him how to get it was unforgettable. Brad would think of the boy and his gigantic sex often when he rubbed himself before sleeping.

Now Brad began to caress between his legs. He was slowly being pushed to the opposite bank and, suddenly, his head hit the leafy earth with a bump, startling him. He stopped his caressing, thinking someone had touched him and discovered what he was doing. He didn't think it was really wrong to stroke himself but somehow, touching that part of his body seemed naughty, something one does only in private.

Brad resumed his caresses while Malc moved in and out of his thoughts. He recalled the very first time he had come. He was thinking of Malc when suddenly there was a new, strange sensation, and he began rubbing himself faster and faster, his actions unexpectedly terminating in a stunning shudder. A small pool of liquid was lying on his stomach. With a look of absolute joy (as if he had created the universe), Brad yelped with delight, staring proudly at the wonderful, wet patch.

Now he needed a more secure base on which to perform his act. Easing himself onto the soft but solid ground, he began the rhythm once more. He concentrated on the one vision that never failed to get him off: Malc fucking Marie, a slut in the village. The idea that Malc would score with this older, previously married woman turned him on uncontrollably and release was swift in coming.

Jumping to his feet he raised his arms high into the sky and proudly shouted, "Yippee!", sending several birds to flight.

He leaped back into the pool and for about half an hour he splashed about, joyfully unaware of just about everything.

Eventually, climbing tiredly from the pool, Brad walked behind what appeared to be a large bush, opening a door secreted among its branches. The coolness of his secret cavern was welcoming and Brad moved over to a camp-bed, covered with dead leaves from lack of recent use, and flopped onto its stiff, canvas surface.

This was his favorite hide-out. There was an oil lamp hanging from the branched roof; a large tree stump doubling as a table or a seat; a rusty kettle but clean on the inside and tin mug. Since his last visit there had been added a large, blue towel. Brad screamed, snatching the offensive object from the branch on which it hung.

Holding the soft, cotton material against his body, he found he could hang it from his shoulders to his feet and it would wrap around him at least twice. It smelled fresh and unused as he rubbed it into his slightly sunburned face, filling him with a strange mixture of extreme anger and increasing excitement. Anger, because someone had discovered this very special, almost sacred, place. But the excitement - he didn't really know why, he just was.

Brad's heart quickened in his chest and he hadn't felt like that since climbing to the very tip of a pine tree, and on another occasion when Malc had got him in a head-lock, Malc's thighs pulling his face into an expanding crotch.

As his anger mounted he racked his brain as to who could possibly own the towel and how they had managed to discover this place. It definitely wasn't his cousins, he hadn't liked him enough to bring him here. Surely someone had discovered it, but who?

He thought long and hard on this and finally decided he would set a trap: He was good at that. A deep hole covered with leaves; and they would break a leg. Or something heavy over the doorway to fall on them and knock them unconscious. Or a spear, like in Indiana Jones; fired as they entered. But what if it was a girl? That was hardly a kindly thing to do to a girl, even if she had invaded his secret space. Even if she was slut Marie. And a grown-up might be too big a prey to handle. But what if it was a boy? That would mean a fight and he might be bigger and stronger than Brad.

Brad suddenly remembered his "safe" (as he called it) and quickly moved the large tree stump; sliding it to one side. Scraping the leaf-mould soil from where the log stood, Brad lifted a foot square piece of wood, revealing an OXO tin lying in the hollow. Kneeling in the soft earth, he lifted the lid on his most personal treasures. To most they were nothing, but to Brad they were special. Each having its own story: his first catapult; several old, lead soldiers; a magnificent multi-colored marble; a naked Polaroid photo of himself taken by the pool, by himself, last year. The objects seemed endless and Brad checked each, and, thankfully, none were missing. Reluctantly, he replaced the lid and slid the log over the wooden cover. He guessed they would remain safe and, anyway, he didn't really want to take them home.

The question was: What should he do now? Should he destroy the towel; weight it down with bricks and throw it to the bottom of the pool or, maybe, burn it? The whole thing required more thought and it was getting late. Disappointed that he had no immediate answers, Brad re-hung the towel exactly where he'd found it and headed home for tea.

. . .

Brad woke early this morning, a cool breeze of many scents wafting through his open window. The sun was beaming in a clear blue sky, the temperature already rising.

His beloved, widowed Mum had already left for work so he fixed himself breakfast of corn flakes, toast and black currant jam.

The towel again entered his mind and, as he munched on his meal, a plan was beginning to formulate in his young mind.

It was a breezy day and that would mean lots of fresh, clean washing hanging on lines. Towels, he guessed, came in sets. Somewhere in the area there would be a towel matching the one in his hide-out. When he had found it, he would have found the intruder.

It was likely to be a long hike, checking out the twenty cottages, so Brad prepared sufficient supplies of food for the strenuous day ahead.

Filled with breakfast and excited about his mission, he headed into the woods in search of the matching towel.

First he checked his hide-out. The towel was still in place and his tin hadn't been touched, so he set off through the woods.

Crouching behind a prickly holly bush at the first cottage, Brad watched a young lady hanging out her morning wash. The breeze quickly catching the clothing sent them fluttering like flags. He couldn't help giggling as she pegged out her panties and bra and almost broke into full laughter when a big pair of bloomers appeared, catching the wind like a huge, double sock at an airport. There were no towels in her wash so he headed onto the next cottage.

The second cottage was a very rich place with a fair-sized swimming pool. But Brad wasn't over-impressed and preferred his secret pool. The occupants were obviously too rich to do their own washing and there wasn't even a line, so he moved on.

As he approached an old, tumble-down cottage deep in a wooded hollow, he noticed something large and blue flipping in the garden. Excitement mounting, he raced down the slope, searching for a vantage point where he wouldn't be seen. Excitement soon subsided when he discovered the item was only a sheet, but he wondered if people had towels which matched them.

Brad's heart was quickly sent racing when a huge, hairy dog came bounding to the fence, teeth flashing beneath its curled lips. Brad almost fell over himself as he raced back up the slope, turning once to check if the dog was in pursuit.

Come midday, he'd covered about half the cottages, without success. Stomach grumbling from lack of food, he climbed halfway up a tree to sit with the birds while he ate a crust of crispy bread and chunk of cheddar cheese. He watched two squirrels playfully chase each other around the trunk of an adjacent tree as he finished his lunch.

Rose Cottage, his next stop, was a wonderful place; almost every variety of flower adorned this peaceful garden. There was no one home. Brad could have sat in the sweet scent all day and for a good fifteen minutes he'd almost forgotten why he was there. There was no washing out and had to be on his way.

He had a quick duel with a couple of bumble bees when they decided he smelled better than the pollen. Or maybe they were attracted to the sweat trickling from his armpits.

Vowing to come back again to Rose Cottage, he stole a couple of apples and a pear from the orchard and continued on.

By the time the sun had dropped to treetop height he still hadn't found a single towel matching that in his hide-out. But he reckoned by the washing he had seen he could calculate who and how many lived in each house, even the size of the people living there. He'd seen jeans, shirts, baby clothes, and even naughty bits (that girls and women wore).

Almost dejected with the failure of his plan Brad decided to make tracks back to the pool. He was boiling from all the walking and filth from climbing through some very tight tangles of bushes, brambles and branches.

He decided to take the pylon path back. It wasn't the most attractive route and noticeably noisy with their constant hum, but as most of the ground had been leveled around their huge, skeleton legs; it allowed him to make good speed.

In fifteen minutes he was at the top of the sharp incline leading down to the pool. It was when he was halfway into the ravine that he saw something move near his hide-out. Like a wild cat stalking its prey, Brad quickly crouched behind a thicket, his breathing increasing rapidly. Yes, it was definitely somebody or something. In a rush of adrenalin-induced excitement he jumped to his feet and began to race toward the hide-out. Speedily his legs carried him down the steep slope, his arms flaying about as he dodged and weaved between bushes and branches, receiving some pretty nasty scratches to both legs and arms. With each yard of ground covered the more he was convinced that it was a person.

Brad's lungs sucked in large amounts of air to fuel his energy-eating legs and his pretty face reddened and dripping large globules of sweat as he raced downward, his body now taking on an uncontrollable momentum of its own.

Within yards of his hideout his foot fell foul of a fallen twig, and with a somersault that any gymnast would have been proud of, his body rotated high in the air then hit the soft earth with a thud, rolling over and over, gathering leaves on his hair, shorts, and T-shirt.

A helpful shrub ceased his untidy descent and his body disappeared into its leafy arms, and became part of it.

Brad dusted himself down and checked all limbs were still attached then limped the remaining distance. At the pool-side there was no sign of anyone, not even a ripple on its glassy surface. He sighed. Perhaps he was mistaken, but he was sure he wasn't. Then again it could have been a fox or even a badger daring to venture out in daylight.

Exhausted, and slightly bruised and battered, he opened the invisible door, stepping into the shaded shelter. Nothing had changed. The towel hung exactly where he had left it.

Feeling that he might cry, having done so much work with so little reward, he flopped onto the bunk. For five minutes he lay, pondering the day, trying hard to convince himself that he had really seen someone, but he knew only too well how the woods can play tricks on the eyes, especially on moonlit nights.

Brad raised himself from the bunk and stepped over to the mystery towel. He stroked his hand along its length. It was wet. The towel was WET! He was right, there had been someone! Joyously he gathered the soft material into his arms rubbing the moisture into his face.

Sucking in the odor he attempted to identify whether it was a boys or girl but couldn't make up his mind. But that wasn't important. What was important was that he was right – and the person was still around.

He was just about to replace the towel and consider his next move when something fell to the ground. He glanced between his feet at the brightly colored object, then scooped it up. Before his excited blue eyes, and bringing a huge smile to his cheeks, was a pair of trunks. But not just any pair of trunks, but a *small* pair of trunks. Trunks that could only fit a BOY perhaps even younger than he! Without even thinking he might look silly, he pulled them over his head and began dancing an Indian-like dance around the den, arms raised high above his head.

Quite suddenly all elation subsided and anger swept through him. Tearing the trunks from his head, he threw them onto the ground, and began stamping on them furiously. Who was this boy who dared enter his den and use his pool? He picked up the trunks and stormed outside, and was just about to heave them into the woods when his anger, as quickly as it started, stopped.

Brad studied the trunks and began to wonder what the boy might look like. How tall, and how old was he? Was he like his cousin? Hopefully not. He obviously liked the countryside and swimming, and may well be a boy similar to himself. Perhaps he was really nice, like Malc. Perhaps, like Malc, the intruder even had a big –

But he shook his head; it was getting late and time for tea. Brad re-entered his den to replace the trunks but then realized if he kept them then the boy would have to bathe nude or, realizing he'd been discovered, might not return. Tucking the trunks into his shorts, he headed home.

Brad lay naked on his bed, the moonlight slicing through his open curtains. He was restless, and glanced at the trunks lying on his bedside cabinet. He began to ponder over the intruder once again. His whole body tingled with a strange sensation, almost as strange as that first time he'd come. Rising from his bed, Brad went to the open window and looked into the starry sky but this unusual sensation was sweeping throughout his body, filling him with a inexplicable excitement.

Lifting the boy's trunks he carefully slipped them up over his legs, thighs and buttocks, pulling them to his waist and just below the navel. They fitted perfectly. Brad looked at himself in his wardrobe mirror, and it was as if his body had been electrified. He began to caress himself over the fabric.

Lying on his bed, his hands went beneath the trunks and he began to rub furiously, focusing on visions of what the boy might look like, but also of Malc. Before he'd even finished his caressing, he fell fast asleep.

. . .

It was another brilliant, sunny day which greeted Brad. His hand was still buried beneath the trunks when he awoke. Jumping from his bed, he stripped them off, washed, dressed, and went to fix his breakfast.

He prepared his usual meal but added a boiled egg. His plans today – after he'd finished his chores – included a visit to the hide-out, where he would sit close by, ready to pounce on the intruder when he appeared.

It was later than expected by the time the chores were complete and cleaning the chicken pens wasn't fun but he was used to it. Having no father, he felt it was his duty to help out and did a good deal more to help his mother than most boys his age.

Within an hour found himself perched high in a tree, looking down on his hide-out and the pool. It was the perfect vantage point: He could see every possible path which led there.

After he'd watched for a good half hour with no sign of life, except wild animals, the urge to swim finally overcame him. Dexterously, he descended through the tree's branches and soon stripped and was floating on the pool's surface.

An hour passed before Brad decided he would lie in the den before resuming his tree top watch, but before opening the secret door he peered through one of several peepholes placed in various parts of his hide-out. He gulped. His heart gave a couple of heavy thuds in his chest and then began to race. Someone was lying on his bunk!

Gingerly, he peered through the peephole a second time. It was definitely a person, although he couldn't see all of him, only his legs and the blue towel lying beside him.

Brad clenched his hand into a fist and ever so quietly opened the secret door, completely forgetting he was naked. Creeping across the twig-covered ground, Brad moved toward the body but his foot snapped a stick and the sound shot through the den with the force of a firecracker.

As a startled bronzed body leapt from the bunk, the nude picture of Brad fell to the ground. Brad jumped back, took all of the scene in. He was angry the boy had found his picture. But as the two stood, silently facing each other, Brad absorbed every detail of the boy's nakedness. The boy also examined, in detail, Brad's own nudity.

Brad's eyes feasted on the intruder's features: the well-defined muscles on both legs and arms; the coppery color of his silken chest; the small tuft of black tight curls above his thick sex. Brad could not help himself; he stared at the boy's sex. It was even bigger than Malc's!

Brad did not notice but the intruder was grinning. Finally, the boy said, "I'm Aaron."

Brad looked away from the cock and into the boy's face. He was incredibly beautiful, Brad thought. So beautiful, in fact, that Brad sighed deeply. All of his anger was gone. All he wanted to do now was get to know this boy better.

Aaron had exactly the same idea. Tentatively, they approached each other. Finally their fingers touched.

"Hi, I'm Brad."

"You are the boy in the picture. This is your hide-out."

Brad nodded. "My secret place, not so secret any more."

They held hands.

"I was hoping you'd come," Aaron said. "It's been so boring since I got here."

Aaron went on to explain he had come to the village to

spend the summer with his Aunt and Uncle who owned Rose Cottage.

"You'll be here *all* summer?"

Aaron nodded. "Yes."

"Then we'd better get along, eh?"

"I don't think that'll be a problem," Aaron said, taking Brad's now erect penis in his hand.

"No, I don't think so either," Brad giggled, bringing his hand to Aaron's rapidly swelling cock. Brad looked down at it and stroked it. "My friend Malc is big, but this is – "

"Do you like it?"

"Oh yes," Brad gushed.

"Then why don't you show me just *how much* you like it."

And there, in his hide-out on the most glorious day of the summer so far, Brad lowered himself to his knees and, guided by the experienced, sure hands of the intruder, began his first blowjob.

To be continued.

THE WRESTLER

David Olivera

Halfway across the Sagamore Bridge to Cape Cod he starts to lose his nerve. His palms are sweaty though the air-conditioning in the car is at full blast; his heart beats like the steady cadence of a train on its way through a canyon.

He considers making a perfectly illegal U-turn and heading back to the anonymity of Boston, hopefully and expectantly into the arms of a stranger who will offer him solace for the night. Except that three cars behind him is a cop cruiser and, after four years behind bars, he doesn't want another encounter with the law. At least not right away, at least not now.

So he feels the reassuring shape of the .38 at his waist inside his jacket and he keeps on going.

He misses Dillingham Avenue on his first drive-by, mainly because the elementary school that had always served as a landmark for residents and visitors no longer exists. In its place is a mini-mall, complete with a food market, a video rental store and a small Sears auto repair shop. Yes, he thinks, progress has come to the Cape, but obviously not with a whole lot of imagination.

He nears 40 Dillingham – the home of his boyhood and young manhood. It lies at the edge of the marshes, with the sand and waters of Cape Cod Bay in the distance. In times past whalers skinned their catches and drained them of their oil among those marshes but the ban on whaling and creeping development had moved the fishermen away.

Forty Dillingham looks pretty much the way it did the day the sheriff's deputies showed up at his door and took him away in handcuffs – painted, neat and ordered.

His sister had sold the house soon after his trial and conviction and moved with her two daughters to Hyannis. In the letter she'd sent to him in prison she wrote her move was dictated both by a good price for the house and the convenience of being in the same town she worked in. Both rational and valid reasons, he knows, but he is also sure she felt great discomfort living across the street from 45 Dillingham, the home of the 15-year-old boy who'd nailed him. Only she hadn't made a point of that.

Life at 45, on the other hand, seemed to have successfully overcome its notoriety and settled back into its semi-suburban rhythms. Some money must have come their way in the past four years too, because the house looks very different from the last time he had seen it

The full house, meaning it has four windows – two on either side of the door – now has an addition built to it. It is no longer white; it is painted Indian red, the other favorite and traditional color for Cape houses.

He also notices that what used to be a scruffy apology for a lawn is now landscaped, and a fence has gone up around it, setting the house attractively apart from the road.

It occurs to him as he passes by that perhaps Steven and his family have moved too, unable to live down the shame and guilt of their family's name being associated with a case that had homosexual overtones. But the lime green Subaru with a portrait of James Dean painted on the hood tells him they are still in town, still in that house.

At Sagamore High – and some of the students were high on the dope and coke brought ashore at Provincetown or New Bedford – Baron had taught Social Studies to 15-year-olds. He was 24 then and for him it had been a dangerous age – too young to know everything, yet too old not to know better. Between those two viewpoints – in that huge pot in which parental anger, accusations, a community's sense of betrayal and judgments of character come to a boil – the jury found a school teacher's encounter with a fifteen-year-old boy sufficient grounds for a four-year sentence.

He had told his story to the jury. He had told them he'd thought nothing of it when Steven came to his door that summer afternoon, wanting, he said, to coach himself on the computer Baron had just bought. The fact that they lived across the street from each other had muted the student-teacher relationship. In fact, Baron and Steven's older brother had studied together, played together, swum in the waters of Cape Cod Bay at the end of Dillingham and explored abandoned clam shacks along the beach. Occasionally they took Steven along with them.

Baron said he had set Steven up in front of the computer and returned to the living room to continue reading Kipling's *Lord Jim*. It could not have been more than fifteen minutes later that Steven had sat himself by him and said, "I'm bored. Want to wrestle? My brother told me you were a good wrestler in school."

"I'm not in school anymore," Baron replied. "And besides, I haven't wrestled since then."

With a speed that astounded him, with a power and strength that was a challenge to his own, Steven had caught his head in a stranglehold and yanked him off the sofa and onto the floor.

Steven left him on the carpet and moved away. Baron reckoned the teen wanted the encounter to be fair, wanted him to get over his surprise, prime himself mentally for a bout Steven obviously had no intention of abandoning. He stood six feet away from Baron, loosening his muscles, crouching this way and that until his body had achieved the sixty-degree angle – the posture wrestlers best like to take at the start of a fight. And he had this smile on his face – a smirk, really – daring and taunting Baron to join the battle.

The fight was on.

In retrospect, Baron was to wonder why he'd forgotten that the reason he had abruptly abandoned high school wrestling in spite of his strength and tactical skills was because of his great fear that the sexual arousal he experienced in such close holds would have revealed his gayness to his opponent. His terror had been that his opponent would use his vulnerability and expose him to ridicule at a time when he wasn't ready for it because he hadn't quite had the chance to solidify his own identity.

The coach had been disappointed – even angry – at what he called Baron's betrayal of the team and the school. But Baron couldn't tell him the real reason, so he'd made one up about how wrestling was taking away from his studies and how he wanted more to be the best student in class. He had other larger, grander ambitions for himself, he'd explained.

He supposed he forgot because he felt secure, in control in his own home. This was, after all, mere horseplay, a short stint. Nothing could possibly go wrong humoring a bored kid.

But things had gone wrong. The security and control he'd

been sure of had only been in his mind. In reality it evaporated and he gave in when the boy, noticing his arousal, said to him in a very, very soothing voice, "It's all right. I know you like guys. I've see you at the Riviera in P-town. You didn't see me because I hid from you. I shouldn't have. But I don't have to hide from you anymore. It's all right. I know. And I like you." His attorney, Laura Reyes, had made a passionate defense, even pulling headlines from the newspapers to make her case for him.

At the time of his trial, a similar episode, from the political life of the Cape was nearing an end. In that, a Congressman had been revealed to have had a liaison with a congressional page, a minor. The shock and confusion the news had been received with was dissipated when the young man involved admitted and acknowledged that he had been a willing participant in that liaison, even to the point of having initiated it.

"Isn't that what really happened between you and your teacher?" Laura Reyes asked Steven sternly. "You seduced him, didn't you? And then, when your mother found those pornographic magazines under your bed, you decided to weasel out of it by saying he gave them to you."

"No, no," Steven answered each question, breaking into a sob, wiping tears from his eyes.

Baron saw the ease with which Steven lied and sobbed on the stand. He knew then that the resolution of his case would be different from that of the Congressman. While the community of fishermen, with the respect and wisdom with which they approached the sea, had returned the Congressman to office, Baron knew that same community would sacrifice him.

It is Sunday morning. Baron sits in his car a few houses up waiting for Steven's parents to leave for church. Some folks don't change their habits – "you can't teach old dogs new tricks" passes through his mind – and he hopes it is so with Steven's parents. He hopes that what he remembers about them from his days as their neighbor is still true.

Sunday was their day together. They were in their car by eight o'clock, ready to make the nine o'clock mass at St. John's in Barnstable, twenty miles away. It had always amused Baron that they set aside a full hour to travel such a short distance and he had once asked them why.

"We don't go straight to church," Steven's mother told him. "We first drive up the coast as far as our fancy takes us. We like to appreciate God's creation. It helps us to offer more thanks than we would otherwise."

They drove as far as their fancy took them after the service too, to early lunch at Wakeby Pond, or John's Pond, or Wequaquet and, if custom holds, Baron knows they won't return to the house until four.

Custom holds this morning. He watches as they get into their car, pull out of the driveway and turn the corner.

Until this moment Baron had felt resolute, but now his heart begins to palpitate. He feels the same rush of nervousness sweep through his body that he'd felt on the drive to the Cape. His conscience is telling him that revenge is a futile emotion, that there is greater virtue in forgiveness. It tells him that punishment is the responsibility of an outside force while redemption is what is provided by the inside. His reason tells him that he is not devious enough to plan the perfect murder, that he will be found out.

Baron shuts his eyes tightly, shakes his head to rid himself of this conflict.

"I will defy both reason and conscience," he says to himself, then gets quickly out of the car, walks up to the door and knocks on it.

He barely recognizes Steven. The young man before him does not look like what a strong, strapping, clean-air-created kid should have grown up to be. This young man is small, almost withered; pale, almost sickly.

"Steven?" he asks.

"Yes. Who are you?"

Baron guesses his newly grown beard has thrown Steven off. So he tells him.

Steven looks him up and down, stops at his eyes. Recognition comes to him then. He looks surprised, even a little frightened. Baron feels Steven probably never believed he'd see him again. He casts a glance up the street and then lets Baron in, hesitantly but without protest.

Baron's heart is pounding again as he is led into the living room, but he knows he must not give in to doubt. He pulls out the .38 and uncocks it. At the sound of the click Steven turns and Baron sees surprise in his eyes, then resignation.

"There were many times when I wondered if you'd come back. To take revenge, you know," Steven says. "But I thought you were too gentle to do something like this." He points to Baron's gun.

"You made me ungentle," Baron answers, surprising himself by how unemotional he is. "I knew there was cruelty in the world, but it hadn't touched me. Until you."

Baron motions with his gun for Steven to sit on a love seat away from the window.

"I know I haven't done well with my life," Steven says. "I know I didn't do good by you. But I don't deserve this."

"No?" Baron asks. "Why not? I didn't deserve four years in jail, but I got it anyway. You destroyed my life and my family's. And you got away scot-free. Now this is pay back time."

"I was frightened."

"Frightened? You weren't frightened to tell all those lies? You were frightened to tell the truth? That it was you who came to my house that afternoon with the intention of having sex with me? That that wrestling match you started with me was a come on?"

"I couldn't help you all right!" Steven shrieks. "Nobody ever helped me so I didn't know how to help anyone else."

"You knew how to help yourself, didn't you?" Baron shoots back. "Didn't you? Did you need somebody to tell you that the way you help yourself is the same way you help others?"

Steven reaches into his pocket for a pack of cigarette, pulls one out and lights it.

"Look," he says, "if you want to shoot me, go ahead. You already killed me once. So if you want to do it a second time, just get it over with."

"What do you mean?"

"I have the plague, man. And you gave it to me. I know you did."

Baron is stunned, incredulous, outraged. The disease explains Steven's gauntness of face, but he also thinks, "The bastard, the son of a bitch."

"Is there nothing you do to others, or to yourself, that you take the responsibility for?" he asks angrily. "Are you so . . . so completely without conscience . . . you bastard . . . is that what you told your parents? That I gave you AIDS? You bastard!"

"There's no other way I could have got it . . . You . . ."

"Oh yes, you could have, you ignorant piece of shit! You must've got it whoring around in P-town. And I tell you why I didn't give you any disease. That prison you sent me to – they tested us every six months. And I am negative – you hear, you liar – negative!"

Baron is hyperventilating. His throat is dry with anger and he gulps saliva down to maintain his equilibrium. His mind is aroar. He searches every part of it to find something in his experience, his learning, his memory that can explain the detachment, the lack of scruples in the young man sitting in front of him. What kind of an amoral monster is this, he thinks. And for some reason he can't place – perhaps it is the proximity to the land he is on – the words of Thoreau go through his mind: the savage in man is never quite eradicated.

"You're right," Steven says almost as though he has read Baron's mind. Then he holds his face in his hands and begins to sob.

Baron feels cheated, conned again. He does not believe the tears, does not accept that they are genuine. He feels sick.

He returns his gun to his jacket, and with a sneer of disgust in his voice says, "I saw you cry like that on the stand in court. That helped you convince the jury you were telling the truth. But I'll tell you this. I don't believe you feel any guilt or remorse, and no matter how human I force myself to be, I don't feel any sorrow for you."

An immense exhaustion overcomes Baron as he lets himself into his car. He rests his forehead against the wheel, slowly deep breathing his way out of his weariness. The sound of the waves beyond the marshes and the saltiness of the air at high tide reminds him he wants to visit the beach once more, one last time, because he has decided that for as long as he lives he'll never come back here again, to this island of his despair.

He walks over the narrow wooden bridge that spans the marshes and leads to the beach. Every few feet, on either side of the bridge, lovers and jilted lovers have carved messages into the wood. One reads: "Melissa, I love you. John." Another, "Todd, why did you leave me? D." Alongside is etched a heart with a large X across it.

About halfway along the bridge he stops and leans over the side. He closes his eyes and raises his face to the nine o'clock sun in the east. Whatever dissolution he experienced is seeping out of him. He feels connected to the desire to live again. For a few moments he ponders the sheer irony of how a young man's inevitable death has saved his own life. He shudders with a chill that even the sun cannot obliterate.

He takes the gun out of his pocket and with one last look at it drops it into the marsh. Except for a dull plop! as it hits the surface, it disappears.

FAXING OFF

David Laurents

I forgot all about Jack Springer until I got an entry-level job, via a trick who'd turned into a friend, at one of those glossy entertainment and fashion magazines. I'd exchanged numbers with him at a bar, and only when I got home and went to write him up in my Little Black Book did I notice he'd given me a fax number. At the time I was waiting tables at a chic French restaurant uptown, so I didn't have access to a fax, but I kept the number anyway. I keep very good records of the men I meet. If only the IRS would audit my Little Black Book instead of my taxes!

On second thought, it's better they don't. I've got a fair chunk of undeclared income in there, and I mean "in cum." I had some heavy-duty student loans to pay off, and its just so hard to dig yourself out of debt, even with a decent job, especially if you like to keep on living while you're doing it. That was my other problem – I had expensive tastes, and wanted to live while I could still enjoy it. I liked to travel and didn't want to be fifty before I could afford it. So I turned my traveling into a working vacation. I not only brought money in, I usually didn't have to pay for a room for the night. And I got laid. Worked out well all around.

Anyway, when my new boss showed me the fax machine on my first day and was explaining where the extra reams of paper were kept and who to call for help if it jammed, I only paid half attention to her. Jack's distinguished profile had leapt into my mind, and I could hardly wait until I went back to my desk, where I could check my Little Black Book. A few weeks after I'd met him at Baxter's, the Sunday paper ran an intelview with him in the magazine section. I had recognized the photo of him right away, and that was the image that came to mind as I was standing beside the fax machine. He wasn't all that handsome, really, at least, not drop-dead handsome. But he was distinguished. He'd aged well, and had an air of high culture about him, which is what had attracted my attention to him in the bar. He photographed well, and this high society air came across in the pictures they ran on him with the interview. I remembered how my estimation of him soared a couple of notches when I saw the profile in the papers. I mean, he was practically famous! I had always meant to pick up one of his books when I was in a bookstore, but I just kept forgetting...

As soon as I could, I sat down at my new desk and checked my notes about him. "Nice Basket" I had written in the same color pen as the fax number, along with "Author" and "Baxter's". The interview had filled in most of the rest of the details. He was a writer, novels mostly, and worked out of his home. That was why he didn't have a phone; too much of a distraction. People calling when he was trying to work. The temptation to call someone up and chat for an hour, or worse, make plans to do something during his working time was too strong for him. With the fax, he didn't need to read messages as they came in, letting them pile up until he had finished a chapter and was ready for a break. In this age of high technology he could still take care of most of his business by fax instead of phone: his editor, many of his friends--even the Chinese food place down the block. He could fax an order over, and 15 minutes later they'd deliver it to his door.

I smiled, pleased that I still could remember so much about him from my notes and the interview I'd read. I wondered if he remembered me as well, and doubted it, which is why, though I still had his fax number, I waited for an excuse to contact him. I resolved to at last get one of his books when I went to lunch and read it that night, so I'd have an excuse to fax him tomorrow. I was excited about connecting with him again, even though there had never seemed to be much chance of our ever sleeping together. Part of it, I think, was having someone to fax to; the novelty of that appealed to me. I hoped he hadn't changed his number in the six months since I'd met him. If he really didn't have a phone, which seemed likely from what the interview had said and the fact that he'd given me his fax number at the bar in the first place, then he would want to keep his number constant so his editors and friends could reach him. I moved the book's little red ribbon to his page and put away my Little Black Book before someone noticed I wasn't working.

I didn't get much work done, though. My desk was out in

the hallway in front of my boss' office, and also across from one of the executive's doors. He'd had his door closed all morning, but just when I settled down to dive into the work my boss had given me he opened it, and there went my ability to keep my mind on my work. He was gorgeous! The kind of blond who tanned with a healthy looking pink glow just exuding from every pore of his body – and I imagined quite a lot of them, undressing him in my head as I watched him sitting behind his desk talking on the phone. He noticed me looking in his direction and flashed me a million dollar smile, blindingly white teeth in an attention-getting grin. My cock was hard as a flagpole and straining against the crotch of my pants as if it meant to burst through the fabric. I wondered if anyone would notice if I unzipped my pants to give my cock some breathing room, but decided against it. I mean, hell, it was my first day.

I didn't know what to do. I couldn't think about the work I'd been given, couldn't think about anything but the guy in the office across from me. I looked away from him, staring at my computer screen, but instead of the terminal all I saw was that smile, his chiseled chest and abs, his cock, hard and waiting for me, his muscled legs up in the air, his pink asshole winking at me, inviting. I wondered if the corporate men's room was busy right then, if I could take five minutes and go jerk off before I creamed in my pants anyway and regretted it. I had to do *something* to get him out of my mind or I would be fired in a few hours, for not being able to work.

I stared across the hallway, trying to read his name off his now-open door, and wished that my boss had done introductions to everyone in the office. No, perhaps it was better that she hadn't, I thought, since I would probably have embarrassed myself somehow upon meeting him. But I had no idea what to call him, and wanted something for my mind to pin down, so I could be done thinking about him and get down to work. I was so turned on by him, I was sitting there fantasizing about his name! I was almost ashamed of myself; it wasn't like I hadn't gotten my rocks off in a few weeks or something. But this guy just really turned my head, and my cock, and I couldn't think about anything else.

I figured if maybe I could talk to someone about him, I would get it out of my system, and could then get back to work. But

I couldn't very well call someone up and say all the things I wanted to do to this guy from my desk; what if my boss came by to ask what was taking me so long on the letters I was supposed to type? And what if he overheard me himself? I didn't, of course, have any friends yet in the office, and frankly, I doubted anyone else in this corporate headquarters was even queer, someone who I could stand with at the water cooler and whisper my fantasies. I looked at my Little Black Book, wondering who I would call if my boss was at lunch and the coast was clear, who I might call in order to have some quick and sweaty sex during my lunch break so I wasn't as distracted during the afternoon, and suddenly I realized what I might do. I would write my fantasies about The Exec (which is how I thought of him since I didn't know his name) and fax them to Jack. I didn't know if he'd remember me, and I had no real excuse for writing to him out of the blue, but it was only 10:37, and there was no way I would last all morning without telling *someone* about The Exec and clearing my head. I'd simply burst.

I opened a new file on the word processor and began to write:

Dear Jack –
You probably don't remember me. We met at Baxter's a few months ago. It was the Friday before the Tribune ran that profile of you in the Magazine section. I really enjoyed reading more about you; it made me want to rush out and read all your books.
I'm writing you now because I just got a new job, where I've got access to a fax machine. Well, I'm really writing you now because I've got nowhere else to turn. See, there's this executive in the office across from my desk, and he's just drop-dead gorgeous. I can't think about anything else but vaulting over my desk and tearing his clothes from him, hungrily running my hands across his well-built, tanned body. He looks like one of those stereotypical California surfers, only hotter, and you know he's got a brain, to boot, because he's a Top Exec at the magazine I now work for! But he's got this body to die for, a body to kill for, a body I can't stop thinking about!
He's got large hands and I keep watching them, curled

around the thick earpiece. I can't hear what he's saying, but I imagine those big hands fisting his own thick cock.

I've never been so turned on by someone before, just from looking at them. I mean, I can get turned on by a lot of things, and even by men who you wouldn't ordinarily think of as attractive, but something in the way the carry themselves, or their mannerisms can do it for me. I don't know what it is about him that hits me so strong, though. It's as if he exudes this masculine sexuality in his every movement. He's probably straight, but that doesn't stop me from fantasizing! It almost makes it even better. I can imagine him fucking me like I was a woman, plowing into me in a workman-like fashion with his huge cock, his large nipples staring down at me from his chiseled torso.

And the idea of fucking him up the ass, that virgin straight ass, makes me so hard I feel I'm about to burst a new fly in these pants, and there goes my best work suit.

It's driving me crazy!

Hope you don't mind my having written to you like this. I had to tell somebody and my boss would've heard me if I called someone. You were the only person I knew with a fax who might understand. But don't write back to me, or I'll get in trouble. Fired my first day at the job for faxing off on the company machine!

Thanks for being a friendly ear. Will try and contact you again when I can be faxed back.

Gotta run.

– Eric

I printed it out and read it over again. Not wonderful prose – and Jack was a writer, so he'd care about things like that – but it would have to do. I started to get up to bring it over to the fax machine and send it to Jack, when I realized my erection was still poking up against the thin fabric of my slacks. I wondered if I should sit back until it went away, but then I looked up and saw The Exec standing behind the desk in his off ice, pacing as he talked on the phone, and I knew my erection wasn't going anywhere. My mind just couldn't seem to imagine this guy in clothes and kept erasing them. I stood and walked to the fax machine, casually holding a folder in front of me, feeling like I was back in high school hiding an erection behind my school books. I felt sure that everyone could tell what I was doing, and stuck one hand into my pocket to hide the bulge. I grabbed hold of my cock, ran my fingers along its throbbing, swollen length, and wished I could just go into The Exec's office, lock the door behind me and fuck until quitting time.

I was all sweaty nervous as I punched Jack's fax number into the machine. Mostly, it was from The Exec, of course, but there was this strange techno-thrill from illicitly using the fax machine like this. Jack's number was for some reason busy, and I wanted to swear at the machine as I waited for it to redial and connect. The longer I stood there, looking guilty and trying to hide my erection, the easier it would be for me to be caught. I tried to look nonchalant, as if I was just faxing something mundane for my boss, and carefully looked everywhere but at the fax machine.

Suddenly, I heard my name called out, and I looked up, startled and guilty. How could my boss have known? She stood at the door of her office, beckoning to me. I looked quickly at the fax machine, planning to grab my letter to Jack and hide it in my folders, to send later, but just then the machine connected, and the sheet of paper began its slow route through the insides of the fax machine. There was no way I could pull it out now, not without tearing it, and I couldn't leave my boss waiting there without her asking what I was doing. Nervous as hell that someone would get to the machine and read it before I had a chance to talk to her and then rush back and get the letter, I walked down the hallway, trying to put on a calm and collected air, as if the world was just peachy keen instead of hanging on the blade of a knife at my throat.

My boss wanted to show me some new trick on my computer. She made me sit down at my desk and stood over my shoulder, giving me directions. I wanted to rush back to the machine, certain that my fax had at last gone through and was just sitting there, waiting for someone to discover it, but I couldn't do anything. I had to sit there, with her leaning over me, the smell of her expensive flowery perfume making me sick, her small breasts brushing against my shoulder every now and then and only reminding me of the totally hot Exec just across the way. I had to forcibly keep my eyes on the screen each time I felt her breast against my shoulder, lest I instinctively look at The Exec, but still my eyes saw him – his bare chest, his naked body spread out before me, so inviting, the slight curve I imagined his cock held. I wondered if my boss had noticed my erection poking up in my lap, and if she did if she thought it was because of her. I tried to lean slightly forward and hide it. And all I could do was smile and nod and "a-hmm" at her directions. She left me to finish the file on my own, going back into her office but leaving the door open in case I needed more help. I was supposed to finish it right then, and to bring it to her when I was done. I raced through it, trying to make the most of my 65 wpm typing skills I'd picked up typing other kids' papers for money in college.

Suddenly, The Exec was standing in front of me! I couldn't help getting an eyeful of his large basket, which sat at my eye level, just past the piece of paper he was holding out to me. I tore my eyes away from his crotch and looked up at his face. God, he was beautiful !

"I think this is yours," he said, and I almost died right there. Of all people to find the transmission I'd left in the fax machine, it had to have been The Exec. I knew he'd read it, how could he not? What must he think of me? I was going to get canned, I felt certain.

"Come into my office."

This was it, I thought as I followed behind him. I'd lasted under three hours at my new job... I couldn't help staring at his ass I trailed after him, though, and imagining working that tight bubble-butt...

The door shut firmly. He stood facing the window, motionless, except for the whir of his fingers drumming against the sill. I waited for him to turn around and fire me, his indignation, his rage. He turned to face me and I closed my eyes, bracing against the shock. I was a wimp. I just couldn't stand there and take it like a man, not knowing what he must think about me after reading that fax. I felt like a prisoner about to be executed, who asks for the blindfold, so he doesn't have to see the gunmen shooting him down.

He didn't say anything.

I waited.

I opened my eyes again, confused, and curious. He stood before me like an imposing blond monolith, silent and immovable. His face was placid and calm, his arms folded across his chest. My eyes continued downwards. His fly was unzipped and his cock thrust boldly from beneath the fabric, swollen and pink. My breath caught in my throat.

I sank to my knees before him, inwardly giving thanks to every deity I could remember. From this vantage I got a chance to examine his thick cock in every detail, from the tiny little piss-hole on the tip of his fat glans to the blond hairs that curled around its base, still lost in the fabric of his pants. I'd been right about the slight curve, but wrong in which direction it went. The vein that ran along the top throbbed as if with impatience, and I leaned forward to take him into my mouth. I flicked my tongue around the swollen crown, stretching my lips further and further as I took more of him into my mouth. I paused, working up saliva to smooth the way. Slowly, my lips slid closer and closer to his crotch, where the fly of his pants loomed like a dark cave.

I reached up and pulled his nuts from his pants, massaging their hefty weight in my palm as I gulped down his cock.

My jaws ached. He grabbed my head and started pumping into my mouth, fucking my face in short quick thrusts. I started to gag as his cock pushed into the back of my throat, but I fought the rising bile and settled back on my knees, bracing myself until I was able to accommodate him.

Now that my hands were free, I unzipped my own pants and reached past my damp jockeys to free my own aching cock. I slicked the head with my own precum, and began whacking off in sync with his thrusting into my face. I'd been so worked up all morning that it wasn't long before my nuts let loose, and I was shooting thick ropes of cum between his legs onto the dark carpet. He didn't stop fucking my face, pumping his huge piece of meat into my mouth with the same even thrusting as before. My jaws had gone beyond aching and were numb, as he battered the back of my throat.

Suddenly he pulled out. A thread of spittle strung between my mouth and the tip of his cock.

"Suck on my nuts," he commanded, as his thick fingers curled about his meat and he began to fist himself as I'd imagined earlier. I eagerly dove into the dark, musky region between his legs and began sucking on his big balls, which were pulling up into his crotch as he got ready to cum. I slobbered from one to the other, getting them both wet, then trying to engulf both of them at once.

Suddenly, both of his balls popped out of my mouth at once and above me he roared. I sent my tongue flicking across the underside of his balls as he bucked forward above me. When he'd stilled, I stood up and zipped myself up. He still hadn't really said anything to me. But as I waited, he merely pulled slowly on his still-swollen cock, lost in a pleasant post-coital haze.

Puddles of cum pooled on the blotter of his desk. I gathered this meant I wasn't about to be fired and, relieved, I began heading for the door, ready to get back to work before my boss got upset.

"Where do you think you're going?"

I looked back, surprised, then smiled. The Exec (I still didn't know his name!) had taken off his shirt, to reveal a torso even more exquisitely sculpted than I'd imagined. A small silver ring glinted in his left nipple. With one hand, he twisted his right nipple, while his other hand drifted across his wash-board stomach with its trail of downy blond hairs pointing towards his crotch.

I turned away from the door, thinking I'd have to write another fax to Jack Springer, thanking him for being there to listen to my fantasies and telling him the incredible things that had happened as a result.

FREE INSTALLATION

L. Amore

The cable company was advertising free installation. I hadn't been at the University a week before I missed having all those channels so I called. "Yes, he can come first thing in the morning," the woman said.

"If I'm lucky maybe we can come together," I muttered.

"What?" she asked.

"Nothing. That'll be fine."

Little did I know how fine.

The small patch on his tan work shirt read "Gary."

"Your mother home?" he asked impatiently.

"My mother?" I bundled my bathrobe around me.

"She called for cable, didn't she?"

"No, I called for cable."

"You?" he chuckled.

"What's so funny?"

"I'm sorry. You look like you're still in high school."

"I've always looked young for my age. Actually, I just started college here. But I prefer living off campus."

"Don't blame you a bit. If you can afford it, it's better. More private. You live here alone?" His eyelashes fluttered. Long, lovely eyelashes, illuminating his steely eyes. The only feminine thing about him. He was about five-ten with sandy brown hair. A strong jawline was covered with a day's growth of beard. And from the way he filled out his uniform he had to have been a professional bodybuilder before he began installing cables. Now his few extra pounds made the rips and definition all the more appealing.

"Yes," I answered. "I'm here all alone."

He nodded. "Yeah, real private. So, where's the TV?"

I showed him to my bedroom and struggled to remain calm.

I sat on the edge of the bed watching him bend over and begin tugging on the cable that was coming up through the floor. His work pants were stretched tight around his thighs but because he had a narrow waist and hips, they were slightly loose on top. As he tugged, I noticed a glimpse of his hairy lower back and a little butt cleavage.

Dead or Alive's "Come Home With Me Baby" was on the stereo and Pete Burns was moaning in would-be ecstasy as Gary knelt on the floor to plug the wires into the VCR and the TV. He came around to the front of the cabinet and turned on the TV, then the VCR. I had forgotten that "Viva Macho" had been left in the machine from the night before. He hit the eject button and it popped out.

"Excuse me but I was just going to jump in the shower when you came. I've only got an hour to make my first class." As I stood up, I tugged the sash of my robe tightly around me but it was impossible to conceal my erection.

"Keep your VCR on channel four and your TV on channel four," he said, his eyes glancing down to where my robe was parted.

"I will. Channel four."

He grinned and began putting away his tools.

"I'll only be a second," I said. I took a quick shower, trying to put the man out of my mind. But it was useless.

"Hey!" he called from the bedroom.

I draped a towel around me and stepped back into the bedroom. "Yeah?"

"Everything seems to be working fine," he chuckled, with the orgy scene from "Viva Macho" playing on the screen. "You sure you're old enough to watch this kinda stuff?"

"You don't have to be twenty-one, you know."

Leaning back with the remote control in his hand, he fast-forwarded the tape. Then let it play. "How does this thing come out?"

"Oh, everybody comes."

"You don't say," he chuckled. "Makes a guy horny to see all of 'em go at each other like that."

I looked at his crotch. "I guess it does."

He saw where my eyes were fixed and started rubbing it. "Yeah, the old lady just doesn't understand I need it at least twice a day."

I walked over and reached down, touching the now stupendous bulge. He moaned and leaned back. I unzipped his pants and drew the swelling cock from its captivity. I didn't waste any time sliding it in my mouth and sucking it. The musky scent of his crotch wafted to my nostrils and I momentarily lost myself in the sheer ecstasy of having him respond to my adoration by moving his hips, sending his cock deeper and deeper down my throat. It seemed to grow longer and thicker with every thrust.

Suddenly he howled. Actually howled. It was as close to a rebel yell as I'd ever heard. I quickly pulled it out and the force with which his sperm hit my face made it feel like I was being bombarded by hot little BB's. I let the cock fall to his thigh and licked it while I jacked off. As I came, he held my head with his calloused hand and forced me down into his crotch. I began sucking him again but he pushed me away. "We both got places we gotta be."

Just then, the phone rang. It was a woman from the cable company, looking for him. "He left here a long time ago," I told her.

As Gary was driving away in his truck, I dialed the cable company again. "I've got a problem," I told the woman. "The TV was working when he left but now it's all fuzzy. I think there must be a loose connection somewhere."

"I'm sorry for the inconvenience. We'll send him back there first thing tomorrow."

"Oh, thank you. Thank you very much."

. . .

"Now what?" Gary said, forcing back a grin.

"The TV just got all fuzzy."

He brushed past me. "Let's have a look."

By the time I reached the bedroom, the TV was on. The picture was perfect.

"Works fine."

"What was the matter?"

"The connector was loose."

"Oh?"

"It was tight when I left."

"It was?"

He shook his head. "You know it was, smart ass. You college kids are all the same. Smart, tight asses."

"Oh?"

"Yeah, I've seen enough of 'em, believe me."

"I'll bet."

"But you're gonna have to pay for this. The installation's free but the service costs ya."

"Oh?"

"And it could cost you a lot. Smart, tight ass college kid like you." He took a length of cable from his tool bag.

"Oh? How much?"

Slowly, he slid the cable up my thigh and brought it to rest where my erection was tenting my robe. He shook his head. "A lot," he said.

Then he brought the cable behind me, across my ass.

Whack.

"Lying to the office, getting me to drive halfway across town..."

"I'm sorry," I said, slipping my robe off my body.

Whack. Whack. On my naked skin.

"Not as sorry as you're gonna be..."

He tied my wrists to the bedposts with cable wire, then bound my legs together at the ankles. Slowly, he began undressing himself, making me watch in delicious agony as he took his time removing his boots, his shirt, and finally his pants.

I moaned as he climbed over me and pressed down on my chest, forcing his now rigid phallus between my lips.

The phone began ringing. "Don't even think about it!" he shouted.

Indeed, answering the phone was the last thing I wanted to do. It rang a few times, then stopped. The only noise was now the slurping noises I was making as he took the back of my head in his strong hands and held it up so that he could fuck my face with his thick horse cock. When I masturbated the previous night, remembering him and his cock and how hard he came, I guessed it had to be ten-inches long. Now I was sure of it. His strokes were long and he plunged all the way down, then pulled almost all the way out. Soft urgent moans and gurgles escaped him.

"Oh, yeah," he grumbled after a few minutes, "you're sure good at that, but I need to find out just how tight an ass you got, college boy."

As he lifted my bound legs high, exposing my puckering hole, I wondered how many others had been in this situation when all they wanted was a free cable installation.

Whack!

I had never been into pain but each blow was like an electric jolt bringing me almost to climax, then slowly subsiding to a warm glow.

He leaned over and rummaged through his pile of clothes. My heart jumped to my throat when the blade of a hunting knife gleamed in the light from the TV screen. He grinned as he cut a piece of wire from the length that was binding my feet. As he threw the knife to the floor, I sighed deeply.

"Oh, yeah, college boy's going to like this," he said as he tied up my balls and my now flaccid penis. Soon my cock was throbbing again and the veins along the shaft were sticking out like those on an addict's arm.

He raised my legs to the level of my shoulders and spit three times into my waiting ass. After he nestled the large cockhead, already well-lubricated with my saliva, in my hole, he began pushing slowly.

"Yeah, tight," he said. "Real tight."

I thought he was going to take it slow, allow me to get used to the enormity of it. Wrong. He plunged into me fiercely and the pain was so deep I couldn't pinpoint it. The skin along my spine went cold as the pain quickly turned into wild sensation as each of his urgent jabs found its mark. He held up my bound legs by the ankles with one hand and spit into his other hand. Then he began jerking my cock in tempo with his assault on my ass. Soon spurt after spurt of my cum was flying into the air, landing on his chest, shoulders, face, even his hair.

Again came the rebel yell. This time it was so loud I feared the neighbors would hear. He pulled out and his cum splattered my ass and balls and, as it ran down my spine, it soaked the sheets.

He let go of me and stood up.

"Wait," I cried.

"Just stay there," he said, chuckling.

Considering I had no choice, I laughed out loud. He dialed the phone. "Hey, I'm having a little trouble with this one. The whole damn apartment building's gone out. You better send Bill over to that one on Riverside. Yeah, I'll call you when I'm done here."

As he hung up the phone, I smiled. "Even you lie to the office."

He climbed over my chest and growled, "Shut up and suck."

TAKE YOUR TIME

Antler

Take your time, what's the rush?
Weeks, months, years you've waited
   for this moment –
Make it last, draw it out,
   there's no hurry.
If the boy has a hard-on
   before you start touching,
Take your time taking his clothes off,
Rub his legs and crotch
   with his pants still on,
And after you take them off
Give him a complete rubdown
   touching everywhere but his cock,
Finally slowly lick his asshole, perineum and balls
   as he lies spreadeagled on his belly.
Now turn him over and begin,
   moving as in slow motion.
Take your time licking his cock.
Some boys like the way it feels
To have their cocks licked
Till they're about to come
And then for the mouth
   to slip gently over
   and suck up down up down
   only two times before blast-off!
Other boys like to be sucked for hours
Reveling in the astounding repertoire
   of gentle sucking nuances
   and play of passionate lips,
And the same with the play of hands
   around belly, balls, thighs, ass,
   cock while sucking,
Or stroking armpits or face or nipples
   at zero-hour.
O what poem could be more beautiful than this?

How can any man, woman, boy, girl
　　not find the prospect of blowing
　　a beautiful boy beautiful?
Take your time, Antler, take your time.
Even if the boy doesn't say "Take your time"
　　take your time.
Inhale the boyish crotch smell
Your nose down there where you love
Doing what so many more boys and men love
　　than anyone realizes –
　Use your lips, tongue, mouth
　The way they were meant to be used.
　Worship God like this.

THE GLORY HOLE

Ken Anderson

I pilgrimaged
to you
as to wonderful Delphi – omphalos
of my splendid college days –
and received the same ambiguous oracle
with thanks.

A quarterback assumed the role
of Apollo's priest. He sat
in the next stall, peeping
through the hole
as through a confessional.

I revealed my sin, then poked the wall
in its eye, where I stuck
till I came, then unplugged myself
with a sigh.

Wall, you are the eye
with its hungry stare, the mouth
with its skillful tongue, the go-between
who brought us together
yet kept us apart.

ROADSIDE STAND

Edmund Miller

A hitchhiker ass-hauls along the highway, on the right.
My truck jerks for a pickup, so, in the night.
He gives me a leg up and in.
I give him a meal. I feel: he's so thin—within.

He goggles at, goes for
The reststop classical floozy
who antedates the hustling that I serve.
I encourage him to drive then
his (he thinks) somethingbetter bargain.

Thumbing, he did take a chance—and get it.
She may smell of pay in advance—and yet it
's true after they do whatever they do,

She'll go home alone,
But he'll have one to go to.

QUICK MIRACLES IN THE ALLEY

Christopher Thomas

He comes, eyes hot with strangers,
jeans slung across his hips,
a touch of talcum at his ankles,
the lanky stance of youth
rolling out his cock like honey

I think of the 30 year old charismatic,
virgin as the day he was born
molesting himself in the mirror,
his eyes crazy, his mouth open,
hands soothing the way to sleep

I've come to rent his skin,
to return to an old motion
where the sweetest swing in Omaha
is warmest on the skin, a place
to root with both sides of pleasure

Hang your alibi on the register tape,
quick miracles in the alley,
where the kneelers,
still glued to their prayers,
put warm mouths around the entire dream.

ALL IN THE FAMILY

"Family is everything. It defines you – the heart of your spirit, the heritage of your smile, not only the color of your eyes but how they see the world. You are bound by kinship. You add your own link to the chain, and that's where you strengthen or weaken what you've been blessed – or burdened – with. That's where you use the indefinable quality that belongs to you, alone..."
– Lola Shiner

TRADITION

Greg Bowden

The thing of it was, I liked it.

I knew I wasn't supposed to like it so I tried not to let on but I'm sure some of the men figured it out. They never said anything, though, except for Ben who kept telling me how good I was at doin' it. He liked his side of it too, more than some of the others, and he kept trying out different things, just for the fun of it.

It happened this way. I turned eighteen in March of 1882, the exact middle of seven brothers and sisters and by that the least useful to the farm. My oldest brother knew some people and he got me hired on as general labor at a logging camp up towards Truckee so I went up there to work and send my money back home. It was hard work but it was okay and I liked life in the lumber camp, living with the men and listening to their stories and all.

I took a special liking to a man called Gatt and he took to me pretty much too 'til one evening settin' around the fire someone said we sure seemed stuck to each other. Gatt didn't like the sound of that at all and the next day when I was out cleaning whips off some felled trees he came and got me.

We walked along the trail up to the lookout and he said that what I'd heard around the fire was pretty much true only he didn't want the responsibility of it. He said he figured I didn't know anything about it anyway and maybe I'd better go off and find out, see if I liked it. He never did say what it was and I didn't like to look stupid and ask.

Anyway, Gatt told me there was this camp he knew, farther up in the mountains, that was real special. They was real particular about who they hired but Gatt said they'd hire me on if he said to. He told me to go up to that other camp, find the foreman and tell him Gatt sent me to be the new stick man if they needed one. I was most especially to tell the foreman to be careful 'cause I'd never once had the stick but I was willing to try it. I didn't know what any of that meant either but I still didn't like to ask. It didn't matter, I'd of done whatever Gatt told me to anyway.

Like they said, I was kind of stuck to him. Gatt said if I still had a wanting for him after my time in the camp I could come back and maybe we'd see about a little farm or something. At the end of the week, after we got paid, Gatt sent me off on the supply wagon that came around with the mail and stuff and the next day I found myself at Kramer Lumber Camp Number Two. One of the men sent me over to a little office where I found the foreman, a big, muscular man named Percy.

When I told him what Gatt had told me to he looked me up and down and got a big grin on his face. "Well, Dan'l, I'm sure if Gatt sent you you'll work out just fine," he said, shaking my hand. "Gatt was stick man here himself, couple of years ago and he liked it fine. I'm sure you will too."

It was a good camp. The bunkhouse was clean, the cots were comfortable and there was even an enclosed shower-bath with room for five or six men to bathe at the same time. The food was good too, better even than Ma made at home. The men in the camp were real friendly and even though the work was about the same as I was used to a lot of them came out to where I was working every day and offered to lend me a hand. They never did that at the other camp and I thought it was real good of them, to want to help the new man out, but I was doin' okay by myself and I told them that. A couple of them helped out anyway and one or two just sat for a while and watched me work.

A man called Clay told me he sure was glad I'd come along because he was sick of being the stick man. He said he looked forward to being on the other side of that with me.

One day in my second week there, about mid-morning, Mr. Percy came out and said he wanted to have a little talk with me. We went down the path a ways to where a little shelter had been made on the bank of the creek and Mr. Percy hopped up to sit on a big old log that had been stripped of its bark and worn smooth from end to end. He had me get up and sit beside him. "Well, Dan'l," Mr. Percy said when we were comfortable, "I don't know if you know all the jobs of the stick man. Did Gatt tell you what all would be expected of you up here?"

"No, sir. He just said I was to do what I was told and see if I liked it. He said to give it some time and be sure either way and that's just what I'm determined to do."

It wasn't my place to say it but in truth I was kind of tired of cleanin' logs and wanted to get on to doin' other things to see what I might like.

"Good for you, boy. I like to hear you say that because there are some things the stick man does that some men might find distasteful and some can't tolerate at all. That's why we don't usually take on a new stick man 'less he comes recommended. And you got a high recommendation, Dan'l. Ol' Gatt ain't never been wrong 'bout a man yet."

He slid off the log and stood looking at me for a moment, his hand resting on my leg. "You know, Dan'l, it's hard on the men, being out here in the forest all the time with no one to make them feel good and, uh, to take care of their needs. You know what I mean? About a man's needs?"

I nodded. My brother Davy had explained it to me once when he'd found me playing with myself out behind the hay barn.

Mr. Percy patted my leg and smiled. "Good boy. Now I suppose you take care of your own needs with your hand and so on but when a man gets to be older it sometimes takes more than just his hand to really bring him satisfaction. That's where the stick man comes in. Part of his job is to see that the others get their needs satisfied as they arise. You understand?"

I nodded again.

"You understand how he does that?"

I'd once seen Gatt down by the log pond with one of the other loggers. I thought they might have been swimming or something because they were both naked except for their boots. Gatt's jock was up hard and he was pushing it in and out of the other man's ass and the man was grunting and swearing and telling Gatt to hurry up. They didn't see me and I let them be. I thought that must be what Mr. Percy meant and I told him so.

"Yeah, that's pretty much the idea, Dan'l," he said. "You ever done that before?"

I shook my head 'cause I hadn't.

"You willing to?"

I nodded, trying not to let him see how anxious I was to try it. I'd thought about it a lot ever since that time I saw Gatt and the other man but I'd never known how to get it started with him. Or anyone for that matter. I wondered though, "Does it really hurt a lot?"

Mr. Percy chuckled. "Can't rightly say, Dan'l. I've never done it, leastways never been the man in front."

Then he got a serious look on his face. "You maybe want to ask Clay about that."

Just about then the man called Clay came into the clearing and Mr. Percy formally introduced us. Clay had been working as the stick man and now I was to take over his duties. He shook my hand and looked me over. "Yeah, big guy like you, you'll make them happy."

"Now, there's a little tradition about this," Mr. Percy said, "about changin' from one stick man to another."

"The tradition," Clay said, interrupting Mr. Percy, "is that you are the very last man in this camp I ever have to take it from and then, when you're through, I'm the first man in this camp that gets to give it to you. Mr. Percy here watches us do it, just to make sure. Then I expect he'll be the second one into you, like he was with me. After that – well, after that it's kind of every man for himself."

"Now don't go scarin' him with that, Clay," Mr. Percy said and then turned to me. "No one will hurt you Dan'l and the men are always real careful of a new stick man for the first week or two, until he gets used to it."

Clay spoke up. "And don't let them tell you you have to do anything else. Like Frank – he's the one with black hair and the big red mustache – Frank's always wantin' to put it in your mouth but you don't have to do that. All you have to give 'em is this." He patted me gently on the butt. "Now, you got anything to say before we get started here?"

He began to unbutton his britches. I could hardly think, watchin' Clay working his buttons and knowin' I was going to put my cock into him.

Finally I remembered what I'd asked Mr. Percy. "Does it hurt a lot?"

Clay looked me in the eye and nodded. "I won't lie to you, Dan'l. It does hurt some at first, 'till your ass gets stretched a bit and you get used to it." He fumbled in his pocket and brought out a stick of wood which he handed to me. "Here. I made it for you myself. It's the reason you're called a stick man."

The stick was about six inches long and maybe an inch and a half in diameter. It was made of white pine, sanded until it was smooth as satin cloth and it had knobs like the uncovered head of a cock carved at each end. It was a handsome thing and I liked the feel of the smooth sanded wood against my fingers but I didn't have any idea what it was for. Clay saw that. "Here," Clay said, "you put it in your mouth and then bite down on it. It helps keep your mind off any pain you might feel." He went back to his buttons. "I pretty much chewed mine up at first but now I hardly ever need it. Just make sure you smear a lot of lard on them before you let them in you."

"We'll find you a little tin you can carry some lard in," Mr. Percy said with a smile. "The cook will fill it for you whenever you want."

Clay pulled off his boots and britches and set them by the log I was sitting on. "Hell, he can have mine," he said. "I'm happy to be rid of it. Now, Dan'l, you going to get down from there so's I can get past the very last fuck I ever have to take?"

I slid off the log and went to get out of my britches. I was kind of self-conscious because my cock was already up hard just thinkin' about what was going to happen but Clay, he looked like he expected it to be that way. He made me get all the way naked 'cause that's the way the men like it he said. "You sure got a big one, don't you Dan'l," he said when he took hold of my cock and smeared some lard over it. "Sure am glad I don't have to take one that size all the time."

I never thought it was any much bigger than anyone else but I also never saw many that were up and hard. I guess maybe I never saw any except for a couple of my brothers and they're just like me.

Anyway, Clay turned away from me and laid himself over the peeled log so his butt was pushed out and his dark little hole was bared to me. He reached back and smeared a little lard on it and told me it was okay, I could go in. I held my cock in my hand and touched the head of it against that dark little pucker and even through all the lard he'd put on me I could feel the heat of it. I pushed a little and it began to open for me, relaxing and letting me in. It was beautiful to watch, like a dark colored bud slowly opening into a flower and taking my cock into the center of it. I put it into Clay real slow, afraid I was going to come even before I got all the way inside him but I finally made it. He was hot inside and I felt the heat saturating my cock, making me forget even where I was or that Mr. Percy was watching what we were doing. He let me rest like that for a little, my cock pushed all the way in him, soaking up his heat and trying not to come. Then he squeezed down on me and told me to go ahead and fuck him. I pulled out a little and pushed back in and I couldn't get over how good it felt. I'd been jacking-off for a good long time but it'd never ever felt like that did. I pulled out again, this time almost all the way, and then pushed in until I was back inside him all the way again.

When I went to pull out one more time Clay squeezed down and I felt the thick edge of his hole drag along my cock and then, just at the end, it grabbed on behind the head of it, keeping me inside.

Clay groaned when I went back into him and I stopped, afraid I was hurting him. It didn't matter anyway because just then I let go and shot off inside him. He rocked back and forth on my cock, pulling the cum out of me and making me weak with how good it felt.

Clay let me stay inside him 'til I began to go soft and then he gently pushed me out. When he turned around I saw he'd gotten hard while I fucked him.

Mr. Percy laughed when he noticed how Clay was. "You want to change your mind about givin' up bein' the stick man?" he asked.

Clay shook his head. "No sir."

He took some lard and began to slick up his erect member with it. "What you see here is anticipation. Been a long while since ol' Piss-Eye has been into anything besides my fist. We both been lookin' forward to this for a some time now." He turned to me and smiled. "I'll try to be gentle on you Dan'l, but you better bite down on that stick I gave you before you bend yourself over that log for me."

Both Clay and Mr. Percy laughed when I put the stick in my mouth. "No son, not like that," Mr. Percy said. "It goes cross-wise, like a horse bit, so you bite down with your back teeth." That embarrassed me and I had to turn away while I seated the stick in my mouth.

"Okay Dan'l, you ready?" Clay bent me over the log and pushed his cock up against my ass. I began to shiver, wanting to feel him inside me, just like that logger had felt Gatt inside him.

I guess Clay thought I was scared 'cause he said, "Now don't you worry none. I'll go in real slow and easy." He pushed gently against my ass and I felt myself opening up to him, letting him in. He did go in real slow and I guess it did hurt a little when he first put the head in but before I knew it I was feeling something wonderful that I'd never felt before. Part of it was how Clay was filling me up with himself and part of it was just the way it felt, his big, hard cock pushing into me. It felt so good I guess I groaned or something because he stopped and waited a bit, rubbing my back and telling me it was going to be okay. I knew somehow that I wasn't supposed to be liking it like I did so I just waited until he pushed some more of himself into me, asking if it was okay. I nodded and wished he'd hurry. I wanted to feel him up against me and know I'd taken all he had to give and it was all up inside me. When it finally was I felt a strange tickling on my balls. I figured out it was Clay's balls, swinging against my own. I thought I might come just from the feel of that. Clay pulled out a little and then pushed back in until his balls were up against mine again. I squeezed down on him and he did it again, pulling out more and pushing in faster.

After a bit he was pulling almost all the way out and then pushing back in so fast it made me moan with how good it felt. "It's okay, Dan'l. Hold on. I'm almost there. Almost," Clay panted in my ear. When he did come it was too much for me and I came too, spraying my spunk out against the log. When he was through he pulled himself out of me, his cock still hard and dripping and gave my butt a gentle pat. I didn't want them to see that I'd come while Clay was fucking me so I let go and peed a little.

Then I stood up and turned away from them, peeing into the bushes so they wouldn't see I'd been hard. Clay looked at the wetness on the log and said I should always pee before taking on one of the men so that wouldn't happen. "You done good

Dan'l," Mr. Percy said, patting my butt while I peed. His voice was low, kind of hoarse sounding, and he was breathing hard.

When I finished and turned around I could see his britches standing out from his cock being hard. "You ready for me?" he asked. He took his suspenders down and let his britches come open.

I said I was but I didn't turn back to the log; I wanted to see what his cock looked like. He let his britches fall and I saw that it wasn't very big. It was kind of pretty though, with the head just barely peaking out from its dark hood of skin. I bent myself over the log again and Clay put the stick in my mouth so I could bite down on it. I was glad of it because Mr. Percy pushed into me and commenced to fuck me in a way that felt so good I couldn't help but cry out a little. Mr. Percy began to whisper in my ear, telling me it would be all right and he was real close and just hang on for a little, stuff like that. Then he let go and started shooting off inside me, fucking me just as hard and fast as he could. I clamped my ass muscle down on him and he shot more and more until he finally collapsed against my back and just lay there, trying to catch his breath.

After Mr. Percy slipped out of me we all three went down to the creek and bathed. There was some soap kept down there and Clay washed me, being real careful of my ass. "You'll be sore for a little," he said when he touched the soap to my ass, "but the men won't be pesterin' you 'til tomorrow and it'll be gone by then." He gave me a hug just for a second and I thought he might be going to kiss me but he just looked me in the eye and smiled. "I guess I'll be one of the ones pesterin' you the most. Like I said, it's been a long time." I guess word got around pretty quick that I was going to take on the position of stick man and most everybody asked me to sit with them at supper. The cook made sure I had the biggest slice of his good berry pie for desert and said I could have more of it any time I wanted. After supper we sat around the fire and swapped stories for a while. Everyone seemed to have his jug of whiskey with him and they all offered me some. There was some sort of card game goin' on too and pretty much everyone tried their hand at for a while and it seemed to me like there was a lot of tension in the air. That went away after a while and the loggers seemed to kind of drift off and then a short, wiry man called

Ben came and sat down next to me. We sat and stared at the fire for a while before he spoke.

"See, Dan'l," he said, "we can't none of us rightly come to you for a, you know, 'til tomorrow so we played a little poker to see who'd get to be first." He smiled proudly at me. "Well, see, I won, so I was wondering if – well, if maybe I could sorta sleep with you tonight so's in the morning I could, uh, I mean we could– you know, get on with it. First thing." He looked at me with shiny eyes.

I'd slept with one or another of my brothers all my life 'til I'd left the farm so I said sure, he could sleep with me. I began to get hard just thinkin' about what we would do in the morning and then I looked at Ben's crotch, saw that he was the same way.

Clay gave up his bunk to me which was a little wider than the others – I guess because of the job – and it was set behind a little curtain at one end the bunkhouse. The other men laughed and pointed at Ben's crotch when we went through but Ben held up his head, even if he did turn a little red in his cheeks. We went to bed without even a nightshirt which I'd never done before and it made me come up hard almost before we got under the sheet.

When we settled down to sleep I wanted to reach out and see how big Ben's cock was but I figured I'd better not 'cause he might think I was kind of anxious and I didn't think that was a good idea. Once the rest of the men had gone off to sleep Ben rolled over and pressed himself up against me. His cock was hard and he pressed it into the crack of my ass, pretending he was asleep. We laid that way for a little while and then he began to rub against me. Finally he put his mouth to my ear and whispered, "Oh, Dan'l, please. Let me inside you, just for a little." His mouth against my ear that way made me weak as water. I took the little can of lard from beside the bed and handed it back to him. Ben's cock was thicker and longer than Clay's but once the big, flaring head was inside me the rest slid in easily.

When he was in all the way Ben put his arms around me and pulled me tight against him. For a while I was afraid his hands might go too low and find that my cock was hard as his but he moved his hands up instead and rubbed his fingers over my chest.

We lay that way for a long time, Ben inside me but not moving, just lying still and holding me. After a while I think he fell asleep but then he stirred in me and I felt his cock begin to swell even larger and it seemed like it got harder, too, like an iron bar. His fingers took hold of my tits and rubbed them gently, sending little lightning bolts down to my cock. Then he let out a ragged kind of sigh and he came in me, his stuff so hot I could feel it against my insides. He didn't move much and I could feel his cock pulsing inside me as he shot. I touched myself and very quickly I came too, biting down on my tongue so I wouldn't cry out with the pleasure of it.

When it was over we went to sleep, Ben still inside me. Ben woke me before the first light of morning by growing hard inside me and beginning to move just a little with short, cautious strokes. He slid his hand down my belly and felt of my cock. I guess he thought it was hard from having to pee because he whispered in my ear, "You got to go too bad to finish this up?"

When I shook my head he whispered, "I'll be real gentle" and rolled me over onto my belly. He was gentle and very quiet about it. I thought maybe he was only supposed to do it once and he hoped when the other men woke they wouldn't know he'd already had his turn. He told me later that was true.

Anyway, it didn't take him long, probably because he'd been inside me all night and every time we'd moved in our sleep it'd brought him up a little further. He did moan a little when he came but it was deep in his throat and could have sounded like a snore to anyone who didn't know what Ben was doing. When he began to go soft he slipped out of me and whispered, "We'll go on outside so's you can piss that thing away."

We crept quietly through the bunkhouse and out into the cool morning air and then we stood next to each other and peed, Ben hitting my stream with his, the splash catching the first light of dawn.

When we were through he led me back into the bunkhouse and back to my bed. "You take it again, Dan'l?" he asked quietly, cupping my butt with his big hands. He was already hard.

I nodded and handed him the lard. I was feeling kind of

empty after spending the night with him inside me.

"Might be a little rougher this time," he said laying down a thin film of lard on his cock and grinning at me. "Gotta wake up the boys." He put me on my belly, careful that my cock was laid out under me, almost like he knew it would get hard when he went into me. "Better have this, just in case," he said, handing me the stick Clay had made for me. I put it between my jaws and bit down on it but I think we both knew I wouldn't need it. He went in fast, shoving his cock into me all at once and making me suck in my breath. He waited a moment and then began to fuck me with long, steady strokes that quickly had me groaning and pushing back against him each time he pushed into me.

After a while he shifted, laying all of his weight on me and fucking me with just the head of his cock, pulling the flair of his cockhead against my ass muscle until it pulled out and then pushing it back in, just enough to do it over again.

I tried to hold myself back but the longer he fucked me the bigger my bubble of pleasure got until I couldn't hold it back anymore. I guess that brought him off because as soon as I started shooting my stuff he did too.

Afterward he stayed inside me until he went soft. When he pulled out he slapped me loudly on the ass and said, "Come on Dan'l, lets go see if Cook has the coffee made."

I waited until he was pulling on his britches before I rolled off the bed and jumped into my own, wiping the cum off my belly as I did. Then I made the bed in a hurry so he wouldn't see the big wet spot I'd made. The bunkhouse smelled like cum as we walked through and Ben paused at the door. "Okay, men, you got yourselves up and off. Now you just got to get yourselves up." He laughed and took my hand, leading me to the cook shack. "Damn I'm the lucky one," he said, "getting to be first." Ben was the most fun, maybe because he liked to do it the most, but the others were good too and they all had their ways. Like Sam, who never could get it all the way in me before he came, and Will, who found out he could make me come and then took great delight in doing it. Ben sometimes liked to make a spectacle of himself, fucking me in the shower room or out at the camp fire where everyone could watch him doing it. He also liked to sneak silently into my bed sometimes and sleep with his cock in me. He was the only one who ever did that and I came to look forward to it.

And then there was Frank. He liked to fuck well enough but what he wanted more than anything in the world was for me to take his cock in my mouth and suck on it.

One Sunday afternoon in the fall I gave in and let his dream come true. We were down at the creek and he made a big show of washing himself and then, standing naked in front of me, wiped his cock with some sweet vanilla extract he'd stolen from the cook shack. When I took him in my mouth he tasted just like candy. I liked doing it too, because he liked it so much. After a while that's all we ever did together. It turned out that Clay liked getting sucked off too. He found me doing it to Frank one afternoon and he just pulled out his cock and stood next to Frank, waiting for me to finish him. When I did he moved right in and put his cock in my mouth. He came in no time at all and then Frank got into an argument with him because he would never let Frank do it to him when he was the stick man. They made up though and came around together a lot, wanting to watch each other get sucked off.

When winter came a lot of the men left the camp but I told Mr. Percy I would stay on until he could find a new stick man in the spring. There wasn't much to do around the camp in winter except shovel snow, sleep, swap stories and play cards. And fuck. We did a lot of that, a couple of times almost all of us together. We'd just get in a mood and it would happen, all of us naked in front of the fire, me and Clay and Sven – who was once a stick man himself – taking on all the rest of them any way they wanted and then taking on each other, sometimes all three of us together, putting on a kind of show for the others.

I learned to carve that winter, too, and I made a stick for whoever the new man was going to be. I made it like the one Clay had made for me only I made the knobs on the ends look like real cockheads. Ben insisted on being the model, so I'd get them just right.

In April a man came around looking for work and after a couple of days Mr. Percy made him the stick man. It was too cold yet for the clearing by the creek so he got initiated in Mr. Percy's office, laid over the desk. He bit down pretty hard on the stick I gave him but I watched when Mr. Percy had his turn and I saw the light go on in his eyes. He was liking it and I knew he'd make a good stick man. After he was settled in I took the supply wagon back down to the camp outside Truckee, to see if Gatt was still around. He was and he was happy to see me, too. "How'd it go, Dan Boy?"

"Good."

"You got your stick?" I handed it to him and he turned it over and over, looking at it. "Not many teeth marks are there? And these ones ain't very deep."

I laughed. "Those are pretty much for show. Fact is, I liked it, being the stick man. Only – "

Gatt looked at me sharply. "Only what?"

"Well, I pretty much had my fill. I think I'd like to settle down with just one man now. The same one all the time."

Gatt smiled. "How 'bout me?"

"That's just what I been thinkin'. You."

Then Gatt did something to me no man ever did before. He took me in his arms and he kissed me and I liked that better than anything. "You want to go look at a little farm I found? Two men could handle it easy."

I nodded. I thought I'd like farming with Gatt. Besides, we could be stick men to each other, keep it in the family.

TIES THAT BIND

Duncan P. Allen

My junior high school in Houston ended its spring semester late in a May and my aunt, who is my father's only sibling, and her husband invited me to take a train over to Beaumont and spend the second week of June with them. The elder Johnsons lived in Beaumont with their two sons, fourteen-year-old Jeff and his brother, Alan, who was not quite two years Jeff's junior.

I had been in Beaumont — a dingy, humdrum little port city in deep Southeast Texas near the Louisiana border — a few times as a child and then as a young teenager, but had never stayed at the home of my aunt and uncle. The reason was that my mother's parents also lived in Beaumont; my parents and my sister and I (or just me alone on a few occasions) had always stayed at the home of my maternal grandparents whenever any of us had traveled to that doleful burgh. "Dan," as my family called my mother's father, was an eminent civil engineer; he and my grandmother lived in a spacious, elegant house they owned in one of the very few stylish areas of Beaumont. My aunt Susan, a pleasant but not an inordinately bright woman, had married about sixteen years earlier my uncle, Gus Johnson, a man about whom the rest of the family had not been pleased, to say the least. Uncle Gus was amiable enough, but the hapless guy was "boring from across the street" — as my father was inclined to remind us frequently. In addition, my poor uncle had never managed to hold onto the same job for any length of time.

As a result of the Johnsons' constantly less-than-affluent state of affairs — they were poor compared to what I'd always been accustomed to – their home was prosaic and slightly decrepit. My aunt and uncle, with help from their boys, even maintained an honest-to-God chicken coop in back of their house—a vile, smelly hutch in which they raised several dozen of those noisy, filthy fowls for food and eggs! My family thought such a practice tasteless at best.

My parents, both cultured and highly educated, had

perpetually been appalled at my aunt's selection of a spouse. Furthermore, even though my father had never specifically *labeled* my uncle "white trash."

On the bright side was the Johnsons' elder son Jeff. I'd experienced, on numerous occasions, vague longings for some variety of bodily contact with him. Although my yearnings had been as a rule indistinct and unfocused, they were nonetheless genuine and powerful.

Jeff and I had invariably been almost alike physically in both size and shape, with the single exception that I'd always been about an inch taller.

When I got off the train and saw Jeff standing on the platform, I was delighted that he was no longer as skinny as I still was, but he was still about an inch shorter than me. Jeff's body — boyishly attractive in concise, tan khaki shorts, a powder-blue T-shirt, and white socks and sneakers – had become extremely well-proportioned. He had told me during the preceding summer that he swam frequently in the Beaumont YMCA's indoor pool; the results now *showed* on him as an almost sculpted musculature.

Jeff's hair was now cut quite short like mine, and was of a light yellowish brown shade, while mine had a dark brown cast. Plus, his eyes were of a bewitching and bright emerald hue, in contrast with mine, which were as dark brown as was my hair. Jeff's nose was a refined little pug, while mine was a straight, relatively large protuberance.

Aunt Susan, Uncle Gus, and Jeff met my train at the Beaumont Southern Pacific Railway depot that Friday afternoon, then drove me in their old Chevy to their house. After we arrived and I'd carried my suitcase in, I discovered Jeff and I would be sharing his *bed* as well as his bedroom! Jeff's room had only a *full*-size bed – not even a double. I knew I was definitely going to have a problem in trying to keep myself on *my* half of the bed, given its narrow width. Adding to my consternation was the fact that I was realizing at this point how physically enticing my cousin appeared to me now. How was I to keep my hands off him?

As I stood there surveying the diminutive bed and picturing myself lying next to Jeff, my dick began to swell in my briefs. I had a difficult time concealing my excitement all through dinner.

That June night was a hot, humid one and Jeff told me he wanted to take a shower. Once we got to his room, Jeff stood by the bed and instantly stripped down to his briefs, Jockey brand, the same as mine.

Jeff's hasty disrobing inspired me to muster all my courage and do the same, even if in a dawdling and *seriously* self-conscious manner; I'd always been paranoid about undressing in front of anyone.

I noticed that Jeff watched me continually as I stood on the other side of the bed from him and removed my sneakers and socks, then my yellow polo shirt and blue Levi's. Yet I wasn't sure what if anything to make of his behavior. I wondered uneasily if the small mound made by my flaccid dick in my briefs looked as insignificant to him as it felt to me. Jeff had exhibited, I felt, a much more impressive-looking protrusion in his Jockeys after he'd taken off his khaki shorts.

He headed for the door on his way toward the only bathroom, which was next door to his room.

Before he left, Jeff paused at the door, idly scratching his buttcheeks with both hands. He smiled warmly at me, then said in a gracious tone, "Mike, go ahead and pick out a magazine from that stack on the bedside table, since I know how much you like to read. Just sprawl out and make yourself at home, and I'll be back in a jiffy."

I returned his smile, thanked him, and then flopped onto the bed, where I attempted to assimilate the Table of Contents of the current issue of *Reader's Digest*; that task, though, proved hopeless, for I was becoming more tense by the minute as I heard the sounds made by Jeff's showering. I speculated curiously about him — surprised both at the persistence and at the wanton nature of my preoccupations.

Wondering lustfully what my cousin's bare, athletic and now pubescent body looked like under the spray of the shower, I pondered whether he might be massaging his full balls and lathering up, then fondling and milking his lengthening pubescent penis in the same way I habitually treated mine while taking a shower. My libidinous daydream about Jeff's genitals stimulated me in fresh and unfamiliar ways, causing me to grow a nearly hard dick. I rolled onto my stomach to hide my growing predicament.

Soon Jeff returned, wearing only a fluffy white towel cinched around his waist. "Hey, you want a shower, too?"

"Hey," I answered, but I became even *more* disquieted than I already was: Jeff pulled his towel off his midsection and began to give his hair a painstaking drying, with his head bent all the way forward. Of course I at once had an unobstructed, covert view, a vista of the totality of his physique — and it was *all* magnificent.

He tossed his head back, shook his hair into place, and then threw his towel onto the dresser, which stood on the opposite side of the room from the bed. Nude, he stood facing me, only about ten feet away. I was spellbound as I gaped at the remarkable attractiveness of the boy I'd known who'd so fast transmuted into an striking adolescent. His dark blond hair was slightly tousled; his pale skin glowed; his limp penis and ample, crinkled scrotum both appeared distinctively grown-up to be those of a fourteen-year-old. His dick was about two, maybe three, inches long in its droopy state, and was moderately thick, as well as circumcised. His dick's crown was slightly fatter than the shaft, and his ball-sac was full and furrowed, albeit as yet hairless.

I was *especially* intrigued, however, to see that Jeff had already sprouted an appealing little thatch of dark blond, almost light brown pubic hair, even if the growth was still fairly sparse compared to mine, and his thicket was of an inverted triangular shape, while mine had more of a rectangular form.

Jeff, now unexpectedly and incredibly enticing to me, opened a dresser drawer and pulled out a pair of Jockey briefs, then pulled them on. He told me he was going to lie down and read a magazine while I showered, to which I replied, "Okay; I'll be back soon." As he fluffed up his pillow, with his back to me, I quickly stood up and went to the dresser, grabbed my shaving kit and fresh briefs, then dashed for the bathroom. My unruly dick was still half-way stiff in my Jockeys.

My cock did its predictable thing in the surroundings: it immediately distended into a powerful erection, pointing toward the ceiling. But after I'd stroked it gently a few times, I managed to ignore its pulsing plea.

Once back in the room, I noticed that Jeff had switched off

the garish overhead light and was lying on his back, reading by the goose-neck lamp on his bedside table. The manner in which my fetching relative looked up at me from his magazine as I swung open his room door sticks with me to this day: He beamed an irresistible smile at me.

"Better now?"

I nodded. He told me to lock the door, then asked me where my pajamas were.

"Yeah, I always do wear p.j.'s at home, and Mother *did* pack a pair of 'em for me. But hell, I feel like the weather's too damn hot to even bother with puttin' 'em on."

"Yeah, it's hot tonight. Let's leave the sheet down, okay?"

"Yeah," I agreed.

I sat on the bed. Jeff was lying beside me on his back, smiling up at me, displaying a plentiful, arching mound in the crotch of his briefs. My crotch and balls tingled hotly, and my dick felt as if it could readily swell into a complete erection in my briefs and then shoot a mammoth load with just the slightest provocation.

Without saying a word, Jeff hit the switch to the goose-neck lamp beside the bed. The reflected, ethereal, bluish-white rays of moonlight bathed the room in lustrous illumination as they streamed in through the room's four lofty, wide-open windows and Venetian blinds.

As I flopped down on my stomach and attempted to get into a comfortable position on the mattress, my cousin rolled over and laid a hand cautiously on my exposed back, right between my shoulder blades.

At once I froze, having no idea *what* to do or say. Jeff stroked my back gently and openly while he confided to me in a quiet voice how he felt about me: "Cousin, I think we're gonna have a *great* time together."

I turned my head. He smiled. "I've really been lookin' forward to spendin' a week with you."

"I noticed. I suppose you noticed, too."

I was speechless as his hand moved down to my briefs, then slid under me to grip my cock. He left it there for a moment, squeezed it, then removed his hand. I moaned. As I slid my hips carefully back toward his body, Jeff mounted me. I was stunned as he rode his stiff cock up and down in my cotton-covered crack. As I rubbed my butt intimately over the sublime stiffness of his cock, his hand gripped my right forearm tighter and pulled my torso even closer to his own, until I knew that the back of my head must be very near his face. Next I felt Jeff shove his pelvis forward, thus increasing his cock's pressure on my inconceivably responsive ass.

I groaned, "Umm" low in my throat while cuddling my body as close to his as I could and relishing the exhilarating, amorous sensations his stalwart hard-on was giving me as it pressed against the crack of my ass.

Before long Jeff's right arm and hand hugged me even tighter as he grazed the tip of his nose on the nape of my neck. He unnerved me by murmured softly onto the back of my ear, "Umm-umm."

He slid his right hand over onto the uppermost area of my chest; he began rubbing me there, using light, circular motions. This drove me *wild* with carnal enjoyment, and I didn't even *think* of trying to halt his caresses, in spite of my fleeting thoughts of our possible wrongdoing. My cousin's hand slipped gently upward onto the front of my neck, and then caressed me there before sliding onto my collar bones and into my right armpit. He stroked and toyed with the patch of sweaty hairs in my pit. I groaned.

Next his hand slipped onto my chest until it reached my nipples. He delicately tweaked and caressed each of the nibs in turn, making effortless, circular motions on them with his fingertips. At last he stroked my tummy and then my right side with subtle gentleness. "Hey cousin, what are you *doin'*?"

Jeff glided his hand from my side down onto my right hip, which he rubbed lightly through my briefs. In reply he whispered softly, his lips making an electrifying contact with the back of my ear, "Well, I was watchin' you and you were as hard as I was, which must mean we want the same thing."

"Yeah," was all I could muster at this point.

His hand persisted in its firm rubbing of my right buttock. My body stiffened.

"Okay," Jeff continued in a quiet voice, "just relax."

Inhaling a deep breath in a vain attempt to calm myself, I said, "Well, I've never slept with anybody before, and I guess just the idea of it turns me on."

"I've never slept with anyone else, either. So my dick just got so damn hard — for *some* strange reason," he added slowly, followed by a little giggle and a firm squeeze of my ass.

Here Jeff paused for a long, meaningful time, but continued the movement of his cock in my crack. "Shit, I even got *real* close to jacking off in the shower."

"Hmm," I murmured, "I'm glad you didn't."

"You are?"

"You know I am."

His hand sought my hard-on again. "Yeah."

"We've both grown a bit, haven't we?"

"Well yeah, and I like to give it plenty of exercise. You too?"

I sniggered uneasily at my cousin's obvious allusion to masturbation, and flexed my butt's muscles

Jeff murmured an abstracted "Umm-*hmm*" as he gradually glided his hand down onto the front of my briefs, pulled out my cock and let his fingers stroke lightly up and down it.

"Ooo, *Jesus!*" I groaned.

I placed my right hand on the back of his hand and wrapped his fingers solidly around my cock's rigid staff. "Oh *yes*, Jeff!"

Then I moved my right hand behind me to the front of his briefs, encircled my fingers around his expanded dick. I moaned. He rolled onto his back, tugged off his briefs, spread his legs at a wide angle, and clasped his hands behind his head, thus allowing me ready access to his genital area. I sat up and used one hand to fondle and then hold tightly his forceful hard-on, and used the other hand to grasp and to caress his balls. Jeff was almost a year younger than me but his cock was *fully* as long, and every bit as thick, as mine. The vision of his exposed, highly aroused privates made my own cock throb responsively in my briefs, its dilated head threatening to jut above their waistband.

Jeff moaned in deep, euphoric tones when I gripped his solid cock with my right hand and masturbated it slowly while I squeezed his flexing scrotum and its twitching, reactive testicles with my left hand. "Man, Jeff," I groaned as I joyfully appreciated the velvety yet dense stiffness of his distended staff in my right hand, and mature ball-sac in my left.

Jeff sighed, "Ohhh yeah!"

I spotted a glistening drop of liquid poised on his cock's tip.

I knew he was close so I stopped. I lay down on my back as Jeff removed my briefs and knelt between my splayed legs. Jeff began moaning in contented tones as he rubbed my armpits, collarbones, chest, tummy, and abdomen with both hands; next he raked his fingers through my pubic thicket. He commented in an aroused voice, "Man, I just *love* all this hair you got."

Jeff then stroked longingly and admiringly the head and shaft of my jerking prick; using both hands, he gripped both my cock's shank and my tautly wrinkled scrotum. He sensitively massaged my testicles with his left hand while he stroked the silken stalk of my taut, convulsing cock with his right. Fondling my genitals, he said, "Wow, I'm *amazed* at how similar your dick looks and feels to *mine* when it's hard!"

He gripped me even tighter, and began to jack me off at a sexy pace.

"Ohh, that feels fuckin' *unreal*," I sighed.

As I felt my balls start to churn and my cock begin to sting from what felt like the huge load of come rising within, I warned him, "Whoa!"

Jeff chuckled softly as he let go of my throbbing cock. "Okay, cousin," he cooed in an engaging tone. Next he astonished me by stretching his body out full-length on top of mine. As I felt his torso, limbs, and rigid cock settle onto me, my excitement was boundless.

"Oh, Jeff!"

Jeff settled his upper body and his legs firmly onto mine. Next he carefully aligned our hard cocks. We lay immobile for a short time, but soon began to entwine and writhe our burning bodies, our heads, and our rigid cocks into every conceivable position. Jeff wrapped his arms around my trunk, and as we rubbed our right cheeks together. He raised himself up a bit and reached down to tuck his rigid spear between my upper thighs.

I squeezed my legs tightly around the shaft of his embedded cock. Without any hesitancy I moaned, "Oh yeah! *Fuck* me, Jeff!"

"You've *got* it, baby," he growled back at me as he plunged his stiff, slick cock in and out of its snug harbor, the upper surface scraping against my balls and my cockroot with maddening sensuality. As the intensity of our mutual moaning and the excitement of our voluptuous cock-to-crotch union increased, Jeff murmured, "Holy sh*it*, I'm gettin' *real* close to comin', and I'll bet *you* are too!"

I lay completely inert under Jeff's weight as I whispered, "Yeah, so let's switch." At that we rolled over together, ending up with me straddling him. I reached down for my cock and positioned it between Jeff's splayed legs; he quickly brought his thighs together to trap my prick.

We ceased all movement, and with me lying comfortably astride him, he asked, "Mike, doesn't this feel *wild*? Go ahead and act as if you're screwin' me — if I were a girl!"

Eagerly doing his bidding, I pumped in and out of Jeff's hot, flexing, thigh-pussy.

Soon the heat and friction produced by Jeff's thighs on my captive dick caused it to pulsate. I stopped; I didn't want to come so soon.

"Hey, shot your load."

After rolling off him so that I could lie next to him on his right side, I began by first gently caressing his arms and armpits, then his chest and nipples, and then his sleek tummy. Next I combed my fingers through his pubic hair; then I cupped and squeezed his heavy balls. Jeff was sighing and groaning.

I slithered the tips of my fingers sensitively up and down the underside of his quivering shaft, then around his cock's head, tracing its flared rim. Gripping his now pulsing, jumping cock a couple of inches below its bulging crown, I began to masturbate him at an unhurried but uniform pace. I slid the taut skin of Jeff's exuberant erection languidly up and down the distance of the shaft; then I moved my hand up to execute mild milking motions on the mushy, dilated, and now purplish-pink head of his solid phallus. As I performed a few pumping squeezes of his corona, a string of pre-cum oozed from his piss slit onto my palm and thumb. Jeff sighed, "Umm! Oh *yeah*."

I smeared the slick juice over his cock's head and rubbed it in as I swirled my wetted palm and fingers over, around, and beneath the ridge of his cock's distended crown. "Umm, *baby*," I whispered.

Wrapping my fist tightly around the strained, energized shaft of his cock and compressing it firmly, I watched its princely head swell. Another healthy string of translucent, glistening pre-cum flowed from the piss-slit and trickled over the head and down onto my thumb. As I grasped the shaft determinedly, I adored feeling Jeff's hot blood pulsing swiftly through the erectile tissues under the velvety, stretched skin of his stiff cock. As I speeded up the rhythm, he began to moan more deeply, twisting and arching his torso under the authority of my skillful stroking. I cuddled and fondled his warm, excitement-tightened balls with my left hand while I used my right fist to beat him off in an ever-quickening tempo.

Jeff groaned and thrashed rapturously on the bed, then cried, "Ooo, beat me *off*, baby! Ohhh, friggin' *Christ*, I'm gonna *come!*"

"Ahh yeahh!" he screamed as he began to squirt. His entire trunk shook and spasmed forcefully when his climax overtook him. He hurled his head back onto the pillow as he soaked both our chests and bellies.

I groaned as the surges of his emissions at last subsided, then ultimately dwindled. I continued my fondling and milking of the top of his shaft and the head of his trembling cock — milking them until I'd finally squeezed every last drop of cum from him. I released his cock and picked up the towel he had worn after his shower.

As I vigilantly mopped up the viscous pools of cum, I whispered, "Hot *damn*, you sure did shoot a *gigantic* load!"

"That really was *fantastic*."

"I'm tickled that you liked my technique, cousin," I told him in a soft voice. Then, without warning, I knew what I *had* to do: I kissed my cousin on his lips. His warm, moist lips tasted so luscious and felt so welcome that I redoubled my fervent efforts.

When I felt his lips part and I sensed the tip of his tongue sliding cautiously into my quickly opening mouth, I requited his tongue's proposition with light-headed eagerness, thinking how altogether fleshly, as well as romantic and fitting, our kissing seemed. Our kisses abruptly became more expressive, sloppier, and more penetrating, with both of our tongues probing ever more intimately into the other's mouth.

Jeff wrapped his left hand around the shaft of my burning dick, squeezed it firmly, and then held onto it tightly. At length we broke off what had progressed into my first-ever deep kiss of anyone, male or female (and most likely his too, I presumed).

"I can't *believe* we *did* that, or that *I* wanted to do it as much as *you* did! And I'm sure *you* want to come *too*, and kissin' each other like we just did *damn* near pushed me over the edge a *second* time! I mean, I still haven't lost my hard-on, and I was gettin' *awfully* close to blastin' another load, *believe* me."

"I do believe you," I assured him.

"Now how 'bout if I get over on your right side?" Jeff proposed. "That way I can use my *right* hand on that tempting cock of yours. I never have been able to jack off with my left hand!"

I chuckled as he crawled over me to position himself to my right and maneuvered himself into position.

Jeff began by using the same stroking and petting motions on my groin, that I'd used on his; then soon he gripped my shaft and went to work in an expert fashion. My cousin's rapidly moving hand, whipping on my rigid cock, quickly set me to sighing, crooning, grunting, and thrashing my body around impetuously on the bed.

After what seemed like a very brief interval, the muscles of my entire anatomy — my chest, stomach, buttocks, arms, legs, and neck — all convulsed and tightened mightily as the inevitable waves of impending gratification washed over me. Swiftly my whole body spasmed and jerked. "Ohhh, *yeahh*, Jeff! Oh *fuck* yeah, baby! I'm gonna shoot my load!" As the first fierce eruption hit me, I raised my head off the pillow to watch in frenzied exhilaration as my first thick ropes of semen gushed from my dick.

The forceful initial stream landed with a soft *plop* on the front of my neck. Jeff bent down and began to French-kiss me greedily as he continued to jerk me. I returned his by now familiar, probing kiss with passionate zeal, clamping my mouth tightly over his and thrusting my tongue between his parted lips, and then far into his mouth.

As I'd done for him, Jeff continued beating me off until he'd drained every last drop of cum.

After he finished blotting my jism off of his and my body with his now well-moistened towel, we promptly found sleep wrapped in each other's arms.

When I awoke the next morning, Jeff was snuggled up against me with his head resting lovingly on my right shoulder. I kissed him sensitively on the lips as he slowly and reluctantly opened his eyes. "Mornin', Mike. Guess what lyin' here snuggled up against your sweet warm body has done to *me*?"

He took my hand and placed it on his stiff cock. Of course, we soon had to reprise our prior feat of jacking each other off to forceful climaxes, except this time we did it to each other concurrently. Jeff spread the towel out under both our midsections; then we lay on our sides facing each other and gripped each other's lance. We each came in record time, and as our climaxes subsided, we blotted off each other's belly, and pubic hair with Jeff's handy towel — that towel which was nowhere near dried out yet from the night before.

As you might expect, during that week in Beaumont, Jeff and I became devoted to each other.

Over the next few months, we saw each other whenever we could and we experimented with fellatio. I have never known greater joy than having Jeff's mouth on my cock and mine on his. We developed a routine of stretching out on the bed fully clothed, then proceeding to remove, slowly, every item of the other's clothing. Once we'd finished stripping each other, we'd lie on our sides and snuggle close, cuddling and stroking comfortably the other's nude body. We'd smooch without reserve, passionately and wetly as we masturbated the other's swelling cock into a burning hard-on.

After a protracted bout of intimate, sopping French-kissing — during which time we'd cuddle the other's balls and massage each other's throbbing erection — one of us would swivel his body 180 degrees, and then we'd indulge in a leisurely sixty-nine until we both arrived right at the brink of climax. At that stinging moment, we'd each withdraw his rampant cock from the other's mouth and then jack each other off to an ecstatic, spurting climax.

Once our bellies and our chests had become soaked with the other's discharge, we'd spin around and French-kiss again. At length we'd climb into the shower and affectionately lather up and scrub every inch of the other's slick but much-relieved body. It surely was the most blissful period of my life.

Jeff eventually married and moved to California. I visited them only once. During that time, I had the opportunity to be with him alone. Over a couple of beers, I was stunned that, in his mind, our sexual adventures were simply convenient methods of first, relieving our sexual tensions, and second, of expressing our deep fondness for another member of the family. I, on the other hand, do not fear to admit the truth.

A FAMILY AFFAIR IN RIO

Daniel Dee

*"I love to sail forbideen seas,
and land on barbarous coasts."*
- Herman Melville, "Moby Dick"

"I made love and was happy."
Joseph Addison, August, 1711

The overnight flight from Miami was full and I felt cramped and tired by the time we finally approached the Brazilian coast at Rio de Janeiro the following morning. But upon my first glimpse of the city, I was suddenly alert and the long flight forgotten. As we descended for our landing I saw the lush, verdant mountains with masses of high-rise hotels wedged between them and the beautiful coastline with their white sandy beaches and clear blue waters. Off in the distance I could see the famous statue of Christ the Redeemer atop the mountain peak at Corcavado and I knew I was approaching paradise. I sat back in my seat, closed my eyes and dreamed of the adventures that lay ahead.

It was August, the winter season in Brazil, not carnival time but I didn't care. After several years of hard work as a senior computer analyst, and fast approaching my thirtieth birthday, I was looking forward to a quiet, but hopefully eventful, vacation. My excitement was building as I eased through customs and looked for my driver. I had decided to spare no expense and arrange for a car and driver during my stay.

Finally, among all the signs being held up, I saw one with my name on it. Carrying the sign was a hunk straight out of one of the Latino sex videos I had been renting lately, sort of boning up for my trip, you might say. The driver's size alone was intimidating. He should have been on a construction crew, stripped to the waist, not driving a car for tourists, with a starched white shirt and black trousers. He was tall, muscular, exceptionally broad-shouldered, and he radiated power, virility, and danger like the sun radiates heat. My gaze dropped to the crotch. I could not believe the enormity of the bulge I saw there. I shuddered, imagining what such a weapon would look like if aroused.

Speaking decent English, the man tipped his little black cap and introduced himself as Hector. I apologized that I didn't speak any Portuguese, and he said he didn't mind, he would take care of everything. To demonstrate this, he took my baggage checks and fetched the luggage, then led me to the exit. His muscles rippled as he walked quickly toward the car and his tight pants crept between his firm, smooth mounds of assflesh as he bent over to stow my bags in the trunk of the ancient, but beautifully maintained, black Cadillac Sedan deVille. I couldn't believe it – here I was in Brazil for the boys and I was being turned-on by a hunk older than I was.

As I settled in the luxurious backseat, Hector asked me to say frankly if I wanted the usual tourist chit-chat. He had a regular spiel, undoubtedly painfully learned and thought to be mostly accurate, that he would be happy to provide if I desired. I told him no thanks, but that if we did pass something of more than ordinary interest I'd appreciate hearing about that.

We began our ride to Copacabana beach where I would be staying and I'd thought the street by which we'd been travelling had been narrow, but the deeper we went into the city the more I got the feeling the huge car was going to hit a point of no return, and we would be stuck like a cork in a bottle. But Hector drove blithely along, honking at pedestrians and shooing them into taking refuge in doorways.

"Short cut," he laughed. "Short cut."

At last, we popped out onto a street that once more had two-way traffic and was lined with shops. Some displayed items aimed at the tourist trade but most were selling groceries and hardware and what people needed to live. I drew a deep breath. "I never thought we'd come out of that," I gasped.

"No more short cuts."

"No, no more." He went on to tell me that he wanted to avoid the slum areas called favelas that rimmed all sections of the city. He warned me to stay out of these areas, filled as they are with pickpockets, prostitutes and transvestites. I told him that I wasn't really interested in the ladies of the evening.

Riding along the beachfront I couldn't get over the great numbers of beautiful men and boys primping and preening in their very skimpy tight briefs. Their bronzed bodies and playful cavorting while playing volleyball and soccer on the sand had me distracted and interested. And my dream state was only encouraged by the fact that Brazil is a country where over half the population is under the age of 25.

In the rearview mirror, Hector observed me ogling the beach boys. He said, "Ah, Rio is a beautiful city filled with many friendly boys."

And friendly drivers, obviously.

At Hotel Bahia Rio, Hector took care of my bags and asked if I would need him any more that day. My eyes dropped to the bulge again and I had to stiffle my urge to extend him an invitation to join me for dinner. "No," I said, swallowing hard, "I am tired. I'll see you in the morning."

As he drove off, I noticed a group of six scantily clad youths leaning against a car across the street from the hotel. They watched me as I walked inside, and made various gestures and noises in an attempt to gain my attention. My god, was all of Rio like this? I turned for a moment to observe a striking teen who stood a short distance away from the group. Suddenly, Hector stopped his car in front of the youth. The boy approached the car and they exchanged words, then Hector drove off. I decided I would ask Hector about the boy in the morning.

Once in my suite, I stepped out onto my balcony, which faced the street in front of the hotel. The group of teens were still standing there. And the boy Hector had spoken briefly to was also still there. He was very slender and delicate in appearance wearing a white T-shirt and a pair of very tight blue shorts, with flared legs and cut up the sides nearly to the waist showing his deeply tanned legs to advantage. As he stepped over to the other boys, I noticed his perfect ass. I sighed deeply. Yes, I would have to ask Hector about him.

I tried taking a nap, but the image of the boys on the street would not let me. Finally, carrying my camera, I left the hotel. The group of teens had vanished. Hector's friend was still there, lurking in the shadows of the late afternoon sun.

As I looked over to him, he smiled at me, straightened his

shorts and ran his hand down over the tidy bulge in his groin.

The connection had been made, but I was reluctant to approach him. Hector said he would take care of everything; perhaps that meant arranging for dates as well. I would wait until morning.

I went up to the corner, crossed the street and walked towards the beachfront. As I strolled down the colorful mosaic walkway along Copacabana beach, I sensed I was being followed but when I turned I could see no one. I did see several beachboys playing and lying in the sand and I discreetly snapped their pictures.

Before long, the sun was beginning to go down and I headed back to the hotel. I again had the feeling I was being followed but when I looked back, I saw no one. I noticed a small building with a sign showing the figure of a man on it. I suddenly felt nature call. Inside there was a long trough along the wall. An elderly man was finishing up as I entered and, nodding to him, I went over to the trough to drain my bladder. As I began to piss, I glanced over my shoulder and saw the group of youths that I had noticed earlier in front of my hotel standing at the entrance of the toilet. They parted to allow the old man to leave and then closed ranks. They looked so menacing, I quickly finished my piss, zipped my fly and turned to leave the restroom. Two of them approached me, and soon the biggest of the group was pushing me back against the wall.

I raised up my hands to protect myself, but before I could fully react, one of the youths punched me in the stomach and the side of my jaw while the other quickly grabbed my arms and held them behind my back. My breath was knocked out of me and I crumpled over into a ball on the urine-soaked tile floor. They were talking and yelling at me in Portuguese so I didn't understand any of it.

One of the youths grabbed my camera and my watch while the other began to rummage through my pockets. All I had taken with me was the key to my suite. This pissed them off and one of them kicked me.

Suddenly, someone was screaming in a high-pitched tone, "*Policia, Policia!*" My attackers ran quickly out of the restroom, leaving me lying on the floor next to the urinal trough. I don't know how long I lay there, but as my dazed mind slowly focused and my eyes finally opened, I noticed Hector's friend standing alone in the doorway. He looked down at me with a quizzical, worried look on his face and cautiously crept towards me. He tried to help me up, speaking softly. I couldn't understand a word he was saying, but I knew that I had nothing to fear from this boy. Struggling, he helped me to my feet and supported me against the wall. I felt blood running down my cheek from a cut at the side of my forehead and from the side of my mouth. I also felt sharp pains in my head and ribs. All I could think of was how stupid I had been.

The youngster lifted my arm and placed it around his shoulder and gestured to me to see if I could walk. He led me out of the toilet and towards the hotel.

Leaning on the boy, I allowed him to lead me across the street and over to my hotel. As we passed through the entrance into the lobby, the elderly bellman, Jorge, and the desk manager, a man named William, came running up to us. They talked with the boy in Portuguese. William suggested that we call the police to report the incident. "No, no, I just want to go to my suite," I said.

They offered to help me, but I said the boy had gotten me this far, so he could certainly see me to my room.

"But – " William said. I waved him off and held onto the boy's tiny waist as he made quite a show of helping me to the elevators.

In the elevator, I smiled at him and said the only Portuguese word that I knew, "*Obrigado*," thank you, and hoped he really understood how grateful I was for his help. He giggled.

"My name is Danny."

He understood, pointed to himself. "Alexander."

"Bless you, Alexander."

As we entered my suite, I motioned for Alexander to help me to the bathroom.

I turned the taps and began to fill the huge tub with hot water. Alexander started to leave as I began getting undressed. "No, don't go," I said, and he understood.

He saw I was having trouble with the buttons of my shirt, and he began to help me. As he removed my shirt, he looked with wide eyes at my pale chest covered with dark blond hair and said, "Papa" while smoothing his hands over his hairless chest. I supposed that his father must also have a hairy chest. I began to open my trousers but he pushed my hands away and opened the belt and button and slid down the zipper, helping me out of the trousers. My head was spinning and my body was aching as he pulled my shorts off of me.

Slowly, I got into the tub. I lay back, luxuriating in warmth. Alex picked up a face cloth and a bar of soap and after sniffing the soap and soaping up the face cloth, he picked up my arm and began to scrub it. After a time, he was getting all wet and sweaty and I gestured for him to join me in the tub.

He grinned and quickly pulled off his T-shirt and dropped his shorts. He wore no underwear. I stared at his luscious cock. It was golden bronze in color like the rest of his body, slightly puffed up and pointing out a little from his groin and had a long, tight foreskin that outlined his helmet-shaped head and rode down beyond his cockhead another half an inch and ended in a beautiful soft fleshy pointed tip.

He saw me staring at it and he pulled the long foreskin forward, stretching it in his fingers far beyond his cockhead so his cock looked even more slender and longer. He twisted, pulled and rolled the soft, fleshy skin in his fingers. "Hmmmm," I murmured.

He grinned and hopped into the tub. He got on his knees facing me, and began to soap up my arms and legs, being careful when going over the areas where there were cuts, abrasions or bruises. I sat up and he started rubbing the soap into my chest and running his bare fingers through the curly hair and rubbing his palms over my taut nipples. He plunged his hands lower and began to scrub my abdomen and with the face cloth wrapped around his hand, he started to wash around my groin. My cock begun to bob up and down, breaking the surface of the water. He motioned for me to turn around in the tub so he could get at my back.

He quickly scrubbed my shoulders and back all the way down to my buttocks. He then poured water over my head and shampooed my hair and scrubbed my neck and ears carefully. He softly washed my face and the bruised areas around my forehead and mouth. While doing this, he pressed his chest against my back and wrapped his arms around my body. As he rubbed against me I felt his steely-hard prong pushing into my back down near my buttocks. By this time my cock was uncontrollably rigid and standing at full attention.

He slid back and I turned around so that I was facing him again. He was kneeling on his haunches and through the cloudy soapy water I could see his long slender cock bobbing up and down in an impatient, frenzied dance. I opened up my arms and he slid forward into them. I wrapped my arms around him. I held him softly, running my arms up and down his slick, warm body, stroking his back and neck as he squirmed and humped against me in pleasure.

Pulling him back a bit, I raised his face and, looking into his soft eyes, kissed him on the lips. He seemed surprised, but unafraid and didn't try to pull away. "*Obrigado, obrigado*, thank you, Alexander," I cooed. I kissed him again softly and rotated his body in my arms so that his back was now pressed against my abdomen. He slid down in the tub with his knees bent up. I spread my legs and he settled down further into the tub so that his bubblebutt was pressed against my groin. I began to soap up his body.

I can't adequately describe the pleasure I was feeling as this boy relaxed against me and allowed me to wash him. As he moved and slid against my slick skin, I felt my cock pushing against and between his ass cheeks. I shampooed his hair and washed his ears, neck and face. I slowly ran my hands down over his chest, feeling his nipples shiver and harden as my fingers twisted them until they stood up hard.

As my hands began to explore further down his body, scrubbing his abdomen and poking into his navel which caused him to buck and roll in the tub. Alex laughed aloud.

I approached his groin slowly, but Alex couldn't wait any longer and grabbed my hand, thrusting it below the water so that my fingers were wrapped around his prick.

He sighed, opening his legs and began to hump and grind against my throbbing cock. I rubbed his balls tenderly as he again settled down and relaxed against me. My fingers delighted in rubbing and squeezing along the length of his cock from its base to its puffy underside and up to its bullet-shaped head. I poked the tip of my finger into the end of his foreskin and stretch its small opening wider and wider feeling its heat and moistness.

He moaned as I rubbed the sensitive head of his cock. His cock lurched in my hand and began to pulse and throb and thicken and his balls began to contract. I knew that he was not far from orgasm. I quickly removed my hands from his crotch and spun him around so that he was facing me. He gave me a questioning look as I pulled him close and give him a long tender kiss on the lips, thrusting my tongue into his mouth and dueling with his tongue. He wrapped his arms around my neck and kissed me back.

I pulled him up by his asscheeks into a standing position before me in order to worship his sex. His cock was sticking straight up, rigidly pulsating against his nearly hairless groin and abdomen. He looked down at me as if pleading with me to do something. I grasped him around the hips, pressing my hands into his buttocks and drawing him closer to my face. I thrust out my lips and nuzzled my mouth against his full, low-hanging scrotal sac. He was almost jumping up and down in the tub as I licked and sucked on his balls. He thrusted his hands down into his groin to grab his anxious cock, but I pushed them away.

Letting the precious balls slide out of my mouth, I began the long, slow pleasurable trip from the base of Alex's cock, along the thick throbbing length and up to the engorged cockhead. The cock was so stiff against his abdomen that I had to pull it loose with my hand in order to bring the pouting circle of flesh down to my mouth.

I licked around the floppy folds of foreskin and tried to worm my way into the small sensitive opening. Using my lips, I pulled the foreskin up over my tongue tip and slowly suctioned it into my mouth. He began to shiver and stabbed his cock quickly into my mouth. The soft tendrils of wispy crotch hair tickled my nose as his hips began a savage dance while thrusting against my face.

He grabbed my head between his hands and began to fuck my face. I wrapped my lips around his cock tighter and tighter as he thrusted into my mouth. I ran the fingers of my one hand down between his asscheeks, searching for and finding the sweaty, puckered opening of his asshole and I wrapped my other hand around his swollen balls. I slowly pushed my finger into his little pink rosette and felt the hot warmth of his inner channel.

As I pushed, his cock stiffened even more, and suddenly he began to moan. He came copiously, the excess dribbling out the corners of my lips. In a final shudder of release, his stiff, arched body became weak and he relaxed over me. I released his cock, and lapped up the last of his jism.

He opened his eyes wide and looked down at me. "*Obrigado*," he whispered and slid down against me, wrapping his arms around my body, hugging me.

In a few moments, he pulled back and gestured for me to kneel up in the tub. With some pain, I rose up and leaned foward. He grasped my cock in his hands. He moved it this way and that and began to jerk it up and down. He wasn't able to completely encircle the shaft with his fingers, but supported it with both hands. He began to torture me with his soft rubbing touch. In moments, unable to hold back any longer, I cried out his name and he looked up at me as my cock erupted, pelting his chest and neck.

The pleasure was so great, I thought I might faint. I slid back down into the water with Alex's hands still grasping my cock. I took one of his hands and pressed it against my chest and he laughed. He gathered thick globs of cum, drew them to his mouth and licked his fingers clean.

By now the water had cooled and we finished rinsing each other off. Alex helped me climb out of the tub. We dried each other with the thick, soft towels and I put on the my terrycloth robe while Alex wrapped one of the large towels around his slim waist.

Back in the living room with Alex sitting close to me on the sofa, I got on the phone and called room service, ordering dinner for the two of us.

When I finished, Alex grabbed the phone and dialed. He had a short conversation while grinning at me. When he got off the phone, he made me understand he had told his mother he was staying at a friend's for dinner.

Alex turned on the television and sat with me on the sofa watching it while we waited for dinner. I put my arm around his shoulder and cuddled with him.

Eventually there was a knock on the door. Alex, looking a bit frightened, leapt off the sofa and ran into the bathroom, closing the door. I opened the door and Jorge brought in our dinner on a rolling table. He efficiently arranged the dinner, I tipped him generously, and he left, wishing me a good evening.

I coaxed Alex out of the bathroom and invited him to sit down at the makeshift table. His eyes were wide as he sat down and saw the dinner laid out before him. He wolfed his food down and, before long his plate was empty. He watched me finish and then went to the bathroom.

After a time, I followed him and found him standing next to the toilet holding his dick and pissing a steady yellow stream into the bowl. Every now and then he would stop the flow by clamping off the opening of his foreskin between his thumb and index finger and the foreskin would balloon out and fill with piss. I could actually see the thin, tender skin stretch and blow up like a balloon until Alex could hold it no longer and he would open his fingers and his piss would flow out of the opening in his foreskin like a pressurized fire hose and the thinned skin of his foreskin would thicken once again and envelope the head of his cock. I was fascinated by this sight as I had never seen anyone do that before.

He was happy and laughing all the time he was emptying his bladder. When it diminished to just a trickle, he pulled the foreskin slowly back from the head so that the skin was pulled all the way behind the flared ridge of his cockhead. He slid the skin back and forth so that it alternately uncovered and hid his cockhead within the fleshy folds of his rumpled foreskin. The head of his cock was moist and bright pink in comparison to the darker skin of his shaft. Somehow he looked even more nude when his cockhead was uncovered and it excited me to watch him. He did this several times till he was completely drained.

As he walked towards me, naked with the towel flung over his shoulders, his cock flopped enticingly back and forth against first one thigh and then the other. He stood before me and I stroked his cock gently. He smiled down at me as I pulled the skin and stretched it far beyond the head. It was soft and smooth, pliable, and I could smell the faint odor of piss as I brought the skin up close to my face and rubbed it under my nose. I spread the tiny opening and, without thinking, I thrust my tongue into the opening and tasted the bitter, acrid taste of a final drop or two trapped there. I kissed it, then sucked it, but I was still aching all over from the beating. All I really wanted to do was sleep. Alex followed me into the bedroom. I climbed in bed and he shut off the lights and lay down beside me.

I turned so that I could observe him in the shadowlight. As he smiled back at me, I realized just how lovely he was. I reached out to him and laid my arm across his side.

As his lips softly touched mine, I kissed him back, then lay there quietly and allowed him to take the initiative. He rolled me over on my back and was soon pressing his body full length upon mine. I wrapped my arms around him and began to caress and fondle him.

He began humping me. I hugged him to me and, rubbing his back with one hand, I slid my other hand down his body so that it was caressing his ass. Despite myself, I was turned on. Never had I met such a sensual being in my life. He released my mouth and slid slowly down my chest, rubbing his hands through the thick mat of my chest hair.

Finding my taut nipples, he began to rub and twist them in his fingers. I moaned. Glancing up at me, he brought his mouth over my left tit and sucked it up into his mouth, softly biting its edges and licking the nipple, causing me to shiver.

I ran my hand between the cheeks of his ass and spread them to allow my fingers access. He helped me by spreading apart his legs. I pushed my hand between our bodies and scooped up a large gob of pre-cum and began to rub it around his puckered asshole.

I moved my other hand down lower so that my fingers were touching and rubbing the back side of his ballsac. He went crazy as I scratched my fingers up and down his balls from behind. As I continued to pet his balls, I felt him relax and my finger slipped easily into him. My finger almost strangled as he flexed and tightened his rectal muscles around it. He groaned as he stiffened and arched up like a cat as I plunged two, then three fingers into the depths of his rectum.

He sat up suddenly and, with my fingers still wedged into his tunnel, he grabbed my now hard cock. I pulled my fingers out of his ass and slid him up on my chest so that his legs were straddling my shoulders. I adjusted my head and, after licking his hairless ball-sac, took his cock in my mouth for a quick suck.

Releasing him, I turned him around so that his ass was now hovering over my face and his upper body was facing my feet. I spread his legs into a frog-like position and, grasping his asscheeks, I pulled them down into my face. He groaned and shuddered and sat down harder on my face. I pulled his cheeks further apart and ran the tip of my tongue into the middle of his tiny opening, pushing it forward until the opening began to give way and my tongue slid up into him.

He leaned forward, laying his body over mine. I felt his hot breath upon my cockhead and his trembling fingers grabbed my cock and held it away from my belly. Soon I felt the feathery touch of his lips upon my cockhead, wrapping around it, engulfing it, sliding into his mouth. He drew in the head, then two inches, then more and more until I felt the tip of my cockhead at the back of his throat.

He was fucking back towards me with his ass and my tongue was licking and sucking his inner channel and chewing on the muscled opening of his ass. Each thrust of his body seemed to bring him greater pleasure. I knew I couldn't last much longer and I wanted to fuck him. I raised his ass from my face and pulled him up towards me and off of my cock till we were facing one another. I made a fucking motion with my pelvis and he seemed to understand. He faced away from me, lying on his side, and folded his legs up so that he was in a fetal position. It was tantalizing to realize that he obviously had been fucked before. But by whom? And how old was he when it happened?

His asshole was still wet from my spit and my cock was drooling ropey strings of pre-cum as I lay down behind the boy. We fit together like two spoons and as I held my cockhead against his small opening. I felt him shudder with anticipation as I pressed against him slowly.

He moaned and I was somewhat reluctant to proceed, but he slowly moved back against me and my cock shaft began to be engulfed into his ass. Soon, with most of my cock embedded deeply within him, I adjusted my position and shoved the rest of it in. He groaned a little, but quickly settled down and, flexing his muscles of his ass, began to massage the full length of my cock.

I began to thrust in a short rhythmic manner, sliding my cock in and out a few inches while I wrapped my arms around his sweaty body. I sucked his neck and pinched and squeezed his nipples as he began to move in synch with me. I wormed my finger tip into his hooded shroud and played havoc with his piss slit and around the widened flange of his cockhead, rubbing deeply into his foreskin.

I pulled out till just my cockhead was still inside him, then drove back into him till my crotch hair was tickling his asscheeks. He groaned as he stiffened up and his cock belched out spurt after spurt of cum into the sheets and onto my hand and wrist. I couldn't hold off any longer. His wild climax brought me over the top and I began to pump my load into him.

As my cock softened in his ass, he rolled over into my arms, and closed his eyes. Wrapped in each other's arms, I was conscious of an enormous sense of comfort, as though all my life was the prelude to this, and then as he drew me closer I knew that for precious minutes my tormented mind was submerged by the surging delight of senses starved too long. If only this would go on forever...

. . .

In the morning, I awoke first and lay there watching the sleeping youngster as he stretched and turned on his side facing me. His cock lay like a long, pointed cigar resting against his thigh, his narrow foreskin with its tiny opening like a small eye winking at me. He opened his eyes and saw that I was watching him. He giggled and hid his head under the pillow. I tickled his ribs and he cried out laughing. As I uncovered his head, he grinned at me mischievously.

He sat up suddenly and pushed the pillow into my face and laughed again. Then, remembering the injuries to my face, quickly removed the pillow and exclaimed, "*Sinto muito*," which I assumed meant that he was sorry.

I called down for breakfast, then followed Alex into the bathroom, where we playfully relieved ourselves at the same time. It was almost as if I were ten years younger.

I was still in my bathrobe when Jorge arrived with the breakfast. Alex hid in the bathroom.

We ate quickly and, as I dressed, I explained I was being picked up by Hector, who was going to take me to visit Corcovado mountain where the famous statue of Christ was dedicated at its very top, and ride through the Tijuca rain forest which was actually within the city of Rio. Alex seemed to understand. He beamed when I gestured that he was to stay with me.

In the elevator I noticed Alex's bare feet and took him into one of the shops in the lobby and bought him a pair of sandals and a brightly colored shirt that he admired. I bought a new camera and several rolls of film. We were now ready to greet the day.

Outside the hotel, Hector was waiting and didn't seem at all surprised by the presence of Alex.

As Hector drove off, I related the story of what had happened the previous afternoon and how Alex had come to my rescue, saving me from more serious harm. This seemed to please Hector immensely. He glanced over his shoulder and winked at Alex. "He a good boy. I tell him to keep an eye on you."

"I will be eternally grateful," I said, rubbing Alex's thigh.

Alex giggled.

As Hector guided us through the streets of the city, Alex clung to my side, his hand often slipping on to my thigh and up into my crotch, teasing my swelling erection. Eventually it became impossible for me not to frequently caress the obvious bulge in his shorts.

Hector drove to a railway station and told us that we should ride the tram up the mountain and that he would meet us at the top. The railway was a narrow gauged funicular that hugged the side of the mountain as it ascended at a very steep angle. As we rode higher up the winding side of the mountain, the entire city of Rio sprawled out below us and the panorama was breathtaking. Near the top of the mountain the railway ended and we got off in order to climb the several hundred stone steps necessary to reach the summit.

At the top, the 30-meter statue with its arms outstretched

towards the city below shone with a pale greenish patina. I stepped back as Alex knelt before the outstretched arms of the beautiful statue and said a silent prayer.

Hector finally arrived and stood by the car, smoking a cigarette. I went over to him and thanked him for having Alex "keep an eye on me." I was slowly warming to Hector, admiring his air of supreme confidence in his masculinity. I wondered what he thought of a "pervert" from America who lusted for boys like Alex. My answer was not long in coming.

Hector tossed his cigarette butt to the ground and leaned back against the car. His hand dropped to his crotch and he "adjusted" it. It was as if he was wearing nothing, so obvious was the heft of it. I couldn't resist it; I had to ask, "My God, how big *is* it, Hector?"

He smiled. "I show you sometime."

Just then, Alex came rushing up and we had to be off.

Leaving Corcovado mountain, we drove down through the Tijuca National Park and rain forest and visited several pools and waterfalls. There was a small zoo located near the base of the mountain, which we explored much to Alex's delight.

We drove along the coastline through the beach areas of Leblon and Ipanema and stopped where a soccer team was practicing. Being with Hector and Alex had made me unbelieveably horny and watching the youngsters at play was more than I could stand. Alex protested but I insisted we leave. I was hungry – in more ways than one.

I didn't feel lost without a watch, but still I asked Hector the time. When he told me, I was stunned, but Hector said four in the afternoon was quite normal for lunch for Brazilians since they usually didn't eat dinner until 9:00 or 10:00 p.m.

We stopped at a small cafe Hector recommended and, all through the meal, Hector pressed his leg against mine. When the time came to pay the check, my hand had taken up residence on Hector's bulge. All the while, Alex and I had been playing footsie with each other. I was in a high state of anxiety, wishing I could have them both at once, right there.

To take my mind off my lust, I began to plan for the next day. Hector translated to Alex that I wanted him to again join me for my excursion. Alex seemed pleased with the idea, but had some problem. I interrupted them and Hector told me that Alex wanted to accompany us very much, but that he had promised one of his brothers, Luis, that he would spend the day with him. Hector suggested perhaps I might want to take the other boy along as well.

"I don't know," I said. "This is very expensive as it is."

"Ah," Hector chuckled, shoving my hand deeper into his crotch, "all included."

"All?" I asked gleefully.

Hector nodded, and when he went on to say Luis was a little over a year younger than Alex and even better looking, I enthusiastically embraced the idea.

As we rode back to the hotel, Alex clung to me in the back seat and played with my aching, over-stimulated cock. As we approached Copacabana beach, he leaned over and gave me a kiss on the cheek. I turned my head towards him and he gave me another kiss, this time on the lips. I looked towards the front seat and saw Hector's face through the rear view mirror. I felt a bit embarrassed by the enthusiastic, unsolicited emotion of Alex, but Hector looked back at me and said, "You very lucky man."

And I couldn't help but agree with him.

At the hotel, Alex ran ahead while I lagged behind to speak to Hector. "You said you would show me sometime – "

He nodded and grinned. "Sometime," he teased, and, as he put the gear into drive, added, "Soon."

I expected the night to be a repeat of the one before, but once in the room, Alex said he could not stay, he had to spend the night at home, but promised to bring Luis with him in the morning. However, he agreed to stay long enough for me to suck his cock to orgasm.

I drew a hot bath after Alex left. The youth had come, gloriously, but I had not. I told him I was tired, but, truth be told, I couldn't get Hector out of my mind. He was such a tease, especially when he shoved my hand into his crotch and told me "all" was included. I lay back and brought myself off simply by recalling the images of Hector's masculinity and the incredibly hefty bulge in his pants.

I called room service and ordered dinner. Shortly thereafter, there was a knock on the door. It couldn't have been my meal so quickly so I approached the door cautiously. Bundled in my robe, I opened the door slightly. "Yes."

"It is me."

Indeed it was. Hector was standing in the hallway. He had changed into a dark blue shirt open to the navel and tight light blue trousers. He looked stunning. "Come in, my friend," I said.

He came into the room. "Join me in a drink?" I asked.

He nodded and I fixed us bourbon and sodas from the bar.

We sat across from each other and talked casually about the events of the day and then I asked how he came to meet Alex.

"Alex is my nephew. I have six nephews."

I nodded. Everything became clear. "And each one very beautiful I'm sure."

"Yes, and very well-trained. I do very well with them. Especially the young ones. You Americans, you are very generous."

"We can be, let me put it that way. If we get what we want, we are very appreciative."

"And what is it you want now?" he asked, standing up. The bulge was growing.

Just then, Jorge appeared with my dinner. I went to the door and told him to just leave the cart in the hallway. He nodded and left, glancing at the big tip added to the check.

I wheeled the cart into the room. Hector stepped over to me and asked if I wanted to eat.

"Yes," I murmured, stroking the bulge. "All included?" I asked, still a bit dubious.

"All," he said, placing his strong hand on my head and shoving me down. I sank to my knees and drew him close to me, wrapping my arms around his hips and nuzzling my face into his crotch. Even through the layers of cloth I could smell the exciting aroma of his dripping cock and raw sensual power. I rubbed my face against his monster cock and breathed deeply of his masculine scent. He ground his crotch into my face while pulling off his shirt. I unfastened his trousers and pulled the zipper down so that they slid down on his legs and lay in a heap near his ankles.

He was wearing white briefs that had long since lost the ability to contain his endowment. I sniffed his ballsac and licked his inner thighs. He began to moan and thrust his pelvis up into my face. I moved up higher and located the base of his lengthening organ. I began licking, making the slow and seemingly never-ending journey up the shaft. As I approached the top of his briefs I realized that his cock had forced itself out of the waistband and continued up towards his navel.

One, two, three, four inches later my lips were approaching the crown of his wide cockhead. His cock was at least 10 inches long and there was no way that I would ever fit it down my throat.

As I approached the summit, I could feel the silky, soft folds of his foreskin enveloping his cockhead. But unlike Alex, Hector's foreskin surrounded his bulbous cockhead and ended near the piss slit in a thick bundle of skin. I could taste a puddle of pre-cum that had collected in the short overhang of cockskin. I slavered and sucked it up, then clasped my lips upon the bulging, bright red knob.

I firmed up the tip of my tongue and pushed it into Hector's huge, wide open piss slit. This caused him to squirm and suddenly more pre-cum emerged. I eagerly lapped it up and dug into the hole for more. I pulled his briefs down, releasing his entrapped cock and balls. I grabbed his pulsating cock in both hands; one hand could hardly contain it. I pulled it away from his body so that it was sticking out and directed right at my open mouth, and hefted his balls with my right hand.

Hector's ripe, musky scent was permeating the air and driving me wild. I drove my head forward and my lips forced his foreskin to slowly slide back. I slid the knob into my mouth and licked all around it, then plunged down on his cock taking perhaps four inches of it before I could handle no more. Hector moaned, then pulled out of my mouth. "No more, no more, I'm about to cum," he cried.

"You're right. That will never do. Not yet," I said, standing up and going to the bedroom. I removed my robe and lay on the bed on my stomach. Hector removed his pants and briefs and followed me into the bedroom. He hovered over me, then began to massage my shoulders and back. Seeing a bottle of lotion, he poured some in his hands and rubbed it into my tense body. Getting behind me, he spread my legs and started to rub the lotion into my lower back and buttocks. He focused his attention on my asscheeks, rubbing and kneading them and delving between them with his long, strong fingers. Soon his fingers were circling and probing around my asshole and down to the back of my scrotal sac, tickling and massaging my balls.

He spread lotion around my asshole and greased up his heavy cock. Sliding forward, he spread my asscheeks apart and pressed. It didn't hurt nearly as much as I anticipated. He was gentle, a true master of the art. I raised my buttocks and pushed back at him allowing several more inches to slide up into me. He settled down some and began a slow but steady drive that soon had almost all of it in me. It wasn't only his length that concerned me, it was his thickness. But I wanted all of him in me and urged him on. "Fuck me," I cried. "Ram it into me to the hilt."

He lay down over my back and began to nibble on my ear and my neck and told me that my ass was grabbing his cock in such a way that he might never get it out. For the time it took him to get it in there, at that moment, that sounded good to me.

After a while, I begged to take it another way. I wanted to watch him as he fucked me. He pulled out completely and I rolled over onto my back. He held my legs as he began a slow, steady, agonizing push into my ass, his cock throbbing. It was hard to adjust to his enormity, but I moved a little, adjusted the height of my buttocks and rode with the flow of his smooth manhood as he screwed me.

Reaching down with his hand, he began to stroke my over-stimulated cock, while continuing to ram me. Soon there was no way I could stop it. My cum spurted up to our faces and spread all over our chests and abdomens. The stud continued to jerk my cock as my orgasm overwhelmed me.

As I climaxed, the muscles of my ass clamped down and squeezed Hector's cock till he was moaning in agony and unleashed his load deep into my ass. Exhausted, he lay upon my chest, panting; his heart was beating rapidly. His cock, still embedded in my ass, began to soften. I told him I had never been fucked so well in all my life.

He got up and went to the bathroom. I could see him

holding his semi-hard cock in his hand and pulling on his foreskin as a stream of piss thundered into the toilet. He stood at the doorway and I asked him if he could stay the night. He apologized, saying he was sorry but he would have to go home to his wife and children. He said he had two little girls of his own.

As he dressed, I begged him to leave his briefs with me. He laughed and tossed them at my face. I caught them and sniffed the pungent crotch as he got into his clothes.

We said our good-byes at the door and I waved at him as he entered the elevator. Closing the door, I realized my dinner was waiting.

And no food ever tasted so good to me as it did that night.

. . .

They were standing beside the Cadillac in front of the hotel. Alex was wearing the shirt and sandals that I had bought him the previous day together with a loose pair of dark blue shorts. Through the wide leg holes I could see the hint of a pair of light blue briefs. He introduced me to Luis, who was wearing an old greyish-white T-shirt and a pair of green silk athletic shorts with a yellow stripe down the side.

"*Bon dia*, Alex," I said, using the words I had learned for good morning. "Hello, Luis," I said. "Como vai?", asking how he was.

To my surprise Luis responded with a boyish voice in halting English, "Hello, Mr. Dan." He looked laughingly over at his brother, and they began a rapid exchange in Portuguese.

As we climbed into the back seat, they positioned me between them. Luis explained he was going to a special school to learn English. It was something his uncle was paying for.

I suddenly realized I had become so engrossed with the two teenagers, I had completely ignored Hector.

"How was your sleep?" Hector had turned his head and was now staring into my eyes.

"Fine," I said. "I never slept better in my life."

"Me, too," he chuckled.

We quickly drove through the lazy morning traffic to the Urca district where the huge monoliths known as Pao de

Acucar or Sugarloaf were located. They were at the edge of the sea and provided an unrestricted view of the coastline, Guanabara bay, the entire city, and to the distance, the mountains including Corcovado with the ever imposing statue of Christ at its summit.

With the boys running on ahead, I purchased the tickets for the Swiss cable car system that had been installed to take you up to the top and Hector and I quickly caught up with them. The cable car ride itself was an adventure as it rode up at a steep angle over open space, swaying and bucking so that it was necessary to hold on to the railing inside the car. At the top of the first rocky mound, we boarded the second cable car that would take us up to the top of Sugarloaf. It was a clear, sunny day and the view from the top was spectacular. We walked all around and Hector and the boys pointed out various sites in the distance including where my hotel was and the area where they lived, which was nearby.

After a snack in the restaurant and the purchase of some postcards, we entered the cable car for the fast, almost frightening descent down the giant monoliths. I felt somewhat relieved when we finally arrived and were back in the car.

Passing the hustle and bustle of Copacabana and Ipanema beaches, we drove until we slowed down after passing a curve to see a quiet expanse of beach in the distance. "This is Leblon beach and it is much more quiet and secluded during this time of the day," Hector said. Before I knew it, Hector was pulling off the main road and slipping down a steeply inclined, unpaved road leading to the coast. We parked not far from the sand and the boys went screaming down to the water's edge. There were little patches of coconut palm trees here and there and we selected a small grove. Hector laid out a blanket and food basket. We stripped off our outer clothes, including Hector, who wore a black bikini swimsuit under his black trousers.

While the boys played and frolicked in the water, Hector and I lay down on the blanket and talked.

"You are very good to the nephews," I said. "A special school for Luis, for instance – "

"Luis is the smartest of my nephews. He deserves it. Alexander for sex, but Luis, he is the smart one. He has worked very hard."

"Speaking of hard," I said, touching the bulge in his bikini tentatively. The sight of his bulge again brought back memories of the night before and my cock was soon jumping up and down in my swim suit. Hector's bikini could hardly contain his heavy weapon and I shuddered with the thought of how well it filled my ass the previous day.

He chuckled and moved away, grabbing the suntan lotion I had brought. He had me lie on my back and began to rub the thick, oily lotion into my skin. He covered my upper torso completely and went down to my legs, rubbing the lotion into my calves and then my thighs.

As his hands approached and then delved under the legs of my swimsuit, rubbing into my groin, my rampant, unyielding cock gave a shudder and popped out of the waistband of the suit.

He grinned and told me to turn over so that he could put sunscreen on my back. I rolled over and, with him sitting astride my buttocks, he began to slather the lotion over my back. I could feel his massive manhood pushing between the cheeks of my ass as he lurched forward and back. I brought my arms around my back and pulled his hips into my buttocks.

God, I thought, how nice it would be to have him fuck me again here in the open.

But suddenly I heard the voices of the youngsters getting louder as they ran back from the water. Hector slid down to my legs and began to apply the sunscreen to them.

The laughing boys enjoyed getting us wet as they dripped water from their sleek bodies and flailed their heads back and forth. They sat down on the sand next to us as Hector finished his massage. I could still feel his bloated cockshaft lunging in his bikini as it struck my legs when he moved. And I was sure that the brothers noticed it too; I saw Alex rubbing the front of his briefs and Luis unashamedly grabbing his cock through his athletic shorts. I got up from the blanket, adjusted the obvious bulge in my swimsuit and ran down toward the water with the others following me.

The water was cool compared with the hot sun and felt good on my baking skin. The sea was fairly calm and the surf quiet. The youngsters jumped on our backs, stood on our shoulders and dove into the water. They swam through our legs. I felt curious, groping fingers pressed into my crotch. Surfacing on the other side of me, they would laugh and quickly swim away from me before I could grab them. They were like two playful dolphins. On one occasion, when Luis surfaced in front of me, while he was rubbing the salty water from his eyes, I grabbed him from behind and pulled him close. My arms encircled him and he made some not-too-serious attempts to escape. My cock rose up against his slim asscheeks and I slide my hand down below the water to press against his crotch. He pushed his ass against my cock and, giggling, he wriggled out of my grasp. I could see that Hector was having a similar experience with Alex as the older boy clasped Hector's waist and hugged his legs around his middle with Hector's hands holding on to his firm asscheeks. It was then I thought that it may well have been Hector who initiated Alex into what he termed "love." I had to agree Alex was a wonderful lover and I silently thanked Hector – for everything.

In a few minutes, Hector suggested that we go back to the blanket and have our lunch. It was about 3:00 p.m. by this time and we were all hungry.

Amid lots of joking and kidding around we ate our lunch. Hector and I lay down on the blanket and the boys relaxed on towels. With his legs spread apart, I could look up into Luis's pant leg and watch the sleepy length of his cock rising and falling with each breath. I lusted for him uncontrollably. Hector noticed the swelling in a swimsuit and suggsted we pack and leave.

In the back seat, the boys leaned against me as we began our drive back to the hotel. I put my arm around Alex as he snuggled his head into my shoulder and adjusted my position to accommodate Luis when he slumped over and rested his head in my lap.

Before long, I sensed a slight movement on my left and watched as Alex nuzzled into my chest and begin licking my sensitive nipple. And then I felt some motion down near my crotch. Luis was twisting his head back and forth in my lap and pressing his face into my groin. I could feel his warm, moist breath permeating my swimsuit, causing my cock to harden and lengthen down the side of my leg. I adjusted my cramped position and saw the knobby head of my cock slip out below the bottom of my swimsuit leg very close to Luis's face. A moment later, his lips were on the pulsing head of my cock. I brought my one arm down and wrapped it around Luis's bottom, rubbing his asscheeks and the divide between them, sliding my fingers in. And with my other arm resting in Alex's crotch, I began to rub and fondle his erection.

Looking at Hector, I tried to carry on a conversation as best I could. He explained that his sister had no husband so he had become like a father to Luis and Alex. He was also close to his other nephews, but not as close.

Before I realized it we were back at the hotel.

I invited the three of them to join me for dinner. Hector said he had an errand to run but would be happy to join us in an hour.

Once in the hotel room, Alex led Luis to the bathroom. Observing his brother, Luis moved over close to the toilet and grasping the sides of his athletic shorts, pulled them down to his thighs revealing his naked mid-section. He was nearly hairless, his groin showing just a sprinkle of dark curly hair around the base of his cock. His cock was nearly as long as his brother's but not quite as thick; he also had a long overhanging foreskin that came to a pouty, narrow point. He held his penis in his hand and directed his pale yellow stream over towards his brother's. As they dueled and played with their now semi-hard cocks, Luis kept sneaking a look over at me. I told them I wanted to take a shower and perhaps they would join me.

After a playful time in the shower, during which they largely ignored my erection, and giggled a great deal, the boys went to the living room and turned on the television. They sat on the sofa, making room for me between them. Luis had a lot more room on the sofa compared with the back seat of the Cadillac and he lay down on his back with his head in my lap. My cock was facing up towards my navel so that the side of Luis's head was pressing into it.

Alex, on the other hand, began to again lick and suck on my nipple. I squeezed his rising cock. I could feel his urgency as it oozed out pre-cum.

Luis turned his face towards my now throbbing cock and

licked the underside of my shaft. Grasping his own hard cock in his hand, he started to squeeze it and masturbate. I quickly slid my hand down his abdomen, fondled his small patch of cock hair, and replaced his hand with mine. His cock was as delightful and I was eager to suck it.

Meanwhile, Luis was doing his best to lap up every drop of the pre-cum seepng from my cockhead.

Alex continued to twist and squeeze my nipples. Then he pulled my head down towards his and began to kiss me.

Eventually I reached the zenith. Not wanting to come, I pulled myself free, stood up and grabbed Luis and pulled him up into my arms. "I want to make love to you," I murmured.

He wrapped his legs around my middle and clung to me. I began slowly walking to the bedroom. Alex followed us, playfully slapping my ass.

I laid Luis on the bed and began kissing and caressing him from his head down to his thighs. He moaned and began to nuzzle his face into my neck, licking and kissing me with an unrestrained ardor to match my own. I ran my hands down to his hard cock.

At the same time, Alex slid his body down the bed, got between my legs and began to spread them apart. He was soon fondling, kissing and licking my heavy ballsac.

Now it was my turn to moan and writhe in the bed. Lowering his hand, Alex searched behind my balls and began to rub my relaxed asshole. Looking over at me, he said, "I fuck you!" And there was no doubt in my mind that he would; and no doubt that I wanted him to. I looked forward to his thick young cock ramming into me.

I slid Luis up higher on my body while responding to Alex's prods by raising my legs up in the air. I pointed to the lotion over on the bedside table and Alex poured some into my asshole and began to probe my opening with his finger. It was quickly inside and he mumbled something like, "Hot." He pushed my legs up higher and centering himself between my legs, plunged his cock deeply into my tunnel. I wasn't really prepared for his sudden thrust and I cried out, but without any prolonged pain, he was in me to his cock hairs.

With his thrusting, he sent Luis flying up towards my chest releasing my cock which began to jump and dance within my crotch. And Luis's cock and ass was now resting between my nipples. I pulled Luis up into a sitting position and found his cock resting on my chin. I grabbed his hips and quickly sucked his foreskin between my lips. I suctioned his very tasty penis and wrapped my tongue around its shaft and tried to control his wild gyrations. He returned my cock to his mouth.

Once deeply embedded in me, Alex began a rapid assault driving his cock back and forth, fucking much like his uncle had, bringing himself to an all-too-premature climax. He screamed as the orgasm swept over him and I felt the powerful jets of his cum filling me.

I thought he would relax and pull out, but his cock didn't soften. Continuing his assult, he cried out, "More, more!"

About this time, I began to erupt into Luis's throat. The poor boy wasn't ready for this and, with a muffled attempt at swallowing, he finally pulled his mouth off my cock and watched as cum spewed all over his face, and his hair and up his nose.

As I continued to explode, my muscles grabbed Alex's probing cock. He cried out in pleasurable agony as his cock began to throb within my well-fucked ass and he began to release his second orgasm.

Now Luis followed suit, pelting the back of my throat with so much pressure that it actually stung.

Alex shuddered against me as his orgasm finally came to an end and he slowly withdrew his tired but still bloated cock from my ass. Luis rolled off to the side and Alex slid up on my body to take his place. He looked into my eyes, smiled and kissed me long and passionately, then fell exhausted onto my chest.

We drifted off to sleep, only to be awakened by a knock on the door. I knew that it must be Hector. I grabbed my robe and made my way to the door. Letting Hector in, I noticed his eyes wandering around the room, finally focusing on my closed bedroom door. "Where are the boys? Did they already leave?"

"No, they are in the bedroom asleep. They were so tired after all the swimming and horsing around."

He took me in his arms. "We let them sleep."

Our kiss was long, all consuming. It literally took my breath away. Then he pushed me down to my knees again and unzipped his trousers, for a repeat of the action I had so much enjoyed the evening before. "All included?" I asked as I held the cock near my lips.

"Suck," he barked. "No more talk. Just suck."

As his cock slid between my lips, it was like coming home.

In a few minutes, after I sucked the incredible cock to full hardness, Hector had me sit on the sofa. He kneeled on the floor. His fingers inspected me gently. "Alex?" he asked, bringing his moist fingers to his nose.

"Yes," I admitted.

"He love to fuck, too."

"Yes, he takes after you."

"You part of the family now," he said.

"Thank you," I murmured.

He nodded, took my buttcheeks in his massive hands and slowly brought my asshole to the head of his cock.

I wrapped my arms around his neck and held him as he slid his erection most of the way in and began to fuck.

I kissed his shoulders and sucked on his neck while he impaled me with the biggest cock I had ever seen.

I leaned back and thoroughly enjoyed the sight of a man who enjoyed his work.

As Hector, his hands clamped on my shins, stretched my legs as wide as they would go, driving deeper in me, he came. I closed my eyes and let the wantonness of the moment envelop me. I could not imagine any moment in my life transcending the quality of this.

It was impossible to recall any moment when I had felt more passionately grateful to the world for its beauty and to life for its infinite possibilities. Just to be in Rio, to be away from my mundane concerns, was gift enough, but here so much else had been added to my life that no prayer of thanks could be ever adequate.

As Hector finished and pulled out, I opened my eyes to see Alex standing next to the sofa stroking his hard-on. Standing beside him was Luis, staring at my asshole, now dripping with his uncle's cum.

Alex looked down into my eyes and said, "I fuck you again, yes?"

"Oh yes," I said, spreading my legs wide. "And Luis too.

It's all included, you know."

"No, no," Hector said, climbing on the sofa next to me and bringing his semi-flaccid cock to my lips. "It's all in the family now."

TRIO

Dan Veen

The night we met, I became infatuated with Craig.
And he soon became my obsession.
I first struck up a conversation with him during intermission at a symphony concert. It looked like the first time this young guy had ever worn a tuxedo, like somebody's nervous dream date for the high school prom. Craig's blond curly hair crested over his collar. His blue eyes sparkled like the cheap champagne we drank.

I started talking music with this stunning creation. Craig remarked how he especially liked the Brahms Horn Trio. The starkness of two instruments felt incomplete to him, Craig said. He preferred chamber music, with several members involved. Chamber music had more texture, he insisted.

I – totally infatuated – agreed totally.

We started lobbing hairpins at each other, exchanging queer culture's telltale passwords: Tchaikovsky, Bernstein, Rorem. Blah-blah Virgil Thomson. Ya-ta-ta Corigliano. I hauled all of literature out of the closet: Somerset Maugham. James Baldwin. Andre Gide. Craig knew them all and upped the ante with Henry James, William Burroughs and Ronald Firbank.

Can you believe my luck?

Knowledge turns me on. Brains attached to such a young functioning cock was irresistible. Was Craig...have-able? I invited him back to my place to view my first editions. He was smart enough to say yes. *Bingo!* An open mind *and* an open fly!

I left the lights off. Moonlight poured in from my courtyard. My hands felt the hard-on growing in Craig's tuxedo pants. The big head warmed like an egg about to hatch.

"Take it out. Play with it. Lick it. Suck on it," he said, a surly sex-charged demand in his voice. He placed his hands on my head, his to control.

I tussled his cock out of his fly. It looked like an exquisite piece of jewelry shown off on black velvet. I sucked it hard.

"Hot fuckin' mouth," he moaned.

We stripped out of our formal clothes, dicks already dripping. Our piss-slits kissed and mixed pre-cum up and down our hot cockshafts, making smacking noises around my balls.

His dangling cock touched his thigh and deposited a wet spot. I licked off every drop. I skimmed his cock's underside, flicking the seam of his prick.

He studied my cock-enraptured face intently. A scientific examination of a horny-assed cocksucker in his native habitat. "You're a real fucking cocksucker! I can tell you like sucking cock. You could suck my cock all night, couldn't you?"

I moved my face between his legs and tasted the perineum while his balls rubbed my chin-stubble. I stuck my nose into young Craig's exquisite pink asshole and inhaled.

"Get your face up in there, ass-licker! Breathe deep, baby!"

He ass reeked of man-sweat and testosterone. Ahhhhh! Ass-amyl, I call it! There's nothing like clean fresh boyhole as an aphrodisiac, I say!

"Lick me! Ram your face into my ass! Use that tongue!"

I burrowed my chin into the blond hairs of his ass. He scrunched his ass over my face just the way he liked, making sure I scratched all those out-of-the-way places for him, with my entire face massaging the muscled depths of his butt. Then Craig jumped on the mattress and trampolined up and down, his cock boinging in the air like a diving board.

"Wow, this bed's big enough for an orgy!"

"Mmm, your *cock's* big enough for an orgy!" I climbed on the bed with him.

While Craig towered above me on the bed, I washed his feet with my tongue, lost among his toes.

"Get your mouth up here," he commanded. "Get up here. between my legs and suck my cock."

The party favor between Craig's legs throbbed too much to ignore. The smooth-slick contours of Craig's meat brushed my cheek. I wanted to gobble the whole cock. My jaw loosened. I held his cock upon my tongue, absorbing the warmth quietly within my mouth.

"Yeah, you're doin' it!" Craig rubbed my head and moaned, his balls wet with my dribble. "You're sucking the whole thing. Love it with your tongue! Work that mouth!"

I chinned the groove beneath his legs. My tongue rippled along the ridges. I tasted the velvet skin of that pink and purple glossy cum-pump of Craig's.

"Yeah, suck on that sucker, suck it!" Craig snarled above me. "Suck my balls. Make 'em pump up some hot cream!"

His cream-steaming prick shoved further into my face. Craig humped my mouth savagely, his hard, long prick soaking in my throat. I applied all the expertise of my lips, snorting against his belly and making a pig of myself on his dick.

"Oooh, that tongue!" Craig's knees nearly buckled. "That tongue is hot for cum. Keep digging it, baby! Slurp my meat like a soda, kid!"

I nibbled his full balls between my teeth, gave tiny bites to the thin skin of his cum cups. His legs tightened around me. My cock humped Craig's shank. The gold blond fuzz of his thigh coaxed a stream of lube from my cock.

Craig's cock dribbled down into my throat while he turned his mouth to my neglected hard-on. He gave my meathead a whirlwind tongue-job.

His mouth worked my cock harder. His taste buds scrubbed me like a goddamn Brillo pad. He sucked my cock all the way down his throat. He stuffed my balls inside his mouth.

Suddenly Craig's meat got iron-stiff. It shoved roughshod over my palate. It grew rigid on my tongue.

"Take it, cocksucker! Eat my load! Swallow my hot load!"

His balls jismed. His cock unloaded like an uncapped fire hydrant. His cum poured down my welcoming throat.

Coming gave him more of an appetite for cocksucking. Craig's tongue slathered like liquid fire on my own cock. He slurped a mouthful of warm saliva all around the sides of my prick. Jets of spit swished around in his cheeks, bathing my cock in his hot mouth. The tingle of imminent ejaculation enflamed my cockhead.

"Suck all that juice out, kid! Here's my load!"

His mouth barely held all the cum I blasted into it. Craig snorted, inhaled my cock to the dregs.

Later, watching the rain shower in my courtyard, we snuggled together. We talked about his studies at the university and how he found little in common with kids his age. He liked people who had other experiences to share. I didn't at all mind sharing a night with a boy who thought sex was a playground ride.

"I'm starving," he complained, stretching like a young lion. "Hungry, famished. Let's order a pizza." Craig kicked his legs playfully up in the air and let his cock flop free.

Pizza arrived. Craig pranced to the door in the nude and tipped the boy five dollars. Then he tiptoed, giggling, back to bed, like a kid playing a Halloween prank.

We ate pizza cross-legged, naked in the middle of the bed. Craig wrapped the stringy cheese around his cock for me to slurp off. "That delivery boy was kind of cute. We should've invited him to join us," he snickered.

With Craig's fresh erection feeding my mouth, there was no way I could answer. Both our cocks were at-large again. We needed to slip into each other. We wanted to hide inside our warm humid holes and stay there till we both were satisfied. We used up a half-dozen rubbers that night.

. . .

Every night Craig "holed up" at my place smacked of wholesome debaucheries. Incestuous hayrides. Slumber parties turned orgies. I wanted Craig every morning. All nine inches of him. But spasmodic tumbles in the sack weren't enough for me.

"I like you a bunch," Craig patiently said every time I broached the C-word: Cohabitation. "But I'm not, you know, monogamous."

Craig joked that he came from an old-fashioned Mormon family. He believed in many husbands. He liked variety. "What's the plural of spouse? *Spice?*"

That got my curiosity up. And my cock. Who else enjoyed Craig's cock and hot ass?

I didn't care if Craig sleazed with twenty men. (That would've been hot as hell.) I just wanted to be with him. Even if his cock shot off in another man's ass, I had to be there, holding Craig's spasming cock for him. I tracked him to job interviews. Stalked him to the university. Who did he look at? Who aroused him?

I found myself loitering outside Craig's dorm at 2:00 a.m.

during a torrential rainstorm. Love, I admitted to myself, was what I was probably in. Then, one month after I bedded Craig, I met his other lover.

At first I only heard him. I had to duck into the rest room of the university cafeteria. Outside my stall, someone whistled while he washed his hands. It sounded like the theme song for Craig and myself! The tune was so familiar that at first I thought it was Craig whistling our Brahms Horn Trio at the sink, the finale, *allegro con brio.*

The guy was surprised to see me suddenly burst out of the john. My cock still hung outside my fly. To Javier, it must have looked like an open invitation. The Latino reeked of machismo and heavy cologne. Javier looked like a twinkling-eyed Don Juan, a gay Casanova, a lewd street urchin hustler-fucker.

I asked him, "What's that you're whistling?"

"For you," Javier flashed a smile like a switchblade, staring hungrily at my cock. "Javier will whistle any song you like."

"No. Just now. What were you whistling?"

"I dunno, *hombre,* just something I picked up."

"I'll bet."

It was plain that this was the stud who had the cock. The cock Craig loved. At first I couldn't figure why Craig would fall for such a gloryhole slut. Then I warmed to the bastard's dirty little mind and his unstoppable libido. His lewd leer and crude sneer. His jockey-sized body, his walnut skin, legs so muscular they were slightly bowlegged. Javier looked like the rollercoaster of fucks. The magnet in his pants tugged at me.

Just to see Javier, this new nasty aspect of Craig, hardened me. Some fresh sexual organ of Craig's sprung to life. A new Q-spot. A heretofore unlicked erogenous zone. Javier disgusted me and turned me on at the same time.

Javier clicked his tongue lasciviously. He leered and licked his lips, watching my swollen cock.

Both my pants and Javier fell down around my knees. He sloshed my cock around in his mouth, let it fill his throat. While Craig's Latino loverboy sucked my balls, I imagined those two going at it. No wonder Craig's cock kept going back to Javier's mouth. Once you stuck it in, you didn't want to leave.

I came right there. Jism drooled down onto my balls. Javier lapped it up. His face snuffled around in my shorts. My knees buckled with the surplus cum Javier sucked out of my balls. It was Javier, his humpy hot-for-Craig body, his stiffstanding cock, that got me off. I felt like I had cheated on Craig, for liking Javier.

"I come here every day to get guys' rocks off." Javier smiled up at me. His voice gurgled happily like a flushed toilet. "This is the best place to be during final exams. The jocks around here get so tense studying. They need me to help them relax. You want I should schedule you for an appointment?"

"Don't you have a boyfriend?"

"Sometimes."

"Does he know you do this?"

"Are you kidding? We met here. Craig likes me to tell him stories about the guys I suck off. But Craig's got the biggest cock. *Grandissimo.* He says he will fuck me with it someday. He loves to lay his ass over my face and jerk off. He cums all over my chest and stomach. Still, it's the hottest cock I've ever sucked on. He's a classy kind of guy, too. Brains. But really great in the cock department, if you know what I mean. . . "

"Yeah I do." Then I had an idea worthy of trash like Javier. "So you like tall blond boys?"

"Yeah, yeah. The blonder the better."

"With big dicks?"

"Yes."

"You like them to fuck you in the ass?"

Javier clutched his crotch and twisted it. He made guttural animal noises.

"Then I've got just the guy for you."

"Where is he?" Javier asked when I brought him back to my place. "I am already *arrecho.* See?"

"Take your clothes off," I snapped. "Get your cock hard. Put your butt up in the air. Make yourself at home."

We stripped for each other. Javier's dark dick looked like a chocolate roll with a pink cherry on top. I told him to suck me.

"What a pale, hairless man," Javier whispered to me. "Just like ivory, smooth as marble. I want to suck on every inch of it. Put your dick in my mouth. Please...put it in...."

Javier, that rascal, proceeded to give me a great blowjob. He brushed my cockhead against the bristles of his Errol Flynn mustache before punching his throat with my dick. While he was down there sucking my cock, I imagined what his face looked like sucking Craig's dick.

"Just keep sucking. When you feel it about to shoot, slow up. I don't know if I want to cream in your slutty little mouth. I want you to get me ready to cum, but I'm going to give it to another guy. Can you do that?"

Javier giggled. That little gutter-stud was game for anything. I phoned Craig.

"Hello."

"Hi," I breathed to our Craig like an obscene phone caller, one hand propped on Javier's bobbing head. "I've been thinking about you. What are you up to?"

"Studying. Big test this Friday. Final exams. A lot of shit."

"Well, would the student body like to come over? Physical Education is on the curriculum at night school."

Javier's mouth nearly popped off my dick, had I not held a firm hand on his head, and my hard dick in his mouth.

"Come to think of it, I do miss you tonight." There was a long silence. "I'll be right over."

"Good. The teacher's always lookin' for a pet."

I lay back. Javier got hotter. He liked getting my cock ready to cum in another guy's mouth. I wouldn't let him taste my cum. I was saving it for Craig.

Craig got there just in time.

"Javier?" Craig's eyes grew wide, his dick hard.

When Craig saw both his boyfriends naked and making it on our bed, his whole body gave off throbs of recognition. Our fuckshow inflamed him.

"Look what I found." I ran my hand across Javier's torso and down to his brown buttcrack.

"Javier!" Craig panted again. An animal look registered on his face. Every muscle in Craig's body hardened. He blushed. With shock. And embarrassment. And lust. Craig's body rippled. Waves of inviting muscles pumped with lust.

"Why don't you come to bed now, Craig?" I called over Javier's slurping mouth. "I see you're still a growing boy."

Craig tore out of his clothes. The boy couldn't wait to join my joint. He stood above us, surveying our outstretched bodies.

"Yeah, Javier, make him cum. Make him cum a lot. Get him hot for me. Get that dick big and hot and ready to bust. Work me up some cream. I want to taste all that hot stuff inside those big nuts." Craig guided Javier's head. He held Javier's ears, rolled the Latino's mouth all around my cock. "Suck it. Suck his cock! Get your tongue all over it. Taste that meat!"

My cock couldn't disappoint Craig's eager face. It broke into orgasm. A deep load of cream spewed up fresh from my balls. "Take it man!" He got it ready, just making a beeline for my fountaining cock, already wet with Javier's hot drool. Craig's eager mouth sucked it up and spit out some more, sliming my cock with his spittle.

Javier kissed and licked all around Craig's mouth, slurping up the cum spillage, while I poured my cream into them both. Javier licked up the excess dribble that slobbered out of Craig's mouth. The two of them together made me shoot off for what seemed like a good five minutes. Then Javier and Craig started smooching with each other, their lips and chins glistening with my blown load.

"Guess you two already know each other," I laughed at the two naked guys between my legs, rummaging around in each other's crotches.

Their mouths were sealed with my cum, pasted together in a froth. Craig, turned on by the sight of both of us, all but crammed Javier's body into the mattress trying to fuck him.

"Mind if I borrow a rubber? I've got to fuck this guy. He's been begging me for months!"

Craig ripped a packet open, scrolled it on to his simmering prick. Craig levered Javier's legs back over his head and told me: "Here, hold these. Keep his ass up in the air so he can see my cock fucking his hole." Then Craig grabbed the lube from the nightstand and nozzled it into Javier's ass.

"*Aye, dios!*"

"Grab on to your *cojones*, Javier," I said. "This stud-baby can throw some rough fucks!"

My asshole twitched as I watched Javier's fucknotch get nonoxynoled to the hilt. Craig pumped Javier full to the brim with that jiffy lube. When Javier's ass couldn't hold more lubricant, Craig got up on his haunches and showed the Latino stud the full length of his cock. Javier quivered over the massive meat size. It was plain that the whole thing was going to go up in him.

Javier groaned.

"I'll let you do the honors." Craig placed my hands on his hard-on.

I held Craig's meat in the palm of my hand like it was a sword I was about to dub Javier with. My eager fingers fed Craig's meat into Javier's open hole. Craig's fat butt-fucker spliced its way through Javier's ooze-lined ass. Then I could hear every inch of it squish through Javier's jellied hole.

Javier howled a thousand Latino curses. I covered his mouth with my ass and that shut him up. Craig's meat was filling him up all right. "What are you yelling about? You're getting exactly what you wanted." I squeezed his face, amazed at the way Javier's tight little hole was taking Craig's cock, making room for all of it. When Craig's cock tunneled more than halfway up his bulging ass, I massaged Javier's splitting ass lips. His hole was stretched to the max, purpled with painful pleasure.

"*Aye! Jesu Cristo!*" Javier's hips twisted to accommodate Craig and his tummy heaved beneath me. His poor stiff dick thrashed wildly. I watched Craig's cock up close, watched it slide in.

I held Javier's legs back through the entire delicate operation. I loved helping Craig fuck Javier just as much as I liked getting my own butt rammed by Craig.

"My ass can't stand being left out of this fuck any longer," I gasped, lubing myself deep with my finger. "Pull out some!"

Craig's dick slid out so just the hot cockhead was clenched by Javier's wide-stretched ass lips.

"Hurry," Craig heaved, "this ass is eating my cock alive!"

I moved into place between them. My bared fuckhole slid slowly and teasingly down Craig's hard sweaty torso. His smooth chest-muscles massaged my rump. I settled on all fours atop Javier.

Javier's legs lodged on my shoulders, grateful for something to hold onto, our assholes exposed for Craig's hot cock to use. We ground our groins together.

"Pussy heaven! Mmm-mmm!" Craig smacked his lips. Usually such a young gentleman, Craig became a hole-rutting wild man during sex. "Sort of makes me wish I had two dicks to fuck you guys with!"

Whenever Craig was busy sticking his dick in me, I quickly

cocked my crotch into Javier's freshly vacated fuckhole, stuffing my own cock into its place. I planted it deep. Ah! His fresh-fucked Latino asshole was all prickly fuzz and friction, like sticking my juicy dick in a warm sweater.

I also had Craig's cock ramming right behind me. His thrusts jammed my cock deeper into Javier's hole. Craig was fuck-mad, a horny doggy-boy. Craig was pure dick now.

When he was ready to fuck Javier's hole, I pulled out.

"Thanks for keeping it warm for me!" Craig's cock sank in fast and heavy. Javier howled with pleasure. I wasn't going to be left out, not as long as Javier's dark juiced-up prong stood out bobbing just beneath my ass.

My hole quickly gobbled up Javier's dark cock, with Craig conducting our fuck-dance.

"*Aye! Dios! Mierda!*" Javier clutched my tits. "*Madre de dios!* He's making me cum! *Chingame!* I'm gonna shoot this thing off inside you!"

"His dick feels great, doesn't it?" I yelled to Javier, "Shoot! Go ahead! Let him fuck it out of you! Fuck me!'

I liked to watch Javier's face. Craig's cockjabs put some crazy expressions on it. One hard long jam would make him go cross-eyed. But my balls burned to shoot their wadding, too.

"Fuck him harder, Craig! He's going to come! Make him shoot his cock in me!"

Craig bit into my shoulder and rammed him hard.

Suddenly, Javier came. It felt like they were both inside me, a pelvis party, because Craig wasn't far behind. He riveted his cock into Javier, slamming us all down into the mattress. When his prick spit its juices, Craig's jolt of cum jiggered my prostate. I would have spasmed right off the bed if I hadn't been mashed between their two cocks.

"Geezus," Javier sighed, kissing us both. "We sure make a fine set of fuck-buddies."

We've had nights like that ever since. Maybe our trio isn't the most traditional family in the world, but for horny studs like us, it's the *best*!

LOVING UNCLE

John Patrick

I'll always be grateful to Uncle Jasper for teaching me all the things he thought I needed to know about life, love and sex. Especially sex.

After my grandmother's demise, Mother took a quasi-maternal concern for her brother Jasper. His gentleness of nature and persistence of sunny common sense moderated some of her inordinate worriment. He charged her often with the sin of soppiness and he told me that while he was not soppy, he was nonetheless a romantic. Mother and he formed a curious contrast, so much yet so little alike. Both were quick, bright, intensely loyal. They laughed at the same things. But while Mother placed a heavy emphasis on what she considered the real values, family and religion, Uncle Jasper seemed more concerned with what he called the "standards of the world."

When Father died, Jasper took over the running of the bank and he urged Mother to become more of a lady of the world. He saw to it that her small fortune was invested well so that she could afford to travel. Then the war came and she plunged into the cause, often leaving me alone with Jasper.

I was to discover Jasper had a fondness for fashionable clubs and parties, cultivating the beautiful people of his generation and, later, of younger generations, but his life was never touched by scandal. It seemed he picked his opportunities carefully; only when he was absolutely sure of himself would he make a move. Near the end of his life he told me he had envisioned my seduction as something that might take months, perhaps years. Indeed, he thought he would never consummate it. It didn't seem to matter: "I enjoyed the fantasy for so long, it seemed almost a sacrilege when it finally happened."

My sexual education really began in the fall of 1944, when I was 15 and staying with him. He had no live-in servants and over the years I had enjoyed tidying up the mansion for him, making meals and serving us. He took to calling me "Jeeves" and I adored it, not understanding why, just knowing that I was giving pleasure to an older man I adored. Little did I realize I was actually deeply involved in a master/slave relationship that could, with the slightest push, have become kinky.

One night, as he indulged in a nightcap in the cool, comfortable, leathery library, with its reassuring rows of books, a bar table of glittering bottles and a crackling fire in the fireplace, I was perfectly at ease, but he noticed I had been suffering from anxiety.

When he asked me about it, I explained it as "girl trouble. " "Strange feelings about sex in general," I elaborated. "I really can't explain it."

"I've been troubled with those strange feelings for thirty years, Freddy!" And then, in a monotone, pausing from time to time to stare at me with what seemed almost defiance, he poured himself out to me. It seemed as if I assumed the role of a judge, listening to his pleading, an act of self-justification. He told me that his lifestyle was not a matter of his choice, he had simply been unable to establish a satisfactory relationship with a woman. He did not accept his fate passively; rather, he went into psychoanalysis and eventually found a doctor who reassured rather than condemned him.

"I found sex with women boring. They wanted me to do all the work and they seemed as disinterested as I was. I began to realize I could enjoy things that other people might not understand, that I could let myself enjoy my feelings toward people, all kinds of people. I stopped going to the doctor because I knew I could make peace with myself and my condition. What did it matter, after all, whether I ever loved or didn't love? I ceased comparing myself to other men. They didn't care what I was. They were perfectly willing to accept me for what I appeared to be. I could be a frustrated homosexual but they didn't care. I made a life of order, routine, work, theater, books, music." He paused, letting it sink in. "Does it shock you?"

"No. You explained to me what homosexuals were a long time ago. And I've read about them. You know how curious I am about life."

He smiled and clenched his fists, as if to stop his hands from touching what I knew, somehow, he desired. He had dropped so many clues over such a long time that I didn't need any explanations.

"But I do not consider myself a homosexual. I guess you could say I'm pansexual, in that I enjoy all kinds of sex."

I crossed the room and lowered myself to the arm of the big wingback chair where he always sat in the library. I told him I was sad that he had to struggle with his moral dilemma for so long. He thanked me and began stroking my thigh, then pinched my knee. There was no question of deception. He knew at all times I knew what he was up to. By this time, there existed between us a kind of symbiosis. He hugged me, drawing me close. My hand fell to his groin and found a firmness there, a firmness that matched my own. He pulled himself up and allowed me to slide into the chair. He began by removing my shoes and socks and fondling my bare feet, kissing them, sucking the toes. I unbuckled my trousers and started unbuttoning the fly but his hand moved to mine to stop me. He wanted me to surrender to him completely. I smiled at him, gently and invitingly. I watched spellbound as he pulled my trousers from me, then kissed my feet again and ran his hands over the smoothness of the hairless skin of my legs and thighs. My feet pressed against his chest; his hands finally came to rest on my crotch. He reached into the opening of my boxers and brought my hard cock into view, followed by my balls. He played with my cock, sliding the foreskin back and forth over the head, driving me to heights of ecstasy I had not known before.

"You will be a great success in life," he said, admiring my erection. "Many times you will be judged by the size of this and you will never fail."

Then he slid my legs over his shoulders and brought his lips to it, then his mouth. He didn't cease sucking until I exploded as never before. He swallowed most of it and continued kissing me all over.

I wanted to lie in bed with him, feel his whole body against mine, so he let me stay in his bedroom. He undressed and it seemed that he knew his power.

His body was thin but strong and I caressed it, caressed it everywhere. His cock grew to meet my hand and I stroked it. He knelt on the bed and I squirmed over to kiss it. It was smaller than mine but still quite sufficient. In my fervent desire to do what he had done, I began to suck it. I fear I scraped it with my teeth because he quickly took it in his hand and held it back from me. "I must teach you," he said softly.

"Yes," I murmured adoringly, "I want you to teach me everything."

"The first thing you must learn is when someone is ready, like now -" And he proceeded to stroke his cock several times and came into his hand.

Later, I made myself small and childlike in his arms and fell asleep.

Jasper had aroused a sexual fever in me so potent that I could never resist his touch. I was sure I could never control myself again. Often, as we sat on the couch together, reading my assignments, our hands wandered over each other's bodies. I responded madly to his teachings and wanted to practice my new techniques on him daily. He taught me to hold back my orgasm until both of us were ready, using slow, rhythmic motions, then quicker, then still quicker, as the temperature of the blood began to boil and the pleasure mounted. Often we would stay in the sixty-nine position, sucking competitively to see who could get the other hard again the quickest. Away from him, I would re-enact the scene in my mind, see his cock quivering as it erupted and I began to learn the meaning of unfulfilled desire.

Mother became concerned over my protracted absences and confronted me with the reality of Jasper. She was quite insensitive to the issue at hand. "I think it's time you knew about your Uncle Jasper," she said, in hushed tones. "He's odd. Not like other men. " She explained that his wit and easy adaptability with people made up in good measure for any deficiency in moral character, for that's what it was called in those days. "But I'm afraid you shouldn't be seeing so much of him," she concluded. "It's not healthy."

But I was not to heed her warnings and when I was not present when she thought I should be, I would be forced to endure long grillings and, while I would never compromise Jasper, I knew she knew where I was.

After the war ended, she told me she had decided to move to Florida. Ostensibly, she wanted to devote her energies to doing something with the thousands of acres of Florida land Father had left her and, she said, it was the best thing for her health. But I knew it was my health, my mental health, that really concerned her.

My last two years of high school were wretched. I missed Uncle Jasper. All the teachers were women and the closest I got to male companionship was when I went to the beach. I happened upon Pass-a-Grille quite by accident. In those days, there was a pavilion where people could change for bathing and I saw men lurking about, making tentative eye contact. I soon came to look upon it as a place where I could relieve myself in more ways than one. At first, I was shocked to see the action and, being just a teen, I was seldom approached directly, which was fine with me because I wanted to do the picking. Often the pickings were slim but on some days the cubicles were filled with adventurers. I learned shortly before sundown was the best time. Most of the bathers had gone and a few of us lingered. The lavatory seemed sordid, dangerous and pathetic and I felt an overwhelming sadness that I lived in a place where men forced men into finding their pleasure in this way, flirting with the authorities, perhaps even courting death. This furtive sex was necessary, I felt, because those men couldn't stand closeness; they didn't look into each other's eyes, preferring to bury themselves into each other's crotches, hiding their shame. Yet I felt compelled to return, intrigued by the strange, erotic darkness of these men.

Late one afternoon, there were seven of us in the place. Two were in cubicles and all you could see was their feet. Four of us stood at the urinals. One acted as a lookout. A man moved next to me. He was old, very old. I put my hand down and felt his cock and he immediately started to play with mine. Another man, a younger one with glasses, moved closer and got behind me, running his hands over my ass. When the old man dropped to his knees and began sucking me, the younger man began sliding his cock up and down the crack of my ass. I pushed him away and backed into the urinal. With that, the younger man dropped down and joined the older one at my cock. A fourth man exposed his cock to me and I took it in my hand and played with it. The man who was acting as a lookout kept puffing on a cigarette, turning back occasionally to watch the action in the dim light. The two men at my cock began sucking like maniacs, almost fighting over it. I came because I knew I could come again. The men then started on the fourth man whose cock I had been stroking. I stepped away and the lookout came over, exposing himself to me. I knelt down and began sucking his hard cock. As he came, I felt at home among these men, at once hopeful and desperate, and I had another orgasm.

A few weeks later, I met a young man who was standing near the entrance. We nodded at each other and I asked him if he worked there, at the pavilion, in one of the shops.

"I don't work," he snarled.

"You don't? What do you do then?"

His face brightened. His teeth were irregular and one was chipped. "I have a good time."

"That's what I want to do. "

"Then come with me."

He was perhaps a couple of years older than I, had curly black hair and his skin was sunburned. I followed him eagerly.

". . . Yeah, I'm fed up with girls," I told him as we walked across the boulevard heading I knew not where. "I take 'em to dances and we go to the parking lot and they let me get my hand inside their panties but they won't let me take them off. They won't touch my cock, they just stare at like it was some kind of strange creature."

"And I'll bet it's a nice one."

I smiled. "You'll see."

He took me back to his tacky furnished room near the beach and began by peeling off my shirt. "Yeah, you've kinda cute," he told me, running his hands all over my hairless chest. "And you got a great tan. "

"I come here a lot."

"Me, I just moved from Jersey." He kissed my nipples. "Hmmm! Yeah, I guess I've found where to go." He dropped to his knees, undid my shorts and pulled them down. "Oh, yeah," he smiled, "it's a nice one, all right."

As he slid back the foreskin and began sucking, I cringed; his ugly teeth were painfully scraping the sensitive skin. "Hey, easy," I cried. He began licking rather than sucking and my cock grew to what seemed, even to me, an enormous degree.

"God, I want that in me," he said finally, stroking my erection, now slick with his spit. He took some Vaseline from a jar on the bureau and coated my cock, then turned around and dropped his trunks, revealing a slim, hairy ass.

"Oh, no," I said emphatically. "I couldn't." I tried to pull away but he held fast.

"Yes, yes," he said, guiding my cock to his crack. He leaned over and brought his hands to his cheeks, spreading them, and shoved backward, forcing my hard cock deep into him.

"Oh God," he cried. "Oh, oh you're hurting me." But it was obvious that was what he wanted. I began to fuck him in earnest. It was tight, incredibly tight. And it felt incredibly right. For some reason, I wanted to hurt him, perhaps in retribution for the way his sucking had pained me, but there was more to it than that. The longer I fucked him, the more violent I got, the more he loved it. He kept begging me to stop, that the pain was killing him, but he kept right on moving his hips with me and when he came he told me not to stop and I kept on hurting him until, at last, I came, gripping his shoulders tightly and jamming it into him as far as I possibly could. I left my prick in after I came, then started again. He shot another load but I continued my assault on his hole. Tears were streaming down his face when I finally came again.

". . . Where'd a little kid like you learn to screw like that?" he asked as we were dressing.

"Oh, along the way, I guess. Along the way." I was not about to tell him it was my first time.

The summer I graduated, Mother let me return to Chicago, ostensibly to see my father's sister Edna. By this time, I had dated girls and brought a few of them home to meet Mother, convincing her she had nothing to fear if I saw Jasper while I was there.

The day I arrived, I went to Aunt Edna's, but I didn't stay. I never warmed to Edna. She, as a debutante, was restrained by the stifling inhibitions of her generation and by her own attraction to just the sort least likely to respond. She had been briefly, unhappily engaged and thereafter her favorite expression seemed to be, "All the evil in the world comes from man!" She could not imagine how Uncle Jasper could've happened to my mother's family and, beyond that, how I could have been so corrupted by him. But there was no stopping me. I couldn't wait to tell my uncle about my adventures. He planned a little welcoming dinner at his house. His housekeeper had left the meal for us and we were alone. I regaled him with my indulgences at the beach and after dinner when we settled in the library with cognacs, I confessed I'd fucked a man. "He was a beach bum," I told him. "He was coarse, just in from New Jersey and talked like it."

"Did he do it to you, too?"

"Oh, no! I wanted to try it but I didn't want it to be him." I stood up and moved next to his chair, laying my hand on top of his. "Uncle, I wanted that to be with you."

He turned away, sighing, "Oh, I couldn't do that."

But before the evening was over, my dear uncle came to realize that I had become an inveterate tease, each new man a challenge and in sex, as in everything else, I was used to getting my own way.

I told him I thought I had to rush it or I'd never get through it. But my problem of receiving it was minor to Jasper's problem of giving it. It was the first time I realized the limitations of a man's erection. As much as he wanted to please me, he couldn't bring himself to it. We'd get it hard, aim it and it would wither.

It was then that I conceived the notion that there was safety in numbers. I calculated that if Jasper saw me about to lose my cherry to someone else, perhaps he would respond.

I went to the beach north of downtown where Jasper had told me boys hung out. There were several possibilities that bright, clear day, but none approaching the appeal of a slim fellow in his early 20s with dark greasy hair. He appeared to be one of those hustlers who once had been extraordinarily good-looking and the tarnished glamour attracted me. I responded to the challenge of his seeming disinterest in me. He kept riding back and forth on the walkway separating the parking lot from the beach until I finally stepped in front of his bike and made him stop. "Hey, I'm looking for work," he said, shaking his head, as if to explain himself to me.

"I'm looking to put you to work."

"Oh yeah? How much does it pay?"

"How much do you need?" In those days, two dollars

bought a lot. Five bought the entire evening. I hailed a cab, stuffed his bike in the trunk, and took off for Jasper's house. The young man, who introduced himself as Jerry, was immediately taken with the place: big, dark, very old-fashioned and stuffy. Upon meeting my uncle, he quickly decided he had hit upon a lode beyond his wildest dreams. Jasper was less taken with him, even going so far as to berate me privately for bringing such riffraff to his house: "These boys will pick your pockets, beat you and leave you for dead in the gutter." Bluffing, I told him I knew what to do with such desperate characters. Jasper calmed down considerably when Jerry, sweaty from all that bicycling, wanted to take a bath. Even more of Jasper's reserve melted when he saw the young man, his weary face flushed from the bath and dressed only in a pair of tattered boxer shorts, return to the library, Jasper's sanctuary away from the eyes of the housekeeper, Mrs. Tyrell.

After appraising the sleek torso replete with tattoos in the oddest places, Jasper reluctantly told me Jerry had to dress for dinner. I loaned him some dressy clothes and we were served elegantly in the dining room, chatting as if we were old friends. The hustler ate as if he hadn't eaten in weeks, pleasing Mrs. Tyrell.

After dinner, we returned to the library. Jasper poured cognacs but I didn't want to waste any more time. Surprisingly, neither did Jerry. He slipped from his clothes almost immediately, sat on the divan and started to stroke his cock. During the long cab ride, I had managed to rub the hustler's crotch, bulging in tight, dirty white pants, to preview the quantity that awaited us. What was not revealed was the quality of it. On close inspection, I marveled that his circumcised cock was the most perfect one I had seen up to that time. The head was of average size and shape but the shaft thickened magnificently as it approached the base. To me, it appeared to be the perfect cock to be fucked by. In my mind, I had created a scenario with Jasper becoming so aroused he would go first, followed by Jerry. But Jasper was still reluctant. He sat stiffly in his chair and watched as I blew Jerry. So captivated was I by my find, I ignored my uncle for several minutes. But Jerry brought him into the action, exhorting him in a deep macho voice to join in, having me suck both at once.

When I had both of their cocks in my mouth, Jasper held the hustler around the waist and said: "Young Freddy's still a virgin. He has brought you here to help cure this condition."

Jerry laughed, saying I wouldn't be his first.

Jasper had explained it to me years before: "Your asshole has a sphincter muscle. It's like a fist, it clamps tight against all invaders but it is weak, it gets tired and relaxes. I'm told that's when you begin to enjoy the sensations."

"You've never done it?" I asked.

"No," he answered, "it's something an older man does to a young protege. I've never allowed myself the luxury of a protege. "

When I got on my knees and Jerry mounted me from behind, a great but soundless and invisible collapse of barriers in my mind began. As his cock slid in, it was as if he was massaging the muscles. He never pulled all the way out, just kept slowly fucking me, pushing into my body all of his marvelous cock. Soon he began in earnest, like a piston in an engine, harder, stronger and as if urgently roaring toward a destination. Jasper moved, positioning himself in front of me so that I could suck him while Jerry blasted his flesh into me.

After I came, I could take no more. Jerry was horny and wouldn't rest until he got off. He told Jasper to lie on the bed in my place. Jasper protested but he was not about to admit he, too, was a virgin. It seemed Jerry sensed that perhaps the old man had not enjoyed a plugging in some years so he took him gently. I watched in awe as my dear uncle began to feel the same sublime sensations I had felt. But he was to enjoy one I hadn't because, after several minutes of gentle probing, Jerry stepped up his assault and came inside my uncle. Jasper moaned so contentedly that I vowed I would feel that ecstasy myself before I took Jerry back to the shore.

Jasper permitted Jerry to stay with me in my room and it was the first time I had slept with another man other than my uncle. It was a sleepless night. I kept waking and watching the stud, listening to his muffled snoring across from me in the huge bed in the guest room.

The next morning, after breakfast, we returned to the room and I told Jerry what I wanted. With an exchange of more cash, he was ready to fulfill my demands. Because my ass was still hurting from its initiation the night before, Jerry gently insinuated himself, bringing me to orgasm almost immediately. But I gripped the mattress and begged him to continue because I wanted to feel the warmth of his ejaculation inside of me. It didn't take long; he lunged into me with a ferociousness that shocked me, finally gasping and pressing his body tight against me. As the wetness entered me, he gained a potent, thoroughly masculine dominance over me, fulfilling my most persistent fantasy.

I was able to see Jasper often during my two month visit that summer and it was as if the hustler had freed each of us to practice sex in every position we could think of. I felt I had finally emerged from the shadows. I considered myself a butterfly that had escaped its drab cocoon to become a more compact version of my adored uncle.

Truth be known, I would have sacrificed anything to be just like Uncle Jasper. In every way. Following his lead, I went on to college and law school and then went into banking as he had. He wanted me to stay in Chicago and work for him. "Only a city has places where someone can hide," he said prophetically. "You'll not be able to lead a double life in St. Petersburg. "

While I had to admit I'd always been attracted to the ambiguity of the city (The Loop, for example, not being the heart of the city, simply a dead center, and surrounding it areas that were dissimilar yet still so very close to each other). I felt my place was with Mother, taking over the reins of the land development company Jasper had helped her found.

Over the years, I would visit Jasper and he would visit us but sex never occurred again between us. I reasoned that I had gotten too old for him. "What was, was," he was fond of saying.

"What it was, was simply wonderful," I countered.

And he would nod and across his face would spread a smile, a knowing, kindly, loving-uncle kind of smile.

GETTING OFF

The Search for Orgasm

An Expose
Edited by
JOHN PATRICK

STARbooks Press
Sarasota, Florida

Contents

Introduction:
Climax in Excelis

1
The Nude Massuer

2
Contact Ads and Fetishes

3
Getting Off Around the World:
Tijuana, Thailand and Fire Island

4
On the Road

5
At the Baths

6
Bars and Bartenders

7
Celebrity Sex

8
A Lust for Leather

9
Solitary Pursuits

10
Beyond Orgasm

INTRODUCTION: CLIMAX IN EXCELIS

The whole point of having gay sex is getting off. As politically incorrect as it may be these days, I fear I must agree with Gore Vidal when he says, "Homosexuality is an *act*, not an identity." I fear I have never been interested in living a "gay lifestyle" and all that involves, which caused me problems when I had live-in lovers. I was trained early on by my older brother that the object was orgasm. To him, it didn't matter whether it was my mouth, my ass, or my hand that brought him off as long as he came, and then he could get on with other things.

With that background, I suppose it was inevitable that my life would be spent in a continuous search for orgasm, *any* orgasm.

Wilhelm Reich had the idea that good orgasms were the key to health and happiness, but bad orgasms depressed him. Tragically, this weird scientist and sex reformer died half-mad at the age of sixty in Lewisburg Federal Penitentiary in 1957, proclaiming to the end that much of human misery was due to the failure to achieve orgasm.

Reich's notions first surfaced in *Function of the Orgasm* in 1927. He was thirty years old at the time and a member of Freud's inner circle in Vienna. Reich dedicated the original manuscript to Freud. Freud was not pleased. Though he praised the book as "rich in observation and thought" in a brief note to his protege, he poked fun at Reich behind his back. Of course, orgasm was important to Freud. After all, he had written in "Sexuality in the Aetiology of the Neuroses" (1905) that "no neurosis is possible with a normal vita *sexualis*." But he did not overly concern himself with the explosive event. As long as men ejaculated in the right orifice and women had vaginal climax, the subject did not materially interest him. "We have Dr. Reich, a worthy but impetuous young man, passionately devoted to his hobby horse, who now salutes in the genital orgasm the antidote to every neurosis," Freud wrote to a mutual friend, Lou Andreas Salome, in 1928.

Where did Reich get his near-apocalyptic concept of orgasm? "As psychoanalysts tend to do," Edward Eichel says in *The*

Perfect Fit, "he beheld the universe in his patients when they confirmed his deepest convictions. Reich started pondering orgasm in a serious way after noticing something unexpected in a group of male patients. When he asked them about their masturbation fantasies he assumed that they would recount pleasant images of intercourse."

Instead, the men reported sadistic or masochistic fantasies that left them discontented after ejaculation. "In not a single patient was the act of masturbation accompanied by the fantasy of experiencing pleasure in the sexual act," Reich wrote in 'The Specificity of Forms of Masturbation' (1922).

Reich next probed the coital attitudes and sensations of hundreds of male and female patients. "What he found," Eichel reports, "apparently convinced him that intercourse would always be a quagmire for neurotics. None of the women had vaginal orgasm; and the most potent men felt something like disgust when they climaxed. Reich concluded that *all* patients suffered from incomplete genital satisfaction.

"His argument was a stretch, and he was forced to admit that not a few patients appeared to have hale and hearty orgasms. Still, he clung to the insight that some orgasms were better than others and, more important, that the quality of release separated the well from the sick. His supposition was reinforced in his private life.

"After a sexually frustrating period in medical school, marked by melancholy after the act, he fell in love with an Italian woman and, at last, had fulfilling sex. ..."

Reich was surely no Alex Comfort, but he gave step-by-step instructions for attaining ultimate orgasms. First, one needed to be "unarmored," that is, "muscularly relaxed and physically unblocked"; but after that it was just a matter of method. Basically, his advice was: don't do what neurotics do in bed. They were fast and frantic, violent and stiff, narcissistic and sad *post coitum*. On the other hand, Reich's lovers were warned to be slow and easy. In "Orgasm as an Electrophysiological Discharge" (1934), Reich referred to "spontaneous and effortless frictions" that focused excitement on the genitals. There was no fear, no fantasy, no rough talk, only surrender to the other.

"However," Eichel maintains, "Reich's blueprint contradicted two historic maxims: that variety is the spice of sexual pleasure and that resistance is the engine of arousal, especially in and around intercourse."

Speaking for erotologists of every era, Comfort observed in *The Joy of Sex* that "being stuck rigidly with one sex technique usually means anxiety."

As for the psychology of excitement, even Freud, who could be something of a fogey, recognized that *tension* was an indispensable aphrodisiac. He knew that an obstacle is required to heighten libido, "and when natural resistances to satisfaction have been insufficient men have at all times erected conventional ones so as to be able to enjoy love," he declared in "On the Universal Tendency to Debasement in the Sphere of Love" (1912).

Nevertheless, Reich's theory of Orgastic Potency and his orgasm formula, like many other erotic myths, have refused to die.

The late sexualist Marco Vassi, when asked about his "Metasex" theories in *A Driving Passion*, said, "If you're having Metasex with someone you love, that's one thing and it's really nice. If you're having Metasex with someone you don't love, that's really fine, too. You might be doing all kinds of things. Love and Metasex needn't have anything to do with each other. Most of the eroticism we involve ourselves in doesn't necessarily have to do with love. Compassion, liking, digging, disliking, are sufficient motivation. So are giving each other Reichian orgasms to get healthy; passing the time when there's nothing on TV, or getting high.

"Eroticism (Metasex) is basically a sensual activity. It includes all the senses, including thought, which the Buddhists list as a sixth sense, and with the kinesthetic sense – the sense of balance and movement of the body – which is the seventh sense. We're so starved in so many of our senses, that sometimes the only way you can get to smell somebody's asshole is to fuck them. Maybe you don't want to fuck them, you just want to smell their asshole, which sounds like a very weird thing, but it isn't."

1
THE NUDE MASSEUR

There's a first time for everything, I told myself as the "masseur" took his $65 and left the room, leaving me agitated and unsatisfied.

In these difficult days when there are few boys on the street anymore, in my travels I tended to rely on "full service" from masseurs. Hustlers available through ads want $150 a call and usually don't provide anywhere near the pleasure of a good masseur. I'll never forget the cute little youngster in Fort Lauderdale who didn't have a massage table in his flower-filled apartment and asked me to just undress and stretch out on the floor in front of his couch. He never even rubbed my back, just proceeded to give me a memorable blowjob.

And there was the guy in New Orleans who, when he finally rolled me over, worked me up and then proceeded to mount me and plunge my cock deep into his ass.

But here I was in Tampa on the last leg of my journey, hitting towns where there were no gay bars, let alone masseurs, and I hungered for a bit of action. A "black stud" included "rubdowns" in his ad and this got me hard, recalling a black who had a massage room set up with posters of porn stars and mirrors. He did his job in the nude and started with my back, which put my face right in his crotch. Even limp the tool was incredibly long and thick. He didn't seem to mind that I licked it and eventually was choking on it. He continued the massage and, when he got to my ass, he greased it up, climbed on the table and gave me a plummeting I shall always cherish. Having had that experience with a black I decided to dial the number. These days, that means pagers. You wait for the return call. He seemed perfectly fine over the phone, offering a rubdown "complete" for $65.

It was only after he rubbed me for a while as I lay on the bed nude that I figured out he was never going to slip out of his jeans. Never, that is, until I agreed to pay his "escort" rate of $150. He looked a bit like Magic Johnson, only shorter, of course, and bulky. He might have played football at some point. But he was definitely not worth $150. Not to me anyway.

The following day, I returned to the classifieds. I was determined to get a massage to remember, even if I was in Tampa. It seemed every advertiser who had possibilities was based in Orlando. Then I came across "ANTONIO . . . My HUGE hands all over you. Hard and/or soft penetration – just let my fingers do the talking. Given by 6 foot two, 200 lb., masculine muscle stud. Discounts to hardbodies or hotel visits. In/Out. $45-$60." Musclebound hunks are not my type but, in my present state, and never one to turn down a "discount rate," I figured it was worth a try.

Antonio's voice purred. I felt better already. He couldn't make it until five. Fine. That gave me all day to relax and get ready.

Antonio was everything promised in the ad – and more. He had served a brief stint in the Marine Corps and had a tattoo to prove it. I don't normally like to see a boy mutilate his body with tattoos either but somehow this worked.

What also worked was Antonio. He brought his own table, his own stereo system and CD's, and a gym bag filled with oils.

"Do you want me dressed or undressed?" he asked when he was all set.

"Oh, undressed," I gushed like a schoolgirl.

"I thought you would," he said, smiling. I had explained to him the situation of the night before and he had said, "See, you should have called me first."

Once he was nude, I knew I was going to enjoy this massage, if for no other reason than being able to look at his hefty cock.

I stretched out on his table and he placed my hands down on my sides. "You can do anything you like as long as it doesn't interfere with my work."

"I understand," I said, lifting my head. His cock was two inches from my lips. I leaned forward and licked. I kept licking while he went about his business. When he moved to the side, he adroitly placed his jewels in my upturned hand. I played with his balls and cock while he massaged by aching body. He really was good. In fact, it was without a doubt the best massage I had ever received.

He went around to the other side and again his thick shaft

was gently placed in my hand. I stroked it while he soothed me.

Eventually he was ready to have me roll over. Then he took my head and positioned it facing his crotch. He began massaging my chest, working his way around and, finally, onto my cock. I was hard by this time because as he leaned over, his cock went deeper into my mouth and throat. Before long he was face-fucking me. It was glorious feeling his practiced fingers working me over while my mouth was stuffed with his prick. I gagged but recovered. He had me on the edge several times, but always knew when to ease up. If I hadn't had his cock in my mouth and if he wasn't enjoying it, I imagined he would have brought me off immediately.

Finally he sensed I could take no more and let me come. After all the built-up tension of the past week, my body was rocked with one of the fiercest orgasms I could remember. He still wasn't through. He moved down and continued massaging my legs.

"You have a pretty cock," he said.

"So do you," I mumbled.

"I love a big, thick, uncut cock," he said, stroking it again.

I shuddered.

"You'll have to call me again."

"Yes, I'll have to." I didn't say it but I was thinking, 'There's a first time for everything.'

Antonio's Story

"I embarked upon massage class with a certain degree of previous experience touching men – well, once or twice anyway," Antonio says. "My experience did not, however, give me the least bit of immunity from trepidation. On the contrary, it gave rise before school actually started, to a rather unpleasant recurring vision: I'm in class, lying on a massage table. This golden Adonis with the face of life and the dick of death (I've no idea how I knew he had the dick of death, but one's allowed leeway when dealing with visions), comes up to me. He rests his warm, massive hands upon my trembling person, and immediately I leap to attention – unmistakably aroused. Amused, he throws me to the floor where I'm set upon by a roomful of redneck ruffians who righteously beat the shit out of me. With every bone in my body pulverized, my massage career is finished before it begins. Obviously it isn't easy being gay either.

"As it turned out, I soon saw my vision to be nothing more than normal, everyday, fanciful paranoia. The icy glare from banks of fluorescent tubes, the stark white towels and sheets and baggy Dr. Kildare jackets we had to wear, the mingled odors of rubbing alcohol and stale mineral oil, and the brusque, business-like demeanor of our teacher combined to produce an atmosphere in the classroom that would have squelched the ardor of the horniest of the horny. Nevertheless, I retained a vague sense of discomfort, a strange feeling that something was amiss. We were a good two months into the course before an incident occurred which reminded me of what it was that had been bothering me.

"The class was structured in a routine pattern: after the instructor had explained and demonstrated a new set of movements, we would pair-off and spend the bulk of the time practicing on each other. This particular day I was approached by a man I'd not yet worked with, who suggested it was about time we teamed-up. My gut reaction was that he was coming from a totally pragmatic position believing that, for the sake of the completeness of his training, he owed it to himself to have the experience of massaging all types, myself included. He was a softly-muscled man, a devotee of the martial arts, whose surface attractiveness had been nullified, in my eyes, by flagrant conceit. In lecture classes he always sat in the very front, answered everyone's questions, questioned everyone's answers, and did his damndest to dominate every general discussion. I, on the other hand, always sat in the very back, remained comparatively silent – content with the self-awareness that I understood as much as anyone else, and was thoroughly pleased with myself for not feeling the need to humble the masses with my intellect. Obviously we were two of a kind who simply chose to manifest our arrogance differently – the ideal circumstances for the ultimate personality conflict.

"It was not, therefore, with the best of attitudes that I first approached this man's body. In turn, I was in no way prepared for what transpired. As I spread the oil over his skin and began to massage him, I felt the involuntary slackening of the hostility that had been clenching my stomach. The antagonism which I had been more than willing to hold on to gradually dissipated. It was replaced with a sense of ease, of comfort, of 'rightness.' I had no consciously intellectual explanation for why it was happening, but I could neither deny nor ignore what I was experiencing. It was as if his flesh was giving itself over to me, his muscles intentionally surrendering themselves. There was none of the implicit reticence at being touched that I had sensed from the other men. Though I alone was expending physical energy, it seemed that we were working together. His body and I were both actively involved in the massage. As my movements fell into a naturally smooth, flowing rhythm, I became totally absorbed – oblivious to my surroundings – as if I were yielding to some sort of hypnotic trance. My focus was solely on what I was feeling: the texture of his sparsely-haired skin, its blood-rich warmth, the pliant resiliency of his muscles, and the awareness of a sharing of some form of fundamental energy – I don't know what else to call it. I had always vehemently taken a position somewhere between skepticism and cynicism in regards to concepts of a spiritualistic or parapsychological nature, and yet my intellect could not overshadow the inner conviction that this man and I were coming together on a level other than the purely corporeal. It was exhilarating; it was intoxicating; it was incredibly sensual.

"When I had finished and we changed places, he worked my body firmly and surely, not once breaking contact with my skin as he moved from part to part. There was never a question of my holding back, his touch was too giving, too open. It was as though his hands were melting against me, as if they were wax softening from the heat. I was awash in luxurious sensation; my body awakening to a glorious self-consciousness. I was unquestionably aroused, but it was not erotic in any conventional terms. The experience demanded no other satisfaction, no other fulfillment, it was complete unto itself. That sense that we were exchanging something not accounted for in clinical massage had grown all the stronger.

"At the end of class we barely spoke a word, but when he bade me good night there was a smile on his face – not suggestive or lurid, simply knowing. I was smiling too. I had come to understand what it was that had been making me uneasy. Until that time the class, for me, had been utterly sterile, determinedly removed from even the slightest suggestion of human sensuality. It was this very lack which had been causing me discomfort. I had not, in all honesty, gone into my training expecting, or wanting, it to be one long bacchanal. I had not been having insurmountable problems with getting laid, and if pseudo-prostitution had been my aim I would not have had to expend either the time or money for schooling. But since my early teens, when I had finally identified my desires, I had viewed the male body in an almost exclusively sexual light. Indeed, I had touched many a man before becoming involved with massage, but it had virtually always been with romantic and/or carnal intent, charged with the understood goal of attaining orgasm. Massage, as I chose to pursue it, demanded dealing with the body from a perspective which did not readily flow from my prior experience. It was this newness, this strangeness that I had been finding unnerving.

"It struck me as wonderfully ironic to realize that while I had been as equally thrown off-balance as many of the heterosexual men, it was for the totally opposite reason. Whereas they had been perceiving our situation as being more intimate, closer to the realm of sexuality, than they'd ever before known; I had been seeing it as colder, more devoid of sexuality, than I'd become used to, from years of prurient preoccupations. That one massage, with a man who I'd been content to detest, had shown me that there existed a wondrous middle-ground. I learned that in massage one could attain a level of sensuality that was positive, comfortable, and fulfilling without it conflicting with or infringing upon, the therapy's utterly valid physiological benefits. Thereafter, I did my best to gently 'test the waters' with each man I paired-off with. I claim no personal responsibility – surely every man went through unique changes as a result of innumerable factors – but I can report that as time went on the work of many of the men, gay and straight alike, became infused with a warmth, an affirmation of the natural sensuality implicit in their task.

"The tension, which had been characteristic of the class at the beginning, eased considerably as more of us came to accept the new dimensions we were discovering within ourselves. These changes seemed to extend beyond massage class itself, with people becoming more open, more approachable, more human. Even my arrogant, know-it-all, karate-trained friend mellowed out appreciably. Of course, I cannot ignore the plain fact that after we'd first laid hands upon one another my judgment of him altered dramatically. I felt that I'd made touch with a part of him that was not readily apparent, so that if, for example, he chose to argue interminably with the anatomy teacher over some inconsequential bit of minutia, I could mollify my resulting irritation in the light of my knowledge of the glowing, sensuous creature who langoured just beneath his domineering intellect.

"Clearly, my objectivity in regards to him was not entirely reliable – I'd have gone to bed with him in a second. Then again, perhaps I wouldn't have: As far as I was concerned we had made love every time we massaged each other, for we had both certainly explored the other's body more completely, more openly, more givingly, more lovingly than I had ever done with a sizeable percentage of the men I had only fucked with. Having sex with him may well have turned out to be anticlimactic. Be that as it may, the evidence would suggest that most of the men in the class made to one degree or another, personal discoveries as to their relationships with other human bodies which affected not only their style of massage, but their basic dealings with their fellow creatures as well.

"A few times a client and I have attained an advanced level of communication, that degree of primal sensuality which was first realized in class, and it has amply compensated for all the massages that have been merely chores.

"I have learned that each individual part of a man's body possesses as much erotic potential as any other part. Massage's structured, deliberate exploration of the body necessitates my concentrating on each component separately. In so doing, my appreciation of the male form as a whole has been greatly enhanced. An ankle, a thigh, the neck, the abdomen are each imbued with the inherent capacity to excite and to be excited. If my own experience is a valid measure, then it is plain that in sex many men place an inordinate emphasis on a comparatively few body parts. I have nothing in the least against qenital stimulation, but I now know that one can make love to the entire body, with his entire body.

"Massage has come to be a far more influential factor in my life than I ever imagined it would be. It provides me with an interesting means of income. It is a source of personal satisfaction. Because of it my understanding of, and respect for, the miraculous structure and intricate functioning of us human animals has grown tremendously I have learned, and am still learning, much about myself and those around me; and through it I have been able to expand and clarify the dimensions of my own sexuality."

— *The editor thanks Stephen Edwards for his contribution to this dialogue.*

. . .

In *Raunch*, Boyd McDonald's 11th volume of true sex histories, a man living in Rhode Island admits, "As a masseur, fooling around with my clients could be construed as prostitution.

"Mind you, I don't believe that I am engaging in prostitution. I just fool around with an occasional client. I don't molest my clients. I admit that when I get an attractive man on my table I may massage a little lower on the abdomen than I should, or a little higher on the thighs than I should. But I don't touch their genitals unless they request it and unless they appeal to me sexually. Also I don't accept any extra money for any sex I may have with a client.

"It turns out that the opportunities for fooling around in the massage profession are legion. I would say that most of the men who come to me enjoy the homo-eroticism of it in one way or another. Some just like being touched by a man, while others want action. When a man (or woman) answers my ad, he has to answer some questions before I will set up an appointment. I ask these questions because I feel that I need to know something about the people I let into my home. He also has to give me his full name and a telephone number at which I can reach him. This screens out the kooks and dangerous ones.

"Last Saturday morning a guy named Steve called and, after checking him out, I set up a one o'clock appointment for him. His answers to my questions were not overly exciting. He said he was 35 (good), worked in the lumber business (maybe good, maybe not), did not engage in any athletic activities (not good), but did do a lot of lifting on the gym (good).

"I was standing at the window when he drove up in his dark green flat-bed truck. He was wearing a navy blue work uniform with a navy blue cap. Having come from an upper middle class family, I found the prospect of massaging this working man fascinating. Steve seemed to be a nice enough guy. He didn't say much but there was no hint of uptightness. He had a moderately thick local accent. He was medium height (about five-nine) and looked stocky. His face was broad and reddish, as was his thick neck, and his hands were calloused and grey from working.

"I led him into the massage room and told him to undress and lie down under the sheet on the massage table and to call me when he was ready. At that point, I still couldn't tell what kind of body he had. When I entered the room I was pleasantly surprised. He was lying with the sheet half-way up his chest and all that stockiness, it turned out, was thick, graceful muscle – with the exception of a moderate beer belly. I was disappointed, however, when I looked at the sheet over his groin and judged that he had kept his underpants on. Nonetheless, the lump in the sheet looked sizable.

"Each person responds differently to a massage, and Steve responded in the way I like best: he became very relaxed and 'lost' to the experience. On the couple of occasions when I spoke to him, he had to rouse himself to respond. When I got to his belly I discovered that he had not kept his underpants on after all. Still, there was no evidence of a hard-on. However, when I got to his right leg, the lump in the sheet definitely grew. I decided to be bold and massaged his inner thighs close to his groin, brushing his balls a bit with my fingers. But his hard-on went down by the time I finished both of his legs.

"When I did his backside I included his butt. (I used to ask my clients if they wanted their buttocks done but now I just go ahead and do them.) He was lying on his dick so I couldn't tell if it was hard.

"When the massage was over (despite all my shenanigans I do give a good massage), he was very relaxed. I wiped the oil off his backside. When he turned over, much to my delight he let the sheet fall partly off his body, so that his dick (flaccid, unfortunately) and balls were mostly exposed. I wiped the oil off one side of his front and then moved the sheet to wipe the other side. In moving the sheet, I inadvertently allowed a corner of it to cover his genitals. In a quick motion (meant not to be noticed), he flicked the sheet off so he was completely exposed.

"That's when I knew he wanted some action. I asked him if the massage lived up to his expectations and he said it was good. Then I asked if I had left anything out and he said, 'I thought maybe you could do...' and motioned toward his dick. I said yes and oiled it up. His genitals were beautiful. His cock swelled to 7 1/2 or 8 inches and, just like his body, was thick (very) and graceful. It was thicker at the middle of the shaft than at the base of head. He was cut but the doctor had mercifully left him with a lot of skin. I told him that he had a big cock and he said, 'Oh, yeah!?' I honestly don't think he knew. After I jerked him for a bit he asked if I would suck it and I said yes.

"Unfortunately, he came quickly, even before I could take a hit of poppers.

"While I was waiting for him to dress, I was mildly fearful that he might get rough now that he had dropped his load.

After all, this was a *real* blue-collar working man, not a gay imitation. But when he came out he was his same, placid self. I asked him not to spread the word around that I had blown him and he said he had no one to tell. Then I said that I enjoyed sucking cock and that he could come back anytime for a free blow job. He told me that he got out of work around 9:00 and was that a good time? I said yes. He called the next day. He sounded tense on the phone and, again, I was a bit apprehensive; but when he walked in he was grinning and I knew everything would be all right.

"It turns out that he's married to a woman he loves but who is semi-frigid (sex once a month). He has no animosity toward gays. In fact he is friendly and talkative and treats me with warmth and respect.

"Again I sucked his cock and sucked his balls, which he loved. For a long time he just lay on the floor and let me rub my hands all over him. He seems to need a lot of human contact. I expect to see a lot of him. There is one small thing wrong with him: he has a bit of trouble getting a hard on. But I think I will always be able to get at least one good hard on (and load) out of him each time I see him.

"One of my massages degenerated into sex even before it was over. The client was a stocky 29-year-old man whom I judged to be gay and who showed a large basket in his pants. The basket looked so good that I decided to throw caution to the winds. Overall, this guy was decent looking, though not as attractive as my working man. When I got to his left thigh I massaged all the way up to his crotch, boldly brushing the back of my hand firmly against his balls. By the way, his balls were round and absolutely huge, probably the biggest I have seen. I commented while I was doing this that it was important to massage the upper thigh muscles, and he said it was fine with him. His cock hung to the right and when I got to his right thigh the back of my hand brushed the tip of his cock as well as his balls, at which point he started getting a hard on. He apologized for the hard-on and I told him it was a normal reaction. Then I touched the glans of his dick and told him that I could 'take care of it" for him if he liked. He said that I could do whatever I wanted. I didn't even wait. I finished that leg and then oiled his genitals and started jerking his cock. Then I sucked it. He ended up sucking me too. It was an exciting experience, although I am not sure he appealed to me enough for me to see him again.

"I have had a lot of attractive men come for massages with whom I did not fool around, but who were a turn-on anyway. The second massage I ever gave was to a young college student. He was a working-class type who spoke in short, elliptical sentences with a heavy local accent. His behavior was reserved and macho. His body was thickly muscled, unusually trim, and well-defined. He sprang a hard-on as soon as I started massaging his belly and sprang another one when I did his legs, and also when I took the oil off his body. I would say that he had a hard-on most of the time. He obviously wanted some action but at that early stage I was still too timid to initiate anything. Also, acting like Sylvester Stallone as he did, I thought it too dangerous to just grab his dick. Unfortunately, he was too macho to ask for what he wanted. Too bad.

"I also had a local racket-sports champion come for a massage. He got a hard-on when I massaged his butt (he pushed it down between his legs so it was visible). When the massage was over, he didn't wait for me to leave the room; he just jumped up and started dressing right in front of me, with his semi-hard-on hanging down. I was certain that I would see him again, but I haven't.

"I had a tall, lanky 'straight' guy show up for a massage. He was more modest about his body than most; when I told him to undress, he said 'everything?' But when I explained that he should remove his underpants if he wanted his buttocks done, he readily took them off. As soon as the massage was over, he asked to make a local call. I brought him the phone and he crouched on the floor, naked, while he made his call. Modestly, he kept his legs tightly together but to no avail, since his large balls and large semi-hard cock hung down between his thighs, quite visible."

2
CONTACT ADS & FETISHES

For those with a particular fetish, contact ads are the likeliest avenue to pursue. For instance, with so many males circumsized at birth, uncut members have become prized in our society and the easiest way to meet those who have what you seek is through the ads.

"*Foreskin Freak. Overhang worshipper. Skin Slave. Uncut a plus. Uncut a MUST.*"

"Whether heading up the salacious text of a contact ad, crouching amidst the academic rhetoric of an American Medical Association dissertation, or topping the agenda of childrens' rights, there's no doubt about it: the male prepuce is increasingly in the news," says J. R. McMillan.

"While our English word *circumcision* derives from the Latin *circum* (around) and *cidere* (to cut, slice or sever), the foreskin itself has been the subject of an acrimonious debate - cultural, social and religious long pre-dating the Romans. For Hindus, the removal of the male foreskin is an abomination, for Muslims a pubescent rite of passage to adulthood, as the Bar Mitzvah is for Jews.

"The ancient Hebrews practiced circumcision as the fulfillment of a Covenant with God, though until the Hellenic Age, this involved the shedding of a drop of blood merely by lopping off the tip of the foreskin, rather than its entire removal. Amputating the entire skin was only adopted at the time when ancient cultures of the Eastern Mediterranean would send their young men to Greece to participate in athletic competitions, forerunners of the modern Olympic Games. The events were played in the nude. As an exposed penis head was considered vulgar and culturally offensive by the Greek hosts, Jewish athletes - and ostensibly non-Jews born with short foreskins - tied the tips of their foreskins with twine to satisfy social convention, thus preventing an embarrassing faux pas should their skin involuntarily retract and expose the glans.

"Devout Hebrew elders promptly condemned what they saw as 'the Hellenization of our youth,' and the ritual practice of severing the entire foreskin began in earnest, surviving to this day. Christianity was more ambivalent about circumcision, though historically the foreskins of Christendom remained intact, by and large, for centuries.

"The first regular circumcisions among European gentiles was in seventeenth-century England. It was practiced only on members of His Majesty's overseas armed forces. The reason involved religion only in an indirect way. Having soundly routed the invading Spanish Armada. In 1588, England stood poised and anxious to overtake Spain as the world's foremost expansionist colonial power. The Royal Navy was dispatched across the globe, not only to settle Jamestown and Plymouth, but also the African and Indian coasts and the Middle East. Muslim sultans and caliphs would have none of it and engaged in battle against the Christian infidels, forcibly converting their European prisoners of war to Islam, as the faith commanded.

"Conversion in this context involved immediate and involuntary circumcision, generally right on the battle field, using the bloody swords of war. The prisoner would be restrained, his genitals extracted from his cod-piece, his foreskin stretched to its limit. Then sword of Islam would fiercely descend, and whoosh! No more foreskin, no more infidel. Scores of humiliated young Englishmen began dying of circumcision wounds on Ottoman battlefields under conditions of appalling hygiene. It was not long before troops destined for service in the Muslim world were routinely shorn of their foreskins as a preventative measure before leaving England.

"Among the civilian British population, circumcision remained extremely rare until the mid-Victorian period, when the temper of British society underwent a significant shift. Mimicking the austere and reclusive decorum of their widowed queen, the public demeanor became staid, dour and determinedly non-sensuous. Prudishness reigned, and even modest and benign expressions of sexuality were viewed at best with disapproval, at worse with moral outrage and censure.

"Against this disapproving backdrop, a frenzied masturbation hysteria developed. At its height, this silliness blamed jerking off on everything from peevish digestion to insanity. To once and for all exorcise the evil of masturbation, the prevailing wisdom thought it best to make it more difficult or painful to masturbate. Circumcision! What more effective way to hinder a boy from the devilish habit of beating off than a tight, radical amputation of those delicious rolls of skin which slide so provocatively up and down his shaft? Circumcision as punishment for not suppressing sexual urges and as a preventative measure against masturbation gained acceptance among the middle and upper classes, whose newborn sons frequently sacrificed their skins to this belief until just after the Second World War.

"In 1948, Britain's National Health Service was launched, financed by taxation, free at delivery point, and guaranteeing medical coverage to all. In reviewing which costs to the new system were worthy and justified, British medical experts concluded that routine neonatal circumcision was unnecessary surgery, being neither medically indicated nor (necessarily) socially desirable. In today's United Kingdom, the practice has fallen into disrepute, the non-religious circumcision rate hovers between one quarter and one half of one percent.

"The more aesthetic continental cultures were never subject to any such dilemma, rejecting the British circumcision mania utterly and absolutely. America was considerably less decisive. Aspiring stateside patricians slavishly imitated British social trends and fancies, from decor to diction, and circumcision was no exception. By the 1920s, routine infant circumcision had become fairly common. It was 'cleaner,' and not at all out of character in a culture profoundly inclined to believe in its ability to improve on nature. The Second World War accelerated this trend, when tens of thousands of enlisted men were ritually clipped upon induction into the military, lest unforeseen 'problems' arise in the hills of Sicily or jungles of Mindanao, miles from medical attention.

"After the war, America largely parted ways with Britain on the issue of circumcision. Solvent, flush with victory, and bursting with an empowering sense of capitalist mission, America saw little need for a nationalized health insurance scheme, still less for informed debate on the fortunes of foreskin. Our national tastes, relentlessly homogenized by omnipresent mass media advertising, tended increasingly towards the squeaky clean, sometimes to the point of obsession. Foreskin was malodorous, and that yellow wax build-up was definitely OUT. Besides, the medical establishment quickly discovered that stripping infant foreskins was not a bad money maker. By the 1960s this logic was so culturally entrenched in modern America that the circumcision trend seemed to settle into permanency. Hospital maternity ward check-in forms routinely included - and often still do - a circumcision authorization clause. In 1971 the US circumcision rate topped 91 percent of newborn male infants. By the 1980s, bagging infant foreskins had ballooned into a $250 million industry. It remains the most commonly performed surgery in America today.

"Fortunately, change is in the air. Parents, doctors and the general public have collectively become more concerned, and more educated, if only marginally. For now we Americans remain unique among nations, a land of social circumcisers."

. . .

So what if you are tired of being cut? Can you go back to the natural state? Porn star Al Parker went through the restoration process a few years before he died and it became another reason for him to star in videos – and make personal appearances. Tim Hammond, a long-standing political activist within the gay men's community, is the co-founder of the National Organization of Restoring Men (NORM). Hammond, who is involved in his own foreskin restoration process, is also the founder of the National Organization to Halt the Abuse and Routine Mutilation of Males (NOHARMM). Tim recalls the time he got Al to appear before his group:

"Men have a whole range of reasons why they want to restore," says Hammond. "Some want to enhance their sexual pleasure. Others literally feel ripped off. They look down, see their scar, and know something was done to them. They don't feel whole or naturally masculine. Gay men who have had experiences with intact men see the superior function of the intact penis over the circumcised penis. My decision to restore is not only about enhancing sexual pleasure or regaining my natural bodily integrity but it's also a political issue. It's taking back my body from the circumciser.

"I'd had experiences with intact men and sensed that they were feeling a higher level of sexual pleasure. They had a whole aspect of sexual function that I was denied and that was the mobility of the shaft skin which I had none. I could also sense from masturbating them that there was this wonderful continuity of feeling with the foreskin that I didn't have.

"Now, the more I get into my foreskin restoration, the more I feel I am benefiting. Before I started this process, I wasn't having bad sex. On a scale of one to ten, I was probably at an eight, which is really good sex. But I wanted to see if I could go further. So I did. I opted for foreskin restoration. Now I'd rate sex at about a 13."

Al Parker showed up at one of Tim's meetings and talked to his group about what he had done for himself. "He really loved talking about his reconstruction," Tim reports. "He said his circumcision was something that he never really accommodated in his life. When he started hearing about restoration he sought out a urologist. Apparently, Al was loosely cut which meant he had a fair amount of foreskin left. So the urologist pulled the foreskin forward over the head, made an incision on the top of the foreskin, and then sewed it together. During the meeting, we did a show and tell kind of thing and that's when Al showed us his restoration."

"Uncut cock, especially if it's sweaty and cheesy, makes me crazy," *Drummer* magazine co-founder Jack Fritscher says. "I spent half my time in high school study hall flipping through my dictionary getting a roaring hard-on looking up words like foreskin, smegma, and prepuce. The other half of my time I spent secretly cruising the locker room and counting off my buddies who were cut and uncut. The most beautiful dicks I saw were the big, chunky cocks that hung long and strong.

"An uncut dick rides different than a piece of meat that's been sliced. Never showing its crown immediately, uncut meat keeps its glistening wet head, thick and full of jutting promises, under its rich rolls. Uncut meat looks different, smells different, and tastes of special man-flavors. It feels like a fucking handful when you grab hold of it. And offers you that special little pucker right at the tip where the skin folds down.

"When an uncut man's foreskin, lipped into foreplay, starts pulling back, a special kind of lube sweetens the taste of the cock. Uncut meat punches out of its foreskin in a way that demands attention, and gets it.

"Check out any hot tub, sauna, steam room, or swimming pool shower room. An uncut stud who's scrubbing down his crotch has to take a long, deliberate time washing his meat – inside and out. He soaps and scrubs, pulls open the foreskin, holds it up to the shower spray and lets the water fill it up. If you hang around long enough you might even catch a glimpse of that supersensitive prick head.

"When I spy a well-hung 'skinster' jerking off at a roadside urinal, I notice a definite difference in his strokes. Because of the extra skin that slides up and down his shaft, I swear his strokes are longer. Even the sound of his uncut dick, as his hand slaps his foreskin up and down his cock, sounds wetter. And hotter. And nothing looks better than a big drop of clear juice hanging just out of tongue's reach on the rich skin-fold of his big, thick foreskin. And then the fucker, with his Wrangler jeans dropped down around his cowboy boots, pulls his foreskin up toward his mouth, and, sure as shit, bends over and almost tongues his own tread!

"Any dick coming through a glory hole is fine, but stripping back an uncut pisser flopping and hanging expectantly is heaven on wheels. There's hardly a manjack on earth who hasn't fallen on his knees at the sight of a big, healthy, juicy, uncut piece of hardening cock stuck through a glory hole. Grabbing hold of a monster like that, feeling the shaft growing thicker, and watching the head start to slip in its own ripe juices is fucking seventh heaven.

"My most amazing crash into a 24-carat foreskin obsession occurred when my buddy, Tom Caserta, and I decided we needed more foreskin in our diet. So we built a glory-hole booth in Tom's garage: three plywood sides with a hole in each side. Then we placed ads in all the Bay Area adult sex papers, straight and gay, offering expert blowjobs and foreskin action (including foreskin worship) to men hung really big (extra bucks for the world's biggest foreskins). Our glory hole had doorbell trade that wouldn't stop! We were totally blown away. We had these big uncut men - blue collar and white collar - sticking their big meat at us with such dripping intensity that we decided to videotape as many as we could."

And speaking of videotape, Gino Colbert tells the tale of Joey Stefano's visit to a porn shoot shortly after he blew into Hollywood with Tony Davis. One of the Gino's uncut co-stars was "unclean" and nobody would blow him. Joey jumped at the chance, and, after doing the deed, Joey passed Gino on his way to the bathroom. Smacking his lips, Joey said, "Tasted just like tacos."

"I've had sex with over one thousand men in my life," Tumbleweed says in *The Lavender Reader*. "Most of it has been outdoor sex: beaches, parks, 'cruising areas.' I've been asked many times 'doesn't it feel weird, to share intimacy with someone you don't know?' But, I don't think so. For me, having sex with another man is kind of like shaking hands. It's impersonal. About half the time, we don't exchange words, and rarely do I know the other guy's name. The only sounds necessary are grunts and moans for pleasure; or 'don't do that' kinds of sounds. Some guys are turned off by any conversation. Many are not consciously acknowledging what they are doing. They may be married or just closeted, so talking is out. Communication beyond sex would be admitting to the act of homosex.

"I've cruised guys all over the world, and that's how I discovered my prime fetish. See, the sex doesn't vary that much from place to place except for one thing: foreskin.

"I love foreskin, the feel and taste and smell of what's under the hood. To me, prepuce makes the man. It's an added erotic turn-on. Strange, that a piece of skin the size of an eyelid makes so much difference. But imagine if eyelids, or lips, were cut off at birth. Then some of us might get an erotic attachment for those few fortunates left with uncut lips or 'lace curtain' eyelids.

"My first complete foreskin experience was at Finnila's Finnish Baths on Market Street (near Cafe Flore) in San Francisco. I was leaving the baths, getting dressed to go home with a friend (my lover was out of town for the week) and this young, uncircumcised gentleman came into my cubicle and stretched his pliant foreskin over the head of my penis and proceeded to jerk me off. I'd never felt anything like it before (this was before the days of lube). It was like a velvet glove.

"Getting fucked by someone with a foreskin is an altogether different experience. No friction. The dick inside you slides in and out of its own skin, not chafing the inside of your rectum. Soft, unobtrusive, almost there, yet not. Of course, condoms changed all of that, now it's latex in your butt, one way or the other, and there's not really much difference, the latex rubs against the inside. But, I get a secret pleasure, anyway, just knowing that I'm getting fucked with an uncut dick.

"Of all the cruising areas I've frequented – Buena Vista Park or Land's End in San Francisco, Ile St. Louis or the Jardins Tuileries in Paris, under the Santa Cruz wharf or along the San Lorenzo (years ago), the beach up by Laguna Creek Road – some of my favorite foreskins have been attached to men in Greece, particularly Mykonos, where there is a decidedly international crowd. I pretend not to speak English, so that I meet only Europeans. Americans are generally circumcised, while the rest of the world, save the Arabs and Jews, are not.

"Back in Mykonos, I'm on the side of a white domed chapel at the edge of the sea. It's after midnight and the boys are out looking for action. Maybe twenty or so, mostly brown- or black-haired gentlemen; probably Italian or French, Spanish or German; not too many Greeks out in these parts. My heart pounds, I'm nervous, a little scared. But, I've done this enough to know I'm safe. If anyone ever acts too rough or rowdy, there's plenty of people around to help.

"I walk to the edge of the cliff on which the chapel perches, and walk down onto the rocks, close to the sea. The dark water reflects strands of lights from cruise ships, and the gas lamps along the crescent of Mykonos's harbor. I pass a few shadows, two or three men assembled in a semi-circle. One is getting jerked off, the other is sucking the jerker. Typically, the sucker would be in his forties or fifties, the suckee in his twenties. But this night it's hard to tell. And there are no hard or fast rules. Every man has his preference. Like me.

"I walk past another guy, but I can tell I don't want to have sex with him. Although I can't see him, I can read his body language. Something isn't there, no attraction. Maybe he seems needy or crazy; maybe I don't meet his standards for a mate. I try to pass unobtrusively. I look out to sea as I near him, and he stares down at his feet.

"I reach the other end of the beach. No one. So I climb back up on the rocks to get a view from the bluff. There is another man in the shadows, I can't really see him – until he comes into the moonlight, and then, yes, I sense lust. I act cool, trying not to appear too interested. Ahhh, this turns him on. I think I've engaged him. He ambles over, penis already out of his pants. Good sign. I reach for it and he gently guides it into my open fist, thrusting his hips, a smile crossing his lips, teeth glinting in the light. I take hold of his dick and *bingo:* foreskin!

"As he moves in closer, I get a faint glimpse into his open shirt, ahhh! Double my pleasure: a hairy chest!

"He leans over and unbuttons my pants, dropping to his knees for closer inspection. He looks up into my eyes and gives me a broad smile. I like this kind of man, the ones who aren't afraid to admit that they are enjoying themselves.

"Both penises are out in the darkness, skin barely glinting in the soft reflection of the boats and the moonlight. I take his penis and stroke it, sliding the loose cuff of skin up and down. We are both breathing heavily, moaning in agreement, anticipation. He's slurping happily, almost hungrily on my dick, moving his eyes every once and again to meet mine, just to connect and let me know that he likes what's going on.

"Soon, one of us comes, then the other. His cum shoots, arching out onto the rocks and down the bluff to the sea. I like it when seed hits the ground; better that than in a Kleenex. My cum he spits out of his mouth, deliberately, thoroughly. He rises to his feet again to kiss me with his tongue. I feel the scrape of his whiskers on my chin. I stroke the black patch of curly hair on his chest. We hold each other for a few minutes as our hearts slow down from pounding, to more like the sound of the waves hitting the rocks below.

"No words are exchanged as we part. Smiles, satisfied looks in our eyes. I wonder if I'll ever see him again. Probably not, but if I did, I get the feeling that we would get along fine."

When it comes to foreskin, a man in Providence summed it up when he wrote to *Drummer*, "Cut men have always been attracted to men who were spared the cruel knife of circumcision. Living in an area where many Portuguese men live, I've made a study of them at the YMCA. All are unclipped and they come in all shapes. There's the funnel type with the long tapered skin (my favorite). Then there's the wide open type with lots of thick skin. I have seen three men who appear to have had blind meat. One man who I was privileged to perform oral sex on loved having his tight nipple worked on. He always came back for more, in fact for many more sessions. Each time it was a treat for me – and him."

3
GETTING OFF AROUND THE WORLD

Tijuana

Getting off depends largely on where in the world you are, or happen to go.

Travelling Brit Mark Simpson reports, "I am in Tijuana, looking at America's youth with its pants down. It ain't pretty but I want a piece of the action. I'm on the prowl, you see, looking to 'recruit' – and this is probably the best place to do it because there isn't a boy here who hasn't drunk the equivalent of a bottle of industrial-strength muscle-relaxant. Tijuana may mean little more than cheery Herb Alpert instrumentals to you, but to kids in the Californian border city and naval base of San Diego, Tijuana spells 'Party on, dude.'

"The reason for this is very simple: the minimum age for imbibing intoxicating liquor in California is 21; in Mexico it is 18. This, and the fact that Tijuana is only a forty-minute drive south, explains why hordes of American teenagers regularly leave leafy suburbs, green campuses and neatly-ordered barracks to party and puke on the pavements of their Third World neighbor.

"Tijuana must be difficult for the American mind to comprehend. Perhaps this is another reason why they drink so much here. Apart from the sheer disorganization of every thing, from street signs to sanitation (particularly shocking after the fastidiousness of well-heeled California), there is the poverty which litters the streets. Four-year-olds sit on the pavement, among their shit and dead cats, with their dirty palms outstretched. Many of the beggars have travelled from the rural interior of Mexico to try and cadge some dollars. 'TJ,' as the kids call it, may be richer for its proximity to the United States than other parts of Mexico. But the image of a town unhooking its bra straps to cater for the apparently limitless hedonism of Yankee youth while its own children sell chewing gum and sleep in its doorways is not an altogether attractive one.

"The main drag for the brattish Yankee invaders is called, with sad Latin American irony, Plaza de la Revolucion. Tonight the square is full of rampaging youths eager to combine the incompatible activities of getting legless and getting their legs over (though not, I hope, incompatible with someone like me getting their leg over them).

"Tonight is also a military payday. Their back-pockets bulging, hundreds of 'squids' and 'jarheads' (sailors and Marines) zig-zag their way up and down the streets, deliberately walking into their sworn enemies, college boys. I came here with the intention of preying upon America's clean-limbed youth while they prey on Mexico. In the sexual food chain I intend to be at the top. But who to choose? Jarheads, squids or college boys?

"It only takes a minute to eliminate the college boys (too smug) and the squids (too geeky) and thus decide on the jarheads. There's a certain irresistible poetic justice in the idea of seducing a U.S. Marine, historically the means of projecting U.S. power in Latin America. But, even more persuasively, Marines have a number of classical features which attract them to the homosexual predator. They are fit, they have short hair, they always suffer from a shortage of women and, best of all, they drink far too much. As a popular American gay joke has it - Q: What's the difference between a straight Marine and a bisexual Marine? A: A six-pack of beer.

"All in all, it's really very thoughtful of the U.S. government to go to the trouble of giving teenage Midwestern boys a decent haircut, making them exercise, depriving them of female company and then sending them to Southern California Fagville U.S.A. - where they can bring a little joy into the lives of lonely homosexuals. The big drawback is that Marines, like nuns, always travel in threes. But that didn't stop me chatting up Troy, a recruiting poster picture come to life, in some bar where he was whooping it up with his two buddies. 'Hey dude, that accent's really cool!' he exclaims, grinning his blond grin and slapping my back with his wide farmboy hands. 'I bet the chicks really go for that!' And so our romance begins...

"As the beers and tequila flow, so does Troy's life story. It turns out that, like many boys, he turned to the U.S. Armed Forces to save him from America. Back in his two-horse town in west Texas, he used to while away the hours mainlining crystal-meth. 'Man, I woulda been dead by now if it wasn't for the Corps,' he tells me. 'They gave me something to live for, y'know?'

"His chaperones, Dusty and Jim, smaller and plainer than Troy, are boyhood buddies who joined up with him. There is something very touching about their friendship. 'He was my protector at school,' confides Jim later. A stutterer, life must have been hard at school and I get the impression that Troy is still his protector in the Corps.

"Nevertheless, their lifelong attachment to one another must end tonight, at least long enough for me to jump on Troy. We march increasingly unsteadily from bar to bar, hassling the college boys along the way. Asked to explain this tribal animosity, Troy just shrugs, 'They're pussies,' he says, adding, 'It's traditional, I guess.'

"But I suspect that the hatred stems from the vague intimation that college boys are going to live the American Dream, whilst boys like Troy are destined only ever to defend it or be its victims. The dark-eyed, long-lashed senoritas who would like a share in the Dream are everywhere, eyeing up their future green cards. But tonight I can afford a sense of solidarity with them; they know that the boys with the short hair who drink their fortnight's pay in two days are not the boys to dream with. Instead they do their best to attract one of the boys spending Pop's money like there was no such thing as an angry long-distance telephone call. Another reason jarheads hate college boys.

"The evening wears on. Trays of sweet-tasting cerveza come and go, as do the neon names of bars and discos. And visits to the john – the only place I seem to have a chance of getting Troy away from his buddies. At last, I find myself answering the call of nature at the same time as him. Standing next to me, Troy has his hands on his hips (I should have known he'd be one of those 'Look, no hands!' pissers). I'm resisting the urge to cop a look at his joint when I catch him checking me out.

"'Hey, Mark,' he says, half in jest, half in wonder, 'so it's true you English guys ain't cut!'

"Now, you might be forgiven for thinking that here was a green light for me, that here was a possibility that this studly young Marine's expression of interest in my dick might somehow be turned into a 'hot scene.' Shamefully, I lose my nerve for tackiness (for example, saying something like 'oh yeah, and look how easy it makes jacking off. . .').

"All I can manage is to mumble 'Er, yes', pull in my pecker and run out of the men's room. Foreskins have never been a major fetish for me, but if you're English and you want to cruise jarheads then you'd better have your rap ready. Despite being programmed at an early age to revile these rather comical flaps of skin as unhygienic and therefore un-American, American men cannot help but experience a dim sense of mutilation and loss when gazing on the untampered-with variety. They think: so it's dirty, but that's what they said about sex, and look how much fun that turned out to be.

"It's also an accessory which they can never have. Now that's what you call a Unique Selling Point. Most of all, the foreskin is a symbol of the Old World and its chaotic messiness. In America roads run straight, air is conditioned, teeth are bleached and foreskins are sliced - God is in his heaven and cinnamon is in apple pie. Americans have everything except smegma, and what Americans don't have, they want very badly. Meanwhile, back at the bar, Troy attempts to recoup some of his virility by suggesting we 'go and cruise some chicks.'

"I wonder if the moment has come to tell him that 'I don't go for dames' but decide that this confession would put the dampers on any chance of persuading him to take a closer look at my foreskin. With boys like Troy, any genital friction with members of the same sex always has to be prefaced with the timeless line 'I'm no fag, understand? I really dig chicks but...' Which is fine by me.

"So I 'cruise some chicks' with him for a couple of hours, to buy some time and to make him feel better. Much later, Troy and I have passed the point at which drunkenness excuses a couple of regular guys who want to get into each other's pants from the duty of pretending to look for women. It also happens to be the same point at which physical expressions of affection cease to be suspect – on the contrary, they become almost compulsory. Troy acknowledges this in the traditional way. 'Hey, man - I'm totally fucked up.' Now he puts his arm around me and begins to recite sketches from Monty Python. I'm happy because I know this is his way of showing me he loves me. To

American youth, Britain means Depeche Mode, Boy George, James Bond and Monty Python. Monty Python, with its anarchic Old World surrealism, is the kind of comedy that American kids were denied until Beavis and Butthead or Ren and Stimpy brought them the smegma they craved.

"Nevertheless, despite scenting victory, I decide to wimp out. I'm too pussy for this. It's 3 a.m. in Tijuana and I'm arm in arm with a drunken teenaged U.S. Marine with the face of an angel and the butt of Beelzebub, who's reciting Monty Python in a Texan accent you could marinate a T-bone with. We met just a few hours ago. Now we're the bestest buddies that there ever was. I can't bring myself to spoil it. The heat, the beer, the game-playing, and now a Texan Marine nudging me and asking 'Is your wife a goer? Know what I mean?' proves a little too much.

"I abdicate my self-appointed position as revenger of Latin America and abandon my fiendish plans to ravish the virtue of the United States Marine Corps. Instead I offer the boys a lift back Stateside. At the border, as we queue to re-enter the neatly-ordered New World, a skinny, ragtag band of Mexican kids - none looking older than ten - wash our windscreen in a determined last-ditch effort to prevent Yankee dollars escaping back over the border. Troy, the simple Texan, is moved enough by this scene of regional deprivation to offer a couple of dollars (all that is left of his pay packet), only to have them snatched out of his hand. By way of thanks, he receives loud demands for more. Truly this evening has blurred the lines between who is the prey and the preyed upon, the fucker and the fucked, more than I care for."

Fire Island

Gay travel writer Peter Palmer says that many guys who frequent Fire Island think of it as "Fantasy Island."

"No," he reminds us, "it's not a little round tropical isle with palm trees swaying in balmy breezes. In fact, it's a barrier island off the southern shore of Long Island, New York. The skyscrapers of NYC are almost within view, and the city glows brightly in the western sky at night. It's a shoestring of a land-mass, 32 miles long but only one-quarter mile wide at its narrowest point. The Island is connected to the mainland on the East and West ends by bridges, but no roads transverse it. Being only a few feet above sea level, the dunes protect the Island and areas that are actually below sea level. It is a very fragile environment which could be wiped out by a major storm at any time. Since it's a barrier island, it protects the southern shore of Long Island from direct assaults from the Atlantic: many times it has taken the full force of hurricanes, softening the blow to the mainland. A few times over the years, huge waves have washed completely over the Island, carrying away almost everything. The hurricanes of 1938 and 1963 almost completely stripped the Island of houses and vegetation. The ocean is a powerful and awesome force which, at times, cannot be reckoned with.

"There is an astonishing amount of sexual activity taking place on Fire Island during the summer. The season starts early in spring and continues until autumn. Cruising takes place 24 hours a day, on the boardwalks, in the clubs and restaurants, in the grocery, on the beach and in the woods. Don't be surprised if every single passerby on the boardwalk looks you in the eye and says 'Hi.' Not everyone is trying to cruise you, it's just that most guys have left their attitudes on the mainland and have adopted a more easy-going manner.

"Most of the legendary cruising and sex takes place in the Meat Rack which is the wild, lush, and undeveloped half-mile-long National Park land between the gay communities of Cherry Grove and the Pines. Since Fire Island is so remote and considerable effort is required to get there, you'll only infrequently be surprised by straights walking through the Meat Rack; police harassment is virtually nonexistent. About the only dangers today are poison ivy and deer ticks.

"Entrance to the Meat Rack (also known as the 'Enchanted Forest' or the 'Judy Garland Memorial Park') is by boardwalk, either over the dunes from the beach or from the communities at either end. Trails meander through the hardwood forest, scrub pines, marshes, thickets, and sandy flats. The trails twist and turn, double back on themselves, disappear into thorny thickets and turn into living-room sized cul-de-sacs. Some old trails are grown over each spring; others are blazed out each summer. While cruising in the woods, you might find a hot number leaning against a tree totally naked, someone sunning himself in a clearing with enough sextoys to open a small boutique, or an all-out orgy taking place in the middle of a major pathway. Some cul-de-sacs are equipped with foam mattresses or old lounge furniture for your reclining pleasure. Rubbers and packets of lube are supplied by local AIDS organizations in mesh bags hanging on trees; many guys take advantage of them.

"Sex takes place at all times of the day and night in the Meat Rack. Popular cruising places at night are the boardwalks over the dunes at either end, right inside the entrances from either community, and the wide open sandy flats behind the dunes, where any moonlight turns the landscape into a lunar fantasy. It's popular after the discos close until the sun comes up. It can be pitch-black on moonless nights, and a full moon brings out the guys in droves. Light clothes or a cigarette glowing help guys to find each other. Just don't mistake a foraging deer rustling in the bushes for your next conquest.

"After the sun comes up, cruising slacks off a little unless you can find one of those horny early risers. The noon fire sirens signal the start of the afternoon hunt. All afternoon, guys wander the woods in search of sex. Many guys take a break from sunning on the beach for some fun in the bushes. The activity goes on until sunset when the mosquitoes come out *en masse* and guys go home for dinner. Evening brings out more guys, spritzed with mosquito repellent, the scent of which can help you track your prey. Late night finds the disco crowd, and the cycle starts all over again.

"The beach on Fire Island is swimsuit optional, especially the stretch between the Grove and the Pines, and lots of overt flirting and playing around goes on. It's a great 'show and tell' area, and an exhibitionist's and voyeur's dream. The infrequent county police patrols are the only thing you have to watch out for; park police don't care what you do. One memorable Sunday afternoon found me involved in a six-way circle-jerk on the beach about fifty feet from the water, with lots of passing beach-goers enjoying the show.

"When you do connect with someone on the beach and want

a little more privacy, you can take the boardwalks over the dunes into the Meat Rack to find a secluded spot.

"Every Friday afternoon in the summer starts the mass exodus from NYC to Long Island with guys packing chartered buses or the Long Island Railroad. No matter how they get there, everyone winds up at the ferry dock in Sayville, waiting to load the ferries to Cherry Grove or the Pines. The ferry acts like a decompression chamber, and the twenty-minute boat ride across the Great South Bay helps shed city workaday facades. Everyone dons a more relaxed Island demeanor. For a more glamorous route to the Island, try the seaplane which takes off from midtown Manhattan and lands in the bay off the Island in just twenty minutes.

"The Grove and the Pines are dotted with houses set up on pilings driven into the sandy soil among the pines, holly, and cherry trees. Each building is raised above ground level, and boardwalks connect everything like a little 'Gay Venice.' The houses in the two communities speak their own architectural language. The Grove, being the older of the two communities, has smaller houses with 'shack-by-the-sea' architecture. The Pines has more 'distinguished' houses, some bordering on being monstrosities. Some houses are owner-occupied, but most are rented by the week, or shared by the season. Some larger houses in the Pines can have eight bedrooms with two guys apiece, which can make for some mean hissy-fits over property and boyfriends! I personally like the Grove better because the architecture makes it smaller and friendlier. The houses in the Pines have addresses, while Grove houses have names such as 'Wounded Knees,' 'Nacho Men,' and 'O Lay!'

"Fire Island draws an international crowd, with many Europeans and South Americans visiting. They all comment that there is no place on earth quite like it. Americans also flock to the Island; one can hear accents from across the country. Many guys from the city come out for the day or for the weekend; if you're lucky enough to come out for an entire week, you'll find it much less populated and even more friendly and relaxing during the week.

"Before the onslaught of AIDS, the Grove was almost exclusively a gay male enclave. Today, there are many lesbians that visit, have bought houses, run businesses, and call Fire

Island their second home."

My own first exposure to the Island was in the films of Wakefield Poole. Who can forget "Boys in the Sand?"

Palmer reminds us, "The '60s and '70s saw the making of many porno movies, the rise of disco, the legends of dusk-to-dawn orgies – and also county police patrols in the discos (watching for 'illegal dancing') and in the Meat Rack, arresting men for illicit sexual activity. Overall, though, this period saw Fire Island become the Gay Mecca of the east coast: an outlet for sexual hedonism.

"There was a brief decline in popularity in the early '80s, at the beginning of the AIDS epidemic. No one knew how it was spread; many thought it was in the water, or transmitted by mosquito bites. Houses went unrented for whole seasons, until the means of transmission was discovered. Sexual activity was also curbed at the Meat Rack.

"Today, Fire Island is more popular than ever. Many weekends throughout the summer are punctuated with little ceremonies. An early May weekend is reserved for the Painting of the Boardwalks: the edges are painted white, so men can see them on those pitchblack nights. The Invasion is usually around the Fourth of July. In the early '70s, several drag queens rented a boat and traveled across the bay into the harbor at the Pines, where drag was not accepted. This custom has increased in popularity, and now each July hundreds of guys in drag rent a huge ferry and 'invade' the Pines for an afternoon. There are other events like the 'Blessing of the Houses,' with guys dressed like an archbishop and nurses raising money door-to-door for the on-call community doctor. The big blowout social event of the season is the Morning Party, benefitting an AIDS organization. Thousands of guys attend this Sunday morning beach party, with performances by a disco diva and other stars in attendance.

"Available only during the summer months and somewhat difficult to reach, it is an isolated and no-holds-barred sexual treat. The rest of the world seems 'on hold' when you are on the Island."

Australia

Speaking of no-holds-barred, consider cruising in the Land of Oz. "Bearing in mind that the legal age of homosexual consent for males is 16 in South Australia, for me there was much more scope to relocate there not long after the law came in," Clive Forsythe, frequent STARbooks contributor and noted gay historian, says. "Nowadays, every night along the Torrens River which divides the city of Adelaide, young, fresh-faced crackers (prostitutes) brazenly saunter the park pathways on the lookout for customers. The going price in 1995 was $50, expensive by some standards for a thirty-minute romp in a cheap hotel room, but even for the fussy, the quality was remarkably good.

"It must be pointed out that Australian youths don't have to work if they feel 'psychologically unconditioned' to earning a living. The Commonwealth Employment Service (thousands of offices spread nationwide), has to find employment for them – employment to suit their particular personalities. If they don't like the sound of a position, they leave the office and return a week later - receiving social security money indefinitely. As Jackie Gleason was so fond of saying, 'How sweet it is!'

"A handsome young cracker can do very nicely with only a small number of clients a week to supplement their government money."

Of course, you can find homosex anywhere in the land of Oz. Tennant Creek gold and copper mines, between Darwin and Alice Springs in the Northern Territory, attract workers who want to earn quick money and get cut. The area is notorious for swarms of flies and high temperatures. I was due to leave after a three months' stint when a cute little number in his late teens arrived as a kitchenman-cleaner. Our eye-contact told each other we were gay, and he related his recent experience of being stranded in Bangkok.

"This came about when he accepted a one-way trip to a Thailand port on a tramp ship, splurged his money on high living when paid off, then in desperation to back to Australia, got in with a gang of junior male prostitutes and 'cracked it' with all and sundry (mainly American servicemen on R&R), for as little as five American dollars. The competition was fierce and a trade war existed with 12-year-olds dropping their prices to two dollars or less. He said that he could charge much more because he was Caucasian, built small, with a good personality. Several of his American customers used to wrap a five- or ten-dollar bill around their cocks on the bone for him to use his anal muscles to suck-off the fee. This was easily done, so he said, if you know what you are doing. It was definitely a buyers' market. He said, 'When I saved enough to get a cheap boat trip back to Darwin, I went down and kissed the ground. At that time, the Americans were leaving for home, and the arse fell out of the arse caper. Boys were going off for a small handful of change money.'

"I managed to have a night with the boy before I left and I paid him handsomely. You see, I don't mind one bit paying for desirable homosex - we both get what we want without hassles. Besides, the subjects always finish with an added wealth of know-how."

Clive reports that in 1995, three thousand sex videos were seized and Sydney's gay brothels, sex shops and escort agencies came under surveillance as part of a police "intelligence probe" into the sex industry. The operation was conducted by the Gaming and Vice Squad, which wanted to gather and collate information on sex businesses. A senior member of the Gaming and Vice Squad Detective Peter George confirmed the police operation, but said: "We're not here to victimise gay businesses or any other operators. We're conducting an intelligence probe to make sure no one is contravening the law.

"We want to know where every vice premise is in the region, we want to gather intelligence on those premises, and then assess what the appropriate police response and strategy should be."

The police action did result in the closure of Alexander's, an infamous brothel in Surrey Hills.

Thailand

"Okay," *Steam* magazine's reporter Hong Kong Al says, "so we all know that even 90-year-old 500-pounders with leprosy can get laid in Bangkok just so long as they have a pocketful of cash. But the problem with Thailand's 'nightlife' scene is that of the five thousand or so boys available, nine-tenths of them are cutesy, hairless, pretty boys with whom you must first engage in an hour of small talk ('Hi, where are you from ... ?') and then have to pay. The other ten percent are older (twenties and thirties), handsome charmers who you'll meet in the bars and discos who will assure you, 'I never take money.' And they don't. What they'll take is your soul. After just one night of the most delicious sex you've ever had with these adonises, you'll be totally in love. After two nights, you'll begin planning how you can get him a visa to America, a job (let's see, what can he be? a brain surgeon? a nuclear physicist?), and, of course, a free ticket.

"After two weeks in heaven, you're back home dying of loneliness and he's writing these wrenching letters to you saying 'You are the only man I've ever really loved ... ' Of course what you don't know is that this is a form letter of which he sends out ten copies to ten different men every day. If you deliver the job visa, and ticket, you get yourself a boy – if you don't then after a few months he drops you like a cold turd.

"Every year, whole planeloads of sophisticated American men who pride themselves on being able to sniff out a hustler from three blocks away fall for these guys. They are professionals! Unless you really enjoy emotional pain, avoid these jerks like the plague.

"Speaking of plague: AIDS is rife in Thailand but about half the guys you meet will tell you, 'Oh, you don't need to use a condom with me, I'm safe.' 'Course you know he said the same thing to the total stranger who fucked him two hours ago!

For a change of menu, Al suggests a trip to Dhaka, Bangladesh. "I know it's a long shot but you never know: some business, your sense of adventure, or a quirky flight itinerary might result in your spending a night or two in Dhaka. Once there, of course, you'll be wondering how you can sample some of the local cuisine. It's not an outrageous thought at all. Bangladeshi men are sexually magnificent. They have that same dark-eyed, mysterious masculinity that Latinos have, and we all know how Latinos get our juices flowing. Bangladeshis are handsome, muscular, and hairy. Unlike the Asians further east

(Japan, Thailand, China, Philippines, etc.), these guys also have real man-sized cocks – and ass-fucking young boys is the national pastime.

"Most of the Bangladeshis are Muslims, which means (unfortunately in my opinion) that they're cut but (fortunately) that there are very few women out and about in public. This creates a lockerroom atmosphere everywhere. I lived in Bangladesh for damn near eight years and I've never seen so much grabbing of balls, goosing, and general sex-play in public anywhere as I've seen there. Clothing is optional for boys until they're about fourteen, and even then you often see them skinny-dipping or just running around buck-ass naked with their little dicks flapping in the breeze.

"On my most recent trip I was in a small boat on a river and a young man of maybe eighteen came to water's edge, stripped down and slowly washed himself. There were lots of other guys around, but nobody minded. I got the whole thing on video, lucky me. Anyway, this sort of public nudity is very common. Once I saw a boy of about fourteen with an enormous hardon jacking off while four even younger boys sat and watched. This was right out on the street for anyone to see; boys will be boys I guess.

"Another refreshing thing about Bangladesh is that there is no boy-hustler scene here, none of the bullshit that surrounds you in a place like Bangkok or Manila."

Al says he's met some gorgeous 25- to 30-year-olds who were very enthusiastic lovers. "In my experience," he says, "they prefer to be the fucker. But they'll all suck with utmost devotion. As I said earlier, most of them are cut, but you may get lucky like I did once and meet a Christian boy (let's just say 'really young' – gulp) who was uncut (Praise Jesus!) and swallowed my whole shaft in one sudden movement – gulp!"

4
ON THE ROAD

In the search for orgasm, some guys have the best luck just getting in their cars and driving. You just never know who you might meet!

A stud from San Jose says, "It was a hot day this first Saturday in August, 1991. I was not looking forward to the heat of the drive from San Jose, California, to La Jolla, near San Diego...

"My course took me down the 101 Freeway to the Pachenco Pass Highway, the connection from the 101 to Interstate 5. As I pulled off the 101 and started up the 'connector' highway, I noticed a young hitchhiker. Needing some company, I pulled my car to the shoulder. The guy, who looked like he was in his late teens, ran to the car like he was on his way to see a long-lost friend. I couldn't figure out why on such a hot day this young man would wear Levi's and a sport shirt, and from what occurred later, I guess he couldn't figure it out either.

"'Hello, my name is Rick,' he said. 'Where are you going?'

"'I'm going to La Jolla,' I replied. 'Get in if you want.'

"'Hey, this is great! I'm going to San Diego,' Rick told me, as he hopped in the passenger seat. I pulled back onto the highway and we were on our way.

"After a few miles, Rick asked, 'Do you mind if I get comfortable?' I jokingly told Rick that my car was a 'clothing-optional vehicle' and he then proceeded to remove his Levi's and shirt, leaving only skimpy bikini briefs on!

"Small talk was the order of the first 15 miles or so of our trip, but it was the last 500 or so miles which makes this story so great!

"Rick's hand started to rub my leg and he noticed that from the bulge in my shorts, his ability to 'turn me on' was very appreciated.

"I reciprocated, and too noticed that the softness which previously inhabited his briefs had turned to hardness.

"It didn't take either one of us long before we removed the last shreds of our clothing, baring complete nudity to our surroundings.

"The balance of the trip was complete ecstasy! It truly was the fastest 500-mile trip that I ever took! I was really sorry when I had to let Rick off at his destination in San Diego, and despite having taken the trip a number of times since, I haven't run into him on the highway since.

"I don't pick up hitchhikers anymore, but I will never forget the best one I *did* pick up!"

A horny motorist from Kansas says, "Every month or so, I drive the Interstate through the Flint Hills, between Wichita and Kansas City. The (mostly) untamed beauty of the Flint Hills is a refreshing change from being in the city all the time. If the weather is nice, I like to roll down the windows and 'commune with nature' (drive nekkid). It's a great way to unwind.

"The first Sunday in August, I had occasion to travel to K.C. It's a three-hour trip each way, and I was just going to pick up supplies and come back that day. Since it would be a quick trip, I packed light. I threw on some loose-fitting cotton terry shorts and tennis shoes, and tossed a pair of jeans and a tank top on the seat beside me. I took along a cooler with some juice to drink on the trip, and I was off.

"This summer was a hot one with many days over 100 degrees, and that weekend was no exception. As soon as I was on the highway, down went the windows, and off came the shorts and shoes. As I approached the Flint Hill, I drove into one of those sudden summer thunderstorms Kansas is famous for: builds fast, lots of dark clouds, lots of lightning, lots of noise, lots of water – and is usually over in half an hour. I love to watch the storms build, the clouds stacking ever higher; and to feel the power of the thunder and lightning. After the storm reaches its climax and is over, the air is so clean and fresh. It always makes me horny!

"In K.C., I slipped on my jeans, picked up the supplies, and had lunch. I killed some time, as I wanted to plan my return trip so I could drive through the Flint Hills at sunset. Finally, I headed back. As soon as I hit the road, off came the clothes again.

"The thunderstorm that morning had cooled the temperature down, but left it very humid in the afternoon. I enjoy hot summer days and seldom use the air conditioning; that day I did. I left the windows down, and directed the vents towards my crotch. The cold air felt great blowing across my cock and balls! I was driving along enjoying the weather and scenery, when I rounded a hill to find a construction zone!

'The 'constriction' zone was about two miles long. The crew had traffic down to one lane, and a flagman was cautioning everyone to drive slow – which people did. Traffic was moderate, so there was no problem merging into one lane, but I had no time to pull on my shorts! Needless to say, the flagman and two hunky construction workers got quite an eyeful when I slowly drove by with nothing on but a smile and a hard-on! I really got a rush out of it, and I hope they did too! A beautiful sunset topped off the day."

My favorite story of finding sex on the open road is recounted by Michael Lane in his book *Pink Highways*:

"...The long roaring sound of my high-powered engine pulls me down the highway toward Grants Pass. The hot spring sun puts me in a hundred-dollar mood. I feel like a rich man going home.

"About ten miles from Gold Beach, I'm going kind of wild around a curve. Double-dot reflectors are going bumpity bump and a twisted line of trees leans over the ditch.

"I see a thumb.

"This thumb pokes out of a fingerless black glove. With a long pair of skintight black tights, the hitchhiker is the very image of a con man in flight. He chews on a candy bar and pours a sixty-cent Coke down his throat from his left hand. His hair stands tall like an afro in the wind.

"I breeze past, ignoring him at first. He flips me the bird, then turns around and moons me, white cheeks and all. I'm watching from the rearview mirror and this gets me to stop because I like what I see.

"If he's advertising it, I'm game.

"I idle by a white-fenced farm with a small herd of billy goats blabbing at the gate. They stand on their back legs looking at me like I'm going to set them free.

"Finally up strolls my hitchhiker. He lugs a heavylooking green-and-orange duffel bag full of clothes and a little string bag full of food. He tosses a candy wrapper to the side of the road and wipes his face on his sleeve. He strolls as if he's got all the time in the world.

'Get the hell in,' I yell as he drags on like a Disney flick at slow speed. 'I'm in a hurry.'

'So where are you going?' he asks before he's in.

'Portland,' I yell.

With his burly black beard, he's a dead ringer for Charles Manson, though considerably younger. He's a short grungemeister with ripped-up clothes, wrinkled seams, a plaid shirt, a pink mouth and thick eyebrows. But his baby-fresh breath smells like mint, or maybe Bazooka gum.

'Name's Atlas,' he says.

'Atlas? I'm sure. Who gave you that name?'

'My uncle. His name was Boots.'

'I don't believe you,' I say.

Atlas is a road babe. Only twenty-two and from Brazil, he's a small man with warm eyes and a lisp that carries like the wind. He's carting too much shit in his bag and I tell him so.

'Got to lighten up if you're going to do the road thing. What are you carrying?'

'Records,' he says.

He opens up his duffel and lets me flip through his albums. Must be twenty pounds of vinyl in there.

'What the hell are you carrying around all that for?'

'I collect,' he says.

'You brought them from Brazil?'

'Yeah. I may never go back.'

'You're nuts.'

We both laugh. He has a funny laugh, half a giggle, but mostly a tease with enough madness thrown in to rattle my cage. He rocks in his seat like he's riding a boat. I smell stink coming up from his shoes and tell him he needs a bath.

'So give me a bath.'

'I don't have a washcloth or water,' I say.

'Just use your hands and my Coke,' he replies.

I study him a second before taking off. His eyes are wide like a deer's. His lashes blink against the steady warm air and I swear he's winking.

'Are you flirting with me?' I ask.

'Maybe,' he says.

"We ride silently and I like it that way. I look at the road up ahead. Patches of sun bright as Wonder Bread slice through the tall forest.

"I keep my mouth shut and don't ask him a thing. I want no story, no life history, no sad tale. I just want his company, nice and quiet, for the ride ahead.

"Our silence continues for miles. But soon, as we come into a town, he's acting all hot and sweaty.

"'Atlas. . . that's really your name?' I ask again.

"'Yes,' he says in his Brazilian accent.

"Young Atlas smells like a skunk, but he is a grungy hunk. He wears a shirt that isn't long enough and his hairy back pokes out the bottom. He scrapes dirt out from his fingernails and ties his hair in little knots. Bubble gum pops out the side of his mouth.

"I pull over for gas in Agness and plan to leave him there on the side of the road, his smell is so bad.

"But it doesn't work. Taking my hints, he jumps out, rips off several lengths of paper towels, leans over the station's radiator water hose and starts hosing himself down. He pulls off his stretch pants and shirt. Hairy as an ape, he stands in his striped jockey underwear with its bulging basket while he takes an impromptu shower next to the pumps.

"This guy is gnarly. But I like his funky style.

"The attendant comes unglued. 'What the hell are you doing? Put your clothes back on.'

"Parents are covering little eyes. Big adult eyes glare heavy with judgment at the nearly naked young Brazilian taking his shower.

"I pay for the gas.

"Atlas pats himself dry, tosses his clothes in the backseat and says he's ready to go.

"'Well, that's an improvement, I must say so.'

"Atlas smiles wide.

"'So where are you going?' I finally ask.

"He's going to Ashland for an off-the-books restaurant job and wants to look fresh. Water drips out of his flattened hair as he pulls dirt balls the size of eggs out of his shoes. His socks lie across the dash to dry.

"We chirp down the road singing a song. Atlas is chewing

on a coffee bean and scraping his knees up under the dash, picking at puckered mosquito bites on the edge of his legs. My eyes follow his woolly mammoth body hair up his thighs. I watch him rocking in his seat and mother lust enters my mind.

"*Long road, no sex, not good,* I think to myself.

"He pulls out a pocket knife and is dipping his toes. I swear that if I see one more knife in a young man's hands on this trip, I am going to bury them all – the knives that is.

"'Knives or guns, knives or guns, everybody's traveling with knives or guns,' I yell my disapproval.

"Atlas looks confused and puts away his knife. He sits back in his seat, sniffing the air. 'Smells like Coppertone,' he says.

"I point to my big bottle of suntan protection, and point at my shiny head.

"'Can't be too careful,' I say.

"I open the cap with one hand and am going to rub some more on when he grabs it from me and squirts a big old glob on top my head.

"'Why'd you do that?' I yell.

"He has no answer.

"I look like a vanilla sundae. I wipe off the glob and in friendly revenge smear it on his face. He wipes it off his face and smears it on my chest. I wipe it off my chest and smear it on his thighs. He wipes it off his thighs and smears it on my lap. I smear it on his groin.

"'You're crazy,' I yell. 'Who the hell are you?'

"'Maybe I'm your boyfriend,' he laughs, his eyes sparkling.

"He is wickedly teasing me, playing with my head. He pulls out a book of matches, lights them off the striker and throws them lit in the backseat.

"'That's enough! You're out of control.' I pull over and tell him to get out, my finger pointed hard to the side of the door.

"'Oh, do I have to?' he baby-doll pleads, mocking me.

"I nod my head and he's about to get out when he wipes off his smile and says with head bowed like a choirboy in need of confession, 'I'll behave. I'll do whatever you want. Whatever...' and he puts his hand on my leg.

"'Do you think I'm gay?' I finally say.

"'Well, aren't you?'

"'What if I weren't?'

"'Well, there's always a first time.' He smiles.

"'Oh my!' I feel through the glove box and pull out a cheap cigar. I light it from the matches and blow a smoke ring over the cheap fuzzy dash.

"'You are a scene. Are you this loose with everyone?'

"He nods.

"I toss back my head and feel my tired hot feet and socks full of sand. He sulks in the corner, his head out the window, wondering what I will do.

"I finally smile, get out of the car and walk toward the woods, expecting he'll follow. He trails me with his wild eyes, then jumps out and tags along. I get far from the road and settle next to a tree. I put out my cigar and watch him coming up the trail.

"'Oregon has laws about this. It's a very Christian place,' I say.

"Atlas smiles a broad, seductive smile. He walks toward me, then leaps down on his knees, squawking like a duck and rubbing his belly. He's a prankster, he is.

"'I don't give a shit about your laws,' he laughs.

"I believe him.

"My thumb presses into the fold of his arm and my fingers follow the bones on his side. My boot rocks like a baby at the base of his groin. I feel the lonely taste of a long bottled-up journey. Desire creases across my head.

"His hair curves off his face and his lips pout up in a kiss. He leans forward as if in prayer and rolls his face across my jeans.

"Then he wrestles me down and bites me till I scream. And I finally get the kiss that I was so long looking for."

5
AT THE BATHS

"*Ed sucking me at the baths, everyone looking, scraped my nipple, hey watch out, then pounded my heart once with his fist. I kiddingly leaned back as if stunned but actually found myself fainting till I blacked out & into a rising and welling & dared myself to follow it though I might be dying & felt reckless & struggled higher into the tumult & roaring thinking at the same time the headline in tomorrow's paper would be about me and sordid. I look down - I'm floating - Ed still sucks the cock of my fainted self, I'm held by this, my cock about 15 feet long & knotted in places & I bob at the end. 'Now I am totally alienated from my body. This might be a good time to stop and think.' In the distance of my distant tip a frail star of sensual feeling.*" - D. Bellamy

In the '40s, gay bars were "dimly lit and generally in unsafe sections of the city," says *Unspeakable* author Roger Steitmatter. "Twenty-five years later, the lights were turned up full beam as gay bars and bathhouses became the twin Goliaths in the gay world, economically as well as culturally. Thick carpets, posh decors, and state-of-the-art sound equipment beckoned the gay dollar. By the mid-1970s, 2,500 bars and 150 bath houses were operating in the United States, with annual receipts in the millions."

Not only did we find the baths a certain kind of paradise, writers did as well. Mark Thompson, a San Francisco State University journalism graduate, joined the staff of *The Advocate* as a feature writer in 1976. "The bath houses were the gay feature writer's dream," he recalled. "They were fantasies literally *oozing* with color and flavor." The large houses transformed individual rooms into exotic settings. One room might simulate a bunk house out of the Old West, the next an army barracks or locker room, the next a rain forest or dungeon or prison cell or fraternity house. A customer paid a single admission fee, placed his clothes in a locker, and entered the world of fantasy. For hours on end, he could wander from room to room wearing nothing but a towel that slipped gently to the floor when he found an appealing partner or partners. The baths contained dozens of small cubicles equipped with beds, as well as larger areas to accommodate nonstop orgies. Thompson recalled, "Sexual pleasure, fantasy, indulgence – it reached an extraordinary level of hedonism."

Because no sex acts were off limits, patrons did not have to sneak into a dark corner to avoid being arrested. The clandestine tenor of previous decades was a dim memory as men, either after or between sex acts, casually played pool, watched television, or grazed the midnight buffet, all of which were part of the bath house experience. *The Advocate* said: "It is not uncommon to find students sitting in the lounge area doing homework or groups of friends taking a few hours off just to relax."

One of my personal favorites in those days was the infamous Continental Baths in New York. Besides providing sex and entertainment facilities, the Continental featured a live stage where performers (Bette Midler with Barry Manilow on the piano was the most famous) played to huge crowds of men wearing nothing but towels.

In 1976 *The Advocate* published a comprehensive business article about the baths. Among the sources was Jack Campbell, who had parlayed a $15,000 investment in a Cleveland steamroom into forty gay bathhouses from coast to coast. Campbell credited the rapid growth of his Club Bath chain to Ohio and other states legalizing sodomy: "Most cities offer a cornucopia of bars. With each passing year, the fantasies get more elaborate."

The gay magazine *Vector* crammed its pages full of ads for bars and bathhouses, surrounded by articles promoting them. One article praised the baths as an oasis from the banalities of life. "The baths are even *spiritual*," Vector wrote, "because raw, glorious sex can be so enlivening, so ego-restoring. Since there's no heaven, the baths will have to do.

"While some men used the baths as a gay community center to meet and socialize with friends, others saw the baths as sexual paradise. After such a visitor entered a bathhouse and placed his street clothes in a locker, he wrapped a towel loosely around his loins and strolled down a long hallway of cubicles with their doors cracked open. Inside each cubicle, a man lay on his stomach. Next to his naked body, the prone figure had placed a tube of K-Y lubricant and a bottle of amyl nitrate that, when inhaled, quickens the heartbeat and intensifies the senses. When the erect man spotted a potential sex partner he liked, he edged his way into the cubicle. If the outstretched man nodded his approval, the visitor quietly closed the door. With no words exchanged, the performance began.

"It was by no means remarkable for a man to receive the semen of a dozen men in a single night, possibly with a couple showers or steam baths in between. For many gay men, an ideal weekend meant three gloriously full nights at the baths."

By July 1981 the *New York Native* was reporting the connection between sex and the disease that later became known as AIDS. As coverage evolved, health experts expressed increasing alarm that the gay male propensity for multiple sex partners placed them at high risk and, therefore, jeopardized their lives. Yet gay activists who had won the battle to be allowed to socialize together – replacing the dingy 1950s bars with the comfortable, well-lighted bathhouses of the 1980s were not eager to take what they saw as a major step backward by shunning either the businesses or the behavior that had come to define their liberation.

George Mendenhall recalls: "The tubs weren't just part of the culture – they *were* the culture. To a large extent, they defined what the gay press was, too. We saw banning sex in the tubs with one stroke, losing everything Stonewall did for us. It meant, at the same time, pushing the gay press back twenty years to the time when we were operating hand-to-mouth. No way we'd let that happen. No way in Hell."

By early 1982 the medical community was describing the baths as death camps. In a front-page article in March, the *Native* stated, "It's probable that sexually transmitted diseases that may be related to the current epidemic are being spread *at* the baths, but not *because* of the baths per se." The *Native* campaigned, therefore, not for sex to be banned from the baths but for gay men to act responsibly by not being promiscuous and not engaging in sexual activity with new partners unless they used condoms – in the baths or anywhere else.

San Francisco papers, on the other hand, continued to

promote the glorious sexual abandon of the baths. The *Sentinel* ridiculed the medical research being conducted. As an April Fool's joke, it published a lead story that played off many gay men's fondness for brunch. The headline read "Brunch Causes 'Gay Cancer,'" and the story began, "Scientists seeking to identify the elusive element of the gay lifestyle that causes 'gay cancer' have named gay brunch as the culprit."

While trivializing the crisis, the papers also continued to encourage promiscuity. BAR published a series of features highlighting the activities available at the Caldron, one of the paper's most frequent advertisers. A first-person article described the sexual activity available nonstop at the popular bath house: "While Man C is being fucked by Man D and sucked off by Man E, Man F places his hand on Man C's left pectoral and starts caressing it. Man C doesn't even look over to see whose hand is touching him. What does he care? It is the experience of raw sexual excitement and sexual pleasure that is of supreme importance."

"I had my first bathhouse experience when I was 19," Philadelphia gay columnist Thom Nickels admits. "I was on Amtrak headed for the New York City gay pride march when a Philadelphia activist noticed my Gay Liberation Now! button and introduced himself. Fred proved to be good company, and so his offer to show me the Village hot spots proved irresistible: Of course I would team up with him for the weekend.

"On the evening of the march, Fred introduced me to the Continental Baths, which he said was the most famous bath house in America at that time. The Continental (ten times as big as other baths and decorated like the Ritz) was equipped with steam rooms, saunas, pools, gyms, snack bars, lounges and floors and floors of unparalleled fun in the form of hundreds of half-naked men. To me, it seemed the Continental was straight out of Coleridge's 'Kubla Khan' or a (gay) Arabian Nights. Where else could you see a 250-pound 'daddy bear' reading Simone de Beauvoir while stroking the back of a blond out-of-work actor?

"Happily dazed, I ambled through the corridors eyeing the small rooms containing naked men on cots in all manner of repose. In the various dark orgy rooms, I couldn't see but had to feel my way through a maze of bodies. Smelling of sweat, freshly showered bodies, poppers and marijuana, they would prove to be some of the handsomest men I'd ever seen.

"During that first evening, I noticed a huge cluster of men near a makeshift amphitheater by the pool. The woman on stage had a funny voice; she was not sexy or pretty but smallish with a big mouth (and nose), but the men were going crazy.

"Bette Midler at this time was still a 'nobody,' so there were no straight society buffs (in gowns and tails) in the audience, just hundreds of semi-naked guys applauding furiously. Standing on the fringes of this mob, I tiptoed to get a glimpse of the future superstar's face, annoyed that show biz antics had temporarily shelved the pursuit of sex. Fred, it appeared, had been swallowed up; after he marched off in pursuit of his room, I never saw him again.

"A few months later, I returned to the Continental and once again witnessed the rush of exhilaration accompanying Bette Midler's act. Still, I was not amused. Actually, I was worried because it seemed to be hard for me to meet men in New York. For one thing, the pandemonium and confusion of Manhattan's streets seemed to rule bathhouse pedestrian traffic and, as an out of towner, this further activated my shy and awkward cruising style. Still, I remember thinking that if straight America could only get a glimpse of the goings-on here they'd be beside themselves with wonder – or outrage. Outrage that so many good-looking men were not going to be dating their daughters.

"I met only one man in a New York bath. This was during Midler's act, when I was wandering the deserted corridors. He was a muscle-bound god.

"He led me on a merry chase and finally I caught him, or he caught me, depending on your view, in the shower stall. He had one of those lanky, muscular bodies with soft skin and not much hair. His nipples were the size of half dollars and made me think of suns on an Inca breastplate: the shock of that chest was something to remember: it was practically immoral the way the sculpted pecs jutted out at such sharp, delicious angles a perfect ridge for a curious tongue. He had a Mediterranean-look and a short haircut which made his face to appear to square, as if it had been 'engineered.' His prominent nose hinted at the power of his penis, which cocked to the left, a bent marvel that kept getting caught between my thighs as it swung pendulum-style every time he moved.

"I don't remember his name; I think it began with a 'J.' His fingers were long and thick and he was big on running them over my lips as he whispered something in his native tongue. I don't know what that language was; perhaps Greek. I do remember I did almost everything he wanted, though the space was tight; we kept colliding against the soap dish and bumping our heads on the shower head. Yet these collisions were nothing compared to the sensation of him pressing into me from behind, his marvel wedged between my crack and sliding gracefully in its own juices.

"He came twice, the first sending a warm spray over my back, the second when he turned me around and held my head to his abdomen. He wanted me to rim the universe of circles inside his navel, a little oval suck that sent him into a major tailspin.

"Finally, he gave me the full golden slope of his back and naked butt, so that my own spray became like a splattering of hot shower soap.

"The fuck was well worth the wait, even though it was over too quickly. Like Peggy Lee, I had to mumble, 'Is that all there is to a Continental connection?'

"Although, in retrospect, I'm probably alive today because I *didn't* score that often at the baths in New York, at the time I couldn't help but feel that the fates were against my meeting people in the Continental as well as other baths I visited, including the seamy St. Mark's, the Tom Waits-style bath house where it was rumored that W.H. Auden rambled around in his bedroom slippers.

"In Boston the baths were more malleable, if a little incestuous. By this I mean you couldn't turn a corner or lie on an orgy cot without meeting an activist friend from the MIT Gay Liberation Front or coming across somebody whose face you'd seen in Harvard Yard.

"And I found that, unlike New York, there was a lot of talk in Boston bath houses. Consciousness-raising sessions took place in the orgy rooms as circles of people gathered to discuss Stonewall. I recall one overweight white guy with a huge Afro drawing cute young things to him because of his powerful rhetoric. Boston was like that. Other things besides the sculpted slope of somebody's butt inspired feelings of lust and attraction.

"In those days, the baths were the classic rite of passage for most urban gay men. Not everybody participated, of course. There were plenty of gay men who objected to the slutty behavior bath houses encouraged. But baths were legendary, and so for the adventurous they had to be experienced. After all, if people like W.H. Auden, Edward Albee, Paul Goodman, Ned Rorem and Tennessee Williams could amble about in towels and then write poems or diary entries about 'the baths,' there must be something to it.

"Most baths were open 24 hours a day. For a meager $7 or less you got a clean cubicle with a cot (clean white sheets and a pillow) with a night stand, towels, soap and a key to lock your valuables in a footlocker. Things like wallets or jewelry were held in the front in manila envelopes with your name on it. Only the clerks knew how many wedding rings were in these envelopes, but rumors circulated (especially in the Philadelphia baths) that Thursday nights was married man's night because of the huge numbers of rings said to be in the envelopes.

"The time limit was seven or eight hours, during which you could sleep, shower, sauna, eat, watch movies or television, meet the person of your dreams or go on a literal erotic rampage, fulfilling a dozen sexual fantasies with different types of men.

"A frequent complaint of the younger men in the baths was that old men followed them around and then, given a moment's opportunity, pounced on them like wolves. Still, there were enough young men willing to experiment outside their immediate age group, since this was a very democratic table and people hooked on specific types tended to hide in their cubicles anyway.

"In a dark orgy room, for instance, the unwritten rule was: never, under any circumstances, keep your hands to yourself (this was the baths, not a church). A guy might protest a come on, but often a 'compromise touch' was okay (a 70-year-old man stroking a young dude's foot as that kid made it with somebody more his type was not an uncommon sight). Egalitarian to the max, as they say.

"With a bath membership card you could go to any chain in

any city (Denver, Salt Lake, Honolulu, Camden, etc.) and stay the night for a few dollars and get clean sheets, a shower and a steam bath. If you wanted (platonic) privacy, you could lock your cubicle door and nobody would bother you. Like the Holiday Inn, you could even arrange to have the clerks wake you at a certain hour.

"For me, going to the baths was like taking a vacation from reality. They had the ability to project one out of a (seemingly) humdrum life, and they had all the healing power of a quick trip to Thailand or the South Pacific. I can remember standing with a towel around my waist after a wonderful sauna and back rub from an agreeable stranger and looking out the bath house windows at the poor slobs walking on 13th Street and thinking how boring and predictable life would be if there weren't baths to escape to.

"At times, conversation came easy in the baths, because erotic tension was usually worked through. When one fulfilled a sexual fantasy regarding an ideal type, there was nowhere else to go. To a calm and relaxed state of mind: After all, once you've seen the lights of Paris, why worry? What we call 'attitude' was very rare.

"For some people, the baths became a home away from home. Regulars populated center stage like Dick Clark's *American Bandstand* dancers of that era. Same people spent weekends there, and it is said that novelist Sloan Wilson holed up in a cubicle with his typewriter and wrote a novel, going out only when he had to eat, shower and find a lover.

"In the '70s, the Philadelphia baths were sometimes raided by the police. I remember the overhead lights going on and a buzzer going off at odd times. This meant to put your towel on and walk around as if you were strolling through Longwood Gardens. I never saw any uniformed officers march through, but rumors flew about hunky undercover cops reclining on wooden benches like Alexander of Macedonia, their hairy legs (and more) extended for caressing.

"New baths cropped up daily. One, Man's County in New York City, had a real tractor trailer truck in one of its rooms to simulate the trucks, an outdoor cruising place near the Hudson with dozens of parked tractor trailers with their back doors open. For me, the baths were a kind of exorcism. In high school and college, I rarely had sex and was so shy about being gay I let many opportunities pass, whereas my heterosexual friends were getting laid every week.

"Do I miss the baths today? No, because I've learned that having sex with lots of people only appears to be satisfying. Actually, it just whets the appetite for more sexual variety. Ann Landers wasn't kidding when she said that sex without emotion or a deep connection leaves one feeling empty. But empty or not, I will never regret – nor forget – my experiences on the steamy side of life."

"Once in a while I got a chance to play around with some of the attendants at the baths," a New York man wrote for Boyd McDonald's *Raunch*. "Often they were young and attractive and of course they knew the score.

"I had several of the attendants at St. Marks. When they were off duty they would sleep in the dormitory along with the customers. Sometimes the attendants would sleep stark naked, sometimes with a towel wrapped around their waist. Often they were so exhausted they didn't know, or didn't care, when I played with their dicks and started sucking on them.

One attendant I sucked fairly regularly – a tall blond guy, good-looking, well hung, good natured – slept profoundly and rarely pushed me away. Only once or twice did he shoot a load. He was probably too tired to come.

There was another attendant there whom I sucked when he was supposedly asleep, but after that he began to want money. Five dollars was the usual fee in those days at that place. On a commercial basis he would come to my room in the baths and let me play around with him as I wished. He was generous with his cream and always delivered a load before he left.

Later on he rented a two-room apartment only a few blocks away from the baths and took me there when he was off duty. The price was higher, of course, but it was worth it. He would let me take his clothes off, play with his feet, kiss his body all over, drink his piss, suck his ass, and fuck him – in other words, the works.

There was another attendant at St. Marks who let me blow him, a rather bully guy with coarse features. He had a heavy-set, powerful body with a thick cock and hot nuts. He took me to a room that had just been vacated and hadn't been made up yet. He unbuttoned his pants, lay on the bed, and let me suck him off. He complimented me on my technique but I never had a chance for a repeat performance. I heard from other customers that he did this with most of the guys who came regularly to the baths.

There used to be a small steam bath in the basement of a fleabag hotel on West 31st Street near Penn Station. Just a bare room with lockers, double-decker beds, a steam room, and showers. Everything was very open and when an orgy began one of the attendants, a young, heavy-set Greek, would join in, opening his pants to let the guys suck him. I had him several times, always giving him a good tip before I left.

"There was one attendant at the Sauna on West 58th Street that I had my eye on for some time. He was a short guy, compactly built, and sexy. Ex-Navy, maybe. Cock appeal at first sight. I saw him sometimes at other baths so I knew he was gay, but he always avoided me. But my opportunity came at long last, early one morning when a violent storm kept people off the streets. The all-night customers at the Sauna had left, so besides the man at the desk, the attendant, and myself, there was no one in the place.

"I followed the attendant about, just making casual conversation, and finally he sat down in a chair in the lounge. I drew up a seat beside him.

"We began talking about the storm, and he told me once he and his brother had spent most of the night stranded in their car because the rain and darkness prevented them from seeing more than a foot or so in front of them. All I had on was a towel wrapped around my waist and while listening to his story I reached under to play with my prick and balls until I got a noticeable hard on.

"When he finished his story I emphasized the fact that we were the only two guys left in the place and that there probably wouldn't be any other customers until the storm slackened. He said he had never before been alone with just one customer in the Sauna.

"He had gradually slouched in his chair, spreading his legs suggestively, while he rubbed his groin with one hand.

"I rose to my feet and he looked up at me with a sly smile

on his lips. He nodded his head, which I took to be an invitation.

He didn't stop me as I knelt between his legs and reached up to unfasten his belt and open his fly. I pulled out his prick and my dream came true at last. His cock rose up immediately. It was a real beauty – long and thick. The head was bright red and a drop of precum glistened in his piss-hole.

"I jerked him off while putting his peter in my mouth. Then I pulled his pants and shorts down to his knees so I could play with his balls and reach up under him and feel his ass. He didn't object when I pulled his loafers off and nuzzled his feet against my cheeks and mouth and massaged them through his socks, enjoying the odor. I reached up under his shirt to tug at his nipples and rub his chest and belly. With all this stimulation, it didn't take long to shoot his load.

"No one came into the baths during our sex play and for some time after we had finished we were still alone. I seldom have had such a good time, and I gave him a large tip when I left.

"Some men have told me that they get bored at the baths and that they prefer the excitement and danger of making conquests on the outside, but I always have a better time at the baths, probably because I don't make friends with strangers on the outside very easily. It takes a certain amount of tact and personal magnetism to persuade a guy on the outside to get into bed with you. The baths gave me experiences that I could never have had anywhere else.

"Some experiences are unforgettable, like the guy from Washington, a magnificent specimen of powerful manhood who said that he liked the way his wife sucked him off but that he had never had a blow job as exciting as the one I gave him.

"I also can't forget the three strapping truck drivers from Jersey who came into Everard's in the early morning hours. I sucked off one after the other. They seemed to be new to the gay scene and it may have been their first time in an all-night steam bath.

"When I asked one of them if he liked to be rimmed, he answered, 'I don't give a shit what you do.'

"And then there was the guy who liked to sit on the edge of the bed while I knelt down at his feet to suck him off. After he had shot his load he used to caress my head and shoulders and tell me, 'You're a natural-born cocksucker. You shouldn't have to do anything but suck men's pricks all day.'"

. . .

"... We don't have anything together. ... We have the ultimate in freedom...and we're abusing it. My sister-in-law does not speak to me, not because I'm a faggot, ...but because she says I'm a coward, I'm not in there pitching to make the world a better place, I'm running away, I'm not relating to anyone successtully, I'm not proving to the world or to myself that I know what to do with this freedom.... If I could be that, then I'd be listened to, respected, not scorned, mocked, feared as something unfit to teach children. But when I look around me, all I see is fucking. All we do is fuck. With dildoes and gallows and in the bushes and on the streets. My sister-in-law doesn't fuck on the streets." – Larry Kramer, Faggots

T.R. Witomski said, "The fear is of inadmissible loneliness, emotional commitment, of relationships, responsibility, of love; the loathing is of the self. These feelings, this homosexual experience, is most acutely ritualized at the baths.

"Paradoxically, it is not self-esteem that is lacking. When the self is reduced to solely sexual terms, one must have a good self-image to function satistactorily, to survive. What matters is not how we look, but how we think we look. But even with a good self-image, there can be self-hatred. Whatever political gains have been made by homosexuals the most salient feature of gay life remains self-hatred.

"The irony of Don Juan: despite all his sexual escapades, he is never satisfied. Often promiscuous people say that if only they could find that one special person, they would stop their promiscuity. It's a naive, impossible view. The excitement *is* the promiscuity. After years on the bath circuit, gay men have lost their ability to relate sexually other than on a "quickie" basis. After the first few thousand tricks, it's hard to act innocent. What remains is fear and loathing."

. . .

Although times have changed and the baths are now called "health clubs," they remain one of the preferred places to go to find sex. One of those gay men surveyed for the book *A Select Body*, by Michael W. Ross, says: "If I wanna have sex I'll go to a sauna . . . where I know I'm going to get it.... I've partied and to go to a recovery party for . . . sex is pointless." Another said, "If I wanted to do sex and drugs that's where I'd go: to the sauna."

Indeed, according to the majority of respondents, the saunas were the most reliable post-party venues for sex. Ross suggests, "Perhaps this was because they were one of the least sexually ambiguous among the diverse range of gay recovery party institutions."

This demonstrates how little things have changed. Consider what Ned Rorem wrote in 1967 in his *New York Diary*:

"A Turkish bath, like the Quaker service, is a place of silent meeting. The silence is shared solely by men, men who come uniquely together not to speak but to act.

"More even than the army, the bath is by definition a male if not a masculine domain . . .

"There are so many varieties of bath as of motel, from the scorpion-ridden hammams of Marrakech, where like Rimbaud in a boxcar you'll be systematically violated by a regiment, to the carpeted saunas of Frisco, where like a corpse in a glossy morgue you'll be a slab of flab on marble with Musak. There is no variety, however, in the purpose served: anonymous carnality.

"As in a whorehouse, you check interpersonal responsibility at the door; but unlike the whorehouse, here a menage might accidentally meet in mutual infidelity. The ethical value too is like prostitution's: the consolation that no one can prove you are not more fulfilled by a stranger (precisely because there's no responsibility to deflect your fantasies – fantasies which now are real) than by the mate you dearly love, and the realization that Good Sex is not in performing as the other person wants but as *you* want."

6
BARS AND BARTENDERS

"The bartenders were wearing leather harnesses about their tanned, muscular bodies, and as we approached the bar I saw they wore jock straps instead of pants. Their bare asses flexed as they bent over to retrieve a glass or empty an ashtray, and a couple were slightly torn in front, giving a glimpse of bulging balls or a spongy dick head. As one of them moved through the crowd carrying a pitcher of beer, he made no objection as he was fondled by the guys he passed. When he got to the group who ordered the pitcher, one of thom actually slid his hand into the bartender's jock and hauled out his long dick, dipped it into the pitcher, then proceeded to lick the beer from it while his buddies cheered him on. The bartender grinned in appreciation, then stood patiently while the sucker stuffed his thickening prick back into his flimsy jockstrap." -Stan Dean, recalling a visit to a leatherbar

For many of us, bartenders can be a main attraction, rivaling porn stars for their fantasy-inducing potential. Some savvy bar owners recognize the fact and advertise "the friendliest bartenders in town." In Tampa, at a place like Angels, the owners get calls asking who is stripping that evening. In Sarasota, where no one takes anything off, even at the beach, the owners get calls asking which bartenders are working.

When I lived in St. Petersburg, a bartender at the Back Door on Madeira Beach fueled many a fantasy. In fact, I even wrote a story about him, inventing a lover so we could have a hot three-way!

Now that I live in an even smaller town, there are fewer bars but there are still some nice bartenders.

One I frequent maintains a stable of six bartenders to work their three rooms: Terry, Hugh, Rob, Fritz, Clayton, Dennis and Devon. On a recent visit, the guys from Florida's own *Encounter* magazine and I were captivated by Devon. The bartender even obliged the intrepid *Encounter* magazine shutterbug by taking off his shirt. Then and there I decided I had to get to know more about Devon!

Over dinner a few nights later, Devon was a tough interview, asking me more questions than I was able to ask him. "I'm used to getting people to talk, not talking about myself," he explained, and therein lies the secret of a great bartender.

Devon's been tending bar for seven years, off and on, starting with a job with a banquet firm when he was 19. Surprisingly, he had not plied his trade in gay establishments until he moved to our town from the Jersey shore. That was a year ago, after coming out of a bad relationship in West Palm Beach (with a bartender there). Knowing the owners of a bar on the beach, he was able to get a job there immediately. He wanted to stay in Florida and was drawn to our area because of the friendliness of the people and our School of Art. Devon attends night classes there even though he has an associate degree in graphic design. "I like to keep up on the latest technology," he says of the computer classes he takes.

At his apartment near the school, Devon maintains an imposing computer set-up. Playing with his computer occupies much of his time when he isn't working at the bar, which isn't often since he keeps a heavy six-day work schedule. When he can manage it, Devon loves to go canoeing and horseback riding.

"The people are so much more down-to-earth here," Devon says, and his bosses are great to work for. "They understand the business," Devon remarks. Devon's ultimate goal is to have his own business – a coffeehouse. And, of course, anyone as attractive as Devon has to have a boyfriend and, yes, he does. His boyfriend works in publishing and, presumably, tolerates Devon's great love, his dog, Casey.

For some reason, the bar doesn't have the busy john that Devon was used to at the beach bar where he worked before.

"One of the advantages of working at the beach was the restroom," Devon confessed. "But for a while, so many guys followed me into the restroom that it got to be a nuisance. Of course, there were times when I was *glad* they did. One time, a dark-haired guy named Bud, who was visiting from West Palm Beach, followed me and we stood side-by-side peeing. Before I knew it, he was stroking my cock, then going down on me.

"We didn't lock the door and another guy came in. Bud knew the guy, who was only a year or so older than me, and called him Jeff. When Jeff pulled out his cock, Bud started sucking both of us. I pulled away from Bud and locked the door. As I turned around, I saw Jeff was now bent over, sucking Bud. Jeff reached out and took my cock in his hand. Stroking it, he began sucking. I played with Bud for a while, then I began sucking him. Soon Jeff stood and I sucked them alternately. They started kissing each other while I knelt and went to work on both their cocks with everything I had in me. I wanted them to come as quickly as possible because I had to return to the bar. Jeff was nearly ready and when I pulled his cock from my mouth, Bud jacked off while Jeff covered my face with his cum. I stood up and began washing myself, only to find the two of them at my cock, sucking me. Bud worked the balls while Jeff nibbled on the head of my cock. It didn't take long for me to come. They left the john after I did and when they came back to the bar, they had another drink, then left together. Bud left me a $5 tip!"

Devon finished telling me this story as we entered his apartment. His Christmas tree with blue lights glowing was still up in the middle of July. I greeted his dog and then he showed me his computer. On the screen flashed a picture of a model I didn't recognize with an incredible hard-on. Then Kevin Dean's image filled the screen. I suddenly knew I had a size-queen on my hands. "Wow!" I said, and asked Devon if he had seen any of Kevin's videos. He hadn't. I promised to get one for him.

I pressed against him and my hand slid down his thigh.

"I bet you have a big one," Devon said, his eyes never leaving the screen, now filled with someone else's image that I didn't recognize.

"I guess."

My hand moved to his crotch. He was hard.

"You show me yours and I'll show you mine," he said.

It was such a delightful line that I couldn't help but laugh.

We both stood and undid each other's pants. I felt like a little kid again. Devon's cock was sublimely hard. The older I get the more impressed I am with hardness. My cock remained semi-flaccid as Devon stroked it. He sensed if he was to see it in its full glory he would have to treat it nice. He sat back down and began kissing my cock, then sucking on the head. I eventually became fully hard and he was suitably impressed with my endowment, even managing to take it down to the pubic hairs. I reached down to stroke his cock. The minute I touched it, Devon started to come. He kept sucking me all through his orgasm.

Now I held Devon's head in my hands and controlled his vigorous sucking of my cock. He was easily worth a $5 tip. I could see why the customers were pleased.

As I prepared to leave, he said, "This is just between us, right?"

"Of course. No one will ever know." And, until now, no one ever has.

. . .

Joseph G. Goodwin, in *More Man Than You'll Ever Be*, says, "The gay bar communicates a number of messages; its lighting, its layout, and its ambience all contribute to this process. Dim, colored lights convey a sense of privacy and intimacy. The floor plan generally allows the patrons easy visual access to people throughout the bar, but it also requires that, when crowded, patrons must come into close contact with one another. Indeed, the proxemics of the gay bar stand in marked contrast to those of social situations in the mainstream white American culture. Western tradition requires us to maintain a certain distance from one another and provides various coping mechanisms in case we find ourselves caught unavoidably close to someone else; in gay bars (and social situations as well), by contrast, these barriers are removed and closeness is encouraged. As one of the men Edmund White interviewed said, 'This place is all about touching . . . they kept fiddling with the design till they got it right, till everyone had to slip and slide against everyone else.' The gay bar makes the statement, 'This place is ours; we can be ourselves; we can openly touch and express affection for one another; we can openly seek sexual partners. We can do these things because this place and this time are ours and are subject to our standards rather than straight values.'

"Stores, streets, cultural events, office parties, churches, most bars, and indeed most places in our society are nongay contexts in whlch gays must be careful about how much information they reveal about themselves. These situations require covert communication strategies if homosexual people are to be able to recognize and communicate with one another without being discovered.

"Finally, there are semi-gay contexts like certain parks, streets, and other places where gay people meet, but since these are public places used by many straight people as well, gays must again rely on covert strategies to avoid detection."

"Going to a bar isn't for everyone; if you're not really ready, you'll probably be really sorry," advises Craig Nelson in *Finding True Love in a Man-Eat-Man World*. "Bars aren't the best places to meet guys, but they are how many men do meet, and going to them is a great way to practice your pickup skills. Most of what you need to know about going to bars will apply to any situation where you might want to meet someone."

However, Nelson says, if you walk into a bar thinking, "Tonight I'm sure I'm going to meet someone great," you're just setting yourself up for disappointment. Nelson feels, "If you go thinking, 'I'll drop in tonight and see what's going on,' you'll be in a much better mood, you'll be less tense, and you'll dramatically improve your chances of meeting someone great.

"Men like possessing their surroundings, and there's nothing like a gay bar in which to practice your chemical urges. Whether it's barside or corner table, find yourself a locale that helps give you presence and makes you feel comfortable and at home. Besides all the psych benefits, staking your claim will mean that, if someone's interested, he'll know where to find you."

I always perch myself on a stool that affords the best view of the bartenders – and the door.

Nelson contends, "A key obstacle to bar pickups is that there can be so many attractive men in one room that you just can't make up your mind. What if you spend time pursuing someone, chat him up, it doesn't work out, and you miss someone else who would have been perfect? The 'so many men, so little time' attitude, celebrated in song and T-shirt slogans, is an epidemic at our bars, making us simultaneously frantic and paralyzed."

Nelson says it's best to be bold, try some empathy, and don't be afraid of rejection. "Sooner or later we all get rejected," he says, "so what? If someone says no, don't push; there's more fish in the sea than you can ever possibly catch. A funny thing: Men who feel inadequate about their looks and constantly fear rejection don't realize that incredible hunks have their own unique problem: Everyone is afraid to approach them. Drop-dead-gorgeous men frequently get ignored because everyone considers them out of their league, and frequently they end up going home alone."

. . .

Nelson says that when you are looking for orgasm, often the first stop is the hottest bar in town, but when you get there, "everyone gives you hostile, appraising glances that make you think you're not good enough for them. You try the newest dance club, but even though everyone's covered in sweat and dancing half naked, the music's so loud and everyone's so cliqued up that it's impossible."

Impossible for most, but not all. The set and setting of the dance party milieu were important co-factors in the overall effectiveness of the drug-induced consciousness and behavior (including sexual behavior), according to a survey conducted in the United Kingdom and published in the book *A Select Body*, by Michael W. Ross. One respondent described the sensual and sexually stimulating effects of the inner-city dance party set and setting: "Getting on the dance floor with other people, releasing energy, a kind of sexual energy, to try and maybe attract people."

Another respondent warned about the possible risk of these eroticizing altered states of cognition: "The drug does tend to heighten sex . . . you put yourself in an environment, where just about anything can happen, and your life can depend on it, that's part of the party scene."

Ross says the ritualized dance phenomenon may be found throughout recorded history and in many belief systems, suggested that the social context (including its norms, values and beliefs) often influenced the effects of the drug and the person's subsequent sexual behavior. One respondent to the survey was concerned about some party patrons' loss of safer-sexual discrimination within these backroom sexual venues at the dance parties: "Drugs have an incredible influence on some people. You see evidence of this at the dance parties in the toilets . . . some people get really carried away and I don't think they know what they're doing, totally out of control."

Ross found that the risk of HIV infection within these back-room sexual venues at the dance parties may have been compounded by four important impairing conditions: an erotic environment, the over-use of consciousness changing substances, the loud background party music and the lack of conveniently placed condom machines or facilities within this context, as described by one of those studied: "In the toilet scene people don't have condoms, it's one great euphoria. You're off your face on drugs so you are definitely not thinking of . . . safe sexuality . . . it is very much a hard sex line.... There's people who do and they talk about it as the greatest aspect of the party scene."

Another respondent said, "It's all to do with sexuality and all the energy needed for dedication to it . . . this became the mascot of Bacchanalia . . . it emphasizes things like sex and drugs."

Ross suggests that this ideology was the essence of the Dionysian tradition with its affirmation of the "whole self through the enactment of ecstatic ritual. The dance parties afforded patrons a novel vehicle for the transformation of their everyday consciousness and reinforcement of their identity through the use of similar mind-altering media. The god Pan was celebrated as the creator of music and dance rituals. He 'was a very sexual Greek god, often having sex with both men and women.... His Roman counterpart was called 'Penetrator' (or more accurately translated, 'Fucker' . . .)'. Many of the patrons' world view was transformed by the introduction of the dance parties, according to the organizers and respondents." Some see the significance and durability of this reality was dependent on the construction of meaningful institutionalized rituals. However, one respondent was concerned about the dissociative effects of these transformed realities: "You see it as the world of bondage. Everything us gays are trying to get away from by taking the mystique out of sex and they're putting it back in there . . . They want their fantasies to come real.... There's too much emphasis on the maleness of the good old Greek gods. The gods with the huge dick; it's all dick-orientated."

Most of the respondents' data suggested that these ritualized celebrations restated on a regular basis the values and principles of the gay dance party institution and how its members should act within this context. This process reaffirmed many of the patrons' and organizers' transformed status and collective world-view which in turn enabled them to transcend the boundaries of their everyday reality and the uncompromising presence of HIV-related issues. "The parties also provided," Ross says, "a 'gateway' or initiation route for some patrons into the gay subculture and often a new or revitalized identity. The dance, music, drugs and sex were all important elements of ritualized behavior."

Some have argued that there were very few opportunities in contemporary western societies for a person to participate in a genuine initiatory ritual. These few exceptions were generally confined to the innovative or creative institutions of urban marginal groups, similar to the inner-city dance party subculture.

"In traditional and modern cultures," Ross says, "an individual generally achieved a state of awareness and identity through social interaction with people who shared a similar world view. This rite of passage was similar to the initiatory ceremony of bar mitzvah which celebrates the Jewish community's legitimation of the thirteen-year-old male's adult status. These rituals reduce ambiguities for all members of the group by making a societal statement of the initiate's changed status and relationship within the community."

One survey respondent described a similar rite of passage in becoming a member of the inner-city gay dance party community: "When I first started going to the dance parties . . . I wasn't used to them. I felt that everyone was more *in* than I was . . . I was a stranger . . . but the more I go to them the more I feel relaxed, dancing with other people and smiling at everyone and having a good time."

Party organizers are, in the words of one, "trying to create a peak experience . . . it means that people on the dance floor or on the seats could forget where they are and transcend their everyday reality . . . overcome your inhibitions and forget where you are in time and space. . . you don't have to think about being a gay person on the street, you always have to think about it no matter where you are . . . it's very Utopian."

If organizers don't provide for sexual behavior the partygoers usually make it, congregating in the darkest most appropriate area.

One respondent described the eroticizing effects of these *en masse* sexual scenes at the dance parties: "There's a lot of raunchy sex going on and it's very erotic . . . I went into the showers in the last dance party to have a look . . . and it was so dark . . . I had a fun grope with somebody: it felt wonderful."

Another said: "In the toilets at the dance parties a lot of them are off their faces and when you're in that state you're vulnerable . . . you're not clear headed ... all your barriers are down.... You could end up having unsafe sex . . . in this moving mass of flesh."

Another said, "I always call them the Romper Roomers. They get so excited they overdose or they mix drug[s] and alcohol, they get caught up in the moment and then all of a sudden they find themselves in a dangerous situation like having unsafe sex or black out . . . and we do everything we can to protect them."

Ross says, "'Romper Room' was the title of a popular and long-running national television program for pre-school children. This patronizing term appeared to reflect a respondent's frustrated attempts, in his role as organizer, to modify some party patrons' recalcitrant risky behaviour. One respondent was also incensed by the irresponsible sexual behaviour of patrons in the backrooms at the dance parties and the homonegative consequences for the inner-city gay community if this behavior became public information. He was particularly concerned about providing ammunition for the Reverend Fred Nile, one of the prime antagonists of the Sydney gay subculture: 'Those people in the back rooms are taking too big a risk for the whole community."

. . .

High risks aside, in today's gay clubs, just being there is, in one boy's words, "one big orgasmic epiphany."

"Little secret rituals bond us together," the club kid says in London's *Gay Times*, September 1994. "Giving boys Olbas Oil blowbacks or smearing Vicks on their tits. Gently blowing on someone's face or spitting a fountain of water over them to cool them down. Kissing boys' lips or twisting their nipples as you bounce past. Trying to freak out your friends when they're tripping. Trekking off to the toilet and looking in the mirror. You're captivated by your own reflection. You think you look so beautiful with your big eyes and glowing skin. You wait here for ages. Boys come out of the cubicles two by two. Others pour out in gangs, Keystone Kops style. Some have been snorting speed. Others having sex. (The speed will make the sex nice and dirty if you cop off.)

"We've got more words to describe how we feel than Eskimo have for snow. We can explain the difference between Phase Fours and Snowballs, or New Yorkers and Rhubarb and Custards, 'til you beg for mercy. You get asked, 'Are you alright?' a hundred times tonight. You could go into detail but usually just give the answer, 'Fab . . . I'm off my tits.' Or, if you're really cunted, just 'Fuck'. If you feel bad - which is often - some stranger will always see you through ('You been sick? Ahh, baby . . . '). In so many gay clubs people only talk to their friends or people they fancy. But here we talk to everyone. Maybe because tonight we're everybody's friend and we fancy everyone. 'Have you come up yet? No? Ha! Just you wait.' Here we go. The rush sneaks up on you. You feel like you're going to fall over, like you might puke at any moment, but it's still glorious. You have to sit down or lean against a wall. 'Are you alright?' You raise your eyes, breathe out really loudly and give a twisted, conspiratorial smile. Then you pull your friend to you and cuddle for a bit. So glad you're here.

"There's nowhere else anything like this place. The club itself is our star. And like any star it has some great rumours. Someone will always assure you that some boy collapsed here last week or some dealer had his face shot off outside. Or that the police are going to raid it tonight or that this is the last week 'cause the council's withdrawn its licence. There's a constant turnover of people. You can't do this regularly for long. Other people spend the weekend recovering from the week. We spend the week recovering from the weekend. Some keep going until Monday morning, only popping back for a shower and a change of clothes. What will you do when it closes at noon? Up the stairs and out blinking into the real world. You put your sunglasses on and ignore the shouts from the mini-cab drivers lying in wait. Drive out to the Vauxhall Tavern and scare all the clones. Then on to one of those places where - thanks to the buffet meal included in the ticket price (which no one touches) - you can carry on dancing until the next club opens in the evening. Some are going mad after being stuck behind a desk all week. But a lot of us don't have the kind of jobs you have to be up for in the morning. We're waiters or barmen or air stewards. Or we sign on or deal or do rent. And some people, well you just don't ask what they do. It's always more fun when a gang of us pile back to someone's house. Coming down, chain smoking, skinning up, drinking tea and chatting. Noticing who's missing and trying to figure out which boy he slinked off with. This mate who deals gives us all another half. It helps put off that dreadful moment of loss when you realize you feel normal again.

"But right now you feel like you've just melted. You're over your rush. You can't really describe what it feels like. The same as you can't describe what it feels like being in love - most of all to someone who's never been in love. You can't stop yourself from dancing. Total joy. Euphoria and empathy. Ecstasy. All the shit disappears and nothing matters but the beauty of being right here, right now. E makes us confident without being arrogant, and it made that scourge of the gay scene, 'attitude', a stranger to this club. Here there's a real sense of belonging, of community. Coming here did me at least as much good as coming out. For a few hours you could glimpse the future - see a different way of doing things - a sort of communism of the emotions. And sometimes you wondered, 'why can't it be like this all the time?' You liked people more yourself included. Of course we didn't really 'love everybody'. There were some people that, no matter how many drugs we or they had taken, would always be 'vile', 'naff' or 'sad'. But even they couldn't phase us.

"I started crying here one time. It was nearly noon and I'm dancing and tripping and looking round at everybody smiling and looking so beautiful and it suddenly hits me that no one in the history of the world could have felt as good as we did right then or could have had this much fun. Or maybe I just knew that my life couldn't get any better.

"And we're such drug pigs. All of us running around with more chemicals inside us than your average Boots. Restraint? Repression? The real world? No, thank you. Release? Yes, please. We're gonna have as much fun with our bodies as we want. And we always want more. Have you got enough for another E? A trip's only three quid. But all you can find are Smileys and they're just *so* pissy. Ask a friend for a line of speed? Some rich queen's bound to start flashing her coke about. You could get something on tick or try and convince your dealer that, even though you've got pupils like saucers, you never came up on that E he sold you.

"The place is heaving now. Behind me is a wall of muscle. Sweat dripping off those beautiful bodies, half hidden by the haze of steam and lights. All swaying in time like some gorgeous nelly army marching to trance. So many men, so little urge. There's all these cute boys here but you don't feel much like pulling. We're all so touchy with each other, so kind - some boy you've never met before will just come up and start massaging your neck muscles and offering you his drink; you're never sure if he means anything more.

"When you're at other clubs you can always tell the boys who come bere by the way they dance. The dances used to slowly evolve over time. These boys dance with their forearms slicing the air, each hand keeping a different beat, or with that sexy shudder that starts in their arse and then grabs their shoulders and head.

"Others just throw themselves all over the place. It's not all queens, though. Some complain it's getting too straight, but pretty much anyone's welcome just so long as they've come to have a good time. There's a fortysomething acid casualty spastic dancing between this heavy dyke and a beautiful skinny black boy who's gracefully spinning round and round. And behind them there's some sweet boy who you'll next see breaking young girls' hearts on *Top of the Pops*.

"All of us ensnared in the rhythm. The night starts off with bright and breezy Garage and House. Kym Sims' 'Too Blind To

See It' and Degrees of Motion's 'Shine On'. But it's the surging, joyous Techno that comes a little later that we really love. Records like Hyper-go-go's 'High', TC 1991's 'Berry', E-Trax's 'Let's Rock', NRG's 'He Never Lost His Hardcore', Bump's 'I'm Rushing', Gat Decor's 'Passion', Glam's 'Hell's Party' and The Age of Love's 'Age Of Love'. They all go 'Bam bam bam BAM!' for a bit, getting harder and faster until 'Whoosh!' A bit like sex really.

"Gay disco had been sentimental. Ours is just mental. These are songs that speak straight to our bodies. Some, like Felix's 'Don't You Want Me?', let us mouth our desires across the dance floor. But usually if they've got words they're no more than a repeated line telling us what a fab time we're having or how great we are. There's one record, though, that's got lots of words and we all know every one of them. The record right now is the big 'fuck you, we're fabulous' of Clivilles and Cole's 'A Deeper Love'. This is our theme tune.

"The DJ teases us by mixing Deborah singing 'deeper love, a deeper love, got a deeper love, a deeper love' into the record he's playing. Real quiet at first, then louder and louder and louder 'til we all know what's coming next. Then there's that 'Whoomph!' like a needle dragged right across the record and we're there. Here we go again . . . 'Well I got love in my heart, it gives me the strength to make it through the day, pride is love, PRIDE is respect for yourself and that's why I'm not looking for . . . ' BAM! The thing explodes. We all explode. 'Now it ain't easy, but I don't need no help. I've got a strong will to survive and I call it pride, pride, PRI-I-DE . . . ' And by this time everybody's going 'Fuck! Fuck! Fuck!' Lost in one big orgasmic epiphany. You live for moments like this. Only when I'm dancing can I feel this free.

"All us boys together clinging. Somehow managing to have a good time in these terrible times. We know the world outside is shit and that all there really is is us. Drugs are just part of the glue that joins us together. What we're really rushing off is each other."

. . .

Of course, if you don't score *inside* the bar, there is always the street out front, or the alley. As John Rechy describes the sexhunt in *Sexual Outlaw*, it's 2:22 AM and it seems that it is business as usual:

"Jim knows where the hunt will shift now, and minutes later he's there. A limbo area: The glittering, slender, decorated young men from the dance bar and the surly posing masculine men from the leather and western bar a block away share overlapping areas for a few minutes. Waiting men line a side street and an alley, stand mutely while cruising cars circle the drowsy streets.

"Removing his vest, Jim walks slowly along the block. His eyes connect with a desirable tall man he wants. That was his purpose, to display himself here, connect, then to be followed across the street, where he is now, away from the dense area; he walks into the alley, moving toward the back of a vacant house.

"Jim and the outlaw who followed him climb the stairless platform. Never completed, the structure has begun to age, a dank odor clings to the naked boards. Stepping carefully to avoid exposed areas on the floor, they move into what would have been an inner room. Skeletal boards randomly dissect the moonless, cloudless sky. An old mattress lies on the patched floor; a mattress brought here by whom? In the gutless house, they remove all their clothes, they lie on the cast-off mattress, head to feet, cock to mouth, mouth to cock.

"Jim feels the gathering at his balls: the rushing feeling spreads, his hips thrust into the other's mouth, which receives the jetting liquid. The other's cock, abandoned at that moment by Jim's mouth, shoots into the warm air.

"Although he just came, the outlaw excitement still rages. Jim drives past Andy's, the all-hours coffee shop. Leathermen, glitterers, hustlers, queens, all are here, milling outside. Jim gets out at the corner, intending to hitchhike, but a man wearing a cowboy hat just circled the block, looking back at him.

"Moments later, they sit in the car, parked on a dim street. The man licks Jim's torso, the tongue nestling under his armpits, pulling at the hairs there.

"(A few minutes later) As he drives to Bierce Place, he glances apprehensively at his watch. Still time before night turns purgatorial purple at dawn.

"Several cars cruise the area, many men roam the alleys. An afterhours club, a bathhouse, a gay theater – these lure the hunters here after two in the morning

"Nearby, neat trim houses slumber cozily, unaware that for a distance of about three blocks and lasting till just before dawn, orgies will recur in their garages, yards; under stairs, unlocked patios, store entryways, open spaces between buildings, and on the street itself.

"In the gray night, Jim walks along the alley. The sexual odor of amyl permeates the misty air. Men lurk gracefully like dark searching ghosts in a silent ballet; flowing forms unite, float away to another, others. In the garages, darker bunched shadows stir. Under a stairway, at least five men devour each other, slowly, slowly. Against walls and in cars bodies connect. Suspended in the dark, forms emerge recurrently beyond the misty scrim. Like in a dream."

7
CELEBRITY SEX

If you think it's difficult for *you* to find orgasm, imagine how hard it must be for celebrities who must hide their passion from the world. Today, the tabloids would be willing to pay a fortune to OUT some hunky star. In the past the studio system protected the actors who wanted to dabble. Still, it was necessary for the star to be discreet, which bothered some stars and excited others.

In Patricia Bosworth's 1978 biography of Montgomery Clift, she quotes Josh, an aspiring actor whose affair with Clift lasted two years (until Josh went into the service in 1942): "Our affair was for me the most beautiful experience in my life. I'll never forget it. We were still sexually pure and innocent. We laughed a great deal. and played together. We hadn't started cruising yet, and neither one of us had ever gone to a public toilet or bathhouse to make contact. We didn't hang out at Forty-second Street movie houses. We'd never seen a drag show, and I for one didn't know what a male hustler was. When we were alone it was like Monty and I were shut away from reality for a couple of hours. It was a disorienting experience. Alone we could be emotional and passionate but outside we had to hide our feelings.

"Naturally we felt guilty about what we were doing, but we couldn't help ourselves. We were violently attracted to each other and knew we had fallen in love . . .

"One of the things that was starting to torture Monty back in 1940 was the fact that he had to hide his sexual feelings. He despised deception, pretense, and he felt the intolerable strain of living a lie. He was scrupulously honest himself, and he had a tremendous sense of morality about what is right and wrong. I think that's one of the reasons he was in such conflict about his homosexualitv. There was no tolerance for it back then. Gays were too oppressed."

At the same time, certain celebrities were better able to deal with their passions. Two who come instantly to mind are Errol Flynn and his sometime lover, Tyrone Power.

When the handsome Flynn was a teenager in Brisbane,

Queensland, he would visit a fortuneteller at the local fairgrounds. She was festooned in beads and wore a robe decorated with the sun, moon, and stars. Usually, she would tell him that his immediate future involved a romance with a woman who had occult powers. He would enter her tent and fulfill her as well as his prophecy.

He also loved the atmosphere at night on the Brisbane Bridge. The girls who were available for a price would sway up and down opposite sides of the bridge, dressed very primly in case the police should see them. When a man approached them, they would say, demurely, "How much will you pay for my flowers?" and hold up a small bouquet. The police could do nothing about it.

Errol would thread his way past the streetcars and automobiles and bicycles across the bridge to confer with the girls on both sides. They would call out to each other over the traffic vying for the favors of the handsome young man with the cheerful grin and money in his pockets. He would return to his roommate Charlie at dawn announcing that he had three "naughties" with the girls of his choice. Then he would empty his pockets of large sums of money which the prostitutes had paid him for his services in bed.

But, as Charles Higham revealed in his biography of the late actor, who fascinated audiences as "Captain Blood" and "Robin Hood," sometimes Errol would suggest a "different" strain. A friend from those days, Charles Pilleau, recalls:

"He said to me one day, 'Have you ever tried having sex with men?' I said, 'No.' He then went on and added, 'Why don't you try it? It's an exciting and unusual adventure.' I told him I had no interest in it whatever. He laughed that laugh of his and shrugged."

When money ran short, the friend remembers, either in Brisbane or Sydney, Errol had several ways of coping. He would move into a rooming house and sell off all the doormats to anyone who would buy them. On rainy days, he and a friend would take the umbrellas people stored in racks at the entrances of the department stores and would sell them in the pubs for a few shillings apiece to people who had been left umbrellaless.

But it was Errol's beauty that most frequently saw him

through. The friend recalls that as a youth Errol was " a little bit stagy, admittedly, when he entered a room and was introduced to people he hadn't met before, he bowed; he rather noticeably attracted attention without perhaps intending to. He was very formal with the 'how do you dos'; he would kiss his hostess' hand which in those days the average man didn't do; some people scoffed; some said, he genuinely means it; to some it seemed like an affectation, but not to many. His behavior was so natural that even to average people it seemed almost normal."

Almost normal is an apt description of Flynn's sexual behavior, both before he became a movie star and after. Higham says: "(Flynn) pursued dangerous pleasures: pleasures which could have destroyed his career had they been discovered. He formed intense brief attachments with both underage girls and young boys. The girls he preferred in the age range from thirteen to sixteen; the boys seventeen to nineteen. He dared not express his homosexual leanings in Hollywood; which explains his frequent visits to Mexico."

A prominent director who worked at Warner Brothers says: "William Haines, the silent star, had been ruined when Louis B. Mayer discovered Haines had been involved with a sailor. (Haines was discovered in the downtown YMCA with a sailor, and MGM dropped him immediately though the matter was never made public.) If Jack Warner, who had a soft spot for Errol, chiefly because of Errol's famous success with women, had found out, he would probably have destroyed Errol's career. Errol discovered when he first went to Mexico that at last there was a safe way of indulging his needs: all he had to do was cross the border. He met an Australian millionaire whom he had known before and who lived in a mansion in Cuernavaca and knew how to obtain boys for small amounts of money. Errol would always go to Cuernavaca for these boys. No one got onto it. Not even the most ardent gossips.

"I knew a boy, a hustler, who was at one of the Australian millionaire's parties. I asked him about it afterward. He told me that Errol invited him to his room and performed fellatio on him and vice versa. The boy said Errol was so handsome, superbly built and passionate that for the first time in his career as a male prostitute he was genuinely turned on by a client. He was amazed by Errol's staying power, virility, and sheer energy in bed.

"For the rest of his life, Errol managed to keep his bisexuality hidden from all except a very small circle. His wives, so far as we know, never suspected it; nor did his very close friend, Jim Fleming. Most of his male friends were – as they are today – so aggressively macho he would never have dared tell them. But there were odd, distorted manifestations of feeling even in his straight relationships: he liked to make love to women while watching other men – often in group – make love at the same time; the men's bodies evidently excited him as much as the women's; later, he installed a two-way mirror in his house so that he could watch men in a lovemaking derby; and he had a strange habit all his life of exhibiting himself in erection to his supposedly heterosexual friends.

"The fact is, Flynn was determined to experience every pleasure to the limit. He wanted to drink deeply of life, and to avoid nothing of what it could offer. He experimented with cocaine, kif, opium, and hashish, not in a spirit of self-destructiveness but in a desire to enhance his senses so intensely that life would seem more brilliantly colorful, less painful and anxiety-inducing than it really was. He lived in a state of acute physical awareness of reality. His nerves tingled with animal vitality. He was aware more than most men of his own physique, his muscles, and the sexual center of his being. Yet, he remained insecure; he needed the reassurance of his sexuality and the admiration of others both on and off the screen. Popular acclaim meant more to him than he pretended; but even more urgently he needed the intimate approval of the boys and girls he shared his bed with. His sexual compulsion was not merely the result of being aggressively healthy and twenty-six years old; it was the result of wanting to be accepted and admired and proven to be a potent male.

"And yet, despite his obsession with sex, he found his deepest satisfactions in the clean life of the sea. Whenever he could, he would drive down to Ensenada, sail with friends to Catalina, fly by amphibian to the same offshore island, and enjoy golden weekends of swimming, fishing, hunting, and sunbathing."

Agent Johnny Meyer revealed another side of Errol's nature when he disclosed that Errol had become involved with the famous and handsome motion picture star Tyrone Power for a few months in 1939. Tyrone Power had recently married the French actress Annabella. She was in Europe. He was moving toward the peak of his career; and he had been a great success in *In Old Chicago, Marie Antoinette,* and *Alexander's Ragtime Band*. His dark hair and eyes and sunburned skin were very attractive to Errol, who of course liked Mexican types. Power was twenty-four; Errol thirty. Annabella never knew about the relationship. It was by no means sustained; the two men were not friends, had met each other socially only at the parties of Jean Howard, the brilliant and charming Hollywood hostess.

The affair was conducted in secret, not because of fear of public exposure – newspapers and magazines would never have reported the story (the subject is still taboo in the press today) – but because of fear of studio reaction.

"Errol and Ty met at obscure motels," Meyer contends, "or at homes of trusted friends. The meetings were extremely sporadic and scattered and known only to a tiny handful of friends Ty had been intensely bisexual from his early teens. At the time Errol met him, he had had several affairs, all with famous stars. He was fascinated by people of his own rank, character, and fame. Errol, by contrast, was interested in obscure people with little or no intelligence, so that his interest in Ty was unusual for him; perhaps he enjoyed the excitement and danger involved.

"In any event, both Errol and Ty had other partners while going to bed with each other....

"I never had any prejudices against homosexuals. I knew that Errol and Tyrone were both concerned to keep their images as macho as possible in the public eye. But the attraction was obvious from the start, and I saw no reason to discourage it. Errol in fact had asked me if it was possible that any of the male teen-age stars he met at parties were homosexuals. He was tired of the furtive desperate flight across the border into Mexico to indulge his appetite.

"Errol was fascinated by Tyrone. In a sense, the relationship should have worked, because of the attraction of opposites. After all, Errol was very much the male in the relationship,

Tyrone very much the female. Errol was incapable of loving anyone. Even himself. Errol was trying to grab as much out of it as he could before the dark night came – and swallowed him up at the end. Ty had a better attitude to life. He enjoyed people, things, events, with an almost puppyish charm.

"They had to meet in complete secrecy. I set up meetings at the home of a director I knew who had homosexual leanings, Edmund Goulding. He had a very sophisticated and sharp sense of humor and was vastly entertained by the idea of two great stars fornicating under his roof. He used to give male orgies to them both, but Ty would not join in. He was too shy and sincere. Errol, who was incapable of being faithful to anyone, whether it was Lili, Tyrone, or anybody else, would enter into the spirit of those orgies with great intensity. Sometimes, the director would even stage bisexual orgies and Errol entered into the scene with a will.

"I think this hurt Ty, who reacted to Errol's ruthlessness, and as a result they drifted apart. They saw each other for only a few months. In fact, they did not meet again until after the war."

Errol talked openly about his relationship with Tyrone with his secretary, Jane Chesis, and his agent, Dick Irving Hyland.

Hyland says, "Tyrone seems to have been fascinated by Errol because of his tremendous masculinity. They slept together on a number of occasions in 1946, at the Hotel Reforma in Acapulco, but the affair did not last. Tyrone wanted things done to him Errol found repellent, for Errol preferred oral sex with men.

"They broke up in 1947, but remained friends. In 1948, Ty married Linda Christian. Errol always laughed with Johnny Meyer about that.

"I will tell you something I have never discussed with anyone before. Howard Hughes, whom I worked for later, was in my opinion, and I was as close to him as anyone, definitely bisexual. That whole image of his, of having women stashed away in apartments that were set up for him was a lot of baloney. In fact, I deliberately set up these women as a disguise for him. In most cases, he never even went to bed with them. He would go by and discuss the latest events and disappear, in the confident knowledge that the press was following to the front door and would report on the period he had spent there, imagining all kinds of macho events going on inside. The fact of the matter is that I doubt if Howard went to bed with these girls more than once or twice, and then only for a quick fuck and departure. I don't think he could satisfy women and I very much doubt if he ever had an orgasm with one.

"On the other hand, he was fascinated by males, and I would arrange assignations for him with boy hustlers. At one time, in a spirit of outrageousness, I actually set him up on a date with Errol. Neither one would ever tell me what took place The meeting was arranged in Santa Barbara. It was very late at night. Errol arrived in his Packard, looking very drunk. Howard arrived in his battered car, much less grand than Errol's, although he could have bought Errol a hundred times over, winding up the windows of his Chevrolet, looking to right and left with terror in case he be seen and creeping into the house under a heavy felt hat, wearing a Humphrey Bogart raincoat. They disappeared into the house. I drove off like a bat out of hell, terrified that the Feds would follow them and the whole thing would be blown. I have no idea whether they went to bed or not but I think it is likely."

According to the late actress Mari Blanchard, Errol was having an affair at the same time with a handsome and well-to-do beach boy, Apollonio (named after Apollo) Diaz. Flynn's wife Nora knew nothing of Errol's interest in Apollonio.

Late in 1943, Errol had a different kind of an escapade. He was at a party in honor of Gloria Vanderbilt in Manhattan with Freddy McEvoy and Johnny Meyer. Meyer remembers, "During the swirl of conversation, he noticed a pretty, eighteen-year-old boy with a cherubic face and a slender, well-male figure. He was deeply attracted. He went over and talked to the boy, asking him what he did for a living. 'My name is Truman Capote,' the boy replied. 'I'm trying to be a writer and I'm living on Gramercy Park.'

"Around midnight, Errol invited Truman to El Morocco, where Errol's friend John Perona was having a late-night party for friends.

"Truman accepted, but the two men had barely reached the lobby when Errol took a deep breath and said, 'Let's forget about El Morocco. Why don't we go to your place?'

"Truman explained he lived in a tiny walkup. Errol didn't care. So long as there was a bed, it would be all right. They spent an enjoyable night; Errol didn't leave until noon the next day.

"Years later, Marilyn Monroe asked Truman whether he enjoyed it. He shrugged. 'If it hadn't been Errol Flynn, I wouldn't even have remembered it,' he said."

In later years, when he was drinking heavily, Flynn would suffer a lapse, Higham reveals. One time Errol gave a party to which he invited his old tennis-playing companion, Jack Kniemeyer, who asked if he could bring a friend of his, a British lawyer named Giles Hernshaw. Errol asked if Hernshaw would come to the phone. Hernshaw did so.

"'What do you look like?' Errol asked.

"Hernshaw was surprised by the question. 'I'm tall and dark.' "'How old are you?'

"'I'm thirty-eight,' Hernshaw replied.

"'Good-looking?'

"'I suppose so.'

"There was a pause. Then Errol said 'How would you like to suck my cock?' Hernshaw was horrified. He went to the party with great reluctance but he made clear he was not interested, and Errol made no further suggestion."

During these days, he picked up a young male hitchhiker and installed him in a cottage on the grounds; but it seems unlikely that the dark intent behind this ever came to anything, and the boy finally left. He seems to have had other, fleeting homosexual experiences during the period but only when he was drunk or drugged.

In explaining how movie stars can succumb to these temptations of the flesh and swing both ways, psychologist Alan Crosland says: "You take people from nothing and rocket them to fame and fortune and they become satiated. They've tried everything and then they go out looking for different kicks. They get involved in homosexuality – they're not strictly homosexuals – but they have had everything else so why not try this? It means nothing; and then they start to feel the guilt well up."

Occasionally, an actor will mask his homosexuality by

involving a woman in the mix in his trysts with other men. One such dabbler is Timothy Hutton, if the revelations in *You'll Never Make Love in This Town Again*, a tell-all by some of Heidi Fleiss' girls, can be believed. Like Liza, a popular L.A. hooker, we found Hutton adorable as the tortured son in "Ordinary People," winning an Oscar, and excellent in the military school-film "Taps."

"Timothy Hutton was the first celebrity I'd ever really dated," Liza says in the book. "...I really liked him. He seemed so innocent, so introverted, so sheltered. But sometimes you can't judge a book by its cover.

"...We rarely went out. Instead we'd stay at his house, leading the simple life. He was the perfect mate. I was the perfect girlfriend. I did everything right. But maybe I was too nice, because one day he decided to test my love for him. It involved those two things I've had a problem with all my life: drugs and sex.

"This particular night, I thought Timothy was going to settle in and read – he was always reading scripts, looking for his next film.

"I was surprised when, as we sat in his kitchen, he took out a Quaalude and asked, 'Do you want to try a 'lude?''

"I thought about it for a second and said, 'Sure, okay.'

"He broke the Quaalude in half and smiled this little boy smile. In a slightly embarrassed tone of voice he remarked, 'Steve will want half of this,' he said.

"I was surprised. 'Oh, is Steve coming over?' I knew Steve pretty well. He was a close friend of Timothy's. Whenever the three of us got together, Steve would act very jealous of me. I never knew if they were more than just friends, but after my experience with Jeff, I knew enough to have suspicions.

"'Yeah, Steve will be over. As a matter of fact, he bought the Quaaludes for us.'

"I wasn't thrilled about Steve's visit. I had hoped to spend time alone with Timothy that evening. In between his usual script reading, I looked forward to making love.

"Before long, the Quaalude hit my brain. My fingers went numb and I felt a tingling sensation in my body. I became very relaxed. Quaaludes are like taking a lot of Valium. Euphoria was kicking in, I was drifting.

"Timothy then said something to me that shocked me sober. Until then I thought he really liked me, and that we had a special connection. All of that went out the window when he told me what was on his mind.

"'Liza, have you ever had a menage a trois?'

"'You mean two girls and a guy?'

"He smiled, as if what I had said was a novel thought to him, but quickly responded, 'No, two guys and a girl.'

"I was surprised. I felt weird. 'No, I haven't thought about being with two men. And I don't want to either.' When it finally hit me what he was talking about, I said, disbelieving, 'Are you talking about you, Steve, and me?'

"'Yes, exactly.'

"'But, I'm not interested in Steve, I'm in love with you!'

"'Oh Liza, if you really loved me, you'd do it for me. Don't worry, it'll be cool. You're going to love it,' he said with a smirk, obviously speaking from experience.

"'Do you guys make love with each other?' I wanted him to validate my suspicions.

"'We've had scenes together.'

"What the hell did that mean, I thought? I was getting pretty angry. 'You mean you want me to make love with another man? I thought we had something special.'

"'We do. It's just that I like to share.' He paused, 'You want to make me happy, don't you?'

"I thought to myself, Liza, there are two ways you can deal with this. You can slap his face and leave, or you can teach him a lesson. I said, 'Okay, fine.'

"Timothy grinned. Within ten minutes, Steve – the jealous Jezebel, the same guy who had given me looks that could kill because I was with Timothy – arrived with his hard-on in his hand.

"Tim immediately told Steve, 'She'll do it.' Steve smiled.

"I felt like a piece of meat. I knew they wanted to use me. Both of them were walking erections. Tim led us into one of the bedrooms. Steve and I sat on the bed as Tim turned to Steve.

"'Liza gives incredible head – you've got to try it.'

"I love giving oral sex. I know Timothy enjoyed my technique because he always used to tell me how good it felt when I did it to him. But just because I do something well doesn't mean I want to do it with just anyone. And I thought I was in love with this fool!"

Liza got her revenge that night, turning the tables on Timothy, locking him in the bathroom while she let Steve – and only Steve – fuck her. Needless to say, that was the last time Liza spent time with Timothy. Now Hutton is rumored to be considering filing suit against the prostitute.

I admit that a menage a trois has always fastened me. The thought of a celebrity getting it on only adds to the thrill. Through the wonders of video, I cannot count the number of times I have gotten off to the sight of Rob Lowe porking a girl in a Paris hotel room while his buddy watches. And then the boys take turns with the whore! As I recounted in my book *Legends*, Rob has turned me on since he stepped out of the shower in "The Outsiders," and to finally see this gorgeous man in all his glory was enough to send me over the edge.

Although Denholm Elliott, the British actor who won an Academy Award nomination for "A Room With a View," died of complications from AIDS in 1992, it took his wife four years to complete her expose of her life with the actor. The book, *Quest for Love*, provides a revealing look at how some actors deal with their desires.

"Elliott met Susan Robinson, almost 20 years his junior, in the early '60s," Peter Galvin reports, "and they married a few months later. The actor told his wife-to-be that he was bisexual soon after he proposed to her, and she writes early that she was never jealous of his later 'fatuations' (which, incidentally, were mostly all with men). Yet after a few years of marriage, when Elliott told her he might have contracted a venereal disease from one of several orgies he engaged in on a Samoan movie set, Susan Elliott asked for a trial separation. The couple eventually got back together with a new understanding: What's good for the gander is good for the goose.

"The pair ultimately learned to live with each other's wayward ways, to the extent that Susan Elliott would often invite the actor's lovers to her dinner parties and he allowed his wife's boyfriend to come live with them in their flat in London for a brief time."

To ultimately "learn to live with it" perhaps identifies the key to happiness for a movie star, actor – or anyone else.

8
A LUST FOR LEATHER

"Fred arrived, all in denim, but with a pair of black boots, belt, and a leather cock ring he had bought somewhere. He dropped his pants to show me. It fitted snugly around the base of his cock and balls making them jut out tightly against his jeans. Not that Fred needed any extra help, his dick is nine inches long and really thick; not what you would expect when you saw his boy-next-door face. He also loved to have it fondled, and didn't object when I hunkered down and quickly slipped it into my warm mouth for a few minutes just to get him going. He was instantly hard and let me suck on it while I tugged at his low hangers. We changed places and he got me hard the same way, then snapped an identical cock ring around my equipment, a surprise gift, he said as he stood up. With difficulty we stuffed our hard dicks back into our jeans and headed for tha leather bar, our crotches bulging between our legs."
– *Stan Ward, getting ready to go out of an evening*

Impresario Ggreg Taylor, leading his dyke and faggot troupe to Disneyland, is not only the insurgent fashion boy flirting with and laughing at Pluto and Cinderella and Alice in Wonderland. Ggreg is always at the edge of becoming another Disneyland animal.

"...Ggreg walks up to Alice. The shameless Orange County sun bounces off her soft golden tresses, illuminates her pleated, puff-shouldered blouse. Beside her stands Cinderella, whose golden hair is arranged in a tight bun, not a single strand dangling loose.

"Are you from Wonderland?" Alice asks Ggreg. As she asks the question, Alice smoothes wrinkles in the mock linen gloves covering the hands of her other companion, a large, black-nosed, six-foot mouse. The mouse wears a yellow Dutch-girl cap.

"N-o-o-h," Ggreg answers with a verbal dip. "I'm from San Francisco. Can't you tell?"

"Well, we simply must talk later," Alice answers, floating off across the asphalt with Cinderella and the mouse.

"Sometimes it's hard to tell who's really queer," Ggreg observes, adjusting his leather biker's cap.

Yes, these days it's hard to tell who's queer, especially now that leather has become a fashion statement for just about everybody.

"There is this new genre of cruising and wardrobe and sexual activity called, LEATHER!" says the editor of *Iniquity*, Sir Charles. "You and I know it has been around forever, but, there are so many outsiders learning that it's okay to wear a biker jacket and black boots instead of a nelly pair of tennies. For generations the gay community has been dictating wardrobe nuances to the rest of the world. Something new, exciting and different will hit the general population and we could always say that we have seen it long before in the gay bars or wherever, wom by gay men. Gay men have controlled the fashion world since Jesus. Finally we have introduced black leather into the market place and you see it everywhere. We know that Madonna takes credit for wearing the bodice and exploiting, but where do you think she saw it? In a gay bar, worn by a drag queen.

"Some video companies that make gay porn movies have always shown clean shaven, muscular, 18-plus-a-day, pretty blond boys in their movies and they sold and rented well. Those same video companies are now allowing a man to have a little hair around his asshole, and, maybe a touch on their chest. Can you believe it? The reaction was incredible. Fans were excited to see that Dallas Taylor had hair everywhere. He did. I remember the switch from the clean shaven blond. I talked to Dallas and he said that in order to get work he had to be clean shaven and had to be blond as well as muscular. Then in January of '94 he showed up for an interview and was told by Doug Davenport that they were looking for men with hair. A few weeks later Dallas returned and won. He had darkened his hair, let the hair grow on his chest, allowed a five o'clock shadow and he got a part in the now famous "Bike Bang" from Palomino Films. Since then he has been working steadily and glad to have his hairy chest.

"Movies with men in leather have until recently been limited to the few companies known for their production. Now it's a different story. ...Forum Studios' 'Leather Obsession' is loaded with leather, chains, men with hairy chests and action. It stars Tom Katt. Tom, when we first met him, was clean-shaven, muscular and didn't look like he was old enough to shave. Now his body is muscular but it is covered with hair. Another new company, Triple XXX, is featuring hot older men you would find driving a truck or cutting timber in Oregon."

Scott, a 41-year-old leatherman from Brooklyn, New York, is attracted to black leather because he sees it as a "psychological tool for entering a psychosexual state."

In his interview with Jack Ricardo for Leathermen Speak Out, Scott said he has made it with non-leather-wearing men who were sadomasochistically inclined. "Countless retail types – actually, I think 70 percent of all men are into some level of S/M."

Scott says that he was eighteen when he had his first adult homosexual experience, receiving blow jobs at the YMCA. Earlier, he had engaged in sex with his brother; he was nine, his brother eleven. Scott was 22 when he realized his S/M bent, and he met a man five years older than he. The man took him home to a dungeon.

Scott is a six-six, 230-pound bodybuilder who likes to be appreciated. He also feels a primal push to fuck and "fill the bottom's emptiness."

Scott himself now has a dungeon, a "black room in my basement." A member of a S/M club, he finds it "moderately easy" to find compatible leathersex partners. He hooks up with some of them at "street gyms." He also enjoys group scenes at "sex clubs, private parties. I also belong to a private military S/M club."

Scott admitted that he has raped. More than once: "A lifeguard at the YMCA who regularly blew me was forced to take my fuck in the sauna. Also, a pizza boy who was acting seductively got raped on my dining room table."

Scott himself has been raped. "When I was 22, by a bodybuilder in a remote bathroom under the University of Minnesota field house."

Scott believes he knows the reason for his S/M inclination. "My size and appearance tend to bring it out in others. It tends to relieve the frustration that most of us gather in our daily lives." The pleasure of pain for Scott is the "intensity of experience, banishment of emptiness, realization of one's self-esteem."

One guy who seemingly had no problems with his self-esteem was Peter Berlin. And I never realized how terribly sexy black leather could be until I saw Berlin in "Nights in Black Leather," one of two classics he made in the seventies. As I mentioned in my book *Legends*, Peter carried exhibitionism to its fullest meaning. After becoming something of a legend in his adopted habitat, the Polk Street section of San Francisco, the German emigre somehow got the money together to finance "Nights in Black Leather," an esoteric film featuring intense scenes of exhibitionist and abuse that are bone-chilling.

The popularity of "Nights" led to the financing of "That Boy," an almost lyrical study in body worship. Sexy Peter gets off on narcissistically posing and letting admirers suck him off. But like all good fiction, there is an irony here. Peter becomes infatuated with a boy who is blind. The boy can't see the splendidly lean, taut body Peter created, he can only feel it.

Oddly, Berlin made a career out of appearing in only two films. They were big at the box office when they were released to theaters and, as videos, remain steady sellers.

As Ted Underwood wrote in *Stallion*: "The opening sequence of 'Nights' remains among the most torrid footage ever committed to film. The cassette, like the film, suffers from muddy sound and color variability, but there has never been anyone quite like Peter. His presence alone makes this a landmark film."

Peter became something of fashion legend, too, because he designed all of his clothes himself.

After the success of the films, he divided his time between San Francisco and New York, where we were able to visit with him. He suggested we meet at one of his favorite venues, the baths. He was barefoot and he wore raspberry-colored pants that clung to his body, a cross between sweats and panty hose. His blond hair was streaked with sun and his skin was deeply tanned from a summer on Fire Island. We asked him how the "Peter Berlin look" came about.

"Very, very sort of natural," he said softly, his voice revealing traces of his German origins. "Before I was Peter Berlin for the public, I was Peter Berlin for myself. When I was seventeen, I started to take in my pants. I felt they didn't show the body like they should. You could buy tight pants but they didn't show the crotch and that was for me, and still is, the nicest part of the male body.

"What I did was to take in the outer seams, straight down. But then I realized I had to redo the entire thing because there was not enough material in certain places to accentuate the crotch, so next I started from scratch and went with the same idea as ballet dancers on stage.

"There are three ways you can wear the cock: left, right, and in the middle. If you wear it in the middle, sort of bundled up, then you might wish to add a cockring, making the whole thing look – um – firm. But if you wear it off to the side, which I think is more sexy, a cockring pushes up the balls in a way that can look funny.

"I find it unfortunate when people say you should leave something to the imagination. Well, most people don't have any so I choose to run around naked-but-not-naked.

"I can get an erection by just looking at myself in the mirror. And I always get dressed for sex rather than undressed. The idea of coming inside your pants by just having pressure or movement is such a different, exciting experience." Reflecting on it, I now consider Peter one of the first true proponents of "safe sex."

"I enjoy sex without ever taking my cock out," he said. "I don't have to penetrate to have completely satisfying sex. I can have sex in the subway, on the street and no one could arrest me for it. I can reach orgasm just by standing on the street corner."

He permitted me to grease his body with oil and then told me, "I am going to dress you for sex." And after adorning me with a sailor suit and cap, he demonstrated just how easily and how quickly I could come in my pants.

Peter also understood that the creation of an image is so much easier for people to deal with than with a real person: "You don't want to have sex with a person with problems, with a mother and father, and this and that. You want an image.

And because of those reasons, I think I fit into many people's fantasies because it is not a person they deal with, but an image that has been beautifully created."

Can such images become boring? Perhaps. Consider the dilemma of one-time leatherman Paul Reed. "One morning I woke up and realized that nearly every bit of interest that I'd had in S/M and leathersex had simply vanished," Reed said in *Black Sheets*. "I looked around my bedroom/playroom and became aware that, somehow, I'd lost all interest in it – so much so that the manacles and restraints, clamps and whips, and other devices were covered in a layer of dust. I just hadn't played that way in a long time, yet I had given it no real thought. It had just withered up and disappeared from my life.

"In the days and weeks that followed, I pondered the situation. One by one I removed the many eye bolts and chains from the playroom walls, floor, and ceiling, and I gave them to a friend who used to earn his living as a professional dominant. Of my formerly favorite whips and toys, I sold some of them, gave others away, and kept but one small cock whip that I had always adored. And as I took these things down, I wondered how it had happened that I had lost interest in something that had been a driving force in my life for years, ever since I was a young teenager beating off to fantasies of crawling naked across the floor...

"As I considered my feelings and thoughts, I realized that a number of things had contributed to this waning passion – years of fulfilling so many fantasies that I had literally run out of ideas; several boring, unsatisfying leather experiences that had left me bruised, sore, and wishing that I just hadn't bothered, and, importantly, the direction in which the 'leather community' had gone with the whole thing (leather beauty pageants, seminars in 'proper technique'" the complete demystification of the S/M experience, as well as the spurious claims by 'leather leaders' about the superiority of S/M sex over vanilla).

"To put it another way, I think that S/M and leathersex was ruined by its practitioners' questionable choice to dogmatize the practice. What was once outlaw sex (rough play, bondage, the simulated rape of dominance and submission games) – and radical physical statements (shaved heads, piercings, tattoos) – not only were absorbed into mainstream culture, the rock culture and MTV's wide-reaching imagery, but were also elevated by leaders of the leather lifestyle to the status of the sacred.

"But of course, that's the age-old rub. As soon as something radical becomes popularized, it ceases to be alternative and becomes, instead, something with rules, regulations, myths and dogma, the right way and the wrong way, whether we're talking about S/M, raving, religion, political action groups like ACT UP, or fashion.

"...I asked myself: which hideous experience transformed my desire? Was it the last links party I attended, a slice-and-dice event that looked more like surgery than sex play? Or was it the fact that my body changed, my tolerance for pain practically nil? Was it the offensiveness of dozens upon dozens of pictures of leather title-holders spread across the pages of the local gay paper week after week, a title for seemingly anything: Mr. Leather Grocery Store, Ms. Leather Nail Care, Mr. and Ms. Leather Hair Relaxer...?

"You get the picture. And I need to be clear that this repulsion has nothing to do with my abiding and continuing passion to be forced roughly to the floor, tied up with phone cord, gagged with dirty socks, and forced to take a big, thick, throbbing stiff prick up my hole. That sort of rough power play remains powerfully attractive.

"For a moment – just a moment – I toyed with the idea that perhaps I had merely outgrown S/M sex, or that maybe S/M is, as some critics suggest, an unhealthy working out of power issues and that I had worked something out and was now in a healthier place because of it. But I dismissed these notions as soon as they entered my mind, because I have never felt that any kind of sex play is inherently more 'grown up' than any other. I've been playing with sex since I was a young child, and for the most part, it's just a ton of fun. As for the neurosis theories, fuck 'em. That whole Stoltenberg/Dworkin thing is a sack of horseshit. Any attempts to psychoanalyze anything, including that will always be met with skepticism by me...

"No, it wasn't anything like that. (It just seems that) there comes a time when one has lived out the fantasy, when the dream has been fulfilled, and it's time for a new dream, a new plan, a new set of goals.

"The problem with sex is that there aren't that many variations on the theme. If one grows bored with a practice, there's not an endless set of options, which is almost an argument for limiting one's exploits, doling them out over time so that one's dance card doesn't get filled up and punched out prematurely.

"There is, lurking deep within me, the suspicion that it might be possible for S/M interests to be revived, given some extraordinary set of circumstances. Let's say, for example, that I were somehow abducted and incarcerated in a vast castle filled with nothing but slaves and masters, like something out of an Anne Rice book. In such a setting, I'll bet that my fantasies would rear their cocky little heads and render me a grovelling slaveboy wiggling my ass in the air for a roomful of gorgeous men and boys wanting to use me for their wild, lusty, animalistic manly pleasures.

"Or, perhaps, I'll meet some cute daddy-master with a bulging crotch who complains to me one evening that he just can't find a bottom boy who really wants to take care of his nine-incher. That might do it. Yes, come to think of it, that just might do it...."

9
SOLITARY PURSUITS

Coming full circle in our pursuit of orgasm, I must confess that at my advanced stage of life, my preferred method of getting off these days is to get a good massage from a naked masseur. The conditional word is *good*.

In my younger days, any sex at all was good. An orgasm is an orgasm, after all.

I was fortunate enough to *come out*, as it were, in the early '70s when gays were enjoying the benefits of the sexual revolution of the '60s. I sampled everything, everywhere. As a married man, I spent hours away from home, cruising the parks, the baths and, when possible, a bar or two. It was on a junket to Pittsburgh that I had occasion to visit a bar and meet Donny, a cute 19-year-old who became my lover for six years.

For the first year, we had sex every day, sometimes twice a day. Eventually, however, it dawned on Donny that I was insatiable. Thus, I had to agree to a schedule: sex three times a week. And the anal intercourse had to be alternated with a blowjob. My friends said I was nuts. At that time it really didn't matter because I was travelling on business most of the week, so my sex with Donny generally occurred on Friday, Saturday and Sunday anyway. Otherwise, my cruising out of town continued unabated. The curious thing was, now that I had a lover and didn't really want all that much sex, I couldn't keep guys away! It was a marvelous time.

It was curious that while Donny would claim he didn't need sex as much as I did, occasionally I would return home to find he had left the dildo in the bathroom, nicely greased up. It got me off just thinking about him in the bathroom, shoving that thing up there as he made love to his own hunky body.

My second lover, Tracy, was a hustler that I was able to – for a time – make respectable. The reason I was willing to indulge him as I never had any other boy was because he was incredible sex, at least for me. Our routine called for sex after lunch and sex before bedtime. He had, as Donny did, his own preferred way of getting off. Tracy would keep Penthouse magazines stashed under our bed and, since he didn't sleep in the bed with me, claiming the mattress was too soft, he would sleep on the floor at the foot of the bed, using the Penthouse Pets as masturbatory fodder before falling asleep. I saw no reason to protest this because I knew as long as he thought he was straight I would remain the only benefactor of his sexual largess. That was true for a year until his addiction to marijuana got out of hand.

Alone, I seek refuge in videos. I've never been turned on by photographs. The images must move. Although I admire a beautiful face and body, I seek relief in watching the real thing right before me. I have, I'll be the first to admit, gotten lazy. I prefer not to use my imagination to get off. I suppose this is because I have to use my imagination so much in composing my books.

To me, video is the greatest boon to the single man ever invented. But it does take a certain amount of effort, at least for me, because just any sex isn't good enough anymore. I can only be turned on by the best, or what I consider the best. Surely, my tastes are not every man's taste, but I have found guys appreciate it when I point out certain videos that contain scenes that have, even after repeated viewings, gotten me off.

Readers familiar with my *Superstars* books know these scenes well since I include them in every issue, adding new ones that always pop up during the year. One of the greatest satisfactions I get these days is when I rent a video and find, without advance billing, a scene that blows me away.

For years, when all else failed, I could count on the final scene from "Kip Noll Superstar," featuring the stud fucking Jon King in several positions, to get me off. A match made in heaven.

One of my personal favorites is Chad Knight, simply because he seems to enjoy so much what he does. For instance, besides featuring a fantastic gang-bang led by Matt Gunther, Falcon's "Buttbusters" features a magnificent coupling of Chad and Matt. In this scene, the two performers were at the top of their form. Chad getting fucked by a group of black studs in "Rich Boy Gang-Bang" was also an incredible turn-on.

Recently Kevin Kramer told me that of all the sex he has had on video, his scene with Chad (in "Tales from the Backlot") was the hottest for him. "Chad is totally into it," Kramer said, "and we did that scene in one long take. There was no stopping and starting like with other scenes. They just let Chad have his way with me and it was great!" And famous bottom boy Chad *topped* Kevin! Kevin says Chad is quiet, shy and committed to his wife and kids, and claims it is true that the only gay sex Chad has is on the set of a video! This might well explain why Chad continues to star for Falcon and others with tremendous results. His scene with Brad Hunt in "Bad Moon Rising" from All Worlds won him an award from *Gay Video News*. His scenes in the "Aspen" sequels sizzle, especially the one with Eric Stone.

The "Aspen" sequel also features Danny Sommers, another legendary bottom, who enjoys the foreskin of Hal Rockland and then lets the stud fuck him.

I have a hunch you will agree that the inventive combo of the TV and VCR was the greatest boon to sexual well-being in history.

...

I've always admired, to a degree, the guy who can get off on himself. "The bodybuilder," Sam Fussell says in his "Bodybuilder Americanus" essay, "(has) balls of energy. He symbolizes force existing through sheer will. He symbolizes the dynamo. Reduced to his purest form, he symbolizes the penis. He glorifies his own glands, just as Jean Genet's muscular Armand, from *The Thief's Journal*, defends his 'immodest attitudes': 'Women walk with their tits bulging, don't they? They parade them, don't they? Well, I've got a right to let my balls stick out so people can see them and even to offer them on a platter.'

"The muscleman is, quite literally, the cock of the walk. He hones his hard body (to be soft is anathema) for the boardwalks and the bedroom. The modern boulevardier is turgid himself, coursing with veins, constantly at attention, ready to explode. Bodybuilder and author Yukio Mishima took priapic delight in his workouts. He could barely contain his excitement at what he calls 'The swelling of muscles encased in a sunlit skin.' This auto-eroticism is a fetishism of form. Don't doubt Arnold Schwarzenegger when he says: 'Seeing new changes in my body, feeling them, turned me on.'

"The sensation is masturbatory, but the roots are homosex past and present. The grandparents of Joe Weider's *Muscle & Fitness* are his *Demi-Gods* and *Young Physique*, the gay porn of its day, featuring basted bodybuilders hanging out in G-strings, caught fresh in the flush of physicality. Today's muscle magazines come wrapped in plastic, with fold-out centerfolds of your favorite flexing bodybuilder. The homosexual undercurrent comes to the surface in the classifieds that end each issue: 'Chest Men of America' Unite, reads the fine print of *Musclemag*. Finally, a club 'for muscular men into pec worship.'"

But solitary confinement, even if you usually get off on yourself, does have its limits. As Craig Nelson says, "Here's the big secret to getting a boyfriend: It doesn't matter what you do, as long as you do *something*."

"How often I hear the refrain, 'All the good ones are taken,'" David Feinberg says. "You know, they're either married or they're dead. During one of those loathsome holiday parties last year, I found myself flirting with a rather attractive young gentleman whom I later discovered was straight. Usually my gaydar isn't *that* off, but in this case my mistake was understandable: He was in advertising, which is so easily confused with prostitution.

"When you're lying like a bored dominatrix on a sofa watching a four-part miniseries based on a bad novel by Stephen King and your testosterone level is so low that masturbation seems like a silly imposition, it's important to remember you used to have sex. You know, sex is what you started to do downstairs in the ladies' room of that gay restaurant with that short hunk from the gym with the tattoo on his left arm who had drunk too much champagne. That short hunk from the gym who was probably with his boyfriend upstairs. He certainly didn't seem dead to me."

Yes, masturbation seems to be the way to go in the age of safe sex. But it doesn't have to always be solitary. "Around the country," Jamie Malanowski says in *Playboy*, "aficionados of the swingers network are singing the praises of masturbation parties to attract new, clean blood, while in New York, businessmen seem to have acquired a taste for Korean massage parlors. (The harried executive can get a relaxing back rub and hand job while waiting for his new Big and Tall suit to be cleaned and pressed.) "

Indeed, New York remains the place you are most likely to find orgasm. I love New York. But over the years I have seen this bastion of sex suffer the same fate as the tiniest burg. Along with the Disney-fying of Times Square, it was doubtful that New York's sex clubs, baths and similar establishments would remain open. Opposition to sex clubs came not only from Mayor Giuliani and the Health Department but also from conservative factions in the gay community. One vocal opponent was politically-correct Gabriel Rotello, a gay columnist for *New York Newsday*.

Drummer has reported, however, that the city was ready to move in on the sex clubs until a budget made it impossible for officials to police the clubs with their own monitors. "Thanks to a deal brokered by the Gay Men's Health Crisis between the Health Department and the Club Owers Coalition, sex clubs are responsible for monitoring the behavior of their clients according to a set of guidelines established by GMHC. This has permitted sex clubs, private parties and monthly events to proceed with less fear of Health Department shut-downs," *Drummer* reported.

"Other sex-oriented business have not fared so well. A new zoning regulation now forbids adult bookstores and stnp clubs from operating within 500 feet of an apartment building, a church, a school or another X-rated business. Sources at the Health Department say the city will soon enforce a new ordinance that forbids doors on cubicles in bookstores and bathhouses. But in early 1996 at least, most bookstores and bathhouses were operating as before."

Drummer recommended many places in the Big Apple to search for orgasm. They liked the East Side Club, where "guys were walking around in towels, some folks in underwear, others keeping shoes on. The men were mostly in their 30's and 40's, racially diverse. My escort was pleased to see many mustaches. More crowded earlier in the evening than after bars closed."

And then there is the unique He's Gotta Have It! "Imagine this," *Drummer* gushes, "A dance studio covered with green garbage bags where guys pay $10 every other week to jack and suck each other off. The Big Dick Contest occurs at 2 a.m. and is simulcast on a video monitor in case you don't get a front row seat. Beer and soda are available for purchase. The music and porno videos are free. Call for schedule."

As always, despite the new conservatism, men on the prowl for sleazy action don't have far to look when they're in New York City. *Drummer* says, "The venues where queers get together for sex are limitless. Getting laid in New York is a matter of knowing where the cock is.

"One good place to start is the narrow streets of Manhattan's meat packing district. By late night, all of the butchers have gone home. All that remains of the day's business is the smell of raw hamburger that lingers in the air and sticks to the sidewalks. It is here that transvestites, jack-booted men in leather, club kids, drug dealers and street people converge to create a meat market of another sort.

"Radiating out north, south and west from the corner of Ninth Avenue and West 14th Street, this neighborhood is home to New York City's leather bars and several of its most popular sex clubs." Of particular interest is The Attic, a New York institution for 10 years, which currently operates out of an old meat locker on 14th Street. "Some of the best sex parties in town are held here," *Drummer* says. "Even though it is a private club, non-members can attend for a higher admission. Patrons check their clothes at the Attic. The most popular events are the twice-monthly piss parties, the Tuesday and Friday Blow Buddies parties, and the Sunday Sleaze parties."

"Meanwhile," *Playboy* says, "fetishists are flourishing, thanks – again – to the Internet (the hot new home of the fetishistic). Whereas once they might have dwelt in loneliness and fear, S&M devotees, foot worshipers, amputee buffs and other enthusiasts of the esoteric now find one another online, where they exchange equipment and techniques and organize support groups and bake sales and defense funds and God knows what else. (Just so you know, the hot old ways of having sex continue to have their adherents.)

"One offshoot of the cyber-revolution is that the hot new

property for nearly anything to have is speed. Souped-up computers were just the beginning; then came Rollerblades, longer tennis rackets that add zip to serves, the Republican mania for cutting red tape, higher speed limits and the continuing rise in the popularity of Dale Earnhardt.

"There are plenty of other ways to partake in the 21st century. You could go to Saigon, a very retro town – so retro, it's once again being called Ho City (with good reason). It's rapidly replacing Prague as the hot new Goa, which, you'll certainly recall, was for a long time the hot new place for disaffected Generation X-patriates to live a sybaritic, bohemian and somehow more authentic existence than was otherwise possible. If you can't get it together to go to Saigon, wait awhile and take a shorter trip to Havana. One day Fidel (essay question: When Castro is rediscovered, will he be retro or camp, and why?) will no longer reign. An explosion of freedom, joy, avarice and greed will fuel an unimaginable number of enterprises. And if you can't get to Cuba, go to Los Angeles, where earthquakes, fires, mudslides, gang wars and riots have turned the old utopia into the hot new dystopia. But if you can't go anywhere, stay home."

My sentiments exactly.

10
BEYOND ORGASM

"The male hustler is seldom called upon only to provide orgasm," John Preston says in *Hustling, A Gentleman's Guide to the Fine Art of Homosexual Prostitution*, (a Richard Kasak Book). Preston agrees that while it may be true when the client seeks only a quick blow job from a street hustler, but even then a contact may be established that is more than one-dimensional.

"The modern male hustler meets his clients through ads or discreet introductions. He doesn't stand on street corners in dangerous neighborhoods. He entertains in his own apartment or visits clients in their hotel rooms or homes. He has more in common with image of the Japanese geisha than with the *National Enquirer's* sensational headlines about white slavery. Expert sensuality is a part of the gay prostitute's reality, but so too are his social skills."

Preston quotes his pal, author and artist Gavin Geoffrey Dillard, a one-time whore: "Now, with mortgage, taxes, garden, and cats to feed, I find myself more behooved than ever to participate in the trials of money-gathering, selling my time, my passions and my sensibilities in more wearisome and much more emotion-consuming manners than ever I did as a paid tart.

"Let's face it, in this exhausted ruin of an industrial society we are all conscripted to prostitute ourselves though seldom do we garner the satisfaction of a good buck, nor even the strokes that accompany the affirmations that one is attractive, sensual, and desired by another.

"As a professional writer, I can find few justifications for the drudgery of word processing, for spreading my creative cheeks for inane corporate policies, for writing a song or an article that in my heart of hearts I know is not worthy of being wntten who is the betterfor it.

"But in a romantic tete-a-tete, even of the basest and most mercenary sort, souls are obliged to touch souls, human energies mingle, and passions, however restrained, do surface. Besides, a hundred bucks for an hour of trolloping beats the heck out of the same wage for a grisly nine-to-five within the toxic air, Muzak and lighting of our modern high-rise whorehouse. And the rest of the day is left available for poetry, prayer and meditation."

Preston says he learned many things from hustling, one of them being that labor in any form can be exploitative and degrading, but the self-employed person can at least have some control over his dignity. "I was a bank teller when I was in my twenties," Preston recalled, "and I held a number of other similar service jobs. Believe me, all of them were much more demeaning than being a hustler.

"The basic problem with being a male prostitute is your own and other people's perceptions of the occupation, not the reality of it. It can be difficult to overcome the internalized interpretation that only people with low self-esteem would sell themselves to a stranger. Forget it. Laugh all the way to the bank and, if your self-image is in bad shape, remember that someone else thought you were hot enough that he was willing to pay for the privilege of sucking your cock. That fact has a lot more reality to it than any New Age bullshit."

Contributors
(Other Than the Editor, John Patrick)

"Randy & Sweet Pete" and "Flecther's Boys"
Grant Adams
Originally from Texas, the author now lives and works in Southern California as a communications consultant. In the past his occupations have included acting, teaching, and real estate. He describes himself as an "obsessive reader and writer" who also enjoys hiking, gardening, and cooking for his friends when time permits. Currently he is working on two novellas.

"Ties That Bind"
Duncan P. Allen
The author lives in Texas and continues to write.

"Free Installation"
L. Amore
The twentysomething author has been in the book business for ten years. He has lived in upstate New York, Boston and New York City and now resides in Connecticut. He is currently working on his first novel, as yet untitled, and finishing a novella called, "The Night John Preston Flogged Me." This story originally appeared in STARbooks' *Big Boys, Little Lies*.

"The Glory Hole"
Ken Anderson
The Intense Lover, a book of Ken's poetry, was published by STARbooks earlier this year. The author lives in Georgia.

"Take Your Time"
Antler
The poet lives in Milwaukee when not traveling to perform his poems or wildernessing. His epic poem *Factory* was published by City Lights. His collection of poems *Last Words* was published by Ballantine. Winner of the Whitman Award from the Walt Whitman Society of Camden, New Jersey, and the Witter Bynner prize from the Academy and Institute of Arts & Letters in New York, his poetry has appeared in many periodicals (including *Utne Reader*, *Whole Earth Review* and

American Poetry Review) and anthologies (including *Gay Roots, Erotic by Nature,* and *Gay and Lesbian Poetry of Our Time).*

"Going Places"
Edward Bangor
The author, an Englishman, is a frequent contributor to the anthologies of Acolyte Press. Under the name of Headbanger, he contributed a piece for the fourth issue of the American gay comic book *Cherubino.*

"The Carriage Boy"
Michael Bates
The author, who lives in Seattle, has had numerous stories published in erotic magazines and a half dozen in Leyland Publications' *True Gay Encounters* series.

"Tradition"
Greg Bowden
The author, who lives in California, has contributed many stories to gay magazines.

"Sex At the Quarry"
Leo Cardini
Author of the best-selling book, *Mineshaft Nights,* Mr. Cardini's stories and theater-related articles have appeared in a variety of magazines. He is the co-author of a musical now being fine-tuned for Broadway.

"Heaven"
Nigel Christopher
The writer lives quietly in England.

"Trucker's Special"
William Cozad
The author is a regular contributor to gay magazines and his startling memoirs are to be published by STARbooks Press in *Lover Boys* and *Boys of the Night.*

"The Full Treatment"
Keith Davis

The author resides in New York and has contributed many stories to gay sex magazines.

"A Family Affair in Rio"
Daniel Dee

A world-traveller, the author now lives in splendid seclusion in Florida.

"Kevin's Ass" and "The Refugee"
John C. Douglas

The author has an enviable track record, having some thirty novels published, and more than twenty screenplays produced. A resident of Alabama, Douglas has a number of works in progress. "Most of the time," he admits, "I don't have a firm plot in mind. I prefer to create the characters and let them do whatever they like. Sometimes, they surprise even me!" A full-length novel, "The Young and the Flawless," appeared in STARbooks Press' most popular anthology of all-time, *Barely Legal*.

"Picking Up Tolly"
Jarred Goodall

When he is not accepting sabbatical appointments abroad, the author teaches English in a Midwestern university. Born in Wisconsin, he loves back-packing, mountain-climbing, chess and Victorian literature. His favorite color: blue-green; favorite pop-star: Leonard Bernstein; favorite car: WWII Jeep; favorite drink: water, preferably recycled; favorite actor: River Phoenix (alas); favorite hobby: "If you want to know that, read my stories."

"Punk's Collateral"
Thomas C. Humphrey

The author, who resides in Florida, is working on his first novel, *All the Difference*, and has contributed stories to First Hand publications.

"Faxing Off"
David Laurents

The writer is the editor of *The Badboy Book of Erotic Poetry*, *Wanderlust: Homoerotic Tales of Travel*, and *Southern Comfort*, among other books. His own stories and poems appear in numerous anthologies, including: *Barely Legal, My Three Boys, The Best of the Superstars 1996, Flashpoint: The Best Gay Male Erotic Writing of 1995, Meltdown!* and *Coming Up: The World's Best Erotic Writing*, and in magazines such as *Drummer, Torso, Mandate, First Hand, Steam*, and others.

"Banjee Boy"
Chris Leslie

The writer is the editor of *Dirty* magazine, published in New York.

"He Didn't Do Virgins"
Bert McKenzie

A free lance writer and drama critic, the Kansan writes a column for a major midwestern newspaper and has contributed erotic fiction to magazines such as *Torso, Mandate*, and *Playguy*. He is a frequent contributor to STARbooks' anthologies and an anthology of his work was published by Badboy, *Fringe Benefits*.

"Roadside Stand"
Edmund Miller

Dr. Miller, the author of the legendary poetry book *Fucking Animals* (recently reprinted by STARBooks), is the chairman of the English Department at a large university in the New York area.

"In the Boy Zone"
Jesse Monteagudo

The author is a regular columnist for *The Gazette* and other gay news journals and is noted for his non-fiction writing, including a passage in John Preston's highly-acclaimed *Hometowns*.

"The Orgasmic Resume"
Thom Nickels
The Cliffs of Aries, the author's first novel, was published in 1988 by Aegina Press. His second book, *Two Novellas: Walking Water & After All This*, was published in 1989 by Banned Books.

"The Wrestler"
David Olivera
The author lives in Boston.

"A Lovely Lad"
Rudy Roberts
The author lives in England.

"The Intruder"
Ken Smith
The author, who lives in England, started life as a simple country lad. At the tender age of 15, he joined the Royal Navy, and says he has "ridden some big ones whilst at sea. Waves mostly." Ken has had several of his stories published in the London-based magazines *Vulcan, Mister,* and *Zipper.*

"Quick Miracles in the Alley"
Christopher Thomas
The poet's work has been published in literary journals.

"Enter The Dragon" and "TRIO"
Dan Veen
The author's first stories were based on his experiences as a hustler in San Francisco and New Orleans. He has written erotic fiction for *Honcho, Mandate, Playguy, Torso, Inches, and First Hand* magazines. He writes regular film articles and erotic video reviews for *Honcho* under the name of V.C. Rand. He has a PhD. in English Literature and Germanic Languages.

"My First Tutor" and "The Tutor, the Tourist & Me"
James Wilton
The author, who resides in Connecticut, has contributed stories to various gay magazines. The stories in this collection were written especially for STARbooks Press.

ACKNOWLEDGEMENTS AND SOURCES

Cover photography by celebrated English photographer David Butt. Our handsome coverboy David Brownstone was revealed in all his natural glory in Prowl issue #32.

Mr. Butt's photographs may be purchased through Suntown, Post Office Box 151, Danbury, Oxfordshire, OX16 8QN, United Kingdom. Ask for a full catalogue.

SPECIAL OFFER

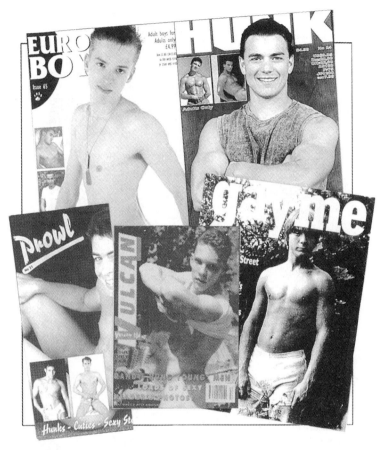

STARbooks Press now offers two very special international gay magazine packages: You can get the hottest American gay magazines, including *GAYME, All-Man, Torso, Advocate Men, Advocate Fresh Men, In Touch,* and *Playguy,* either singly for $6.95, or in a very special deluxe sampler package for only $25 for six big issues.

We also offer the sizzling British and European magazines, including *Euros, Euroboy, Prowl, Vulcan, HUNK,* and *Steam* for $9.95 each or only $49.95 for sampler of six fabulous issues.

Please add $2.75 post per issue or sampler. Order from: STARbooks, P.O. Box 2737-B, Sarasota FL 34230-2737 USA.

ABOUT THE EDITOR

John Patrick is a prolific, prize-winning author of fiction and non-fiction. One of his short stories, "The Well," was honored by PEN American Center as one of the best of 1987. His novels and anthologies, as well as his non-fiction works, including *Legends* and *The Best of the Superstars* series, continue to gain him new fans every day. One of his stories appears in the Badboy collection *Southern Comfort*.

A divorced father of two, the author is a longtime member of the American Booksellers Association, the Florida Publishers' Association, American Civil Liberties Union, and the Adult Video Association. He resides in Florida.